The Enchanted Wanderer
and Other Stories

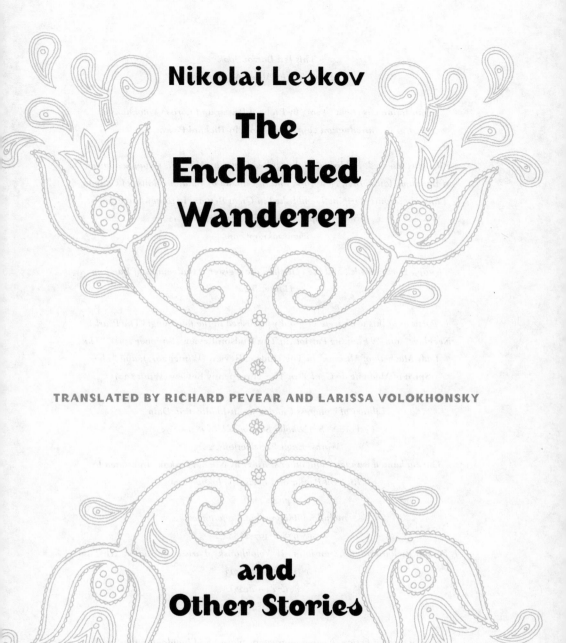

Nikolai Leskov

The Enchanted Wanderer

TRANSLATED BY RICHARD PEVEAR AND LARISSA VOLOKHONSKY

and Other Stories

Alfred A. Knopf New York 2013

This Is a Borzoi Book
Published by Alfred A. Knopf

Portions of this work were originally published in the following: "The Pearl
Necklace" and "A Flaming Patriot" in The Hudson Review (Summer 2011); "The
Lady Macbeth of Mtsensk" in The Hudson Review (Winter 2012); and "The
Spirit of Madame de Genlis" in The Threepenny Review (Winter 2013).

Library of Congress Cataloging-in-Publication Data
Leskov, N. S. (Nikolai Semenovich), 1831–1895.
[Works. English. Selections. 2013]
The enchanted wanderer and other stories / by Nikolai Leskov ; translated by
Richard Pevear and Larissa Volokhonsky.
pages ; cm
Includes bibliographical references.
ISBN 978-0-307-26882-2
I. Pevear, Richard, [date], translator. II. Volokhonsky, Larissa, translator. III. Title.
PG3337.L5A255 2013
891.73'3—dc23
2012025416

Jacket design by Peter Mendelsund
Manufactured in the United States of America
First American Edition

Contents

Contents

Introduction

> *Leskov is a writer who yields enormous pleasure, breaking past
> sectarian literary and ideological premises. But more: we live in
> a moment of lowered cultural and emotional expectations, after
> the fall of modernism but with nothing very strong to replace it.
> To go back to certain earlier writers is to regain a sense of human
> possibility. To go back to Leskov is to regain a sense of the passion,
> sometimes the joy, that can be part of the human enterprise.*
>
> IRVING HOWE, "JUSTICE FOR LESKOV"

I

nikolai Leskov, a younger contemporary of Dostoevsky and Tolstoy and one of the great masters of Russian fiction, is a writer who keeps being discovered. The first to discover him was Leskov himself. He was in his late twenties and working as a business agent for his uncle, a Russianized Scotsman named Alexander Scott, whose firm managed the vast estates of two noble Russian families. Leskov later described those years, from 1857 to 1859, as the best period of his life. He traveled all over Russia, "from the Black Sea to the White and from Brod to Krasny Yar," and sent back reports in the form of letters to his uncle. "I had no need to clear myself a path to the people through books and ready-made ideas," he later wrote. "I studied them in place. Books were a precious help to me, but I was the helmsman. Hence I'm not rooted in any school, because it was not in school that I learned, but on Scott's barges." These travels gave him a great store of impressions that he drew upon all his life.

Scott was struck by the literary quality of Leskov's reports and used to read them aloud to his neighbors, one of whom praised them so highly that it gave Leskov the idea of becoming a writer. As he commented rather drily in a third-person "Note on Himself" thirty years later: "His writing began by chance."

He was born in the village of Gorokhovo, near the town of Orel (pronounced "Oryól"), in 1831. Orel, located in the Russian heartland, the so-called "wooden Russia," some two hundred and twenty miles southwest of Moscow, is the setting of five of the seventeen stories in the present collection. Another is set in Mtsensk, which is in the Orel region, and five more take place in other provincial Russian towns. This preponderance of the provincial is typical of Leskov's work as a whole, though, as the reader will see, he could also tell sophisticated and witty stories set in Petersburg, Moscow, Vienna . . .

On his father's side, Leskov came from several generations of priests serving the village of Leski, which gave them their family name. His father, too, received a seminary education, but he broke with tradition and entered government service in the Orel courts, eventually attaining the rank of collegiate assessor, which conferred hereditary nobility. His mother was from an impoverished aristocratic family: her father, a Moscow nobleman who had lost everything during the French invasion in 1812, worked as an estate manager in Gorokhovo; her mother, of whom Leskov gives us a fine portrait in the last chapter of "Deathless Golovan," was of Moscow merchant stock and, as Leskov says, "was taken in marriage into a noble family 'not for her wealth, but for her beauty.'" Leskov thus combined in himself the three estates—noble, mercantile, and clerical—but in oddly mixed and attenuated forms.

He first came to know the fourth estate, the peasants (serfs at that time), in 1839, when his father gave up his position as a magistrate in Orel and bought the small country estate of Panino, in the Kromy district, twenty miles from Orel. This move and some of the experiences it led to are described in the opening chapters of his story "The Spook." The knowledge of peasant life he acquired then, later enriched by his travels for Alexander Scott, differed greatly from the abstractions of radical social theory that were becoming fashionable in Moscow and Petersburg.

Leskov's formal schooling was limited to the five years, from 1841 to 1846, he spent at the secondary school in Orel. He later wrote that he was "terribly bored but studied well," but in fact he was a mediocre student, and at the age of fifteen he left school without finishing and went into civil service as a clerk in the Orel criminal court. In 1848 his father died during an outbreak of cholera, leaving his mother to manage the little estate at Panino and raise seven children, of whom he was the eldest. In 1849 his maternal uncle, Sergei Petrovich Alferiev, a doctor in Kiev and a professor at the university, invited him to visit. Leskov was greatly impressed by the city and decided to stay. He took a leave from his post in Orel and by February of 1850 had been accepted as a junior clerk in the Kiev military recruitment office. This close experience of the workings of Russian bureaucracy and of the fate of conscripts (the term of military service at that time was twenty-five years) would reappear again and again in his writing.

Leskov spent eight years in Kiev, made friends with students and professors at the university through his uncle, sat in on courses, read widely, learned Ukrainian and Polish, and incidentally witnessed the building of the famous Nikolaevsky Chain Bridge over the Dniepr River, designed by the Anglo-Irish engineer Charles Blacker Vignoles. This was the first multi-span suspension bridge in Europe and at the time the longest in the world. The workers and the work on the bridge have a central place in his story "The Sealed Angel" (1873), and though he deliberately avoids naming the city, the setting is vividly evoked. The directors of the actual project were English, as in Leskov, and Vignoles's letters and papers (which, of course, Leskov never saw) describe the same natural disasters, the floods and ice damage, that play such a major part in the story. In 1853, the year that the bridge was officially opened, Leskov married Olga Smirnova, the daughter of a Kiev merchant.

The suffering and the corruption Leskov witnessed daily in the system of military conscription under the emperor Nicholas I were counterbalanced by the intellectual breadth and moral idealism he met with in the people of his uncle's circle. He was profoundly influenced by a number of them, in particular by a man he refers to in an autobiographical note as "the well-known statistician-abolitionist Dmitri Petrovich Zhuravsky." Zhuravsky (1810–1856) was an economist who not only advocated the abolition of serfdom in theory but also practiced it in reality, buying out house serfs and setting them free. At his death, he left his small inheritance for the continuation of that practice. Writing to his friend the Slavophile publicist Ivan Aksakov on December 2, 1874, Leskov said of Zhuravsky: "he was all but the first living person who, in the days of my youth in Kiev, made me understand that virtue exists not only in abstractions."

Another of his Kievan acquaintances, and one closer to him in age, had an even stronger influence on the young Leskov. This was Stepan Stepanovich Gromeka (1823–1877), a nobleman from Poltava who was attached to the governor-general's staff when they met in 1852. Gromeka had a rather strange career. Politically he began as a liberal, advocating reform rather than revolution. He defended the monarchy while hoping to improve it. In 1857–1858 he published a series of satirical articles on the police in the prominent Moscow journal *The Russian Messenger*. He also contributed to the liberal Petersburg monthly *Notes of the Fatherland,* and to the radical journal *The Bell,* edited in London by the expatriate Alexander Herzen. But his journalistic career was confined to some five or six years. By 1862 he had turned against Herzen, and in the later 1860s he went back into government service, ending as governor of Siedlce province in Russian Poland, where he campaigned for the absorption of the Uniate (Eastern Roman Catholic) Church into the Russian Orthodox Church and was notorious for his brutal treatment of peasants who resisted.

Leskov followed a very different path from Gromeka's, but in his "Note on Himself" he acknowledged that their friendship during his years in Kiev "had a decisive influence on Leskov's subsequent destiny. The example of Gromeka, who abandoned his government service and went to work for the Russian Society of Shipping and Trade, induced Leskov to do the same." So it was that Leskov left his position in the recruiting office and went to work for Alexander Scott. But in 1860 Scott's firm suffered reverses and he could no longer keep his nephew employed. Leskov returned to Kiev, and here the influence of Gromeka again proved crucial. Gromeka had preceded Leskov into business; he had also preceded him into journalism. In the early 1860s it was Gromeka who connected Leskov with such prominent Moscow and Petersburg editors as Mikhail Katkov of *The Russian Messenger,* Stepan Dudyshkin and Andrei Kraevsky of *Notes of the Fatherland,* Mikhail and Fyodor Dostoevsky of *Time* and *Epoch* ("The Lady Macbeth of Mtsensk" was first published in *Epoch* in 1865). In the same "Note on Himself," he confessed that

"Leskov's decisive enslavement to literature was again the work of that same Gromeka. He has been writing ever since."

Leskov's earliest article, "Sketches of the Distilling Industry (Penza Province)," was published in April 1861 in *Notes of the Fatherland*. By then the thirty-year-old author had moved to Petersburg himself. It was his first taste of life in the capital, and it was a heady moment for Russian society. In 1855 the repressive emperor Nicholas I had died and his son, Alexander II (1818–1881), had taken the throne. In March 1861, Alexander II released a manifesto proclaiming the emancipation of the serfs, for which he became known as the "tsar-liberator." In 1864 came a far-reaching judicial reform, for the first time establishing open courts, trial by jury, and a bar association. There were also military reforms shortening the length of service and eliminating corporal punishment, among other things. But this was also the time of the nihilists, the so-called "new people," who were not satisfied with Alexander's reforms or with liberalism in general and called for far more radical changes. The term "nihilist" first entered Russian literature in a novel by another writer from Orel—Ivan Turgenev. In his *Fathers and Sons,* published in 1862, it is applied to Evgeny Bazarov, whom Turgenev conceived as "a new type of hero." Arkady Kirsanov, a close friend of Bazarov, explains the meaning of the term to his father: "A nihilist is a man who does not bow down before any authority, who does not take any principle on faith, whatever reverence that principle may be enshrined in." The radical journalist Dmitri Pisarev (1840–1868) put it more bluntly: "Whatever can be smashed, must be smashed." It was a time of fierce polemics, clandestine publications, the first experiments with communes, and also of several attempts to assassinate the tsar-liberator, the last of which, in March 1881, was successful.

With his move to Petersburg, Leskov was caught up in the contradictions of the time, and as a journalist he quickly found himself embroiled in them. Writing about "Leskov's Literary Beginnings," the French scholar Jean-Claude Marcadé observed: "Leskov's articles are interesting because they show the same temperament in the publicist as would be that of the writer throughout his career. It was impossible for him to compose accommodating works, to hide the truth as he felt it."* Near the end of his life, in an interview with V. V. Protopopov, Leskov said of himself:

---

* "Les débuts littéraires de Leskov," in *Cahiers du monde russe et soviétique,* vol. 22, no. 1 (1981).

Introduction

I love literature as a means enabling me to express what I hold to be true and good. If I cannot do that, literature is of no value to me: looking upon it as art is not my point of view. I absolutely cannot understand the concept of "art for art's sake." No, art must be useful. Only then does it have a precise meaning. I do not acknowledge the art of painting naked women. It is the same for literature. If one cannot serve the true and the good by means of art, it is useless to write, and one ought to abandon the occupation.[*]

He was a prolific journalist and remained one all his life, producing over six hundred articles in all. But in 1862 he also published his first fiction in *The Northern Bee*, which, in tune with the times, had turned from a reactionary to a liberal journal.

The progressives were divided into two camps, the "gradualist" and the "impatient." Leskov remained with the gradualists, he said, because he found their moderation more trustworthy. Besides, he was somewhat older than most of the "new people" and had behind him a much deeper and more varied experience of Russian realities. But he had a number of good friends among the "impatient," and when student unrest broke out in Petersburg and then in Moscow in 1861–62, he sympathized with their cause. From them he arrived at the notion, to be embodied in his polemical novel *No Way Out* (1864), that there were good nihilists and bad nihilists, and that the good would soon distinguish themselves from the "nihilizing babblers."

In Moscow, on May 18, 1862, a clandestine proclamation entitled "Young Russia" appeared, calling upon the radical youth to "pick up their axes" and "strike the imperial party" wherever it might be—"in the public squares . . . the streets, the fields, the villages"—and with each blow to cry: "Long live the social and democratic Republic of Russia!" The "imperial party" meant not only the emperor and his family, but the nobility, the merchants, the functionaries, the landowners—they were all to be included in the bloodbath. Copies of the proclamation were handed out in the streets and courtyards, sent by mail, stuffed into coat pockets, distributed in churches, pasted up on walls. It caused great alarm among the inhabitants of both capitals, and all sorts of rumors began to spread. In the midst of that agitation, towards the end of May, a series of fires broke out in Petersburg. The conservatives immediately blamed them on the students and revolutionaries. The progressives countered by saying

---

[*] *The Petersburg Gazette*, November 27, 1894.

they had been set by the police as a provocation. (Some also suggested they were simply the work of property owners who wanted to collect on their insurance. To this day, in fact, no one knows whether the fires were deliberate or accidental.) The fire in the Apraksin and Shchukin markets on May 28 caused the greatest panic and destruction. Two days later Leskov published an editorial in *The Northern Bee* responding to the rumors about arson, noting that "the public also points to what sort of people the incendiaries are, and hatred of that sort of people [he carefully avoids mentioning students] is growing with unheard-of speed." He voiced his concern about the danger "the members of that body" might face as a result of the rumors. He did not presume to judge how well-founded the suspicions were and to what extent they might be connected to "the latest abominable and revolting proclamation calling for the overthrow of the entire civil order of our society." But to avoid worse disorders, he called on the police to make public at once all the solid information they had. "They should boldly say whether the rumors circulating in the capital about the fires and the incendiaries have the least substance. The ignoble villains must not be spared; but neither is it fitting to risk a single hair on a single head living in the capital and exposed to the accusations of a totally frightened population."

The editorial is somewhat awkwardly worded, but it is clear that Leskov wanted to get at the truth, so that the rumors would not continue to grow and threaten innocent people. He did not believe the students were responsible for the fires. He condemned the "Young Russia" proclamation in the strongest terms and meant to separate it from the majority of the students, but to the minds of the radicals, he was in fact connecting them with the fires and even inciting the police against them. The violence of their reaction astonished Leskov and wounded him deeply. He was accused of being a government agent and, worse than that, a turncoat. Dmitri Pisarev, the spokesman of the nihilists, anathematized him, calling him both reactionary and dishonest, and virtually banned him from the pages of the liberal press. What was more, the emperor was also said to be displeased with the editorial. Though he never recanted, and in fact had nothing to recant, Leskov's attempts to explain himself in subsequent articles only made matters worse both on the right and on the left. He even received death threats. On September 6, 1862, to escape the turmoil and clear his head, Leskov went abroad as foreign correspondent for *The Northern Bee*. Choosing to travel by stagecoach rather than train,* he passed through the Ukraine, Poland, Bohemia, and finally settled in Paris, where he spent four months, returning to Russia only the next March.

Among the liberal intelligentsia Leskov bore the totally misplaced stigma of a reactionary all his life, and it lingered on into Soviet times. In a letter to his friend Pyotr Shchebalsky dated November 10, 1875, he mimicked the general editorial opinion of him: "He has marked himself off so clearly . . . and besides they say he's close to the Third Section" (i.e., the secret police). A reviewer who praised the language of "The Sealed Angel" in 1873 added, "Leskov has such a reputation that it takes a sort of audacity to praise him." As a result, though he always had readers, more and more of them as time went on, he suffered during his lifetime from an almost total critical neglect. Even his admirers among the critics were reluctant to write about him because of the suspicions he aroused. He was considered a minor writer, and the great originality of his work was overlooked. He remained, in that sense, undiscovered.

In the 1880s that situation began to change. A younger generation of writers, artists, and thinkers, who had themselves rejected the violent and doctrinaire judgments of nihilism, turned to Leskov as a master. This was his second discovery. In 1881 the new weekly humor magazine *Fragments* published Leskov's story "The Spirit of Madame de Genlis." Two years later the same magazine published "A Little Mistake." Meanwhile, the stories of the young Anton Chekhov had begun to appear there. Chekhov was in medical school and earned his living by placing comic sketches wherever he could (*Fragments* published two hundred and seventy of them between 1882 and 1887). In 1883 he met Leskov in Moscow. "Leikin brought along with him my favorite writer, the famous N. S. Leskov," he wrote in a letter to his brother. He was twenty-three, Leskov fifty-two. After a night of carousing, they wound up in a cab together. "Leskov turns to me half-drunk," Chekhov wrote in the same letter, "and asks: 'Do you know what I am?' 'I do.' 'No, you don't. I'm a mystic.' 'I know.' He stares at me with his old man's popping eyes and prophesies: 'You will die before your brother.' 'Maybe so.' 'I shall anoint you with oil as Samuel did David . . . Write.' The man is a mixture of an elegant Frenchman and a defrocked priest. But he's considerable." Chekhov

---

* See the opening of "The Pearl Necklace."

took this consecration by Leskov more seriously than it sounds. And in fact they had much in common: they shared a broad experience of Russia and Russian life and an unidealized knowledge of the people. And something more important as well. In his biography of Chekhov,* Donald Rayfield speaks of "a mystic side of Chekhov—his irrational intuition that there is meaning and beauty in the cosmos," which "aligns him more to Leskov than to Tolstoy in the Russian literary tradition."

Another new discoverer of Leskov was the painter Ilya Repin (1844–1930), one of the major Russian artists of the later nineteenth century. He had met Leskov and had illustrated some of his stories. In September 1888, in a letter asking permission (unsuccessfully) to paint Leskov's portrait, he wrote: "Not only I but the whole of educated Russia knows you and loves you as a very outstanding writer of unquestionable merits, and at the same time as a thinking man." The poet and philosopher Vladimir Soloviev (1853–1900), a central intellectual figure then and now, also championed Leskov's work. They became personal friends in 1891 and met frequently. Soloviev hand-carried the manuscript of Leskov's novella "Night Owls" to M. M. Stasyulevich, editor of the liberal, pro-Western *Messenger of Europe,* who had declared once that Leskov was "someone I will never publish," and persuaded him to change his mind. When Leskov died in February 1895, Soloviev published an obituary notice:

In his will, Leskov wrote: "I know there was much bad in me; I deserve no praise and no pity. As for those who want to blame me, they should know that I have already done so myself." But it is impossible to fulfill such wishes when it is a question of such a remarkable man. Therefore I will conform myself to the spirit rather than the letter of this will, and allow myself to express in a few words what I think of the person of the dead man and of his work.

What was striking above all in Nikolai Semyonovich was his passionate nature; at an advanced age, and though seemingly inactive, he was still prey to a constant seething of the soul. He needed a quite uncommon spiritual force to keep his ardent character within bounds. Besides, in his works one felt a passionate and restless attitude towards the things he described, which, if his talent had been less, might have turned into an obvious partiality. But in Leskov,

---

* *Chekhov: A Life* (New York: Henry Holt, 1997).

as in every great writer, that passion is tempered and betrays itself only secretly, though here and there in his writings there still remains some trace of ideological engagement . . .

It is likely that Leskov's compositions will elicit critical judgments as serious as they are profound; and then, despite what is written in his will, the late writer will become the object of much praise and much blame. But they will all certainly acknowledge in him the brilliance and extraordinary originality of a talent that never remained buried, like the keen yearning for the truth that ruled his being and his work.

II

In 1889–90 the first collected edition of Leskov's works was published in ten volumes, seen through the press by the author himself. An eleventh volume was added in 1893, and a twelfth in 1896, posthumous but prepared by Leskov. This edition was reprinted twice, with the addition of an interesting, somewhat hagiographic preface by Rostislav Sementkovsky. In 1902–03 a thirty-six-volume *Complete Collected Works* (also not complete) was published and became the standard edition. Twenty years later the formalist critic Boris Eikhenbaum (1886–1959) finally accorded Leskov his rightful place in Russian literature, looking at his writing in itself rather than in its ideological context, and showing that the attempt to set his work beside that of Dostoevsky, Tolstoy, and Turgenev was mistaken, because he equaled them not by resembling them, but by being totally unlike them. In a tribute published in 1945, on the fiftieth anniversary of Leskov's death, Eikhenbaum wrote:

Without him our literature of the nineteenth century would have been incomplete, first and foremost because it would not have captured to an adequate degree the depths of Russia with its "enchanted wanderers," it would not have revealed with sufficient fullness the souls and fates of the Russian people with their daring, their scope, their passions and misfortunes . . . Neither Turgenev, nor Tolstoy, nor Dostoevsky could have accomplished this as Leskov did.[*]

---

[*] Quoted in *The Organic Worldview of Nikolai Leskov,* by Irmhild Christina Sperrle (Evanston, IL: Northwestern University Press, 2002), p. 6 (slightly revised).

Here Eikhenbaum was looking back at Leskov in his own time. In 1924, looking at the present and the writers of the early twentieth century, in an article entitled "In Search of a Genre," Eikhenbaum wrote: "The influence of Tolstoy and Dostoevsky has been replaced in an unexpected way by the influence of Leskov, as much in stylistic tendency as in that of genre." By way of example, he cites the "memoirs and autobiographical stories" of Maxim Gorky, who declared himself Leskov's disciple, then the major figures of the new Russian prose—Alexei Remizov, Andrei Bely, Evgeny Zamyatin, Mikhail Zoshchenko, Boris Pilnyak, Isaac Babel, and others. (Incidentally, in 1926 Evgeny Zamyatin made a stage version of what may be Leskov's most famous story, "Lefty," entitling it "The Flea.") Their work showed the influence of Leskov's art in two seemingly contradictory things: an "ornamentalism" of style, giving value to words, wordplay, puns, popular etymology; and a return to the primitive sources of storytelling, to speech, the voice of the storyteller, the act of telling. "We often forget," Eikhenbaum wrote, "that the word in itself has nothing to do with the printed letter, that it is a living, moving activity, formed by the voice, articulation, intonation, joined with gestures and mimicry."

Tolstoy once remarked cryptically, "Leskov is a writer for the future, and his life in literature is profoundly instructive." Eikhenbaum shows that Leskov's storytelling was indeed not a return to the past, a nostalgic imitation of old ways, but a new joining of past and future, a synthesis and interpenetration of old and new. In his preface to the critical anthology *Russian Prose* (1926), he refers to this fusion of archaism and innovation as "the dynamic of traditions": "We must become aware of the historical dynamic of traditions. We have forgotten far too many things and have blindly accepted far too many things. We have need of *culture*."

This third discovery of Leskov, by the modernist writers and then by the new criticism, also reached beyond the borders of Russia. We feel the same sense of excitement in Walter Benjamin's well-known essay, "The Storyteller: Reflections on the Works of Nikolai Leskov," published in 1936, and in the fine chapter on Leskov in D. S. Mirsky's *History of Russian Literature*, written in English and first published in 1926, the same year as *Russian Prose*. Mirsky ends with an admonition to his readers:

The Anglo-Saxon public have made up their mind as to what they want from a

Introduction

Russian writer, and Leskov does not fit in to this idea. But those who really want to know more about Russia must sooner or later recognize that Russia is not all contained in Dostoevsky and Chekhov, and that if you want to know a thing, you must first be free of prejudice and on your guard against hasty generalizations. Then they will perhaps come nearer to Leskov, who is generally recognized by Russians as the most Russian of Russian writers and the one who had the deepest and widest knowledge of the Russian people as it actually is.[*]

It is true that we meet people, see places, and witness events in Leskov's work that we do not find anywhere else in Russian literature. It is also true that, fantastic as they may often seem, they are almost always grounded in reality. In an open letter to his friend P. K. Shchebalsky, editor of the *Warsaw Journal*, dated December 10, 1884, Leskov wrote:

In the articles in your newspaper it is said that I have mainly *copied* living persons and recounted actual incidents. Whoever the author of those articles is—he is *perfectly right*. I have a gift for observation and perhaps a certain aptitude for analyzing feelings and motives, but I have *little fantasy*. I invent painfully and with difficulty, and therefore I have always needed living persons whose spiritual content interested me. They would take possession of me, and I would try to incarnate them in stories, which I also quite often based on real events.

In 1862, during his stay in Paris, away from the troubles that had overwhelmed him in Petersburg, Leskov wrote "The Musk-ox." He dated it very precisely on the final page: "Paris, November 28, 1862," as if he were marking an important moment in his life. In it for the first time he found his way as an artist; that is, he found his own manner of constructing and narrating a story, "perching it," as Hugh McLean has written, "neither solidly in the realm of reality nor in that of fiction, even realistic fiction, but in the no-man's-land between them."[†] The story portrays people from Leskov's own past (his maternal grandmother appears here for the first time and under her real name; the hero is modeled on a school friend from Orel); it includes seemingly irrelevant digressions, and is told in the first person by a narrator who may or may not be the author.

---

[*] *A History of Russian Literature from Its Beginnings to 1900* (New York: Alfred A. Knopf, 1926, 1927, 1949, 1958; Evanston, IL: Northwestern University Press, 1999), p. 333.

[†] *Nikolai Leskov: The Man and His Art* (Cambridge, MA: Harvard University Press, 1977), p. 110.

Leskov wrote other important stories during the sixties, among them his first real masterpiece, "The Lady Macbeth of Mtsensk," which in its single focus and sustained objectivity is unique among his works. But he gave most of his time to writing three long and more conventional novels, *No Way Out* (1864), *The Bypassed* (1865), and *At Daggers Drawn* (1870–71). All three were anti-nihilist and entered into the polemics that had begun with the editorial of 1862, so that while they are by far the longest of Leskov's works, they are also the most limited—"hasty, journalistic jobs," as he acknowledged later. Leskov's genius was not suited to the genre of the novel and he knew it, or he came to know it after *At Daggers Drawn*. While he was writing this last novel, he was already at work on something very different, a "novelistic chronicle," as he first called it, entitled *Cathedral Folk*, which was published in 1872. After *Cathedral Folk*, Leskov went on steadily producing works in his own genre, or genres, for the rest of his life.

The form of the chronicle appealed to Leskov because of its freedom from the artificial restrictions of plot, its seemingly unselective inclusiveness, its way of unrolling like a ribbon or a scroll. In a letter to the philologist and art historian Fyodor Buslaev, on June 1, 1877, he spoke of this "expanded view of the memoir form as a fictional work of art. To tell the truth, this form seems very convenient to me: it is more alive, or, better, more earnest than depicting scenes, in the grouping of which, even in such great masters as Walter Scott, the forcing is obvious—which is what simple people mean when they say, 'It happened just like in a novel.'"

The free form of the chronicle allowed Leskov to bring all sorts of materials into *Cathedral Folk*, including the notes of one of the book's heroes, the elderly archpriest Father Savely Tuberozov, written in his own churchly, slightly old-fashioned, but forceful style. In one passage, Father Savely "involuntarily" recalls reading *The Life and Opinions of Tristram Shandy*, by "the very witty pastor Sterne," and jots down his conclusion that, "as our patented nihilism is coming to an end among us, *Shandyism* is now beginning . . ." ("Shandyism," as Sterne himself defined it, is "the incapacity for fixing the mind on a serious object for two minutes together.") Laurence Sterne was one of Leskov's favorite writers, and the narrative form of many of his works besides *Cathedral Folk* is indebted to *Tristram Shandy* and *A Sentimental Journey*. At the end of his life, discussing his last story in a letter to Stasyulevich (January 8, 1895), he says: "I've written this piece in a whimsical manner, like the narrations of Hoffmann and Sterne, with digressions and ricochets."

The form of the journey as a narrative structure is embodied most fully in "The Enchanted Wanderer," which Leskov began in 1872, after journeying himself around Lake Ladoga, an area of ancient monasteries, fishing villages, and isolated peasant communities north of Petersburg. The full title in its first magazine publication in 1873 was "The Enchanted Wanderer: His Life, Experiences, Opinions, and Adventures," which clearly echoes the titles of works in the picaresque tradition, but in its "opinions" also gives a nod to *Tristram Shandy*. Here again Leskov chose a loose, accumulative form of storytelling, looped together by the "enchantment" that leads his hero in his wanderings from one chance encounter to another and one part of Russia to another, until it finally brings him to the place he was intended for by his mother's prayers before he was born. The story is told by the hero himself in response to questions from his fellow passengers as they sail across Lake Ladoga to the monastery of Valaam.

Leskov made use of various other forms of storytelling, giving them names like memoir, potpourri, paysage and genre, rhapsody, sketch, stories apropos ("I very much like this form of story about what 'was,' recounted 'apropos,'" he once wrote to Leo Tolstoy), and sometimes subtitling them "a story told on a grave," "a Moscow family secret," "a fantastic story," "a spiritualistic occurrence." Later in life, when he allied himself with Tolstoy, he wrote fables for publication by the Tolstoyan popular press, *The Mediator,* and he also wrote a series of legends set in the ancient Near East, Egypt, Byzantium, in early Christian times. He wrote a number of Christmas stories, and also a series of what he called "stories of righteous men," several of which are included in this collection ("Singlemind," "Deathless Golovan," "The Spook," "The Man on Watch," "The Enchanted Wanderer," "Lefty"). Leskov considered these last the most important part of his work. "The real strength of my talent lies in the positive types," he boasted in a letter to a friend. "Show me such an abundance of positive Russian types in another writer."* As Walter Benjamin says in "The Storyteller": "The righteous man is the advocate for created things and at the same time he is their highest embodiment."

---

* See note 26 to "Singlemind" for Leskov's account of how he came to write the stories of righteous men.

All of these forms are based essentially on the anecdote, which serious critics tend to scorn. Mirsky enthusiastically defends Leskov's practice:

His stories are mere anecdotes, told with enormous zest and ability, and even in his longer works his favorite way of characterizing his characters is by a series of anecdotes. This was quite contrary to the traditions of "serious" Russian fiction and induced the critics to regard Leskov as a mere jester. His most original stories are packed with incident and adventure to an extent that appeared ludicrous to the critics, who regarded ideas and messages as the principal thing.

Boris Eikhenbaum, in his essay "An 'Excessive' Writer," published in 1931 in honor of Leskov's hundredth birthday, says: "the anecdote . . . can be considered a sort of atom in Leskov's work. Its presence and action are felt everywhere." The anecdote is the most elementary form of story, told for its own sake or apropos of some more general topic of discussion in a group of friends, at a Christmas party, or among travelers stranded at an inn during a blizzard. This last is the occasion for the telling of "The Sealed Angel," a fine example of Leskov's composition at its most complex. The story is held together by the event of the title, the official "sealing" of an old icon, but it includes much else besides. The storyteller, who is also the central character, is an orphaned peasant who has worked all his life as a stonemason; the action, as I have already mentioned, involves the construction of the Nikolaevsky suspension bridge in Kiev, which Leskov witnessed in the early 1850s. The masons who build the bridge belong to the Old Believers, a group that separated from the official Russian Orthodox Church in 1666, in protest against the reforms of the patriarch Nikon. The Old Believers were anathematized by the Church and deprived of civil rights; they were often persecuted and tended to live in the more remote parts of the empire. They had their own ways of speaking, which had fascinated Leskov since his youth in Kiev, and which he captures in his narrator's voice. In 1863, soon after his return to Petersburg from Paris, Leskov was sent on an official mission to inspect the schools of the Old Believers in Riga, an experience that deepened his knowledge of and sympathy for their condition. The masons he portrays in "The Sealed Angel" are very devout, but have no priests or sacraments; their piety is centered on their collection of old icons, the most beautiful of which is the angel of the title. Leskov himself had become interested in icon painting, and particularly in the icons of the Old Believers, in the later 1860s. At around that time he made the acquaintance of an icon painter and restorer by the name of Nikita Sevastianovich Racheiskov, who was an Old Believer himself and lived in a shabby quarter of Petersburg inhabited mainly by Old Believers. Leskov visited him often, and in a tribute to him written after Racheiskov's death in 1886, he claimed that "The Sealed Angel" had been "composed entirely in Nikita's hot and stuffy workroom."* The icon painter who comes to help the masons in the story is named Sevastian, from Racheiskov's patronymic; he has enormous hands like Racheiskov's, and yet, like Racheiskov, he sometimes paints with brushes made of only three or four hairs. Much of the discourse on icon painting that plays so important a part in the story was noted down by Leskov from his talks with the master.

The construction of the Nikolaevsky bridge, the ways and speech of the Old Believers, the icon painter Racheiskov and his art—these are the realities Leskov builds on. And yet the story has nothing of the documentary about it. On the contrary, the storyteller's voice transforms it all into an intensely personal, human story, with touches of the visionary and fantastic. What calls up the story is a question one of the guests at the inn asks tauntingly at the beginning: "So you saw an angel, and he led you—is that it?" "Yes, sir," the stonemason replies, "I saw him, and he guided me."

In his letter to Shchebalsky, Leskov wrote of his need for living persons whose *spiritual content* interested him. That content is revealed in the spoken word. This sort of "oral writing" is known in Russian as *skaz*, from the verb *skazat*, to speak or tell. A story in Russian is a *rasskaz*, a folktale is a *skazka*. *Skaz* includes the teller in the tale, so that we do not simply read the printed word, but also hear the speaking voice; we listen to the telling and even begin to mouth the words ourselves. George Orwell's dictum "Good prose is like a window pane" does not apply here. On the contrary, language becomes physically present in *skaz*; we are as conscious of it as we are of the events it narrates. In "The Sealed Angel," the author, who places himself among the listeners, creates the frame setting; other listeners occasionally interrupt to ask questions; but the story itself

---

* Quoted in McLean, *Nikolai Leskov*, p. 233.

is told by the stonemason in his own particular language. *Skaz* is not merely an imitation of old-fashioned storytelling; it is a new form of written expression, even a "modern" one, which draws on the qualities of oral recitation.

Leskov's comic masterpiece, "Lefty," is subtitled "The *Skaz* of Cross-eyed Lefty from Tula and the Steel Flea." Its speech is the most richly and playfully misspoken Leskov ever invented. The first separate edition of the story, published in 1882, included a preface in which Leskov declared:

I wrote this legend down in Sestroretsk from the *skaz* of an old gunsmith there, a native of Tula, who had moved to the Sestra River back in the reign of the emperor Alexander I. Two years ago the storyteller was still of sound body and fresh memory; he gladly recalled the old days, greatly honored the sovereign Nikolai Pavlovich, lived "by the Old Belief," read sacred books, and bred canaries. People treated him with respect.

This was a mystification, meant simply to introduce his narrator, but readers and critics took him seriously. Whether they admired his "stenography" or thought he might have distorted the language somewhat in copying it down, they all believed the story was an actual transcription, and even said it was a well-known legend, heard long ago. But "Lefty" had cost him a lot of work (in a letter to Sergei Shubnitsky of September 19, 1887, he confessed: "This language . . . does not come easily, but with much difficulty, and only love of the task can make a man take up such mosaic work"), and Leskov decided to clarify things and reclaim his story by publishing an explanation in a prominent journal, declaring: "I made up the whole story last May, and Lefty is a character of *my own invention.*" He insisted on it several more times in various places, but that did little to dispel the illusion. Finally, when he prepared the story for his collected works in 1889, he cut the preface, leaving the fictional Tula gunsmith out entirely. But he is still there, because the whole adventure of the steel flea is told in his voice. The author himself appears only in the brief final chapter.

The question of the author's presence in Leskov's stories is a complicated one, because Leskov most often screens himself behind the figure of a narrator who stands for the author. We meet this "author" among the guests at the snowbound inn in "The Sealed Angel," on the boat with the enchanted wanderer, or taking down the story of the steel flea from the old gunsmith's dictation. There is no direct authorial commentary, no analysis, no psychological interpretation in Leskov's work ("it is half the art of storytelling to keep a story free of explanation," as Walter Benjamin observed). Yet Leskov insisted that art must serve the true and the good and that art for art's sake did not interest him at all. And in fact the real author's point of view does come through quite forcefully, though it takes some discernment to see what he sees. The conservative Slavophiles praised "Lefty" as a paean to deep Russia and the noble Russian craftsman. The scathing commentary on the conditions of Russian life passed them by. But it is not a matter of either/or: both are there.

Not all of Leskov's stories are composed in the language of *skaz*, but they are all *told*, as memoirs, stories apropos, or simply amusing and sophisticated anecdotes like "The Spirit of Madame de Genlis," "The Pearl Necklace," or "A Flaming Patriot," which are also far from simple. He always includes the situation of their telling, and they all share the complex relation of author and teller. In "The Spook," for instance, we see everything simultaneously through a boy's eyes and a man's. "The Voice of Nature," inconsequential as it might seem, prompted Benjamin to exclaim: "The way the profundity of this story is hidden beneath its silliness conveys an idea of Leskov's magnificent humor." "The White Eagle" has been interpreted in various ways: as a mockery of the vogue of spiritualism in Russia of the late 1870s, as an unmasking of an ambitious bureaucrat driven to hallucinations by his desire for a new decoration, as an exposure of deceit and conspiracy among provincial government officials. But the fantastic keeps evolving in this "fantastic story"; it refuses to be reduced to political satire or psychodrama, and ends in an almost mystical irresolution, as the hero admits in his last words. Even the clipped, objective report of "The Man on Watch" shifts in its brief chapters from one point of view to another, one character to another, setting them side by side—again with no commentary, no single resolving voice, until the author steps in at the end.

We have arranged the stories chronologically. The earliest, "The Lady Macbeth of Mtsensk," was written in 1864; the latest, "A Robbery," in 1887. We have not included works dealing with specifically churchly subjects, fine as they are, or the parables and legends of the 1890s, or any of the last darkly satirical stories, which were admirably translated (along with "Lefty," "Singlemind," and others) by William Edgerton and Hugh McLean, in *Satirical Stories of Nikolai Leskov* (New York: Pegasus, 1969). Our aim has been to bring together in one volume a broad and representative selection of Leskov's best work, so that a new generation of English-speaking readers may discover him for themselves.

RICHARD PEVEAR

Translators' Note

Leskov is notoriously difficult to translate. He wrote to his German translator: "'The Flea' is much too Russian and hardly translatable (on account of its language)" (October 26, 1888). A month later he softened a little: "If you translate 'Lefty,' you're the 'foremost magician.'" But a few days later he cautioned: "You will have a hard time with 'Lefty and the Flea.' A knowledge of colloquial German is not enough. What will you do with the sound effects and the plays on words?" In the face of these warnings, we have tried all the same to keep the whole story, including its sound effects and plays on words. And we have done the same with all the stories in this collection. That is not only the challenge, but also the delight of translating Leskov. The philosopher Jacques Maritain wrote to Pope Paul VI about a new French translation of the Bible (which he did not like): "The first duty of a translator . . . is always to respect the *word* itself that the author has used . . . and to seek its exact equivalent." He was not advocating a slavish literalism; he was defending the full meaning, meaning also the way of meaning, of the original.

The Enchanted Wanderer
and Other Stories

The Lady Macbeth of Mtsensk

A Sketch

The first song brings a blush to the cheek.

A SAYING

I

in our parts such characters sometimes turn up that, however many years ago you met them, you can never recall them without an inner trembling. To the number of such characters belongs the merchant's wife Katerina Lvovna Izmailova, who once played out a terrible drama, after which our gentlefolk, in someone's lucky phrase, started calling her "the Lady Macbeth of Mtsensk."

Katerina Lvovna was not born a beauty, but she was a woman of very pleasing appearance. She was only twenty-three years old; not tall, but shapely, with a neck as if carved from marble, rounded shoulders, a firm bosom, a fine, straight little nose, lively black eyes, a high and white brow, and very black, almost blue-black hair. She was from Tuskar in Kursk province and was given in marriage to our merchant Izmailov, not out of love or any sort of attraction, but just so, because Izmailov sent a matchmaker to propose, and she was a poor girl and could not choose her suitors. The house of Izmailov was not the least in our town: they traded in white flour, kept a big rented mill in the district, had orchards outside town, and in town had a fine house. Generally, they were well-to-do merchants. Besides, the family was very small: the father-in-law, Boris Timofeich Izmailov, was already nearly eighty, a longtime widower; his son, Zinovy Borisych, Katerina Lvovna's husband, was a little over fifty; then there was Katerina Lvovna, and that was all. In the five years of Katerina Lvovna's marriage to Zinovy Borisych, she had had no children. Nor did Zinovy Borisych have children from his first wife, with whom he had lived for some twenty years before becoming a widower and marrying Katerina Lvovna. He thought and hoped that God might grant an heir to his merchant name and capital from his second marriage; but in that he was again unlucky with Katerina Lvovna.

This childlessness greatly distressed Zinovy Borisych, and not only Zinovy Borisych, but also old Boris Timofeich, and even Katerina Lvovna herself was much grieved by it. For one thing, exceeding boredom in the merchant's locked-up tower, with its high walls and watchdogs running loose, had more than once filled the merchant's young wife with pining, to the point of stupefaction, and she would have been glad, God knows how glad, to nurse a little child; and for another thing, she was also sick of reproaches: "Why marry, what's the point of marrying; why bind a man's fate, barren woman?"—as if she really had committed some crime against her husband, and against her father-in-law, and against their whole honorable merchant family.

For all its ease and plenty, Katerina Lvovna's life in her father-in-law's house was most boring. She went visiting very little, and if she did go with her husband to call on his merchant friends, that was also no joy. They were all strict people: they watched how she sat, and how she walked, and how she stood. But Katerina Lvovna had an ardent nature, and when she had lived in poverty as a young girl, she had been accustomed to simplicity and freedom, running to the river with buckets, swimming under the pier in nothing but a shift, or showering sunflower husks over the garden gate on some young fellow passing by. Here it was all different. Her father-in-law and husband got up as early as could be, had their tea at six o'clock, and went about their business, while she dilly-dallied from room to room alone. It was clean everywhere, it was quiet and empty everywhere, icon lamps shone before the icons, and nowhere in the house was there a living sound, a human voice.

Katerina Lvovna would wander and wander about the empty rooms, start yawning with boredom, and climb the stairs to her marital bedroom in the small, high mezzanine. There, too, she sat, looked at how they hung up hemp or poured out flour by the storehouse—again she would start to yawn, and she was glad of it: she would doze off for an hour or two, then wake up—again the same Russian boredom, the boredom of a merchant's house, from which they say you could even happily hang yourself. Katerina Lvovna was not a lover of reading, and besides there were no books in their house except for the lives of the Kievan saints.[1]

Katerina Lvovna lived a boring life in the rich house of her father-in-law during the five years of her marriage to her unaffectionate husband; but, as often happens, no one paid the slightest attention to this boredom of hers.

II

In the sixth spring of Katerina Lvovna's marriage, the Izmailovs' mill dam burst. At that time, as if on purpose, a lot of work had been brought to the mill, and the breach proved enormous: water went under the lower sill, and to stop it up slapdash was impossible. Zinovy Borisych drove people to the mill from all around and sat there constantly himself; the business in town was managed by the old man alone, and Katerina Lvovna languished at home for whole days as alone as could be. At first she was still more bored without her husband, but then it came to seem even better to her: she felt freer by herself. Her heart had never really gone out to him, and without him there was at least one less commander over her.

Once Katerina Lvovna was sitting at the window on her upper floor, yawning, yawning, thinking of nothing in particular, and she finally felt ashamed to be yawning. And the weather outside was so wonderful: warm, bright, cheerful, and through the green wooden lattice of the garden various birds could be seen flitting from branch to branch in the trees.

"What in fact am I yawning for?" thought Katerina Lvovna. "I might at least get up and go for a walk in the yard or a stroll in the garden."

Katerina Lvovna threw on an old damask jacket and went out.

Outside it was so bright and the air was so invigorating, and in the gallery by the storehouses there was such merry laughter.

"What are you so glad about?" Katerina Lvovna asked her father-in-law's clerks.

"You see, dearest Katerina Lvovna, we've been weighing a live sow," an old clerk replied.

"What sow?"

"This sow Aksinya here, who gave birth to a son, Vassily, and didn't invite us to the christening," a fine fellow with a handsome, impudent face framed in jet-black curls and a barely sprouting beard told her boldly and merrily.

At that moment the fat mug of the ruddy cook Aksinya peeked out of a flour tub hung on a balance beam.

"Fiends, sleek-sided devils," the cook swore, trying to catch hold of the iron beam and climb out of the swinging tub.

"Weighs two hundred and fifty pounds before dinner, and once she's eaten a load of hay, there won't be weights enough," the handsome young fellow again explained, and, overturning the tub, he dumped the cook out onto the sacking piled in the corner.

The woman, cursing playfully, began putting herself to rights.

"Well, and how much might I weigh?" Katerina Lvovna joked, and, taking hold of the ropes, she stepped onto the plank.

"A hundred and fifteen pounds," the same handsome young Sergei said, throwing weights onto the balance. "Amazing!"

"What's amazing?"

"That you weigh over a hundred pounds, Katerina Lvovna. I figured a man could carry you around in his arms the whole day and not get tired out, but only feel the pleasure it gave him."

"What, you mean I'm not a human being or something? You'd get tired for sure," Katerina Lvovna replied, blushing slightly, not used to such talk and feeling a sudden surge of desire to loosen up and speak her fill of merry and playful words.

"God, no! I'd carry you all the way to happy Araby," Sergei replied to her remark.

"Your figuring's off, young fellow," said the little peasant doing the pouring. "What is it makes us heavy? Is it our body gives us weight? Our body, my dear man, means nothing in the scales: our strength, it's our strength gives us weight—not the body!"

"In my girlhood I was awfully strong," Katerina Lvovna said, again not restraining herself. "It wasn't every man who could beat me."

"Well, then, your hand please, ma'am, if that's really true," the handsome fellow asked.

Katerina Lvovna became embarrassed, but held out her hand.

"Aie, the ring, it hurts, let go!" Katerina Lvovna cried, when Sergei pressed her hand in his, and she shoved him in the chest with her free hand.

The young man let go of his mistress's hand, and her shove sent him flying two steps back.

"Mm—yes, and you figured she's just a woman," the little peasant said in surprise.

"Then suppose we try wrestling," Sergei retorted, tossing back his curls.

"Well, go on," replied Katerina Lvovna, brightening up, and she cocked her elbows.

Sergei embraced the young mistress and pressed her firm breasts to his red shirt. Katerina Lvovna was just trying to move her shoulders, but Sergei lifted her off the floor, held her in his arms, squeezed her, and gently sat her down on the overturned measuring tub.

Katerina Lvovna did not even have time to show her vaunted strength. Getting up from the tub, red as could be, she straightened the jacket that had fallen from her shoulders and quietly started out of the storehouse. Sergei coughed dashingly and shouted:

"Come on, you blessed blockheads! Pour, look sharp, get a move on; if there's a plus, the better for us."

It was as if he had paid no attention to what had just happened.

"He's a skirt-chaser, that cursed Seryozhka," the cook Aksinya was saying as she trudged after Katerina Lvovna. "The thief's got everything—the height, the face, the looks. Whatever woman you like, the scoundrel knows straight off how to cajole her, and he cajoles her and leads her into sin. And he's fickle, the scoundrel, as fickle as can be!"

"And you, Aksinya . . ." said the young mistress, walking ahead of her, "that is, your boy, is he alive?"

"He is, dearest, he is—what could happen to him? Whenever they're not wanted, they live."

"Where did you get him?"

"Ehh, just from fooling around—you live among people after all—just from fooling around."

"Has he been with us long, this young fellow?"

"Who? You mean Sergei?"

"Yes."

"About a month. He used to work for the Kopchonovs, but the master threw him out." Aksinya lowered her voice and finished: "They say he made love to the mistress herself . . . See what a dare-devil he is, curse his soul!"

III

A warm milky twilight hung over the town. Zinovy Borisych had not yet returned from the dam. The father-in-law, Boris Timofeich, was also not at home: he had gone to a friend's name-day party and had even told them not to expect him for supper. Katerina Lvovna, having nothing to do, had an early meal, opened the window in her room upstairs, and, leaning against the window frame, was husking sunflower seeds. The people in the kitchen had supper and went their ways across the yard to sleep: some to the sheds, some to the storehouses, some up into the fragrant haylofts. The last to leave the kitchen was Sergei. He walked about the yard, unchained the watchdogs, whistled, and, passing under Katerina Lvovna's window, glanced at her and made a low bow.

"Good evening," Katerina Lvovna said softly to him from her look-out, and the yard fell silent as a desert.

"Mistress!" someone said two minutes later at Katerina Lvovna's locked door.

"Who is it?" Katerina Lvovna asked, frightened.

"Please don't be frightened: it's me, Sergei," the clerk replied.

"What do you want, Sergei?"

"I have a little business with you, Katerina Lvovna: I want to ask a small thing of your honor; allow me to come in for a minute."

Katerina Lvovna turned the key and let Sergei in.

"What is it?" she asked, going back to the window.

"I've come to you, Katerina Lvovna, to ask if you might have some book to read. I'm overcome with boredom."

"I have no books, Sergei: I don't read them," Katerina Lvovna replied.

"Such boredom!" Sergei complained.

"Why should you be bored?"

"For pity's sake, how can I not be bored? I'm a young man, we live like in some monastery, and all I can see ahead is that I may just waste away in this solitude till my dying day. It sometimes even leads me to despair."

"Why don't you get married?"

"That's easy to say, mistress—get married! Who can I marry around here? I'm an insignificant man: no master's daughter will marry me, and from poverty, as you're pleased to know yourself, Katerina Lvovna, our kind are all uneducated. As if they could have any proper notion of love! Just look, if you please, at what notion there is even among the rich. Now you, I might say, for any such man as had feeling in him, you would be a comfort all his own, but here they keep you like a canary in a cage."

"Yes, it's boring for me" escaped Katerina Lvovna.

"How not be bored, mistress, with such a life! Even if you had somebody on the side, as others do, it would be impossible for you to see him."

"Well, there you're . . . it's not that at all. For me, if I'd had a baby, I think it would be cheerful with the two of us."

"As for that, if you'll allow me to explain to you, mistress, a baby also happens for some reason, and not just so. I've lived among masters for so many years now, and seen what kind of life women live among merchants, don't I also understand? As the song goes: 'Without my dearie, life's all sad and dreary,' and that dreariness, let me explain to you, Katerina Lvovna, wrings my own heart so painfully, I can tell you, that I could just cut it out of my breast with a steel knife and throw it at your little feet. And it would be easier, a hundred times easier for me then . . ."

Sergei's voice trembled.

"What are you doing talking to me about your heart? That's got nothing to do with me. Go away . . ."

"No, please, mistress," said Sergei, trembling all over and taking a step towards Katerina Lvovna. "I know, I see very well and even feel and understand, that it's no easier for you than for me in this world; except that now," he said in the same breath, "now, for the moment, all this is in your hands and in your power."

"What? What's that? What have you come to me for? I'll throw myself out the window," said Katerina Lvovna, feeling herself in the unbearable power of an indescribable fear, and she seized hold of the windowsill.

"Oh, my life incomparable, why throw yourself out?" Sergei whispered flippantly, and, tearing the young mistress from the window, he took her in a firm embrace.

"Oh! Oh! Let go of me," Katerina Lvovna moaned softly, weakening under Sergei's hot kisses, and involuntarily pressing herself to his powerful body.

Sergei picked his mistress up in his arms like a child and carried her to a dark corner.

A hush fell over the room, broken only by the measured ticking of her husband's pocket watch, hanging over the head of Katerina Lvovna's bed; but it did not interfere with anything.

"Go," said Katerina Lvovna half an hour later, not looking at Sergei and straightening her disheveled hair before a little mirror.

"Why should I leave here now?" Sergei answered her in a happy voice.

"My father-in-law will lock the door."

"Ah, my soul, my soul! What sort of people have you known, if a door is their only way to a woman? For me there are doors everywhere—to you or from you," the young fellow replied, pointing to the posts that supported the gallery.

IV

Zinovy Borisych did not come home for another week, and all that week, every night till dawn, his wife made merry with Sergei.

During those nights in Zinovy Borisych's bedroom, much wine from the father-in-law's cellar was drunk, and many sweetmeats were eaten, and many were the kisses on the mistress's sugary lips, and the toyings with black curls on the soft pillow. But no road runs smooth forever; there are also bumps.

Boris Timofeich was not sleepy: the old man wandered about the quiet house in a calico nightshirt, went up to one window, then another, looked out, and the red shirt of the young fellow Sergei was quietly sliding down the post under his daughter-in-law's window. There's news for you! Boris Timofeich leaped out and seized the fellow's legs. Sergei swung his arm to give the master a hearty one on the ear, but stopped, considering that it would make a big to-do.

"Out with it," said Boris Timofeich. "Where have you been, you thief you?"

"Wherever I was, I'm there no longer, Boris Timofeich, sir," replied Sergei.

"Spent the night with my daughter-in-law?"

"As for where I spent the night, master, that I do know, but you listen to what I say, Boris Timofeich: what's done, my dear man, can't be undone; at least don't bring disgrace on your merchant house. Tell me, what do you want from me now? What satisfaction would you like?"

"I'd like to give you five hundred lashes, you serpent," replied Boris Timofeich.

"The guilt is mine—the will is yours," the young man agreed. "Tell me where to go, and enjoy yourself, drink my blood."

Boris Timofeich led Sergei to his stone larder and lashed him with a whip until he himself had no strength left. Sergei did not utter a single moan, but he chewed up half his shirtsleeve with his teeth.

Boris Timofeich abandoned Sergei to the larder until the mince-meat of his back healed, shoved a clay jug of water at him, put a heavy padlock on the door, and sent for his son.

But to go a hundred miles on a Russian country road is not a quick journey even now, and for Katerina Lvovna to live an extra hour without Sergei had already become intolerable. She suddenly unfolded the whole breadth of her awakened nature and became so resolute that there was no stopping her. She found out where Sergei was, talked to him through the iron door, and rushed to look for the keys. "Let Sergei go, papa"—she came to her father-in-law.

The old man simply turned green. He had never expected such insolent boldness from his sinful but until then always obedient daughter-in-law.

"What do you mean, you such-and-such," he began shaming Katerina Lvovna.

"Let him go," she said. "I swear on my conscience, there's been nothing bad between us yet."

"Nothing bad!" he said, gnashing his teeth. "And what were you doing during the nights? Plumping up your husband's pillows?"

But she kept at it: "Let him go, let him go."

"In that case," said Boris Timofeich, "here's what you'll get: once your husband comes, you honest wife, we'll whip you in the stable with our own hands, and I'll send that scoundrel to jail tomorrow."

So Boris Timofeich decided; but his decision was not to be realized.

V

In the evening, Boris Timofeich ate a bit of kasha with mushrooms and got heartburn; then suddenly there was pain in the pit of his stomach; he was seized with terrible vomiting, and towards morning he died, just as the rats died in his storehouses, Katerina Lvovna having always prepared a special food for them with her own hands, using a dangerous white powder entrusted to her keeping.

Katerina Lvovna delivered her Sergei from the old man's stone larder and, with no shame before people's eyes, placed him in her husband's bed to rest from her father-in-law's beating; and the father-in-law, Boris Timofeich, they buried without second thoughts, according to the Christian rule. Amazingly enough, no one thought anything of it: Boris Timofeich had died, died from eating mushrooms, as many had died from eating them. They buried Boris Timofeich hastily, without even waiting for his son, because the weather was warm, and the man sent to the mill for Zinovy Borisych had not found him there. He had had the chance to buy a woodlot cheaply another hundred miles away: he had gone to look at it and had not properly told anyone where he was going.

Having settled this matter, Katerina Lvovna let herself go entirely. She had not been a timid one before, but now there was no telling what she would think up for herself; she strutted about, gave orders to everyone in the house, and would not let Sergei leave her side. The servants wondered about it, but Katerina Lvovna's generous hand managed to find them all, and the wondering suddenly went away. "The mistress is having an intriguery with Sergei, that's all," they figured. "It's her business, she'll answer for it."

Meanwhile, Sergei recovered, unbent his back, and, again the finest of fellows, a bright falcon, walked about beside Katerina Lvovna, and once more they led a most pleasant life. But time raced on not only for them: the offended husband, Zinovy Borisych, was hurrying home after his long absence.

VI

In the yard after lunch it was scorching hot, and the darting flies were unbearably annoying. Katerina Lvovna closed the bedroom shutters, covered the window from inside with a woolen shawl, and lay down to rest with Sergei on the merchant's high bed. Katerina Lvovna sleeps and does not sleep, she is in some sort of daze, her face is bathed in sweat, and her breathing is hot and heavy. Katerina Lvovna feels it is time for her to wake up, time to go to the garden and have tea, but she simply cannot get up. At last the cook came and knocked on the door: "The samovar's getting cold under the apple tree," she said. Katerina Lvovna turned over with effort and began to caress the cat. And the cat goes rubbing himself between her and Sergei, and he's so fine, gray, big, and fat as can be . . . and he has whiskers like a village headman. Katerina Lvovna feels his fluffy fur, and he nuzzles her with his nose: he thrusts his blunt snout into her resilient breast and sings a soft song, as if telling her of love. "How did this tomcat get here?" Katerina Lvovna thinks. "I've set cream on the windowsill: the vile thing's sure to lap it up. He should be chased out," she decided and was going to grab him and throw him out, but her fingers went through him like mist. "Where did this cat come from anyway?" Katerina Lvovna reasons in her nightmare. "We've never had any cat in our bedroom, and look what a one has got in!" She again went to take hold of him, and again he was not there. "Oh, what on earth is this? Can it really be a cat?" thought Katerina Lvovna. She was suddenly dumbstruck, and her drowsiness and dreaming were completely driven away. Katerina Lvovna looked around the room—there is no cat, there is only handsome Sergei lying there, pressing her breast to his hot face with his powerful hand.

Katerina Lvovna got up, sat on the bed, kissed Sergei, kissed and caressed him, straightened the rumpled featherbed, and went to the garden to have tea; and the sun had already dropped down quite low, and a wonderful, magical evening was descending upon the thoroughly heated earth.

"I slept too long," Katerina Lvovna said to Aksinya as she seated herself on the rug under the blossoming apple tree to have tea. "What could it mean, Aksinyushka?" she asked the cook, wiping the saucer with a napkin herself.

"What's that, my dear?"

"It wasn't like in a dream, but a cat kept somehow nudging into me wide awake."

"Oh, what are you saying?"

"Really, a cat nudging."

Katerina Ivanovna told how the cat was nudging into her.

"And why were you caressing him?"

"Well, that's just it! I myself don't know why I caressed him."

"A wonder, really!" the cook exclaimed.

"I can't stop marveling myself."

"It's most certainly about somebody sidling up to you, or something else like that."

"But what exactly?"

"Well, *what exactly*—that's something nobody can explain to you, my dear, what exactly, only there will be something."

"I kept seeing a crescent moon in my dream and then there was this cat," Katerina Lvovna went on.

"A crescent moon means a baby."

Katerina Lvovna blushed.

"Shouldn't I send Sergei here to your honor?" Aksinya hazarded, offering herself as a confidante.

"Well, after all," replied Katerina Lvovna, "you're right, go and send him: I'll have tea with him here."

"Just what I say, send him here," Aksinya concluded, and she waddled ducklike to the garden gate.

Katerina Lvovna also told Sergei about the cat.

"Sheer fantasy," replied Sergei.

"Then why is it, Seryozha, that I've never had this fantasy before?"

"There's a lot that never was before! Before I used to just look at you and pine away, but now—ho-ho!—I possess your whole white body."

Sergei embraced Katerina Lvovna, spun her in the air, and playfully landed her on the fluffy rug.

"Oh, my head is spinning!" said Katerina Lvovna. "Seryozha, come here; sit beside me," she called, lying back and stretching herself out in a luxurious pose.

The young fellow, bending down, went under the low apple tree, all bathed in white flowers, and sat on the rug at Katerina Lvovna's feet.

"So you pined for me, Seryozha?"

"How I pined!"

"How did you pine? Tell me about it."

"How can I tell about it? Is it possible to describe how you pine? I was heartsick."

"Why is it, Seryozha, that I didn't feel you were suffering over me? They say you can feel it."

Sergei was silent.

"And why did you sing songs, if you were longing for me? Eh? Didn't I hear you singing in the gallery?" Katerina Lvovna went on asking tenderly.

"So what if I sang songs? A mosquito also sings all his life, but it's not for joy," Sergei answered drily.

There was a pause. Katerina Lvovna was filled with the highest rapture from these confessions of Sergei's.

She wanted to talk, but Sergei sulked and kept silent.

"Look, Seryozha, what paradise, what paradise!" Katerina Lvovna exclaimed, looking through the dense branches of the blossoming apple tree that covered her at the clear blue sky in which there hung a fine full moon.

The moonlight coming through the leaves and flowers of the apple tree scattered the most whimsical bright spots over Katerina Lvovna's face and whole recumbent body; the air was still; only a light, warm breeze faintly stirred the sleepy leaves and spread the subtle fragrance of blossoming herbs and trees. There was a breath of something languorous, conducive to laziness, sweetness, and obscure desires.

Receiving no answer, Katerina Lvovna fell silent again and went on looking at the sky through the pale pink apple blossoms. Sergei, too, was silent; only he was not interested in the sky. His arms around his knees, he stared fixedly at his boots.

A golden night! Silence, light, fragrance, and beneficent, vivifying warmth. Far across the ravine, beyond the garden, someone struck up a resounding song; by the fence, in the bird-cherry thicket, a nightingale trilled and loudly throbbed; in a cage on a tall pole a sleepy quail began to rave, and a fat horse sighed languidly behind the stable wall, and outside the garden fence a merry pack of dogs raced noiselessly across the green and disappeared into the dense black shadow of the half-ruined old salt depots.

Katerina Lvovna propped herself on her elbow and looked at the tall garden grass; and the grass played with the moonbeams, broken up by the flowers and leaves of the trees. It was all gilded by these intricate bright spots, which flashed and trembled on it like live, fiery butterflies, or as if all the grass under the trees had been caught in a lunar net and was swaying from side to side.

"Ah, Seryozhechka, how lovely!" Katerina Lvovna exclaimed, looking around.

Sergei glanced about indifferently.

"Why are you so joyless, Seryozha? Or are you already tired of my love?"

"Why this empty talk!" Sergei answered drily, and, bending down, he lazily kissed Katerina Lvovna.

"You're a deceiver, Seryozha," Katerina Lvovna said jealously. "You're insubstantial."

"Such words don't even apply to me," Sergei replied in a calm tone.

"Then why did you kiss me that way?"

Sergei said nothing at all.

"It's only husbands and wives," Katerina Lvovna went on, playing with his curls, "who shake the dust off each other's lips like that. Kiss me so that these young apple blossoms over us fall to the ground. Like this, like this," Katerina Lvovna whispered, twining around her lover and kissing him with passionate abandon.

"Listen to what I tell you, Seryozha," Katerina Lvovna began a little later. "Why is it that the one and only word they say about you is that you're a deceiver?"

"Who's been yapping about me like that?"

"Well, people talk."

"Maybe I deceived the unworthy ones."

"And why were you fool enough to deal with unworthy ones? With unworthy ones there shouldn't be any love."

"Go on, talk! Is that sort of thing done by reasoning? It's all temptation. You break the commandment with her quite simply, without any of these intentions, and then she's there hanging on your neck. That's love for you!"

"Now listen, Seryozha! How it was with those others I don't know and don't want to know; only since you cajoled me into this present love of ours, and you know yourself that I agreed to it as much by my own will as by your cunning, if you deceive me, Seryozha, if you exchange me for anybody else, no matter who, then—forgive me, friend of my heart—I won't part with you alive."

Sergei gave a start.

"But Katerina Lvovna, my bright light!" he roused himself. "Look at how things are with us. You noticed just now that I'm pensive today, but you don't consider how I could help being pensive. It's like my whole heart's drowned in clotted blood!"

"Tell me, Seryozha, tell me your grief."

"What's there to tell? Right now, first off, with God's blessing, your husband comes back, and you, Sergei Filipych, off with you, take yourself to the garden yard with the musicians, and watch from under the shed how the candle burns in Katerina Lvovna's bedroom, while she plumps up the featherbed and goes to sleep with her lawful Zinovy Borisych."

"That will never be!" Katerina Lvovna drawled gaily and waved her hand.

"How will it never be? It's my understanding that anything else is even quite impossible for you. But I, too, have a heart in me, Katerina Lvovna, and I can see my suffering."

"Ah, well, enough about all that."

Katerina Lvovna was pleased with this expression of Sergei's jealousy, and she laughed and again started kissing him.

"And to repeat," Sergei went on, gently freeing his head from Katerina Lvovna's arms, bare to the shoulders, "and to repeat, I must say that my most insignificant position has made me consider this way and that way more than once and maybe more than a dozen times. If I were, so to speak, your equal, a gentleman or a merchant, never in my life would I part with you, Katerina Lvovna. But as it is, consider for yourself, what sort of man am I next to you? Seeing now how you're taken by your lily-white hands and led to the bedroom, I'll have to endure it all in my heart, and maybe I'll turn into a man who despises himself forever. Katerina Lvovna! I'm not like those others who find it all the same, so long as they get enjoyment from a woman. I feel what a thing love is and how it sucks at my heart like a black serpent."

"Why do you keep talking to me about all this?" Katerina Lvovna interrupted him.

She felt sorry for Sergei.

"Katerina Lvovna! How can I not talk about it? How? When maybe it's all been explained to him and written to him already, and maybe in no great space of time, but even by tomorrow there'll be no trace of Sergei left on the premises?"

"No, no, don't speak of it, Seryozha! Never in the world will it happen that I'm left without you," Katerina Lvovna comforted him with the same caresses. "If things start going that way . . . either he or I won't live, but you'll stay with me."

"There's no way that can follow, Katerina Lvovna," Sergei replied, shaking his head mournfully and sadly. "I'm not glad of my own life on account of this love. I should have loved what's worth no more than me and been content with it. Can there be any permanent love between us? Is it any great honor for you having me as a lover? I'd like to be your husband before the pre-eternal holy altar: then, even considering myself as always lesser than you, I could still show everybody publicly how I deserve my wife by my honoring her . . ."

Katerina Lvovna was bemused by these words of Sergei's, by this jealousy of his, by this wish of his to marry her—a wish that always pleases a woman, however brief her connection with the man before marriage. Katerina Lvovna was now ready, for the sake of Sergei, to go through fire, through water, to prison, to the cross. He made her fall so in love with him that her devotion to him knew no measure. She was out of her mind with happiness; her blood boiled, and she could no longer listen to anything. She quickly stopped Sergei's lips with her palm and, pressing his head to her breast, said:

"Well, now I know that I'm going to make a merchant of you and live with you in all propriety. Only don't upset me for nothing, while things still haven't gotten there."

And again there were kisses and caresses.

The old clerk, asleep in the shed, began to hear through his sound sleep, in the stillness of the night, now whispering and quiet laughter, as if mischievous children were discussing some wicked way to mock feeble old age; now ringing and merry laughter, as if mermaids were tickling somebody. It was all Katerina Lvovna frolicking and playing with her husband's young clerk, basking in the moonlight and rolling on the soft rug. White young blossoms from the curly apple tree poured down on them, poured down, and then stopped pouring down. Meanwhile, the short summer night was passing; the moon hid behind the steep roofs of the tall storehouses and looked askance at the earth, growing dimmer and dimmer; a piercing cat duet came from the kitchen roof, then spitting, angry snarling, after which two or three cats, losing hold, tumbled noisily down a bunch of boards leaning against the roof.

"Let's go to sleep," Katerina Lvovna said slowly, as if worn out, getting up from the rug and, just as she had lain there, in nothing but her shift and white petticoat, she went off across the quiet, the deathly quiet merchants' yard, and Sergei came behind her carrying the rug and her blouse, which she had thrown off during their mischief-making.

VII

As soon as Katerina Lvovna blew out the candle and lay down, completely undressed, on the soft featherbed, sleep drew its cloak over her head. Having had her fill of play and pleasure, Katerina Lvovna fell asleep so soundly that her leg sleeps and her arm sleeps; but again she hears through her sleep how the door seems to open again and last night's cat drops like a heavy lump on the bed.

"What, really, is this punishment with the cat?" the tired Katerina Lvovna reasoned. "I just now locked the door on purpose, with my own hands, the window is shut, and he's here again. I'll throw him out right now." Katerina Lvovna went to get up, but her sleepy arms and legs refuse to serve her; and the cat walks all over her, and purrs in such a peculiar way, as if he were speaking human words. Katerina Lvovna even got gooseflesh all over.

"No," she thinks, "the only thing to do is make sure to bring some holy water to bed tomorrow, because this peculiar cat has taken to me."

But the cat goes purr-murr in her ear, buries his snout, and then speaks clearly: "What sort of cat am I! As if I'm a cat! It's very clever of you, Katerina Lvovna, to reason that I'm not a cat at all, but the distinguished merchant Boris Timofeich. Only I'm feeling bad now, because my guts are all burst inside me from my daughter-in-law's little treat. That's why I've been reduced down like this," he purrs, "and now seem like a cat to those with little understanding of who I really am. Well, how's life going for you, Katerina Lvovna? Are you keeping faithfully to your law? I've come from the cemetery on purpose to see how you and Sergei Filipych warm your husband's bed. Purr-murr, but I can't see anything. Don't be afraid of me: you see, my eyes rotted out from your little treat. Look into my eyes, my friend, don't be afraid!"

Katerina Lvovna looked and screamed to high heaven. Again the cat is lying between her and Sergei, and the head of this cat Boris Timofeich is as big as the dead man's, and in place of eyes there are two fiery circles spinning, spinning in opposite directions!

Sergei woke up, calmed Katerina Lvovna, and fell asleep again; but sleep had totally deserted her—luckily.

She lies with open eyes and suddenly hears a noise as if someone has climbed the gate in the yard. Now the dogs come rushing, then quiet down—must have started fawning. Now another minute passes, and the iron latch clicks downstairs, and the door opens. "Either I'm imagining it all, or it's my Zinovy Borisych come home, because the door's been opened with the spare key," thought Katerina Lvovna, and she hurriedly gave Sergei a shove.

"Listen, Seryozha," she said, and she propped herself on her elbow and pricked up her ears.

Someone was indeed coming up the stairs, stepping carefully on one foot after the other, approaching the locked door of the bedroom.

Katerina Lvovna quickly leaped out of bed in nothing but her shift and opened the window. At the same moment, barefoot Sergei jumped out onto the gallery and twined his legs around the post, which he had more than once used to climb down from his mistress's bedroom.

"No, don't, don't! Lie down here . . . don't go far," Katerina Lvovna whispered and threw his shoes and clothes out to him, and herself darted back under the blanket and lay waiting.

Sergei obeyed Katerina Lvovna: he did not slide down the post, but huddled on the gallery under a bast mat.

Meanwhile, Katerina Lvovna hears her husband come to the door and listen, holding his breath. She even hears the quickened beating of his jealous heart; but it is not pity but wicked laughter that is bursting from Katerina Lvovna.

"Go searching for yesteryear," she thinks to herself, smiling and breathing like an innocent babe.

This lasted for some ten minutes; but Zinovy Borisych finally got tired of standing outside the door and listening to his wife sleeping: he knocked.

"Who's there?" Katerina Lvovna called out, not at once and as if in a sleepy voice.

"It's me," replied Zinovy Borisych.

"Is that you, Zinovy Borisych?"

"Yes, me! As if you don't hear!"

Katerina Lvovna jumped up just as she was, in her shift, let her husband into the room, and dove back into the warm bed.

"It's getting cold before dawn," she said, wrapping herself in the blanket.

Zinovy Borisych came in looking around, said a prayer, lit a candle, and glanced around again.

"How's your life going?" he asked his spouse.

"Not bad," answered Katerina Lvovna, and, getting up, she began to put on a calico bed jacket.

"Shall I set up the samovar?" she asked.

"Never mind, call Aksinya, let her do it."

Katerina Lvovna quickly slipped her bare feet into her shoes and ran out. She was gone for about half an hour. During that time she started the samovar herself and quietly fluttered out to Sergei on the gallery.

"Stay here," she whispered.

"How long?" Sergei asked, also in a whisper.

"Oh, what a dimwit you are! Stay till I tell you."

And Katerina Lvovna herself put him back in his former place.

From out there on the gallery, Sergei could hear everything that went on in the bedroom. He hears the door open again and Katerina Lvovna return to her husband. He hears every word.

"What were you doing there so long?" Zinovy Borisych asked his wife.

"Setting up the samovar," she replied calmly.

There was a pause. Sergei hears Zinovy Borisych hang up his coat on the coat rack. Now he is washing, snorting and splashing water all over; now he asks for a towel; the talk begins again.

"Well, so how is it you buried papa?" the husband inquires.

"Just so," says the wife, "he died, we buried him."

"And what an astonishing thing it was!"

"God knows," Katerina Lvovna replied and rattled the cups.

Zinovy Borisych walked mournfully about the room.

"Well, and how have you passed your time here?" Zinovy Borisych again began asking his wife.

"Our joys here, I expect, are known to everybody: we don't go to balls, nor to theaters likewise."

"And it seems you take little joy in your husband," Zinovy Borisych hazarded, glancing out of the corner of his eye.

"We're not so young as to lose our minds when we meet. How do you want me to rejoice? Look how I'm bustling, running around for your pleasure."

Katerina Lvovna ran out again to fetch the samovar and again sprang over to Sergei, pulled at him, and said: "Look sharp, Seryozha!"

Sergei did not quite know what it was all about, but he got ready anyhow.

Katerina Lvovna came back, and Zinovy Borisych was kneeling on the bed, hanging his silver watch with a beaded chain on the wall above the headboard.

"Why is it, Katerina Lvovna, that you, in your solitary situation, made the bed up for two?" he suddenly asked his wife somehow peculiarly.

"I kept expecting you," replied Katerina Lvovna, looking at him calmly.

"I humbly thank you for that . . . And this little object now, how does it come to be lying on your bed?"

Zinovy Borisych picked up Sergei's narrow woolen sash from the sheet and held it by one end before his wife's eyes.

Katerina Lvovna did not stop to think for a moment.

"Found it in the garden," she said, "tied up my skirt with it."

"Ah, yes!" Zinovy Borisych pronounced with particular emphasis. "We've also heard a thing or two about your skirts."

"What is it you've heard?"

"All about your nice doings."

"There are no such doings of mine."

"Well, we'll look into that, we'll look into everything," Zinovy Borisych replied, moving his empty cup towards his wife.

Katerina Lvovna was silent.

"We'll bring all these doings of yours to light, Katerina Lvovna," Zinovy Borisych went on after a long pause, scowling at his wife.

"Your Katerina Lvovna is not so terribly frightened. She's not much afraid of that," she replied.

"What? What?" cried Zinovy Borisych, raising his voice.

"Never mind—drop it," replied his wife.

"Well, you'd better look out! You're getting a bit too talkative!"

"Why shouldn't I be talkative?" Katerina Lvovna retorted.

"You'd better watch yourself."

"There's no reason for me to watch myself. Wagging tongues wag something to you, and I have to take all kinds of insults! That's a new one!"

"Not wagging tongues, but certain knowledge about your amours."

"About what amours?" cried Katerina Lvovna, blushing unfeignedly.

"I know what."

"If you know, then speak more clearly!"

Zinovy Borisych was silent and again moved the empty cup towards his wife.

"Clearly there's nothing to talk about," Katerina Lvovna answered with disdain, defiantly throwing a teaspoon onto her husband's saucer. "Well, tell me, who have they denounced to you? Who is my lover according to you?"

"You'll find out, don't be in such a hurry."

"Is it Sergei they've been yapping about?"

"We'll find out, we'll find out, Katerina Lvovna. My power over you no one has taken away and no one can take away . . . You'll talk yourself . . ."

"Ohh, I can't bear that!" Katerina Lvovna gnashed her teeth and, turning white as a sheet, unexpectedly rushed out the door.

"Well, here he is," she said a few seconds later, leading Sergei into the room by the sleeve. "Question him and me about what you know. Maybe you'll find out a lot more than you'd like!"

Zinovy Borisych was at a loss. He glanced now at Sergei, who was standing in the doorway, now at his wife, who calmly sat on the edge of the bed with her arms crossed, and understood nothing of what was approaching.

"What are you doing, you serpent?" he barely brought himself to utter, not getting up from his armchair.

"Question us about what you know so well," Katerina Lvovna replied insolently. "You thought you'd scare me with a beating," she went on, winking significantly. "That will never be; but what I knew I would do to you, even before these threats of yours, that I am going to do."

"What's that? Get out!" Zinovy Borisych shouted at Sergei.

"Oh, yes!" Katerina Lvovna mocked.

She nimbly locked the door, put the key in her pocket, and again sprawled on the bed in her little jacket.

"Now, Seryozhechka, come here, come, darling," she beckoned the clerk to her.

Sergei shook his curls and boldly sat down by his mistress.

"Oh, Lord! My God! What is this? What are you doing, you bar-

barians!?" cried Zinovy Borisych, turning all purple and getting up from his chair.

"What? You don't like it? Look, look, my bright falcon, how beautiful!"

Katerina Lvovna laughed and passionately kissed Sergei in front of her husband.

At the same moment, a deafening slap burned on her cheek, and Zinovy Borisych rushed for the open window.

VIII

"Ah . . . Ah, so that's it! . . . Well, my dear friend, thank you very much. That's just what I was waiting for!" Katerina Lvovna cried. "Now it's clear . . . it's going to be my way, not yours . . ."

In a single movement she pushed Sergei away from her, quickly threw herself at her husband, and before Zinovy Borisych had time to reach the window, she seized him by the throat from behind with her slender fingers and threw him down on the floor like a damp sheaf of hemp.

Having fallen heavily and struck the back of his head with full force against the floor, Zinovy Borisych lost his mind completely. He had never expected such a quick denouement. The first violence his wife used on him showed him that she was ready for anything, if only to be rid of him, and that his present position was extremely dangerous. Zinovy Borisych realized it all instantly in the moment of his fall and did not cry out, knowing that his voice would not reach anyone's ear, but would only speed things up still more. He silently shifted his eyes and rested them with an expression of anger, reproach, and suffering on his wife, whose slender fingers were tightly squeezing his throat.

Zinovy Borisych did not defend himself; his arms, with tightly clenched fists, lay stretched out and twitched convulsively. One of them was quite free; the other Katerina Lvovna pinned to the floor with her knee.

"Hold him," she whispered indifferently to Sergei, turning to her husband herself.

Sergei sat on his master, pinning down both his arms with his knees, and was about to put his hands around his throat under Katerina Lvovna's, but just then he cried out desperately himself. Seeing his offender, blood vengeance aroused all the last strength in Zinovy Borisych: with a terrible effort, he tore his pinned-down arms from under Sergei's knees and, seizing Sergei by his black curls, sank his teeth into his throat like a beast. But that did not last long: Zinovy Borisych at once uttered a heavy moan and dropped his head.

Katerina Lvovna, pale, almost breathless, stood over her husband and her lover; in her right hand was a cast-iron candlestick, which she held by the upper end, the heavy part down. A thin trickle of crimson blood ran down Zinovy Borisych's temple and cheek.

"A priest," Zinovy Borisych moaned dully, throwing his head back with loathing as far as he could from Sergei, who was sitting on him. "To confess," he uttered still more indistinctly, trembling and looking from the corner of his eye at the warm blood thickening under his hair.

"You'll be all right like this," Katerina Lvovna whispered.

"Well, no more dawdling with him," she said to Sergei. "Squeeze his throat well and good."

Zinovy Borisych wheezed.

Katerina Lvovna bent down, pressed her own hands to Sergei's hands, which lay on her husband's throat, and put her ear to his chest. After five quiet minutes, she stood up and said: "Enough, he's had it."

Sergei also stood up and let out a long breath. Zinovy Borisych lay dead, with a crushed throat and a gashed temple. Under his head on the left side was a small spot of blood, which, however, was no longer pouring from the clotted wound stopped up with hair.

Sergei carried Zinovy Borisych to the cellar under the floor of the same stone larder where he himself had been locked up so recently by the late Boris Timofeich and returned to the room upstairs. Meanwhile, Katerina Lvovna, having rolled up the sleeves of her bed jacket and tucked her skirt up high, was carefully washing off with a soapy sponge the bloodstain left by Zinovy Borisych on the floor of his bedroom. The water was not yet cold in the samovar from which Zinovy Borisych had steamed his little merchant's soul in poisoned tea, and the stain was washed away without a trace.

Katerina Lvovna took the copper basin and soapy sponge.

"Light, here," she said to Sergei, going to the door. "Lower, hold it lower," she said, carefully studying all the floorboards over which Sergei had dragged Zinovy Borisych to the cellar.

In only two places on the painted floor were there two tiny spots the size of a cherry. Katerina Lvovna rubbed them with the sponge and they disappeared.

"That'll teach you to sneak up on your wife like a thief and spy on her," said Katerina Lvovna, straightening up and glancing in the direction of the larder.

"Finished off," said Sergei, and he jumped at the sound of his own voice.

When they returned to the bedroom, a thin red strip of dawn was cutting across the east and, lightly gilding the blossom-covered apple trees, peeked through the green slats of the garden fence into Katerina Lvovna's room.

The old clerk, a short coat thrown over his shoulders, crossing himself and yawning, came trudging through the yard from the shed to the kitchen.

Katerina Lvovna carefully drew the shutter closed and looked Sergei over attentively, as if she wished to see into his soul.

"So now you're a merchant," she said, laying her white hands on Sergei's shoulders.

Sergei made no reply.

His lips were trembling, he was shaking feverishly. Katerina Lvovna's lips were merely cold.

After two days, Sergei had big calluses on his hands from the pick and heavy spade; but Zinovy Borisych was laid away so nicely in his cellar that, without the help of his widow or her lover, no one would have been able to find him before the general resurrection.

IX

Sergei went around with his neck wrapped in a crimson scarf and complained of a swelling in his throat. Meanwhile, before the traces left on Sergei by Zinovy Borisych's teeth had healed, Katerina Lvovna's husband was missed. Sergei himself began speaking of him even more often than others. He would sit by the gate in the evening with other young fellows and say: "Really, lads, how is it the master hasn't turned up yet?"

The young fellows were also wondering.

And then news came from the mill that the master had hired

horses and gone home long ago. The driver who had taken him said that Zinovy Borisych had seemed to be in distress, and had dismissed him somehow strangely: about two miles from town, near the monastery, he got off the cart, took his bag, and walked away. Hearing this story, everybody wondered still more.

Zinovy Borisych had vanished, and that was that.

A search was made, but nothing was discovered: the merchant had vanished into thin air. From the testimony of the arrested driver, it was learned only that the merchant had gotten out by the monastery on the river and walked away. The matter was never clarified, but meanwhile Katerina Lvovna, in her position as a widow, lived freely with Sergei. There were random surmises that Zinovy Borisych was here or there, but Zinovy Borisych still did not return, and Katerina Lvovna knew better than anyone that it was quite impossible for him to return.

A month went by like that, and another, and a third, and Katerina Lvovna felt herself heavy.

"The capital will be ours, Seryozhechka; I have an heir," she said to Sergei, and she went to complain to the town council that, thus and so, she felt she was pregnant, and the business was stagnating: let her take charge of it all.

A commercial venture should not go to waste. Katerina Lvovna was her husband's lawful wife: there were no apparent debts, which meant they ought to let her. And so they did.

Katerina Lvovna lived like a queen; and at her side Sergei was now called Sergei Filipych; and then smack, out of nowhere, came a new calamity. Somebody wrote to the town headman from Livny saying that Boris Timofeich had not traded all on his own capital, that more money than his own had been invested in the business, the money of his young nephew Fyodor Zakharovich Lyamin, and that the matter had to be looked into and not left in the hands of Katerina Lvovna alone. The news came, the headman talked about it with Katerina Lvovna, and then a week later, bang, an old lady arrives from Livny with a little boy.

"I am the late Boris Timofeich's cousin," she says, "and this is my nephew, Fyodor Lyamin."

Katerina Lvovna received them.

Sergei, watching this arrival from the courtyard, and the reception Katerina Lvovna gave the new arrivals, turned white as a sheet.

"What's wrong?" asked his mistress, noticing his deathly pallor, when he came in after the arrivals and stopped in the front room, studying them.

"Nothing," the clerk replied, turning from the front room to the hallway. "I'm just thinking, how lovely is Livny," he finished with a sigh, closing the door to the hallway behind him.

"Well, what are we to do now?" Sergei Filipych asked Katerina Lvovna, sitting with her at night over the samovar. "Now our whole business together is turned to dust."

"Why to dust, Seryozha?"

"Because now it will all be divided. Why sit here managing a futile business?"

"Won't it be enough for you, Seryozha?"

"It's not about me; I only doubt we'll be as happy as before."

"Why is that? Why won't we be happy, Seryozha?"

"Because, loving you as I do, Katerina Lvovna, I'd like to see you as a real lady, and not as you've lived so far," replied Sergei Filipych. "But now, on the contrary, it turns out that with reduced capital we'll have to descend to an even lower level than before."

"What do I care about that, Seryozha?"

"It may be, Katerina Lvovna, that you're not at all interested, but for me, since I respect you, and again looking at it with other people's eyes, base and envious as they are, it will be terribly painful. You may think as you like, of course, but I, having my own considerations, will never manage to be happy in these circumstances."

And Sergei played over and over on that same note for Katerina Lvovna, that because of Fedya Lyamin he had become the unhappiest of men, deprived of the opportunity to exalt and distinguish her before the entire merchant estate. Sergei wound up each time by saying that, if it were not for this Fedya, the child would be born to Katerina Lvovna less than nine months after her husband disappeared, she would get all the capital, and then there would be no end or measure to their happiness.

X

And then Sergei suddenly stopped talking about the heir altogether. As soon as the talk of him ceased on Sergei's lips, Fedya Lyamin came to lodge in Katerina Lvovna's mind and heart. She became pensive and even less affectionate towards Sergei. Whether she slept, or tended the business, or prayed to God, in her mind there was one and the same thing: "How can it be? Why should I be deprived of capital because of him? I've suffered so much, I've taken so much sin upon my soul," thought Katerina Lvovna, "and he comes and takes it from me without any trouble . . . Well and good if he was a man, but he's a child, a little boy . . ."

There was an early frost outside. Of Zinovy Borisych, naturally, no word came from anywhere. Katerina Lvovna was getting bigger and went about deep in thought; in town there was much beating of drums to do with her, figuring out how and why the young Izmailov woman, who had always been barren, thin as a pin, had suddenly started swelling out in front. And the young co-heir, Fedya Lyamin, walked about the yard in a light squirrel-skin coat, breaking the ice on the potholes.

"Hey, Fyodor Ignatych! Hey, you merchant's son!" the cook Aksinya would shout at him, running across the yard. "Is it fitting for you, a merchant's son, to go poking in puddles?"

But the co-heir, who troubled Katerina Lvovna and her beloved object, kicked up his feet serenely like a little goat and slept still more serenely opposite his doting old aunt, never thinking or imagining that he had crossed anyone's path or diminished anyone's happiness.

Fedya finally ran himself into the chicken pox, with a cold and chest pains attached, and the boy took to his bed. First they treated him with herbs and balms, and then they sent for the doctor.

The doctor came calling, prescribed medications, the old aunt herself gave them to the boy by the clock, and then sometimes asked Katerina Lvovna.

"Take the trouble, Katerinushka," she would say, "you're big with child yourself, you're awaiting God's judgment—take the trouble."

Katerina Lvovna never refused her. When the old woman went to the evening service to pray for "the child Fyodor who is lying in sick-bed" or to the early liturgy so as to include him in the communion,[2] Katerina Lvovna sat with the sick boy and gave him water and his medications at the proper time.

So the old woman went to the all-night vigil on the eve of the feast of the Entrance[3] and asked Katerinushka to look after Fedyushka. By then the boy was already getting better.

Katerina Lvovna went into Fedya's room, and he was sitting on his bed in his squirrel-skin coat, reading the lives of the saints.

"What are you reading, Fedya?" Katerina Lvovna asked, sitting down in the armchair.

"I'm reading the *Lives,* auntie."

"Interesting?"

"Very interesting, auntie."

Katerina Lvovna propped her head on her hand and began watching Fedya's moving lips, and suddenly it was as if demons came unleashed, and all her former thoughts descended on her of how much evil this boy had caused her and how good it would be if he were not there.

"But then again," thought Katerina Lvovna, "he's sick; he's being given medications . . . anything can happen in illness . . . All you have to say is that the doctor prescribed the wrong medicine."

"Is it time for your medicine, Fedya?"

"If you please, auntie," the boy replied and, having swallowed the spoonful, added: "It's very interesting, auntie, what's written about the saints."

"Read, then," Katerina Lvovna let fall and, passing her cold gaze around the room, rested it on the frost-patterned windows.

"I must tell them to close the shutters," she said and went out to the drawing room, and from there to the reception room, and from there to her room upstairs, and sat down.

Some five minutes later Sergei silently came to her upstairs, wearing a fleece jacket trimmed with fluffy sealskin.

"Have they closed the shutters?" Katerina Lvovna asked him.

"Yes," Sergei replied curtly, removed the snuff from the candle with a pair of snuffers, and stood by the stove.

Silence ensued.

"Tonight's vigil won't be ending soon?" asked Katerina Lvovna.

"It's the eve of a great feast; they'll make a long service of it," replied Sergei.

Again there was a pause.

"I must go to Fedya: he's there alone," Katerina Lvovna said, getting up.

"Alone?" asked Sergei, glancing sidelong at her.

"Alone," she replied in a whisper. "What of it?"

And between their eyes flashed something like a web of lightning, but they did not say a word more to each other.

Katerina Lvovna went downstairs, walked through the empty rooms: there was total silence everywhere; the icon lamps burned quietly; her own shadow flitted over the walls; the windows behind their closed shutters began to thaw out and weep. Fedya sits and reads. Seeing Katerina Lvovna, he only says:

"Auntie, please take this book, and give me, please, that one from the icon shelf."

Katerina Lvovna did as her nephew asked and handed him the book.

"Won't you go to sleep, Fedya?"

"No, auntie, I'll wait for my old aunt."

"Why wait for her?"

"She promised to bring me some blessed bread from the vigil."

Katerina Lvovna suddenly went pale, her own child turned for the first time under her heart, and she felt a chill in her breast. She stood for a while in the middle of the room and then went out, rubbing her cold hands.

"Well!" she whispered, quietly going into her bedroom and finding Sergei again in the same position by the stove.

"What?" Sergei asked, barely audibly, and choked.

"He's alone."

Sergei scowled and started breathing heavily.

"Let's go," said Katerina Lvovna, abruptly turning to the door.

Sergei quickly took off his boots and asked:

"What shall I take?"

"Nothing," Katerina Lvovna replied under her breath and quietly led him after her by the hand.

XI

The sick boy gave a start and lowered the book to his knees when Katerina Lvovna came into his room for the third time.

"What's wrong, Fedya?"

"Oh, auntie, I got frightened of something," he said, smiling anxiously and pressing himself to the corner of the bed.

"What are you frightened of?"

"Who is it that came with you, auntie?"

"Where? Nobody came, dearest."

"Nobody?"

The boy leaned towards the foot of the bed and, narrowing his eyes, looked in the direction of the door through which his aunt had come, and was reassured.

"I probably imagined it," he said.

Katerina Lvovna stood leaning her elbow on the headboard of her nephew's bed.

Fedya looked at his aunt and remarked that for some reason she was very pale.

In reply to this remark, Katerina Lvovna coughed deliberately and glanced expectantly at the door to the drawing room. A floorboard creaked softly there.

"I'm reading the life of my guardian angel, St. Feodor Stratilatos, auntie.[4] There was a man pleasing to God."

Katerina Lvovna stood silently.

"Sit down if you like, auntie, and I'll read it over to you," her nephew tried to make up to her.

"Wait, I'll just go and tend to that icon lamp in the reception room," Katerina Lvovna replied and went out with hurried steps.

There was the softest whispering in the drawing room; but amidst the general silence it reached the child's keen ear.

"Auntie, what is it? Who are you whispering to there?" the boy cried with tears in his voice. "Come here, auntie, I'm afraid," he called a second later, still more tearfully, and he thought he heard Katerina Lvovna say "Well?" in the drawing room, which the boy took as referring to him.

"What are you afraid of?" Katerina Lvovna asked him in a slightly hoarse voice, coming in with bold, resolute strides and standing by his bed in such a way that the door to the drawing room was screened from the sick boy by her body. "Lie down," she said to him after that.

"I don't want to, auntie."

"No, Fedya, you listen to me: lie down, it's time, lie down," Katerina Lvovna repeated.

"What's the matter, auntie? I don't want to at all."

"No, you lie down, lie down," Katerina Lvovna said in a changed, unsteady voice, and, picking the boy up under the arms, she laid him at the head of the bed.

Just then Fedya screamed hysterically: he had seen the pale, barefoot Sergei come in.

Katerina Lvovna put her hand over the frightened child's mouth, gaping in terror, and shouted:

"Quick now, hold him straight so he doesn't thrash!"

Sergei held Fedya by the arms and legs, and Katerina Lvovna, in one movement, covered the sufferer's childish face with a big down pillow and pressed it to him with her firm, resilient breasts.

For about four minutes there was a sepulchral silence in the room.

"It's all over," Katerina Lvovna whispered and was just getting up to put everything in order when the walls of the quiet house that concealed so many crimes shook with deafening blows: the windows rattled, the floors swayed, the chains of the hanging icon lamps quivered and sent fantastic shadows wandering over the walls.

Sergei trembled and broke out running for all he was worth; Katerina Lvovna rushed after him, and the noise and din followed them. It seemed as though some unearthly powers were shaking the sinful house to its foundations.

Katerina Lvovna was afraid that, driven by terror, Sergei would run outside and give himself away by his fright; but he dashed straight upstairs.

Having run up the stairs, Sergei struck his head against the half-open door in the darkness and fell back down with a moan, totally crazed by superstitious fear.

"Zinovy Borisych, Zinovy Borisych!" he muttered, flying headlong down and dragging Katerina Lvovna with him, having knocked her off her feet.

"Where?" she asked.

"He just went flying over us with a sheet of iron. There, there he is again! Aie, aie!" Sergei cried. "It's thundering, it's thundering again!"

By now it was quite clear that many hands were banging on the windows from outside and someone was breaking down the door.

"Fool! Stand up!" cried Katerina Lvovna, and with these words she herself went flitting back to Fedya, arranged his dead head on the pillow in a most natural sleeping position, and with a firm hand unlocked the door through which a crowd of people was about to crash.

The spectacle was frightening. Katerina Lvovna looked over the heads of the crowd besieging the porch, and there were whole ranks of unknown people climbing the high fence into the yard, and outside there was a hum of human voices.

Before Katerina Lvovna managed to figure anything out, the people surrounding the porch overran her and flung her inside.

XII

This whole alarm came about in the following way: for the vigil before a major feast in all the churches of the town where Katerina Lvovna lived, which, though provincial, was rather large and a trading center, a numberless multitude of people always gathered, and in the church named for that feast, even the yard outside had no room for an apple to fall. Here a choir consisting of young merchants usually sang, led by a special director who also belonged to the lovers of vocal art.

Our people are pious, zealous for God's church, and, as a result of that, are to a certain extent artistic people: churchly splendor and harmonious "organ-drone" singing constitute one of their loftiest and purest delights. Wherever the choir sings, almost half of our town gathers, especially the young tradesmen: shopkeepers, errand boys, factory workers, and the owners themselves, with their better halves—everybody packs into one church; everybody wants to stand if only outside on the porch or by the window, in scorching heat or freezing cold, to hear how the octave drones and the ecstatic tenor pulls off the most intricate grace notes.

The Izmailovs' parish church was dedicated to the Entrance of the Mother of God into the Temple, and therefore, on the eve of this feast, just at the time of the episode with Fedya described above, all the young folk of the town were in that church and, on leaving in a noisy crowd, were discussing the virtues of a well-known tenor and the accidental blunders of an equally well-known bass.

But not everyone was interested in these vocal questions: there were people in the crowd who were concerned with other things.

"You know, lads, strange things are told about the young Izmailov woman," said a young mechanic, brought from Petersburg by a merchant for his steam mill, as they approached the Izmailovs' house. "They say," he went on, "that she and their clerk Seryozhka make love every other minute . . ."

"Everybody knows that," replied a fleece-lined blue nankeen coat. "And, by the way, she wasn't in church tonight."

"Church, ha! The nasty wench has turned so vile, she has no fear of God, or conscience, or other people's eyes."

"Look, there's light in their place," the mechanic noticed, pointing to a bright strip between the shutters.

"Peek through the crack, see what they're up to," several voices called out.

The mechanic propped himself on the shoulders of two of his comrades and had just put his eye to the narrow gap when he screamed at the top of his voice:

"Brothers, friends, they're smothering somebody, they're smothering somebody in there!"

And the mechanic desperately banged on the shutters with his hands. Some dozen men followed his example and, running to the windows, began applying their fists to them.

The crowd grew every moment, and the result was the siege of the Izmailov house already known to us.

"I saw it, with my own eyes I saw it," the mechanic testified over the dead Fedya. "The child was lying on the bed, and the two of them were smothering him."

Sergei was taken to the police that same evening, and Katerina Lvovna was led to her upstairs room and two guards were placed over her.

It was freezing cold in the Izmailovs' house: the stoves were not lit; the door was never shut; one dense crowd of curious people replaced another. They all came to look at Fedya lying in his coffin and at the other big coffin, its lid tightly covered with a wide shroud. There was a white satin crown on Fedya's forehead, covering the red scar left by the opening of the skull. The forensic autopsy had discovered that Fedya died of suffocation, and Sergei, when brought to his corpse, at the priest's first words about the Last Judgment and the punishment of the unrepentant, burst into tears and not only confessed openly to the murder of Fedya, but also asked them to dig up Zinovy Borisych, whom he had buried without a funeral. The corpse of Katerina Lvovna's husband, buried in dry sand, was not yet completely decomposed: it was taken out and laid in a big coffin. As his accomplice in both these crimes, to the general horror, Sergei named his young mistress. Katerina Lvovna, to all questions, answered only: "I know nothing about it." Sergei was forced to expose her at a confrontation. Having heard his confession, Katerina Lvovna looked at him in mute amazement, but without anger, and then said indifferently:

"If he's willing to tell about it, there's no point in my denying it: I killed them."

"What for?" she was asked.

"For him," she answered, pointing to Sergei, who hung his head.

The criminals were put in jail, and the terrible case, which attracted general attention and indignation, was decided very quickly. At the end of February, the court announced to Sergei and the widow of the merchant of the third guild, Katerina Lvovna, that it had been decided to punish them by flogging in the marketplace of their town and then to send them both to hard labor. At the beginning of March, on a cold, frosty morning, the executioner counted off the appointed number of blue-purple weals on Katerina Lvovna's bare white back, and then beat out his portion on Sergei's shoulders and branded his handsome face with three convict's marks.

During all this time, Sergei for some reason aroused much more general sympathy than Katerina Lvovna. Smeared and bloody, he stumbled as he came down from the black scaffold, but Katerina Lvovna came down slowly, only trying to keep the thick shirt and coarse prisoner's coat from touching her torn back.

Even in the prison hospital, when they gave her her baby, all she said was: "Oh, away with him!" and turning to the wall, without a moan, without complaint, she laid her breast on the hard cot.

XIII

The party in which Sergei and Katerina Lvovna found themselves set out when spring had begun only by the calendar, while, as the popular proverb says, "there was lots of sun, but heat there was none."

Katerina Lvovna's child was given to Boris Timofeich's old sister to be brought up, because, being counted as the legitimate son of the criminal woman's murdered husband, the infant was now left the sole heir to the entire Izmailov fortune. Katerina Lvovna was very pleased with that and surrendered the baby quite indifferently. Her love for the father, like the love of many all too passionate women, did not extend in the least to the child.

Anyhow, nothing in the world existed for her: neither light, nor darkness, nor good, nor bad, nor boredom, nor joy; she did not understand anything, did not love anyone, did not love herself. She waited impatiently for the party to set out on its way, when she hoped to be able to see her darling Sergei again, and she even forgot to think about the baby.

Katerina Lvovna's hopes were not deceived: heavily bound in chains, branded, Sergei came out of the prison gates in the same group with her.

Man accustoms himself as far as possible to any abominable situation, and in every situation preserves as far as possible his capacity to pursue his meager joys; but for Katerina Lvovna there is nothing to adjust to: she sees her Sergei again, and with him even the convict's path blossoms with happiness.

Katerina Lvovna took very few valuable things with her in her canvas sack and even less money. But long before they reached Nizhny she had given it all away to the convoy soldiers in exchange for the possibility of walking beside Sergei or standing for a little hour embracing him on a dark night in a cold corner of the narrow transit prison corridor.

Only Katerina Lvovna's branded young man somehow became very reserved towards her: he did not so much talk as snap at her; his secret meetings with her, for which, not thinking of food or drink, she gave the necessary twenty-five kopecks from her lean purse, he did not value very highly; and more than once he even said:

"You'd do better to give me the money you gave the soldier, instead of us rubbing against corners in the corridor."

"All I gave him was twenty-five kopecks, Seryozhenka," Katerina Lvovna justified herself.

"As if twenty-five kopecks isn't money? Did you pick up a lot of these twenty-five kopecks on the way, that you hand them out so freely?"

"That's how we could see each other, Seryozha."

"Well, where's the joy of seeing each other after such suffering! I could curse my whole life, not just these meetings."

"And for me it makes no difference, as long as I get to see you."

"That's all foolishness," replied Sergei.

Katerina Lvovna sometimes bit her lips until they bled hearing such replies, and sometimes her eyes, not given to weeping, filled with tears of anger and vexation in the darkness of their nighttime meetings; but she endured it all, kept silent, and wished to deceive herself.

Thus, in these new relations with each other, they reached Nizhny

Novgorod. Here their party merged with another party that was going to Siberia from the Moscow highway.

In this big party, among a multitude of people of all sorts in the women's section, there were two very interesting persons. One was Fiona, a soldier's wife from Yaroslavl, a splendid, magnificent woman, tall, with a thick black braid and languorous brown eyes, curtained as with a mysterious veil by thick eyelashes; and the other was a sharp-faced seventeen-year-old blonde with tender pink skin, a tiny little mouth, dimples on her fresh cheeks, and golden-brown locks, which stubbornly strayed across her forehead from under her convict's kerchief. In the party they called this girl Sonetka.

The beautiful Fiona was of a soft and lazy disposition. Everyone in her party knew her, and no one among the men rejoiced especially at achieving success with her, and no one was upset at seeing her grant the same success to another suitor.

"Our Aunt Fiona is a kindly wench, she doesn't offend anybody," the convicts all joked unanimously.

But Sonetka was of a completely different sort.

Of her they said:

"An eel: slips through your fingers, and never lingers."

Sonetka had taste, chose her dishes, and maybe even chose very strictly; she wanted passion to be offered to her, not blandly, but with a piquant, spicy seasoning, with sufferings and sacrifices; while Fiona was Russian simplicity, who is even too lazy to say "Go away," and who knows only one thing, that she is a woman. Such women are very highly valued in robber bands, convict parties, and the social-democratic communes of Petersburg.[5]

The appearance of these two women in one combined party with Sergei and Katerina Lvovna had tragic consequences for the latter.

XIV

From the first days of the combined party's movement from Nizhny Novgorod to Kazan, Sergei openly began to seek the favors of the soldier's wife Fiona, and suffered no lack of success. The languid beauty Fiona did not make Sergei languish, as, in her kindness, she did not make anyone languish. At the third or fourth halting place, in the early dusk, Katerina Lvovna set up a meeting with Seryozhechka by means of bribery, and lay there without sleeping: she kept waiting for the guard on duty to come at any moment, nudge her slightly, and whisper "Run quickly." The door opened once, and a woman darted out to the corridor; the door opened again, and another woman prisoner quickly jumped up from another cot and also disappeared after the guard; finally there came a tug at the coat with which Katerina Lvovna covered herself. The young woman hurriedly got up from the cot, well polished by the sides of convicts, threw the coat over her shoulders, and gave a push to the guard standing before her.

As Katerina Lvovna went down the corridor, in one place faintly lit by a dim lamp, she came across two or three couples who could not be made out from a distance. As Katerina Lvovna passed the male convicts' room, she seemed to hear restrained laughter through the little window cut out in the door.

"Having fun," Katerina Lvovna's guard growled, and, taking her by the shoulders, he pushed her into the corner and withdrew.

Katerina Lvovna felt a coat and a beard with her hand; her other hand touched the hot face of a woman.

"Who's that?" Sergei asked in a half whisper.

"And what are you doing here? Who is that with you?"

In the darkness, Katerina Lvovna pulled the headcloth from her rival. The woman slipped aside, rushed off, stumbled against someone in the corridor, and fell.

From the men's quarters came a burst of guffawing.

"Villain!" Katerina Lvovna whispered and hit Sergei across the face with the ends of the kerchief she had torn from the head of his new girlfriend.

Sergei raised his hand; but Katerina Lvovna flitted lightly down the corridor and took hold of her door. The guffawing from the men's quarters that followed her was repeated so loudly that the guard, who had been standing apathetically next to the lantern and spitting at the toe of his boot, raised his head and barked:

"Quiet!"

Katerina Lvovna lay down silently and went on lying like that until morning. She wanted to say to herself: "I don't love him," and felt that her love for him was still greater, still more ardent. And now before her eyes she keeps picturing again and again how his palm trembled under *that woman's* head, how his other arm embraced her hot shoulders.

The poor woman wept and unwillingly called upon the same palm to be under her head that minute and his other arm to embrace her hysterically trembling shoulders.

"Well, give me back my kerchief anyhow," the soldier's wife Fiona woke her up in the morning.

"Ah, so that was you? . . ."

"Give it back, please!"

"But why did you come between us?"

"How have I come between you? Is it some sort of love or real interest, that you should be angry?"

Katerina Lvovna thought for a second, then took the kerchief she had torn off at night from under her pillow and, throwing it at Fiona, turned to the wall.

She felt relieved.

"Pah," she said to herself, "am I going to be jealous of that painted tub? She can drop dead! It's nasty even comparing myself to her."

"The thing is this, Katerina Lvovna," said Sergei, as they walked down the road the next day. "Please understand that, first of all, I'm no Zinovy Borisych to you, and, second, that you're no great merchant's wife now: so kindly don't get so puffed up. There's no market for butting goats with us."

Katerina Lvovna said nothing to that, and for a week she walked without exchanging a word or a glance with Sergei. As the offended party, she stood firm and did not want to make the first step towards reconciliation in this first quarrel with him.

In the meantime, while Katerina Lvovna was angry, Sergei began making eyes at and flirting with the blond Sonetka. Now he greets her "with our particular honor," now he smiles, now, meeting her, he tries to embrace and squeeze her. Katerina Lvovna sees it all and her heart seethes all the more.

"Shouldn't I maybe make peace with him?" Katerina Lvovna thinks, stumbling and not seeing the ground under her feet.

But her pride now forbids her more than ever to go to him first and make peace. And meanwhile Sergei attaches himself to Sonetka ever more persistently, and it seems to everyone that the inaccessible Sonetka, who slipped away like an eel, is suddenly growing more tame.

"Here you wept over me," Fiona once said to Katerina Lvovna, "but what did I do to you? With me it came and went, but you'd better watch out for Sonetka."

"Perish my pride: I absolutely must make peace today," Katerina

Lvovna decided, now only pondering how to set about the reconciliation most adroitly.

Sergei himself helped her out of this difficulty.

"Lvovna!" he called to her as they made a halt. "Come and see me tonight for a moment: it's business."

Katerina Lvovna said nothing.

"What, maybe you're still angry and won't come?"

Katerina Lvovna again said nothing.

But Sergei and all who observed Katerina Lvovna saw that, as they approached the transit prison, she started moving closer to the chief guard and gave him seventeen kopecks she had saved up from alms.

"I'll give you another ten once I save more," Katerina Lvovna begged him.

The soldier put the money behind his cuff and said:

"All right."

Once these negotiations were concluded, Sergei grunted and winked at Sonetka.

"Ah, Katerina Lvovna!" he said, embracing her as they went up the steps of the transit prison. "Compared to this woman, lads, there's not another such in the whole world."

Katerina Lvovna blushed and choked with happiness.

That night, as soon as the door quietly opened a crack, she ran out at once: she was trembling and felt for Sergei with her hands in the dark corridor.

"My Katya!" said Sergei, embracing her.

"Ah, my villain!" Katerina Lvovna answered through her tears and clung to him with her lips.

The guard paced the corridor and, stopping, spat on his boots, and paced again; behind the door the tired inmates snored, a mouse gnawed at a feather, under the stove crickets chirped away one louder than the other, and Katerina Lvovna was still in bliss.

But the raptures wore off, and the inevitable prose began.

"I'm in mortal pain: my bones ache from the ankles right up to the knees," Sergei complained, sitting with Katerina Lvovna on the floor in a corner of the corridor.

"What can we do, Seryozhechka?" she asked, huddling under the skirt of his coat.

"Maybe I can ask to be put in the infirmary in Kazan?"

"Oh, is it as bad as that, Seryozha?"

"Like I said, it's the death of me, the way it hurts."

"So you'll stay, and I'll be driven on?"

"What can I do? It chafes, I'm telling you, it chafes, the chain's cut almost to the bone. If only I had woolen stockings or something to put under," Sergei said a moment later.

"Stockings? I still have a pair of new stockings, Seryozha."

"Well, never mind!" Sergei replied.

Without another word, Katerina Lvovna darted to the cell, shook her sack out on the cot, and hastily ran to Sergei again with a pair of thick, dark blue woolen stockings with bright clocks on the sides.

"Now it should be all right," said Sergei, parting from Katerina Lvovna and accepting her last stockings.

The happy Katerina Lvovna returned to her cot and fell fast asleep.

She did not hear how, after she came back, Sonetka went out to the corridor and quietly returned just before morning.

This happened only a two days' march from Kazan.

XV

A cold, gray day with gusty wind and rain mixed with snow drearily met the party as they stepped through the gates of the stuffy transit prison. Katerina Lvovna started out quite briskly, but she had only just taken her place in line when she turned green and began to shake. Everything became dark in her eyes; all her joints ached and went limp. Before Katerina Lvovna stood Sonetka in those all too familiar dark blue stockings with bright clocks.

Katerina Lvovna moved on more dead than alive; only her eyes looked terribly at Sergei and did not blink.

At the first halt, she calmly went up to Sergei, whispered "Scoundrel," and unexpectedly spat right in his eyes.

Sergei was about to fall upon her; but he was held back.

"Just you wait!" he said and wiped his face.

"Nice, though, how bravely she treats you," the prisoners mocked Sergei, and Sonetka dissolved in especially merry laughter.

This little intrigue Sonetka had yielded to was perfectly suited to her taste.

"Well, you won't get away with that," Sergei threatened Katerina Lvovna.

Worn out by the bad weather and the march, her heart broken,

Katerina Lvovna slept uneasily that night on her cot in the next transit prison, and did not hear how two men entered the women's barrack.

When they came in, Sonetka got up from her cot, silently pointed to Katerina Lvovna, lay down again, and wrapped herself in her coat.

At the same moment, Katerina Lvovna's coat flew up over her head, and the thick end of a double-twisted rope let loose with all a man's strength on her back, covered only by a coarse shirt.

Katerina Lvovna screamed, but her voice could not be heard under the coat that covered her head. She thrashed, but also without success: a stalwart convict sat on her shoulders and held her arms fast.

"Fifty," a voice, which it was not hard for anyone to recognize as Sergei's, finally counted off, and the night visitors disappeared through the door.

Katerina Lvovna uncovered her head and jumped up: there was no one there; only not far away someone giggled gleefully under a coat. Katerina Lvovna recognized Sonetka's laughter.

This offense was beyond all measure; also beyond all measure was the feeling of spite that boiled up at that moment in Katerina Lvovna's soul. Oblivious, she rushed forward and fell oblivious onto the breast of Fiona, who took her in her arms.

On that full breast, where so recently Katerina Lvovna's unfaithful lover had enjoyed the sweetness of debauchery, she was now weeping out her unbearable grief, and she clung to her soft and stupid rival like a child to its mother. They were equal now: both were equal in value and both were abandoned.

They were equal—Fiona, subject to the first opportunity, and Katerina Lvovna, acting out the drama of love!

Katerina Lvovna, however, was by now offended by nothing. Having wept out her tears, she turned to stone, and with a wooden calm prepared to go to the roll call.

The drum beats: ratta-tat-tat; chained and unchained prisoners pour out into the yard—Sergei, Fiona, Sonetka, Katerina Lvovna, an Old Believer[6] fettered with a Jew, a Pole on the same chain with a Tartar.

They all bunched together, then pulled themselves into some sort of order and set off.

A most cheerless picture: a handful of people, torn away from the world and deprived of any shadow of hope for a better future, sinking into the cold black mud of the dirt road. Everything around them is horribly ugly: the endless mud, the gray sky, the leafless, wet broom, and in its splayed branches a ruffled crow. The wind now moans, now rages, now howls and roars.

In these hellish, soul-rending sounds, which complete the whole horror of the picture, one hears the advice of the biblical Job's wife: "Curse the day you were born and die."[7]

Whoever does not want to listen to these words, whoever is not attracted but frightened by the thought of death even in this dismal situation, must try to stifle these howling voices with something still more hideous. The simple man understands this perfectly well: he then unleashes all his animal simplicity, begins to be stupid, to jeer at himself, at people, at feeling. Not very tender to begin with, he becomes doubly malicious.

◆◆◆◆◆◆

"What, then, merchant's wife? Is your honor in good health?" Sergei impudently asked Katerina Lvovna, as soon as the party went over a wet hillock and lost sight of the village where they had spent the night.

With these words, he turned at once to Sonetka, covered her with the skirts of his coat, and sang in a high falsetto:

A blond head flashes in the dark outside the window.
So you're not asleep, my tormentress, you're not asleep, sweet cheat.
I'll cover you with my coat skirts, so that none can see.[8]

With these words, Sergei embraced Sonetka and kissed her loudly in front of the whole party . . .

Katerina Lvovna saw and did not see it all: she walked on like an utterly lifeless person. They started nudging her and pointing to Sergei's outrageous behavior with Sonetka. She became an object of mockery.

"Let her be," Fiona defended her, when somebody in the party tried to laugh at the stumbling Katerina Lvovna. "Don't you devils see that the woman's quite ill?"

"Must have got her feet wet," a young prisoner cracked.

"She's of merchant stock, you know: a pampered upbringing," Sergei responded.

"Of course, if she at least had warm stockings, it would be better," he went on.

It was as if Katerina Lvovna woke up.

"Vile serpent!" she said, unable to restrain herself. "Keep jeering, scoundrel, keep jeering!"

"No, merchant's wife, I'm not jeering at you at all, but Sonetka here has some very nice stockings for sale, so I thought our merchant's wife might buy them."

Many laughed. Katerina Lvovna strode on like a wound-up automaton.

The weather was turning stormy. From the gray clouds that covered the sky, snow began to fall in wet flakes, which melted after barely touching the ground and made the mud still deeper. Finally a dark, leaden strip appears; its other side cannot be seen. This strip is the Volga. Over the Volga a rather stiff wind is blowing, driving the slowly rising, dark, gape-jawed waves back and forth.

The party of drenched and chilled prisoners slowly came to the crossing and stopped, waiting for the ferry.

The wet, dark ferry came; the crew began loading the prisoners.

"They say somebody has vodka on this ferry," one prisoner observed, when the ferry, under the downpour of wet snowflakes, cast off and rocked on the big waves of the storm-tossed river.

"Yes, right now a little nip wouldn't do any harm," Sergei responded, and, persecuting Katerina Lvovna for Sonetka's amusement, he said: "Merchant's wife, for old friendship's sake, treat me to a little vodka. Don't be stingy. Remember, my sweet, our former love, and what a good time you and I had, my joy, sitting together of a long autumn evening, sending your relations off to their eternal rest without priests or deacons."

Katerina Lvovna was trembling all over with cold. But, besides the cold that pierced her to the bone under her soaked dress, something else was going on in Katerina Lvovna's whole being. Her head burned as if on fire; the pupils of her eyes were dilated, alive with a sharp, roving glitter, and peered fixedly into the rolling waves.

"And I'd like a little vodka, too: the cold's unbearable," Sonetka's voice rang out.

"Come on, merchant's wife, treat us!" Sergei kept rubbing it in.

"Ah, you've got no conscience!" said Fiona, shaking her head reproachfully.

"That does you no credit at all," the prisoner Gordyushka seconded the soldier's wife.

"If you're not ashamed before her, you should be before others."

"You common snuffbox!" Sergei yelled at Fiona. "Ashamed, is it! What should I be ashamed of! Maybe I never loved her, and now . . . Sonetka's worn-out shoe is dearer to me than her mangy cat's mug; what do you say to that? Let her love skew-mouthed Gordyushka; or—" he glanced at a runty fellow on horseback in a felt cape and military cap with a cockade and added, "or, better still, let her cuddle up to this transport officer: at least his cape will keep her from the rain."

"And she'll be called an officer's wife," Sonetka chimed in.

"Right you are! . . . and she'll easily get enough to buy stockings," Sergei seconded.

Katerina Lvovna did not defend herself: she looked more and more intently into the waves and moved her lips. Through Sergei's vile talk she heard the rumble and moan from the opening and slamming waves. And suddenly the blue head of Boris Timofeich appears to her out of one breaking wave; her husband, rocking, peers out of another, holding Fedya with a drooping head. Katerina Lvovna wants to remember a prayer, and she moves her lips, but her lips whisper: "What a good time you and I had, sitting together of a long autumn evening, sending people out of this world by a cruel death."

Katerina Lvovna was trembling. Her roving gaze became fixed and wild. Her arms reached out somewhere into space once or twice and dropped again. Another moment—and she suddenly began to sway all over, not taking her eyes from the dark waves, bent down, seized Sonetka by the legs, and in one sweep threw the girl and herself overboard.

Everyone was petrified with amazement.

Katerina Lvovna appeared at the top of a wave and sank again; another wave tossed up Sonetka.

"A hook! Throw them a hook!" they shouted on the ferry.

A heavy hook on a long rope soared up and fell into the water. Sonetka could no longer be seen. Two seconds later, borne away from the ferry by the swift current, she again flailed her arms; but at the same moment, out of another wave, Katerina Lvovna rose up almost to the waist, threw herself on Sonetka like a strong pike on a soft-finned little roach, and neither of them appeared again.

The Sealed Angel

I

It happened during Christmastime, on the eve of St. Basil's.[1] The weather was raging most unmercifully. A severe, ground-sweeping blizzard, of the kind for which the winters of the Transvolga steppe are famous, drove a multitude of people into a solitary inn that stood like an old bachelor in the midst of the flat and boundless steppe. Here gentlefolk, merchants, and peasants, Russians, and Mordovians, and Chuvashes, all ended up in one heap. To observe grades and ranks in such night lodgings was impossible: wherever you turned, it was crowded, some drying off, others warming themselves, still others looking for a bit of space to huddle up in; the dark, low cottage, crammed with people, was stuffy and filled with dense steam from the wet clothes. There was no free space to be seen: on the bunks, on the stove,[2] on the benches, and even on the dirty earth floor—people were lying everywhere. The innkeeper, a stern muzhik, was glad neither of the guests nor of the gains. Angrily slamming the gate after the last sleigh, carrying two merchants, forced its way in, he locked it with a padlock and, hanging the key in the icon corner, said firmly:

"Well, now whoever wants to can beat his head on the gate—I won't open."

But he had barely managed to say that and, having taken off his vast sheepskin coat, to cross himself with a big, old-style cross and prepare to get onto the hot stove, when someone's timid hand knocked on the windowpane.

"Who's there?" the innkeeper called in a loud and displeased voice.

"It's us," a muffled reply came from outside the window.

"Well, what do you want?"

"Let us in, for Christ's sake, we're lost . . . frozen."

"Are there many of you?"

"Not many, not many, eighteen in all, just eighteen," a man, obviously completely frozen, said outside the window, stammering and his teeth chattering.

"There's no room for you, the whole cottage is packed with people as it is."

"At least let us warm up a little!"

"What are you?"

"Carters."

"Empty or loaded?"

"Loaded, dear brother, we're carrying hides."

"Hides! You're carrying hides, and you ask to spend the night in the cottage? What's become of the Russian people! Get out of here!"

"But what are they to do?" asked a traveler lying under a bearskin coat on an upper bunk.

"Pile up the hides and sleep under them, that's what," the innkeeper replied, and, giving the carters another good cursing out, he lay motionless on the stove.

From under his bearskin, the traveler reprimanded the innkeeper for his cruelty in tones of highly energetic protest, but the man did not honor his remarks with the slightest response. Instead of him, a small, red-haired man with a sharp, wedge-shaped little beard called out from a far corner.

"Don't condemn our host, my dear sir," he began. "He takes it from experience, and what he says is true—with the hides it's safe."

"Oh?" a questioning response came from under the bearskin.

"Perfectly safe, sir, and it's better for them that he doesn't let them in."

"Why is that?"

"Because now they'll get themselves useful experience from it, and meanwhile if some helpless person or other comes knocking here, there'll be room for him."

"Who else would the devil bring here now?" said the fur coat.

"Listen, you," the innkeeper put in. "Don't spout empty words. Can the foul fiend bring anybody to where there's such holy things?

Don't you see the icon of the Savior and the face of the Mother of God here?"

"That's right," the red-haired little man seconded. "Every saved person is guided by an angel, not by the dark one."

"That's something I've never seen, and since I find this a vile place, I don't want to think my angel brought me here," replied the garrulous fur coat.

The innkeeper only spat angrily, but the little redhead said good-naturedly that not everybody could behold the angel's path, and you could only get a notion of it from real experience.

"You speak of it as if you've had such experience yourself," said the fur coat.

"Yes, sir, I have."

"So you saw an angel, and he led you—is that it?"

"Yes, sir, I saw him, and he guided me."

"What, are you joking, or making fun?"

"God keep me from joking about such things!"

"So what precisely was it that you saw: how did the angel appear to you?"

"That, my dear sir, is a whole big story."

"You know, it's decidedly impossible to fall asleep here, and you'd be doing an excellent thing if you told us that story now."

"As you wish, sir."

"Please tell it, then: we're listening. But why are you kneeling over there? Come here to us, maybe we can make room and all sit together."

"No, sir, I thank you for that! Why crowd yourselves? And besides, the story I'm going to tell you is more properly told kneeling down, because it's a highly sacred and even awesome thing."

"Well, as you wish, only tell us quickly, how could you see an angel and what did he do to you?"

"If you please, sir, I'll begin."

II

As you can undoubtedly tell from my looks, I'm a totally insignificant man, nothing more than a muzhik, and the education I received was most village-like, as suited that condition. I'm not from hereabouts, but from far away; by trade I'm a mason, and I was born into the old Russian faith.[3] On account of my orphanhood, from a young age I went with my countrymen to do itinerant work and worked in various places, but always with the same crew, under our peasant Luka Kirilovich. This Luka Kirilovich is still alive: he's our foremost contractor. His business was from old times, established by his forefathers, and he didn't squander it, but increased it and made himself a big and abundant granary,[4] but he was and is a wonderful man and not an offender. And where, where didn't our crew go with him! Seems we walked all over Russia, and nowhere have I seen a better and steadier master than him. We lived under him in the most peaceful patriarchy, and he was our contractor and our guide in trade and in faith. We followed him to work the way the Jews followed Moses in their wanderings in the desert; we even had our own tabernacle with us and never parted with it: that is, we had our own "God's blessing" with us. Luka Kirilovich passionately loved holy icons, and, my dear sirs, he owned the most wonderful icons, of the most artful workmanship, ancient, either real Greek, or of the first Novgorod or Stroganov icon painters.[5] Icon after icon shone not so much by their casings as by the keenness and fluency of their marvelous artistry. I've never seen such loftiness anywhere since!

There were various saints, and Deisises, and the Savior-not-made-by-hands with wet hair,[6] and holy monks, and martyrs, and the apostles, and most wondrous were the multifigured icons with different deeds, such as, for instance, the Indictus, the feasts, the Last Judgment, the Saints of the month, the Council of Angels, the Paternity, the Six Days, the Healers, the Seven Days of the Week with praying figures, the Trinity with Abraham bowing down under the oak of Mamre, and, in short, it's impossible to describe all this beauty, and nowadays such icons aren't painted anywhere, not in Moscow, not in Petersburg, not in Palekh;[7] and there's even no talking about Greece, because the know-how has long been lost there. We all passionately loved these holy icons of ours, and together we burned lamps before them, and at the crew's expense we kept a horse and a special cart in which we transported this blessing of God in two big trunks wherever we went. We had two icons in particular, one copied from the Greek by old Moscow court masters: our most holy Lady praying in the garden, with all the cypress and olive trees bowing to the ground before her; and the other a guardian angel, Stroganov work. It's impossible to express what art there was in these two holy images!

You look at Our Lady, how the inanimate trees bow down before her purity, and your heart melts and trembles; you look at the angel . . . joy! This angel was truly something indescribable. His face—I can see it now—is most brightly divine and so swiftly succoring; his gaze is tender; his hair is tied with a fine ribbon, its ends curling around his ears, a sign of his hearing everything from everywhere; his robe is shining, all spangled with gold; his armor is feathery, his shoulders are girded; on his chest the face of the infant Emmanuel; in his right hand a cross, in his left a flaming sword. Wondrous! Wondrous! . . . The hair on his head is wavy and blond, curly from the ears down, and traced hair by hair with a needle. His wings are vast and white as snow, but azure underneath, done feather by feather, and on each shaft barb by barb. You look at those wings, and where has all your fear gone to? You pray, "Overshadow me," and you grow all quiet at once, and there's peace in your soul. That's what kind of icon it was! And for us these two icons were like the holy of holies for the Jews, adorned by the wonderful artistry of Bezaleel.[8] All the icons I mentioned earlier were transported by horse in special trunks, but these two we didn't even put in the cart, but carried: Luka Kirilovich's wife, Mikhailitsa, always carried Our Lady, and Luka himself kept the image of the angel on his breast. He had a brocade pouch made for this icon, lined with dark homespun, and with a button, and on the front side there was a scarlet cross made from real damask, and there was a thick green silk cord to hang it round the neck. And so this icon that was always kept on Luka's breast preceded us wherever we went, as if the angel himself were going before us. We used to go from place to place for new work over the steppe, Luka Kirilovich ahead of us all, waving his notched measuring stick instead of a staff, Mikhailitsa behind him in the cart with the icon of the Mother of God, and behind them the whole crew of us marching, and there in the field there's grass, meadow flowers, herds pasturing here and there, a shepherd playing his reed . . . a sheer delight for heart and mind! Everything went beautifully for us, and wondrous was our success in all things: we always found good work; there was concord among us; peaceful news kept coming to us from our folks at home; and for all that we blessed the angel who went before us, and it seemed to us it would be harder to part with his most wonderful icon than with our own lives.

And could we have thought that somehow, by some chance or other, we would be deprived of our most precious and holy thing?

And yet that grief awaited us, and was arranged for us, as we perceived only later, not through people's perfidy, but through the providence of our guide himself. He himself wished to be insulted, in order to grant us the holy ordeal of sorrow, and through it to show us the true path, before which all the paths we had trodden were like a dark and trackless wilderness. But allow me to inquire whether my story is interesting and I am not troubling your attention for nothing?

"Not at all, not at all: be so kind as to continue!" we exclaimed, having become interested in what he was telling.

"Very well, sirs, I obey, and will begin, as best I can, to set forth the wondrous wonders that came to us from our angel."

III

We came to do big work near a big city on a big stream of water, the Dniepr River, to build there a big and now highly famous stone bridge.[9] The city stands on the steep right bank, and we settled on the low left bank covered with meadows, and a beautiful peosage opened before us: old churches, holy monasteries with the relics of many saints; lush gardens and trees such as are pictured in the frontispieces of old books, that is, sharp-pointed poplars. You look at it all and it's as if somebody's plucking at your heart—it's so beautiful! You know, of course, we're simple people, but all the same we do feel the all-graciousness of God-created nature.

And so we fell so cruelly in love with this place that, on the very first day, we started building ourselves a temporary dwelling there. We first drove in long piles, because the place was low-lying, right next to the water, then on those piles we set about constructing a room, with an adjacent storeroom. In the room we set out all our holy icons as they ought to be by our forefathers' rules: along the length of one wall we opened a folding iconostasis of three levels, the lowest for big icons, and the two upper shelves for smaller ones, and thus we built a stairway, as it should be, up to the crucifix itself, and we put the angel on the lectern on which Luka Kirilovich read the Scriptures. Luka Kirilovich and Mikhailitsa set up house in the storeroom, and we closed off a little barrack for ourselves beside it.

On looking at us, the others who came to work for a long stretch began building for themselves in the same way, and so, across from the great, established city, we had our light little town on piles. We got down to work, and everything went as it ought to! The money counted out by the Englishmen in the office was reliable; God sent us such good health that we didn't have a single sick man all summer, and Luka's Mikhailitsa even started complaining, "I'm not glad, myself, I've grown so plump in all quarters." What we Old Believers especially liked about it was that, while we were subjected to persecution everywhere back then, we had an easy time of it here: there were no town or district authorities, no priests; we didn't set eyes on anybody, and nobody was concerned or interfered with our religion . . . We prayed our fill: put in our hours of work and then gathered in the room, and there the holy icons shone so much from all the lamps that your heart even got to glowing. Luka Kirilovich would begin by pronouncing the blessing, and then we'd all join in and sing praises so that sometimes, in calm weather, it could be heard far beyond our settlement. And our faith didn't bother anybody, and many even seemed to fall in with our way, and it pleased not only simple people, who were inclined to worship God in Russian fashion, but even those of other faith. Many churchgoers of pious disposition, who had no time to go to church across the river, used to stand under our windows and listen and begin to pray. We didn't forbid them this standing outside: we couldn't drive them all away, because even foreigners who were interested in the old Russian rite came more than once to listen to our singing and approved of it. The head of the English builders, Yakov Yakovlevich, would even come and stand under the window with a piece of paper and kept trying to take down our chanting in notes, and then he'd go around the works humming to himself in our way: "God is the Lord and has revealed Himself to us"—only for him, naturally, it all came out in a different style, because this singing, which is set down in the old notation, can't be accurately recorded in the new Western notes. The English, to do them credit, were most reliable and pious people themselves, and they liked us very much, considered us good people, and praised us. In short, the Lord's angel brought us to a good place and opened to us all the hearts of people and all the peosage of nature.

In this same peaceful spirit as I've represented to you, we lived nigh onto three years. Everything went swimmingly, successes poured down on us as from Amalthea's horn,[10] when we suddenly perceived that among us there were two vessels chosen by God for our punishment. One such was the blacksmith Maroy, and the other the accountant Pimen Ivanovich. Maroy was quite simple, even illiterate, which is even a rarity among the Old Believers, but he was a peculiar man: of clumsy appearance, like a camel, and stout as a boar—an armful and a half in girth, and his brow all overgrown with a thick mane like an old antlion,[11] and in the middle of his head, on top, he used to shear a bare patch. He was dull and incomprehensible of speech, he maundered with his lips, and his mind was slow and inept at everything, so that he couldn't even learn prayers by heart and used to repeat just some one word, but he could foresee the future and had the gift of prophecy, and could give intimations of what was to come. Pimen, on the other hand, was a foppish man: he liked to behave with great swagger and spoke with such a clever twisting of words that you could only wonder at his speech; but then he was of a light character and easily carried away. Maroy was an elderly man, in his seventies, but Pimen was middle-aged and refined: he had curly hair parted down the middle; bushy eyebrows; a pink-cheeked face—Belial, in a word.[12] In these two vessels there was suddenly fermented the vinegar of that bitter draft we were to drink.

IV

The bridge we were building on eight granite piers was already rising high above the water, and in the summer of the fourth year we were starting to put iron chains on those piers. At that point there was a little hitch: as we started sorting out the links and fitting steel rivets to each hole by measure, it turned out that many of the bolts were too long and had to be cut, and each of those bolts—steel rods all made in England—was cast of the strongest steel and thick as a grown man's arm. To heat up these bolts was impossible, because it softens the steel, and no tool could saw through them: but our blacksmith Maroy suddenly came up with this method: he'd coat the place where it had to be cut with thick axle grease mixed with coarse sand, and then stick the whole thing into the snow, and crumble salt around it, and turn it, spin it; then snatch it out of there all at once, put it on a hot anvil, and give it such a whack with a sledge that it would get cut off like a wax candle with snips. All the Englishmen and Germans came to look at Maroy's cleverness, stared and stared, then suddenly laughed and started talking among themselves first, and then said in our language:

"So, Russ! You fine fellow; you goot understand physic!"

But what sort of "physic" could Maroy understand? He had no understanding of science at all, and simply did it with the wisdom the Lord gave him. And our Pimen Ivanovich went and started boasting about it. So it went badly on both sides: some ascribed it to science, of which this Maroy of ours had no notion, and others started saying that a visible blessing of God was upon us, working wonders such as had never been seen. And this last thing was worse for us than the first. I've already told you that Pimen Ivanovich was a weak man and a sensualist, and I will now explain why we nevertheless kept him in our crew. He went to town after provisions for us, made whatever purchases were necessary; we sent him to the post office to mail passports and money back home, and to retrieve the new passports when they came.[13] Generally, it was that sort of thing he took care of, and, to tell the truth, in that sense he was a necessary and even very useful man. A real, solid Old Believer, naturally, always shuns that sort of vanity, and flees from dealings with officials, for we saw nothing but vexation from them, but Pimen was glad of the vanity, and had acquired a most abundant acquaintance across the river in town: merchants and gentlefolk he had to do with on the crew's business—everybody knew him and considered him the first man among us. We, naturally, chuckled at that, but he was terribly fond of having tea with gentlefolk and showing off his eloquence: they called him our chief, and he only smiled and spread his beard on his chest. In short, an empty fellow! And this Pimen of ours wound up at a certain not unimportant person's, whose wife was born in our parts, also a wordy one, and she had read herself up on some new books about Old Believers, in which we've no notion what's written about us, and suddenly, I don't know why, it entered her head that she had a great liking for us. The surprising thing was why she chose to be such a vessel! Well, if she liked us, she liked us, and whenever our Pimen came to her husband for something, she immediately sat him down to tea, and Pimen was glad of it and immediately rolled out his scrolls before her.

She pours out her woman's vain talk, that you Old Believers are this and that, holy people, righteous, ever-blessed, and our Belial goes cross-eyed with pleasure, head bowed, beard smooth, voice soothing:

"Of course, madam. We observe the law of our forefathers, we're this and that, we hold to these rules, and keep an eye on each other for the purity of our customs," and, in a word, he says all sorts of things to her that don't belong to a conversation with a worldly woman. And yet, just imagine, she's interested.

"I've heard," she says, "that God's blessing is manifested visibly to you."

And the man chimes in at once:

"Of course, my dear lady," he replies, "it is manifested; it is manifested quite ocularly."

"Visibly?"

"Visibly," he replies, "visibly, madam. Just a couple of days ago one of our men snipped off stout steel like a cobweb."

The little lady just clasped her sweet little hands.

"Ah," she says, "how interesting! Ah, I love miracles terribly, and I believe in them! Listen," she says, "please ask your Old Believers to pray that God will give me a daughter. I have two sons, but I absolutely must have a daughter. Is that possible?"

"It is, ma'am," Pimen replies. "Why not? It's perfectly possible! Only," he says, "in such cases you must always have sacrificial oil burning."

With the greatest pleasure, she gives him ten roubles for the oil, and he puts the money in his pocket and says:

"Very well, ma'am, be of good hope, I'll tell them."

Naturally, Pimen tells us nothing about it, but the lady gives birth to a daughter.

Pah, what a noise she made! She's barely recovered from the delivery when she summons our empty fellow and honors him as if he was a wonderworker, and he accepts that as well. Such was the vanity of the man, and the darkening of his mind, and the freezing of his feelings. A year later, the lady again had a request for our God, that her husband should rent her a summer house—and again everything was done according to her wishes, and Pimen got more offerings for candles and oil, and he disposed of those offerings as he saw fit, without sending them our way. And incomprehensible wonders indeed got done: this lady's elder son was in school, and he was the foremost hooky player, and a lazy dunce, and didn't study at all, but when it came time for examinations, she sent for Pimen and gave him a commission to pray that her son pass to the next class. Pimen says:

"That's hard. I'll have to get all our men together to pray all night and call out by candlelight till morning."

But she didn't bat an eye. She handed him thirty roubles—only pray! And what do you think? This wastrel son of hers runs into such luck that he passes to the upper class. The lady nearly went out of her mind with joy that our God showed her such kindness! She started giving Pimen commission after commission, and he had already petitioned God and obtained health for her, and an inheritance, and high rank for her husband, and so many decorations that there was no more room on his chest and they say he carried one in his pocket. Wondrous, that's all, and we knew nothing about it. But the time came for all that to be revealed and for some wonders to be exchanged for others.

V

Trouble was brewing in the commercial dealings among the Jews in one of the Jewish towns of that province. I can't tell you for sure whether it was about some wrong money or some duty-free trading, but it had to be looked into by the authorities, and here there was the prospect of a mighty reward. So the lady sends for our Pimen and says:

"Pimen Ivanovich, here's twenty roubles for oil and candles; tell your people to pray as zealously as they can that my husband gets sent on this mission."

Nothing to it! He's already acquired a taste for collecting this oil tax and replies:

"Very well, my lady, I'll tell them."

"And they should pray good and proper," she says, "because it's very necessary for me!"

"As if they dare to pray badly on me, my lady, when I order them," Pimen reassured her. "I'll have them go hungry till their prayer's answered." He took the money and was off, and that same night the lady's husband got the job she wished for him.

Well, this time the blessing went to her head so much that she wasn't satisfied with having us pray, but absolutely desired to go and pray to our holy images herself.

She said so to Pimen, but he turned coward, because he knew our people wouldn't let her go near our holy images. But the lady wouldn't leave off.

"Say what you like," she said, "but I'll take a boat towards evening today and come to you with my son."

Pimen tried to talk her out of it. "It's better," he says, "if we pray by ourselves. We have this guardian angel, you donate for the oil to burn before him, and we'll entrust him with safeguarding your spouse."

"Ah, splendid," she replies, "splendid. I'm very glad there's such an angel. Here's for the oil. Be sure to light three lamps before him, and I'll come and look."

Trouble caught up with Pimen. He came to us and started saying, "Thus and so, it's my fault, I didn't contradict this vile heathen woman in her wishes, because her husband is somebody we need." And so he told us a cock-and-bull story, but still didn't tell us all he'd done. Well, unpleasant as it was for us, there was nothing else to do. We quickly took our icons off the walls and hid them away in the trunks, and replaced them with some substitutes we kept for fear the authorities might come and inspect us. We put them on the shelves and waited for the visitor. And she came, spiffed up something awful, sweeping around with her long, wide skirts, looking at our substitute icons through a lorgnette and asking: "Tell me, please, which one is the wonderworking angel?" We didn't even know how to get her off the subject:

"We have no such angel," we said.

And no matter how she insisted and complained to Pimen, we didn't show her the angel and quickly took her away to have tea and whatever little treats we could give her.

We disliked her terribly, and God knows why: her look was somehow repulsivous, for all that she was considered beautiful. Tall, you know, with such spindly legs, thin as a steppe goat, and straight-browed.

"You don't like that kind of beauty?" the bearskin coat interrupted the storyteller.

"Good grief, what's likeable in such snakiness?" he replied.

"Do your people consider it beautiful if a woman looks like a hump or something?"

"A hump?" the storyteller repeated, smiling and not taking offense. "Why do you suggest that? In our true Russian understanding concerning a woman's build, we keep to a type of our own, which we find much more suitable than modern-day frivolity, and it's nothing like a hump. We don't appreciate spindliness, true; we prefer that a woman stand not on long legs, but on sturdy ones, so that she doesn't get tangled up, but rolls about everywhere like a ball and makes it, where a spindly-legged one will run and trip. We also don't appreciate snaky thinness, but require that a woman be on the stout side, ample, because, though it's not so elegant, it points to maternity in them. The brow of our real, pure Russian woman's breed is more plump, more meaty, but then in that soft brow there's more gaiety, more welcome. The same for the nose: ours have noses that aren't hooked, but more like little pips, but this little pip itself, like it or not, is much more affable in family life than a dry, proud nose. But the eyebrows especially, the eyebrows open up the look of the face, and therefore it's necessary that a woman's eyebrows not scowl, but be opened out, archlike, for a man finds it more inviting to talk with such a woman, and she makes a different, more welcoming impression on everybody coming to the house. But modern taste, naturally, has abandoned this good type and approves of airy ephemerality in the female sex, only that's completely useless. Excuse me, however, I see we've started talking about something else. I'd better go on."

Our Pimen, being a vain man, notices that we, having seen the visitor off, have begun to criticize her, and says:

"Really, now! She's a good woman."

And we reply: what kind of good is she, if there's no goodness in her appearance? But God help her: whatever she is, let her be. We were glad enough to be rid of her, and we hastened to burn some incense so that there would be no smell of her in our place.

After that we swept all traces of the dear guest's visit from the room, put the substitute images back into the trunks behind the partition, and took out our real icons, placed them on the shelves as they had been before, sprinkled them with holy water, said some initial prayers, and went each to his own night's rest, only, God knows why and wherefore, we all slept poorly that night and felt somehow eerie and restless.

VI

In the morning we all went to work and set about our tasks, but Luka Kirilovich wasn't there. That, judging by his punctuality, was surprising, but it seemed still more surprising to me that he turned up after seven all pale and upset.

Knowing that he was a self-possessed man and did not like giving way to empty sorrows, I paid attention to that and asked: "What's the matter with you, Luka Kirilovich?" And he says: "I'll tell you later."

But, being young then, I was awfully curious, and, besides, a premonition suddenly came to me from somewhere that this was something bad to do with our faith; and I honored our faith and had never been an unbeliever.

And therefore I couldn't stand it for long, and, under some pretext or other, I left work and ran home. I think: while nobody's home, I'll worm something out of Mikhailitsa. Though Luka Kirilovich hadn't revealed anything, she, in all her simplicity, could still somehow see through him, and she wouldn't conceal anything from me, because I had been an orphan from childhood, and had grown up like a son to them, and she was the same to me as a second mother.

So I rush to her, and I see she's sitting on the porch, an old coat thrown over her shoulders, and herself as if sick, sad, and a sort of greenish color.

"My second mother," I say, "why are you sitting here of all places?"

And she says:

"And where am I to huddle up, Marochka?"

My name is Mark Alexandrovich, but she, having maternal feelings for me, called me Marochka.

"What's she giving me this nonsense for," I think, "that she's got nowhere to huddle up?"

"Why don't you lie down in your closet?" I say.

"I can't, Marochka," she says, "old Maroy's praying in the big room."

"Aha!" I think. "So it's true that something's happened to do with our faith." And Aunt Mikhailitsa begins:

"You probably don't know what happened here during the night, do you, Marochka, my child?"

"No, second mother, I don't."

"Ah, terrible things!"

"Tell me quickly, second mother."

"Ah, I don't know how I can tell you."

"How is it you can't tell me?" I say. "Am I some kind of stranger to you, and not like a son?"

"I know, my dearest," she replies, "that you're like a son to me, only I don't trust myself to put it in the right words for you, because I'm stupid and untalented, but just wait—uncle will come back at quitting time, he'll surely tell you everything."

But there was no way I could wait, and I pestered her to tell me, tell me right now, what it was all about.

And I see she keeps blinking, blinking her eyes, and her eyes get all filled with tears, and she suddenly brushes them away with her shawl and softly whispers to me:

"Our guardian angel came down last night, child."

This revelation threw me into a fit of trembling.

"Say quickly," I ask, "how did this wonder happen and who were the beholders of it?"

And she replies:

"It was an unfathomable wonder, child, and nobody beheld it but me, because it happened in the deepest midnight hour, and I was the only one not asleep."

And this, my dear sirs, is the story she told me:

"I fell asleep having said my prayers," she says. "I don't remember how long I slept, but suddenly in my dreams I see a fire, a big fire: as if everything here is burning down, and the river carries the ashes and whirls them around the piers, and swallows them, sucks them into the depths." And as for herself, it seemed to Mikhailitsa that she ran out in a threadbare nightshirt, all holes, and stood right by the water, and across from her, on the other bank, a tall red pillar thrust itself up, and on that pillar was a small white cock, and he kept flapping his wings. And it was as if Mikhailitsa said: "Who are you?"—because her feeling told her that he was announcing something. And the cock suddenly exclaimed "Amen" as if in a human voice, and drooped, and was no longer there, and around Mikhailitsa it became quiet and there was such spentness in the air that Mikhailitsa became frightened and couldn't breathe, and she woke up and lay there, and she heard a lamb start bleating outside the door. And she can hear from its voice that it's a very young lamb that still hasn't shed its newborn wool. Its pure, silvery little voice rings out "Ba-a-a," and suddenly Mikhailitsa senses that it's walking about the prayer room, its little hooves beating out a quick tap-tap-tap on the floorboards, as if it's looking for someone. Mikhailitsa reasons to herself: "Lord Jesus Christ! What is it? There are no sheep in our whole settlement and no lambing either, so where has this little one dropped from?" And at the same time she gives a start: "How, then, did it end up in the house? It means that, with all last night's bustle, we forgot to bolt the front door. Thank God," she thinks, "it's just a lamb that's wandered in, and not a yard dog getting at our holy icons." And she tries to wake up Luka with it: "Kirilych!" she calls him. "Kirilych! Wake up quick, dearest, we've left the door open and some little lamb's wandered in." But Luka Kirilovich, as bad luck would have it, was wrapped up in a dead sleep. No matter what Mikhailitsa did, she couldn't wake him up: he groaned, but didn't speak. The harder Mikhailitsa shook and shoved him, the louder he groaned, and that was all. Mikhailitsa began asking him at least "to remember the name of Jesus," but she had barely uttered that name herself when something in the room squealed, and at the same moment Luka tore himself from the bed and went rushing forward, but in the middle of the room it was as if a metal wall suddenly flung him back. "A light, woman! A light, quickly!" he shouted to Mikhailitsa, and he himself couldn't move from the spot. She lit a candle and ran out, and saw him, pale as a condemned man, trembling so much that not only was the clasp moving on his neck, but even his pants were shaking on his legs. The woman turned to him again. "My provider," she said, "what is it?" And he just pointed his finger at the empty spot where the angel used to be, while the angel himself was lying on the floor by Luka's feet.

Luka Kirilovich went at once to old Maroy and said, thus and so, this is what my woman saw and what happened to us. Come and look. Maroy came and knelt before the angel lying on the floor and stayed motionless over him for a long time, like a marble tombstone. Then, raising his hand, he scratched the bare patch on the crown of his head and said softly:

"Bring me twelve clean, newly fired bricks."

Luka Kirilovich brought them at once, Maroy looked them over and saw that they were all clean, straight from the fiery furnace, and told Luka to stack them one on top of the other, and in that way they erected a pillar, covered it with a clean towel, raised the icon up on it, and then Maroy, bowing to the ground, exclaims:

"Angel of the Lord, may thy footsteps be poured out wheresoe'er thou wishest!"

And he had only just uttered these words, when there suddenly comes a rap-rap-rap on the door, and an unfamiliar voice calls out:

"Hey, you schismatics, which of you is the chief here?"

Luka Kirilovich opens the door and sees a soldier with a badge standing there.

Luka asks what chief he wants, and the soldier replies:

"The one who visited the lady and calls himself Pimen."

Well, Luka sent his wife for Pimen at once, and asked the soldier what was the matter. Why had he been sent at night to find Pimen?

The soldier says:

"I don't know for certain, but the word is that the Jews set up some awkward business with the gentleman."

But precisely what it was, he couldn't tell.

"I heard," he says, "that the gentleman sealed them, and they put a seal on him."

But how it was that they sealed each other, he couldn't tell coherently.

Meanwhile Pimen came over and, like a Jew himself, rolled his eyes this way and that: obviously, he didn't know what to say. Luka says:

"What are you standing there for, you spielman, go on now and bring your spielmaning to an end!"

Pimen and the soldier got into the boat and left.

An hour later our Pimen comes back and puts up a cheerful front, but it's clear he's cruelly out of sorts.

Luka questions him:

"Tell me, featherbrain," he says, "and you'd better tell me in all frankness, what were you up to there?"

And he says:

"Nothing."

Well, so it was left at nothing, and yet it was by no means nothing.

VII

A most astonishing thing had happened with the gentleman our Pimen supposedly had us pray for. As I told you, he set out for the Jewish town and arrived there late at night, when nobody was thinking about him, and at once sealed every one of the shops, and informed the police that he would come and inspect them the next morning. The Jews, naturally, found it out at once and came to him at once that night asking to make a deal, meaning they had no end of illegal goods. They come and shove ten thousand roubles at the gentleman straight off. He says: "I can't, I'm a big official, invested with confidence, and I don't take bribes," and the Jews psht-psht-psht among themselves and offer him fifteen. He says again: "I can't." They offer twenty. He says: "What is it, don't you understand that *I can't,* I've already let the police know about going there together tomorrow to inspect." They psht-psht again, and then say:

"Vel, Your Excellency, dat's nothing dat you let the police know, here ve're giffing you twenty-five tousend, and you jes gif us your seal till morning and go peacefully to bed, and ve don't need anyting else."

The gentleman thought and thought: he considered himself a big person, but, obviously, even big persons don't have hearts of stone. He took the twenty-five thousand and gave them his seal, with which he had done the sealing, and went to bed. During the night, the Jews, naturally, dragged everything they had to out of their cellars and sealed them again with the same seal, and the gentleman was still asleep when they were already psht-pshting in his front hall. Well, so he lets them in; they thank him and say:

"And now, Your Honor, you're velcome to inspect."

Well, he makes as if he doesn't hear that, and says:

"Give me back my seal, quickly."

And the Jews say:

"And you gif us back our money."

"What? How's that?" says the gentleman. But they stand their ground:

"Ve left you de money as a pledge."

"What do you mean, as a pledge?"

"Dat's right, zir," they say, "it vas a pledge."

"You're lying," he says, "scoundrels that you are, Christ-sellers, you gave me that money to keep."

They nudge each other and chuckle:

"Hörst-du," they say, "you hear, ve supposedly gafe it outright . . . Hm, hm! Oy vey, as if ve could be so shtupid, just like some muzhiks mitout politics, to gif such a big person a khabar." ("Khabar" is their word for a bribe.)

Well, sirs, can you imagine anything better than this story? The gentleman, naturally, should have given back the money, and that would have been the end of it, but he held out a little longer, because he was sorry to part with it. Morning came; all the shops in town were locked; people came and marveled; the police demand the seal, and the Jews shout: "Oy vey, vat kind of gofernment is dis! De high autorities vant to ruin us." A terrible uproar! The gentleman locks himself in and sits there almost out of his mind till dinnertime, but in the evening he summons those clever Jews and says: "Take your money, curse you, and give me back my seal!" But they no longer want that. They say: "How can you do dat! In de whole town ve did no business all day: now Your Honor muss gif us fifty tousend." You see what came of it! And the Jews threaten: "If you don't gif fifty tousend today, tomorrow it vill cost you anoder twenty-fife tousend more!" The gentleman didn't sleep all night, and in the morning he sent for the Jews again, gave them back all the money he had taken from them, and wrote a promissory note for another twenty-five thousand, and went ahead with the inspection anyhow; found nothing, naturally, quickly went home to his wife, and stormed and raged before her: where was he to get twenty-five thousand to buy back the promissory note from the Jews? "We'll have to sell the estate that came as your dowry." But she says: "Not for anything in the world—I'm attached to it." He says: "It's your fault, you prayed through some schismatics that I be sent on this mission and assured me their angel would help me, and yet see how nicely he's helped me." But she replies: "No, the fault is yours. Why were you so stupid that you didn't arrest those Jews and declare that they stole the seal from you? But, in any case," she says, "never mind: just listen to me and I'll set things right, and others will pay for your injudiciousness." And she suddenly shouted out to whoever happened to be there: "Quick, hurry, go across the Dniepr and bring me the schismatics' headman."

Well, the envoy, naturally, went and brought our Pimen, and the lady says directly, not beating about the bush: "Listen, I know you're an intelligent man and will understand what I need: there's been a little unpleasantness with my husband, some scoundrels have robbed him . . . Jews . . . you understand, and now we absolutely must have twenty-five thousand today or tomorrow, and there's nowhere I can get it that quickly; but I've called you in and am at peace, because Old Believers are intelligent and rich people, and, as I've become convinced, God Himself helps you in all things, so kindly give me twenty-five thousand, and I, for my part, will tell all the ladies about your wonderworking icons, and you'll see how much you get for wax and oil."

I suppose it's not hard for you to imagine, my dear sirs, what our spielman felt about such a turn of events. I don't know what words

he used, but only—and I do believe him—that he began hotly vowing and swearing, testifying to our poverty in the face of such a sum,
but she, this new Herodias,[14] didn't even want to know about it. "No,"
she says, "I know very well that the Old Believers are rich, and for
you twenty-five thousand is nonsense. When my father was serving
in Moscow, the Old Believers did him such favors more than once
and for more than that. No, twenty-five thousand is a trifle."

Here, too, naturally, Pimen tried to explain to her that the Moscow Old Believers were capital people, while we were simple, hardworking hayseeds and had no place competing against Muscovites.
But she must have had good Muscovite lessons in her and suddenly
cut him short:

"What's this?" she says. "What's this you're telling me? Don't I
know how many wonderworking icons you've got, and weren't you
telling me yourself how much they send you for wax and oil from
all over Russia? No, I don't want to listen. I must have the money
right now, otherwise my husband will go to the governor today and
tell him all about how you pray and seduce people, and it'll be bad
for you." Poor Pimen nearly fell off the porch; he came home as I
told you, and just kept repeating the one word "Nothing," and he
himself was all red, like from the steambaths, pacing up and down
and blowing his nose. Well, Luka Kirilovich finally got a little something out of him, only the man, naturally, didn't reveal everything to
him, but just gave away the most insignificant part of the essence,
like saying: "This lady demands of me that I get you to lend her five
thousand." Well, hearing that, Luka, naturally, flies into a temper:
"Ah, you spielman, you," he says, "you just had to go dealing with
them and then bring them here! What, are we so rich, are we, that
we can raise that kind of money? And why should we give it to them?
And where is it, anyway? . . . Since you dealt yourself into it, you
can deal yourself out of it—we can't get five thousand anywhere."
With that, Luka Kirilovich went on his way to work and arrived, as
I told you, pale as a condemned man, because, going by the night's
events, he anticipated trouble for us; and Pimen himself went the
other way. We had all seen him emerge from the bulrushes in a little
boat and cross over to town, and now, once Mikhailitsa had told me
everything in order, how he'd dunned them for the five thousand,
I figured he was probably in a rush to sweeten up the lady. In such
reflections, I was standing by Mikhailitsa, thinking whether something harmful for us might come of it, and whether measures ought

to be taken against this possibly occurring evil, when I suddenly saw
it was too late for the whole undertaking, because a big boat had
come to shore, and just behind my back I heard the noise of many
voices, and, turning, I saw a number of different officials, in various
corresponding uniforms, and with them no small number of policemen and soldiers. And, my dear sirs, before Mikhailitsa and I had
time to blink, they all poured past us straight to Luka's room, and
at the door they placed two sentries with drawn sabers. Mikhailitsa
started throwing herself at these sentries, not so much to be allowed
in as to endure suffering. They, naturally, pushed her away, but she
threw herself at them still more fiercely, and their combat went so
far that one of the gendarmes finally hurt her badly, so that she went
rolling head over heels off the porch. I rushed to the bridge to fetch
Luka, but I saw Luka himself already running towards me, and our
whole crew after him, they had all risen up, and with whatever they
had in their hands, one a crowbar, another a mallet, came running
to save our holy icons . . . Those who didn't catch a boat and had
no way of reaching the shore dove off the bridge into the water,
in all their clothes, as they had been at work, and swam one after
another through the cold waves . . . It was terrible even to think how
it would end. About twenty guardsmen came there, and they were all
in various bold attire, but ours numbered more than fifty, and all of
them animated by lofty, ardent faith, and they all swam through the
water like sea dogs, and though they might be bashed on the head
with mallets, they reached the bank where their holy icons were,
and suddenly, all soaking wet, marched forward like your living and
indestructible stones.

VIII

Now kindly remember that, while Mikhailitsa and I were talking on
the porch, old Maroy was praying in the room, and the gentlemen
officials and their sbirri found him there. He told us later that, as
soon as they came in, they bolted the door and threw themselves
straight at the icons. Some were putting out the lamps, others were
tearing the icons from the walls and piling them on the floor, shouting to him: "Are you the priest?" He says: "No, I'm not." They say:
"Who is your priest, then?" He replies: "We have no priest." And

they say: "What do you mean, no priest! How dare you say you have no priest!" Here Maroy began explaining to them that we don't have priests, but since he spoke badly, mumblingly, they didn't try to make out what he meant. "Bind him," they said, "he's under arrest!" Maroy let them bind him: it was nothing to him that a common soldier tied his hands with a piece of string, but he stood there and, accepting it all for the sake of the faith, watched for what would follow. And the officials meanwhile lit candles and started placing seals on the icons: some placed the seals, others wrote them down on a list, still others bored holes in the icons and strung them on iron rods like kitchen pots. Maroy looked at all this blasphemous outrage and didn't even flinch, because, he reasoned, it was probably God's will to allow such savagery. But just then Uncle Maroy heard one gendarme cry out, and another after him: the door flew open, and our sea dogs, wet as they were, straight from the water, pushed their way into the room. Fortunately, Luka Kirilovich found himself at the head of them. He shouted at once:

"Wait, Christian folk, don't brazen it out!" And he himself turned to the officials and, pointing to the icons strung on rods, said: "Why, gentlemen superiors, have you damaged the holy images like this? If you have the right to take them from us, we do not resist authority—take them; but why do you damage the rare artwork of our forefathers?"

But that husband of Pimen's lady acquaintance, who was there at the head of them all, shouted at Uncle Luka:

"Silence, scoundrel! How dare you argue!"

And Luka, though he was a proud man, humbled himself and said softly:

"Permit me, Your Honor, we know the procedure. We have some hundred and fifty icons in this room. Allow us to pay you three roubles per icon, and take them, only don't damage our ancestral art."

The gentleman flashed his eyes and shouted loudly:

"Away with you!" But in a whisper he whispered: "Give me a hundred roubles apiece, or else I'll torch them all."

Luka could not give or even consider giving such big money, and said:

"In that case, God help you: ruin it all however you like, we don't have that kind of money."

But the gentleman started yelling wrathfully:

"Ah, you bearded goat, how dare you talk about money in front of us?"—and here he suddenly started rushing about, and all the divine images he saw, he strung together, and they screwed nuts onto the ends of the rods and sealed them, too, so that it was impossible to take them off and exchange them. And it was all gathered up and ready, they were about to leave for good: the soldiers took the rods strung with icons on their shoulders and carried them to the boat; but Mikhailitsa, who had sneaked into the room with the other folk, had meanwhile quietly stolen the angel's icon from the lectern and was carrying it to the closet under her shawl, but as her hands were trembling, she dropped it. Saints alive, how the gentleman flew into a temper! He called us thieves and knaves, and said:

"Aha! You knaves wanted to steal it so that it wouldn't end up on the bolt; well, then it won't end up there, but here's what I'm going to do to it!" And heating the stick of sealing wax, he jabbed the boiling resin, still flaming, right into the angel's face!

My dear sirs, don't hold it against me if I can't even try to describe what happened when the gentleman poured the stream of boiling resin onto the face of the angel and, cruel man that he was, raised the icon up, so as to boast of how he'd managed to spite us. All I remember is that the bright, divine face was red and sealed, and the varnish, which had melted slightly under the fiery resin, ran down in two streams, as if it were blood mixed with tears . . .

We all gasped and, covering our eyes with our hands, fell on our faces and groaned as if we were being tortured. And we went on groaning, so that the dark night found us howling and lamenting over our sealed angel, and it was here, in this darkness and silence, over the devastated holiness of our fathers, that a thought occurred to us: we would keep an eye out for where they put our guardian, and we swore to steal him back, even at the risk of our lives, and unseal him, and to carry out this resolve, they chose me and a young fellow named Levonty. In years this Levonty was still a downright boy, no more than seventeen, but he was big of body, good of heart, God-fearing from childhood, and obedient and well-behaved, just like your ardent white, silver-bridled steed.

A better co-thinker and co-worker couldn't have been asked for in such a dangerous deed as tracking down and purloining the sealed angel, whose blinded appearance was unbearable for us to the point of illness.

IX

I'm not going to trouble you with the details of how I and my co-thinker and co-worker passed through the eyes of needles, going into all this, but I'll tell you directly of the grief that came over us when we learned that our icons, drilled through by the officials and strung on rods as they were, had been piled up in the basement of the diocesan office. This was a lost cause, as if they had been buried in the grave, and there was no use thinking about them. The nice thing, however, was that they said the bishop himself did not approve of such savagery of behavior and, on the contrary, said: "Why that?" and even stood up for the old art and said: "It's ancient, it must be cherished!" But here was the bad thing, that the disaster of irreverence had only just passed, when a new, still greater one arose from his very reverence: this same bishop, it must be supposed, not with bad but precisely with good consideration, took our sealed angel, studied him for a long time, then averted his eyes and said: "Disturbing sight! How terribly they've disfigured him! Don't put this icon in the basement," he says, "but set it up in the sanctuary, on the windowsill behind the altar." The bishop's servants did as he ordered, and I must tell you that such attention on the part of a Church hierarch was, on the one hand, very agreeable to us, but, on the other—we could see that any plan we had of stealing our angel had become impossible. There remained another means: to bribe the bishop's servants and with their help substitute for the icon an artfully painted likeness of itself. In this our Old Believers had also succeeded more than once, but to do it one first of all needed a skillful and experienced icon painter, who could make a substitute icon with precision, and we did not anticipate finding such an icon painter in those parts. And from then on a redoubled anguish came over us all; it spread through us like dropsy under the skin: in our room where only the praise of God had been heard, only laments began to ring out, and in a short time we had all lamented ourselves sick and our tear-filled eyes couldn't see the ground under our feet, and owing to that, or not owing to that, an eye disease attacked us and began to spread through all our people. What had never happened before, happened now: there was no end of sick people! Talk went around among all the working people that all this was not for nothing, but on account of the Old Believers' angel: "He was blinded by the sealing," they said, "and now we're all going blind." And at this explanation not only we but all church-going people rose up, and however many doctors the English bosses brought, nobody went to them or took their medicine, but cried out as one:

"Bring us the sealed angel, we want to pray to him, and he alone will heal us."

The Englishman Yakov Yakovlevich, having looked into the matter, went to the bishop himself and said:

"Thus and so, Your Grace, faith is a great thing, and to him who has faith, it is given according to his faith: let the sealed angel come to us on the other bank."

But the bishop did not heed him and said:

"This should not be indulged."

These words seemed cruel to us then, and we condemned the bishop with much vain talk, but afterwards it was revealed to us that this was all guided not by cruelty, but by divine providence.

Meanwhile the signs seemed unceasing, and the chastising finger sought out on the other bank the chief culprit of the whole thing, Pimen himself, who, after our calamity, fled from us and joined the Church. I met him in town once. He bowed to me, so I bowed to him, and he said:

"I have sinned, brother Mark, by going from you to a different faith."

And I replied:

"Who is of what faith—that's God's business, but that you sold a poor man for a pair of boots, that, naturally, is not good, and, forgive me, but for that, as the prophet Amos ordered,[15] I convict you in brotherly fashion."

At the name of the prophet, he began to tremble.

"Don't talk to me about prophets," he says. "I remember the Scriptures myself and feel that 'the prophets torment the dwellers on earth,'[16] and I even have a sign of it," and he complained that he had bathed in the river the other day and after that his whole body became piebald, and he unbuttoned his chest and showed me, and in fact he had spots on him, like on a piebald horse, covering his chest and creeping up on his neck.

Sinful as I was, I had a mind to tell him, "Beware of him whom God hath marked," but I quashed these words on my lips and said:

"Pray, then, and rejoice that you've been stamped like that in this world—perhaps you'll present yourself clean in the next."

He started lamenting to me about how unhappy he was because of it and what it would cost him if the piebaldness spread to his face, because the governor himself, seeing Pimen when he was received into the Church, had admired his beauty and said to the mayor that, when important persons passed through town, Pimen should unfailingly be placed in front with the silver platter. Well, and how are they going to place him there if he's piebald? But, anyhow, as there was no point in my listening to the vanity and futility of this Belial, I turned and left.

And with that we parted ways. His spots became ever more clearly marked, and we had no lack of other signs, at the end of which, in the fall, the ice had only just set in, when suddenly there was a thaw, all that ice was scattered and came to wreck our constructions, and from then on damage followed upon damage, until suddenly one granite pier gave way, and the deeps swallowed up all the work of many years, worth many thousands . . .

Our English bosses themselves were struck by that, and then word from someone reached their chief, Yakov Yakovlevich, that to be delivered from it all he had to drive out us Old Believers, but since he was a man of good soul, he didn't listen to it, but, on the contrary, sent for me and Luka Kirilovich and said:

"Give me your advice, lads: isn't there some way I can help you and comfort you?"

But we replied that, as long as the image of the angel, which was sacred to us and had gone before us everywhere, was sealed with fiery resin, we could not be comforted and were wasting away from sorrow.

"What do you hope to do?" he asks.

"We hope in time to replace him with a substitute and to unseal his pure face, scorched by the godless hand of an official."

"Why is he so dear to you?" he asks. "Can't you get hold of another one like him?"

"He's dear to us," we reply, "because he has protected us, and to get hold of another is impossible, because he was painted by a pious hand in times of firm faith and was blessed by an old-time priest according to the complete prayer book of Pyotr Mogila,[17] and now we have neither priests nor that prayer book."

"But how will you unseal him," he asks, "if his whole face is burnt with resin?"

"Well," we reply, "Your Honor needn't worry on that account: it will be enough to have him in our hands; then our protector will stand up for himself. He wasn't made by commercial painters, he's real Stroganov work, and Stroganov and Kostroma varnish is boiled up so that it has no fear of fiery seals and won't let the resin through to the delicate paint."

"Are you sure of that?"

"We are, sir. That varnish is as strong as the old Russian faith itself."

Here he swore at those who were unable to cherish such art, gave us his hands, and said once more:

"Well, don't grieve, then: I'll help you, and we'll get hold of your angel. Do you need him for long?"

"No," we say, "just for a short time."

"Well, then I'll say I want to have a rich gold casing made for your sealed angel, and once they give him to me, we'll put a substitute in his place. I'll get started on it tomorrow."

We thanked him, but said:

"Only don't do anything, sir, either tomorrow or the next day."

"Why not?" he asks.

And we reply:

"Because, sir, first of all we've got to have a substitute icon made, as like the real one as two drops of water, and there are no such masters here, and none to be found anywhere nearby."

"Nonsense," he says. "I'll bring a painter from town myself; he paints not only copies but portraits excellently well."

"No, sir," we reply, "kindly don't do that, because, first of all, improper rumors may start up through this worldly artist, and, second of all, such a painter cannot carry out the work."

The Englishman didn't believe it, but I stepped forward and explained the whole difference to him: that nowadays the work of worldly artists is not the same; they work in oils, but for icons the colors are delicate, being mixed with egg; in oil painting the work is done in brushstrokes and looks natural only from a distance, but here the paint is applied in thin layers and is clear even close up. Besides, a worldly artist, I say, can't transfer the drawing satisfactorily, because they're trained to represent the flesh of the earthly, life-loving man, while in sacred Russian icon painting there is portrayed the heavenly type of the face, concerning which a material man cannot even have any real notion.

He became interested.

"But where are there such masters," he asked, "who still understand that special type?"

"Nowadays they are very rare," I tell him (and at that time they lived in the strictest hiding). "In the village of Mstera there's a certain master Khokhlov, but he's now very advanced in years, he can't be taken on a long journey. There are two men in Palekh; they, too, are unlikely to come, and besides that," I say, "neither masters from Mstera nor masters from Palekh are any good for us."

"Why is that, now?" he persists.

"Because," I reply, "they don't have the right knack: Mstera icons are drawn big-headed and the painting is muddy, and in Palekh icons there's a turquoise tinge, everything tends towards pale blue."

"In that case," he says, "what's to be done?"

"Myself," I say, "I don't know. I've often heard that there's a good master in Moscow named Silachev: he's known among our folk all over Russia, but his work is more in the style of the Novgorodians and the court painters in Moscow, while our icon is done in the Stroganov manner, with the brightest and richest colors, and only the master Sevastian from the lower Dniepr can please us, but he's a passionate wanderer: he walks all over Russia doing work for the Old Believers, and where to look for him nobody knows."

The Englishman listened with pleasure to all these reports of mine and smiled, and then replied:

"You're quite astonishing people, and, listening to you, it's even gratifying to realize that you know so well everything that touches on your ways and can even understand art."

"Why shouldn't we understand art, sir?" I say. "Artwork is a divine thing, and we have such fanciers from among the simplest muzhiks as can not only distinguish, for example, between different schools of icon painting—Ustiug or Novgorod, Moscow or Vologda, Siberia or Stroganov—but even within one and the same school can distinguish without error between the work of one well-known old Russian master and another."

"Can it be?" he asks.

"Just like you telling one person's handwriting from another's," I reply, "so they look and see at once who painted it: Kuzma, Andrei, or Prokofy."

"By what signs?"

"There's a difference in the way the outline is transferred, and in the layering, and in the highlighting of the face and garments."

He goes on listening; and I tell him what I know about Ushakov's work, and about Rublev's, and about the most ancient Russian artist Paramshin, whose icons our pious tsars and princes gave to their children as blessings and instructed them in their wills to cherish these icons like the apple of their eye.[18]

The Englishman straightaway snatched out his notebook and asked me to repeat the name of the painter and where his works could be seen. And I reply:

"It's no use, sir, to go looking for them: there's no memory of them left anywhere."

"What's become of them?"

"I don't know," I say, "maybe they turned them into chibouks or traded them to the Germans for tobacco."

"That can't be," he says.

"On the contrary," I reply, "it's quite possible, and there are examples of it: in Rome the pope in the Vatican has folding icons painted in the thirteenth century by the Russian icon painters Andrei, Sergei, and Nikita. This miniature with multiple figures is so astonishing, they say, that even the greatest foreign artists, looking at it, go into raptures over its wondrous workmanship."

"But how did it end up in Rome?"

"Peter the Great made a gift of it to a foreign monk, and he sold it."[19]

The Englishman smiled and fell to thinking, and then said softly that in England they keep every painting from generation to generation, and that makes clear who comes from which genealogy.

"Well, but with us," I say, "there's most likely a different education, and the connection with the traditions of our ancestors is broken, so that everything seems new, as if the whole Russian race had been hatched only yesterday by a hen in a nettle patch."

"But if your educated ignorance is such," he says, "then why are those who preserve a love for your own things not concerned with maintaining your native art?"

"We have no one to maintain it, my good sir," I reply, "because in the new art schools everywhere a corruption of the senses is developed and the mind is given over to vanity. The model of lofty inspiration is lost, and everything is taken from the earth and breathes of earthly passion. Our newest artists started by portraying the warrior-angel Michael as Prince Potemkin of Taurida, and now they've gone so far that Christ the Savior is depicted as a Jew.[20] What can be expected from such people? Their uncircumcised hearts may portray something even worse and worship it as a deity: in Egypt, after all, they worshipped a bull and a red onion; but we're not going to bow down before strange gods, or take a Jewish face for the image of our Savior, and we even consider these portrayals, however artful they may be, as shameful ignorance, and we turn away from them, because our fathers said that 'distraction of the eyes destroys the purity of reason, as a broken water pump spoils the water.'"

I finished with that and fell silent, but the Englishman says:

"Go on: I like the way you reason."

"I've already said everything," I reply, but he says:

"No, tell me what you mean by your notion of inspired representation."

The question, my dear sirs, was quite difficult for a simple man, but, no help for it, I went ahead and told him how the starry sky is painted in Novgorod, and then I began to describe the decoration of St. Sophia in Kiev, where seven winged warrior-angels, who naturally do not resemble Potemkin, stand to the sides of the God of Sabaoth; and just below are the prophets and forefathers; on a lower level, Moses with the tables; still lower, Aaron in a miter and with a sprouting rod; then come King David in a crown, the prophet Isaiah with a scroll, Ezekiel with a shut gate, Daniel with a stone; and around all these who stand before God, showing us the way to heaven, are depicted the gifts through which man can reach that glorious path, namely: a book with seven seals—the gift of wisdom; a seven-branched candelabra—the gift of reason; seven eyes—the gift of counsel; seven trumpets—the gift of fortitude; a right hand amidst seven stars—the gift of vision; seven censers—the gift of piety; seven lightning bolts—the gift of the fear of God. "There," I say, "is an uplifting picture!"

And the Englishman replies:

"Forgive me, my good man, but I don't understand you. Why do you consider it uplifting?"

"Because this picture says clearly to the soul what a Christian ought to pray and yearn for, in order to ascend from earth to the unutterable glory of God."

"But," he says, "anyone can comprehend that from the Scriptures and prayers."

"By no means, sir," I reply. "It is not given to everyone to comprehend the Scriptures, and the uncomprehending mind can be darkened even in prayer: a man hears the exclamation, 'Awaiting Thy great and rich mercies,' and immediately thinks it's about money and starts bowing greedily. But when he sees the picture of heavenly glory before him, then he thinks on the lofty prospects of life and understands how that goal is to be reached, because here everything is simple and reasonable: a man should first pray that his soul be given the gift of the fear of God, and then it will proceed lightly from step to step, assimilating at each step the superabundance of higher gifts, and in those moments of prayer, money and all earthly glory will seem to a man no more than an abomination before the Lord."

Here the Englishman stands up and says merrily:

"And what do you odd birds pray for?"

"We," I reply, "pray for a Christian ending to our life and a good defense before the dread judgment seat."

He smiled and suddenly pulled a green curtain open by a golden cord, and behind that curtain his English wife was sitting in an armchair, knitting on long needles by a candle. She was a fine, affable lady, and though she didn't speak much of our language, she understood everything and had probably wanted to hear our conversation about religion.

And what do you think? When the curtain that hid her was pulled aside, she stood up at once, seemed to shudder, and came, the dear woman, to me and Luka, offered both hands to us muzhiks, and there were tears glistening in her eyes, and she pressed our hands and said:

"Goot people, goot Russian people!"

Luka and I kissed both her hands for those kind words, and she put her lips to our muzhik heads.

The storyteller stopped and, covering his eyes with his sleeve, wiped them discreetly, and murmured in a whisper: "A touching woman!" and with that he straightened up and went on again.

·   ·   ·

Having begun with these affectionate acts of hers, the English-woman said something to her husband in their language, which we didn't understand, but we could tell by her voice that she was probably speaking on our behalf. And the Englishman—this kindness in his wife evidently pleased him—gazes at her, beaming all over with pride, and strokes his wife's little head, and coos like a dove in his language: "Goot, goot," or however they say it, only it's clear that he's praising her and confirming her in something. Then he goes to his desk, takes out two hundred-rouble bills, and says:

"Here's money for you, Luka: go and look where you know for an artful icon painter of the kind you need, let him do what you need and also paint something of the same sort for my wife—she wants to give such an icon to our son—and my wife is giving you this money for all your trouble and expenses."

And she smiles through her tears and says quickly:

"No, no, no: that's from him, mine's separate," and so saying, she fluttered out the door and came back with a third hundred-rouble bill.

"My husband gave it to me for a dress, but I don't want a dress, I donate it to you."

We, naturally, started to refuse, but she wouldn't even hear of it and ran away, and he says:

"No, don't you dare refuse; take what she's giving you," and he turns away and says, "And get out, you odd birds!"

Naturally, we weren't in the least offended by this expulsion, because, though the Englishman turned away from us, we saw that he did it to conceal the fact that he was deeply moved himself.

So it was, my dear sirs, that our own native people treated us unjustly, but the English nation comforted us and lent zeal to our souls, just as if we'd received the bath of regeneration!

Now from here on, my dear sirs, the second half of my story begins, and I'll tell you briefly how, taking my silver-bridled Levonty, I set out after an icon painter, and what places we went to, what people we saw, what new wonders were revealed to us, and, finally, what we found, and what we lost, and what we came back with.

X

For a man going on a journey, the first thing is a companion; cold
and hunger are easier with an intelligent and good comrade, and
this blessing was granted me in that wonderful youth Levonty. We
set out on foot, taking with us our shoulder bags and a sufficient
sum of money, and to protect it and our own lives we took with us an
old, short-bladed saber with a broad back, which we always carried
in case of danger. We made our way like tradespeople, inventing
errands at random as the supposed causes for our traveling, and
all the while, naturally, with an eye on our business. At the very
beginning we visited Klintsy and Zlynka, then called on some of our
people in Orel, but did not obtain any useful results: nowhere did we
find any good icon painters, and so we got to Moscow. But all I can
say is: Woe to thee, Moscow! Woe to thee, most glorious queen of
the ancient Russian people! We of the old belief were not comforted
by thee either.

I'm not eager to say it, but it's impossible to keep silent: we did
not meet in Moscow the spirit we were thirsting for. We found that
the old ways there no longer stood upon piety and love of the good,
but only upon obstinacy, and becoming more and more convinced
of it every day, Levonty and I began to be ashamed of each other,
for we both saw things that were insulting to a peaceful follower of
the faith, but, being ashamed in ourselves, we kept silent about it all
with each other.

Naturally, we found icon painters in Moscow, and quite artful
ones, but what use was that, since all these people were not of the
spirit which the tradition of our forefathers tells us about? In olden
times, pious painters, when taking up their holy artwork, fasted and
prayed, and worked in the same way for big money or for little, as the
honor of the lofty task demands. But these paint one slap, another
dash, to last a short time, not for long years; they lay a weak ground
of chalk, not of alabaster, and, being lazy, they flow the paint on
all at once, not like in the old days, when they flowed on four or
even five layers of paint, thin as water, which produced that wonderful delicacy unattainable nowadays. And, aside from carelessness in
their art, they're all of lax behavior, and boast before each other, and

say anything at all to humiliate another painter; or, worse still, they band together, carry out clever deceptions, gather in pot-houses and drink and praise their own art with conceited arrogance, and blasphemously call other painters' work "infernography," and there are always junkmen around them, like sparrows around owls, who pass various old icons from hand to hand, alter them, substitute them, make fake boards, smoke them in chimneys, giving them a decrepit and worm-eaten look; they cast bronze folding icons from old molds and coat them with antiquated patina; they refashion copper bowls into baptismal fonts and put old-fashioned splayed eagles on them as in the time of Ivan the Terrible, and sell them to inexperienced buyers as genuine fonts from that period, though there's countless numbers of these fonts going the rounds in Russia, and it's all a shameless lie and deception. In a word, as swarthy Gypsies cheat each other with horses, so all these people do with holy objects, and they treat it all in such a way that you feel ashamed for them and see in it all only sin and temptation and abuse of faith. For those who have acquired the habit of this shamelessness, it's nothing, and among Moscow fanciers there are many who are interested in such dishonest trading and boast that so-and-so cheated so-and-so with a Deisis, and this one stuck that one with a Nicholas, or fobbed off a fake Our Lady in some scoundrelly manner: and they all cover it up, and vie with each other in how best to hoodwink the trustful inexperienced with God's blessing, but to Levonty and me, being of simple village piety, all this seemed unbearable to such a degree that we both even felt downcast and fear came over us.

"Can it be," we thought, "that in these times our ill-fated Old Belief has come to this?" But, though I thought that, and I could see that he harbored the same thing in his grieving heart, we didn't reveal it to each other, and I only noticed that my youth kept seeking some solitary place.

I looked at him once and thought to myself: "What if in his confusion he decides on something improper?" So I say:

"What is it, Levonty, are you sorrowing over something?"

And he replies:

"No, uncle, it's nothing: never mind."

"Then let's go to the Erivan Tavern in Bozheninova Street to chat up the icon painters. There are two who promised to come there and bring old icons. I've already bartered for one, and I'd like to obtain another today."

But Levonty replies:

"No, uncle, you go by yourself, I won't go."

"Why won't you?" I ask.

"I'm just not feeling myself today," he replies.

Well, once I didn't insist, and twice I didn't insist, but the third time I called him again:

"Let's go, Levontiushka, let's go, my lad."

And he bows meekly and pleads:

"No, dear uncle, my white dove: allow me to stay home."

"What is it, Levonty?" I say. "You came with me as my co-worker, but you sit at home all the time. I don't get much help from you this way, my dove."

And he:

"My own, my dearest Mark Alexandrych, my lord and master, don't call me to where they eat and drink and make unsuitable speeches about holy things, or I may be drawn into temptation."

This was his first conscious word about his feelings, and it struck me to the very heart, but I didn't argue with him and went alone, and that evening I had a big conversation with the two icon painters, and they put me in terrible distress. It's frightful to say what they did to me! One sold me an icon for forty roubles and left, and then the other said:

"Watch out, man, don't venerate that icon."

"Why not?" I ask.

And he says:

"Because it's infernography," and he picked off a layer of paint at the corner with his nail, and under it a little devil with a tail was painted on the priming! He picked the paint off in another place, and underneath there was another little devil.

"Lord!" I wept. "What does it mean?"

"It means," he says, "that you shouldn't order from him, but from me."

And here I already saw clearly that they were one band and aimed to deal wrongly and dishonestly with me, and, abandoning the icon to them, I left with my eyes full of tears, thanking God that my Levonty, whose faith was in agony, had not seen it. But I was just drawing near our house, and I saw there was no light in the window of the room we rented, and yet a high, delicate singing was coming from it. I recognized at once that it was Levonty's pleasant voice singing, and singing with such feeling as if he were bathing each word in tears. I came in quietly, so that he wouldn't hear me, stood by the door, and listened to how he intoned Joseph's lament:[21]

> *To whom will I tell my sorrow,*
> *Who will share in my weeping?*

This chant, if you happen to know it, is so pitiful to begin with that it's impossible to listen to it calmly, but Levonty himself also wept and sobbed as he sang:

> *My brothers they have sold me!*

And he weeps and weeps, singing about seeing his mother's coffin and calling upon the earth to cry out for his brothers' sin! . . .

These words can always stir a man, and especially me at that moment, as I came running from the brother-baiting. They moved me so much that I began to snivel myself, and Levonty, hearing it, stopped singing and called to me:

"Uncle! Hey, uncle!"

"What," I say, "my good lad?"

"Do you know," he says, "who this mother of ours is, the one that's sung about here?"

"Rachel," I reply.

"No," he says, "in ancient times it was Rachel, but now it should be understood mysteriously."

"What do you mean, mysteriously?" I ask.

"I mean," he replies, "that this word signifies something else."

"Beware, child," I say. "Aren't you reasoning dangerously?"

"No," he replies, "I feel in my heart that Christ is being crucified for us, because we don't seek him with one mouth and one heart."[22]

I was frightened still more by what he was aiming at and said:

"You know what, Levontiushka? Let's get out of this Moscow quickly and go to the country around Nizhny Novgorod, to seek out the icon painter Sevastian. I hear he's going about there now."

"Well, let's go then," he replies. "Here in Moscow some sort of needy spirit irks me painfully, but there there are forests, the air is cleaner, and I've heard there's an elder named Pamva, a hermit totally envyless and wrathless. I would like to see him."

"The elder Pamva," I reply sternly, "is a servant of the ruling Church. Why should we go looking at him?"

"Where's the harm in it?" he says. "I'd like to see him, in order to comprehend the grace of the ruling Church."

I chided him, saying, "What sort of grace could there be?"—yet I felt he was more right than I was, because he wished to test things out, while I rejected what I didn't know, but I insisted on my rejection and talked complete nonsense to him.

"Church people," I say, "look at the sky not with faith, but through the gates of Aristotle, and determine their way in the sea by the star of the pagan god Remphan, and you want to have the same view as theirs?"[23]

But Levonty replies:

"You're inventing fables, uncle: there was no such god as Remphan, and everything was created by one wisdom."

That made me feel even more stupid and I said:

"Church people drink coffee!"

"Where's the harm in that?" Levonty replies. "The coffee bean was brought to King David as a gift."

"How do you know all that?" I ask.

"I've read it in books," he says.

"Well, know then that not everything is written in books."

"And what isn't written in them?" he says.

"What? What isn't written in them?" I myself have no idea what to say, and blurt out to him:

"Church people eat hare, and hare is unclean."

"Don't call God's creature unclean," he says. "It's a sin."

"How can I not call hare unclean," I say, "when it is unclean, when it has an ass's constitution and a male-female nature and generates thick and melancholy blood in man?"

But Levonty laughs and says:

"Sleep, uncle, you're saying ignorant things!"

I admit to you that at the time I had not yet discerned clearly what was going on in the soul of this blessed young man, but I was very glad that he did not want to talk anymore, for I myself understood that in my anger I say God knows what, and so I fell silent and only lay there thinking:

"No, such doubts in him come from anguish, but tomorrow we'll get up and go, and it will all disperse in him." But just in case, I decided in my mind that I would walk silently with him for some time, in order to make a show of being very angry with him.

But my inconstant character totally lacked the firmness for pretending to be angry, and Levonty and I soon began talking again, only not about divine things, because he was very well read compared to me, but about our surroundings, for which we were hourly given a pretext by the sight of the great, dark forests through which our path led. I tried to forget about my whole Moscow conversation with Levonty and decided to observe only one precaution, so that we would not somehow run across that elder Pamva the hermit, to whom Levonty was attracted and of whose lofty life I myself had heard inconceivable wonders from Church people.

"But," I thought to myself, "there's no point in worrying much, since if I flee from him, he's not going to find us himself!"

And once again we walked along peacefully and happily and, at last, having reached a certain area, we heard that the icon painter Sevastian was in fact going about in those parts, and we went searching for him from town to town, from village to village, and we were following right in his fresh tracks, we were about to catch up with him, but we couldn't catch up with him. We ran like hunting dogs, making fifteen or twenty miles without resting, and we'd come, and they'd say:

"He was here, he was, he left barely an hour ago!"

We'd go rushing after him, and not catch up with him!

And then suddenly, during one of these marches, Levonty and I got to arguing. I said, "We must go to the right," and he said, "To the left," and in the end he almost argued me down, but I insisted on my way. But we went on and on, and in the end I saw we'd wound up I don't know where, and further on there was no path, no trail.

I say to the youth:

"Let's turn back, Levonty!"

And he replies:

"No, I can't walk anymore, uncle—I have no strength."

I get all in a flutter and say:

"What's the matter, child?"

And he replies:

"Don't you see I'm shaking with fever?"

And I see that he is, in fact, trembling all over, and his eyes are wandering. And how, my good sirs, did all this happen so suddenly? He hadn't complained, he had walked briskly, and suddenly he sits down on the grass in the woods, puts his head on a rotten stump, and says:

"Ow, my head, my head! Oh, my head's burning with fiery flames!

I can't walk, I can't go another step!" And the poor lad even sinks to the ground and falls over.

It happened towards evening.

I was terribly frightened, and while we waited to see if he'd recover from his ailment, night fell; the time was autumnal, dark, the place was unknown, only pines and firs all around, mighty as an archaic forest, and the youth was simply dying. What was I to do? I say to him in tears:

"Levontiushka, dear heart, make an effort, maybe we'll find a place for the night."

But his head was drooping like a cut flower, and he murmured as if in sleep:

"Don't touch me, Uncle Mark; don't touch me, and don't be afraid."

I say:

"For pity's sake, Levonty, how can I not be afraid in such a deep thicket?"

And he says:

"He who sleeps not and watches will protect."

I think: "Lord, what's the matter with him?" And, fearful myself, all the same I started listening, and from far away in the forest I heard something like a crunching . . . "Merciful God," I think, "that must be a wild beast, and he's going to tear us to pieces!" And I no longer call to Levonty, because I see it's like he's flown out of himself and is hovering somewhere, but only pray: "Angel of Christ, protect us in this terrible hour!" And the crunching is coming nearer and nearer, and now it's right next to us . . . Here, gentlemen, I must confess to you my great baseness: I was so scared that I abandoned the sick Levonty where he lay and climbed a tree more nimbly than a squirrel, drew our little saber, and sat on a branch waiting to see what would happen, my teeth clacking like a frightened wolf's . . . And suddenly I noticed in the darkness, which my eyes had grown used to, that something had come out of the forest, looking quite shapeless at first—I couldn't tell if it was a beast or a robber—but I began to peer and made out that it was neither a beast nor a robber, but a very small old man in a skullcap, and I could even see that he had an axe tucked in his belt, and on his back a big bundle of firewood, and he came out into the clearing. He sniffed, sniffed the air several times, as if he were picking up scents all around, and suddenly threw the bundle on the ground and, as if he'd scented a man, went straight to my comrade. He went up to him, bent over, looked in his face, took him by the hand, and said:

"Stand up, brother!"

And what do you think? I see him raise Levonty, lead him straight to his bundle, and place it on his shoulders. And he says:

"Carry it behind me!"

And Levonty carries it.

XI

You can imagine, my dear sirs, how frightened I must have been by such a wonder! Where had this commanding, quiet little old man appeared from, and how was it that my Levonty, who had just been as if given over to death and unable to raise his head, was now carrying a bundle of wood!

I quickly jumped down from the tree, put the saber behind my back on its cord, broke off a young tree for a big stick just in case, went after them, and soon caught up with them and saw: the little old man goes on ahead, and looks exactly as he had seemed to me at first—small and hunched over, his wispy little beard like white soapsuds; and behind him walks my Levonty, stepping briskly in his footsteps and not looking at me. I tried several times to address him and to touch him with my hand, but he paid no attention to me and went on walking as if in his sleep.

Then I run to the little old man from the side and say:

"My good-honest man!"

And he replies:

"What is it?"

"Where are you leading us?"

"I don't lead anyone anywhere," he says. "The Lord leads us all!"

And with that word he suddenly stopped: and I saw before us a low wall and a gateway, and in the gateway a little door, and the old man began to knock on this door and call out:

"Brother Miron! Hey, brother Miron!"

And an insolent voice rudely replies:

"Again you drag yourself here at night. Sleep in the forest! I won't let you in!"

But the old man begged again, entreating gently:

"Let me in, brother!"

The insolent fellow suddenly opened the door, and I saw it was a man in the same kind of skullcap as the old man's, only he was very stern and rude, and just as the old man stepped across the threshold, he shoved him so that he almost fell.

"God save you, brother mine, for your service!" said the old man.

"Lord," I thought, "where have we landed!" And suddenly it was as if lightning struck me and lit me up.

"Merciful Savior," it dawned on me, "if this isn't Pamva the wrathless! It would be better," I think, "for me to perish in the thick of the forest, or to come upon some beast's or robber's den, than to be under his roof."

And once he had led us into the small hut and lit a yellow wax candle, I guessed straight off that we were indeed in a forest hermitage, and, unable to stand it any longer, I said:

"Forgive me, pious man, for asking you: is it good for me and my comrade to remain here where you've brought us?"

And he replies:

"All the earth is the Lord's and blessed are all who dwell in it[24]—lie down, sleep!"

"No, allow me to inform you," I say, "that we are of the old belief."

"We're all members of the one body of Christ! He will gather us all together!"

And with that he led us to a corner, where a meager bed of bast matting had been made on the floor, with a round block of wood covered with straw at the head, and, now to us both, he again says:

"Sleep!"

And what then? My Levonty, as an obedient youth, falls onto it at once, but I, pursuing my apprehensions, say:

"Forgive me, man of God, one more question . . ."

He replies:

"What is there to ask? God knows everything."

"No," I say, "tell me: what is your name?"

And he, with a totally unsuitable, womanish singsong, says:

"My name is lucky: they call me ducky"—and with these frivolous words he crawled off with his candle stub to some tiny closet, small as a wooden coffin, but the insolent one shouted at him again from behind the wall:

"Don't you dare light a candle! You'll burn down the cell! You pray enough from books in the daytime; now pray in the dark!"

"I won't, brother Miron," he replies, "I won't. God save you!"
And he blew out the candle.
I whisper:
"Father, who's that yelling at you so rudely?"
And he replies:
"That's my lay brother Miron . . . a good man, he watches over me."

"Well, that's that!" I think. "It's the hermit Pamva! It's none other than him, the envyless and wrathless. Here's real trouble! He's found us, and now he's going to rot us the way gangrene rots fat. There's only one thing left, to carry Levonty away from here early tomorrow morning and flee the place, so he won't know where we've been." Holding to this plan, I decided not to sleep and watch for the first light, so as to waken the youth and flee.

And so as not to doze off and oversleep, I lay there and repeated the Creed, in the old way as it should be, and after each repetition I would add: "This is the apostolic faith, this is the catholic faith, on this faith the universe stands firm,"[25] and then I'd start all over. I don't know how many times I recited the Creed so as not to fall asleep, but it was many; and the little old man went on praying in his coffin, and it was as if light came through the cracks between the boards, and I could see him bowing, and then suddenly it was as if I began to hear a conversation and . . . a most inexplicable one: as if Levonty had come in, and he and the elder were talking about faith, but without words, just looking at each other and understanding. And this vision lasted for a long time, and I forgot to repeat the Creed, but it was as if I heard the elder say to the youth: "Go and purify yourself," and the youth reply: "I will." And I can't say now whether this was in a dream or not, only afterwards I slept for a long time, and finally woke up and saw it was morning, fully light, and the elder, our host, the hermit, was sitting and poking with a spike at a bast shoe on his knee. I began to look closely at him.

Ah, how good! Ah, how spiritual! As if an angel were sitting before me and plaiting bast shoes, so as to appear simple to the world.
I gaze at him and see that he looks at me and smiles, and says:
"Enough sleeping, Mark, it's time to go about your business."
I answer:
"What is my business, godly man? Or do you know everything?"
"I do," he says, "I do. When did a man ever make a long journey

without any business? Everyone, brother, everyone is seeking the Lord's path. May the Lord help you, help your humility!"

"What is my humility, holy man?" I say. "You are humble, but what humility is there in my vanity!"

But he replies:

"Ah, no, brother, I'm not humble: I'm a most impudent man, I wish for a share in the heavenly kingdom."

And suddenly, having acknowledged his crime, he pressed his hands together and wept like a little child.

"Lord," he prayed, "do not be angry with me for this willfulness: send me to the nethermost hell and order the demons to torment me as I deserve!"

"Well, no," I think, "thank God, this isn't Pamva, the sagacious hermit, this is just some mentally deranged old man." I decided that, because who in his right mind could renounce the kingdom of heaven and pray that the Lord send him to be tormented by demons? Never in my life had I heard such a desire from anyone, and, counting it as madness, I turned away from the elderly weeping, considering it idolatrous grief. But, finally, I reasoned: what am I doing lying down, it's time to get up, but suddenly I look, the door opens, and in comes my Levonty, whom I seem to have forgotten all about. And as soon as he comes in, he falls at the old man's feet, and says:

"I have accomplished everything, father: bless me now!"

The elder looks at him and replies:

"Peace be unto you: rest."

And my youth, I see, again bows down to him and leaves, and the hermit again starts plaiting his bast shoe.

Here I jumped up at once, thinking:

"No, I'll go quickly and take Levonty, and we'll flee from here without looking back!" And with that I went out to the little entryway and saw my youth lying flat on his back on a plank bench with his arms crossed on his chest.

I asked him loudly, so as not to look alarmed:

"Do you know where I can get a splash of water to wash my face?" and in a whisper I added: "I adjure you by the living God, let's get out of here quickly!"

Then I look closely at him and see that Levonty isn't breathing . . . He's passed away! . . . He's dead! . . .

I howled in a voice not my own:

"Pamva! Father Pamva, you've killed my youth!"

But Pamva came out quietly to the porch and said with joy:

"Our Levonty's flown off!"

I was even seized with rage.

"Yes," I replied through my tears, "he's flown off. You let his soul go like a dove from a cage!" And, throwing myself down at the dead boy's feet, I lamented and wept over him all the way till evening, when monks came from the monastery, tidied up his remains, put them in a coffin, and carried them off, because that morning, while I slept like a sluggard, he had joined the Church.

Not one word more did I say to Father Pamva, and what could I have said to him? Treat him rudely and he blesses you; beat him and he bows down to you. A man of such humility is invincible! What has he to be afraid of, if he even prays to be sent to hell? No, it was not for nothing that I trembled and feared he would rot us the way gangrene rots fat. He could drive all the demons of hell away with his humility, or convert them to God! They'd torment him, and he'd beg: "Torture me harder, for I deserve it." No, no! Even Satan couldn't bear that humility! He'd bruise his hands on him, break all his claws, and realize his impotence before the Maker who created such love, and be ashamed.

So I decided to myself that this elder with the bast shoe was created to destroy hell! And I wandered all night in the forest, not knowing why I didn't go further, and I kept thinking:

"How does he pray, in what manner, and with what books?"

And I remembered that I hadn't seen a single icon in his cell, only a cross of sticks tied together with bast, and hadn't seen any fat books . . .

"Lord," I dared to reason, "if there are only two such men in the Church, we're lost, for this one is all animated by love."

And I kept thinking and thinking about him, and suddenly, before morning, I began to yearn to see him, if only for a moment, before leaving there.

And I had only just thought it, when suddenly I again heard the same crunching, and Father Pamva came out again with his axe and a bundle of wood and said:

"Why are you tarrying so long? Aren't you in a hurry to build Babylon?"

These words seemed very bitter to me, and I said:

"Why do you reproach me with such words, old man? I'm not building any Babylon, and I shun the Babylonian abomination."

And he replies:

"What is Babylon? A pillar of pride. Don't be proud of the truth, lest the angel withdraw."

I say:

"Father, do you know why I am going about?"

And I told him all our grief. And he listened, listened, and replied:

"The angel is gentle, the angel is meek, he clothes himself in whatever the Lord tells him to; he does whatever is appointed to him. That is the angel! He lives in the human soul, sealed by vain wisdom, but love will shatter the seal . . ."

And with that I saw him withdraw from me, and I couldn't take my eyes from him and, unable to master myself, I fell prostrate on the ground behind him, and when I raised my face, I saw he was no longer there—either he went off into the trees, or . . . Lord knows what became of him.

Here I started ruminating on the sense of his words: "The angel lives in the soul, but sealed, and love will free him"—and suddenly I thought: "What if he himself is the angel, and God orders him to appear to me in another guise: I'll die, like Levonty!" Having imagined that, I crossed the little river on some sort of stump, I don't remember how myself, and broke into a run: forty miles I went without stopping, all in a fright, thinking whether I had seen an angel, and suddenly I stopped at one village and found the icon painter Sevastian. We talked everything over right then and decided to set out the next day, but we talked coldly and traveled still more coldly. And why? For one thing, because the icon painter Sevastian was a pensive man, and still more because I was no longer the same myself: the hermit Pamva hovered in my soul, and my lips whispered the words of the prophet Isaiah, that "the spirit of God is in this man's nostrils."[26]

XII

My return trip with the icon painter Sevastian went quickly and, arriving at the construction site at night, we found everything there in good order. After seeing our own people, we appeared at once before the Englishman Yakov Yakovlevich. Curious as he was, the man was interested in seeing the icon painter at once, and he kept looking at his hands and shrugging, because Sevastian's hands were huge as rakes, and dark, inasmuch as he himself had the look of a swarthy Gypsy. Yakov Yakovlevich finally says:

"I'm surprised, brother, that you can paint with such huge hands."

And Sevastian replies:

"How so? What's unsuitable about my hands?"

"You can't trace anything small with them," he says.

"Why?" the man asks.

"Because the finger joints aren't flexible enough to allow it."

But Sevastian says:

"That's nonsense! How can my fingers allow or not allow me something? I'm their master, and they're my servants and obey me."

The Englishman smiles.

"So," he says, "you'll copy the sealed angel for us?"

"Why not?" the man says. "I'm not one of those masters who fears work, it's work that fears me. I'll copy it so you can't tell it from the real one."

"Very well," says Yakov Yakovlevich, "we'll immediately set about getting hold of the real one, and in the meantime, to convince me, you show me your artistry: paint an icon for my wife of the ancient Russian sort, and one that she'll like."

"Of what type?"

"That I don't know," he says. "Paint what you know how, it makes no difference to her, so long as she likes it."

Sevastian pondered a moment and then asked:

"And about what does your spouse pray to God the most?"

"I don't know, my friend," he says, "I don't know what, but I think most likely about the children, that the children grow up to be honest people."

Sevastian pondered again and replied:

"Very well, sir, I can satisfy that taste as well."

"How will you satisfy it?"

"I'll paint it so that it will be contemplative and favorable to the increase of your wife's prayerful spirit."

The Englishman ordered that he be given all comfort in his own upstairs rooms, but Sevastian would not work there, but settled by the window in the attic above Luka Kirilovich's room and went into action.

And what he did, sirs, was something we couldn't imagine. As it had to do with children, we thought he would portray the wonderworker Roman, whom people pray to about infertility, or the slaughter of the innocents in Jerusalem, which is always pleasing to mothers who have lost children, for there Rachel weeps with them for their little ones and will not be comforted;[27] but this wise icon painter, realizing that the Englishwoman had children and poured out her prayers not about the having of children, but about the rightness of their morals, went and painted something completely different, still more suitable to her purposes. He chose for it a very small, old board of a hand's length in size, and began to exercise his talents upon it. First of all, naturally, he gave it a good priming with sturdy Kazan alabaster, so that the priming came out smooth and hard as ivory, and then he divided it into four equal spaces, and in each space he marked out a separate little icon, and he reduced each of them still more by placing borders of gold leaf between them, and then he started painting. In the first space he painted the nativity of John the Baptist—eight figures, the newborn baby, and the chamber; in the second, the nativity of our most holy Lady, the Mother of God—six figures, the newborn baby, and the chamber; in the third, the most pure nativity of our Savior, the stable, the manger, Our Lady and Joseph standing, and the God-guided Magi prostrating, and the wise-woman Salomé, and various kinds of livestock: oxen, sheep, goats, and asses, and the dry-legged heron, which the Jews are forbidden to eat,[28] included to signify that this comes not from Judaism, but from God, the creator of all. And in the fourth section was the nativity of St. Nicholas, and here again was the saint in infancy, and the chamber, and many standing figures. And the point here was that you see before you the raisers of such good children, and with what art it was done, all the figures the size of a pin, yet you can see their animation and movement! In the nativity of the Mother of God, for instance, St. Anne, as prescribed by the Greek original, lies on her bed; before her stand maidens with timbrels, and some hold gifts, and others sun-shaped fans, and others candles. One woman supports St. Anne by the shoulders; Joachim looks into the upper chamber; the wise-woman washes the Mother of God, who is in a font up to her waist; another girl pours water from a vessel into the font. The chambers are all laid out with a compass, the upper chamber is greenish blue and the lower crimson, and in this lower chamber sit Joachim and Anne on a throne, and Anne holds the most holy Mother of God, and around them there are stone pillars dividing the chambers, the curtains are red, and the surrounding fence is white and ochre . . . Wondrous, wondrous was all that Sevastian depicted, and in each miniature face he expressed divine contemplation, and he inscribed the image "Good Childbearing," and brought it to the Englishmen. They looked, started examining, and just threw up their hands: "Never," they say, "did we expect such fantasy, and such fineness of meagroscopic depiction is unheard-of." They even looked through a meagroscope and found no mistakes, and they gave Sevastian two hundred roubles for the icon and said:

"Can you do still finer work?"

Sevastian replies:

"I can."

"Then make a copy of my wife's portrait for a signet ring."

But Sevastian says:

"No, that I cannot do."

"Why not?"

"Because," he says, "first of all, I've never tried that kind of work, and, second, I cannot humiliate my art for the sake of it, lest I fall under the condemnation of our forefathers."

"That's rubbish!"

"By no means is it rubbish," he replies. "We have a statute from the good times of our forefathers, and it is confirmed by patriarchal decree, that 'If anyone is found worthy to undertake this sacred work, which is the painting of icons, then let this artist be of goodly life and paint nothing except holy icons!'"

Yakov Yakovlevich says:

"And if I give you five hundred roubles for it?"

"Though you promise me five hundred thousand, all the same they will remain with you."

The Englishman beamed all over and said jokingly to his wife:

"How do you like that? He considers painting your face a humiliation for him!"

And he added in English: "Oh, goot character." But in the end he said:

"Watch out, brothers, we now undertake to bring this whole thing off, and I see you've got your own rules for everything, so make sure nothing's omitted or forgotten that could hinder it all."

We replied that we foresaw nothing of the kind.

"Well, watch out, then," he says, "I'm beginning." And he went to the bishop with the request that he wanted out of zealousness to gild the casing and embellish the crown on the sealed angel. The bishop said neither yes nor no to that: he neither refused nor ordered it. But Yakov Yakovlevich did not give up and persisted; and we were now waiting like powder for the match.

XIII

With all that, let me remind you, gentlemen, that since this affair began, no little time had passed, and Christmas was at the door. But don't compare Christmas in those parts with ours here: the weather there is capricious, and one time this feast is celebrated in the winter way, but another time who knows how: in rain, in wetness. One day there's a light frost, on the next it all melts away; now the river's covered with sheet ice, then it swells and carries off the broken ice, as in the high water of spring . . . In short, the most inconstant weather, and in those parts it's not called weather, but simply *snow-slush*— and snow-slush it is.

In the year my story belongs to, this inconstancy was most vexing. Since I returned with the icon painter, I can't even count for you the number of times our crew set themselves up now for winter, now for summer conditions. And that was the hottest time, in terms of work, because we already had seven piers done and were putting up chains from one bank to the other. Our bosses, naturally, would have liked very much to have those chains linked up quickly, so that by the high water some sort of temporary bridge could be hung for the delivery of materials, but that didn't work out: we had just stretched the chains across, when we were hit by such a frost that we couldn't lay any planks. And so it remained: the chains were hung, but there was no bridge. Instead God made another bridge: the river froze over, and our Englishman crossed the Dniepr on the ice to see about our icon, and he comes back from there and says to me and Luka:

"Tomorrow, lads, just wait, I'll bring you your treasure."

Lord, how that made us feel then! At first we wanted to keep it a secret and only tell the icon painter, but how could the human heart endure it! Instead of keeping the secret, we ran around to all our people, knocking on all the windows and whispering it to each other, running from cottage to cottage not knowing why, helped by the bright, magnificent night, the frost scattering precious stones over the snow, and Hesperus blazing in the clear sky.

Having spent the night in such joyful rushing about, we greeted the day in the same delighted expectation, and from morning on never left our icon painter's side and couldn't do enough to please him, because the hour had come when everything depended on his artistry. If he told us to give him or fetch him something, ten of us flew off together, and so zealously that we knocked each other down. Even old Maroy ran around so much that he tripped over something and tore off his boot heel. Only the icon painter himself was calm, because it wasn't the first time he'd done such work, and therefore he prepared everything without any fuss: diluted the egg with kvass, inspected the varnish, prepared the primed canvas, set out some old boards to see which was the right size for the icon, tuned up a little saw like a string in its sturdy bow, and sat by the window, rubbing in his palm the pigments he foresaw would be necessary. And we all washed ourselves in the stove, put on clean shirts, and stood on the bank, looking at the city refuge from where our light-bearing guest was to visit us; and our hearts now trembled, now sank . . .

Ah, what moments those were, and they went on from early dawn until evening, and suddenly we saw the Englishman's sleigh racing across the ice from the city and straight towards us . . . A shudder went through us all, we all threw our hats at our feet and prayed:

"God, father of spirits and angels: have mercy on Thy servants!"

And with that prayer we fell on our faces in the snow, eagerly stretching out our arms, and suddenly we hear the Englishman's voice above us:

"Hey, you Old Believers! See what I've brought you!"—and he handed us a little bundle in a white handkerchief.

Luka took the bundle and froze: he felt it was something small and light! He opened a corner of the handkerchief and saw it was just our angel's casing, and the icon itself wasn't there.

We flung ourselves at the Englishman and said to him in tears:

"Your Honor's been deceived, there's no icon, they just sent the silver casing."

But the Englishman was no longer the one he had been to us till then. This long affair must have vexed him, and he yelled at us:

"You confuse everything! You yourselves told me to ask for the casing, and so I did: you just don't know what you want!"

We saw that he was seething, and were carefully beginning to explain to him that we needed the icon in order to make a copy, but he no longer listened to us, drove us out, and only showed us one mercy, that he ordered the icon painter sent to him. The icon painter Sevastian came to him, and he treated him in the same seething manner.

"Your muzhiks," he says, "don't know themselves what they want: first they asked for the casing, said you only had to take the dimensions and outline, and now they're howling that that's not what they need; but I can't do any more for you, because the bishop won't give me the icon. Imitate the icon quickly, we'll put the casing on it and give it back, and my secretary will steal me the old one."

But the icon painter Sevastian, as a reasonable man, tried to charm him with gentle speech and made answer:

"No, Your Honor, our muzhiks know their business, and we really must have the original icon first. It's been thought up only in offense to us," he says, "that we copy icons as if by stencils. What we have is rules about the originals, but in executing the icon, there is room for free artistry. According to the original, for example, we must depict St. Zosima or Gerasim with a lion, but there's no restriction on the painter's fantasy in how he paints the lion. The rule is to paint St. Neophytus with a dove, Konon the Gardener with a flower, Timothy with a coffer, George and Sabbas Stratilatos with spears, Photius with his jerkin, and Kondraty with clouds, for he taught the clouds, but every icon painter is free to portray them as his artistic fantasy permits, and therefore again I cannot know how the angel that is to be replaced was painted."

The Englishman listened to all that and chased Sevastian out, as he had us, and there were no further decisions from him, and so, my dear sirs, we sat over the river like crows on a ruin, and didn't know whether to be in total despair, or to expect something more, but we no longer dared go to the Englishman; moreover, the weather was again of like character to us: a terrible thaw set in, and it poured rain, the sky at midday was like a smokehouse, and the nights were so dark that even Hesperus, which never leaves the heavenly firmament in December, hid and refused to come out . . . A prison for the soul, that's what! And so Christmas came, and right on the eve there was thunder, a downpour, and it poured and poured without stopping for two or three days: the snow was all washed away into the river, and the ice on the river began to turn blue and swell, and suddenly, two days before the New Year, it burst and was carried away . . . Block upon block shot up and hurtled over the turbid waves, clogging the whole river around our constructions: mountains of ice arose chunk upon chunk, and whirled and crashed, God forgive me, like demons. How the constructions stood and endured such inconceivable pressure was even astonishing. Frightful millions might have been destroyed, but we were past worrying, because our icon painter Sevastian, seeing that there was nothing for him to do, rose up—he started packing his bags and wanted to go to other parts, and there was no way we could hold him back.

The Englishman was also past worrying, because something happened to him during this foul weather, so that he nearly went out of his mind. He kept going about, they say, asking everybody: "What am I to do? What am I going to do?" And then he suddenly mastered himself, called Luka, and said:

"You know what, my muzhik? Why don't we go and steal your angel?"

"Agreed," says Luka.

Luka's observation was that the Englishman apparently wished to experience danger and had decided to go the next day to the bishop in the monastery, to take the icon painter with him in the guise of a goldsmith, and ask to be shown the icon of the angel, so that he could make a detailed outline of it, as if for a casing; and meanwhile the man would examine it the best he could and paint an imitation of it at home. Then, when the real goldsmith had the casing ready for us, he would bring it to us across the river, and Yakov Yakovlevich would go to the monastery again and say that he wanted to see the festal episcopal service, and would go into the sanctuary and stand in his overcoat in the darkness by the altar, where our icon was kept on the windowsill, and would hide it under the skirt of his coat, and, giving the coat to his servant, as if from the heat, would take it away. And in the yard behind the church, our man would at once take the icon out of the overcoat and fly to our side with it, and there, during the time that the vigil lasted, the icon painter would have to remove the old icon from its old board, replace it with the copy, cover it with the casing, and send it back, so that Yakov Yakovlevich could return it to the windowsill as if nothing had happened.

"Why not, sir?" we say. "We agree to everything!"

"Only watch out," he says. "Remember that I'll be standing there in the role of the thief, and I want to have faith in you, that you won't give me away."

Luka Kirilovich says:

"We're not the sort of people who deceive their benefactors, Yakov Yakovlevich. I'll take the icon and bring both back to you, the real one and the copy."

"Well, and if something prevents you?"

"What can prevent me?"

"Well, if you suddenly die or drown?"

Luka thinks: why should there be such a hindrance? But then he figures that it does sometimes happen that while digging a well you discover treasure, or you go to the market and meet a rabid dog, so he replies:

"In that case, sir, I'll leave a man with you, one of ours, who will take all the blame on himself in case I fail you, and will suffer death rather than give you away."

"And who is this man you rely on so much?"

"The blacksmith Maroy," replies Luka.

"That old man?"

"True, he's not young."

"But it seems he's stupid?"

"His mind we don't need, but the man has a worthy spirit."

"What kind of spirit can a stupid man have?" he says.

"The spirit, sir," Luka answers, "does not go according to reason: the spirit bloweth where it listeth,[29] the same as one person has long and luxuriant hair and another scarcely any."

The Englishman ponders and says:

"Very well, very well: these are all interesting sensations. But how will he bail me out if I get caught?"

"Here's how," Luka replies. "You'll stand in the church by the window, and Maroy will stand outside under the window, and if I don't come with the icons before the end of the service, he'll break the glass, climb through the window, and take all the blame on himself."

The Englishman liked that very much.

"Curious," he said, "very curious! And why should I trust that your stupid man with spirit won't just run away?"

"Well, that is a matter of mutual trust."

"Mutual trust," he repeats. "Hm, hm, mutual trust! Either I go to hard labor for a stupid muzhik, or he goes under the knout for me? Hm, hm! If he keeps his word . . . it's under the knout . . . That's interesting."

We sent for Maroy and explained to him what it was about, and he says:

"Well, what of it?"

"And you won't run away?" says the Englishman.

And Maroy replies:

"Why should I?"

"So as not to be flogged and sent to Siberia."

And Maroy says:

"Oh, that!"—and wouldn't talk anymore.

The Englishman was overjoyed: he got all livened up.

"Delightful," he says. "How interesting!"

XIV

Right after this discussion, the action began. We hung oars on the Englishman's big longboat the next morning and transported him to the city side. There he and the icon painter Sevastian got into a carriage and drove to the monastery, and after a little more than an hour, we see our icon painter come running, and in his hand there's a sheet of paper with the tracing of our icon.

We ask:

"Did you see it, dear man, and can you now copy it nicely for us?"

"Yes, I saw it," he replies, "and I can do it, except that it may come out a bit more vivid. But that doesn't matter. When the icon gets here, I can then tone down the brightness in a minute."

"Dear heart," we beg him, "do your best."

"Don't worry," he replies, "I will!"

And as soon as we brought him back, he immediately sat down to work and by the end of the day had an angel ripe on the canvas, as like our sealed one as two drops of water, except that the colors seemed a bit fresher.

By evening the goldsmith had also sent the new casing, because it had been commissioned earlier on the model of the old silver one.

The most dangerous time of our thievery was coming.

We were all prepared, naturally, and had prayed before evening, and were waiting for the right moment; and as soon as the first bell rang for vigil in the monastery on the other side, the three of

us—myself, old Maroy, and Uncle Luka—got into a small boat. Old
Maroy brought along an axe, a chisel, a crowbar, and a rope, so as
to look more like a thief, and we headed straight for the monastery
wall.

At that time of year, naturally, twilight came early, and the night,
despite the full moon, was pitch-dark, really thievish.

Having crossed, Maroy and Luka left me at the bank in the boat
and went sneaking into the monastery themselves. I shipped the
oars, caught hold of the end of the rope, and waited impatiently, so
as to cast off as soon as Luka set foot in the boat. The time seemed
terribly long to me, out of anxiety for how it was all going to turn
out and whether we would succeed in covering up our thievery while
the vespers and vigil were still going on. And it seemed to me that
God knows how much time had already passed; it was frightfully
dark, the wind was fierce, and instead of rain wet snow began to
pour down, the boat rocked slightly in the wind, and I, the wicked
servant, gradually warming up in my coat, began to doze off. But
suddenly there came a shove to the boat, and it began to pitch about.
I roused myself and saw Uncle Luka standing in it, and he says in a
stifled voice, not his own:

"Row!"

I took the oars, but couldn't get them into the oarlocks from fear.
I managed with great effort and pushed off from the shore, and then
asked:

"Did you get the angel, uncle?"

"He's with me. Row harder!"

"Tell me," I persist, "how did you get him?"

"Just the way we said."

"And we'll have time to bring him back?"

"We should. They've just sung the great prokeimenon.[30] Row!
Where are you rowing to?"

I turned around. Oh, Lord! True enough, I was rowing in the
wrong direction: it seemed I kept steering across the current, as I
ought to, but our settlement wasn't there—it was because there was
such snow and wind, it was awful, and it blinded your eyes, and all
around there was roaring and heaving, and the surface of the river
seemed to breathe ice.

Well, anyway, by God's mercy we made it, jumped out of the boat,
and ran. The icon painter was ready: he acted coolly, but firmly. He

took the icon in his hands, and once the people had fallen down and venerated it, he let them all cross themselves before the sealed face, while he looked at it and at his forgery and said:

"Fine work! Only it has to be toned down a bit with dirt and saffron!" And then he clamped the icon by the edges, tuned up his saw, which he had put into the tight bow, and . . . the saw went into a flutter. We all stood there seeing if he'd damage it! Awful, sirs! Can you picture him to yourselves, with his enormous hands, sawing a layer from the board no thicker than a sheet of the finest writing paper? . . . It's a short step to sin: if the saw goes off by a hair, it will tear through the image and come out the other side! But the icon painter Sevastian performed the whole action with such coolness and artistry that, looking at him, we felt more at peace in our souls every minute. And indeed, he sawed off the image on its paper-thin layer, then in one minute he cut the image out, leaving a border, and glued the border back onto the same board. Then he took his copy and crumpled it, crumpled it in his fists, scraped it on the edge of the table, and rubbed it between his palms, tearing at it as if he wanted to destroy it, and finally held it up to the light, and the whole of this new copy was full of cracks like a sieve . . . Then Sevastian took it at once and glued it onto the old board inside the border, filled his palm with some sort of dark pigment, he knew which, added old varnish and saffron, mixed it with his fingers into a sort of paste, and rubbed it hard into the crumpled copy . . . He did it all very briskly, and the newly painted icon became quite old and looked just like the real one. In a moment, this copy was varnished, and our people were putting the casing on it, while the icon painter put the real icon he had sawed out onto the prepared board and quickly demanded a scrap of an old felt hat.

This was the beginning of the most difficult action—the unsealing.

They gave the icon painter a hat, he immediately tore it in half on his knee and, covering the sealed icon with it, shouted:

"Give me the hot iron!"

On the stove, at his orders, a heavy tailor's iron had been heated burning hot.

Mikhailitsa picked it up with tongs and gave it to him, and Sevastian wrapped the handle with a cloth, spat on the iron, and passed it quickly over the scrap of hat! . . . An evil stench arose from the felt at once, and the icon painter did it again, and pressed, and snatched it away. His hand flew like lightning, and a column of smoke already rose from the felt, but Sevastian went on scorching: with one hand he turned the felt a little, with the other he worked the iron, and each time more slowly and pressing harder, and suddenly he set both the iron and the felt aside and held the icon up to the light, and it was as if the seal had never been: the strong Stroganov varnish had held out, and the sealing wax was all gone, only a sort of fiery red dew was left on the image, but the whole brightly divine face was visible . . .

Here some of us prayed, some wept, some tried to kiss the painter's hands, but Luka Kirilovich did not forget what he was about and, treasuring every minute, handed the painter his forged icon and said:

"Well, finish quickly!"

The man replies:

"My action is finished, I've done everything I promised."

"What about placing the seal?"

"Where?"

"Why, here on the face of this new angel, like on the other one."

Sevastian shook his head and replied:

"Oh, no, I'm no official, I wouldn't dare do such a thing."

"Then what are we to do now?"

"That I don't know," he says. "You ought to have had an official or some German on hand, but since you failed to supply them, you'll have to do it yourselves."

Luka says:

"What? We wouldn't dare do that!"

And the icon painter replies:

"I don't dare either."

And in those brief moments of great turmoil, Yakov Yakovlevich's wife suddenly comes flying into the cottage, all pale as death, and says:

"Aren't you ready yet?"

"Ready and not ready," we say. "The most important thing is done, but the paltry one we can't do."

And she babbles in her language:

"What are you waiting for? Don't you hear what's going on outside?"

We listened and turned paler than she was: amidst our cares, we had paid no attention to the weather, but now we heard the noise: the ice was moving!

I sprang outside and saw it had already covered the whole river—block heaving upon block like rabid beasts, whirling into each other, and crashing, and breaking up.

Forgetting myself, I rushed to the boats, but there wasn't a single one left: they had all been swept away . . . My tongue went stiff in my mouth, I couldn't move it, and my ribs sank one after another, as if I was going down into the earth . . . I stand there, and don't move, and don't give voice.

But while we were rushing around in the dark, the Englishwoman stayed in the cottage alone with Mikhailitsa, found out what had caused the delay, snatched up the icon and . . . a moment later rushed out to the porch with it, holding a lantern, and cried:

"Here, it's ready!"

We looked: the new angel had a seal on his face!

Luka immediately put both icons in his bosom and shouted:

"A boat!"

I let on that there were no boats, they'd been swept away.

And the ice, I tell you, came thronging like a herd, smashing against the icebreakers and shaking the bridge, so that even the chains, for all that they were thick as good floorboards, could be heard rattling.

The Englishwoman, when she understood that, clasped her hands, shrieked "James!" in an inhuman voice, and fell as if dead.

And we stand there, all feeling the same thing:

"What of our word? What will happen to the Englishman now? What will happen to old Maroy?"

Just then the bells in the monastery bell tower rang for the third time.

Uncle Luka suddenly roused himself and exclaimed to the Englishwoman:

"Come to your senses, lady, your husband will be safe, and maybe our old Maroy will just have his decrepit hide torn by the executioner and his honest face dishonored by a brand, but that will happen only after my death!" And with those words he crossed himself, stepped out, and left.

I cried out:

"Uncle Luka, where are you going? Levonty perished, and you're going to perish!"—and I rushed after him to hold him back, but he picked up an oar that I thrown down when we came and, brandishing it at me, cried:

"Away, or I'll strike you dead!"

Gentlemen, I have rather openly confessed my faintheartedness to you in my story, how I abandoned the late youth Levonty on the ground that time and climbed a tree, but really and truly I say to you, this time I would not have feared the oar and retreated before Uncle Luka, but—believe it or not, as you like—at that moment, just as I remembered Levonty's name, the youth Levonty appeared in the darkness between me and him and shook his hand at me. This terror I couldn't bear, and I drew back. Meanwhile, Luka was already standing at the end of the chain and, having set his foot firmly on it, suddenly said through the storm:

"Start singing!"

Our choir director, Arefa, was standing right there and obeyed at once and struck up "I will open my mouth," the others joined in, and we shouted out the hymn, fighting against the howling of the storm, and Luka, fearless of this deadly terror, walked along the chain of the bridge. In one minute he had walked the first span and descended into the next . . . And further on? Further on the darkness enveloped him, and we couldn't see whether he was still walking or had already fallen and the cursed blocks of ice had whirled him into the abyss, and we didn't know whether to pray for his safety or weep for the repose of his firm and honor-loving soul.

XV

Now, sirs, what was happening on the other bank? His grace the bishop, according to his rule, was celebrating the vigil in the main church, knowing nothing about the robbery being carried out at the same time in the side chapel. With his permission, our Englishman, Yakov Yakovlevich, stood in the chapel sanctuary, and, having stolen our angel, sent it out of the church, as he had intended, in his overcoat, and Luka raced off with it. Meanwhile old Maroy, keeping his word, remained outside by the same window, waiting till the last moment, so that, in case Luka did not come back, the Englishman could retreat, and Maroy would break the window and get into the church with a crowbar and a chisel, like a real villain. The Englishman didn't take his eyes off him, and he saw that old Maroy was standing strictly by his duty, and the moment he saw the Englishman press his face to the window so as to see him, he nodded at once, meaning, "I'm here to answer for the theft—I'm here!"

And in this manner the two showed each other their nobility, and would not allow one to outdo the other in mutual trust, but with these two trusts a third, still stronger trust was at work, only they didn't know what this third trust was doing. But then, as soon as the last bell of the vigil was rung, the Englishman quietly opened the casement, to tell Maroy to climb in, and he himself prepared to retreat, when he suddenly saw old Maroy had turned away and wasn't looking at him, but was staring fixedly across the river and repeating:

"God, bring him over! God, bring him over! God, bring him over!" and then he suddenly jumped up and danced as if he were drunk, and shouted: "God brought him over, God brought him over!"

Yakov Yakovlevich was thrown into the greatest despair, thinking:

"Well, that's it: the stupid old man has gone crazy, and I'm done for." Then he looks, and Maroy and Luka are already embracing.

Old Maroy muttered:

"I watched the way you walked along the chain with those lanterns."

And Uncle Luka says:

"I didn't have any lanterns."

"Then where did the light come from?"

Luka replies:

"I don't know, I didn't see any light, I just made a run for it and don't know how I didn't fall as I ran . . . it was as if somebody held me up under both arms."

Maroy says:

"It was angels—I saw them, and for that I'll now die before noon today."

But Luka had no time to talk much. He didn't reply to the old man, but quickly gave the Englishman both icons through the window. He took them and handed them back.

"What's this?" he says. "There's no seal?"

Luka says:

"There isn't?"

"No, there isn't."

Well, here Luka crossed himself and said:

"That's it! Now there's no time to fix it. The Church angel performed this miracle, and I know why."

And Luka rushed to the church at once, pushed his way to the sanctuary, where the bishop was being divested, fell at his feet, and said:

"Thus and so, I've blasphemed, here's what I've just done: order me put in chains and taken to jail."

But the bishop, more honor to him, listened to it all and replied:

"That should bring home to you now where the true faith is at work: you took the seal off your angel by deceit, but ours took it off himself and brought you here."

Luka says:

"I see, Your Grace, and I tremble. Order me to be handed over quickly for punishment."

But the bishop replies with an absolving word:

"By the power granted me by God, I forgive and absolve you, child. Prepare yourself to receive the most pure body of Christ tomorrow morning."[31]

Well, gentlemen, I think there's nothing further to tell you: Luka Kirilovich and Maroy came back in the morning and said:

"Fathers and brothers, we have seen the glory of the angel of the ruling Church and all the divine Providence of it in the goodness of its hierarch, and we have been anointed unto it with holy chrism, and today at the liturgy we partook of the body and blood of our Savior."

And I, who for a long time, ever since I was the elder Pamva's guest, had been drawn to become one in spirit with all of Russia, exclaimed for us all:

"And we shall follow you, Uncle Luka!" And so all of us gathered together in one flock, with one shepherd, like lambs, and only then did we realize where and to what our sealed angel had brought us, first bending his steps away and then unsealing himself for the sake of the love of people for people, manifested on that terrible night.

XVI

The storyteller had finished. The listeners remained silent, but one of them finally cleared his throat and observed that everything in the story was explicable—Mikhailitsa's dreams, and the vision she had imagined half awake, and the fall of the angel, whom a dog or a cat running in had knocked to the floor, and the death of Levonty, who had been ill even before meeting Pamva. Explicable, too, were all the chance coincidences in the words spoken by Pamva in some sort of riddles.

"And it's understandable," the listener added, "that Luka crossed on the chain with an oar: masons are known to be good at walking and climbing anywhere, and the oar was for balance; it's also understandable, I think, that Maroy could see a light around Luka, which he took for angels. Under great strain, a badly chilled man can start seeing all kinds of things. I'd even find it understandable if, for example, Maroy had died before noon, as he predicted . . ."

"He did die, sir," Mark put in.

"Splendid! There's nothing astonishing in an eighty-year-old man dying after such agitation and cold. But here's what I really find totally inexplicable: how could the seal disappear from the new angel that the Englishwoman had sealed?"

"Well, that's the simplest thing of all," Mark replied cheerfully, and he told how, soon after that, they had found the seal between the icon and the casing.

"How could it happen?"

"Like this: the Englishwoman also didn't dare spoil the angel's face, so she made a seal on a piece of paper and tucked it under the edges of the casing . . . It was done very cleverly and skillfully, but when Luka carried the icons in his bosom, they shifted on him, and that made the seal fall off."

"Well, now, that means the whole affair was simple and natural."

"Yes, many people suggest that it all took place in the most ordinary way. And not only the educated gentlemen who know of it, but even those of our brothers who have remained in the schism laugh at us, saying the Englishwoman slipped us into the Church on a scrap of paper. But we don't argue against such reasoning: each man judges as he believes, and for us it's all the same by which paths the Lord calls a man to Him and from what vessel He gives him to drink, so long as He calls him and quenches his thirst for unanimity with the fatherland. But here come our peasant lads, crawling out from under the snow. Looks like they've had a rest, the dear hearts, and will soon be on their way. Perhaps they'll give me a ride. St. Basil's night has gone by. I've wearied you and led you around to many places with me. But to make up for it I have the honor of wishing you a happy New Year, and forgive me, for Christ's sake, ignorant as I am!"

The Enchanted Wanderer

I

We were sailing over Lake Ladoga from the island of Konevets to Valaam and stopped for a shipyard necessity at the wharf in Korela.[1] Here many of us were curious to go ashore and ride on frisky Finnish horses to the deserted little town. Then the captain made ready to continue on our way, and we sailed off again.

After the visit to Korela, it was quite natural that our conversation should turn to that poor, though extremely old, Russian settlement, than which it would be hard to imagine anything sadder. Everyone on the boat shared that opinion, and one of the passengers, a man inclined to philosophical generalizations and political jesting, observed that he could in no way understand why it was customary that people objectionable in Petersburg should be sent to some more or less remote place or other, which, of course, incurred losses to the treasury for transportation, when right here, near the capital, on the shore of Ladoga, there is such an excellent place as Korela, where no freethinking or liberal-mindedness would be able to withstand the apathy of the populace and the terrible boredom of the oppressive, meager natural life.

"I'm sure," this traveler said, "that in the present case the fault must lie with the routine, or in any case, perhaps, with a lack of pertinent information."

Someone who often traveled here replied to this, that some exiles had apparently lived here, too, at various times, but none of them had been able to stand it for long.

"One fine fellow, a seminarian, was sent here as a clerk on account of rudeness (that kind of exile I cannot even understand). So, having come here, he played it brave for a long time and kept hoping to start some sort of litigation; but then he took to drinking, and drank so much that he went completely out of his mind and sent in a petition saying it would be best, as soon as possible, to order him 'shot or sent for a soldier, or, failing that, to hang him.'"

"And what decision followed from it?"

"Hm . . . I . . . I really don't know; only he didn't wait for the decision in any case: he hanged himself without leave."

"And he did very well," the philosopher responded.

"Very well?" repeated the storyteller, evidently a merchant, a solid and religious man.

"Why not? At least he died and put a lid on it."

"How do you mean, a lid, sir? And how will it be for him in the other world? Suicides will be tormented for all eternity. No one can even pray for them."

The philosopher smiled venomously, but made no reply, but instead a new opponent stepped forward against him and against the merchant, unexpectedly defending the clerk who had carried out the death sentence on himself without official permission.

This was a new passenger, who had come on board at Konevets without any of us noticing him. He had been silent until then, and no one had paid any attention to him, but now everyone turned to look at him, and everyone probably wondered how he could have gone unnoticed until then. He was a man of enormous stature, with an open and swarthy face and thick, wavy hair of a leaden color: so strangely was it streaked with gray. He was wearing a novice's cassock, with a wide monastic leather belt and a tall, black broadcloth cap. Whether he was a novice or a tonsured monk it was impossible to tell, because the monks of the Ladoga islands do not always wear monastic headgear, not only when traveling, but even on their own islands, and in country simplicity limit themselves to caps. This new companion of ours, who later turned out to be an extremely interesting man, looked as if he might be a little over fifty; but he was a mighty man in the fullest sense of the word, and a typical, artless, kind Russian mighty man at that, reminiscent of old Ilya Muromets in the beautiful painting by Vereshchagin and in the poem by Count

A. K. Tolstoy.[2] It seemed that he should not be going around in a cas-sock, but riding through the forest in huge bast shoes, mounted on his "dapple gray," and lazily scenting "how the dark thicket smells of resin and wild strawberry."

But for all this kindly artlessness, it did not take much keenness of observation to see in him a man who had seen much and, as they say, "had been around." He behaved boldly, self-assuredly, though with-out unpleasant casualness, and he began speaking with accustomed ease in a pleasant bass voice.

"That all means nothing," he began, lazily and softly letting out word after word from under his thick gray mustaches, twirled upwards Hussar fashion. "What you say concerning the other world for suicides, that they will supposedly never be forgiven, I don't accept. And that there's supposedly no one to pray for them—that, too, is nonsense, because there is a man who can quite simply mend the situation for them all in the easiest way."

He was asked who this man was who can deal with and amend things for suicides after their death.

"Here's who, sir," replied the black-cassocked mighty man. "There is in the Moscow diocese a certain little village priest—a most hard-ened drunkard, who had been all but defrocked—it's he who han-dles them."

"How do you know that?"

"Good heavens, sir, I'm not the only one who knows, everybody in the Moscow region knows it, because it went through his grace the metropolitan Filaret himself."[3]

There was a brief pause, then someone said it was all rather dubious.

The black-cassocked man was not offended in the least by this observation and replied:

"Yes, sir, at first glance it looks that way—dubious, sir. And what's surprising about it seeming dubious to us, when even his grace him-self didn't believe it for a long time, but then, receiving sure proofs of it, saw that it was impossible not to believe it, and finally believed it?"

The passengers badgered the monk with requests that he tell them this wondrous story, and he did not refuse them and began as follows:

The story goes that a certain archpriest supposedly wrote once to his grace the bishop that, thus and so, there's this little priest, a terrible drunkard—he drinks vodka and is no good in his parish. And it, this report, was essentially correct. The bishop ordered the priest to be sent to him in Moscow. He looked him over and saw that the priest was indeed a boozy fellow, and decided to remove him from his post. The priest was upset and even stopped drinking, and kept grieving and weeping: "What have I brought myself to," he thinks, "and what else can I do but lay hands on myself? That's all that's left to me," he says. "Then at least the bishop will take pity on my unfortunate family and give my daughter a husband, so that he can replace me and feed my family."[4] So far so good. He firmly resolved to do away with himself and set a day for it, but since he had a good soul, he thought: "Very well, suppose I die, but I'm not a brute, I'm not without a soul—where will my soul go after that?" And from then on he began to grieve still more. Well, so he grieves and grieves, but the bishop decided to remove him from his post on account of his drunkenness, and he lay down with a book once to rest after a meal and fell asleep. Well, so he fell asleep or else just dozed off, when suddenly he seemed to see the door of his cell opening. He called out "Who's there?" because he thought the attendant had come to announce someone; but no—instead of the attendant, he saw a most kindly old man come in, and the bishop recognized him at once—it was St. Sergius.[5]

The bishop says:

"Is that you, most holy Father Sergius?"

And the holy man replies:

"It is I, servant of God Filaret."

The bishop asks:

"What does your purity want of my unworthiness?"

And St. Sergius replies:

"I want mercy."

"Upon whom do you want it shown?"

The holy man named that little priest deprived of his post on account of drunkenness, and then withdrew; and the bishop woke up and thought: "What shall I count that as: a simple dream or fancy, or an inspiring vision?" And he began to reflect and, as a man known to the whole world for his intelligence, figured that it was a simple dream, because how on earth could it be that St. Sergius, an ascetic and observer of the good, strict life, would intercede for a weak priest who lived a life of negligence? Well, sir, so his grace decided that way, and left this whole matter to take its natural course, as it had begun, and passed the time as was suitable to him, and at the proper hour lay down to sleep again. But no sooner had he nodded off than another vision came, and of such a sort that it plunged the bishop's great spirit into still worse confusion. Imagine, if you can: noise . . . such a frightful noise that nothing can convey it . . . They come riding . . . so many knights, there's no counting them . . . racing, all in green attire, breastplates and feathers, their steeds like lions, raven-black, and at their head a proud stratopedarchos[6] in the same attire, and wherever he waves his dark banner, there they ride, and on the banner—a serpent. The bishop doesn't know what this procession means, but the proud one commands them: "Tear them apart," he says, "for now they have no one to pray for them"—and he galloped on; and after this stratopedarchos rode his warriors, and after them, like a flock of scrawny spring geese, drew dreary shades, and they all nodded sadly and pitifully to the bishop and moaned softly through their weeping: "Let him go! He alone prays for us." As soon as the bishop got up, he sent at once for the drunken priest and questioned him about how and for whom he prays. And the priest, from poverty of spirit, became all confused before the hierarch and said: "Master, I do as is prescribed." And his grace had a hard time persuading him to confess: "I am guilty," he says, "of one thing: that I am weak of spirit, and thinking it better to do away with myself out of despair, I always pray when preparing the communion for those who passed away without confession or who laid hands on themselves . . ." Well, here the bishop understood what those shades were that floated past him like scrawny geese in his vision, and he did not want to please the demons who sped before them to destruction, and he gave the little priest his blessing: "Go," he said, "and do not sin in that other thing, but pray for those you prayed for"—and sent him back to his post. So you see, such a man as he can always be useful for such people as cannot endure the struggle of life, for he will never retreat from the boldness of his calling and will keep pestering the Creator on their account, and He will have to forgive them.

"Why 'have to'?"

"Because of the 'knock'[7]—you see, He ordered it Himself, so that's never going to change, sir."

"And tell us, please, does anybody else pray for suicides besides this Moscow priest?"

"I don't rightly know how to fill you in on that. They say you supposedly shouldn't petition God for them, because they followed their own will, though maybe there are some who don't understand that and do pray for them. On the Trinity, or on the day of the Holy Spirit,[8] though, it seems everybody's allowed to pray for them. Some special prayers are even read then. Wonderful, moving prayers; I think I could listen to them forever."

"And they can't be read on other days?"

"I don't know, sir. For that you'd have to ask somebody who's studied up on it; I suppose they should know; since it's nothing to do with me, I've never had occasion to talk about it."

"And you've never noticed these prayers being repeated sometimes during services?"

"No, sir, I haven't; though you shouldn't take my word for it, because I rarely attend services."

"Why is that?"

"My occupation doesn't allow me to."

"Are you a hieromonk or a hierodeacon?"[9]

"No, I just wear a habit."

"But still, doesn't that mean you're a monk?"

"Hm . . . yes, sir; generally that's how it's considered."

"Indeed it is," the merchant retorted to that, "only even in a habit they can still call you up as a soldier."

The black-cassocked mighty man was not offended in the least by this observation, but only reflected a little and replied:

"Yes, they can, and they say there have been such cases; but I'm too old now, I'm in my fifty-third year, and then military service is nothing unusual for me."

"You mean you've already been in military service?"

"That I have, sir."

"What, as a corporal, was it?" the merchant asked again.

"No, not as a corporal."

"Then what: a soldier, an orderly, a noodle—the whole caboodle?"

"No, you haven't guessed it; but I'm a real military man, involved in regimental doings almost since childhood."

"So you're a cantonist?"[10] the merchant persisted, getting angry.

"No again."

"Then what the deuce are you?"

"I'm a *conosoor*."

"A wha-a-at?"

"A conosoor, sir, a conosoor, or, as plain folk put it, a good judge of horseflesh, and I served as an adviser to the remount officers."

"So that's it!"

"Yes, sir, I've selected and trained a good few thousand steeds. I've broken such wild beasts as, for example, the ones that rear up and then throw themselves backwards with all their might, and the rider can have his chest crushed right then against the pommel, but with me not one of them could do that."

"How did you tame that kind?"

"I—it was very simple, because I received a special gift for it from nature. When I jump into the saddle, straightaway, without giving the horse time to collect its wits, I pull its ear to the side as hard as I can with my left hand, and with my right fist I bash it between the ears, and I grind my teeth at it something terrible, so that sometimes you even see brains come out its nostrils along with blood—and it quiets down."

"And then?"

"Then you dismount, stroke it, let it look you in the eye and admire you, so that a good picture stays in its memory, and then you mount up again and ride."

"And the horse goes quietly after that?"

"It goes quietly, because a horse is smart, it feels what sort of man is handling it and what he's thinking about it. Me, for instance, by that same reasoning, every horse loved me and felt me. In Moscow, in the manège, there was one horse that got completely out of hand, and he learned this heathenish trick of biting off a rider's knee. The devil simply caught the kneecap in his big teeth and tore it off whole. Many men were done in by him. At that time the Englishman Rarey visited Moscow[11]—the 'furious breaker,' as he was called—and the lowdown horse nearly ate him, too, and put him to shame in any case; they say the only thing that saved him was that he wore a steel knee guard, so, though the horse did bite his leg, he couldn't bite through, and so he bucked him off; otherwise it would have been the death of him; but I straightened him out good and proper."

"Tell us, please, how did you do that?"

"With God's help, sir, because, I repeat, I have a gift for it. This Mister Rarey, known as the 'furious tamer,' and the others who took on this steed, used all their art against his wickedness to keep him bridled, so that he couldn't swing his head to this side or that. But I invented a completely opposite means to theirs. As soon as this

Englishman Rarey renounced the horse, I said: 'Never mind, it's all futile, because this steed is nothing if not possessed by a devil. The Englishman can't fathom that, but I can, and I'll help you.' The superiors agreed. Then I say: 'Take him out the Drogomilovsky Gate!' They took him out. Right, sir. We led him by the bridle down to a hollow near Fili, where rich people live in their summer houses. I saw the place was spacious and suitable, and went into action. I got up on him, on that cannibal, without a shirt, barefoot, in nothing but balloon trousers and a visored cap, and I had a braided belt around my naked body, brought from the brave prince St. Vsevolod-Gavriil of Novgorod,[12] whom I believed in and greatly respected for his daring; and embroidered on the belt was *'My honor I yield to none.'* I had no special instruments in my hands, except that in one I had a stout Tartar whip topped with a lead head of no more than two pounds, and in the other a simple glazed pot of liquid batter. Well, sir, I sat him, and there were four men pulling the horse's bridle in different directions so that he wouldn't hurl himself at anybody with his teeth. And he, the demon, seeing that we're all up in arms against him, whinnies, and shrieks, and sweats, and trembles all over with wickedness, wanting to devour me. I see that and tell the stablemen: 'Quick, tear the bridle off the scoundrel.' They don't believe their ears, that I'm giving them such an order, and they gape at me. I say: 'What are you standing there for! Don't you hear? What I order you to do, you should do at once!' And they answer: 'But, Ivan Severyanych' (my name in the world was Ivan Severyanych, Mr. Flyagin), 'how can you tell us to take the bridle off?' I began to get angry at them, because I could see and feel in my legs that the horse was raging with fury, and I pressed him hard with my knees, and shouted to them: 'Take it off!' They were about to say something, but by then I was in a complete frenzy and gnashed my teeth so hard that they pulled the bridle off at once, in an instant, and made a dash for it wherever their feet would take them, while in that same moment I first off did something he wasn't expecting and smashed the pot on his head; the pot broke and the batter ran down over his eyes and nose. And he got frightened, thinking: 'What's that?' And I quickly snatched the cap from my head and with my left hand began to rub the batter into the horse's eyes still more, and I gave him a whack on the side with my whip . . . He surged forward, and I kept rubbing him on the eyes with my cap, to blear his eyesight completely, and gave him a whack on the other side . . . And I keep laying it on hotter and hotter. I don't let him catch his breath or open his eyes, and keep smearing the batter over his muzzle with my cap, blinding him, gnashing my teeth to make him tremble, scaring him, and flogging him on both sides with the whip, so he'll understand this is no joke . . . He understood it and didn't stay stubbornly in one place, but raced off with me. He carried me, the dear heart, carried me, and I thrashed and thrashed him, and the more zealously he carried me, the more ardently I plied the whip, and at last we both began to get tired of this work. My shoulder ached and I couldn't raise my arm, and he, I could see, also stopped looking sideways and stuck his tongue out of his mouth. Well, here I saw he was begging for mercy. I quickly dismounted, wiped his eyes, took him by the forelock, and said: 'Don't move, dog meat, bitch's grub!' and pulled him down—he fell to his knees before me, and after that he became so meek, you couldn't ask for anything better: he let people mount him and ride around, only he dropped dead soon after."

"So he dropped dead?"

"Dropped dead, sir. He was a very proud creature, behaved humbly, but clearly couldn't subdue his character. But Mr. Rarey, when he heard about it, invited me to work for him."

"So, then, did you work for him?"

"No, sir."

"Why not?"

"How can I put it to you! First, because I was a conosoor and was more used to that line—to selecting, and not to breaking, and he only needed furious taming—and second, because on his side, as I suppose, it was just a crafty ploy."

"Of what sort?"

"He wanted to get my secret."

"Would you have sold it to him?"

"Yes, I would have."

"So what was the matter?"

"Must be he just got frightened of me."

"Will you be so kind as to tell us that story as well?"

"There was no special story, only he said: 'Reveal your secret to me, brother—I'll pay you a lot and take you to be my conosoor.' But since I was never able to deceive anybody, I answered: 'What secret? It's just foolishness.' But he looked at everything from his English, learned point of view, and didn't believe me. He says: 'Well, if you don't want to reveal it, have it your way, let's go and drink rum together.' After that we drank a lot of rum together, so much that he turned all red and said, as well as he was able: 'Well, go on and tell me now, what did you do to the horse?' And I answered: 'Here's what . . .'—and I threw him as scary a look as I could and gnashed my teeth, and since I had no pot of batter around just then, I took a glass, as an example, and swung it, but seeing that, he suddenly ducked his head, got under the table, and then made a dash for the door, and that was it, and there was no going looking for him. We haven't set eyes on each other since."

"That's why you didn't go to work for him?"

"That's why, sir. How could I work for him, when from then on he was even afraid to meet me? And I was quite willing to go to him then, because, while we were competing over that rum, I got to like him very much, but, right enough, there's no sidestepping your path, and I had to follow a different calling."

"And what do you consider your calling?"

"I really don't know how to tell you . . . I've done all kinds of things, had occasion to be on horses, and under horses, and was taken prisoner, and made war, and beat people myself, and was made a cripple, such that maybe not everybody could have stood it."

"And when did you go to the monastery?"

"That wasn't long ago, sir, just a few years after all my past life."

"And you also felt a calling for that?"

"Mm . . . I . . . I don't know how to explain it, sir . . . though it must be assumed I did."

"How is it that you speak of it as . . . as if you're not certain?"

"Because how can I say for certain, when I can't even embrace all my extensive past living?"

"Why is that?"

"Because much that I did wasn't even by my own will."

"And by whose, then?"

"By a parental promise."

"And what happened to you by this parental promise?"

"I kept dying all my life, and could never die."

"Really?"

"Precisely so, sir."

"Then please tell us your life."

"What I remember, I can tell you if you like, only I can't do it otherwise than from the very beginning."

"Do us the favor. That will be all the more interesting."

"Well, I don't know if it will be of any interest at all, but listen if you like."

II

The former connoisseur Ivan Severyanych, Mr. Flyagin, began his story thus:

I was born a serf and come from the household staff of Count K——of Orel province.[13] Now, under the young masters, these estates have been broken up, but under the old count they were very sizeable. In the village of G——, where the count himself lived, there was a great, huge mansion, with wings for guests, a theater, a special skittles gallery, a kennel, live bears sitting chained to posts, gardens; his singers gave concerts, his actors performed various scenes; there were his own weavers, and he kept workshops for various crafts; but most attention was paid to the stud farm. Special people were appointed for each thing, but the horse department received still more special attention, and as in military service in the old days cantonists descended from soldiers in order to fight themselves, so with us little coachmen came from coachmen in order to drive themselves, from stablemen came little stablemen to tend the horses, and from the fodder peasant—the fodder boy, to carry fodder from the threshing floor to the cattle yard. My father was the coachman Severyan, and though he wasn't among the foremost coachmen, because we had a great many, still he drove a coach-and-six, and once, during the tsar's visit, he came in seventh and was awarded an old-style blue banknote.[14] I was left an orphan of my mother at a very young age and I don't remember her, because I was her *prayed-for son*, meaning that, having no children for a long time, she kept asking God for me, and when she got what she asked for, having given birth to me, she died at once, because I came into the world with an unusually big head, for which reason I was called not Ivan Flyagin, but simply *Golovan.** Living with my father in the coachmen's yard, I spent my

* Russian for "big head." *Trans.*

whole life in the stables, and there I comprehended the mystery of animal knowing and, you might say, came to love horses, because as a little boy I crawled on all fours between horses' legs, and they didn't hurt me, and once I got a little older, I became quite intimate with them. Our stud farm was one thing, the stables were another, and we stable folk had nothing to do with the farm, but we received horses ready to be taught and trained them. Every coachman and postillion drove a coach-and-six, and of all different breeds: Vyatka, Kazan, Kalmyk, Bitiug, Don—these were all horses bought at fairs and brought to us. There were more of our own from the stud farm, naturally, but they're not worth talking about, because stud-farm horses are placid and have neither strong character nor lively fantasy, but these wild ones were terrible beasts. The count used to buy up whole shoals of them, entire herds outright, cheap, at eight or ten roubles a head, and once we drove them home, we immediately set about schooling them. They were terribly headstrong. Half of them would even drop dead rather than submit to training: they stand there in the yard—they're bewildered and even shy away from the walls, and only keep their eyes turned to the sky, like birds. You'd even feel pity looking at them, because you see how the dear heart would like to fly away, save that he has no wings . . . And from the very start he won't eat or drink for anything, neither oats nor water from the trough, and so he pines away, until he wears himself out completely and drops dead. Sometimes we lost half of what we spent, especially on Kirghiz horses. They love steppe freedom terribly. And of those who get habituated and stay alive, no small number get crippled during training, because against their wildness there's only one means—strictness; but then those that survive all this training and learning come out as such choice horses, no stud-farm horse can compare to them in driving quality.

My father, Severyan Ivanych, drove a Kirghiz six, and when I grew up, they set me on that same six as a postillion. They were cruel horses, not like some of the cavalry horses taken for officers nowadays. We called these officer's horses *Kaffeeschenks*,[15] because there was no pleasure in riding them, since even officers could sit them, but ours were simply beasts, asps and basilisks at once: their muzzles alone were worth something, or their bared teeth, or else their legs, or their manes . . . that is, to put it simply, sheer terror! They never knew fatigue; to do not only fifty, but even seventy or eighty miles from the village to Orel and back again without a rest was nothing

to them. Once they got going, you had to watch out that they didn't
fly right by. At the time when they sat me in the postillion's saddle,
I was all of eleven years old, and my voice was just the kind that, by
the custom of that time, was required of a nobleman's postillion:
most piercing, resounding, and so long-drawn-out that I could keep
that "hhhi-i-i-ya-a-ahhh" ringing for half an hour; but my strength
of body wasn't great enough yet for me to keep myself freely sitting
up for long journeys, and they would tie me to the saddle and harness with straps, so that I was all twined around and couldn't fall.
I was jolted to death, and even passed out and lost consciousness
more than once, but still rode in my upright position, and, sick of
dangling, would come to my senses again. It was no easy duty; on
the way, these changes would occur several times, I'd grow faint,
then straighten up, and at home they'd untie me from the saddle
like a dead man, lay me out, and make me sniff horseradish. Well,
but later I got used to it, and it all became like nothing to me. I even
kept aiming to give some passing peasant a hot one over the shirt as
we drove—that's a well-known postillion's prank. So, once we were
taking the count visiting. The weather was beautiful, summery, and
the count and his dog were sitting in the open carriage, father was
driving a four-in-hand, and I was blowing about in front, and here
we turned off the main road and went along a special byway for
some ten miles to a monastery called the P—— hermitage. This
little road was tended by the monks, to make it more enticing to go
to them: naturally, on the state road there were weeds and broom
and twisted branches sticking out everywhere; but the monks kept
the road to the hermitage clean, all swept and cleared, with young
birches planted along both sides, and these birches were so green
and fragrant, and the wide view of the fields in the distance . . . In
short—it was so good, I was about to cry out to it all, but, of course,
I couldn't cry out for no reason, so I controlled myself and galloped
on. Then suddenly, two or three miles before the monastery, the
road began to slope downwards a bit, and I suddenly saw a little
speck ahead of me . . . something was creeping along the road like a
little hedgehog. I was glad of the chance and struck up with all my
might: "Hhhhi-i-i-i-ya-a-a-ahh!" and kept it going for almost a mile,
and got so fired up that when we began to overtake the hay wagon
I was shouting at, I rose in the stirrups and saw a man lying on the
hay in the wagon, and it was probably so pleasant for him, warmed
by the sun in the fresh breeze, that he lay there fast asleep, fearing

nothing, sweetly sprawled facedown, and even with his arms spread wide, as if embracing the wagon. I could see he wasn't going to pull over, so I went alongside, and, drawing even with him, stood up in the stirrups, gnashed my teeth for the first time in my life, and hit him across the back as hard as I could with my whip. His horses lunged forward down the hill, and he gave a start—he was a little old man in a novice's cap, like the one I'm wearing now, and his face was pitiful, like an old woman's, all frightened, with tears running down, and he thrashed on the hay like a gudgeon in a frying pan, and suddenly, probably half-asleep, not knowing where the edge was, he tumbled off the wagon under the wheels, and went sprawling in the dust . . . his legs tangled in the reins . . . At first my father and I, and even the count himself, found it funny the way he tumbled off, but then I saw that, down there by the bridge, the horses had caught one of the wheels on a post and stopped, but *he* didn't get up and didn't move . . . We came closer, I looked, he was all gray, covered with dust, and on his face there was no nose to be seen, only a crack, and blood coming from it . . . The count ordered us to stop, got out, looked, and said: "Dead." He threatened to give me a good thrashing for that at home and ordered us to drive quickly to the monastery. From there people were sent down to the bridge, and the count talked things over with the father superior, and in the fall a whole train of gifts went there from us, with oats, and flour, and dried carp, and father gave me a whipping behind a shed in the monastery, not a real thrashing, but over the trousers, because it was my duty to mount up again right away. The matter ended there, but that same night the monk I had whipped to death comes to me in a vision and again weeps like a woman. I say:

"What do you want from me? Get out!"

But *he* replies:

"You took my life before I could confess."

"Well, it happens," I reply. "What am I to do with you now? I didn't do it on purpose. And what's so bad for you now?" I say. "You're dead, and it's all over."

"It's all over," he says, "that's true enough, and I'm very grateful to you for it, but I've come now from your own mother to ask you, do you know you're her *prayed-for son*?"

"Of course, I've heard that," I say. "My grandmother Fedosya has told me so more than once."

"But do you know," he says, "that you're also a *promised son*?"

"Meaning what?"

"Meaning," he says, "that you're promised to God."

"Who promised me to Him?"

"Your mother."

"Well," I say, "then let her come and tell me that herself, because maybe you're making it up."

"No," he says, "I'm not making it up, but she can't come herself."

"Why not?"

"Because," he says, "here with us it's not like with you on earth: here not everybody can speak or go places, but each of us does what he has a gift for. But if you like," he says, "I can give you a sign to confirm it."

"I'd like," I say, "only what sort of sign?"

"Here is the sign for you," he says, "that you'll be dying many times, but you won't die until real death comes for you, and then you'll remember your mother's promise and go to be a monk."

"Wonderful," I say. "I accept and I'll be waiting."

He disappeared, and I woke up and forgot all about it and didn't foresee that all these deaths would begin right away one after another. But a short while later I went with the count and countess to Voronezh—to the newly revealed relics there,[16] to cure the little countess, who had been born pigeon-toed—and we stopped in the Elets district, in the village of Krutoe, to feed the horses, and I fell asleep again by the trough, and I see—again that little monk comes, the one I did in, and says:

"Listen, Golovan, I feel sorry for you, quickly ask your masters to go to the monastery—they'll let you."

I answer:

"Why should I?"

And he says:

"Well, look out, you're going to suffer a lot of evil."

I thought, all right, you've got to caw about something, since I killed you, and with that I got up, hitched the horses with my father, and we drove out, and the mountain here was steep as could be, with a sheer drop on one side, where who knows how many people had perished by then. The count says:

"Watch out, Golovan, be careful."

I was good at it, and though the reins of the shaft horses, which had to make the descent, were in the coachman's hands, I could do much to help my father. His shaft horses were strong and reliable:

they could make the descent simply by sitting on their tails, but one of them, the scoundrel, was into astronomy—you only have to rein him in hard, and straightaway he throws his head up and starts contemplating deuce knows what in the sky. There's no worse harness horses than these astronomers—and they're most dangerous especially between the shafts, a postillion always has to watch out for horses with that habit, because an astronomer doesn't see where he puts his feet, and who knows where they'll land. Naturally, I knew all about our astronomer and always helped my father: I'd hold the reins of my saddle horse and his mate under my left elbow, and place them so that their tails were just in front of the shaft horses' muzzles and the shafts were between their croups, and I always held the whip ready in front of the astronomer's eyes, and the moment I see him looking up in the sky, I hit him on the nose and he lowers his head, and we make the descent perfectly well. So it was this time: we're taking the carriage down, and I'm fidgeting around in front of the shaft and controlling the astronomer with the whip, when suddenly I see that he no longer feels either my father's reins or my whip, his mouth is all bloody from the bit and his eyes are popping, and behind me I suddenly hear something creak and crack, and the whole carriage lurches forward . . . The brakes have snapped! I shout to my father: "Hold up! Hold up!" And he also yells: "Hold up! Hold up!" But what is there to hold up, when all six are racing like lunatics and don't see a thing, and something suddenly goes whizzing before my eyes, and I see my father fly off the box—a rein has broken . . . And ahead is that terrible abyss . . . I don't know whether I felt sorry for my masters or for myself, but seeing death was inevitable, I threw myself off of the lead horse right onto the shaft and hung from the end of it . . . Again I don't know how much weight was in me then, only I must have been much heavier in the overbalance, and I choked the two shaft horses till they wheezed and . . . I see my lead horses aren't there, as if they've been cut off, and I'm hanging over the abyss, and the carriage is standing propped against the shaft horses that I had throttled with the shaft.

Only then did I come to my senses and get frightened, and my hands lost their grip, and I went flying down and don't remember anything more. I don't know how long it was before I came to and saw that I'm in some cottage, and a stalwart muzhik says to me:

"Well, can it be you're alive, lad?"

I answer:

"Must be I am."

"And do you remember what happened to you?" he asks.

I began to recall and remembered how the horses had bolted on us and I had thrown myself onto the end of the shaft and was left hanging over the abyss; but what happened next I didn't know.

The muzhik smiles:

"And where could you know that from," he says. "Your lead horses didn't make it to the bottom of that abyss alive, they got all broken up, but it's like you were saved by some invisible force: you dropped onto a lump of clay and slid down on it like on a sled. We thought you were quite dead, then we see you're breathing, only the air has stopped your breath. Well," he says, "now get up if you can, hurry quick to the saint: the count left money to bury you if you died, and to bring you to him in Voronezh if you should live."

So I went, only I didn't say anything all the way, but listened to how that muzhik who was taking me kept playing "Mistress Mine" on the concertina.

When we came to Voronezh, the count summoned me to his rooms and said to the countess:

"So, my dear countess," he says, "we owe this boy our lives."

The countess only nodded her head, but the count said:

"Ask me whatever you like, Golovan—I'll do it all for you."

I say:

"I don't know what to ask!"

And he says:

"Well, what would you like to have?"

I think and think, and then say:

"A concertina."

The count laughs and says:

"Well, you're a real fool, but anyhow, it goes without saying, I'll remember you when the time comes. And," he says, "buy him a concertina right now."

A footman went to a shop and brought me a concertina in the stables:

"Here," he says, "play."

I took it and started to play, but only saw that I didn't know how and dropped it at once, and the next day some wanderers[17] stole it on me from where I'd hidden it under the shed.

I ought to have taken advantage of the count's favor on that occasion and asked to go to a monastery right then, as the monk had advised; but, without knowing why myself, I had asked for a concertina, and had thereby refuted my very first calling, and on account of that went from one suffering to another, enduring more and more, yet didn't die of any of them, until everything the monk had predicted to me in my vision came true in real life because of my mistrust.

III

I barely had time, after this show of benevolence from my masters, to return home with them on new horses, from which we again put together a six in Voronezh, when the fancy took me to acquire a pair of crested pigeons, a male and a female, which I kept on a shelf in the stables. The male had clay-colored feathers, but the female was white and with such red legs, a real pretty little thing! . . . I liked them very much: especially when the male cooed in the night, it was so pleasant to listen to, and in the daytime they'd fly among the horses and land in the manger, pecking up food and kissing each other . . . It was comforting for a young boy to see it all.

And after this kissing children came along; they hatched one pair, and they were growing up, and they went kiss-kissing, and more eggs got laid and hatched . . . They were such tiny little pigeons, as if all furry, with no feathers, yellow as the little chamomile known as "cat's communion," but they had beaks on them worse than on a Circassian prince, big and strong . . . I started examining them, these pigeon chicks, and so as not to squash them, I picked one up by the beak and looked and looked at it, and got lost in contemplating how tender it was, and the big pigeon kept driving me away. I amused myself with them—kept teasing him with the pigeon chick; but then when I went to put the little bird back in the nest, it wasn't breathing anymore. What a nuisance! I warmed it in my hands and breathed on it, kept trying to revive it; but no, it was dead, that's all! I got angry and threw it out the window. Well, never mind; the other one was left in the nest, and the dead one got snatched up and carried off by some white cat that ran past from who knows where. And I made good note of this cat then, that she was all white and had a black spot on her forehead like a little hat. Well, I thought to myself, darn it all, let her eat the dead one. But that night I was asleep, and suddenly I heard the pigeon on the shelf above my bed fighting angrily with someone. I jumped up and looked, and it was a moonlit night, and I saw it was the same white cat carrying off my other pigeon chick, the live one.

"Well," I thought, "no, why should she do that?" and I threw my boot after her, only I missed, and she carried off my pigeon chick and no doubt ate it somewhere. My two pigeons were left childless, but they didn't pine for long and began kissing again, and again they had a pair of children ready, but that cursed cat was there again . . . Deuce knows how she managed to spy it all out, only I look once, and in broad daylight she's dragging off another pigeon chick, and just when I had nothing to fling after her. But for that I decided to pull a fast one on her and set a trap in the window, so that as soon as she showed her face at night, it slammed shut on her, and she sat there complaining and miaowing. I took her out of the trap at once, stuffed her head and front paws into a boot to keep her from scratching, held her back paws and tail in my left hand, with a mitten on it, took a whip from the wall with my right hand, and began teaching her a lesson on my bed. I think I gave her some hundred and fifty hot ones, with all my might, so that she even stopped struggling. Then I took her out of the boot, wondering: is she done in or not? How, I wonder, can I test whether she's alive or not? And I put her on the threshold and chopped her tail off with a hatchet: she went "Mia-a-a-ow," shuddered all over, spun around ten times or so, and then ran off.

"Good," I thought, "now you're sure not to come here after my pigeons again." And to make it still scarier for her, the next morning I nailed the chopped-off tail outside over my window, and was very pleased with that. But an hour later, or two hours at the most, I look, and the countess's maid comes running in, though she's never set foot in our stable in all her born days, and she's holding a parasol over herself, and she screams:

"Aha, aha! So that's who, that's who!"

I say:

"What's the matter?"

"It's you," she says, "who mutilated Zozinka! Confess: it's her tail you've got nailed over the window!"

I say:

"Well, what's so important about a nailed-up tail?"

"How dared you?" she says.

"And how dared she eat my pigeons?"

"Well, what's so important about your pigeons!"

"Your cat's no great lady either."

You see, I was already old enough for back talk.

"She's just a crummy cat," I say.

And the fidget says:

"How dare you speak that way: don't you know that she's my cat and the countess herself has petted her?" And with that she slaps me across the cheek with her hand, but I, since I had also been quick with my hands since childhood, not thinking twice, grabbed a dirty broom that was standing by the door and hit her across the waist with it . . .

My God, here everything blew up! I was taken to the German steward's office to be judged, and he decided I should be given the severest possible thrashing and then be taken from the stables and sent to the English garden, to crush gravel for the paths with a hammer . . . They gave me a terribly severe hiding, I couldn't even pick myself up, and they took me to my father on a bast mat, but that would have been nothing to me; but then there was this last punishment, of going on my knees and crushing stones . . . That tormented me so much that I kept thinking and thinking how to get out of it, and decided to put an end to my life. I provided myself with a stout cord, having begged it from a houseboy, and went for a swim in the evening, then to the aspen grove behind the threshing floor, got on my knees, prayed for all Christians, tied the cord to a branch, made a noose, and put my head in it. It only remained for me to jump, and the story would be all told . . . Given my character, I could have done it quite easily, but I had only just swung, jumped off the branch, and hung down, when I saw that I was lying on the ground, and in front of me stood a Gypsy with a knife, laughing—his bright white teeth flashing against his swarthy mug in the night.

"What's this you're up to, farmhand?" he says.

"And you, what do you want with me?"

"Or," he persisted, "is your life so bad?"

"Seems it's not all sweetness," I say.

"Instead of hanging by your own hand," he says, "come and live with us, maybe you'll hang some other way."

"But who are you and what do you live by? I'll bet you're thieves."

"Thieves we are," he says, "thieves and swindlers."

"There, you see," I say, "and, on occasion, I'll bet you put a knife in people?"

"Occasionally," he says, "we do that, too."

I thought over what to do: at home it would be the same thing again tomorrow and the day after, going on your knees in the path, and tap, tap, crushing little stones with a hammer, and I already had lumps growing on my knees from the work, and all I had in my ears was people jeering at me, that the fiend of a German had condemned me to make rubble of a whole mountain of stones on account of a cat's tail. Everybody laughed: "And yet they call you a savior: you saved the masters' lives." I simply couldn't stand it, and figuring that, if I didn't hang myself, I'd have to go back to the same thing, I waved my hand, wept, and went over to the robbers.

IV

That sly Gypsy gave me no time to collect my wits. He said:

"To convince me you won't go back on it, you must bring me a pair of horses from the master's stable right now, and take the best ones, so that we can gallop far away on them before morning."

I grieved inwardly: Lord knows I didn't want to steal; but then it was sink or swim; and, knowing all the ins and outs of the stables, I had no trouble leading two fiery steeds, the kind that knew no fatigue, out beyond the threshing floor, and the Gypsy had already taken wolves' teeth on strings from his pocket, and he hung them on each horse's neck, and the Gypsy and I mounted them and rode off. The horses, scenting wolves' teeth on them, raced so fast I can't tell you, and by morning we were seventy miles away, near the town of Karachev. There we sold the horses at once to some innkeeper, took the money, went to the river, and began settling our accounts. We had sold the horses for three hundred roubles—in banknotes, of course, as it was done then—but the Gypsy gave me one silver rouble and said:

"Here's your share."

I found that insulting.

"How come?" I say. "I stole the horses and could suffer more for it than you—why is my share so small?"

"Because," he says, "that's how big it grew."

"That's nonsense," I say. "Why do you take so much for yourself?"

"And again," he says, "it's because I'm a master and you're still a pupil."

"Pupil, hah!" I say. "What drivel!" And one word led to another, and we got into a quarrel. Finally, I say:

"I don't want to go any further with you, because you're a scoundrel."

And he replies:

"Do leave me, brother, for Christ's sake, because you've got no passport,[18] and I could get in trouble with you."

So we parted ways, and I was about to go to the local justice and turn myself in as a runaway, but when I told my story to his clerk, the man says to me:

"You fool, you: why go turning yourself in? Have you got ten roubles?"

"No," I say, "I've got one silver rouble, but not ten."

"Well, then maybe you've got something else, maybe a silver cross on your neck, or what's that in your ear—an earring?"

"Yes," I say, "it's an earring."

"A silver one?"

"Yes, a silver one, and I've also got a silver cross from St. Mitrofan's."[19]

"Well," he says, "take them off quickly and give them to me, and I'll write you out a release, so you can go to Nikolaev—they need people there, and hordes of vagrants flee there from us."

I gave him my silver rouble, the cross, and the earring, and he wrote out the release, put the court seal on it, and said:

"I should have added something for the seal, like I do with everybody, but I pity your poverty and don't want papers of my making to be imperfect. Off you go," he says, "and if anybody else needs it, send him to me."

"Well," I think, "a fine benefactor he is: takes the cross from my neck and then pities me." I didn't send anybody to him, I only went begging in Christ's name without even a penny in my pocket.

I came to that town and stood in the marketplace so as to get myself hired. There were very few people up for hire—three men in all—and all of them must have been the same as me, half vagrants, and many people came running to hire us, and they all latched onto us and pulled us this way and that. One gentleman, a great huge one, bigger than I am, fell on me, pushed everybody away, seized me by both arms, and dragged me off with him: he led me along, making his way through the others with his fists and cursing most foully, and there were tears in his eyes. He brought me to his little house, hastily slapped together from who knows what, and asked me:

"Tell me the truth: are you a runaway?"

"I am," I say.

"A thief," he says, "or a murderer, or just a vagrant?"

I answer:

"Why do you ask me that?"

"The better to know what kind of work you're good for."

I told him all about why I ran away, and he suddenly threw himself into kissing me and said:

"Just the one I need, just the one I need! If you felt sorry for your pigeons," he says, "surely you'll be able to nurse my baby: I'm hiring you as a nanny."

I was horrified.

"How do you mean," I say, "as a nanny? I'm not at all suited to that situation."

"No, that's trifles," he says, "trifles: I see you can be a nanny; otherwise I'm in a bad way, because my wife, out of boredom, ran off with a remount officer and left me a baby daughter at the breast, and I've got no time and no way to feed her, so you'll nurse her, and I'll pay you a salary of two roubles a month."

"For pity's sake," I reply, "it's not a matter of two roubles, but how am I to manage that kind of work?"

"Trifles," he says. "Aren't you a Russian? Russians can manage anything."

"Well, all right, so I'm a Russian, but I'm also a man, and what's needed for nursing a baby at the breast, I'm not endowed with."

"But," he says, "to help you in that regard, I'm going to buy a goat from a Jew: you'll milk her and nurse my daughter with the milk."

I thought it over and said:

"Of course, why not nurse a baby with a goat," I say, "only it seems to me you'd be better off having a woman do this work."

"No, kindly don't talk to me about women," he replies. "All the scandals here are caused by women, and there's nowhere to get them, and if you don't agree to nurse my baby, I'll call the Cossacks at once and order you bound and taken to the police, and you'll be sent back under convoy. Choose now what's better for you: to crush stones again on the count's garden path or nurse my baby?"

I thought: no, I won't go back, and agreed to stay on as a nanny. That same day we bought a white goat with a kid from a Jew. The kid I slaughtered, and my master and I ate it with noodles, and I milked the goat and started giving her milk to the baby. The baby was little, and so wretched, so pathetic: she whined all the time.

My master, her father, was a Pole, an official, and the rogue never stayed home, but ran around to his comrades to play cards, and I stayed alone with this charge of mine, this little girl, and I began to be terribly attached to her, because it was unbearably boring for me, and having nothing to do, I busied myself with her. I'd put her in the tub and give her a good washing, and if she had a rash somewhere, I'd sprinkle it with flour; or I'd brush her hair, or rock her on my knees, or, if it got very boring at home, I'd put her on my bosom and go to the estuary to do laundry—and the goat, too, got used to us and would come walking behind us. So I lived until the next summer, and my baby grew and began to stand on her feet, but I noticed that she was bowlegged. I pointed it out to the master, but he wasn't much concerned and only said:

"What's that got to do with me? Go and show her to the doctor: let him look her over."

I took her, and the doctor says:

"It's the English disease, she must sit in the sand."

I began doing that. I chose a little spot on the bank of the estuary where there's sand, and whenever the day was nice and warm, I took the goat and the girl and went there with them. I'd rake up the warm sand with my hands and cover the girl with it up to the waist and give her some sticks and pebbles to play with, and our goat walks around us, grazing on the grass, and I sit and sit, my arms around my knees, and get drowsy, and fall asleep.

The three of us spent whole days that way, and for me it was the best thing against boredom, because, I repeat again, the boredom was terrible, and that spring especially, when I started burying the girl in the sand and sleeping over the estuary, all sorts of confused dreams came to me. I'd fall asleep, and the estuary is murmuring, and with the warm wind from the steppe fanning me, it's as if some kind of sorcery flows over me, and I'm beset by terrible fantasies. I see a wide steppe, horses, and somebody seems to be calling me, luring me somewhere. I even hear my name shouted: "Ivan! Ivan! Come, brother Ivan!" I rouse myself, give a shake, and spit: "Pah, hell's too good for you, what are you calling me for?" I look around: dreariness. The goat has wandered far off, grazing in the grass, and the baby sits covered with sand, and nothing more . . . Ohh, how boring! The emptiness, the sun, the estuary, and again I fall asleep, and this current of wafting wind gets into my soul and shouts: "Ivan, let's go, brother Ivan!" I even curse and say: "Show yourself, deuce

take you, who are you to call me like that?" And once I got bitterly
angry and was sitting half asleep, looking across the estuary, and a
light cloud rose up from there and came floating straight at me. I
thought: "Whoa! Not this way, my good one, you'll get me all wet!"
Then suddenly I see: it's that monk with the womanish face standing over me, the one I killed with my whip long ago when I was a
postillion. I say: "Whoa there! Away with you!" And he chimes out
so tenderly: "Let's go, Ivan, let's go, brother! You still have much to
endure, but then you'll attain." I cursed him in my sleep and said:
"As if I had anywhere to go with you or anything to attain." And suddenly he turned back into a cloud and through himself showed me
I don't know what: the steppe, some wild people, Saracens, like in
the tales of Eruslan and Prince Bova,[20] in big, shaggy hats and with
bows and arrows, on terrifying wild horses. And along with seeing
that, I heard hooting, and neighing, and wild laughter, and then suddenly a whirlwind . . . a cloud of sand rose up, and there is nothing,
only a thin bell softly ringing somewhere, and a great white monastery all bathed in the scarlet dawn appears on a height, and winged
angels with golden lances are walking on its walls, all surrounded by
the sea, and whenever an angel strikes his shield with his lance, the
sea around the monastery heaves and splashes, and from the deep
terrible voices cry: "Holy!"

"Well," I think, "it's this monkhood getting at me again!" and from
vexation I wake up and am astonished to see that someone of the
gentlest appearance is kneeling in the sand over my little mistress
and pouring out floods of tears.

I watched this for a long time, because I kept thinking it was my
vision going on, but then I saw that it didn't vanish, and I got up and
went closer: I see the lady has dug my little girl out of the sand, and
has picked her up in her arms, and is kissing her and weeping.

I ask her:

"What do you want?"

She rushes at me, pressing the baby to her breast and whispering:

"This is my baby, this is my daughter, my daughter!"

I say:

"Well, what of it?"

"Give her to me," she says.

"Where did you get the idea," I say, "that I'd give her to you?"

"Don't you feel sorry for her?" she weeps. "See how she clings
to me."

"She clings because she's a silly baby—she also clings to me, but as for giving her to you, I'm not going to do that."

"Why?"

"Because," I say, "she's been entrusted to my keeping—and that goat there walks with us, and I must bring the baby back to her father."

The lady began to weep and wring her hands.

"Well, all right," she says, "so you don't want to give me the baby, but at least don't tell my husband, your master, that you saw me," she says, "and come here to this same place again tomorrow with the baby, so that I can fondle her more."

"That," I say, "is a different matter. I promise and I'll do it."

And just so, I said nothing about it to my master, but the next morning I took the goat and the child and went back to the estuary, and the lady was there waiting. She was sitting in a little hollow, and when she saw us, she jumped out and came running, and wept, and laughed, and gave the baby toys in each hand, and even hung a little bell on a red ribbon around our goat's neck, and for me there was a pipe, and a pouch of tobacco, and a comb.

"Kindly smoke the pipe," she says, "and I'll mind the baby."

And we kept meeting in this way over the estuary: the lady with the baby all the time, and me asleep, and occasionally she would start telling me that she was sort of . . . given in marriage to my master by force . . . by a wicked stepmother, and this husband of hers she sort of . . . never could come to love. But . . . that one . . . the other . . . the remount officer . . . or whatever . . . that one she loves, and she complained that, against her will, she says, "I've given myself to him. Because my husband," she says, "as you know yourself, leads an irregular life, but this one with the—well, how is it called?—the little mustache, or whatever, deuce knows, is very clean," she says, "he's always well dressed, and he pities me, only once again," she says, "for all that I still can't be happy, because I'm sorry about this baby. And now," she says, "he and I have come here and are staying in one of his friends' lodgings, but I live in great fear that my husband will find out, and we'll leave soon, and again I'll suffer over the baby."

"Well," I say, "what's to be done? If you've scorned law and relidgin, and changed your ritual, then you ought to suffer."

And she began to weep, and from one day to the next she started weeping more and more pitifully, and she bothered me with her complaints, and suddenly, out of the blue, she started offering me money. And finally she came for the last time, to say good-bye, and said:

"Listen, Ivan"—by then she knew my name—"listen to what I tell you," she says. "Today," she says, "*he* himself will come to us here."
I ask:
"Who's that?"
She replies:
"The remount officer."
I say:
"Well, what's that got to do with me?"
And she tells me that the night before he supposedly won a lot of money at cards and said he wanted to please her by giving me a thousand roubles—that is, provided I give her her daughter.
"Well, that," I say, "will never happen."
"Why not, Ivan? Why not?" she insists. "Aren't you sorry for both of us that we're separated?"
"Well," I say, "sorry or not, I've never sold myself either for big money or for small, and I won't do it now, and therefore let all the remounter's thousands stay with him, and your daughter with me."
She began to weep, and I said:
"You'd better not weep, because it's all the same to me."
She says:
"You're heartless, you're made of stone."
And I reply:
"I'm not made of stone at all, I'm the same as everybody else, made of bones and sinews, but I'm a trustworthy and loyal man: I undertook to keep the baby, so I'm looking after her."
She tries to convince me, says, "Judge for yourself, the baby will be better off with me."
"Once again," I reply, "that's not my business."
"Can it be," she cries out, "can it be that I must part with my baby again?"
"What else," I say, "since you've scorned law and relidgin . . ."
But I didn't finish what I wanted to say, because I saw a light uhlan coming towards us across the steppe. Back then regimental officers went about as they ought, swaggering, in real military uniform, not as nowadays like some sort of clerks. This remount uhlan walks towards us, so stately, arms akimbo, and his greatcoat thrown over his shoulders—there may not be any strength in him, but he's full of swagger . . . I look at this visitor and think: "It would be an excellent thing to have some fun with him out of boredom." And I decided that the moment he said so much as a word to me, I'd be

as rude as possible to him, and maybe, God willing, we'd have the satisfaction of a good fight. That, I exulted, would be wonderful, and I no longer listened to what my little lady was saying and tearfully babbling to me, I only wanted to have fun.

V

Once I had decided to provide myself with such amusement, I thought: how can I best tease this officer into attacking me? And I sat myself down, took the comb out of my pocket, and started combing my hair; and the officer walks straight up to this little lady of his.

She goes blah, blah, blah—that is, all about me not giving her the baby.

But he strokes her head and says:

"It's nothing, dear heart, nothing: I'll find a means against him right now. We'll spread out the money for him, he'll be dazzled; and if that means has no effect, then we'll simply take the baby from him"—and with those words, he comes over to me and hands me a wad of banknotes.

"Here," he says, "this is exactly a thousand roubles—give us the baby, take the money, and go wherever you like."

But I was being deliberately impolite, I didn't answer him at once: first I slowly got to my feet; then I hung the comb on my belt, cleared my throat, and finally said:

"No, Your Honor, this means of yours has no effect"—and I tore the money from his hand, spat on it, threw it down, and said:

"Here, boy, here, good doggy, come fetch!"

He got angry, turned all red, and flew at me; but me, you can see how I'm built—dealing with a uniformed officer takes me no time: I just gave him a little shove and that was it: he went sprawling, spurs up, and his saber stuck out sideways. I stamp my foot down on the saber.

"Take that," I say, "and your bravery I trample underfoot."

But though he wasn't much for strength, he was a courageous little officer: he saw he couldn't get his saber from me, so he unbuckled it and instantly rushed at me with his little fists . . . Naturally, that way he got himself nothing but bodily injury from me, but I liked it that he had such a proud and noble character. I didn't take his money, and he also wasn't about to pick it up.

Once we stopped fighting, I shouted:

"Pick up the money, Your Serenity, to cover your traveling expenses!"

And what do you think: he didn't pick it up, but ran straight to the baby and grabbed her; but, naturally, he takes the baby by one arm, and I immediately grab her by the other and say:

"Well, let's pull: we'll see who tears off the bigger half."

He shouts:

"Scoundrel, scoundrel, monster!"—and with that he spits in my face and lets go of the child, and now only draws that little lady away, and she's in despair and howls pathetically, and drawn away by force, she follows him, but her eyes and arms reach out to me and the baby . . . and I see and feel how she's torn in two alive, half to him, half to the baby . . . And that same minute I suddenly see my master, whose service I was in, come running from town with a pistol in his hand, and he fires the pistol and shouts:

"Hold them, Ivan! Hold them!"

"Well, now," I think to myself, "should I go holding them for you? Let them love each other!"—and I caught up with the little lady and the uhlan, gave them the baby, and said:

"Take the little scamp with you! Only now you'll have to take me, too," I say, "or else he'll hand me over to justice for having an illegal passport."

She says:

"Come along, Ivan dearest, come along, you can live with us."

So we galloped off, and took the little girl, my charge, with us, and that gentleman was left with the goat, the money, and my passport.

I sat on the box of the tarantass and rode all the way to Penza with these new masters of mine, thinking: was it a good thing I did, beating an officer? He's taken an oath, and in war he defends the fatherland with his saber, and maybe the sovereign himself addresses him formally, according to his rank, and I, fool that I am, offended him so! . . . And then, having thought that over, I began thinking about something else: what is fate going to allot me now? And there was a fair in Penza then, and the uhlan says to me:

"Listen, Ivan, I think you know that I can't keep you with me."

I say:

"Why's that?"

"Because," he replies, "I'm in the service, and you haven't got any sort of passport."

"No, I had a passport," I say, "only it was a false one."

"Well, you see," he replies, "and now you don't even have that. Here, take these two hundred roubles for the road, and go with God wherever you like."

I confess I was terribly unwilling to leave them, because I loved that baby; but there was nothing to be done.

"Well, good-bye," I say. "I humbly thank you for your reward— only there's just one thing."

"What's that?" he asks.

"It's that I'm guilty before you," I reply, "for fighting with you and being rude."

He laughed and said:

"Well, what of it, God be with you, you're a good fellow."

"No, sir," I reply, "never mind my being good, it can't be left like this, because it may weigh on my conscience: you're a defender of the fatherland, and maybe the sovereign himself addresses you formally."

"That's true," he replies. "When we're given our rank, it's written in the document: 'We grant unto you and order that you be honored and respected.'"

"Well, please, then," I say, "I can't stand it any longer . . ."

"But what can we do about it now?" he says. "You're stronger than I am, and you gave me a beating—that can't be taken back."

"To take it back is impossible," I say, "but at least to ease my conscience, think what you like, but kindly hit me a few times"—and I puffed up both cheeks before him.

"But what for?" he says. "What should I beat you for?"

"Just like that," I reply, "for my conscience, so that I don't go unpunished for insulting my sovereign's officer."

He laughed, and again I puffed up my cheeks as full as I could and again stood there.

He asks:

"Why this puffing yourself up, what are you making faces for?"

And I say:

"I'm preparing myself soldier-like, according to the rules," I say. "Kindly hit me on both sides"—and again I puffed up my cheeks; but instead of hitting me, he suddenly tore from his place and started kissing me, and he says:

"Enough, Ivan, enough, for Christ's sake: I wouldn't hit you even once, not for anything in the world, only go away quickly, while

Mashenka and her daughter aren't home, otherwise they'll weep very much over you."

"Ah, now that's another matter. Why upset them?"

And, though I didn't want to go, there was nothing to be done: so I left quickly, without saying good-bye, went out the gate, and stood, and thought:

"Where do I go now?" And in truth, so much time had passed since I ran away from my masters and started rambling, and yet nowhere had I warmed up a place for myself . . . "That's it," I think, "I'll go to the police and turn myself in, only," I think, "again it's awkward now that I have money, the police will take it all away: why don't I spend at least some of it, have tea and sweet rolls in a tavern for my own good pleasure?" So I went into a tavern at the fair, asked for tea and sweet rolls, and drank it for a long time, but then I saw that I couldn't drag it out any longer, and went for a stroll. I went across the river Sura to the steppe, where herds of horses stood, and here there were also Tartars in kibitkas.[21] The kibitkas were all identical, but one was multicolored, and around it there were many different gentlemen occupied with trying out saddle horses. Civilians, military, landowners come for the fair—these different men all stood smoking their pipes, and in the midst of them, on a multicolored rug, sat a tall, dignified Tartar, thin as a rail, in a fancy robe and a golden skullcap. I look around and, seeing a man who was having tea when I was in the tavern, I ask him who this important Tartar is, to be the only one sitting down among them all. And he replies:

"Don't you know him? He's Khan Dzhangar."

"Who is this Khan Dzhangar?"

And the man says:

"Khan Dzhangar is the foremost horse breeder of the steppe, his herds go from the Volga all the way to the Ural over the whole Ryn Sands, and he himself, this Khan Dzhangar, is the same as a tsar of the steppe."[22]

"Isn't that steppe ours?" I say.

"Yes," he replies, "it's ours, but we can't have any hold on it, because all the way to the Caspian it's either salt marshes or just grass and birds wheeling under the heavens, and there's nothing for an official to get out of it," he says, "and that's the reason why Khan Dzhangar rules there, and there in the Ryn Sands he's got his own sheikhs, and sheikh-zadas, and malo-zadas, and imams, and dervishes, and uhlans, and he orders them around as he likes, and they gladly obey him."

I was listening to those words, and at the same time I saw a Tartar boy bring a small white mare before this khan and start to babble; and the man stood up, took a long-handled whip, placed himself right in front of the mare's head, put the whip to her forehead, and stood there. But how did the brigand stand there? I'll describe to you: a magnificent statue, that's how, you couldn't have enough of looking at him, and you see at once that he spies out all that's in a horse. And since I've been observant in these matters from childhood, I could see that the mare herself perceived the expert in him and stood at attention before him: here, look at me and admire! And this dignified Tartar looked and looked at the mare like that, without walking around her the way our officers do, who bustle and fidget around a horse, but kept gazing at her from one point, and suddenly he lowered the whip and silently kissed his fingertips, meaning *perfect!*—and again sat cross-legged on the rug, and the mare at once twitched her ears, snorted, and began to act up.

The gentlemen who were standing there got into a haggling match for her: one offered a hundred roubles, another a hundred and fifty, and so on, raising the price higher and higher against each other. The mare was, in fact, wonderful—of smallish stature, like an Arabian, but slender, with a small head, a full, apple-like eye, pricked-up ears; her flanks were ringing, airy, her back straight as an arrow, and her legs light, finely shaped, swift as could be. As I was a lover of such beauty, I simply couldn't tear my eyes off this mare. And Khan Dzhangar, seeing that a hankering for her has come over them all, and the gentlemen are inflating the price for her like they're possessed, nods to the swarthy little Tartar, and the boy leaps on her, the little she-swan, and starts her off—sits her, you know, in his own Tartarish way, working her with his knees, and she takes wing under him and flies just like a bird and doesn't buck, and when he leans down to her withers and whoops at her, she just soars up in one whirl with the sand. "Ah, you serpent!" I think to myself, "ah, you kestrel of the steppe, you little viper! Wherever could you have come from?" And I feel that my soul yearns for her, for this horse, with a kindred passion. The Tartar came riding back, she puffed at once through both nostrils, breathed out, and shook off all fatigue, and didn't snort or sniff anymore. "Ah, you darling," I think, "ah, you darling!" If the Tartar had asked me not just for my soul, but for my own father and

mother, I'd have had no regrets—but how could I even think of getting such a wingèd thing, when who knows what price had been laid
down for her by the gentlemen and the remount officers, but even
that would have been nothing, the dealing still wasn't over, and no
one had gotten her yet, but suddenly we see a swift rider come racing
on a black horse from beyond the Sura, from Seliksa, and he waves
his broad-brimmed hat and comes flying up, jumps off, abandons his
horse, goes straight to the white mare, stands by her head, like that
first statue, and says:

"It's my mare."

And the khan replies:

"She's not yours: the gentlemen are offering me five hundred coins
for her."

And that rider, an enormous, big-bellied Tartar, his mug sun-
burned and all peeling, as if the skin had been torn off, his eyes
small, like slits, bawls at once:

"I give a hundred coins more!"

The gentlemen flutter themselves up, promise still more, and the
dry Khan Dzhangar sits and smacks his lips, and from the other side
of the Sura another Tartar horseman comes riding on a long-maned
sorrel horse, this time a skinny and yellow one, his bones barely
holding together, but a still greater rascal than the first one. This one
slips off his horse and sticks himself like a nail in front of the white
mare and says:

"I tell you all: I want this mare to be mine!"

I ask my neighbor what this business depends on for them. And
he replies:

"This business depends on Khan Dzhangar's very great understanding. More than once," he says, "and maybe each time, he has
pulled this trick at the fair: first he sells all the ordinary horses, the
horses he brings here, but then, on the last day, he produces, devil
knows from where, as if pulling it out of his sleeve, such a horse, or
two, that the connoisseurs don't know what to do; and he, the sly
Tartar, watches it and amuses himself, and makes money as well for
all that. Knowing this habit of his, everybody expects this last twist
from him, and that's what's happened now: everybody thought the
khan would leave today, and, in fact, he will leave tonight, but just
see what a mare he's brought out . . ."

"It's a wonder," I say, "such a horse!"

"A real wonder, and they say he drove her to the fair in the middle of the herd, so that nobody could see her behind all the other horses, and nobody knew about her except the Tartars who came with him, and them he told that the horse wasn't for sale, she's too precious, and during the night he separated her from the others and drove her to a forest near a Mordovian village and had her pastured there by a special herdsman, and now he suddenly brought her and put her up for sale, and you just watch what antics go on here and what that dog will make from her. Want to wager on who's going to get her?"

"But what's the point in us betting on it?"

"The point is," he says, "that passions are going to break loose, the gentlemen are all sure to back out, and the horse will be bought by one of these two Asians."

"Are they very rich or something?" I ask.

"They're both rich," he replies, "and shrewd horse fanciers: they've got their own big herds, and never in their lives will either of them yield a fine, precious horse to the other. Everybody knows them: this big-bellied one with the peeling mug, his name is Bakshey Otuchev, and the skinny one, nothing but bones, is Chepkun Emgurcheev—they're both wicked horse fanciers. Just watch what a show they'll put on."

I fell silent and watched: the gentlemen who had been haggling for the mare had already quit and were only looking on, and the two Tartars keep pushing each other aside and slapping Khan Dzhangar's hands and taking hold of the mare, and they're shaking and shouting. One shouts:

"Besides the coins, I also give five head for her" (meaning five horses)—and the other screams:

"You lying gob—I give ten."

Bakshey Otuchev shouts:

"I give fifteen head."

And Chepkun Emgurcheev:

"Twenty."

Bakshey:

"Twenty-five."

And Chepkun:

"Thirty."

And evidently neither of them had any more . . . Chepkun shouted thirty, and Bakshey also offered only thirty, and no more; but then Chepkun offers a saddle on top, and Bakshey a saddle and a robe, so Chepkun also takes off his robe, and again they have nothing to outbid each other with. Chepkun cries: "Listen to me, Khan Dzhangar: when I get home, I'll send you my daughter"—and Bakshey also promises his daughter, and again they have nothing to outvie each other with. Here suddenly all the Tartars who had been watching the haggling started yelling, yammering in their own language; they parted them, so that they wouldn't drive each other to ruin, pulled them, Chepkun and Bakshey, to different sides, poked them in the ribs, trying to persuade them.

I ask my neighbor:

"Tell me, please, what's going on with them now?"

"You see," he says, "these princes who are parting them feel sorry for Chepkun and Bakshey, that they overdid the haggling, so now they've separated them, so they can come to their senses and one of them can honorably yield the mare to the other."

"But," I ask, "how can one of them yield her to the other, if they both like her so much? It can't be."

"Why not?" he replies. "Asiatic folk are reasonable and dignified: they'll reason that there's no use losing all they've got, and they'll give Khan Dzhangar as much as he asks, and agree on who gets the horse by flogging it out."

I was curious:

"What does 'flogging it out' mean?"

And the man replies:

"No point asking, look, it's got to be seen, and it's beginning right now."

I look and see that Bakshey Otuchev and Chepkun Emgurcheev seem to have quieted down, and they tear free of those peace-making Tartars, rush to each other, and clasp hands.

"Agreed!"—meaning, it's settled.

And the other one says the same thing:

"Agreed: it's settled."

And at once they both throw aside their robes and beshmets and shoes, take off their cotton shirts, and remain in nothing but their wide striped trousers; they plop down on the ground facing each other, like a pair of steppe ruffs, and sit there.

This was the first time I'd had occasion to see such a wonder, and I watched for what would come next. They gave each other their left hands and held them firmly, spread their legs and placed them foot to foot, and shouted: "Bring 'em on!"

What it was they wanted "brought on," I couldn't guess, but the Tartars from the bunch around them replied:

"At once, at once."

And a dignified old man stepped from this bunch of Tartars, and he had two stout whips in his hands and held them up together and showed them to the public and to Chepkun and Bakshey: "Look," he says, "they're the same length."

"The same length," the Tartars cried, "we all see it's honorably done, the lashes are the same length! Let them sit up and begin."

Bakshey and Chepkun were just dying to get hold of those whips.

The dignified Tartar said "Wait" to them, and gave them the whips himself, one to Chepkun and the other to Bakshey, and then quietly clapped his hands, one, two, and three . . . And just as he clapped for the third time, Bakshey, with all his might, lashed Chepkun with the whip over the shoulder on his bare back, and Chepkun replied to him in the same way. And they went on regaling each other like that: they look each other in the eye, their foot soles are pressed together and their left hands firmly clasped, and with their right hands they deal out lashes . . . Oh, how expertly they whipped! One gives a good stroke, the other still better. The eyes of both became glassy, and their left hands didn't move, and neither of them would yield.

I ask my new acquaintance:

"So what they're doing is like when our gentlemen fight a duel?"

"Yes," he says, "it's a kind of duel, only not for the sake of honor, but so as not to spend their money."

"And can they keep whipping each other like this for a long time?" I ask.

"As long as they like," he says, "and as long as they have the strength."

And they go on lashing each other, and an argument starts among the people around them. Some say, "Chepkun will outflog Bakshey," and others argue, "Bakshey will outwhip Chepkun," and they place bets, if they want to—some for Chepkun, others for Bakshey, whoever they think is stronger. They look knowingly in their eyes, in their teeth, at their backs, and seeing by some tokens which one is surer, they stake on him. The man I had been talking with was also an experienced spectator and began by staking on Bakshey, but then said:

"Ah, drat, my twenty kopecks are lost: Chepkun will beat Bakshey."

And I say:

"How do you know? Nothing's sure yet: they're sitting the same way."

And the man replies:

"They're sitting the same way, but they lash differently."

"Well," I say, "in my opinion, Bakshey lashes more fiercely."

"And that," he replies, "is what's wrong. No, my twenty kopecks are lost: Chepkun will finish him off."

"What a remarkable thing," I think. "How can my acquaintance reason so incomprehensibly? And yet," I reflect, "he must understand this practice rather well, since he placed a bet!"

And, you know, I got very curious, and I started badgering my acquaintance.

"Tell me, my dear man," I say, "what makes you fear for Bakshey now?"

And he says:

"What a stupid bumpkin you are! Look at the back on Bakshey."

I look: all right, it's a good enough back, manly, big and plump as a pillow.

"And do you see how he hits?"

I look and see that he beats fiercely, his eyes are even popping out, and with each stroke he draws blood.

"Well, and now consider, what is he doing to his insides?"

"Who knows about his insides? I see one thing, that he's sitting up straight, and his mouth is wide open, and he's quickly taking in air."

And my acquaintance says:

"That's the bad thing: his back is big, there's lots of room for lashing; he beats quickly, huffing and puffing, and breathing through his open mouth, he'll burn up all his insides with air."

"So," I ask, "that means Chepkun is surer?"

"Certainly he's surer," he says. "See, he's all dry, nothing but skin and bones, and his back's as warped as a shovel, the blows don't land full on it, but only in places, and see how he pours it out on Bakshey measuredly, not rapidly, but with little pauses, and doesn't pull the lash away at once, but lets the skin swell under it. That's why Bakshey's back is all swollen and blue as a stew pot, but there's no blood, and all the pain stays in his body now, but on Chepkun's lean back the skin crackles and tears, like on a roast pig, and his pain will all come out in blood, and he'll finish Bakshey off. Do you understand now?"

"Now," I say, "I understand." And, in fact, here I understood this whole Asiatic practice all at once and became extremely interested in it: what in that case was the most useful way to act?

"And another most important thing," my acquaintance points out. "Notice how well this cursed Chepkun keeps the rhythm with his mug. See, he strikes and suffers the reply and blinks his eyes correspondingly—it's easier than just staring the way Bakshey stares, and Chepkun clenches his teeth and bites his lips, and that's also easier, because owing to that reticence there's no unnecessary burning inside him."

I bore in mind all these curious examples and looked closely at Chepkun and Bakshey myself, and it became clear to me, too, that Bakshey was bound to collapse, because his eyes already looked quite stupefied, and his lips were drawn thin and revealed his bare teeth . . . And, in fact, we look: Bakshey gives Chepkun some twenty more lashes, weaker and weaker each time, and suddenly flops backwards, letting go of Chepkun's left hand, but still moving his right as if lashing, only unconsciously now, completely passed out. Well, here my acquaintance said: "That's it: my twenty kopecks are gone." Here all the Tartars started talking, congratulating Chepkun, shouting:

"Ai, clever Chepkun Emgurcheev, ai, clever head—completely outwhipped Bakshey. Mount up—the mare is yours now."

And Khan Dzhangar himself got up from the rug and strode about, and smacked his lips, and also said:

"Yours, Chepkun, the mare is yours: mount up, ride, you can rest on her."

And Chepkun got up: blood streamed down his back, but he didn't show any pain; he put his robe and beshmet on the mare's back, threw himself on his belly over her, and rode off that way, and I again felt bored.

"There," I think, "it's over now, and thoughts about my situation will start coming into my head again"—and Lord knows I didn't want to think about that.

But, thanks be, this acquaintance of mine says to me:

"Wait, don't leave, there's sure to be something more here."

I say:

"What more can there be? It's all over."

"No," he says, "it's not over. Look how Khan Dzhangar's pipe is burning. See, it's smoking away: he's sure to be thinking something over to himself, something most Asiatic."

And I thought to myself: "Ah, if there's going to be more of the same sort, then just let somebody wager on me and see if I back down."

VI

And what do you think? It all came out just as I wished: Khan Dzhangar's pipe was smoking away, and another little Tartar comes racing towards him from the open, this one not on a mare like the one Chepkun peaceably took from Bakshey, but on a dark bay colt impossible to describe. If you've ever seen how a corncrake—in Orel we call him a twitcher—runs along a boundary through the wheat: he spreads his wings out wide, but his behind doesn't spread in the air, as with other birds, but hangs down, and he lets his legs dangle, too, as if he doesn't need them—it comes out as if he's really riding on air. So this new horse, just like the bird, raced as if by a power not his own.

I truly won't be telling a lie if I say that he didn't even fly, but the ground behind him just kept increasing. Never in my life had I seen such lightness, and I didn't know how to put a price on a horse like that, in what treasure, and whom he was fated for, what kind of prince, and still less did I ever think that this horse would become mine.

"So he became yours?" the astonished listeners interrupted the storyteller.

"Yes, sir, mine, by all rights mine, but only for one minute, and kindly listen to how it happened, if you want."

The gentlemen, as was their habit, began haggling over this horse as well, and my remount officer, to whom I had given the baby, also mixed into it, but against them, like their equal, the Tartar Savakirey stepped in, a short fellow, small but sturdy, well-knit, head shaven as if turned on a lathe and round as a firm young cabbage, and his mug red as a carrot, and the whole of him like some sort of healthy and fresh vegetable. He shouts: "Why empty your pockets for nothing? Whoever wants to can lay down his money, as much as the khan asks, and flog it out with me for who gets the horse."

For the gentlemen, naturally, that was unseemly, and they backed away from it at once: why should they go thrashing with this Tartar—the rascal would outwhip them all. And by then my remount officer wasn't rolling in money, because in Penza he had lost at cards again, but I could see he wanted the horse. So I tugged his sleeve from behind and said: "Thus and so, don't offer anything extra, but give what the khan asks, and I'll sit down to contend peaceably with Savakirey."

At first he didn't want to, but I persuaded him. I said:

"Do me the favor: I want it."

Well, and so we did.

"What . . . you and that Tartar . . . whipped each other?"

"Yes, sir, we also thrashed it out peaceably in the same way, and the colt went to me."

"So you beat the Tartar?"

"Beat him, sir, not without difficulty, but I overcame him."

"Yet it must have been terribly painful."

"Mmm . . . how shall I put it . . . Yes, to begin with it was; I really felt it, especially since I was unaccustomed, and he, that Savakirey, also had a trick of hitting so that it swelled and didn't let the blood out, but against that fine art of his I applied my own clever trick: as he lashed me, I hitched my back up under the whip and adjusted it so that the skin got torn at once, that way it was safe, and I finished Savakirey off."

"How, finished him off? You mean to death?"

"Yes, sir, through his stubbornness and through his politics, he stupidly let himself go so far that he was no longer in the world," the storyteller replied good-naturedly and impassively, and, seeing that all his listeners were looking at him, if not with horror, then with dumb bewilderment, he seemed to feel the need to supplement his story with an explanation.

"You see," he went on, "that came not from me, but from him, because he was considered the foremost battler in the whole Ryn Sands, and on account of that ambition he didn't want to yield to me for anything, he wanted to endure nobly, so that shame wouldn't fall on his Asiatic nation on account of him, but he wilted, the poor fellow, and couldn't hold out against me, probably because I kept a copper in my mouth. That helped me terribly, and I kept biting it so as not to feel the pain, and to distract my mind I counted the strokes, so it was all right for me."

"And how many strokes did you count?" they interrupted the storyteller.

"I can't say for certain. I remember that I counted up to two hundred and eighty-two, but then I suddenly reeled in something like a swoon and lost count for a moment, and then went on without counting, but soon after that Savakirey swung at me for the last time, but couldn't hit anymore, and fell over onto me like a doll: they looked, and he was dead . . . Pah, what a fool! To hold out that long! I almost landed in jail on account of him. It was nothing to the Tartars: well, if you killed him, you killed him, those were the conditions, because he could have beaten me to death as well, but our own folk, our Russians, it's even annoying how they didn't understand and got riled up. I said:

"'Well, what is it to you? What are you after?'

"'But,' they say, 'you killed the Asiatic, didn't you?'

"'Well, what if I did? It was all done amicably. Would it have been better if he beat me to death?'

"'He could beat you to death,' they say, 'and it would be nothing to him, because he's of another faith, but you,' they say, 'have got to judge by Christianity. Come along,' they say, 'let's go to the police.'

"Well, I think to myself: 'All right, brothers, chase the wind in the field.' And since, in my opinion, there's nothing more pernicious than the police, I dodged behind one Tartar, then behind another. I whisper to them:

"'Save me, princes: you saw it was all a fair fight . . .'

"They pressed together and pushed me from one to the other, and concealed me."

"Excuse me . . . but how did they *conceal* you?"

"I cleared out with them all the way to their steppe."

"To the steppe even!"

"Yes, sir, right to the Ryn Sands."

"And did you spend long there?"

"A whole ten years: I was twenty-three when they brought me to the Ryn Sands and thirty-four when I escaped and came back."

"So, did you like living in the steppe or not?"

"No, what could you like there? Boredom, and nothing else; only it was impossible to get away earlier."

"Why's that? Did the Tartars keep you in a pit or under guard?"

"No, they're kind, they didn't allow themselves such meanness with me as to put me in a pit or in the stocks, but simply said: 'Be our friend, Ivan; we like you very much, and you'll live with us in the steppe and be a useful man—treat our horses and help our women.'"

"And did you treat them?"

"Yes, I was like a doctor to them, and I attended to them, and all their cattle, and horses, and sheep, and most of all their wives, the Tartar women."

"So you know how to treat people?"

"How shall I put it . . . Well, I mean, what's so clever about it? When somebody was sick, I gave them aloe or galingale root, and it would go away, and they had a lot of aloe—in Saratov one of the Tartars found a whole sack of it and brought it back, but before me they didn't know what it was meant for."

"And you felt at home with them?"

"No, sir, I always longed to go back."

"And can it really have been so impossible to leave them?"

"No—why? If my feet had been in good shape, I'd most likely have gone back to the fatherland long before."

"And what happened to your feet?"

"They bristled me up after the first time."

"How's that? . . . Forgive us, please, we don't quite understand what you mean by 'bristled up.'"

"It's a most ordinary means with them: if they like somebody and want to keep him, but the man pines away or tries to escape, they do it to him so he doesn't get away. So with me, after I got lost trying to escape once, they caught me and said: 'You know, Ivan, you be our friend, and to make it so you don't leave us again, we'd better cut open your heels and stuff a few bristles in them.' Well, they ruined my feet that way, so I had to crawl on all fours all the time."

"Tell us, please, how do they do this terrible operation?"

"Very simply. Some ten men threw me down on the ground and said: 'Shout, Ivan, shout louder when we start cutting. It'll be easier for you.' And they sat on me, and in a trice one master craftsman of theirs cut the skin open on my soles, put in some chopped-up horse-hair, covered it with the skin, and sewed it up with string. After that they kept my hands tied for a few days, for fear I'd harm my wounds and the bristles would come out with the pus; but once the skin healed, they let me go: 'Now,' they say, 'greetings to you, Ivan, now you're our real friend and you'll never go away and leave us.'

"I only just got to my feet then, when I went crashing to the ground again: the chopped-up hair sewn under the skin of my heels pricked the live flesh with such deadly pain that it was not only impossible to take a step, but there was even no way to stand on my feet. I had never cried in my life, but here I even howled out loud.

"'What have you done to me, you cursed Asiatics?' I say. 'You'd have done better to kill me outright, you vipers, than to make me a cripple like this for all time, so that I can't take a step.'

"But they say:

"'Never mind, Ivan, never mind, don't upset yourself over a trifle.'

"'What kind of trifle is it?' I say. 'You ruin a man like this, and then say he shouldn't upset himself?'

"'You'll get the knack of it,' they say. 'Don't step square on your heels, but walk bowlegged on the little bones.'

"'Pah, you scoundrels!' I thought to myself and turned my back on them and didn't talk, but made up my mind that I'd rather die than follow their advice about walking bowlegged on my anklebones; but then I went on lying there—a deadly boredom came over me, and I began to get the knack of it, and gradually hobbled around on my anklebones. But they didn't laugh at me in the least for that, and kept saying:

"'How well you walk, Ivan, see how well you walk.'"

"What a misfortune! And how was it you tried to escape and got caught?"

"It was impossible, sir; the steppe is flat, there are no roads, and you get hungry . . . I walked for three days, grew feeble as a fox, caught some sort of bird barehanded and ate it raw, then got hungry again, and there was no water . . . How could I go on? . . . So I fell down, and they found me and took and bristled me up."

One of the listeners remarked, apropos of this bristling up, that it must have been devilishly awkward to walk on your anklebones.

"At the outstart it was even very bad," Ivan Severyanych replied, "and later on, though I managed better, all the same I couldn't go far. But then again, I'll tell you no lies, those Tartars took good care of me after that.

"'Now, Ivan,' they say, 'it's going to be pretty hard for you to fetch water, and to cook for yourself will also be awkward. Take yourself a Natasha now, brother,' they say, 'we'll give you a nice Natasha, choose whichever one you like.'

"I say:

"'What's there to choose: they're the same use one and all. Give me whichever you like.' Well, so they married me off at once without any argument."

"What? Married you to a Tartar woman?"

"Yes, naturally, to a Tartar woman. First to one who'd been the wife of that Savakirey that I outwhipped, only she, this Tartar woman, wasn't to my taste at all: she was a bit off and always seemed very afraid of me and didn't delight me in the least. She missed her husband, maybe, or had something weighing on her heart. Well, so they noticed that I began to feel burdened by her and right away brought me another, this one a young little girl, no more than thirteen years old . . . They said to me:

"'Take this Natasha, too, Ivan, this one will be more fun.'

"So I took her."

"And was she really more fun for you?" the listeners asked Ivan Severyanych.

"Yes," he replied, "this one turned out to be more fun, only sometimes she amused me, and sometimes she annoyed me with her pranks."

"What sort of pranks?"

"All sorts . . . Whatever she happened to think up; she'd jump onto my knees; or I'd be asleep, and she'd flick the skullcap off my head with her foot and throw it away somewhere and laugh. I'd start scolding her, and she'd laugh loud, merrily, running around like a nymph, and I couldn't catch her on all fours—I'd fall down and burst out laughing myself."

"So you shaved your head there on the steppe and wore a skullcap?"

"That I did, sir."

"What for? Most likely you wanted to please your wives?"

"No, more for cleanliness, because there are no bathhouses there."

"So you had two wives at once?"

"Yes, sir, two in that steppe; and then with another khan, with Agashimola, who stole me from Otuchev, they gave me two more."

"Excuse me," one of the listeners inquired again, "but how could they steal you?"

"By trickery, sir. I ran away from Penza with the Tartars of Chepkun Emgurcheev, and for some five years on end I lived in Emgurcheev's horde, and all the princes, and uhlans, and sheikh-zadas, and malozadas used to get together with him there for festivities, and Khan Dzhangar would be there, and Bakshey Otuchev."

"The one Chepkun whipped?"

"Yes, sir, the very same."

"But how's that . . . Wasn't Bakshey angry with Chepkun?"

"What for?"

"For outwhipping him and winning the horse away from him?"

"No, sir, they never get angry with each other for that: whoever wins out by amicable agreement takes it, and that's all; though once, in fact, Khan Dzhangar reproached me . . . 'Eh, Ivan,' he says, 'eh, you numbskull, Ivan, why did you sit down for the whipping with Savakirey in place of the Russian prince? I wanted to have a laugh,' he says, 'seeing a Russian prince take his shirt off.'

"'You'd have had a long wait,' I replied to him.

"'How so?'

"'Because,' I say, 'our princes are fainthearted and unmanly, and their strength is quite negligible.'

"He understood.

"'I could see,' he says, 'that they had no real passion, and if they wanted to get something, they'd pay money for it.'

"'True enough: they can't do anything without money.' Well, but Agashimola, he was from a far-off horde, his herds roamed about somewhere near the Caspian; he loved medical treatment and invited me to cure his wife and promised Emgurchey many head of cattle for it. Emgurchey let me go with him: I took along a supply of aloe and galingale root and went. But as soon as Agashimola took me, he hied himself off with his whole band, and we galloped for eight days."

"And you rode on horseback?"

"That I did, sir."

"But what about your feet?"

"What about them?"

"The chopped-up horsehair that was in your heels didn't bother you?"

"Not at all. They've got it worked out nicely: when they bristle a man up like that, he can't walk very well, but such a bristled-up man sits a horse better than anybody, because, walking on his anklebones all the time, he's used to being bowlegged and grips the horse so tight he can't be knocked off for anything."

"Well, and how was it for you afterwards in the new steppe with Agashimola?"

"I was dying again even more cruelly."

"But you didn't die?"

"No, sir, I didn't."

"Will you be so kind as to tell us what you endured after that with Agashimola?"

"If you like."

VII

"As soon as Agashimola's Tartars brought me to their camp, they hied themselves off to another one, in a new place, and wouldn't let me leave.

"'Why should you live with Emgurchey's people, Ivan?' they say. 'Emgurchey's a thief. Live with us, we'll gladly respect you and give you nice Natashas. There you had two Natashas in all, but we'll give you more.'

"I refused.

"'Why should I have more?' I say. 'I don't need more.'

"'No,' they say, 'you don't understand, more Natashas are better: they'll bear you more Kolkas, they'll all call you daddy.'

"'Well,' I say, 'I have no need to bring up little Tartars. If they could be baptized and take communion, that would be a different matter, but now what: as many of them as I multiply, they'll all be yours, not Orthodox, and they'll cheat Russian peasants when they grow up.' So again I took two wives, and wouldn't have more, because when there's a lot of women, even if they're Tartars, the foul things will get to quarreling, and you have to discipline them all the time."

"Well, sir, and did you love these new wives of yours?"

"What's that?"

"These new wives of yours—did you love them?"

"Love? . . . Ah, so that's what you mean? Yes, one that I had from Agashimola was very obliging to me, so I just . . . took pity on her."

"And that girl, the young one who had been married to you before—most likely she pleased you more?"

"She was all right. I took pity on her, too."

"And you probably missed her when you were stolen by one horde from the other?"

"No, I didn't miss her."

"But still, you most likely had children there, from your first wives?"

"Of course I did: Savakirey's wife bore two Kolkas and a Natasha, and the young one gave birth to six in five years, because once she had two Kolkas at the same time."

"Allow us to ask you, though: why do you keep calling them 'Kolkas' and 'Natashas'?"

"That's the Tartar way. For them, if it's a grown Russian man—it's *Ivan,* if it's a woman—it's *Natasha,* and boys they call *Kolka,* and so my wives, though they were Tartars, were counted as Natashas because of me, and the boys were Kolkas. Though all this, naturally, was only superficial, because they had no Church sacraments, and I didn't consider them my children."

"So you didn't consider them yours? Why was that?"

"How could I, when they weren't baptized or anointed with oil?"

"And your parental feelings?"

"What's that, sir?"

"Can it be that you didn't love these children at all and never caressed them?"

"Why should I caress them? Naturally, if I happened to be sitting alone and one of them came running up, well, I'd just pat him on the head and tell him: 'Go to your mother'—only that rarely happened, because I couldn't be bothered with them."

"Why couldn't you be bothered: did you have so much to do?"

"No, sir, I had nothing to do, but I was pining away: I wanted very much to go home to Russia."

"So in ten years you still didn't get used to the steppe?"

"No, sir, I wanted to go home . . . I pined for it. Especially in the evenings, or even at midday, when it was fair weather, hot, the camp was quiet, the Tartars had all dropped off to sleep in their tents from the scorching heat, and I raise the flap of my tent and look at the steppe . . . to this side and to that—it's all the same . . . Scorching hot, a cruel sight; the expanse boundless; a riot of grass; feather-grass white, fluffy, billowing like a silver sea; and a smell borne on the breeze, the smell of sheep, and the sun beats down, burning hot, and the steppe, like a burdensome life, has no foreseeable end, and there's no bottom to the depths of your anguish . . . You gaze off somewhere, and suddenly out of the blue a monastery or a church appears, and you remember your baptized land and start to weep."

Ivan Severyanych paused, sighed deeply at his memories, and went on:

"Or even worse than that was on the salt marshes near the Caspian: the sun glows, bakes, and the salt marsh glitters, and the sea glitters . . . You get befuddled by that glitter even worse than by the feather-grass, and you don't know anymore what part of the world you're in, that is, whether you're still alive or dead and suffering for your sins in hopeless hell. Where there's more feather-grass on the steppe, all the same it's more heartening; at least you find gray-blue sage here and there on a low rise, or small clusters of wormwood and thyme, colorful in all that whiteness, but here there's nothing but glitter . . . If fire runs scorching through the grass somewhere, there's a great bustle: bustards, kestrels, steppe snipe fly up, and the hunt for them begins. We'd overtake the bustards on horseback, surround them, and bring them down with long whips; but then we and our horses would have to flee from the fire ourselves . . . All this was a diversion. And then strawberries would grow again on the old burnt places; birds of all sorts would come flying, mostly small ones, and there'd be chirping in the air . . . And then you'd occasionally come upon a little bush: meadowsweet, wild peach, or broom. And when the mist falls as dew at sunrise, it's as if there's a breath of coolness, and the plants give off their scents . . . Of course, it's boring even with all that, but still you can endure it, but God keep anyone from staying long on a salt marsh. A horse is content there for a while: he licks the salt, which makes him drink a lot and get fat, but for a man it's the end. There's not a living thing there, there's only, as if in mockery, one little bird, the redbill, like our swallow, quite unremarkable, only it has a red edging on its bill. Why it comes to that seashore, I don't know, but since there's nothing for it to light on, it drops onto the salt, lies there for a while on its behind, and then flutters up and flies off again, but you're deprived even of that, for you've got no wings, and so here you are again, and you've got neither death, nor life, nor repentance, and if you die, they'll put you in the salt like mutton, and you can lie there salted till the end of the world. And it's still more wearisome in winter; it snows a little, just enough to cover the grass, and hardens. Then the Tartars all sit by the fire in their yurts and smoke . . . And here, out of boredom, they often have whipping contests among themselves. Then you go out, and there's nothing to look at: the horses are all sullen and go around hunched up, so skinny that only their tails and manes flutter in the wind. They can barely drag their feet and dig through the snowy crust with their hooves to nibble on the frozen grass, which is all they feed on . . . Unbearable. The only distraction is when they notice one of the horses has grown very weak and can no longer break the snow with his hoof and get at the frozen roots with his teeth, so they slit his throat with a knife at once, skin him, and eat the meat. It's vile-tasting meat, though: sweet, like cow's udder, but tough; you eat it, of course, because you have to, but it turns your stomach. Thankfully, one of my wives knew how to smoke horse ribs; she'd take a rib with meat on both sides, put it in the large intestine, and smoke it over the fire. That wasn't too bad, you could eat it more readily, because at least it smelled something like ham, but even so the taste was vile. So here you are gnawing on this foul thing, and you suddenly think: Ah, at home now in the village they're plucking ducks and geese for the feast, slaughtering pigs, cooking cabbage soup with the nice, fatty necks, and soon now Father Ilya, our priest, a most kindly old man, will lead the procession glorifying Christ, and the deacons and their wives walk with him, and the seminarians, and they're all tipsy, but Father Ilya himself can't drink much; the butler in the manor house offers him a little glass; the steward sends the nanny with a bit more from the office; Father Ilya goes limp, he can barely drag his feet to us in the yard from drunkenness: he'll manage to sip another little glass at the first cottage on his way, but after that he can't take any more and pours it all into a bottle under his chasuble. He does it all in a family-like way, even with regard to food. If he sees something that looks appetizing, he asks: 'Wrap it up in newspaper for me, I'll take it along.' They usually reply: 'We have no newspaper, Father'—he doesn't get angry, but takes it as it is, unwrapped, gives it to his wife, and goes on just as peaceably. Ah, gentlemen, when all that life remembered since childhood comes to mind, and it suddenly weighs on your soul and suddenly begins to press on your liver that you've been perishing in this place, separated from all that happiness, and haven't been to confession for so many years, and are living without a Church marriage, and will die without a Church funeral, you're overcome with anguish and . . . you wait for night, quietly crawl outside the camp, so that neither your wives, nor the children, nor any of the infidels can see you, and you begin to pray . . . and you pray . . . pray so hard that the snow even melts under your knees, and where your tears fall you see grass the next morning."

The storyteller fell silent and hung his head. No one disturbed him; they all seemed filled with respect for the sacred sorrow of these last memories; but a moment went by, and Ivan Severyanych himself sighed, as if waving it away; he took his monastery hat from his head and, crossing himself, said:

"But that's all past, thank God!"

We let him rest awhile and then ventured upon some new questions about how he, our enchanted mighty man, had cured his heels ruined by the chopped-up horsehair, and by what paths he had escaped from his Natashas and Kolkas on the Tartar steppe and ended up in a monastery.

Ivan Severyanych satisfied this curiosity with complete frankness, which he was obviously quite unable to abandon.

VIII

Valuing the sequence of development in Ivan Severyanych's story, which had caught our interest, we asked him first of all to tell us by what extraordinary means he had rid himself of his bristles and left captivity. He gave the following account of it:

I utterly despaired of ever returning home and seeing my fatherland. The thought of it even seemed impossible to me, and my anguish itself even began to fade. I lived like an insensible statue and nothing more; and sometimes I'd think how, in church at home, that same Father Ilya who asked for newspaper used to pray during services "for travelers by land and by sea, for the suffering and for *captives*," and I used to listen and think: "If there's no war now, why pray for captives?" But now I understood why they prayed like that, but I didn't understand why all those prayers were no use to me, and, to say the least, though not an unbeliever, I became confused and did not pray myself.

"Why pray," I think, "if nothing comes of it?"

And meanwhile one day I suddenly hear the Tartars are in a commotion about something.

I say:

"What is it?"

"Nothing," they say. "Two mullahs have come from your country. They have a safe conduct from the white tsar and are going far and wide to establish their faith."

I hurriedly said:

"Where are they?"

They pointed to one yurt, and I went where they pointed. I come and see there's a gathering of many sheikh-zadas, and malo-zadas, and imams, and dervishes, and they're all sitting cross-legged on rugs, and in the midst of them are two unknown men dressed for traveling, but you can see they're some sort of clerics. The two are standing in the midst of this Tartar riffraff and teaching them the word of God.

When I caught sight of them, I rejoiced at seeing Russians, and my heart throbbed inside me, and I fell at their feet and wept. They also rejoiced at my bowing and both exclaimed:

"Well, well! So you see how grace works! It has already touched one of yours, and he is turning away from Mohammed!"

The Tartars replied that nothing was working: this is your Ivan, he's from you Russians, only he's living here with us as a prisoner.

The missionaries were very displeased at that. They didn't believe I was Russian, so I butted in myself:

"No," I say, "I really am Russian! Spiritual fathers, have mercy on me! Rescue me from this place! It's already the eleventh year I've been languishing here in captivity, and see how crippled I am: I can't walk."

But they didn't pay the slightest attention to my words, turned away, and went on with their business of preaching.

I think: "Well, what's there to grumble about: they're on official business, and maybe it's awkward for them to treat me differently in front of the Tartars"—and I left off, and chose a time when they were alone in their separate quarters, and I flung myself at them and told them everything in all frankness, how I was suffering from the cruelest lot, and I begged them:

"My father-benefactors, threaten them with our beloved white tsar: tell them that he does not allow Asiatics to hold his subjects captive by force, or, better still, pay them a ransom for me, and I'll serve you for it. Living here," I say, "I've learned their Tartar language very well and can be a useful man to you."

But they reply:

"We have no ransom for you, my son, and we are not permitted to threaten the infidels, because they are devious and disloyal people even without that, and we maintain a courteous policy towards them."

"So, then," I say, "it means that on account of that policy I'm to perish with them here for all time?"

"Well," they say, "it makes no difference where you perish, my son, but you must pray: God's mercy is great, perhaps He will deliver you."

"I've already prayed," I say, "but I have no strength left, and I've laid aside all hope."

"Do not despair," they say, "because that is a great sin!"

"I don't despair," I say, "only . . . how is it that you . . . it pains me very much that you are Russians and my countrymen, and you don't want to help me at all."

"No, child," they reply, "don't mix us into this, we are in Christ, and in Christ there is neither Greek nor Jew: whoever listens to us is our countryman. For us all are equal, all are equal."

"All?" I say.

"Yes," they reply, "all—that is the teaching we have from the apostle Paul.[23] Wherever we go, we do not quarrel . . . it is not befitting for us. You are a slave and, no help for it, you must endure, for, according to the apostle Paul, slaves should obey. But remember that you are a Christian, and therefore with you we have nothing to worry about, since even without us the gates of paradise are open to your soul, while these people will be in darkness if we don't join them up, so we must worry about them."

And they show me a book:

"Here," they say, "see how many names we've got written down in this register—that's how many people we've joined to our faith!"

I didn't talk with them anymore and didn't see any more of them, except for one of them, and that by chance: one of my little sons came running from somewhere and said:

"Daddy, there's a man lying over there near the lake."

I went to look: I see that his legs have been skinned from the knees down like stockings, and his arms from the elbows down like gloves. The Tartars do it skillfully: they make an incision around and pull the skin off in one piece. The man's head was lying nearby, with a cross cut on the forehead.

"Eh," I thought, "you didn't want to concern yourself with me, your countryman, and I condemned you, and here you've been found worthy of a martyr's crown. Forgive me now for Christ's sake!"

I made a cross over him, put his head together with his body, bowed to the ground, buried him, and sang "Holy God"[24] over him— and what became of his comrade I don't know, but most likely he also ended by receiving the crown, because afterwards the Tartar women of the horde turned up with lots of little icons like the ones these missionaries had with them.

"So these missionaries even get as far as the Ryn Sands?"

"Of course they do, only it's all no use."

"Why so?"

"They don't know how to handle them. The Asiatic has to be brought to faith by fear, so that he's shaking with fright, but they preach the meek God to him. At the outstart that's no good at all, because without threats an Asiatic will never respect a meek God for anything and will kill the preachers."

"And the main thing, it must be supposed, when going to the Asiatics, is that you should have no money or valuables with you?"

"You shouldn't, sir, though all the same they won't believe that somebody came and brought nothing with him; they'll think you buried it somewhere in the steppe, and start torturing you, and torture you to death."

"The bandits!"

"Yes, sir, that's what happened in my time with a certain Jew: an old Jew turned up from who knows where and also talked about faith. He was a good man, and obviously zealous for his faith, and all in such rags that you could see his whole body, and he started talking about faith so that it even seemed you could listen to him forever. At the outstart I began to argue with him, saying what kind of faith is it if you haven't got any saints, but he said, 'We do,' and he began reading from the Talmud about the saints they have . . . very entertaining. 'And this Talmud,' he says, 'was written by the rabbi Jovoz ben Levi, who was so learned that sinful people couldn't look at him; as soon as they looked, they all died straightaway, on account of which God called him before Him and said: "You, learned rabbi, Jovoz ben Levi! It's good that you're so learned, but it's not good that because of you all my Jews may die. It was not for that," he says, "that I drove them over the steppe with Moses and made them cross the sea. For that, get out of your fatherland and live somewhere where nobody can see you."' And so the rabbi Levi left and went straight to the place where paradise was, and he buried himself up to the neck in the sand there, and stayed in the sand for thirteen years, and even though he was buried up to the neck, he prepared a lamb for himself every Saturday, cooked by a fire that came down from heaven. And if a mosquito or a fly landed on his nose to drink his blood, they were consumed at once by a heavenly fire . . .' The Asiatics liked this story about the learned rabbi very much, and they listened to the Jew for a long time; but then they got after him and began questioning him about where he buried his money before coming to them. The Jew swore up and down that he had no money, that God had sent him with nothing but wisdom, but they didn't believe him, and raking up the coals where the campfire had been burning, they spread a horsehide over the hot coals, put the Jew on it, and started shaking it. 'Tell us, tell us, where is the money?' But when they saw that he had turned all black and didn't speak, they said:

"'Wait, let's bury him up to the neck in the sand: maybe that will bring him around.'

"And so they buried him, but the Jew just died buried like that, and his head stuck up black from the sand for a long time afterwards, but the children began to be afraid of it, so they cut it off and threw it into a dry well."

"There's your preaching to them!"

"Yes, sir, it's very hard, but all the same that Jew did have money."

"He did?!"

"He did, sir. Later on wolves and jackals began worrying him, and they dug him out of the sand bit by bit, and finally got to his boots. Once his boots fell apart, seven coins came out of the soles. They were found later."

"Well, but how did you break free of them?"

"I was saved by a miracle."

"Who performed this miracle that delivered you?"

"Talafa."

"Who is this Talafa—also a Tartar?"

"No, sir, he's of another race, an Indian, and not a simple Indian at that, but one of their gods who comes down to earth."

Prevailed upon by his listeners, Ivan Severyanych Flyagin told the following about this new act in the tragicomedy of his life.

IX

After the Tartars got rid of our missaneries, again nearly a year went by, and again it was winter, and we drove our herds to graze further south, towards the Caspian, and there suddenly one day before evening two men came to us, if they could be called men. Nobody knew who they were and where from and of what sort and rank. They didn't even have any real language, neither Russian nor Tartar, but they spoke a word in ours, a word in Tartar, and between themselves in who knows what. They weren't old. One was dark, with a big beard, in a robe, something like a Tartar, only his coat wasn't multicolored but all red, and on his head he had a conical Persian hat. The other one was red-haired, also in a robe, but a tricky fellow: he had all sorts of little boxes with him, and as soon as there was a moment when nobody was looking at him, he'd take off his robe and remain just in trousers and a little jacket, and these trousers and jacket were of the same fashion as what Germans wear in factories in Russia. And he kept turning over and sorting out something in those boxes, but what it was that he had in them—deuce knew. They said they came from Khiva[25] to buy horses and wanted to make war on somebody at home, but who it was they didn't say, they just kept stirring the Tartars up against the Russians. I heard him, this red-haired one—he couldn't say much, but just brought out something like "soup-perear" in Russian and spat; but they had no money with them, because these Asiatics know that if you come to the steppe with money, you won't leave with a head on your shoulders, and they urged our Tartars to drive the herds of horses to their river, the Darya, and settle accounts there. The Tartars were of two minds about that and didn't know whether to agree or not. They thought and thought, as if they were digging gold, and were obviously afraid of something.

They tried persuading them honorably, and then also began to frighten them.

"Drive them," they say, "or it may go badly for you: we have the god Talafa, who has sent his fire with us. God forbid he should get angry."

The Tartars didn't know this god and doubted that he could do anything to them with his fire on the steppe in winter. But that black-bearded man from Khiva, the one in the red robe, says, "If you have doubts, Talafa will show you his power this very night, only if you see or hear anything, don't run outside, or he'll burn you up." Naturally, this was all terribly interesting amidst the boredom of the winter steppe, and we were all a bit afraid of this terrible thing, but eager to see what this Indian god could do and how, by what miracle, he would manifest himself.

We crawled into our tents early with our wives and children and waited . . . All was dark and quiet, as on any other night, but suddenly, during my first sleep, I heard something on the steppe hiss like a strong wind and explode, and through my sleep I fancied there were sparks falling from the sky.

I roused myself and saw my wives stirring and my children crying. I say:

"Shh! Stop their gullets, get them sucking instead of crying."

The children started smacking away, and it became quiet again, and on the dark steppe a fire suddenly went hissing up again . . . hissed and burst again . . .

"Well," I think, "anyhow it's clear this Talafa is no joke!"

And a little later he hissed again, but now in quite a different way—like a fiery bird fluttering up, and with a tail of fire as well, and the fire is of an extraordinary color, red as blood, and when it bursts, it all suddenly turns yellow and then blue.

In the camp, I can hear, it's like everything has died. It was impossible, of course, for anybody not to hear such a cannonade, but it meant they were all frightened and lying under their sheepskins. You can only hear the earth tremble, start shaking, and stop again. That, you could figure, was the horses shying and huddling close together, and you could also hear those Khivians or Indians running somewhere, and all at once fire again shot over the steppe like a snake . . . The horses got terrified and bolted . . . The Tartars forgot their fear and all came jumping out, shaking their heads, howling "Allah! Allah!"—and set off in pursuit, but the Khivians vanished without a trace, just leaving one of their boxes behind as a souvenir . . . Now, when all our fighting men had gone in pursuit of the herd, and only women and old men were left in the camp, I took a look at that box: what's in there? I see there are various powders, and mixtures, and paper tubes: I started examining one of the tubes close to the fire, and it burst, almost burned my eyes out, and flew upwards, and there—bang!—scattered in little stars . . . "Aha," I thought, "so it's not a god, it's just fiverworks like they set off in our public garden." I went bang with another tube, and saw that the Tartars, the old ones who had stayed here, had already fallen down and were lying on their faces where they fell, and only jerking their legs . . . At first I was scared myself, but when I saw them jerking like that, I suddenly acquired a completely different attitude, and for the first time since I fell into captivity, I gnashed my teeth and started uttering random, unfamiliar words at them. I shouted as loud as I could:

"Parley-bien-cumsa-shiray-mir-ferfluchter-min-adiew-moussiew!"

Then I sent up a spinning tube . . . Well, this time, seeing how the fire went spinning, they all nearly died . . . The fire went out, and they were all lying there, and only one of them raised his head every once in a while, and then put it mug-down again, while beckoning to me with his finger. I go up to him and say:

"Well, so? Confess what you want, curse you: death or life?"— because I can see they're terribly afraid of me.

"Forgive us, Ivan," they say, "don't give us death, give us life."

And the others also beckon to me from their places in the same way, and ask for forgiveness and life.

I see my case has taken a good turn: I must have suffered enough for all my sins, and I prayed:

"Mother of us, most holy Lady, St. Nicholas, my swans, my little doves, help me, my benefactors!"

And I myself sternly ask the Tartars:

"For what and to what end should I forgive you and grant you life?"

"Forgive us," they say, "for not believing in your God."

"Aha," I think, "see how I've frightened them," and I say: "Ah, no, brothers, that's rubbish, I'm not going to forgive you for your opposition to relidgin!" And I gnashed my teeth again and unsealed one more tube.

This one turned out to have a rawcket . . . Terrible fire and crackling.

I shout at the Tartars:

"So, one more minute, and I'll destroy you all, if you don't want to believe in my God."

"Don't destroy us," they reply, "we all agree to go under your God."

Then I stopped setting off fiverworks and baptized them all in the river.

"You baptized them right then and there?"

"That same minute, sirs. Why put it off for long? It had to be so they couldn't think it over. I wetted their heads with water from a hole in the ice, recited 'in the name of the Father and the Son,' and hung those little crosses left from the missaneries on their necks, and told them to consider that murdered missanery a martyr and pray for him, and I showed them his grave."

"And did they pray?"

"That they did, sir."

"But I don't suppose they knew any Christian prayers, or did you teach them?"

"No, I had no chance to teach them, because I saw the time had come for me to flee, but I told them: 'Pray like you always prayed, the old way, only don't you dare call on Allah, but instead of him name Jesus Christ.' So they adopted that confession."

"Well, but all the same, how did you escape from these new Christians then with your crippled feet, and how did you cure yourself?"

"Then I found some caustic earth in those fiverworks; as soon as you apply it to your body, it starts burning terribly. I applied it and pretended to be sick, and meanwhile, lying under the rug, I kept irritating my heels with this caustic stuff, and in two weeks I irritated them so much that the flesh on my heels festered and all the bristles the Tartars had sewn in ten years earlier came out with the pus. I got better as soon as I could, but gave no signs of it, and pretended that I was getting worse, and I ordered the women and old men to pray for me as zealously as they could, because I was dying. And I imposed a penitential fast on them and told them not to leave their yurts for three days, and to intimidate them even more I shot off the biggest fiverwork and left . . ."

"And they didn't catch you?"

"No, and how could they catch me? With all the fasting and fear I put into them, they were probably only too glad to keep their noses inside their yurts for three days, and when they peeked out later, I was already too far away to go looking for. My feet, once I got all the bristles out, dried up and became so light that, when I started running, I ran across the whole steppe."

"All on foot?"

"How else, sir? There's no road there, nobody to meet, and if you do meet somebody, you won't be glad of what you've acquired. On the fourth day, a Chuvash appeared, alone, driving five horses. 'Mount up,' he said.

"I felt suspicious and didn't."

"Why were you afraid of him?"

"Just so . . . he somehow didn't look trustworthy to me, and besides that it was impossible to figure out what his religion was, and without that it's frightening in the steppe. And the muddlehead shouts:

"'Mount up—it's merrier with two riding.'

"I say:

" 'But who are you? Maybe you've got no god?'

" 'How, no cod?' he says. 'It's the Tartar has no cod, he eats horse, but I have a cod.'

" 'Who is your god?' I say.

"For me,' he says, 'everything is cod: sun is cod, moon is cod, stars are cod . . . everything is cod. How I have no cod?'

"Everything! . . . Hm . . . so everything is god for you,' I say, 'which means Jesus Christ is not god for you?'

" 'No,' he says, 'he is cod, and his mother is cod, and Nikolach is cod . . .'

" 'What Nikolach?' I ask.

" 'Why, the one who lives once in winter, once in summer.'

"I praised him for respecting our Russian saint, Nicholas the Wonderworker.[26]

" 'Always honor him,' I said, 'because he's Russian'—and I was quite ready to approve of his faith and quite willing to ride with him, but, thankfully, he went on babbling and gave himself away.

" 'As if I don't honor Nikolach,' he says. 'Maybe I don't bow to him in winter, but in summer I give him twenty kopecks to take good care of my cows. Yes, and so as not to trust in him alone, I also sacrifice a bullock to the Keremet.'[27]

"I got angry.

" 'How dare you not trust in Nicholas the Wonderworker,' I say, 'and give him, a Russian, only twenty kopecks, while you give your foul Mordovian Keremet a whole bullock! Away with you,' I say, 'I don't want . . . I won't go with you, if you have such disrespect for Nicholas the Wonderworker.'

"And I didn't go: I strode on with all my might, and before I realized it, towards evening on the third day, I caught sight of water and people. I lay in the grass out of apprehension and spied out what kind of people they were. Because I was afraid of falling again into a still worse captivity, but I see that these people cook their food . . . They must be Christians, I thought. I crawled closer: I saw them crossing themselves and drinking vodka—well, that means Russians! . . . Then I jumped up from the grass and showed myself. They turned out to be a fishing crew out fishing. They received me warmly, as countrymen should, and said:

" 'Have some vodka!'

"I reply:

"'From living with the Tartars, brothers, I'm completely unused to it.'

"'Well, never mind,' they say, 'here it's your nation, you'll get used to it again: drink!'

"I poured myself a glass and thought:

"'Well then, with God's blessing, here's to my return!'—and I drank, but the crewmen—nice lads—persisted.

"'Have another!' they say. 'Look how scrawny you've grown without it.'"

I allowed myself one more and became very outspoken: I told them everything, where I'm from and where and how I'd lived. I spent the whole night sitting by the fire, telling it all and drinking vodka, and it was so joyful to me that I was back in Holy Russia, only towards morning, when the fire began to go out and almost all the listeners had fallen asleep, one of the crew members says to me:

"And do you have a passport?"

I say:

"No, I don't."

"If you don't," he says, "it means jail for you."

"Well, then," I say, "I'm not going to leave you. I suppose I can live with you here without a passport."

And he replies:

"You can live with us without a passport," he says, "but you can't die without one."

I say:

"Why's that?"

"How's the priest going to register you," he says, "if you've got no passport?"

"What'll happen to me in that case?"

"We'll throw you into the water," he says, "as fish food."

"Without a priest?"

"Without a priest."

Being a little tipsy, I was terribly frightened at that and began weeping and lamenting, but the fisherman laughed.

"I was joking with you," he says. "Die fearlessly, we'll bury you in your native soil."

But I was already very upset and said:

"A fine joke. If you joke with me like that very often, I won't live to see the next spring."

And as soon as this last crewman fell asleep, I quickly got up and went away and came to Astrakhan, earned a rouble doing day labor and went on such a drinking binge that I don't remember how I wound up in another town, and by then I was sitting in jail, and from there they sent me under escort to my own province. I was brought to our town, given a whipping at the police station, and delivered to my village. The countess who had ordered me whipped for the cat's tail was dead by then, only the count was left, but he had grown very old and pious and didn't hunt on horseback any more. They reported to him that I had arrived, he remembered me, ordered me to be whipped once again at home, and to go to the priest, Father Ilya, for confession. Well, they gave me a whipping the old-fashioned way, in the village lockup, and I went to Father Ilya, and he heard my confession and forbade me to take communion for three years . . .

"Why so, Father? I've gone . . . so many years without communion . . . I've been waiting . . ."

"Well, no matter," he says. "So you've been waiting, but how is it you kept Tartar women around you instead of wives? . . . Be it known to you," he says, "that I'm showing mercy in only forbidding you communion, and if you were handled according to the rules of the holy fathers, you'd have all your clothes burnt off you alive. Only don't be afraid of that," he says, "because the police laws don't allow it now."

"Well, there's nothing to be done," I thought, "so I'll just stay like this, without communion, living at home, resting after my captivity." But the count didn't want it. He said:

"I will not tolerate having an excommunicated man near me."

And he told the steward to whip me once more publicly as an example for everybody and then to release me on quitrent. And so they did: I was flogged in a new way this time, on the porch, before the office, in front of all the people, and then given a passport. I was delighted that, after so many years, I was a completely free man, with legal papers, and I left. I had no definite intentions, but it was my fate that God sent me employment.

"What sort?"

"The same thing again, in the horse line. I started from nothing, without a penny, but soon reached a very well-to-do state, and could have managed even better, if it hadn't been for a certain matter."

"What was it, if we may ask?"

"I fell into the great possession of various spirits and passions and yet another unseemly thing."

"What was this unseemly thing that possessed you?"

"Magnetism, sir."

"What? Magnetism?!"

"Yes, sir, the magnetic influence of a certain person."

"How did you feel this influence upon you?"

"A foreign will worked in me, and I fulfilled a foreign destiny."

"Was it then that *your own* ruin came upon you, after which you decided that you ought to fulfill your mother's promise and go into a monastery?"

"No, sir, that came later, but meanwhile many other adventures of all sorts befell me, before I was granted real conviction."

"Would you mind telling us those adventures, too?"

"Not at all. It will be a great pleasure for me."

"Please do, then."

X

Taking my passport, I went off without any intentions for myself, and came to the fair, and there I see a Gypsy trading horses with a muzhik and deceiving him godlessly. He started testing their strength, and hitched his own nag to a cart loaded with millet, and the muzhik's horse to a cart loaded with apples. The loads, naturally, were of equal weight, but the muzhik's horse got in a stew, because the smell of the apples stupefied it, since horses find that smell terribly repulsive, and, besides that, I could see that the Gypsy's horse was prone to fainting, and you could tell it at once, because it had a mark on its forehead where it had been seared by fire, but the Gypsy said, "It's a wart." But I, naturally, felt sorry for the muzhik, because it would be impossible for him to work with a fainting horse, since it would fall over and that would be that, and besides I had a mortal hatred of Gypsies then, because it was from them that I first got tempted to ramble, and I probably also had a presentiment of things to come, which proved true. I revealed this flaw in the horse to the

muzhik, and when the Gypsy began to argue that it wasn't a mark
from searing but a wart, to prove I was right I jabbed the horse in the
kidney with a little awl, and it flopped to the ground and thrashed.
Then I went and chose the muzhiks a good horse according to my
understanding, and for that they treated me to food and drink and
gave me twenty kopecks, and we had some good carousing. And it
went on from there: my capital was growing and so was my zeal for
drinking, and before the month was out, I saw that things were good.
I hung myself all over with badges and horse doctor's trappings and
began going from fair to fair, giving guidance to poor people everywhere, and collecting income for myself, and wetting the good deals;
and meanwhile I became just like the wrath of God for all the horse-
trading Gypsies, and I learned indirectly that they intended to beat
me up. I tried to avoid that, because they were many and I was one,
and never once could they catch me alone and give me a sound beating, and with muzhiks around they didn't dare, because they always
stood up for me on account of the good I'd done them. Then they
spread a bad rumor about me, that I was a sorcerer and it was not
through my own powers that I knew about animals, but, naturally,
that was all nonsense: as I told you, I have a gift for horses, and I'm
ready to teach it to anybody you like, only the main thing is that it
won't be of use to anybody.

"Why won't it be of use?"

"Nobody will understand it, sir, because for that nothing else but
a natural gift will do, and more than once I've had the same experience, that I teach, but it's all in vain. But, excuse me, we'll get to
that later."

When my fame was noised around the fairs, that I could see right
through a horse, a certain remount officer, a prince, offered me a
hundred roubles:

"Reveal the secret of your understanding, brother," he says. "It's
worth a lot of money."

And I reply:

"I have no secret, I have a natural gift for it."

But he persists:

"Reveal to me, anyway, how you understand these things. And so you don't think I want it just like that—here's a hundred roubles for you."

What to do? I shrugged my shoulders, tied the money up in a rag, and said:

"All right, then, I'll tell you what I know, but please learn and follow it; and if you don't learn and you get nothing useful from it, I won't answer for it."

He was content with that, anyway, and said:

"How much I learn is not your problem, just tell me."

"The very first thing," I say, "if it's a matter of knowing a horse and what goes on inside it, is that you've got to have a good position for examining it and never depart from it. From the first glance you have to look intelligently at the head and then at the whole horse down to the tail, and not paw it all over the way officers do. They touch it on the withers, the forelock, the nose bridge, the chest artery, the breastbone, or whatever they land on, and all senselessly. Horse dealers love cavalry officers terribly for this pawing. When a horse dealer spots such a military pawer, he immediately starts twisting and twirling the horse, turning it in all directions, and whichever part he doesn't want to show, he won't show for anything, and it's there that the flaw lies, and there's no end to these flaws. Say a horse is lop-eared—they cut away a strip of skin on the crown, pull the edges together, sew them up, and paint the seam over. The horse's ears perk up, but not for long: the skin stretches and the ears droop again. If the ears are too big, they cut them, and to make them stand up, they put little props in them. If somebody's looking for a match for his horse, and if, for instance, his horse has a star on its forehead, the dealers make sure to fix him up with another that has the same star: they rub the hide with pumice, or apply a hot baked turnip to the right spot, so that white hair will grow, and it does at once, only if you bother to look closely, hair that's been grown that way is always slightly longer than normal, and it frizzes up like a little tuft. Horse dealers offend against the public even more over eyes: some horses have little hollows above their eyes, and it's not pretty, but the dealer punctures the skin with a pin and then puts his lips to the place and blows, and the skin inflates, and the eye looks more fresh and pretty. That's easy to do, because a horse likes the feel of warm breath on its eyes, and it stands there without moving, but then the air leaks out and there are hollows above the eyes again. There's one remedy for that: to feel around the bone and see whether air is coming out. But it's still funnier when they sell blind horses. That's a real comedy. Some little officer, for instance, is stealing up to the horse's eye with a straw, to test whether the horse can see the straw, but he himself doesn't see that, just when the horse should shake its head, the dealer punches it in the belly or the side with his fist. Or another is stroking the horse quietly, but has a little nail in his glove, and while he seems to be stroking it, he pricks it." And I explained this to the remount officer ten times more than I've been telling you now, but none of it proved any use to him: the next day I see he's bought such horses that one nag's worse than the other, and then he calls me over to look and says:

"Come, brother, look at my expert knowledge of horses."

I glanced, laughed, and replied that there was nothing to look at:

"This one's got fleshy shoulders—it'll catch its hooves in the dirt; this one tucks its hoof under its belly when it lies down—in a year at most it'll work itself up a hernia; and this one, when it eats oats, stamps its foreleg and knocks its knee against the trough"—and I criticized his whole purchase away like that, and it came out that I was right.

The next day the prince says:

"No, Ivan, I really can't understand your gift. You'd better work for me as a conosoor and do the choosing, and I'll just pay out the money."

I agreed and lived excellently for a whole three years, not like a hired servant, but more like a friend and helper, and if these outings hadn't got the better of me, I might even have saved up some capital for myself, because, in remounting practice, whenever a breeder comes to make the acquaintance of a remount officer, he sends a trusty man to the conosoor, so as to cajole him as much as possible, because breeders know that the real power is not with the remount officer, but in his having a real conosoor with him. And I was, as I told you, a natural conosoor and fulfilled that natural duty conscientiously: not for anything would I deceive the man I worked for. And my prince felt that and had great respect for me, and we lived together with full openness in everything. If he happened to lose at cards somewhere during the night, he would get up in the morning and come to me in the stable, still in his robe, and say:

"Well, now, my almost half-esteemed Ivan Severyanych! How are things with you?" He always joked that way, calling me "almost half-esteemed," though, as you'll see, he esteemed me fully.

I knew what it signified when he came with such a joke, and I'd reply:

"Not bad. Things are fine with me, thank God, but I wonder about Your Serenity—how are your circumstances?"

"Mine," he says, "are so vile, you couldn't even ask for worse."

"What you mean to say, I suppose, is that you blew it all again yesterday, like the other time?"

"A good guess, my half-esteemed fellow," he replies. "I blew it, sir, I blew it."

"And how much lighter is Your Honor now?" I ask.

He would tell me at once how many thousands he had lost, and I would shake my head and say:

"Your Serenity needs a good spanking, but there's nobody to do it."

He would laugh and say:

"That's just it, there's nobody."

"Lie down here on my cot," I say, "and I'll put a clean little sack under your head and whip you myself."

He, naturally, starts getting around me, so that I'll lend him money for the revanche.

"No," he says, "better not thrash me, but give me some of our spending money for a little revanche: I'll go, win everything back, and beat them all."

"Well, as to that," I reply, "I humbly thank you, playing is one thing, winning back is another."

"Hah, you thank me!" he begins by laughing, but then he gets angry: "Well, I'll thank you not to forget yourself," he says. "Stop playing the guardian over me and bring me the money."

We asked Ivan Severyanych if he ever gave his prince money for the revanche.

"Never," he said. "I either deceived him, saying I'd spent all the money on oats, or I simply quit the premises."

"I suppose he got angry with you for that?"

"That he did, sir. He'd announce straight off: 'It's all over, sir. You no longer work for me, my half-esteemed fellow.'

"I'd reply:

"'Well, that's just fine. My passport, please.'

"'Very well, sir,' he says. 'Kindly make your preparations: you'll get your passport tomorrow.'

"Only there was never any more talk about that tomorrow between us. In no more than an hour or so, he'd come to me in a totally different state of mind and say:

"'I thank you, my greatly insignificant fellow, that you stood firm and did not give me money for the revanche.'

"And he always had such feelings about these things that, if anything happened to me during my outings, he also made allowances for me like a brother."

"And what happened to you?"

"I already explained to you that I used to have these outings."

"And what do you mean by 'outings'?"

"I'd go carousing, sir. Having learned about drinking vodka, I avoided drinking it every day and never just took it in moderation, but if I happened to be troubled, then I'd get a terrible zeal for drinking, and I'd immediately go on an outing for several days and disappear. And you'd never notice why it came over me. For instance, we'd let go of some horses, and it's not that they're brothers to you, but I'd miss them and start drinking. Especially if you send away a very handsome horse, then the scoundrel just keeps flashing in your eyes, so you hide from him like some sort of obsession and go on an outing."

"Meaning you'd start drinking?"

"Yes, sir, I'd go and drink."

"And for how long?"

"Mmm . . . they're not all the same, sir, these outings: sometimes you drink until you've drunk up everything, and either somebody gives you a beating, or you give somebody a beating, but another time it turns out shorter, you just get taken to the police station or sleep it off in a ditch, and it's enough, the mood goes away. On such occasions I went by the rules, and if I happened to feel I needed an outing, I'd go to the prince and say:

"'Thus and so, Your Serenity, kindly take the money from me, and I'll disappear.'

"He never argued, he'd just take the money, and sometimes ask:

"'Does Your Honor contemplate being at it for a long time?'

"So I'd give him a reply depending on how zealous I felt, for a big outing or a short one.

"And I'd leave, and he'd run things by himself and wait until my outing was over, and it all went quite well; only I was terribly sick of this weakness of mine, and I resolved suddenly to get rid of it; and it was then that I went on such a last outing that even now it's frightening to remember it."

XI

We naturally insisted that Ivan Severyanych crown his amiability by telling us all about this new ill-fated episode in his life, and he, in his goodness, of course did not refuse us that, and of his "last outing" told the following:

We had a mare named Dido that we bought from a stud farm, a young golden bay for an officer's saddle. A marvelous beauty she was: pretty little head, comely eyes, nostrils delicate and flared—just breathe away; light mane; chest sitting smartly, like a boat, between her shoulders; supple in the flanks; and her legs light in their white stockings, and she flings them out as if she's playing . . . In short, if you were a fancier and had an understanding of beauty, the sight of such a creature could make you ponder. As for me, she was so much to my liking that I never even left her stable and kept caressing her from joy. I'd brush her and wipe her all over with a white handkerchief, so that there wasn't a speck of dust anywhere on her coat, and I'd even kiss her right on the forehead, where her golden hair turned into a little swirl . . . At that time we had two fairs going on at once, one in L——, the other in K——, and the prince and I separated: I did one, and he went to the other. And suddenly I received a letter from him, saying: "Send such-and-such horses and Dido to me here." I didn't know why he was sending for my beauty, in whom my fancier's eyes rejoiced. But I thought, of course, that he had traded or sold my darling to someone, or, still more likely, had lost her at cards . . . And so I sent Dido off with the stablemen and started pining away terribly and longed to go on an outing. And my situation at that moment was quite unusual: I told you I had made it a rule that, whenever the zeal for an outing came over me, I would present myself to the prince, give him all my money, since I always had large sums on my hands, and say: "I'm going to disappear for this many or that many days." Well, but how was I going to arrange it this time, when my prince wasn't with me? And so I thought to myself: "No, I'm not going to drink anymore, because my prince isn't here, and it's impossible for me to go on a regular outing, because I have no one to give my money to, and I've got a considerable sum on me, more than five thousand." So I decided it was not to be done, and I held firmly to that decision, and did not give way to my zeal for going on an outing and disappearing good and proper, but all the same I felt no weakening of that desire, but, on the contrary, craved more and more to go on an outing. And, finally, I came to be filled with a single thought: how can I arrange things so as both to fulfill my zeal for an outing and to safeguard the prince's money? And with that aim I began hiding it and kept hiding it in the most incredible places, where it would never occur to anyone to put money . . . I thought: "What to do? It's clear that I can't control myself. I'll put the money in a trustworthy place, to keep it safe, and then I'll do my zeal, I'll go on an outing." Only I was overcome by perplexity: where should I hide this cursed money? Wherever I put it, the moment I stepped away from the place, the thought would at once come to my head that someone was stealing it. I'd go and quickly take it again and hide it again . . . I simply wore myself out hiding it, in haylofts, and in cellars, and under the eaves, and in other such unsuitable hiding places, and as soon as I stepped away, it immediately seemed to me that someone had seen me hide it and would certainly find it, and I would go back again, and get it again, and carry it around with me, and again think: "No, basta, I'm clearly not fated to fulfill my zeal this time." And suddenly a divine thought occurred to me: it's the devil who keeps tormenting me with this passion, so I'll go and drive the scoundrel away with holiness! And I went to an early liturgy, prayed, and as I was leaving the church, I saw the Last Judgment painted on the wall, and there in a corner the devil in Gehenna being beaten with flails by angels. I stopped, looked, and prayed zealously to the holy angels, and, spitting on my fist, shoved it into the devil's mug.

"Here's a fig for you, buy what'll do, and a lot of it, too"—and after that I suddenly calmed down completely and, having given all the necessary orders at home, went to a tavern to have tea . . . And there in the tavern I saw some rascal standing among the customers. The most futile of futile men. I had seen the man before, too, and considered him some sort of charlatan or clown, because he kept dragging himself around to the fairs and begging gentlemen for a handout in French. He was supposedly of the nobility and had served in the army, but had squandered all he had and gambled it away at cards, and now went around begging . . . There, in that tavern I came to, the waiters wanted to throw him out, but he refused to leave and stood there saying:

"Do you know who I am? I'm no equal of yours, I had my own serfs, and I've whipped a great many fine fellows like you in the stable just because I felt like it, and if I've lost everything, it's because there was some special divine will for it, and there's a seal of wrath upon me, which is why nobody dares to touch me."

They didn't believe him and laughed at him, but he told them how he used to live, and rode around in carriages, and drove all the civilians out of the public garden, and once came naked to the governor's wife, "and now," he says, "I've been cursed for my willfulness, and my whole nature has turned to stone, and I have to wet it constantly, so give me vodka! I've got no money to pay for it, but instead I'll eat the glass."

One of the customers ordered vodka for him, so as to watch how he would eat the glass. He tossed off the vodka at once, and, as promised, honestly began to crunch the glass with his teeth and ate it right in front of us, and everybody was amazed at it and laughed heartily. But I felt sorry for him, because here was a nobleman who, from his zeal for drink, would even sacrifice his insides. I thought he should be given something to rinse the glass out of his guts, and I ordered him another shot at my expense, but I didn't make him eat the glass. I said: never mind, don't eat it. He was touched by that and gave me his hand.

"I suppose," he says, "you come from a gentleman's household?"

"Yes, I do," I say.

"One can see at once," he says, "that you're not like these swine. Gramercy to you for that."

I say:

"It's nothing, go with God."

"No," he replies, "I'm very glad to converse with you. Move over a bit, I'll sit down beside you."

"Please do," I say.

He sat down beside me and began to tell me about his noble origins and grand upbringing, and again he says:

"What's this . . . you're drinking tea?"

"Yes, tea. Want to have some with me?"

"Thanks," he replies, "but I can't drink tea."

"Why not?"

"Because," he says, "my head's not for tea, my head's for a spree: better order me another shot of vodka! . . ." And once, and twice, and three times he asked me for vodka like that, and it was beginning to make me very annoyed. But I found it still more repugnant that he said very little that was true, but kept showing off all the time and making up God knows what about himself, and then would suddenly turn humble and weep, and all over vanities.

"Just think," he says, "what sort of man am I? I was created by God Himself in the same year as the emperor. I'm his coeval."

"Well, what of it?"

"And, despite all that, what sort of position am I in? Despite all that," he says, "I'm not distinguished in the least and live in insignificance, and, as you just saw, I'm despised by everybody." And with those words, he again asked for vodka, but this time for a whole decanter, and started telling me an enormous story about merchants in taverns making fun of him, and in the end he says:

"They're uneducated people. Do they think it's easy to bear such responsibility, to be eternally drinking vodka and nibbling the glass? It's a very difficult calling, brother, and for many even completely impossible; but I've accustomed my nature to it, because I see that one must do one's part, and I bear with it."

"Why be so zealous about this habit?" I argue. "Just drop it."

"Drop it?" he replies. "Ah, no, brother, it's impossible for me to drop it."

"Why can't you?" I ask.

"I can't," he says, "for two reasons. First, because, unless I'm drunk, I'm quite unable to go to bed, and I'll keep wandering about; and the second, the main reason, is that my Christian feelings won't allow it."

"What on earth does that mean? That you don't go to bed is understandable, because you keep looking for drink; but that your Christian feelings won't allow you to drop such harmful vileness—that I refuse to believe."

"So," he replies, "you refuse to believe it . . . That's what everybody says . . . But suppose I drop this habit of drunkenness and someone else picks it up and takes it: will he be glad of it or not?"

"God save us! No, I don't think he'll be glad of it."

"Aha!" he says. "There we have it, and if it must be that I suffer, you should at least respect me for that and order me another decanter of vodka!"

I rapped for another little decanter, and sat, and listened, because I was beginning to find it entertaining, and he went on in these words:

"It ought to be so that this torment ends with me, rather than going on to someone else, because," he says, "I'm from a good family and received a proper upbringing, so that I even prayed to God in French when I was still very little; but I was merciless and tormented people: I gambled my serfs away at cards; I separated mothers and children; I took a rich wife and hounded her to death; and finally, being guilty of it all myself, I also murmured against God: why did He give me such a character? And He punished me: he gave me a different character, so that there's no trace of pride in me, you can spit in my eye, slap me in the face, if only I'm drunk and oblivious of myself."

"And now," I ask, "aren't you murmuring against that character as well?"

"No, I'm not," he says, "because even though it's worse, it's still better."

"How can that be? There's something I don't understand: how can it be worse, but better?"

"It's like this," he answers. "Now I know only one thing, that I'm ruining myself, but then I can't ruin others, for they're all repulsed by me. I'm now the same as Job on his dung heap," he says, "and in that lies all my happiness and salvation"—and again he finished the vodka, and asked for another decanter, and said:

"You know, my kind friend, you should never scorn anyone, because no one can know why someone is tormented by some passion and suffers. We who are possessed suffer, but that makes it easier for others. And if you yourself are afflicted by some sort of passion, do not willfully abandon it, lest another man pick it up and suffer; but seek out such a man as will voluntarily take this weakness from you."

"Well," I say, "but where can such a man be found? No one would agree to it."

"Why not?" he replies. "You don't even have to go far: such a man is here before you, I myself am such a man."

I say:

"Are you joking?"

But he suddenly jumps up and says:

"No, I'm not joking, and if you don't believe it, test me."

"How can I test you?" I say.

"Very simply: do you wish to know what my gift is? I do have a great gift, brother. You see, I'm drunk now . . . Yes or no, am I drunk?"

I look at him and see that he has gone quite blue in the face and is all bleary-eyed and swaying on his feet, and I say:

"Yes, of course, you're drunk."

And he replies:

"Well, now turn towards the icon for a moment and recite the 'Our Father' to yourself."

I turn and, indeed, I've no sooner recited the "Our Father" to myself while looking at the icon, than this drunken gentleman again commands me:

"All right, look at me now: am I drunk or not?"

I turn and see that he's sober as a judge and standing there smiling. I say:

"What does this mean? What's the secret?"

And he replies:

"It's not a secret, it's called magnetism."

"What's that?" I say. "I don't understand."

"It's a special will," he says, "which resides in man, and can neither be drunk away, nor slept away, because it's freely given. I demonstrated it to you, so that you would understand that, if I wanted to, I could stop right now and never drink again, but I don't want to have someone else start drinking for me, while I, having recovered, go and forget about God. But I'm ready and able to remove the drinking passion from another man in a moment."

"Do me a favor," I say. "Remove it from me!"

"Can it be," he says, "that you drink?"

"Yes," I say, "and at times I even drink very zealously."

"Well, then, don't be timid," he says. "It's all work for my hands, and I'll repay you for your treating me: I'll remove it all from you."

"Ah, do me the favor, I beg you, remove it!"

"Gladly, my friend, gladly," he says. "I'll do it for your treating me; I'll remove it and take it upon myself"—and with that he called again for vodka and two glasses.

I say:

"What do you want two glasses for?"

"One," he says, "for me, the other—for you!"

"I'm not going to drink."

But he suddenly seems to get angry and says:

"Hush! *S'il vous plaît!* Keep quiet! Who are you now? A patient."

"Well, all right, have it your way: I'm a patient."

"And I'm a doctor," he says, "and you must obey my orders and take your medicine"—and with that he pours a glass for me and for himself and begins waving his hands in the air over my glass like a church choirmaster.

He waves and waves, and then orders:

"Drink!"

I was doubtful, but since, to tell the truth, I myself wanted very much to sample the vodka, and he ordered me to, I thought: "Go on, if for nothing else, then for the sake of curiosity, drink up!"—and I drank up.

"How does it taste," he asks, "good or bitter?"

"I'm unable to tell you."

"That means you didn't have enough," he says, and he pours a second glass and again moves his hands to and fro over it. He moves them, moves them, then shakes them off, and he makes me drink this second glass and asks: "How was this one?"

I say jokingly:

"This one seemed a bit heavy."

He nods his head, and at once starts waving over a third, and again commands: "Drink!" I drink it and say:

"This one was lighter"—and after that I took the decanter myself, and treated him, and poured for myself, and went on drinking. He didn't hinder me in that, only he wouldn't let me drink a single glass simply, without waving over it. The moment I put my hand to it, he'd take it from me and say:

"Hush, *s'il vous plaît . . . attendez,*" and would first wave his hands over it, and then say:

"Now it's ready, you can *take it as prescribed.*"

And I went on curing myself in that fashion with that gentleman there in the tavern right until evening, and I was quite at peace, because I knew I was drinking not for the fun of it, but in order to stop. I patted the money in my breast pocket, and felt that it was all lying there safely in its place, as it should be, and went on.

The gentleman who was drinking with me told me all about how he had caroused and reveled in his life, and especially about love, and after all that he started to quarrel, saying that I didn't understand love.

I say:

"What can I do if I'm not attracted to these trifles? Let it be enough for you that you understand everything and yet go around as such a scallywag."

And he says:

"Hush, *s'il vous plaît*! Love is sacred to us!"

"Nonsense!"

"You," he says, "are a clod and a scoundrel, if you dare laugh at the sacred feelings of the heart and call them nonsense."

"But nonsense it is," I say.

"Do you understand," he says, "what 'beauty nature's perfection' is?"

"Yes," I say, "I understand beauty in horses."

He jumps up and goes to box my ear.

"Can a horse," he says, "be beauty nature's perfection?"

But since the hour was rather late, he couldn't prove anything to me about it, and the barman, seeing that we were both drunk, winked to his boys, and some six of them made a rush at us and begged us to "kindly clear out," while holding us both under the arms, and they put us outside and locked the door tightly behind us for the night.

Here such bedevilment began that, though it was many, many years ago, to this day I cannot understand what actually happened and by what power it must have been worked on me, but it seems to me that such temptations and happenings as I endured then are not to be found in any saint's life in the Menaion.[28]

XII

First thing, as I came flying out the door, I put my hand into my breast pocket to make sure that my wallet was there. It turned out that I had it on me. "Now," I think, "the whole concern is how to bring it home safely." The night was the darkest imaginable. In summer, you know, around Kursk, we have such dark nights, but very warm and very mild: the stars hang like lamps all across the sky, and the darkness under them is so dense that it's as if someone in it is feeling and touching you . . . And there's no end of bad people at the fairs, and occasions enough when people are robbed and killed. And though I felt myself strong, I thought, first of all, that I was drunk, and second of all, that if ten or more men fell upon me, even with my great strength I couldn't do anything against them, and they would rob me, and, despite my bravado, I remembered that more than once, when I got up to pay and sat down again, my companion, that little gentleman, had seen that I had a fat lot of money with me. And therefore, you know, it suddenly came to my head: wasn't there some sort of treachery on his part that might be to my harm? Where was he, in fact? We had been chucked out together. Where had he gotten to so quickly?

I stood there quietly looking around, and, not knowing his name, quietly called to him like this:

"Do you hear me, magnetizer? Where are you?"

And suddenly, like some devil, he rises up right before my eyes and says:

"I'm here."

But it seemed to me that it wasn't his voice, and in the dark even the mug didn't look like his.

"Come closer," I said. And when he did, I took him by the shoulders and began to examine him, and for the life of me I couldn't make out who he was. The moment I touched him, suddenly, for no reason at all, my entire memory was blotted out. All I could hear was him jabbering something in French: *"Di-ka-ti-li-ka-tipé,"* and I didn't understand a word of it.

"What's that you're jabbering?" I say.

And he again in French:

"Di-ka-ti-li-ka-tipé."

"Stop it, you fool," I say. "Answer me in Russian who you are, because I've forgotten you."

He answers:

"Di-ka-ti-li-ka-tipé: I'm the magnetizer."

"Pah," I say, "what a little rogue you are!"—and for a moment I seemed to recall that it was him, but then I took a good look and saw he had two noses! . . . Two noses, that's what! And reflecting on that—I forgot all about who he was . . .

"Ah, curse you," I think, "what makes you stick yourself to me, you rascal?"—and I ask him again:

"Who are you?"

He says again:

"The magnetizer."

"Vanish from me," I say. "Maybe you're the devil?"

"Not quite," he says, "but close to it."

I rap him on the forehead, and he gets offended and says:

"What are you hitting me for? I do you a good turn and deliver you from zealous drinking, and you beat me?"

And, like it or not, again I can't remember him and say:

"But who are you?"

He says:

"I'm your eternal friend."

"Well, all right," I say, "but even if you're my friend, maybe you can do me harm?"

"No," he says, "I'll present you with such a *p'tit-comme-peu* that you'll feel yourself a different man."

"Well," I say, "kindly stop lying."

"Truly," he says, "truly: such a *p'tit-comme-peu* . . ."

"Don't babble to me in French, you devil," I say. "I don't understand what a *p'tit-comme-peu* is!"

"I," he says, "will give you a new understanding of life."

"Well, that may be so," I say, "only what kind of new understanding can you give me?"

"It's this," he says, "that you'll perceive beauty nature's perfection."

"How am I going to perceive it all of a sudden like that?"

"Let's go," he says, "you'll see at once."

"Very well, then, let's go."

And we went. We both walk along, staggering, but walking all the same, and I don't know where, only suddenly I remember that I don't know who I've got with me, and again I say:

"Stop! Say who you are, otherwise I won't go."

He tells me, and I seem to remember for a moment, and I ask:

"Why is it that I keep forgetting who you are?"

And he replies:

"That's the effect of my magnetism; but don't let it frighten you, it will pass straightaway, only let me give you a bigger dose of magnetism right now."

He suddenly turned me around, so that he was facing my back, and started feeling with his fingers in the hair on my nape . . . So strange: he rummaged there as if he wanted to climb into my head.

I say:

"Listen, you . . . whoever you are! What are you burrowing for there?"

"Wait," he replies, "stand still: I'm transferring my magnetic power into you."

"It's fine," I say, "that you're transferring your power, but maybe you want to rob me?"

He denies it.

"Well, wait then," I say, "I'll feel for the money."

I felt—the money was all there.

"Well, now," I say, "it's likely you're not a thief"—but who he was I again forgot, only now I no longer remembered how to ask about it, but was taken up with the feeling that he had already climbed right inside me through my nape and was looking at the world through my eyes, and my eyes were just like glass for him.

"See," I think, "what a thing he's done to me—and where's my eyesight now?" I ask.

"Yours," he says, "is no longer there."

"What kind of nonsense is that—not there?"

"Just so," he replies, "with your own eyesight you can now see only what isn't there."

"What a strange thing! Well, then, let me give it a try!"

I peel my eyes for all I'm worth, you know, and it's as if I see various vile mugs on little legs gazing at me from all the dark corners, and running across my path, and standing at the intersections, waiting and saying: "Let's kill him and take the treasure." And my disheveled little gentleman is there before me again, and his mug is all lit up, and behind me I hear a frightful din and disorder, voices, and clanging, and hallooing, and shrieking, and merry guffawing. I look around and realize that I'm standing with my back up against some house, and its windows are open, and there's light inside, and from it come those various voices, and the noise, and the twanging of a guitar, and my little gentleman is there before me again, and he keeps moving his palms in front of my face, then passes his hands over my chest, stops at my heart, pushes on it, then seizes my fingers, shakes them a little, then waves again, and he's working so hard that I see he's even all in a sweat.

But only here, as the light began to shine on me from the windows of the house, and I felt I was regaining consciousness, did I stop being afraid of him and say:

"Well, listen, whoever you are—devil, or fiend, or petty demon—do me a favor: either wake me up, or dissolve."

And to that he answers me:

"Hold on, it's still not time: it's still dangerous, you still can't bear it."

I say:

"What is it I can't bear?"

"What's happening now in the ethereal spheres," he says.

"Then how is it I don't hear anything special?"

But he insists that I'm supposedly not listening right, and says to me in divine language:

"That thou mayest hear, follow thou the example of the psaltery player, who inclineth low his head and, applying his ear to the singing, moveth his hand over the instrument."

"No," I think, "what on earth is this? That's even nothing at all like a drunk man's speech, the way he's started talking!"

And he gazes at me and slowly moves his hands over me, all the while continuing to talk in the same way.

"Thus," he says, "from its strings all together, artfully struck one with the others, the psaltery giveth out its song, and the psaltery player rejoiceth at its honeyed sweetness."

I'll tell you, it was simply like I was listening not to words, but to living water flowing past my hearing, and I thought: "There's a drunkard for you! Look how well he can talk about things divine!" And my little gentleman meanwhile stops fidgeting and comes out with these words:

"Well, now it's enough for you; wake up now," he says, "and fortify yourself!"

And with that he bent a little and spent a long time searching for something in his trouser pocket, and finally took something out of it. I looked: it was a teeny-weeny little piece of sugar, and dirty all over, obviously because it had been wallowing there for a long time. He picked the dirt off with his fingernail, blew on it, and said:

"Open your mouth."

I say:

"What for?"—and gape my mouth open. And he pushes the bit of sugar between my lips and says:

"Suck fearlessly; it's magnetic sugar-mentor: it will fortify you."

I realized, though he had said it in French, that it was about magnetism, and didn't question him anymore, but got busy sucking the sugar, but the one who had given it to me I no longer saw. Whether he had stepped away somewhere in the dark just then or had simply vanished somewhere, deuce knew, but I was left alone and completely in my right mind, and I think: Why should I wait for him? What I have to do now is go home. But again a problem: I don't know what street I'm on, and what house I'm standing by. And I think: Is this really a house? Maybe it all only seems so to me, and it's all a bedevilment . . . It's night now—everyone's asleep, so why is there light here? . . . Well, better test it out . . . go in and see what's up: if there are real people, then I'll ask them the way home, and if it's only a delusion of the eye and not living people . . . then what's the danger? I'll say: "Our place is holy: get thee gone"—and it will all dissolve.

XIII

With that bold resolution, I went up to the porch, crossed myself, and did a get-thee-gone—nothing happened: the house stood, didn't waver, and I see: the door is open, and before me is a big, long front hall, and on the far wall a lamp with a lighted candle. I look around and see two more doors to the left, both covered with matting, and above them again these candleholders with mirrors shaped like stars. I think: What kind of house is this? A tavern? No, not a tavern, but clearly some kind of guest house, but what kind—I can't tell. Only suddenly I begin to listen, and I hear a song pouring out from behind that matted door . . . as languorous as could be, heartfelt, and the voice singing it is like a mellow bell, plucking the soul's strings, taking you prisoner. I listen and don't go any further, and just then the far door suddenly opens, and I see a tall Gypsy come out of it, in silk trousers and a velvet jacket, and he is quickly seeing someone out through a special door, which I hadn't noticed at first, under the far lamp. I must say, though I didn't make out very well who he was seeing out, it seemed to me that it was my magnetizer, and the Gypsy said after him:

"All right, all right, my dear fellow, don't begrudge us these fifty kopecks, but come by tomorrow: if we get any benefit *from him,* we'll add more for your having brought him to us."

And with that he slid the bolt shut and ran to me as if inadvertently, opened a door under one of those mirrors, and said:

"Please come in, mister merchant, kindly listen to our songs! There are some fine voices."

And with that he quietly flung the door wide open before me . . . My dear sirs, a wave of something poured over me, I don't know what, but it was something so akin to me that I suddenly found myself all the way inside. The room was spacious but low, the ceiling all uneven, hanging belly down, everything was dark, sooty, and the tobacco smoke was so thick that the light from the chandelier above was barely visible. And below, in this great smoke, there were people . . . very many, terribly many people, and before them a young Gypsy girl was singing with that voice I had heard. Just as I came in, she was finishing the last piece on a high, high note, tenderly drawn out and trailing off, and her voice died away . . . Her voice died away, and with it at the same instant everything seemed to die . . . Yet a moment later everyone jumped up like mad, clapping their hands and shouting. I was simply amazed: where did all these people come from, and aren't there more and more of them emerging from the smoke? "Oh-oh," I thought, "maybe they're some kind of wild things instead of people?" Only I saw various gentlemen acquaintances, remount officers and stud-farm owners, or rich merchants and landowners I recognized, who were horse fanciers, and amidst all this public such a Gypsy girl goes walking . . . she can't even be described as a woman, but just like a bright-colored snake, moving on her tail and flexing her whole body, and with a burning fire coming from her dark eyes. A curious figure! And in her hands she held a big tray, with many glasses of champagne standing around the edge, and in the middle an awful heap of money. There was no silver, but there was gold, and there were banknotes: blue titmice, gray ducks, red heath cocks—only white swans were missing.[29] Whoever she offered a glass to drank the wine at once and flung money on the tray, gold or banknotes, as much as his zeal prompted him to; and she would then kiss him on the lips and bow to him. She went along the first row, and the second—the guests seemed to be sitting in a semicircle— and then passed along the last row, where I was standing behind a chair, and was about to turn back without offering me wine, but the old Gypsy who came behind her suddenly cried: "Grusha!"—and indicated me with his eyes. She fluttered her eyelashes at him . . . by God, what eyelashes they were, long, long and black, and as if they had a life of their own and moved like some sort of birds, and in her eyes I noticed that, when the old man gave her that order, it was as if wrath breathed all through her. Meaning she was angry that she had been ordered to serve me, but nevertheless did her duty, went behind the last row to where I was standing, bowed, and said:

"Drink to my health, dear guest!"

And I couldn't even reply to her: that's what she had made of me all at once! All at once, that is, as she bent before me over the tray, and I saw how, amidst the black hair on her head, the parting ran like silver and dropped down her back, I got bedeviled and all reason left me. I drank what she offered me, and looked through the glass at her face, and I couldn't tell whether she was dark or fair, but I could see how color glowed under her fine skin, like a plum in sunlight, and a vein throbbed on her tender temple . . . "Here's that real beauty," I think, "which is called nature's perfection. The magnetizer was telling the truth: it's not at all like in a horse, a beast for sale."

And so I drained the glass to the bottom and banged it down on the tray, and she stood there waiting to see what she'd get for her attention. To that end I quickly put my hand in my pocket, but in my pocket all I found were twenty- and twenty-five-kopeck pieces and other small change. Too little, I think; not enough to give such a stinging beauty, and it would be shameful in front of the others! And I hear the gentlemen say none too softly to the Gypsy:

"Eh, Vassily Ivanovich, why did you tell Grusha to serve this muzhik? It's offensive to us."

And he replies:

"With us, gentlemen, every guest finds grace and a place, and my daughter knows the customs of her own Gypsy forefathers; and there's nothing for you to take offense at, because you don't know as yet how a simple man can appreciate beauty and talent. Of that there are various examples."

And hearing that, I think:

"Ah, let the old wolf eat you all! Can it be that if you're richer than I am, you have more feeling? No, what will be, will be: afterwards I'll earn it back for the prince, but now I'm not going to disgrace myself and humiliate this incomparable beauty by stinginess."

And with that I thrust my hand into my breast pocket, took a hundred-rouble swan from the wad, and slapped it down on the tray. And the Gypsy girl, holding the tray in one hand, at once took a white handkerchief in the other, wiped my mouth, and with her lips did not even kiss so much as lightly touch my lips, and it was as if she smeared them with some poison, and then stepped away.

She stepped away, and I would have stayed where I was, but that old Gypsy, Grusha's father, and another Gypsy took me under the arms, and dragged me forward, and seated me in the frontmost row next to the police chief and other gentlemen.

That, I confess, I had no wish for: I didn't want to go on, I wanted to get out of there; but they begged me and wouldn't let me leave, and called out:

"Grusha! Grunyushka, keep our welcome guest here!"

And she came up and . . . deuce knows what she was able to do with her eyes: she glanced as if she were putting some venom in mine, but said:

"Don't offend us: be our guest here a while longer."

"Well," I said, "as if anyone could offend you"—and sat down.

And she kissed me again, and again the sensation was the same: as if she was touching my lips with a poisoned brush and all the blood in me right down to my heart was burning with pain.

And after that the singing and dancing began again, and another Gypsy woman went around again with champagne. This one was also good-looking, but nothing next to Grusha! She didn't have half her beauty, and for that I raked up some twenty- and twenty-five-kopeck pieces and poured them onto the tray . . . The gentlemen started laughing at that, but it was all the same to me, because I was only looking out for her, this Grushenka, and waiting until I heard her voice alone, without any chorus, but she didn't sing. She was sitting with some others, singing along, but not giving a solo, and I didn't hear her voice, but only saw her pretty little mouth with its white teeth . . . "Ah, well," I think, "this is my orphan's lot: I came in for a minute and lost a hundred roubles, and she's the only one I won't get to hear!" But, luckily for me, I wasn't alone in wanting to hear her: other important gentlemen visitors all shouted out together after one of the breaks:

"Grusha! Grusha! 'The Skiff,' Grusha! 'The Skiff!' "[30]

The Gypsies cleared their throats, her young brother took up a guitar, and she began to sing. You know . . . their singing usually gets to you and touches the heart, but when I heard that voice of hers, the same that had lured me from outside the door, I melted away. I liked it terribly! She began as if a bit coarsely, manfully: "Ho-o-owls the se-e-ea, mo-o-oans the se-e-ea." It's as if you really hear the sea moaning, and in it a sinking little skiff struggling. And then suddenly there's a complete change of voice, as it addresses the star:

"Golden one, dear one, herald of the day, with you earthly trouble can never come my way." And again a new turnabout, something you don't expect. With them everything's in these turnabouts: now she weeps, torments you, simply takes your soul out of your body, and then suddenly she strikes up something completely different, and it's as if she puts your heart right back in place again . . . Now, too, she stirred up this "sea" with its "skiff," and the others all just squealed in chorus:

> *Ja-lá-la. Ja-la-la.*
> *Ja-lá-la pringalá!*
> *Ja-la-la pringa-la.*
> *Hey da chepuringalya!*
> *Hey hop-high, ta gara!*
> *Hey hop-high-ta gara!*

And then Grushenka again went around with the wine and the tray, and again I pulled a swan from my breast pocket for her . . . Everyone started looking at me, because I had placed them all beneath me with my gifts: they were even ashamed to give after me, but I was decidedly unsparing now, because it was my own free will, to express my heart, to show my soul, and I showed it. Each time Grusha sings, I give her a swan, and I'm no longer counting how many I've loosed, I just give and that's it, but when the others all ask her to sing, she doesn't, to all their requests she says "I'm tired," but I have only to nod to the Gypsy: Can't we make her?—and he at once gives her a look, and she sings. And she sang a lot, one song more powerful than the other, and I had already handed over a lot of swans to her, a countless number, and in the end, I don't know what time it was, but it was already dawn, and it seemed she really was worn out, and tired, and, looking at me as if hintingly, she began to sing: "Go away, don't look, quit my sight." These words seemed to be driving me out, but others were as if asking: "Or do you want to toy with my lion's soul and feel all the joy of beauty's burning coal?"[31] And I gave her another swan! She unwillingly kissed me again, as if stinging me, and there seemed to be a dark flame in her eyes, and the others, in this canny hour, began to shout:

> *You must feel, my nearest,*
> *How I love you, dearest!*

And they all joined in and looked at Grusha, and I looked and joined in: "You must feel!" And then the Gypsies struck up "Dance, cottage, dance, stove; the master has nowhere to go"—and suddenly they all started dancing . . . The Gypsy men danced, and the Gypsy women danced, and the gentlemen danced: all together in a whirl, as if the whole cottage really were dancing. The Gypsy women flit about before the gentlemen, who try to keep up with them, the young ones with a whistle, the older ones with a groan. I look: no one has stayed seated. Even dignified men, from whom you'd never in your life expect such clowning, all rose to it. One of the more staid ones would sit and sit, and, obviously very ashamed at first, go and only follow with his eyes, or pull at his mustache, and then it was as if a little imp would get him to twitch his shoulder, another to move his leg, and see, suddenly he jumps up and, though he doesn't know how to dance, starts cutting such capers as you've never seen. A police chief, fat as can be, and with two married daughters, is there with his two sons-in-law, huffing and puffing like a catfish and kicking up his heels, but a hussar captain, a remount officer, a fine fellow and a rich one, a rollicking dancer, is the most brilliant of all: hands on hips, stamping his heels, going out in front of everybody, saluting, scraping the floor—and when he comes face-to-face with Grusha, he tosses his head, drops his hat at her feet, and shouts: "Step on it, crush it, my beauty!"—and she . . . Oh, she too was a dancer! I've seen how actresses in theaters dance, and it's all, pah, the same as when an officer's horse, without any fantasy, prances at a parade just to show off, grandstanding for all he's worth, but with no fire of life. This beauty, once she sets off, goes floating like some pharaoh, smooth as can be, and inside her, the snake, you hear the cartilage crunch and the marrow flow from bone to bone, then she stands, curves her body, heaves a shoulder, and brings her brow into line with the point of her toe . . . What a picture! Simply from the sight of her dancing, they all seem to lose their minds: they rush to her madly, obliviously; one has tears in his eyes, another bares his teeth, but they all cry out:

"We'll spare nothing: dance!" They simply fling money under her feet, one gold, another banknotes. And here everything starts whirling thicker and thicker, and I'm the only one sitting, and I don't know how long I can bear it, because I can't look at how she steps on the hussar's hat . . . She steps on it, and a devil gives me a tweak; she steps on it again, and he gives me another tweak, and finally I think: "Why should I torment myself uselessly like this! Let my soul revel all it wants"—and I jump up, push the hussar away, and break into a squatting dance before Grusha . . . And to keep her from stepping on the hussar's hat, I invent this method, thinking, "So you all shout that you'll spare nothing, that doesn't surprise me: but that I will spare nothing, I'll prove by my true deeds"—and I leap over and fling a swan from my breast pocket under her feet and shout: "Crush it! Step on it!" She didn't care . . . Though my swan was worth more than the hussar's hat, she wasn't even looking at the swan, but kept aiming at the hussar; only the old Gypsy, bless him, noticed it and stamped his foot at her . . . She understood and went after me . . . She's sailing towards me, her eyes lowered, burning the ground with her anger like the dragon Gorynych,[32] and I'm capering before her like some sort of demon, and each time I leap, I fling a swan under her feet . . . I respect her so much that I think: "Was it you, cursed thing, who created earth and heaven?"—and I brazenly shout at her: "Move faster!" and go on flinging down the swans, and then I put my hand into my breast pocket to get one more, and I see that there are only about a dozen left . . . "Pah!" I think, "devil take you all!" I crumpled them all into a bunch and threw them under her feet, then took a bottle of champagne from the table, broke the neck off, and shouted:

"Step aside, my soul, you'll get wet!" and I drank it off to her health, because after that dancing I was terribly thirsty.

XIV

"Well, and what then?" we asked Ivan Severyanych.

"Then everything actually followed as *he* promised."

"Who promised?"

"Why, the magnetizer who put it on me: he promised to make the demon of drink leave me, and so he did, and I've never drunk a single glass since. He made a very good job of it."

"Well, sir, and how did you and the prince finish this business of the loosed swans?"

"I don't know myself, somehow very simply: how I got myself home from those Gypsies I don't remember, nor how I went to bed, only I hear the prince knocking and calling, and I want to get up from my

cot, but I simply can't find the edge and climb off. I crawl one way—
no edge; I turn the other way—no edge there either . . . I'm lost on
the cot, of all things! . . . The prince cries: 'Ivan Severyanych!' And
I respond: 'Just a minute!'—and I'm crawling in all directions and
still don't find the edge, and finally I think: 'Well, if I can't get off, I'll
jump,' and I reared back and hurled myself as far as I could, and felt
as if I'd been smashed in the mug, and around me something's jingling and pouring down, and behind me it's also jingling and pouring down, and the prince's voice says to his orderly: 'Quick, bring a
light!'

"And I stand there, I don't move, because I don't know whether I'm
seeing all this awake or in a dream; and I think I still haven't reached
the edge of the cot, but instead, when the orderly brings the light, I
see that I'm standing on the floor and that I've rammed my mug into
the master's cabinet of crystal and broken it all . . ."

"How did you lose your bearings like that?"

"Very simply: I thought I was sleeping on my cot, as had always
been my habit, but most likely, on coming back from the Gypsies, I
lay down on the floor, and crawled all over searching for the edge,
and then jumped . . . and jumped right into the cabinet. I lost my
bearings because that . . . magnetizer, having rid me of the demon
of drink, provided me with the demon of straying . . . I remembered
at once the words he had spoken: 'It may be worse if you stop drinking'—and I went looking for him—I wanted to ask him if he hadn't
better demagnetize me to the old way, but I didn't find him. He, too,
had taken a lot on himself and couldn't bear it, and right there, in a
pot-house across from the Gypsies, had drunk so much that he died."

"And so you remained magnetized?"

"So I did, sir."

"And did this magnetism work on you for long?"

"Why for long? Maybe it's still working."

"But all the same it would be interesting to learn how things went
between you and the prince . . . Can it be that you never had it out
over those swans?"

No, sir, we had it out, only it wasn't much. The prince also came
home having lost at cards and began asking me for money to win it
back. I say:

"Forget about that: I have no money at all."

He thinks I'm joking, but I say:

"No, it's true, I had a big outing while you were gone."

He asks:

"What could you have done with five thousand on one outing?"

I say:

"I threw it all to a Gypsy girl . . ."

He doesn't believe me.

I say:

"Well, don't believe me, then; but I'm telling you the truth."

He got angry and said:

"Lock the door, I'm going to give it to you for throwing my money away"—and then he suddenly cancelled it and said: "No, never mind, I myself am as wayward as you are."

And he went to his room to finish his night's sleep, and I also went to sleep again in the hayloft. I came to my senses in a hospital and heard them saying that I had had delirium tremens and had wanted to hang myself, only, thank God, I'd been swaddled in a long shirt. Then I got better and went to the prince on his country estate, because in the meantime he had resigned his commission, and I said:

"Your Serenity, I have to earn the money back for you."

He says:

"Go to the devil."

I see he's very offended at me, go up to him, and bend down:

"What does this mean?" he says.

"At least," I beg, "give me a good, sound thrashing."

And he replies:

"And why do you think I'm angry at you? Maybe I don't consider you guilty at all."

"For pity's sake," I say, "how am I not guilty, when I squandered a whole province of money? I myself know that hanging's too good for such a scoundrel as me."

And he replies:

"No help for it, brother, since you're an artist."

"How's that?" I ask.

"It is," he replies, "that you, dearest Ivan Severyanych, my half-esteemed fellow, are an artist."

"That," I say, "I can't understand."

"Don't think anything bad," he says, "because I'm also an artist myself."

"Well, that's clear enough," I think. "Obviously, I'm not the only one who has made a pursuit of delirium tremens."

He stood up, flung his pipe on the floor, and said:

"No wonder you threw all you had before her: I, brother, gave for her what I don't have and never did have."

I stared at him goggle-eyed.

"Merciful heavens," I say, "Your Serenity, my dear man, what are you saying? It's even dreadful for me to hear it."

"Well," he replies, "don't be very frightened: God is merciful, and perhaps I'll get out of it somehow, only I gave the Gypsy camp fifty thousand for this Grusha."

I gasped.

"What?" I say. "Fifty thousand? For a Gypsy girl? Can the snake be worth it?"

"Well, there," he replies, "my half-esteemed fellow, you are talking most stupidly and inartistically . . . Is she worth it? A woman is worth everything in the world, because she can inflict such a wound that you won't be cured of it for a whole kingdom, but she alone can cure you of it in a single moment."

I keep thinking it's all true, and keep shaking my head and saying:

"Such a sum! A whole fifty thousand!"

"Yes, yes," he says, "and don't go on repeating it, because thankfully they took it, otherwise I'd have given more . . . as much as you like."

"You should have spat on it," I say, "and left it at that."

"I couldn't, brother," he says, "I couldn't spit on it."

"Why not?"

"She stung me with her beauty and talent, and I need to be cured, otherwise I'll go out of my mind. But tell me: she is beautiful, isn't she? Eh? Isn't she? Enough to drive you out of your mind? . . ."

I bit my lips and only nodded silently:

"Right, right."

"You know," says the prince, "I could even die for a woman, it would be nothing to me. Can you understand that I think nothing of dying?"

"What's there not to understand?" I say. "It's beauty, nature's perfection."

"How do you understand that?"

"Like this," I reply, "that beauty is nature's perfection, and from that ravishment a man can perish—even joyfully!"

"Good for you," my prince replies, "good for you, my almost half-esteemed and most greatly insignificant Ivan Severyanych! Precisely, sir, precisely, it is joyful to perish, and it now feels sweet to me that I overturned my whole life for her: resigned my commission, mortgaged my estate, and from now on I'll live here, seeing nobody, but only looking in her face."

I lowered my voice still more and whispered:

"How are you going to look in her face?" I say. "You mean she's here?"

And he answers:

"What else? Of course she's here."

"Can it be?" I ask.

"Wait here," he says, "I'll bring her right now. You're an artist—I'm not going to hide her from you."

And with that he left me and went out the door. I stood there, waiting and thinking:

"Eh, it's not good your insisting that you only want to look at her face! You'll get bored!" But I didn't reason about it in detail, because when I remembered that she was there, I immediately felt that my sides were even getting hot, and my mind became addled, and I thought: "Can it be that I'm going to see her now?" And suddenly they came in: the prince came first, carrying a guitar on a broad red ribbon in one hand, and with the other dragging Grusha by both hands, and she walked downcast, reluctantly, without looking, and only those huge eyelashes of hers fluttered against her cheeks like a bird's wings.

The prince led her in, picked her up in his arms, and seated her like a child, with her legs tucked under, in the corner of a wide, soft sofa; he put one velvet pillow behind her back, another under her right elbow, threw the ribbon of the guitar over her shoulder, and placed her fingers on the strings. Then he himself sat on the floor by the sofa, leaned his head against her red morocco bootie, and nodded for me to sit down, too.

I quietly lowered myself to the floor by the doorway, also tucked my legs under, and sat looking at her. It became as quiet as if the room were empty. I sat and sat, my knees even began to ache, and I glanced at her, she was still in the same position, and I looked at the prince: I see he's gnawing his mustache from languor, but he doesn't say a word to her.

I nod to him, as if to say: tell her to sing! And in response he does me a pamtomine, meaning: she won't listen to me.

And again we both sit on the floor and wait, but suddenly it's as if she starts raving, sighing, and sobbing, and a little tear flows from her lashes, and her fingers crawl and murmur over the strings like wasps . . . And suddenly she begins to sing very, very softly, as if she's weeping: "Good people, listen to my heartfelt grief."

The prince whispers: "What?"

And I whisper back in French:

"P'tit-comme-peu"—and have nothing more to say, but at that same moment she suddenly cries out: "And for my beauty they'll sell me, they'll sell me," and she flings the guitar far from her knees, and tears the kerchief from her head, and falls facedown on the sofa, covers her face with her hands, and weeps, and I weep, looking at her, and the prince . . . he, too, begins to weep, and he takes up the guitar, and, not really singing but more like intoning in church, moans: "If you but knew all the fire of love, all the anguish in my ardent soul"—and he bursts into sobs. He sings and sobs: "Comfort me, the comfortless one, make me happy, the unhappy one." As he becomes so cruelly shaken, I see that she begins to heed his tears and singing and grows quieter, calmer, and she suddenly takes her hand quietly from under her face and, like a mother, tenderly embraces his head . . .

Well, here it became clear to me that she had pitied him this time and would now comfort him and heal all the anguish of his ardent soul, and I got up quietly, inconspicuously, and left.

"And it was probably then that you entered the monastery?" someone asked the storyteller.

"No, sir, not then, but later," replied Ivan Severyanych and added that he was still to see much from that woman in this world, before all that was destined for her was fulfilled and crossed him out.

His listeners naturally fell upon him with requests that he tell them Grusha's story, if only briefly, and Ivan Severyanych did so.

XV

You see (Ivan Severyanych began), my prince had a good heart, but a changeable one. Whatever he wanted, he had to get at all costs on the spot—otherwise he'd go out of his mind; and in that state, he wouldn't spare anything in the world to attain it, but then, once he got it, he wouldn't appreciate his good luck. That's how it was with this Gypsy girl, and Grusha's father and all the Gypsies of the camp right away understood that very well about him and asked him God knows what price for her, more than all his domestic property allowed, because though he did have a nice country estate, it was ruined. The prince did not have on hand then the kind of money the camp was asking for Grusha, and he went into debt for it and could no longer serve in the army.

Knowing all his habits, I didn't expect much good from him for Grusha, and it came out as I thought. He kept clinging to her, endlessly gazed at her and sighed, and suddenly he started yawning and kept inviting me to keep them company.

"Sit down," he'd say, "and listen."

I'd take a chair, sit somewhere near the door, and listen. This happened often: he'd ask her to sing, and she'd say:

"Who am I going to sing for! You've turned cold, and I want my song to make someone's soul burn and suffer."

The prince would at once send for me again, and the two of us would listen to her; later Grusha herself started reminding him to invite me, and began to treat me very amiably, and more than once after her singing I had tea in her rooms together with the prince, though, naturally, either at a separate table or somewhere by the window, but when she was alone, she always simply sat me down beside her. Some time passed this way, and the prince was becoming more and more troubled, and once he said to me:

"You know, Ivan Severyanych, thus and so, things are very bad with me."

I say:

"What's so bad about them? Thank God, you live as one ought to, and you've got everything."

He suddenly became offended.

"How stupid you are, my half-esteemed fellow," he says. "I've 'got everything'? And what is it I've *got*?"

"Why," I say, "everything a man needs."

"Not so," he says. "I've become poor, I now have to calculate whether I can have a bottle of wine with dinner. Is that a life? Is that a life?"

"So," I think, "that's what you're upset about," and I say:

"Well, if there's not wine enough, that's still no great trouble, it can be endured, since there's something sweeter than wine and honey."

He understood I was hinting at Grusha and seemed to be ashamed, and he paced about, waved his arm, and said:

"Of course . . . of course . . . naturally . . . only . . . I've been living here for half a year now and haven't set eyes on another human being . . ."

"And what do you need another human being for," I say, "when you've got your heart's desire?"

The prince flared up.

"You understand nothing, brother," he says. "All's well when you've got the one and the other."

"Aha!" I think, "so that's your tune, brother?"—and I say:

"What do we do now?"

"Let's take up horse trading," he says. "I want to have remount officers and horse breeders come to me again."

Horse trading is a futile and ungentlemanly business, but, I think, "So long as baby's amused and doesn't cry," and I say: "If you like."

And we began to set up a corral. But we had barely started work, when the prince got carried away by this passion: whenever a little money came in, he at once bought horses, and he took them, he snatched them up senselessly; he wouldn't listen to me . . . We bought a slew of them, but there were no sales . . . He couldn't stand it, dropped the horses, and gave himself to whatever happened along: first he threw himself into building an extraordinary mill, then he started a saddler's shop, and all of it brought losses and debts, and worst of all it deranged his character . . . He was never at home, but flew now here, now there, looking for something, and Grusha was alone and in a certain condition . . . expecting. She was bored. "I see little of him," she said—but she forced herself to be tactful. The moment she noticed that he was bored at home for a day or two, she would say at once:

"My ruby-jewel, why don't you go out and have some fun? What should you sit with me for? I'm simple and uneducated."

At these words he would at once feel ashamed, and kiss her hands, and hold himself back for two or three days, but then he would just go off in a whirl and leave me in charge of her.

"Take care of her, my half-esteemed Ivan Severyanych," he'd say. "You're an artist, you're not a whippersnapper like me, but a real high-class artist, and therefore you're somehow able to talk to her so that you both have a nice time, while those 'ruby-jewels' just put me to sleep."

I say:

"Why so? They're loving words."

"Loving," he says, "but stupid and tiresome."

I made no reply, but from then on started visiting her without ceremony: when the prince wasn't there, I'd go to her wing twice a day to have tea and amuse her the best I could.

And I had to amuse her because, if she happened to start talking, she always complained:

"My dear Ivan Severyanych, friend of my heart," she'd say, "jealousy, my darling one, torments me bitterly."

Well, naturally, I reassured her:

"Why be so tormented?" I'd say. "Wherever he goes, he always comes back to you."

She would burst into tears, beat her breast, and say:

"No, tell me . . . don't conceal it from me, friend of my heart: where does he go?"

"To gentlefolk," I say, "in the neighborhood or in town."

"But isn't there some woman," she says, "who has come between us? Tell me: maybe he loved someone before me and has now gone back to her—or might my wicked one be thinking of marrying?" And her eyes blaze so as she says it that it's even terrible to see.

I comfort her, but I think to myself:

"Who knows what he's up to?"—because we saw little of him at that time.

Once it occurred to her that he wanted to marry, she got to begging me:

"Go to town, Ivan Severyanych, my darling, my this-and-that; go, find out the whole truth about him, and tell me everything without any secrets."

She badgered me about it more and more and made me feel so sorry for her that I thought:

"Well, come what may, I'll go. Though if I find out anything bad about betrayal, I won't tell her everything, but I'll see and clear things up for myself."

I chose as a pretext that I supposedly had to go to buy medicine for the horses from the herbalists, and so I went, but I went not simply, but with a cunning design.

Grusha didn't know, and the servants were under the strictest orders to conceal from her, that the prince, before this occasion with Grusha, had had another love in town: Evgenia Semyonovna, a gentlewoman, an official's daughter. She was known to the whole town as a great piano player and a very kindly lady, and was also very good-looking, and she had a daughter by my prince, but she gained weight, and people said that was why he left her. However, as he still had considerable capital at that time, he bought a house for this lady and her daughter, and they lived on the income from this house. After bestowing it upon Evgenia Semyonovna, the prince never visited her, but our people, remembering old times, recalled her kindliness, and on each trip to town they would all drop in on her, because they loved her and she was terribly affectionate towards them all and was interested in the prince.

So on coming to town I went straight to her, to this good lady, and said:

"My dear Evgenia Semyonovna, I am going to stay with you."

She replies:

"Well, of course, I'm very glad. But why aren't you going to the prince's place?"

"Ah," I say, "is he here in town?"

"Yes, he is," she replies. "It's already the second week he's been here, setting up some kind of business."

"What kind of business?" I ask.

"He wants to lease a fulling mill," she says.

"Lord," I say, "what will he think up next?"

"Why," she says, "is there something wrong with it?"

"Not at all," I say, "only it surprises me a little."

She smiles.

"No," she says, "but here's something that will really surprise you: the prince has sent me a letter asking me to receive him today, because he wants to have a look at his daughter."

"And you, my dearest Evgenia Semyonovna," I say, "are going to let him?"

She shrugs her shoulders and replies:

"Why not? Let him come and look at his daughter"—and with that she sighs and turns thoughtful; she sits with her head lowered, and she's still so young, fair and full-bodied, and her manners are quite unlike Grusha's . . . who knows nothing besides her "ruby-jewel," while this one's quite different . . . I became jealous for her.

"Oh," I think, "while he's here looking at his child, his greedy heart may notice you as well! Not much good will come of that for my Grushenka." And in such reflections I was sitting in Evgenia Semyonovna's nursery, where she had told the nanny to serve me tea, when I suddenly heard the doorbell, and the maid ran in all joyful and said to the nanny:

"Our dear prince has come!"

I was about to get up and go to the kitchen, but the nanny Tatyana Yakovlevna was a talkative old woman from Moscow: she passionately loved to tell all and on account of that didn't want to be deprived of a listener, so she said:

"Don't leave, Ivan Golovanych, let's go to the dressing room there behind the wardrobes, she'll never bring him there, and we can chat some more."

I agreed, because, given Tatyana Yakovlevna's talkativeness, I hoped to find out something useful for Grusha from her, and since Evgenia Semyonovna had sent me a little lodicolone bottle of rum to have with tea, but by then I was no longer drinking, I thought: "If I lace the blessed old woman's tea with a bit of chat from this little bottle, maybe, in her goodness, she'll let slip to me something she wouldn't tell otherwise."

We left the nursery and went to sit behind the wardrobes, and that little dressing room was so narrow it was more like a corridor with a door at the end, and that door gave directly onto the room where Evgenia Semyonovna was receiving the prince, and even right onto the sofa they were sitting on. In short, all that separated me from them was that closed door with its cloth curtain on the other side, so that I heard everything just like I was sitting in the same room with them.

As soon as he comes in, the prince says:

"Greetings, my old friend, tried and true!"

And she replies:

"Greetings, Prince! To what do I owe the pleasure?"

And he to her:

"Of that we shall speak later, but first let me greet you and allow me to kiss you on your little head"—and I hear him give her a smacking kiss on the head and ask about their daughter. Evgenia Semyonovna replies that she is at home.

"Is she well?"

"Quite well," she says.

"And grown, most likely?"

Evgenia Semyonovna laughs and replies:

"Naturally, she's grown."

The prince asks:

"You'll show her to me, I hope?"

"Why not?" she replies. "With pleasure"—and she gets up, goes to the nursery, and calls for this same nanny, Tatyana Yakovlevna, with whom I'm having tea.

"Nanny," she says, "bring Lyudochka to the prince."

Tatyana Yakovlevna spits, puts the saucer down on the table, and says:

"Oh, dash it all! You just sit down, in the right appetite for talking with a man, and they're sure to interrupt you, they never let you enjoy anything the way you'd like to!" And she quickly covers me with her mistress's skirts, which are hanging on the walls, and says: "Sit here"—and she herself goes out with the girl, and I'm left there alone behind the wardrobes, and suddenly I hear the prince kiss the girl a couple of times and dandle her on his knee and say:

"My anfan, would you like to go for a ride in the carriage?"

The girl makes no reply. He says to Evgenia Semyonovna:

"Zhe voo pree, please let her and the nanny go out for a ride in my carriage."

She also says something to him in French, what for and poorkwa, but he says something like "It's absolutely necessary," and so they exchange words some three times, and then Evgenia Semyonovna reluctantly says to the nanny:

"Get her dressed and go for a ride."

They left, and these two remained alone, with me there listening in secret, because I couldn't come out from behind the wardrobes, and I thought to myself: "My time has come, and now I'll really discover if anyone has bad thoughts against Grusha."

XVI

Having come to this decision to eavesdrop, I didn't content myself with that, but wanted to see what I could with my own eyes, and I succeeded in that as well: I quietly climbed onto a stool, and at once found a little chink above the door and put my greedy eye to it. I see the prince sitting on the sofa, and the lady standing by the window and probably looking at her child being put in the carriage.

The carriage drives off; she turns and says:

"Well, Prince, I've done everything as you wanted: tell me now, what business do you have with me?"

And he replies:

"Ah, why talk of business! . . . It won't run away. Come here to me, first: we'll sit next to each other and talk nicely, like the old times, like we used to."

The lady stands there, hands behind her back, leaning against the window, and says nothing. She is frowning. The prince asks:

"What's the matter? I beg you: we must talk."

She obeys, goes to him; seeing that, he at once jokes again:

"Well, let's sit, let's sit like the old times"—and he goes to embrace her, but she pushes him away and says:

"Business, Prince, talk business: what can I do for you?"

"What's this?" asks the prince. "You mean I should just lay it out openly, without any preamble?"

"Of course," she says, "explain straight out what the business is. You and I are close acquaintances—there's no need to stand on ceremony."

"I need money," says the prince.

She says nothing and looks at him.

"Not a lot of money," he says.

"How much?"

"Just twenty thousand this time."

Again she doesn't reply, and the prince starts painting it on, saying: "I want to buy a fulling mill, but I don't have a penny. If I buy it, though, I'll be a millionaire. I'll redo the whole thing," he says. "I'll throw all the old stuff out and start making bright-colored fabrics and sell them to the Asiatics in Nizhny.[33] From the most trashy materials," he says, "but dyed bright colors, and it will sell well, and I'll make big money, but now I need only twenty thousand in down payment for the mill."

Evgenia Semyonovna says:

"Where are you going to get it?"

The prince says:

"I don't know myself, but I must get it, and then my calculations are quite correct: I have a man, Ivan Golovan, an army connoisseur, not very bright, but a solid gold muzhik—honest, and zealous, and he was held captive for a long time by the Asiatics and knows all their tastes very well, and now there's the Makary fair, I'll send Golovan there to take orders and bring samples, and there'll be down payments . . . then . . . first thing, I'll immediately pay back the twenty thousand . . ."

And he fell silent, and the lady said nothing for a moment, then sighed and began:

"Your calculations are correct, Prince."

"Aren't they, though?"

"Correct," she says, "correct. Here's what you'll do: you'll pay the down payment for the mill, after which you'll be considered a mill owner; there'll be talk in society that your affairs have improved . . ."

"Right."

"Right. And then . . ."

"Golovan will take a lot of orders and down payments at the fair, and I'll return my debt and become rich."

"No, please, don't interrupt me: first, you'll use all that to flimflam the marshal of the nobility,[34] and, while he thinks you're rich, you'll marry his daughter, and then, having taken her dowry along with her, you'll indeed become rich."

"You think so?" the prince says.

And the lady replies:

"And do you think otherwise?"

"Ah, well, if you understand everything," he says, "then God grant we see it all come true."

"*We?*"

"Of course," he says, "then it will be good for all of us: you'll mortgage the house for me now, and I'll give our daughter ten thousand in interest on the twenty thousand."

The lady replies:

"The house is yours: you gave it to her, take it if you need it."

He starts saying: "No, the house isn't mine; you're her mother, I ask you . . . of course, only in the event that you trust me . . ."

But she replies:

"Ah, enough, Prince, I trusted you with more than that! I entrusted you with my life and honor."

"Ah, yes," he says, "you mean that . . . Well, thank you, thank you, excellent . . . So, then, tomorrow I can send you the mortgage papers for signing?"

"Send them," she says, "I'll sign them."

"You're not afraid?"

"No," she says, "after what I've already lost, I'm not afraid of anything."

"And you're not sorry? Tell me: you're not sorry? It must be that you still love me a tiny bit? What? Or you simply pity me? Eh?"

She merely laughs at these words and says:

"Stop babbling nonsense, Prince. Wouldn't you like it better if I served you some steeped cloudberries with sugar? Mine came out very tasty this year."

He must have been offended: he had clearly expected something else. He gets up and smiles:

"No," he says, "you eat your cloudberries yourself, I can't be bothered with sweets now. Thank you and good-bye"—and he started kissing her hands, and just then the carriage came back.

Evgenia Semyonovna gave him her hand in farewell and said:

"And how are you going to deal with your dark-eyed Gypsy girl?"

He suddenly slapped himself on the forehead and cried out:

"Ah, true! What a smart one you've always been! Believe it or not, I always remember your intelligence, and I thank you for reminding now of that ruby!"

"And you had forgotten her just like that?" she says.

"By God," he says, "I had. She'd gone clean out of my head, but I really do have to set the foolish girl up."

"Set her up," Evgenia Semyonovna replies, "only good and proper: she's got no cool Russian blood half mixed with milk, she won't be meekly pacified, and she won't forgive anything for the sake of the past."

"Never mind," he says, "she'll be pacified somehow."

"She loves you, doesn't she, Prince? They say she even loves you very much?"

"I'm awfully sick of her; but, thank God, luckily for me, she and Golovan are great friends."

"What do you gain by that?" asks Evgenia Semyonovna.

"Nothing. I'll buy them a house and register Ivan as a merchant, they'll get married and start a life."

But Evgenia Semyonovna shakes her head, smiles, and says:

"Ah, dear Prince, dear Prince, dear muddleheaded Prince: where is your conscience?"

But the prince replies:

"Kindly leave my conscience out of it. By God, I can't be bothered with it now: I've somehow got to bring Ivan Golovan here today."

The lady told him that Ivan Golovan was in town and was even staying with her. The prince was very gladdened by that, told her to send me to him as soon as possible, and left her house at once.

After that everything went at a spanking pace, like in a fairy tale. The prince gave me warrants and certificates that the mill was his, taught me how to talk about the fabrics he produced, and sent me straight from town to the fair, so that I couldn't even see Grusha, only I was all offended at the prince over her: how could he say she'd be my wife? At the fair I had a run of good luck: I gathered up orders, and money, and samples from the Asiatics, and I sent all the money to the prince, and came back myself and couldn't recognize his place . . . It was as if everything there had been changed by some kind of magic: it was all done up new, like a cottage decorated for a feast, and there was no trace of the wing where Grusha used to live: it had been torn down, and a new house had been built in its place. I just gasped and went rushing around: where's Grusha? But nobody knew anything about her. And the servants were all new, hired, and very haughty, so that I no longer had my former access to the prince. He and I used to deal with each other in military fashion, simply, but now it had all become politics, and if I had to say something to the prince, I could only do it through his valet.

I detest that sort of thing so much that I wouldn't have stayed there for a minute and would have left at once, only I felt very sorry for Grusha, and I couldn't find out what had become of her. I asked some of the old servants—they all said nothing: clearly they were under strict orders. I finally managed to get out of an old serving woman that Grushenka had been there still recently, and it was only ten days ago that she had gone off somewhere in a carriage with the prince and hadn't come back since. I went to the coachmen who had driven them: I started questioning them, but they wouldn't tell me anything. They said only that the prince had changed horses at a station and sent his own back, and he and Grusha had gone on somewhere with hired ones. Wherever I rushed, there was no trace, and that was it: the villain might have put a knife in her, or shot her and thrown her into a ditch somewhere in the forest and covered her with dry leaves, or drowned her . . . From a passionate man, all that could easily be supposed; and she was a hindrance to his marrying, because Evgenia Semyonovna had spoken truly: Grusha loved this villain with all her passionate, devastating Gypsy love, and she was incapable of enduring and submitting like Evgenia Semyonovna, a Russian Christian, who burned her life like an icon lamp before him. In her, I thought, that great Gypsy flame had flared up like a smoldering bonfire when he told her about his wedding, and she must have made the devil's own row, and so he finished her off.

The more I entertained this thought in my head, the more convinced I was that it couldn't be otherwise, and I couldn't look at any of the preparations for his marriage to the marshal's daughter. And when the wedding day came, and the servants were all given bright-colored neckerchiefs and new clothing, each according to his duties, I put on neither the neckerchief nor the outfit, but left it all in my closet in the stables, and went to the forest in the morning, and wandered about, not knowing why myself, till evening, thinking all the while: maybe I'll happen upon her murdered body? Evening fell, and I came out on the steep riverbank and sat there, and across the river the whole house is lit up, shining, and the feast is going on; guests are making merry, music resounds, echoing far away. And I go on sitting and looking, not at the house now, but into the water, where that light is all reflected and ripples in streams, as if the columns are moving, like watery chambers opening out. And I felt so sad, so oppressed, that I began to speak with the invisible power—something that hadn't happened to me even in captivity—and, as it's told in the tale of little sister Alyonushka, whose brother called out to her,[35] I called out to my little orphan Grunyushka in a pitiful voice:

"My dear sister, my Grunyushka! Answer me, call out to me; answer me; show yourself to me for one little moment!"—And what do you think: I moaned these words three times, and I began to feel eerie, and fancied somebody was running towards me, was coming close, was fluttering around me, whispering in my ears, and peeking over my shoulder into my face, and suddenly, out of the darkness of night, something comes shooting at me! . . . And hangs right onto me and throbs against me . . .

XVII

I almost fell down from fright, but I was not quite unconscious, and I felt something alive and light, like a shot-down crane, fluttering and sighing, but saying nothing.

I recited a prayer to myself—and what then? Right in front of my face I see Grusha's face . . .

"My own!" I say. "My little dove! Are you alive, or have you come to me from the other world? Don't hide anything," I say. "Tell me the truth: I won't be afraid of you, my poor orphan, even if you're dead."

And she sighs deeply, deeply, from deep down in her breast, and says:

"I'm alive."

"Well, thank God for that."

"Only," she says, "I've escaped in order to die here."

"What are you saying, Grunyushka?" I say. "God help you: why should you die? Let's go and live a happy life: I'll work for you, and I'll set up a special little chamber for you, my dearest orphan, and you'll live with me like my own sister."

And she replies:

"No, Ivan Severyanych, nó, my gentle one, dear friend of my heart, accept from me, an orphan, my eternal respect for your words, but it's impossible for me, a bitter Gypsy, to live any longer, because I might destroy an innocent soul."

"Who are you talking about?" I ask. "Whose soul do you pity so?"

And she replies:

"It's her, my villain's young wife, that I pity, because she's a young soul, not guilty of anything, but even so my jealous heart can't bear it, and I'll destroy her and myself."

"What are you saying? Cross yourself," I say. "You're baptized: what will become of your soul?"

"No-o-o," she says, "I won't be sorry for my soul, let it go to hell. The hell here is worse!"

I could see that the woman was all upset and in a frenzied state of mind: I took her hands and held them, and I looked closely and marveled at how awfully changed she was. Where had all her beauty gone? There was even no flesh on her, only eyes burning in a dark face, like a wolf's eyes at night, and they seemed to have grown twice bigger than before, and her womb had swollen, because her term had almost come; her little face was clenched like a fist, and strands of black hair hung on her cheeks. I looked at the dress she was wearing—it was a dark cotton dress, all in tatters, and her feet were bare in her shoes.

"Tell me," I say, "where have you come here from? Where have you been, and how is it you're so unsightly?"

And she suddenly smiled and said:

"What? . . . So I'm not beautiful? . . . Beautiful! The dear friend of my heart adorned me like this because of my faithful love for him: because I forgot for his sake the one I loved more than him and gave him my all, without mind or reason. For that he hid me away in a sure place and set guards to keep strict watch on my beauty . . ."

And at that she suddenly burst out laughing and said wrathfully:

"Ah, you fool of a little prince: is a Gypsy girl a young lady to be kept under lock and key? If I like, I'll throw myself at your young wife right now and bite through her throat."

I could see she was shaking all over from the torments of jealousy, and I thought: "Let me distract her from it, not by the fear of hell, but by a sweet memory," and I said:

"But how he loved you! Oh, how he loved you! How he kissed your feet . . . He used to kneel by the sofa while you sang and kiss your red slipper all over, even on the sole . . ."

She listened to that, and her black eyelashes moved on her dry cheeks, and, looking into the water, she began in a hollow, quiet voice:

"He loved me, he loved me, the villain, he loved me, he spared nothing, as long as my heart wasn't his, but when I came to love him— he abandoned me. And for what? . . . Is she, my interloper, better than I am, or is she going to love him more? . . . Foolish, foolish man! Winter's sun gives no heat compared to summer's, and he'll never ever see a love to compare with my love for him; you tell him that: So Grusha, dying, foretold for you, and as your fate it will hold true."

I was glad she had started talking, and I joined in, asking:

"What was it that went on between you and what brought it all about?"

And she clasped her hands and said:

"Ah, nothing brought it about, it all came from betrayal alone . . . I ceased to please him, that's the whole reason"—and as she said it, she became tearful. "He had dresses made for me that were to his own taste, but that a pregnant woman has no need of: narrow in the waist. I'd put them on, show him, and he'd get angry and say: 'Take it off, it doesn't suit you.' If I didn't wear them and showed myself in a loose dress, he'd get twice as upset and say: 'What a sight you are!' I understood then that I couldn't win him back, that I disgusted him . . ."

And with that she burst into sobs and, looking straight ahead, whispered to herself:

"I'd long been feeling that I was no longer dear to him, but I wanted to try his conscience. I thought: I won't vex him in anything, I'll see if he feels pity. And here's how he pitied me . . ."

And she told me that her last break with the prince had occurred on account of such a trifle that I didn't even understand, and don't understand to this day, why the perfidious man parted with this woman forever.

XVIII

Grusha told me how, "when you," she says, "went and disappeared," that is, when I went off to the fair, "the prince stayed away from home for a long time, and rumors reached me that he was getting married . . . These rumors made me cry terribly, and my face got all pinched . . . My heart ached and the child turned over in me . . . I thought: it's going to die in my womb. Then suddenly I hear them say: 'He's coming!' . . . Everything inside me trembled . . . I rushed to my rooms in the wing to dress up the best I could for him, put on my emerald earrings, and pulled from under a sheet on the wall his favorite blue moiré dress, trimmed with lace, with an open neck . . . I was in a hurry, I put it on, but couldn't get it buttoned in the back . . . so I didn't button it, but quickly threw a red shawl over it so that you couldn't see it was unbuttoned, and ran out to meet him on the porch . . . Trembling all over and forgetting myself, I cried out:

"'My golden one, my ruby-jewel!'—threw my arms around his neck, and went numb . . ."

She had fainted.

"When I came to in my room," she says, "I lay on the sofa and tried to remember: was it in a dream or awake that I embraced him? Only," she says, "there was a terrible weakness in me"—and she didn't see him for a long time . . . She kept sending for him, but he didn't come.

At last he shows up, and she says:

"Why have you abandoned me and forgotten me so completely?"

And he says:

"I have things to do."

"What things?" she replies. "Why didn't you have any before? Oh, my ruby-diamond!"—and she held out her arms again to embrace him, but he frowned and pulled the string of the cross on her neck with all his might . . .

"Luckily for me," she says, "the silk string on my neck wasn't strong, it was worn out and broke, because I'd been wearing an amulet on it for a long time, otherwise he'd have strangled me; and I suppose that's precisely what he wanted to do, because he went all white and hissed:

"'Why do you wear such a dirty string?'

"And I say:

"'What's my string to you? It used to be clean, but it has turned black on me from the heavy sweat of grief.'

"And he spat—'Pah, pah, pah'—spat and left, but before evening he came back angry and said:

"'Let's go for a carriage ride!' And he pretended to be tender and kissed my head, and, fearing nothing, I got in with him and went. We drove for a long time and changed horses twice, yet I couldn't get out of him where we were going, but I saw we'd come to a place in the forest—swampy, unlovely, wild. And we arrived at some beehives, and beyond the beehives—a yard, and there we were met by three strapping young peasant wenches in red linen skirts, and they called me 'lady.' As soon as I got out of the carriage, they took me under the arms and hustled me straight to a room that was all prepared.

"Something about all this, and especially about these wenches, made me sick at once, and my heart was wrung.

"'What kind of stopping place is this?' I asked him.

"And he replied:

"'You're going to live here now.'

"I began to weep, to kiss his hands, so that he wouldn't abandon me there, but he had no pity: he pushed me away and left . . ."

Here Grushenka fell silent and looked down, then sighed and said:

"I wanted to escape, tried a hundred times—impossible: those

peasant wenches were on guard and never took their eyes off me . . .
I languished, then I finally got the notion to pretend I was carefree,
merry, as if I wanted to go for a walk. They took me for a walk in the
forest, watched me all the time, and I watched the trees, noticing by
the treetops and the bark which way was south, and I planned how
I'd escape from these wenches, and yesterday I did it. Yesterday after
lunch I went to a clearing with them, and I said:

"'Come, my sweet ones, let's play blind man's buff in the clearing.'

"They agreed.

"'But instead of our eyes,' I say, 'let's tie each other's hands behind
our backs and play catch from behind.'

"They agreed to that, too.

"And so we did. I tied the first one's hands very tightly behind
her back, and with the second one I ran behind a bush, and that
one I hobbled there, and the third one came running at her cries,
and I trussed her up by force before the eyes of the other two. They
shouted, but I, heavy with child as I am, started running faster than
a frisky horse through the forest, right through the forest, and I ran
all night and in the morning I fell down by some old beehives in
the dense second growth. There a little old man came up to me and
mumbled something I couldn't understand, and he was all covered
with wax and smelled of honey, and bees were crawling in his yellow
eyebrows. I told him that I wanted to see you, Ivan Severyanych, and
he says:

"'Call to him, young one, first with the wind, and then against
the wind: he'll start pining and come looking for you—and you'll
meet.' He gave me water to drink and a cucumber with honey to
fortify myself. I drank the water and ate the cucumber and went on
again, and I kept calling you, as he told me to, now with the wind,
now against the wind—and so we met. Thank heaven!" And she
embraced me, and kissed me, and said:

"You're the same as a dear brother to me."

I say:

"And you're the same as a dear sister to me"—and I'm so moved
that tears come to my eyes.

And she weeps and says:

"I know, Ivan Severyanych, I know and understand it all; you're
the only one who loved me, dear friend of my heart, my gentle one.
Prove to me now your final love, do what I ask of you in this terrible
hour."

"Tell me what you want," I say.

"No," she says, "first swear by the most dread thing in the world that you'll do what I'm going to ask."

I swore by the salvation of my soul, but she says:

"That's not enough: you'll break it for my sake. No," she says, "swear by something more dreadful."

"Well," I say, "I can't think of anything more dreadful than that."

"Well," she says, "I've thought of it for you. Quickly repeat after me, and don't hesitate."

I promised, fool that I was, and she says:

"Damn my soul the same as you've damned your own if you don't obey me."

"Very well," I say—and I damned her soul.

"Well, now listen," she says. "You must quickly become the savior of my soul. I have no strength left to live like this and suffer, seeing his betrayal and his outrages against me. If I live a day longer, I'll settle it for *him* and for *her,* but if I take pity on them and settle it for myself, I'll destroy my poor soul forever . . . Take pity on me, my own, my darling brother: strike me once through the heart with a knife."

I turned aside, made a cross over her, and backed away, but she embraced my knees, weeping, bowing at my feet, and pleading:

"You'll live, you'll pray to God for my soul and for your own, don't be the ruin of me, don't make me raise my hand against myself . . . W—w—well? . . ."

Ivan Severyanych frowned dreadfully and, chewing his mustaches, breathed out as if from the depths of his heaving breast.

She took the knife from my pocket . . . opened it . . . straightened out the blade . . . and put it into my hand . . . And she . . . began pouring out such talk, I couldn't stand it . . .

"If you don't kill me," she says, "I'll become a shameful woman, and that will be my revenge on all of you."

I started trembling all over, and told her to pray, and didn't stab her, but just pushed her over the steep riverbank . . .

.   .   .

All of us, on hearing this latest confession from Ivan Severyanych, began for the first time to doubt the truthfulness of his story and kept silent for a rather long while, but, finally, someone cleared his throat and said:

"Did she drown?"

"She went under," replied Ivan Severyanych.

"And how was it for you after that?"

"What do you mean?"

"You must have suffered?"

"Of course, sir."

XIX

I ran away from that place, beside myself, and only remember that somebody seemed to be pursuing me, somebody terribly big and tall, and shameless, naked, and his body was all black, and his head was small, and he was all overgrown with hair, and I figured that if it wasn't Cain, it was the demon of destruction himself, and I kept trying to run from him and called out to my guardian angel. I came to my senses somewhere on a high road under a bush of broom. And the day was autumnal, dry, the sun was shining, but it was cold, and there was dust in the wind, and yellow leaves were whirling; and I didn't know what time it was, or what place it was, or where the road led, and there was nothing in my soul, no feeling, no notion of what I should do; and I could think of only one thing, that Grusha's soul is lost now, and it's my duty to suffer for her and deliver her from hell. But how to do it—I don't know and I'm in anguish over it, and then something touches my shoulder: I look—a twig has fallen from the broom and goes swirling, swirling into the distance, and suddenly it's Grusha walking, only small, no more than six or seven years old, and with little wings on her shoulders. But as soon as I notice her, she flies away from me like a shot, and only dust and dry leaves billow up behind her.

I thought: that must surely be her soul following me; she's probably beckoning to me and showing me the way. And I set off. All day I walked, not knowing where myself, and I became unbearably tired, and suddenly people overtook me, an old man and woman in a cart and pair, and they say:

"Get in, poor man, you can ride with us."

I get in. They drive, and they grieve:

"Woe to us," they say, "our son's being taken as a soldier, and we have no money, we can't pay to replace him."

I felt sorry for the old people and said:

"I'd go for you just like that, without pay, but I have no papers." They say:

"That's a trifle: leave it to us; you only have to give our son's name, Pyotr Serdyukov."

"Well," I reply, "it's all the same to me: I'll pray to my saint, John the Baptist, and call myself anything you like."

That was the end of it, and they took me to another town and handed me over as a recruit instead of their son, and gave me twenty-five roubles in cash for the road, and promised their help as long as they lived. The money I took from them, the twenty-five roubles, I placed with a poor monastery, as a contribution for Grusha's soul, and I started asking my superiors to send me to the Caucasus, where I could die quickly for the faith. So they did, and I spent more than fifteen years in the Caucasus and never revealed my real name or condition to anyone, and was always called Pyotr Serdyukov, and only on St. John's day I prayed for myself through my saint, the Baptist. And I forgot about my former existence and condition, and was serving out my last year that way, when suddenly, right on St. John's day, we were pursuing the Tartars, who had done some nastiness and withdrawn across the Koysa River. There were several Koysas in those parts: the one that flows through Andia, and is called the Andian Koysa, another through Avaria, called the Avarian Koysa, and there's also the Korikumuiskian and the Kuzikumuiskian, and they all flow together, and at the confluence the Sulak River begins. But each of them is swift and cold, especially the Andian, which the Tartars had crossed. We killed countless numbers of those Tartars, but the ones who crossed the Koysa sat behind the rocks on the other bank and kept firing at us the moment we showed ourselves. But they fired so skillfully that they never wasted a shot, but saved their powder for doing sure harm, because they knew we had much more ammunition than they had, and so they caused us real harm, because though we all stood in full view of them, the rogues never just popped off at us. Our colonel was a man of valiant soul and liked to imitate Suvorov,[36] saying "Merciful God" all the time and giving us courage by his example. So here, too, he sat down on the bank, took his boots off, put his legs up to the knees into that terribly cold water, and boasted:

"Merciful God, how warm the water is: just like your fresh-drawn milk in the bucket. Which of you, my benefactors, is willing to swim to the other side with a cable, so we can throw a bridge across?"

The colonel sat and gibble-gabbled with us like that, and on the other shore the Tartars put two gun barrels through a crack, but didn't shoot. But as soon as two willing soldiers volunteered and started swimming, flames flashed, and both soldiers sank into the Koysa. We pulled out the cable, sent two more, and started showering bullets on the stones where the Tartars were hiding, but couldn't do them any harm, because our bullets hit the stones, but they, the cursed ones, spat fire at the swimmers, the water clouded with blood, and again the two soldiers plunged down. A third pair went after them, but before they reached the middle of the Koysa, the Tartars sank them, too. After the third pair, there was a lack of volunteers, because it was obvious that this wasn't war, but simple murder. Yet it was necessary to punish the villains. The colonel says:

"Listen, my benefactors. Isn't there someone among you who has a mortal sin on his soul? Merciful God, how good it would be for him now to wash his iniquity away with his own blood."

And I think:

"Why wait for a better occasion than this to end my life? Lord, bless my hour!"—and I stepped forward, undressed, recited the "Our Father," bowed in all directions before my superior and my comrades, and said to myself: "Well, Grusha, my adopted sister, accept the blood I give for you!"—and with that I took a thin string in my mouth, the other end of which was tied to the cable, made a run to the bank, and dove into the water.

The water was awfully cold: I even got stitches in my armpits, and my chest went numb, cramps seized my legs, but I kept swimming . . . Above me flew our bullets, and around me Tartar bullets smacked into the water without touching me, and I didn't know if I was wounded or not, but I did reach the bank . . . There the Tartars could no longer hit me, because I stood just under the ridge, and in order to shoot at me they would have had to lean out over it, and our men were raining bullets on them like sand from the other bank. So I stood under the rocks and pulled the cable, and pulled it all the way, and the bridge got thrown across, and suddenly our men are coming, and I go on standing there as if taken out of myself, I don't understand anything, because I'm thinking: did anybody else see what I saw? Because as I was swimming I saw Grusha flying over me, and she was like a girl of about sixteen, and her wings were enormous now, bright, stretched across the whole river, and she shielded me with them . . . However, I see nobody says a word about it: well, I think, I'll have to tell it myself. So when the colonel started embracing me, and kissing me, and praising me, saying:

"Oh, merciful God, what a fine fellow you are, Pyotr Serdyukov!"

I replied:

"I'm no fine fellow, Your Excellency, but a great sinner, and neither the earth nor the water wants to take me."

He asks:

"What is your sin?"

And I reply:

"In my time, I've been the ruin of many innocent souls"—and that night in the tent I told him all that I've just told you.

He listened, listened, then pondered, and said:

"Merciful God, you've been through a lot, but above all, brother, whether you like it or not, you must be made an officer. I'll send in a request for it."

I say:

"As you please, but also send to find out whether it's true, as I've testified, that I killed the Gypsy girl."

"Very well," he says, "I'll ask about that, too."

And he did, but the paper went around and around and came back with wrong information. It said there had never been such an incident with any Gypsy girl, and Ivan Severyanovich, though he had existed and had served the prince, had bought himself out and was freed in absentia, and after that had died in the house of the crown peasants, the Serdyukovs.[37]

Well, what more could I do here? How could I prove my guilt?

But the colonel says:

"Don't you dare to lie about yourself anymore, brother: when you swam across the Koysa, your mind got a bit addled from the cold water and the fear, and I," he says, "am very glad that what you accused yourself of is all not true. Now you'll be an officer, and, merciful God, that's a good thing."

Here I myself even got confused in my thoughts: had I really pushed Grusha into the water, or had I imagined it all so intensely then out of my terrible longing for her?

And they made me an officer for my bravery, only since I stood by my own truth, wanting to reveal my past life, they decided, so as to have no more bother from me about that, to award me the St. George Cross and retire me.

"Congratulations," the colonel said, "you're a nobleman now and can go into government service. Merciful God, how peaceful!" And he gave me a letter to some big personage in Petersburg. "Go," he said. "He'll be the making of your career and well-being." With that letter I made my way to Petersburg, but I had no luck with a career.

"Why is that?"

"I was without a post for a very long time, and then I landed on theta, and that made everything worse."

"On *theta*? What does that mean?"

"That patron I'd been sent to about a career appointed me as a consultant in the address bureau, where each consultant is responsible for a single letter. Some letters are very good, like, for instance, B, or P, or S. Many last names begin with them, and that brings the consultant income. But I was put in charge of Θ. It's the most insignificant letter, very few names begin with it, and even those that should belong to it all deviously shirk it: as soon as anybody wants to ennoble himself a bit, he highhandedly puts F in place of Θ. You search and search for him under Θ, only it's wasted work, he's registered himself under F. There's no use at all, yet you sit there. Well, I saw things were bad, and out of old habit I tried to get myself hired as a coachman, but nobody would take me; they said: 'You're a noble officer, and with a decoration, it's improper to yell at you or hit you . . .' I was fit to hang myself, but, thank God, even in my despair I didn't let myself go that far, and so as not to perish from hunger, I up and became an actor."

"What sort of actor were you?"

"I played roles."

"In what theater?"

"In a show-booth on Admiralty Square.[38] They don't scorn the nobility, they take everybody: there are officers, and clerks, and students, and especially many scribes from the Senate."

"And did you like that life?"

"No, sir."

"Why not?"

"For one thing, the memorizing and rehearsals all take place during Holy Week or just before Lent, when 'Open to me the doors of repentance' is sung in church—and, for another, my role was very difficult."

"What was it?"

"I played the devil."

"Why was that especially difficult?"

"I'll tell you, sir: in both acts I had to dance and turn somersaults, and turning somersaults was awfully uncomfortable, because I was sewn into the shaggy skin of a hoary billy goat, fur side out, and I had a long tail strung on a wire, which was constantly getting tangled between my legs, and the horns on my head kept catching on everything, and I was no longer as young as before and had no lightness; and then it was specified that I was to be beaten all through the performance. That was terribly annoying. Granted, the sticks were hollow, made of canvas, and with flakes inside, but even so it was terribly boring to endure it, because they keep slapping you and slapping you, and some of them, whether because of the cold or just for the fun of it, manage to hit you quite painfully. Especially the Senate scribes, who have experience at it and act together: they stand up for each other, and when a military man comes along, they annoy him terribly, and it all goes on for a long time, because they start beating before the whole public at noontime, when the police flag is raised, and go on beating till night falls, and each of them, to please the public, tries to produce a louder slap. Nothing pleasant about it. And on top of it all, I was involved in an unpleasantness there as a consequence, after which I had to give up my role."

"What happened to you?"

"I dragged a certain prince by the forelock."

"A prince?"

"Not a real prince, but a theatrical one: he was a collegiate secretary from the Senate, but he played a prince."

"Why did you give him a beating?"

"He deserved more than that, sir. He was a wicked jeerer and contriver, and kept contriving all sorts of pranks against everybody."

"And against you?"

"Against me, sir, he played many pranks: he ruined my costume; he would sneak up to me in the warming room, where we warmed ourselves by a coal fire and drank tea, and fasten my tail to my horns, or do some other stupid thing for the fun of it, and I wouldn't notice and would run out to the public like that, and the owner would get angry. For my own part I let it all go, but he suddenly started to offend one of the fairies. She was a young girl, from poor nobility; she played the goddess Fortuna for us and had to save that prince from my clutches. And her role was such that she had to go around in nothing but sparkling tulle with wings, and it was very cold, the poor girl's hands were completely blue and numb, and he badgered her, thrust himself at her, and in the apapheosis, when the three of us fell through the trapdoor, he kept pinching her. I felt very sorry for her, so I thrashed him."

"And how did it end?"

"With nothing. In the cellarage there were no witnesses, except for that same fairy, but our Senate boys rose up and refused to have me in the company; and since they were the foremost performers there, the owner threw me out to please them."

"What happened to you then?"

"I would have been left with no roof or food at all, but that noble fairy fed me, only I felt ashamed, because the poor girl had a hard enough time providing for herself, and I kept thinking how to resolve this situation. I didn't want to go back to the Θ, and, besides, another poor man was already sitting and suffering on it, so I up and went to the monastery."

"Only for that?"

"Why, what was I to do, sir? I had nowhere to go. And it's nice there."

"Have you come to like monastery life?"

"Very much, sir; I like it very much—it's peaceful there, just like in the regiment; there's a lot of similarity, everything's prepared for you: you're dressed, and shod, and fed, and the superiors keep an eye out and demand obedience."

"And isn't that obedience sometimes a burden to you?"

"Why should it be? The more obedient a man is, the more peacefully he lives, and in my particular obedience there's nothing offensive: I don't go to church services except when I want to, and I perform my duties as I'm accustomed to: if they say 'Hitch up, Father Ishmael' (I'm now called Ishmael)—I hitch up; and if they say: 'Father Ishmael, unhitch'—I undo the harness."

"Excuse us," we say, "so it turns out that in the monastery you're still . . . with the horses?"

"I'm a permanent coachman. In the monastery they don't worry about my officer's rank, because, though I've only taken the initial vows, I'm already a monk and equal to them all."

"Will you take your solemn vows soon?"

"I won't be taking that on, sir."

"Why not?"

"I just . . . don't consider myself worthy."

"Is that still because of old sins or errors?"

"Y-y-yes, sir. And generally, why should I? I'm very pleased with my obedience, and I live in peace."

"And have you told anyone your whole story before, as you've now told it to us?"

"Of course, sir, more than once, but to no avail, since there are no records . . . they don't believe me, as if I've brought a worldly lie into the monastery, and there I'm counted as a nobleman. But it's all the same how I live my life out: I'm getting old."

The story of the enchanted wanderer was obviously coming to an end; there remained only one thing we were curious about: what was it like in the monastery?

XX

Since our wanderer had sailed in his story to his life's last haven—the monastery—which, in his deepest belief, had been his destination from birth, and since everything there seemed favorable to him, one might think that Ivan Severyanych no longer ran into any adversities there. However, it turned out quite otherwise. One of our fellow travelers recalled that, according to everything told about them, monks constantly suffered very much from the devil, and he asked:

"Tell us, please, has the devil not tempted you in the monastery? They say he constantly tempts monks."

Ivan Severyanych cast a calm glance at the speaker from under his brows and replied:

"How could he not tempt me? Naturally, if Paul the Apostle himself didn't escape him and writes in his epistle that 'a messenger of Satan was given me in the flesh,'[39] how could I, a sinful and weak man, not suffer his torments?"

"What have you suffered from him?"

"Many things, sir."

"Of what sort?"

"All kinds of dirty tricks, and at first, before I overcame him, there were even temptations."

"But you also overcame *him*, the devil himself?"

"How could it be otherwise? That's the monastic calling. But I'll tell you in all conscience, I wouldn't have been able to do it myself, but one perfect elder taught me how, because he was experienced and could deal with any temptation. When I confessed to him that Grusha kept appearing to me, as alive as if the air around me was breathing nothing but her, he at once cast about in his mind and said:

"'In the apostle James it is told: "Resist the devil and he will flee from you"[40]—so resist.' And here he admonished me about what to do: 'If you feel your heart softening and remember her,' he says, 'you should understand that it is the messenger of Satan accosting you, and you should prepare at once to act against him. Kneel, first of all. Man's knees are the first instrument: as soon as you kneel, your soul at once soars up, and there, being thus elevated, you must bow down to the ground, as many times as you can, till you are exhausted, and wear yourself out with fasting, to mortify yourself, and when the devil sees you striving for a great deed, he will not endure it and will run away at once, for fear that with such a man his machinations will drive him still more directly to Christ, and he will think: "Better to leave him alone and not tempt him, perchance he will forget himself the sooner."' I started doing that, and indeed everything went away."

"Did you torment yourself like that for a long time before the messenger of Satan withdrew?"

"A long time, sir. And it was only by wearing him down that I got the better of such an enemy, because he's not afraid of anything else: to begin with, I made up to a thousand bows and didn't eat or drink water for four days, and then *he* realized that he wasn't up to vying with me, and he grew timid and weak. As soon as he saw me throw my pot of food out the window and take up my beads so as to count the bows, he understood that I wasn't joking and was setting out on my great deed, and he ran away. It's terrible how afraid he is of bringing a man to the joy of hope."

"All right, let's suppose . . . *he* . . . So you overcame him, but how much did you suffer from him yourself?"

"It's nothing, sir; what of it? I oppressed the oppressor, and didn't take any constraints on myself."

"And now you're completely rid of him?"

"Completely, sir."

"And he no longer appears to you at all?"

"He never comes anymore in the seductive form of a woman, and if he still shows himself now and then somewhere in a corner of the cell, it's in the most pitiful guise: he squeals like a little pig at his last gasp. I don't even torment the scoundrel now, I just cross him once and make a bow, and he stops grunting."

"Well, thank God you've dealt with it all like that."

"Yes, sir, I've overcome the temptations of the big devil, but I'll tell you—though it's against our rule—I'm more bothered by the nasty tricks of the little devils."

"So little devils pester you as well?"

"What else, sir? Granted they're of the most insignificant rank, but they constantly get at you . . ."

"What is it they do to you?"

"You see, they're children, and what's more, there are a great many of them there in hell, and since the grub's provided, they've got nothing to do, so they ask to learn how to cause trouble on earth, and they do mischief, and the more a man wants to stand firm, the more they vex him."

"What, for instance, do they . . . How can they vex you?"

"For instance, they put something in your way or under your feet, and you tip it over or break it, and somebody gets upset and angry, for them that's the foremost pleasure and fun. They clap their hands and run to their chief, saying: 'We, too, cause trouble, give us a kopeck for it.' That's why they do it . . . Children."

"Precisely how, for instance, did they manage to cause you trouble?"

"There was, for instance, this case with us, when a Jew hanged himself in the forest near the monastery, and the novices all started saying he was Judas, and that he went about the place sighing during the night, and there were many witnesses to it. I wasn't even distressed about him, because I thought: as if we don't have enough Jews left. Only one night I'm sleeping in the stable, and suddenly I hear somebody come up and stick his muzzle over the crossbar in the doorway and sigh. I say a prayer—no, he's still standing there. I make a cross at him: he goes on standing there and sighs again.

'What am I to do with you? I can't pray for you, because you're a Jew, and even if you weren't a Jew, I have no blessing to pray for suicides. Leave me, go away to the forest or the desert.' I laid that injunction on him, and he went away, and I fell asleep again, but the next night the blackguard came again and sighed again . . . disturbed my sleep, and that was it. I couldn't stand it! 'Pah, you lout,' I think, 'don't you have enough room in the forest or on the church porch, that you have to come bursting into my stable? Well, no help for it, I've clearly got to invent some good remedy against you.' The next day I took a clean piece of coal and traced a big cross on the door, and when night came, I lay down peacefully, thinking to myself: 'He won't come now,' but I had only just fallen asleep, and there he was again, standing there and sighing! 'Pah, you jailbird, what am I to do with you!' All that night he scared me like that, but in the morning, at the first sound of the bell for the liturgy, I quickly jumped up and ran to complain to the superior, and met the bell ringer, Brother Diomed, and he says:

"'Why are you so frightened?'

"I say:

"'Thus and so, I've been bothered all night, and I'm going to the superior.'

"And Brother Diomed replies:

"'Drop it, and don't go. The superior put leeches in his nose last night, and now he's *very angry* and won't be of any help to you in this matter, but, if you want, I can help you much better than he can.'

"I say:

"'It makes absolutely no difference to me: only be so good as to help me—for that I'll give you my old warm mittens, they'll be very good for ringing the bells in winter.'

"'All right,' he says.

"And I gave him the mittens, and he brought me an old church door from the belfry, on which the apostle Peter was painted with the keys to the kingdom of heaven in his hand.

"'These *keys*,' he says, 'are the most important thing: just close yourself behind this door, and nobody will get through it.'

"I all but bowed to his feet from joy, and I think: 'Rather than just closing myself behind the door and then removing it, I'd better attach it fundamentally, so that it will always be a protection for me,' and I hung it on very secure, strong hinges, and for more safety I also attached a heavy pulley to it with a cobblestone as counterweight, and I did it all quietly in one day, before evening, and when nighttime came, I went to bed at the proper hour and slept. But what would you think: I hear him breathing again! I simply can't believe my ears, it's impossible, but no: he's breathing. And not just that! That was nothing, that he was breathing, but he also pushed the door . . . My old door had a lock inside, but with this one, since I was relying more on its holiness, I didn't put a lock on it, because I had no time, and so he just pushes it, and more boldly each time, and finally I see something like a muzzle poking in, but then the door swung on the pulley and knocked him back with all its might . . . And he backed up, evidently scratched himself, waited a little, came even more boldly, and again the muzzle, but the pulley smacks him even harder . . . It must have been painful, he grew quiet and stopped pushing, and I fell asleep again, but only a short time went by, and I see the scoundrel is at it again, and with new artfulness. He doesn't butt straight on now, but gradually opens the door with his horns, brazenly pulls off the sheepskin jacket I've covered my head with, and licks me on the ear. I couldn't stand this insolence any longer: I reached under the bed, grabbed an axe, and bashed him with it. I heard him grunt and drop down on the spot. 'Well,' I think, 'serves you right'—but instead of him, in the morning, I look, and there's no Jew at all. Those scoundrels, those little devils, had put our monastery cow there for me instead of him."

"And you had wounded her?"

"I'd hacked her to death with the axe, sir! It caused a terrible stir in the monastery."

"And you probably got into trouble on account of it?"

"That I did, sir. The father superior said I'd imagined it all because I don't go to church enough, and he gave me a blessing that, once I was finished with the horses, I should always stand by the screen in front to light candles, but here those nasty little demons contrived things even better and thoroughly did me in. It was on the Wet Savior,[41] at the vigil, during the blessing of bread according to the rite, the father superior and a hieromonk were standing in the middle of the church, and one little old woman gave me a candle and said:

"'Put it before the icon of the feast, dearie.'"

"I went to the icon stand where the icon of the 'Savior on the Waters' lay, and was putting that candle in place, when another fell. I bent down to pick it up, started putting it back in place—and two more fell. I started replacing them—and four fell. I just shook my head: 'Well,' I think, 'that's bound to be my little imps vexing me again and tearing things out of my hands . . .' I bent down, quickly picked up the fallen candles, and on straightening up hit the back of my head against the candle stand . . . and the candles just came raining down. Well, here I got angry, and I knocked all the rest of the candles off with my hand. 'Why,' I think, 'if there's such insolence going on, I'd better just throw it all down myself.'"

"And what did you get for that?"

"They wanted to try me for it, but our recluse, the blind elder Sysoy, who lives with us in an underground hermitage, interceded for me.

"'What would you try him for,' he says, 'when it's Satan's servants who have confounded him?'

"The father superior heeded him and gave his blessing that I be put in an empty cellar without trial."

"How long did you spend in the cellar?"

"The father superior didn't give his blessing for a precise length of time, he simply said 'Let him sit there,' and I sat there all summer right up to the first frost."

"It must be supposed that the boredom and torment in the cellar were no less than on the steppe?"

"Ah, no, how can you compare them? Here the church bells could be heard, and comrades visited me. They came, stood over the pit, and we talked, and the father bursar ordered a millstone lowered to me on a rope, so that I could grind salt for the kitchen. There's no comparison with the steppe or anywhere else."

"And when did they take you out? Probably with the frost, because it got cold?"

"No, sir, it wasn't on account of the cold at all, but for a different reason: because I started to prophesy."

"To prophesy!?"

"Yes, sir, in the cellar I finally fell to pondering what an utterly worthless spirit I had, and how much I'd endured because of it, and without any improvement, and I sent a novice to a certain teaching elder, to inquire if I could ask God to give me a different, more appropriate spirit. And the elder ordered him to tell me: 'Let him pray as he should, and then expect what cannot be expected.'

"I did just that: three whole nights I spent on this instrument, my knees, in my pit, praying fervently to heaven, and I began to expect something else to be accomplished in my soul. And we had another monk, Geronty, he was very well read and had various books and newspapers, and once he gave me the life of St. Tikhon of Zadonsk[42] to read, and whenever he happened to pass by my pit, he'd throw me a newspaper he had under his cassock.

"'Read,' he says, 'and look for what's useful: that will be a diversion for you in your ditch.'

"In expectation of the impossible answer to my prayer, I meanwhile began to occupy myself with this reading: once I finished grinding all the salt it was my task to grind, I'd start reading, and first I read about St. Tikhon, how our most holy Lady and the holy apostles Peter and Paul visited him in his cell. It was written that St. Tikhon then started asking the Mother of God to prolong peace on earth, and the apostle Paul answered him loudly about the sign of the cessation of peace: 'When everyone talks of peace and stability,' he says, 'then suddenly will the all-destroyer come upon them.' And I thought a long time about these apostolic words, and at first I couldn't understand: why had the saint received these words of revelation from the apostle? Finally I read in the newspapers that at home and in foreign lands tireless voices were constantly proclaiming universal peace. And here my prayer was answered, and all at once I understood that the saying, 'If they talk of peace, suddenly will the all-destroyer come upon them,' was coming true, and I was filled with fear for our Russian people and began to pray and with tears exhorted all those who came to my pit to pray for the subjugation under the feet of our tsar of all enemies and adversaries, for the all-destroyer was near. And I was granted tears in wondrous abundance! . . . I kept weeping over our native land. They reported to the father superior that 'our Ishmael in his cellar has started weeping a lot and prophesying war.' For that the father superior gave me a blessing to be transferred to the empty cottage in the kitchen garden and given the icon 'Blessed Silence,' which shows the Savior with folded wings, in the guise of an angel, but with the Sabaoth's eight-pointed halo, and his arms crossed meekly on his breast. And I was told to bow down before this icon every day, until the prophesying spirit in me fell silent. So I was locked up with this icon, and remained locked up there till spring and stayed in that cottage and kept praying to the 'Blessed Silence,' but as soon as I caught sight of a man, the spirit rose up in me again and I spoke. At that time the superior sent a doctor to me to see if my wits were addled. The doctor sat in my cottage for a long time, listened, like you, to my whole story, and spat:

"'What a drum you are, brother,' he says. 'They beat and beat on you, and still can't beat you down.'

"I say:

"'What to do? I suppose it's got to be so.'

"And he, having heard it all, says to the superior:

"'I can't figure him out. Is he simply a good soul, or has he gone mad, or is he a true soothsayer? That,' he says, 'is your department, I'm not versed in it, but my opinion is: chase him somewhere far away to get some air, he may have sat too long in one place.'

"So they released me, and now I have a blessing to go to Solovki and pray to Zosima and Sabbatius, and I'm on my way there.[43] I've been all over, but them I haven't seen, and I want to bow down to them before I die."

"Why 'before I die'? Are you ill?"

"No, sir, I'm not. It's still on this same chance that we'll soon have to go to war."

"Sorry, but it seems you're talking about war again?"

"Yes, sir."

"So the 'Blessed Silence' didn't help you?"

"That's not for me to know, sir. I try my best to keep silent, but the spirit wins out."

"What does he say?"

"He keeps exhorting me to 'take up arms.'"

"Are you prepared to go to war yourself?"

"What else, sir? Certainly: I want very much to die for my people."

"So you mean to go to war in your cowl and cassock?"

"No, sir, I'll take the cowl off and put on a uniform."

Having said that, the enchanted wanderer seemed to feel prophetic inspiration coming upon him anew and lapsed into quiet concentration, which none of his interlocutors ventured to interrupt with any new question. And what more could they have asked him? He had divulged the story of his past with all the candor of his simple soul, and his predictions remained in the hands of Him who conceals their destinies from the wise and prudent and only sometimes reveals them unto babes.

Singlemind

I

during the reign of Catherine II,[1] to a certain couple of the clerkly sort by the name of Ryzhov, a son was born named Alexashka. This family lived in Soligalich, one of the chief towns of Kostroma province, located on the rivers Kostroma and Svetitsa. Prince Gagarin's dictionary[2] mentions it as having seven stone churches, two religious schools and one secular, seven factories and mills, thirty-seven shops, three taverns, two pot-houses, and 3,665 inhabitants of both sexes. The town had two annual fairs and weekly markets; besides that, there is mention of "a rather brisk trade in lime and tar." In our hero's lifetime there was also a saltworks.

All this must be known in order to form an idea of how the small-time hero of our story, Alexashka, or, later, Alexander Afanasyevich Ryzhov, known around town as "Singlemind," could and actually did live.

Alexashka's parents owned their own house—one of those little houses which in that forest area were *worth nothing*, but, anyhow, provided a roof. Apart from Alexashka, the clerk Ryzhov had no other children, or at least I was told nothing about them.

The clerk died soon after the birth of this son and left his wife and son with nothing except that little house, which, as we said, was "worth nothing." But the clerk's widow herself was worth a lot: she was one of those Russian women who "in trouble helps and does not fear, stops a horse that gallops off, boldly enters a hut on fire"[3]—a simple, sensible, sober-minded Russian woman, strong of body, valiant of soul, and with a tender capacity for ardent and faithful love.

When she was widowed, there were still pleasing qualities in her, suitable for an unpretentious everyday life, and people sent matchmakers to her, but she declined any new matrimony and busied herself with the baking of savory pies. On non-fast days her pies were stuffed with cottage cheese or liver, on fast days with kasha or peas; the widow carried them on trays to the town square and sold them for five copper kopecks apiece. On the earnings from her pie production she fed herself and her son, whom she sent to a "tutoress" for lessons; the tutoress taught Alexashka what she knew herself. Further, more serious lessons were taught him by a scribe with a braid and a leather pouch in which he kept snuff for a known use without any snuffbox.

The scribe, having "taught up" Alexashka, took a pot of kasha for his labors, and with that the widow's son went among people to earn his keep and all the worldly blessings allotted to him.

Alexashka was then fourteen, and at that age he can be introduced to the reader.

The young Ryzhov took after his mother's kind: he was tall, broad-shouldered—almost an athlete, of boundless strength and indestructible health. In his adolescent years he was already among the foremost strongmen, and so successfully took the lead in the "wall" during fistfights that whichever side Alexashka Ryzhov was on was considered invincible. He was capable and hardworking. The scribe's schooling had given him an excellent, rounded, clear, beautiful handwriting, in which he wrote a multitude of memorial notices for old women[4] and with that commenced his self-subsistence. But more important were the qualities given him by his mother, whose living example imparted a strict and sober disposition to his healthy soul, dwelling in a strong and healthy body. He was moderate in everything, like his mother, and never resorted to any outside help.

At the age of fourteen he already considered it a sin to eat his mother's bread; memorial notices brought in little, and besides, this income, dependent on chance, was not steady; Ryzhov had an inborn aversion to trade, and he did not want to leave Soligalich, so as not to part from his mother, whom he loved very much. And therefore he had to provide himself with an occupation here, and provide it he did.

At that time permanent postal communication was only beginning to take shape in Russia: weekly runners were established between neighboring towns, who *carried* a bag of mail. This was known as the foot mail. The pay fixed for this job was not big: around a rouble and a half a month, "on your own grub and with your own boots." But those for whom even such maintenance was attractive hesitated to take up carrying mail, because for the sensitive Christian conscience of Russian piety it seemed dubious: did such a futile undertaking as carrying paper not contain something heretical and contrary to true Christianity?

Anyone who happened to hear of it pondered to himself whether he might destroy his soul that way and for an earthly recompense lose eternal life. And it was here that common compassion arranged things for Alexashka Ryzhov.

"He's an orphan," they said. "The Lord will forgive him more—especially on account of his young years. If while he's carrying he gets mauled to death on the road by a bear or a wolf, and he appears at the Judgment, he'll answer just one thing: 'Lord, I didn't understand,' and that's all. At his age no more could be asked of him. And if he stays whole and in time grows up, he can perfectly well go to a monastery and most excellently pray it away, with no expenses for candles or incense. What better can be expected for his orphanhood?"

Alexashka himself, whom this concerned most of all, was on good terms with the world and had no bone to pick with it: with a bold hand he hoisted the mail bag, slung it over his shoulder, and began carrying it from Soligalich to Chukhloma and back. Working in the foot mail was perfectly suited to his taste and to his nature: he walked alone through forests, fields, and swamps, and thought to himself his orphan's thoughts, as they composed themselves in him under the vivid impression of everything he met, saw, and heard. In such circumstances a poet the likes of Burns or Koltsov[5] might have come of him, but Alexashka Ryzhov was of a different stamp—not poetical but philosophical—and all that came of him was a remarkably odd "Singlemind." Neither the length of the tiring way, nor the heat, nor the cold, nor wind or rain frightened him;[6] the mail bag was so negligible for his powerful back that, besides that bag, he always carried another gray canvas bag with him, in which lay a thick book of his, which had an irresistible influence on him.

This book was the Bible.

II

It is not known to me how many years he performed his job in the foot mail, constantly toting his bag and Bible, but it seems it was a long time and ended when the foot mail was replaced by horse mail, and Ryzhov was "upped in rank." After these two important events in our hero's life, a great change took place in his destiny: an eager walker with the mail, he had no wish to ride with it and started looking for another job—again nowhere else but there in Soligalich, so as not to part from his mother, who by then had become old and, with dimming eyesight, now baked worse pies than before.

Judging by the fact that promotions for low-ranking postal work did not come along very often—for instance, once in twelve years—it must be thought that Ryzhov was by then about twenty-six or even a little more, and in all that time he had only walked back and forth between Soligalich and Chukhloma, and, while walking or resting, had read nothing but his Bible in its well-worn binding. He read it to his heart's content and acquired a great and firm knowledge of it, which laid the foundation for all his subsequent original life, when he started to philosophize and to apply his biblical views in practice.

Of course, there was considerable originality in all this. For instance, Ryzhov knew by heart whole writings by many of the prophets and especially loved Isaiah, whose vast knowledge of God answered to his own state of soul and made up all his catechesis and all his theology.

An elderly man, who in the time of his youth had known the eighty-five-year-old Ryzhov, when he was already famous and had earned the name of "Singlemind," told me how the old man recalled some "oak tree in the swamp," where he had especially liked to rest and "cry out to the wind."

"I'd stand," he said, "and howl into the air:

"'The ox knoweth his owner, and the ass his master's crib, but my people doth not consider. A seed of evildoers, children that are corruptors! Why should ye be stricken any more? ye will revolt more and more: the whole head is sick, and the whole heart faint. To what purpose is the multitude of your sacrifices unto me? I delight not in the blood of bullocks, or of lambs, or of he goats. When ye come to appear before me, bring no vain oblations; incense is an abomination unto me; the new moons and sabbaths, the calling of assemblies, I cannot away with; it is iniquity, even the solemn meeting. Your new moons and your appointed feasts my soul hateth. And when ye spread forth your hands, I will hide mine eyes from you: yea, when ye make many prayers, I will not hear. Wash you; put away the evil of your doings; learn to do well. Come now, and let us reason together: though your sins be as scarlet, they shall be as white as snow. Thy princes are rebellious, and companions unto thieves: every one loveth gifts, and followeth after rewards. Therefore saith the Lord, the Lord of hosts: woe to the mighty—mine enemies will not stand against my fury.' "[7]

And the orphan boy cried out this "woe, woe to the mighty" over the deserted swamp, and he imagined to himself that the wind would take Isaiah's words and carry them to where the "dry bones" of Ezekiel's vision lie without stirring;[8] living flesh does not grow on them, and the decayed heart does not come to life in their breast.

The oak and the reptiles of the swamp listened to him, while he himself became half mystic, half agitator in a biblical spirit—in his own words, "breathed out love and daring."

All this had ripened in him long ago, but it revealed itself in him when he obtained rank and started looking for another job, not over the swamp. Ryzhov's development was now completely finished, and the time for action was coming, in which he could apply the rules he had created for himself on a biblical ground.

Under the same oak, over the same swamp where Ryzhov had cried out in the words of Isaiah, "Woe to the mighty," he finally received the spirit which gave him the thought of becoming mighty himself, in order to shame the mightiest. And he accepted this consecration and carried it along all of his nearly hundred-year path till the grave, never once stumbling, never going lame either in the right knee, or in the left.

Enough examples await us further on of his astonishing strength, stifled in narrowness, and at the end of the story an unexpected act of daring fearlessness, which crowned him, like a knight, with a knightly reward.

III

In that far-off time which the story I am passing on about Ryzhov goes back to, the most important person in every small Russian town was the mayor. It has been said more than once and disputed by no one that, in the understanding of many Russian people, every mayor was "the third person of the state." From its primary source—the monarch—state power in the popular notion ramifies like this: the first person in the state is the sovereign, who rules over the whole state; second after him is the governor, who rules over a province; and then, right after the governor, immediately follows the third—the mayor, who "sits over a town." There were no district police chiefs then, and therefore no opinion was offered about them in this division of powers. However, it remained that way later on as well: the police chief was a traveling man, and he whipped only country people, who then still had no independent notion of hierarchy, and no matter who whipped them, twitched their legs in the same way.

The introduction of new legal institutions, limiting the former theocratic omnipotence of local administrators, has spoiled all that, especially in the towns, where it has contributed significantly to the decline not only of the mayor's, but even of the governor's prestige, which can no longer be raised to its former heights—at least for the mayor, whose high authority has been replaced by innovation.

But back then, when "Singlemind" pondered and decided his fate, all this was still in its well-established order. Governors sat in their centers like little kings: access to them was difficult, and appearing before them was "attended by fear"; they aimed at being rude to everybody, everybody bowed down before them, and some, in their zeal, even bowed very low; archpriests "came forth to meet" them with crosses and holy water at the entrances to churches, and the second-rate nobility honored them with expressions of base fawning and barely dared, in the persons of a few of their chosen representatives, to ask them to "stand godfather at the font." And even when they agreed to condescend to such a favor, they behaved in kingly fashion: they did not come to the baptism themselves, but in their place sent special envoys or adjutants, who drove up with the "trappings" and accepted the honor "in the person of the sender." Back then everything was majestic, dignified, and earnest, as befitted that good and earnest time, often contrasted with our present time, which is neither good nor earnest.

Ryzhov came upon an excellent line of approach to the source of local power and, without leaving his native Soligalich, of stepping onto the fourth rung in the state: the old police constable died in Soligalich, and Ryzhov thought of asking for his post.

IV

The post of police constable, though not a very high one, despite the fact that it constituted the first rung below the mayor, was nevertheless rather advantageous, if only the man who filled it was good at filching a piece of firewood, a couple of turnips, or a head of cabbage from every cart; but if he wasn't, things were bad for him, because the official salary for this fourth officer of the state amounted to ten roubles a month in banknotes, which is about two roubles and eighty-five kopecks by today's rates. On this the fourth person of the state was supposed to maintain himself and his family decently, but since that was impossible, every constable "tacked on" from those who turned to him for some "matter of concern." Without this "tacking on" it was impossible to get by, and even the Voltaireans themselves did not rise up against it.[9] No one ever thought of a "non-taking" constable, and therefore, since all constables took, Ryzhov also had to take. The authorities themselves could not wish for or tolerate his spoiling of the official line. Of that there could be no doubt, and there could be no talk of it.

The mayor, to whom Ryzhov had applied for the post of constable, naturally did not ask himself any questions about his ability to take bribes. He probably thought that Ryzhov would be like all the others, and therefore there were no special agreements between them on that score. The mayor took into consideration only his immense height, imposing figure, and the great fame he enjoyed for his strength and tirelessness in walking, which Ryzhov had demonstrated by his carrying the mail on foot. These were all qualities very suitable for the police work Ryzhov was seeking—and he was made the Soligalich constable, while his mother went on baking and selling her pies at that same market where her son was supposed to establish and maintain good order: to watch over the correct weight and the full, shaken-down measure.

The mayor made him only one admonition:

"Beat without crippling and don't poke your fingers into matters of my concern."

Ryzhov promised to fulfill that and went into action, but soon began to awaken strange doubts about himself, which started to worry the third person of the state, and put the former Alexashka himself, now Alexander Afanasyevich, through some quite painful ordeals.

From his first day on the job, Ryzhov proved zealous and correct in his duties: coming to the market, he positioned the carts and seated the women with their pies differently, not putting his mother in the best place. Some drunken muzhiks he brought to reason, and some he taught with his powerful hand, but with pleasantness, as nicely as if he were doing them a great favor, and he took nothing for the lesson. On that same day he also turned down an offering from the cabbage women, who came begging to him on a matter of concern, and declared further that on matters of concern there was nothing owing to him from anybody, because for all his matters of concern "the tsar pays him a salary, and God forbids the taking of bribes."

Ryzhov spent the day well, and the night better still: he patrolled the whole town, and whoever he caught out walking at a late hour, he questioned: where from, where to, and on what necessity? He had a talk with a nice man, even accompanied him and gave him advice, but he boxed the ears of one or two drunkards, and locked up a sentry's wife who went around putting spells on cows, and in the morning he appeared before the mayor to report that in the sentries he saw nothing but a hindrance to his work.

"They spend their time in idleness," he said, "and needlessly go about half asleep, pestering people on matters of concern and corrupting themselves. Better remove them from lazy emptiness and send them to Your Excellency to weed the kitchen-garden beds, and I'll manage everything alone."

The mayor had no objections to that, and it was quite to the liking of his thrifty wife; only the sentries might not like it, and it was not in accordance with the law; but who thought of asking the sentries, and as for the law . . . the mayor judged that in a Russian way: "The law is like a horse: wherever you want to go, you turn its head so." But Alexander Afanasyevich placed highest of all the law:

"In the sweat of thy face shalt thou eat bread,"[10] and from that law it followed that any superfluous "hangers-on" were an unnecessary burden, which had to be unhung and rehung to some other real, "sweaty" work.

And the matter was arranged as Ryzhov indicated, and it was pleasing in the eyes of the ruler and the people, and it turned the hearts of the grateful populace towards Ryzhov. And Ryzhov himself went about town during the day, went about alone at night, and little by little his good managerial supervision began to be felt everywhere, and again this was pleasing in the eyes of all. In short, everything went well and promised imperturbable peace, but that was just the trouble: if folks don't heat up, generals don't eat up—there was nothing of concern from anywhere, and apart from weeding the kitchen garden, there was no profit for the ruler, neither big, nor medium, nor small.

The mayor became roused in spirit. He looked into the matter, saw that it was impossible like that, and raised up a bitter persecution against Ryzhov.

He asked the archpriest to find out whether there was not in the "concernless" Ryzhov some sort of unorthodoxy, but the archpriest replied that he did not perceive any obvious unorthodoxy in Ryzhov, but noticed only a certain pride, proceeding, of course, from the fact that his mother baked pies and gave some to him.

"I advise putting a stop to this trade, improper for her now on account of her son, and his boundless pride will then be done away with, and he will become concerned."

"I'll put a stop to it," replied the mayor, and he told Ryzhov: "It's not fitting for your mother to sit in the market."

"Very well," Ryzhov replied, and he took his mother with her trays from the market, but kept up the same reprehensible behavior as before—he did not become concerned.

Then the archpriest pointed out that Ryzhov had not provided himself with a dress uniform, and on Easter Sunday, having stingily congratulated only his near and dear ones, had not appeared with his congratulations before any of the distinguished citizens, for which, however, they bore him no grudge.

The two things turned out to be dependent on each other. Ryzhov had not taken up a holiday collection, and therefore had no money for a uniform, but the uniform was necessary and the previous constable had had one. Everyone had seen him in a tunic with a collar, breeches, and boots with tassels, but this one remained the same as when he had gone around with the mail, in a beshmet of striped ticking with hooks,[11] yellow nankeen trousers, and a simple peasant hat, and for winter he had a raw sheepskin coat, and he had acquired nothing else, and could not acquire anything on a monthly salary of two roubles and eighty-seven kopecks, which he lived on, serving faithfully and truly.

Besides that, an incident occurred that required money: Ryzhov's mother died, having been left with nothing to do on earth once she could no longer sell pies on it.

Alexander Afanasyevich gave her, in the general opinion, a "niggardly" funeral, and thereby showed his lack of love. He paid the clergy a little for it, but the pie baker had no pies baked at her funeral, and the forty-day prayers were not ordered.

A heretic! And it was the more plausible in that, though the mayor did not trust him and the archpriest had doubts about him, both the mayor's wife and the priest's wife stood like a rock for him—the first for driving the sentries to her kitchen garden, and the second for some mysterious reason that lay in her "resistant character."

In these persons Alexander Afanasyevich had his protectors. The mayor's wife herself sent him two measures of potatoes from the earth's yield, but he, without untying the sacks, brought the potatoes back on his shoulders and said briefly:

"I thank you for the intention, but I don't accept gifts."

Then the priest's wife, a nervous woman, offered him two calico shirtfronts of her own making from ancient times, when the archpriest was still a layman, but the odd fellow did not take them either.

"It's forbidden to take gifts," he said, "and besides, since I dress simply, I find no use for such finery."

And here the priest's wife spoke a maliciously provocative word to her husband:

"He's the one who ought to stand at the altar," she said, "and not you clerical finaglers."

The archpriest was angry. He told his wife to be quiet, but he himself went on lying there and thinking:

"This is some Masonic novelty, and if I track it down and uncover it, I may get some big distinction and may even be transferred to Petersburg."

So he raved about it and in his raving made up a plan of how to lay bare Ryzhov's conscience even to the point of separating soul from body.

V

The Great Lent was approaching,[12] and the archpriest saw as in the palm of his hand how he was going to lay bare Ryzhov's soul to the point of separation, and would then know how to deal with him for his wicked deviation from the truths of Orthodoxy.

With that aim he openly advised the mayor to send the striped constable to him for confession in the very first week. He promised to examine his soul well and, frightening him with the wrath of God, to worm out of him all that he kept secret and hidden and why he shunned all matters of concern and did not accept gifts. And then he said: "By the sight of his conscience laid open by fear, we'll see what's to be done with him, and we'll put him through it, that the spirit may be saved."[13]

Having mentioned the words of St. Paul, the archpriest calmly began to wait, knowing that each seeks out his own in them.

The mayor also did his share.

"You and I, Alexander Afanasyevich, as prominent persons in town," he said, "must set folk a religious example and show respect for the Church."

Ryzhov replied that he agreed.

"Be so good, brother, as to prepare and go to confession."

"Agreed," said Ryzhov.

"And since we're both people in everybody's sight, we should also do that in everybody's sight, and not somehow in hiding. I go to our archpriest for confession—he's the most experienced of our clergy— you go to him, too."

"I'll go to the archpriest."

"Right. You go in the first week, and I'll go in the last—that's how we'll divide it up."

"I agree to that, too."

The archpriest thoroughly confessed Ryzhov and even boasted that he raked him over the coals, but he did not find any mortal sins in him.

"He confessed," he said, "to this and that and the other—he's not quite a saint—but his sins are all simple, human, and he has no especially ill thoughts against the authorities and isn't thinking of denouncing either you or me for 'matters of concern.' And that he 'doesn't accept gifts' comes from harmful fantasy alone."

"All the same, that means there's harmful fantasy in him. What does it consist in?"

"He's read up the Bible."

"What a fool thing to do!"

"Yes, he read it out of boredom and can't forget it."

"A real fool! Now what are we to do with him?"

"There's nothing we can do: he's already very far into it."

"Can it be he's got to Christ himself?"

"All of it, he's read all of it."

"So it's the kibosh!"

They felt sorry for Ryzhov and started being more charitable to him. All Orthodox people in Russia know that, if someone has read through the Bible and "gone as far as Christ," he cannot very well be expected to act reasonably; such people are rather like holy fools—they behave oddly, but harm nobody, and are not to be feared. However, so as to be more secure with regard to the strange correcting of Ryzhov on "matters of concern," the father archpriest offered the mayor a wise but cruel piece of advice: to get Alexander Afanasyevich married.

"For a married man," the archpriest expounded, "even if he has 'read as far as Christ,' it's hard to preserve his honesty: his wife will light a fire under him, and in one way or another will drive him until he yields to her and lets the whole Bible leave his head, and becomes amenable to gifts and devoted to the authorities."

This advice accorded with the mayor's thinking, and he gave orders to Alexander Afanasyevich that in one way or another he must marry without fail, because bachelors are unreliable in political positions.

"Say what you like, brother," he said, "but I find you good from all points of view except one, and from that one point of view you're unfit."

"Why so?"

"You're a bachelor."

"Where's the reproach in that?"

"The reproach is that you may do something treacherous and flee to another province. What is it to you now? Just grab your Bibbel and that's it."

"That's it."

"There's just what's untrustworthy."

"And is a married man more trustworthy?"

"No comparison. A married man," he says, "I can twist like a rope, and he'll suffer it all, because he's got his nestlings to tend to, and his woman to feel sorry for, but a bachelor's like a bird himself—it's impossible to trust him. So either you walk off, or you get married."

The enigmatic fellow, having heard this argument, was not put out in the least and replied:

"Well, marriage is a good thing, too, it's indicated by God: if need be, I'll get married."

"Only cut down a tree that suits you."

"Yes, one that suits me."

"And choose quickly."

"I've already chosen: I only have to go and see if anybody else has taken her."

The mayor laughed at him:

"Look at you," he said, "you little sinner—makes out like there's never been any sin on him, yet he's already spied out a wife for himself."

"Who hasn't got sin on him!" replied Alexander Afanasyevich. "The vessel's brimming with abomination, only I haven't asked her to be my bride yet, but I do indeed have my eye on her and ask permission to go and see what's what."

"Not a local girl, probably—is she from far away?"

"Not local and not from far away—she lives by the stream near the swamp."

The mayor laughed again, dismissed Ryzhov, and, intrigued, began to wait, wondering when the odd fellow would come back to him and what he would say.

VI

Ryzhov indeed cut down a tree that suited him: a week later he brought a wife to town—a big woman, white-skinned, ruddy-cheeked, with kindly brown eyes and submissiveness in every step and movement.

She was dressed in peasant clothes, and the two spouses walked one behind the other, carrying a yoke on their shoulders from which a decorated bast box containing a dowry hung on a canvas strap.

Veterans of the marketplace recognized this person at once as the daughter of old Kozlikha, who lived in a solitary hut by the stream beyond the swamp and passed for a wicked witch. Everyone thought that Ryzhov had taken the witch's wench to keep house for him.

That was partly true, only before bringing her home, Ryzhov had married her in church. Conjugal life cost him no more than bachelorhood; on the contrary, now it became even more profitable for him, because, having brought home a wife, he immediately dismissed the hired woman he had paid no less than a copper rouble a month. From then on the copper rouble remained in his pocket, and the house was better kept; his wife's strong hands were never idle: she spun and wove, and also turned out to be good at knitting stockings and growing vegetables. In short, his wife was a simple, capable peasant woman, faithful and submissive, with whom the biblical eccentric could live in a biblical way, and apart from what has been said, there is nothing to say about her.

Alexander Afanasyevich's treatment of his wife was most simple, but original: he addressed her informally, and she addressed him formally; he called her "woman," and she called him Alexander Afanasyevich; she served him, and he was her master; when he spoke to her, she replied—when he was silent, she did not dare ask. At the table, he sat and she served, but they shared a common bed, and that was probably the reason why their marriage bore fruit. There was just one fruit—an only son, whom the "woman" reared, and in whose education she did not interfere.

Whether the "woman" loved her biblical husband or not is not clear from anything in their relations, but that she was faithful to her husband was unquestionable. Besides that, she feared him as a person placed above her by divine law and having a divine right over her. That did not disturb her peaceful life. She was illiterate, and Alexander Afanasyevich did not wish to fill this gap in her education. They lived, naturally, a Spartan life, of the strictest moderation, but they did not consider it a misfortune; in that, perhaps, they were much helped by the fact that many others around them lived in no greater prosperity. They did not drink tea and kept none at home, and they ate meat only on days of major feasts—the rest of the time they lived on bread and vegetables, preserved or fresh from their kitchen garden, and most of all on mushrooms, which grew abundantly in their forested area. In summertime the "woman" picked these mushrooms in the forest herself and prepared them for keeping, but, to her regret, the only way of preparing them was by drying. There was nothing to salt them with. The expense for salt in the necessary amount for such a supply was not included in Ryzhov's calculations, and when the "woman" once prepared a small barrel of mushrooms with a little sack of salt given to her by a tax farmer, Alexander Afanasyevich, on learning of it, gave the "woman" a patriarchal beating and took her to the archpriest to have a penance laid on her for disobeying her husband's precepts; and he rolled the whole barrel of mushrooms to the tax farmer's yard with his own hands and told them to "take it wherever they liked," and he gave the tax farmer a reprimand.

Such was this odd fellow, of whom for all the length of his days there is also not much to say; he sat in his place, did his little job, which did not enjoy anyone's special sympathy, nor did he ever seek any special sympathy; the Soligalich ringleaders considered him "deranged by the Bible," and simple people judged that he was simply "this-that-and-the-other."

Which rather unclear definition had for them a clear and plain meaning.

Ryzhov did not care in the least what people thought of him: he served everyone honestly and did not play up to anyone in particular; in his thoughts he gave his accounting to the one he believed in immutably and firmly, calling him the author and master of all that exists. Ryzhov's pleasure consisted in fulfilling his duty, and his highest spiritual comfort in philosophizing about the highest questions of the spiritual world and about the reflection of the laws of that world in phenomena and in the destinies of particular persons and of entire kingdoms and peoples. Whether Ryzhov shared the common weakness of many self-taught men in considering himself more intelligent than anyone else is not known, but he was not proud, and he never thrust his beliefs and views on anyone or even shared them, but only wrote them into big blue-paged notebooks, which he filed under one cover with the significant inscription: *Singlemind*.

What was written in this whole enormous manuscript by the policeman-philosopher remained hidden, because at Alexander Afanasyevich's death his *Singlemind* perished, and no one can say much about it from memory. Only a bare two or three passages from the whole of *Singlemind* were shown by Ryzhov to an important person on an extraordinary occasion in his life, which we are now approaching. The rest of *Singlemind*'s pages, the existence of which almost all Soligalich knew about, were used to paper walls, or perhaps were even burned to avoid unpleasantness, because these writings contained much incoherent raving and religious fantasy, for which, in those times, both the author and his readers might have been sent to pray in the Solovetsky Monastery.[14]

The spirit of this manuscript became known with the following incident, so memorable in the annals of Soligalich.

VII

I cannot recall for certain and do not know where to find out in precisely what year Sergei Stepanovich Lanskoy, later a count and a well-known minister of the interior, was named governor of Kostroma.[15] This dignitary, according to the apt observation of a contemporary, "was of strong mind and haughty bearing," and this brief characterization is correct and perfectly sufficient for the notion our reader needs to have of him.

One may, it seems, add only that Lanskoy respected honesty and fairness in people and was kind himself, and he also loved Russia and the Russian man, but understood him in a lordly way, as an aristocrat, having a foreign view and a Western measure for everything.

The appointment of Lanskoy as governor of Kostroma occurred at the time of Alexander Afanasyevich Ryzhov's eccentric service as Soligalich's constable, and under certain peculiar circumstances besides.

On entering into his duties as governor, Sergei Stepanovich, following the example of many functionaries, first of all made a "clean sweep of the province," that is, threw out of office a great many negligent civil servants who abused their positions, among them the mayor of Soligalich, under whom Ryzhov was constable.

In throwing unsuitable persons out of office, the new governor did not rush to replace them with others, so as not to fall upon the same sort, and maybe on still worse. To select worthy people, he wanted to have a look around, or, as we now say in Russian, to "orient himself."

With that aim, the duties of the removed persons were entrusted temporarily to substitutes from among the junior officials, and the governor soon undertook a tour of the whole province, which trembled with a strange trembling at the mere rumors of his "haughty bearing."

Alexander Afanasyevich assumed the duties of mayor. What he did in this substitution that differed from the former "standing" order, I don't know; but, naturally, he did not take bribes as mayor, just as he had not taken bribes as constable. Ryzhov also did not change his manner of living or his relations with people—he did not even sit in the mayor's chair before the zertsalo,[16] but signed "for the mayor" seated at his ink-stained little desk by the front door. For this last obstinacy Ryzhov had an explanation, which was connected with the apotheosis of his life. After many years of service, just as in the first days of his constableship, Alexander Afanasyevich *had no uniform*, and he governed "for the mayor" wearing the same greasy and much-mended beshmet. And therefore, to all the appeals of the chief clerk that he take the mayor's seat, he replied:

"I can't: my garment betrays me as unfit for the wedding feast."[17]

This was all duly written down in his own hand in his *Singlemind*, with the addition that the chief clerk suggested that he "take the seat in his beshmet, but remove the eagle from the zertsalo." However, Alexander Afanasyevich "ignored this indecency" and went on sitting in the former place in his beshmet.

This non-uniformity did not interfere with the business of policing the town, but the question became completely different when news arrived of the coming of the "haughty bearing." In his quality as the town's mayor, Alexander Afanasyevich was supposed to meet the governor, receive him, and report to him on the welfare of Soligalich, and also to answer all the questions Lanskoy was going to ask him and introduce him to all the town's points of interest, from the cathedral to the prison, the vacant lots, the ravines, which nobody knew what to do with.

Ryzhov indeed had a problem: how was he to perform all that in his beshmet? But he did not worry about that in the least; instead all the others worried about it, because Ryzhov, by his unsightliness, might anger the "haughty bearing" from the first step. It did not occur to anyone that it was precisely Alexander Afanasyevich who was going to astonish and even *delight* the all-terrifying "haughty bearing" and even prophesy his promotion.

The generally conscientious Alexander Afanasyevich was not

embarrassed in the least by how he looked, and did not share the general bureaucratic fear at all, on account of which he was subject to disapproval and even hatred and fell in the opinion of his compatriots, but he fell in order to rise afterwards higher than all and leave behind him a heroic and almost legendary memory.

VIII

It is not superfluous to recall once again that, in those recent but deeply vanished times to which the story of Ryzhov dates, governors were not at all as in our evil days, when the grandeur of these dignitaries has fallen significantly, or, in the expression of a certain ecclesiastical chronicler, has "cruelly deteriorated." Back then governors traveled "fearsomely," and were received "tremblingly." Their progress was accomplished in a grandiose bustle, to which not only all the lesser principalities and powers,[18] but even the rabble and the four-footed brutes contributed. By the time of the governor's arrival, towns would have received an anointing with chalk, soot, and ochre; the tollgates would be newly adorned with the national motley of official tricolors; the sentries in their booths and the invalids would be admonished to "wax their heads and mustaches," the hospitals would set about intensifying the discharge of the "healthified." Everything to the ends of the earth took part in the general animation; peasant men and women were driven from their villages to the roadways, shifting about for months repairing swamped roads, log roads, and bridges; at the posting stations even special couriers and various lieutenants hurrying on countless official errands were detained. During such periods stationmasters revenged themselves on these restless people for their insufferable offenses and with steadfast inner firmness made them drag along on any old nags, because the good horses were "kept resting" for the governor. In short, no one could walk or drive anywhere without feeling with some one of his senses that in the nature of all things something extraordinary was going on. Thanks to that, back then, without any empty babble from the garrulous press, each person, old or young, knew that the one than whom there was none greater in the province was passing through, and on that occasion, each as he was able, they all expressed to their intimates their manifold feelings. But the most

exalted activity went on in the central nests of the district lordship—
in the court offices, where things began with the tedious and boring
checking of lists, and ended with the merry operation of dusting the
walls and scrubbing the floors. The floor scrubbing was something
like the classical orgies in the days of the grape harvest, when everything was intensely exultant, having only one concern: to live, before
the hour of death comes. Following a small convoy of crooked invalids, female prisoners, bored with a deadly boredom, were delivered
from jail to the offices, where, snatching at a brief moment of happiness, they enjoyed the captivating rights of their sex—to delight
the lot of mortals. The *décolletés* and *manches courtes*[*] with which
they set about their work had such an arousing effect on the young
clerks busy with their papers that the consequence in the jails, as is
known, was not infrequently the coming into the world of so-called
"floor-scrubbing children"—of unacknowledged but undoubtedly
noble origin.

At home during those same days dress boots were blackened,
breeches were whitened, and long-folded-away, moth-eaten tunics
were spruced up. This, too, enlivened the town. The tunics were
first *hung out* on a hot day in the sun, on lines stretched across the
yard, which attracted multitudes of the curious to every gate; then
the tunics were laid on pillows or felt and *beaten out* with rods; after
that they were *shaken out,* then *darned, ironed,* and, finally, *spread
out* on an armchair in a drawing room or some other reception room,
and at the conclusion of it all—in the final end, they were surrepti-
tiously sprinkled with Theophany water from holy bottles, which, if
kept near an icon in a wax-sealed vessel, does not go bad from one
year to the next, and does not lose a bit of the wonderworking power
imparted to it at the moment when the cross is immersed in it, to the
singing of "O, Lord, save Thy people and bless Thine inheritance."[19]

Stepping forth to meet the personages, the officials vested themselves in their besprinkled uniforms and, in their quality as the
Lord's inheritance, would be saved. Many reliable stories are told
about this, but given the present-day universal lack of faith and the
particularly Offenbachian mood[20] that reigns in the bureaucratic
world, all this has by now been discredited in the general opinion,
and, among many other things sanctified by time, is light-mindedly

---

[*] Low necklines and short sleeves. *Trans.*

called into question; but to our forefathers, who had genuine, firm faith, it was given according to their faith.

Waiting for the governor in those times was long and agonizing. There were as yet no railroads, with trains coming on schedule at an appointed hour, delivering the governor along with all other mortals, but a high road was specially prepared, and after that no one knew with certainty either the day or the hour when the dignitary would be pleased to appear. Therefore the weary waiting was prolonged and filled with a special, solemn anxiety, at the very zenith of which stood the guard on duty, who had to watch the high road from the tallest belfry in town. He was not supposed to doze off, protecting the town from an unexpected arrival, but of course it happened that he would doze and even sleep, and on such unfortunate occasions there would be various unpleasantnesses. Sometimes the negligent watchman rang the little bell when the governor was already at too close a distance, so that the officials did not all have time to uniform themselves and rush out, nor the archpriest to vest himself and come out with the cross, and sometimes the mayor even had no time to ride out to the town gates standing on a cart. To avoid this, the sentry was obliged to walk around the belfry and on each side make a bow in the corresponding direction.

This served the sentry as a diversion and the general public as a guarantee that the one keeping vigil over them was not sleeping or dozing. But this precaution did not always help; it would happen that the sentry mastered the ability of the albatross: he would sleep while walking and bowing, and, half-awake, would ring a false alarm, having taken a landowner's carriage for the governor's, and then a useless commotion would arise in town, ending with the officials un-uniforming themselves again and the mayor's troika being unharnessed, while the imprudent watchman would get a light or not so light whipping.

Suchlike difficulties occurred frequently and were not easy to overcome, and, besides, their whole weight lay chiefly on the mayor, who had to go galloping off to the meeting ahead of them all, was the first to take upon himself the superior's glares and growls, and then again, standing up, galloped ahead of the governor's carriage to the cathedral, where the fully vested archpriest, with the cross and a sprinkler in a bowl of holy water, was waiting by the porch. Here the mayor, unfailingly with his own hand, flipped down the governor's footboard and in that way, so to speak, with his own hand let the arriving exalted personage out of his traveling ark onto our native soil. Nowadays this is all no longer so, it has all been spoiled, and that not without the participation of the governors themselves, among whom there were those eager to "sell themselves short." Now they may even repent of it, but what's slipped away can't be brought back: no one flips down footboards for them except lackeys and policemen.

But the mayor of old fulfilled his duty unabashedly and served as a first touchstone for everyone; he was the first to find out whether the arriving governor was ferocious or benign. And, truth to tell, much depended on the mayor: he could spoil things straight off, because one awkwardness of any sort on his part could anger the governor and throw him into a rage; but with one nimble leap, turn, or other fitting caper he could also bring his excellency to a benign disposition.

Now every reader, even one ignorant of these patriarchal customs, can judge how natural was the anxiety of the Soligalich officialdom, who came to have as their representative such an original, awkward, and stubborn mayor as Ryzhov, who, besides all his inconvenient personal qualities, had a wardrobe consisting of nothing but a beshmet of striped ticking and a shaggy peasant hat.

These would be the first things to strike the eye of the "haughty bearing," of whom idle tongues had already brought the most terrible news to Soligalich . . . What good could come of it?

IX

Alexander Afanasyevich could indeed drive anyone you like to despair; he did not worry about anything, and, in waiting for the governor, behaved as if the impending terrible event did not concern him at all. He did not demolish a single fence of a single citizen, did not paint anything either with chalk or with ochre, and generally took no measures not only towards beautifying the town, but also towards changing his incongruous costume, and continued to go about in his beshmet. To all projects proposed to him, he replied:

"Folk mustn't be put to any loss: is the governor to lay waste the land? Let him pass through, and let the fence remain." The requests concerning his uniform Ryzhov parried by saying that he had no means, and, he said, "I appear in what I have: before God I'll stand completely naked. The point isn't in clothes, it's in reason and conscience—in clothes they find you, in thought they mind you."

Nobody hoped to out-stubborn Ryzhov, and yet it was very important, not so much for the stubborn Ryzhov, for whom it might have been nothing, from his biblical point of view, if the second person in the state drove him from his sight in his beshmet; but it was important for all the others, because the governor, of course, would become incensed, seeing such a spectacle as a mayor in a beshmet.

Worried about the expected visitor's first impression, the Soligalich officials strove for only two things: (1) that the tollgate at which Alexander Afanasyevich was to meet the governor be repainted, and (2) that on that occasion Alexander Afanasyevich wear, not his striped beshmet, but a uniform suited to his rank. But how achieve it?

Opinions differed, but everyone was more inclined to pitch together for the painting of the tollgate and the dressing of the mayor. With regard to the tollgate that was, of course, convenient, but with regard to Ryzhov's outfitting it was no good at all.

He said, "That is a gift, and I don't accept gifts." Then the suggestion offered by the father archpriest of mature judgment triumphed over all. He saw no need for any pitching in either for painting the tollgate or for the mayor's uniform, and said that it should all lie upon the one who was guiltiest of all, and the guiltiest of all, in his opinion, was the tax farmer. It should all fall on him. He alone was obliged, at his own expense, not through any force, but out of zeal, to paint the tollgate, for which the archpriest promised to recall it in a brief oration at the greeting of the governor, and, besides that, to include the donor in a secretly uttered prayer before the altar. Besides that, the father archpriest decided that the tax farmer had to give the assessor, on top of the usual offering, a triple portion of rum, French vodka, and home brew, of which the assessor was a great fancier. And for that let the assessor report himself sick and drink this additional offering at home alone and not go outside, but lend his uniform, which was the same as a policeman's, to Ryzhov, which the latter would probably find no reason to refuse, and then the sheep would be safe and the wolves sated.

This plan was the more fortunate in that the permanent assessor somewhat resembled Ryzhov in height and bulk, and besides, having recently married a merchant's daughter, he had a two-piece uniform in perfect order. Consequently, it only remained to prevail upon him, for the general good, to take to his bed at the time of the superior's arrival, under the pretext of a grave illness, and surrender his ammunition on this occasion to Ryzhov, whom the father archpriest, relying on his spiritual authority, also undertook to persuade—and did persuade. Seeing neither a gift nor a bribe in it, the righteous Alexander Afanasyevich agreed, for the general happiness, to don the uniform. The assessor's two-piece uniform was tried on and fitted for Ryzhov, and after some letting out of the double seams on all sides of the tunic and breeches, the matter was brought to a satisfactory conclusion. Alexander Afanasyevich, though he felt a highly inconvenient constraint in the uniform, could still move and all the same was now a tolerable representative of authority. It was decided to cover the small white gap between the tunic and the linen breeches with a piece of linen of the same color, which camouflaged the gap quite successfully. In short, Alexander Afanasyevich was now so well fitted out that the governor could turn him in all directions and admire him this way and that. But ill fate was pleased to mock all this and leave Alexander Afanasyevich suitably presentable from one side only, and to spoil the other completely, and that in such an ambiguous way that it could give grounds for the most arbitrary interpretation of his political way of thinking, mysterious as it was even without that.

X

The tollgate was painted in all the bright national colors, consisting of black and white stripes with red in between, and had had no time to get dusty before the news arrived that the governor had left the neighboring town and was making straight for Soligalich. At once signalmen were posted everywhere, and a restive postal troika stood champing at the bit by the fence of Ryzhov's poor hut, hitched to a cart into which Alexander Afanasyevich was supposed to leap at the first signal and gallop to meet the "haughty bearing."

In this last stipulation there was an extraordinary amount of inconvenient complexity, which filled everything around with uneasy anxiety—something the self-possessed Ryzhov disliked very much.

He decided "to be always in his place": he moved the troika from his fence to the town gates, and sat right there himself on the painted bar of the tollgate, in full dress—tunic and white breeches—with a report in his breast pocket, installing himself like a saint on a pillar, while the curious gathered around him, whom he did not send away, but, on the contrary, conversed with, and in the midst of this conversation it was granted him to see a cloud of dust billowing up on the road, in which the lead pair and postillion, adorned with brass plates, outlined themselves. It was the governor rolling along.

Ryzhov quickly leaped into the cart and was about to gallop off, when he was suddenly struck by the general moan and gasp of the crowd calling out to him:

"Dear man, take off your trousers!"

"What's that?" asked Ryzhov.

"Your trousers, take off your trousers," the people replied. "Look at your white behind, the whole tollgate's printed on it."

Ryzhov looked over his shoulder and saw that all the undried stripes of the national colors from the tollgate were indeed printed on his breeches with astonishing distinctness.

He winced, but then sighed at once and said: "No need for superiors to go looking there," and sent the troika galloping to meet the "haughty personage."

The people just waved their hands:

"Desperate man! What's he in for now?"

XI

Runners from that same crowd quickly managed to inform the clergy and superiors in the cathedral of the ambiguous guise in which Ryzhov would be meeting the governor, but by then it was each man for himself.

The archpriest was the most frightened of all, because the officials were lurking in the church, while he stood on the steps with the cross in his hands. He was surrounded by a very small number of clergy, among whom two figures stood out: a squat deacon with big head and a lanky beadle in a vestment, who was holding holy water in an "applicated" bowl, which tossed and trembled in his timorous hands. But now the quaking of fear turned to petrifaction: on the square, drawn by a briskly galloping troika, appeared the post cart, on which Ryzhov's gigantic figure towered up with remarkable dignity. He was wearing a hat, a tunic with a red collar, and white breeches with linen sewn over the gap, which from a distance decidedly spoiled nothing. On the contrary, he appeared to everyone like something majestic, and indeed that was how he ought to have appeared. Standing firmly on the galloping cart, on the box of which the driver bounced up and down, Alexander Afanasyevich swayed neither right nor left, but sailed on his chariot like a triumphator, his mighty arms folded on his chest, and sending a whole cloud of dust onto the coach-and-six and the light tarantass that followed him. In the tarantass rode the officials. Lanskoy sat alone in the coach and, despite the grave importance he was noted for, was evidently much intrigued by Ryzhov, who flew ahead of him, standing up, in a short, tight tunic, not concealing in the least the pattern of the national colors on his white breeches. It is very likely that a considerable portion of the gubernatorial attention was drawn precisely to that oddity, the meaning of which was not at all easy to understand and determine.

In due course the cart pulled up to one side, and in due course Alexander Afanasyevich jumped off and opened the door of the governor's carriage.

Lanskoy stepped out, having, as always, his invariable "haughty bearing," which, however, enclosed a rather kind heart. The archpriest, raising the cross over him, said: "Blessed be he that cometh in the name of the Lord,"[21] and then sprinkled him slightly with holy water.

The dignitary planted a kiss on the cross, wiped away the drops that had landed on his haughty brow with a cambric handkerchief, and entered the church *first*. All this went on right in front of Alexander Afanasyevich and displeased him in the extreme—it was all "haughty." The unfavorable impression was intensified still more when, having entered the church, the governor did not cross himself or bow to anyone—neither the altar, nor the people—but walked straight as a pole right to the front, without bending his head.

This was against all of Ryzhov's rules regarding reverence for God and the obligation of the superior to set an example for their inferiors—and his pious spirit was stirred and rose to an incredible height.

Ryzhov went on walking behind the governor and, as Lanskoy approached the front, Ryzhov shortened the distance between them more and more and suddenly seized him unexpectedly by the arm and uttered in a loud voice:

"Servant of God Sergius! Enter the church of the Lord not haughtily but humbly, presenting yourself as the greatest of sinners—like this!"

And with that he placed his hand on the governor's back, slowly bent him into a full bow, released him again, and stood at attention.

XII

The eyewitness who passed on this anecdotal story of the Soligalich eccentric said nothing about how the people and authorities who were in the church then took it. All that is known is that no one had the courage to defend the bent-down governor and stop Ryzhov's dauntless hand, but of Lanskoy he communicated something more detailed. Sergei Stepanovich did not give the least occasion for prolonging the disorder, but, on the contrary, "exchanged his proud haughtiness for intelligent self-control." He did not cut Alexander Afanasyevich short, or even say a word to him, but crossed himself and, turning around, bowed to all the people, and after that quickly left and headed for the quarters that had been prepared for him.

There Lanskoy received the officials—both crown and elected—and those of them who seemed deserving of greater trust he questioned about Ryzhov: what sort of man he was and how he was tolerated in society.

"He's our Constable Ryzhov," the headman answered him.

"He's . . . mad, probably?"

"Not at all: he's just always *like that*."

"But why keep somebody *like that* in service?"

"He's good at it."

"An insolent man."

"The meekest of the meek: if a superior sits on his neck, he reasons, 'Then he's got to be carried,' and carry him he does, only he's read up the Bible and it's deranged him."

"What you say is absurd: the Bible is a divine book."

"That's exactly right, only it's not suitable reading matter for everybody: monks get into a wild passion over it, and worldly people have their wits addled."

"What nonsense!" Lanskoy objected and went on questioning:

"And how is he in the matter of bribes: moderate?"

"Good heavens," said the headman, "he doesn't take anything at all . . ."

The governor's disbelief grew still more.

"That," he said, "I won't believe for a moment."

"No, he really doesn't take bribes."

"In that case," he says, "what does he live on?"

"He lives on his salary."

"You're telling me a lot of rubbish: there's no such man in all Russia."

"Right," he replies, "there isn't; but one has turned up among us."

"And how much does he get as a salary?"

"Ten roubles a month."

"Why," he says, "you couldn't keep a sheep on that."

"It really is tricky to live on it," he says, "but he does."

"But if it's impossible for everybody, how does he manage it?"

"He's read up the Bible."

"Very well, so 'he's read up the Bible,' but what does he eat?"

"Bread and water."

And here the headman told about how Ryzhov was in all his doings.

"Then this is quite a remarkable man!" Lanskoy exclaimed and asked that Ryzhov be summoned to him.

Alexander Afanasyevich appeared and stood by the doorpost, in accordance with subordination.

"Where are you from?" Lanskoy asked him.

"I was born here, on Nizhnaya Street," replied Ryzhov.

"And where were you brought up?"

"I had no upbringing . . . I grew up with my mother. She baked pies."

"Did you study anywhere?"

"With the scribe."

"What is your confession?"

"Christian."

"You act very strangely."

"Not that I notice: each of us finds strange what's not peculiar to him."

Lanskoy thought that this was a challenging, impudent allusion, and, glancing sternly at Ryzhov, he asked sharply:

"Do you belong to some sort of sect?"

"There are no sects here: I go to the cathedral."

"Do you confess?"

"I confess to God before the archpriest."

"Do you have a family?"

"A wife and a son."

"Do you receive a small salary?"

The never-laughing Ryzhov smiled.

"I get ten roubles a month," he said, "but I don't know if that's big or small."

"It's not big."

"Report to the sovereign that for a wicked servant it's little."[22]

"And for a faithful one?"

"It's enough."

"They say you don't profit from your position?"

Ryzhov looked at him and said nothing.

"Tell me in all conscience: can that really be so?"

"And why can't it be?"

"You have very small means."

"If you have great self-control, you can get by on small means."

"But why don't you ask for another post?"

"And who's going to fill this one?"

"Somebody else."

"Will he manage better than I do?"

Now it was Lanskoy who smiled: the constable greatly interested his soul, which was no stranger to warmth.

"Listen," he said, "you're an odd fellow; I beg you to sit down."

Ryzhov sat down vis-à-vis the "haughty" one.

"They say you're an expert on the Bible?"

"I read it as much as time permits, and advise you to do the same."

"Very well; but . . . allow me to assure you that you may speak with me quite candidly and in all truth."

"Lying is forbidden by the commandments—I'm not going to lie."

"Very well. Do you respect the authorities?"

"No, I don't."

"Why not?"

"They're lazy, greedy, and duplicitous towards the throne," replied Ryzhov.

"Yes, you are candid. Thank you. Do you also prophesy?"

"No. But I conclude what clearly follows from the Bible."

"Could you show me at least one of your conclusions?"

Ryzhov replied that he could—and at once fetched a whole sheaf of papers with the inscription *Singlemind*.

"Is there anything here from the past that was prophetic and has come true?" asked Lanskoy.

The constable leafed through the familiar pages and read: "In her correspondence with Voltaire, the empress called him a second Chrysostom. For this incongruous comparison, our monarch's life will not have a peaceful end."

In the margin by this place it was noted: "Fulfilled with the grievous marriage of Pavel Petrovich."[23]

"Show me something else."

Ryzhov again flipped through the pages and pointed to another place, which consisted only of the following: "An ukase issued on stump duties. Henceforth the cold will intensify in poor cottages. A special punishment is to be expected." And again a note in the margin: "Fulfilled—see page such-and-such," and on that page was reported the death of the baby daughter of the emperor Alexander I, with the note: "This followed the imposition of the tax on timber."[24]

"Excuse me," asked Lanskoy, "but doesn't timber constitute property?"

"Yes, but to heat the air in a dwelling constitutes a necessity."

"Are you against property?"

"No, I only want people to be warm when it's cold out. Timber shouldn't go to those who are warm anyway."

"And how do you judge about taxes: should taxes be imposed on people?"

"They should, and there should be an additional tax on everything that's a luxury, so that the rich pay into the treasury for the poor."

"Hm, hm! Have you drawn that teaching from somewhere?"

"From Holy Scripture and my conscience."

"You haven't been led to it by some other source from modern times?"

"All other sources are impure and filled with vain thinking."

"Now tell me one last thing: how is it that you're not afraid either of writing what you write, or of doing what you did to me in church?"

"What I write, I write for myself, and what I did in church had to be committed to protect the tsar's authority."

"Why the tsar's?"

"So that everybody could see his servant showing respect for the people's faith."

"But I could have dealt with you quite differently than I'm doing."

Ryzhov looked at him "with pity" and replied:

"And what harm can be done to a man who is able to live with his family on ten roubles a month?"

"I could have you arrested."

"They eat better in jail."

"You could be exiled for this insolence."

"Where could I be exiled where I'd be worse off and where my God would abandon me? He's with me everywhere, and besides Him I fear no one."

The haughty neck bent, and Lanskoy's left hand reached out to Ryzhov.

"Your character is honorable," he said and told him to leave.

But apparently he still did not quite trust this biblical socialist and personally asked several simple people about him.

Twirling their hands in the air, they all answered in the same way: "He's this-that-and-the-other."

None of them knew anything more definite about him.

On bidding him farewell, Lanskoy said to Ryzhov:

"I won't forget you, and I'll take your advice—I'll read the Bible."

"Only that's not enough, you must also learn to live on ten roubles a month," Ryzhov added.

But that advice Lanskoy did not promise to take, but only laughed, gave him his hand again, and said:

"An odd fellow, an odd fellow!"

Sergei Stepanovich left, and Ryzhov carried his *Singlemind* home and went on writing in it whatever poured out from his observations and prophetic inspiration.

XIII

Quite some time had gone by since Lanskoy's visit, and the events that had accompanied his passing through Soligalich were already largely forgotten and rubbed out by the everyday hurly-burly, when suddenly out of the blue, a wonder of wonders not only for Soligalich but for all enlightened Russia, the inspected town received some absolutely incredible news, even impossible in an orderly system of government: Constable Ryzhov had been awarded the St. Vladimir's Cross, which confers nobility[25]—the first St. Vladimir's Cross ever bestowed on a police constable.

The decoration itself arrived along with instructions for putting it on and wearing it according to the rules. Both the cross and the diploma were handed to Alexander Afanasyevich with an announcement that he had been vouchsafed this honor and this bestowal on the recommendation of Sergei Stepanovich Lanskoy.

Ryzhov took the decoration, looked at it, and said aloud:

"An odd fellow, an odd fellow!" and noted in the *Singlemind* next to Lanskoy's name: "Will be made a count," which, as we know, was fulfilled. As for wearing the decoration, Ryzhov had *nothing to wear it on*.

The chevalier Ryzhov lived to be almost ninety, noting everything down precisely and originally in his *Singlemind*, which was probably expended on papering the walls in some local restoration. He died, having carried out all the Christian rites according to the prescriptions of the Orthodox Church, though his Orthodoxy, by general observation, was "questionable." In his faith, too, Ryzhov was a this-that-and-the-other sort of man, but for all that, it seems to me that we can see in him something besides "mere trash"—for which he should be remembered at the very beginning of a search into "three righteous men."[26]

The Devil-Chase

I

It is a rite that can be seen only in Moscow, and then not otherwise than with special luck and patronage.

I saw a devil-chase from beginning to end thanks to a lucky concurrence of circumstances, and want to record it for true connoisseurs and lovers of what is serious and majestic in our national taste.

Though I'm a nobleman on one side, on the other I'm close to "the people": my mother is from the merchant estate. She left a very wealthy house to marry, but left it by eloping, out of love for my father. My late father had a way with the ladies, and what he intended, he achieved. Thus he also succeeded with my mother, but for that adroitness my mother's parents gave her nothing except, of course, her wardrobe, linens, and God's mercy, which were obtained along with forgiveness and the parental blessing, forever inviolable. My old folks lived in Orel, lived in want, but proudly, asked nothing of my mother's rich relations, and had no contacts with them. However, when it came to my going to university, my mother began to say:

"Please, go to Uncle Ilya Fedoseevich and pay him my respects. It's not humiliating, one should honor one's older relations—and he's my brother, and a pious man at that, and carries great weight in Moscow. At all the official greetings, he always brings the bread and salt . . . always stands in front of the others with the dish or the icon . . . is received at the governor general's and the metropolitan's . . .[1] He may give you good advice."

I did not believe in God at that time, having studied Filaret's catechism,[2] but I did love my mother, and one day I thought: "Here I've been in Moscow for about a year and still haven't carried out my mother's will. Why don't I go right now to Uncle Ilya Fedoseich, convey my mother's respects to him, and see what he really has to teach me?"

By childhood habit I was respectful of my elders—especially those who were known to both the metropolitan and the governor general.

I rose, brushed myself off, and went to Uncle Ilya Fedoseich.

II

It was somewhere around six in the evening. The weather was warm, mild, and grayish—in short, very nice. My uncle's house was well-known—one of the foremost houses in Moscow—everybody knew it. Only I had never gone there, and had never seen my uncle, even from afar.

I boldly went, however, reasoning: if he receives me, good, and if he doesn't, he doesn't.

I come to the courtyard; by the porch stand horses, fierce, raven black, their manes flying loose, their hide shining like costly satin, and they are hitched to a carriage.

I go up to the porch and say: thus and so, I'm his nephew, a student, I ask to be announced to Ilya Fedoseich. And the servants reply:

"He'll be coming down presently—to go for a ride."

A very simple figure appears, a Russian one, but quite majestic—there is a resemblance to my mother in his eyes, but the expression is different—what's known as a solid man.

I introduced myself; he heard me out silently, quietly gave me his hand, and said:

"Get in, we'll go for a ride."

I was about to decline, but somehow faltered and got in.

"To the park," he ordered.

The fierce horses galloped off at once, with only the rear of the carriage bouncing, and when we left town, they raced even more swiftly.

We sat there not saying a word, only I could see that the edge of my uncle's top hat was cutting into his forehead, and on his face there was that sort of wry scowl that comes from boredom.

He looked this way and that, and once cast a glance at me and, out of the blue, said:

"No life at all."

I didn't know what to reply, and said nothing.

We rode on and on. I think, "Where's he taking me?" and I begin to suspect that I've landed in some sort of adventure.

And my uncle suddenly seems to have made up his mind about something and starts giving orders to the coachman one after another:

"Turn right, turn left. Here at the Yar—stop!"[3]

I see many waiters pouring out of the restaurant to meet us, and they all bend almost double before my uncle, but he does not stir from the carriage and summons the owner. They run off. A Frenchman appears—also very respectful, but my uncle does not stir: he taps the ivory knob of his cane against his teeth and says:

"How many superfluous ones are there?"

"Up to thirty in the main rooms," replies the Frenchman, "and three private rooms are occupied."

"Out with them all!"

"Very good."

"It's now seven," my uncle says, looking at his watch. "I'll come back at eight. Will you be ready?"

"No," he replies, "by eight is difficult . . . there are many reservations . . . but by nine, if you please, there won't be a single stranger in the restaurant."

"Very well."

"And what shall we prepare?"

"Gypsies, naturally."

"What else?"

"An orchestra."

"One?"

"No, better two."

"Send for Ryabyka?"

"Naturally."

"French ladies?"

"No need for them!"

"The cellar?"

"All of it."

"From the kitchen?"

"The *carte*!"

They brought the menu for the day.

My uncle glanced and, it seems, did not really see anything, and perhaps did not wish to. He tapped the paper with his stick and said:

"All of it, for a hundred persons."

And with that he rolled up the menu and put it in his kaftan.

The Frenchman was both glad and hesitant:

"I can't serve it all to a hundred persons," he said. "There are very expensive things here, of which there are only five or six portions in the whole restaurant."

"And how am I to sort out my guests? Whoever wants something should get it. Understand?"

"Yes."

"Otherwise, brother, even Ryabyka won't help. Drive!"

We left the restaurateur with his lackeys at the entrance and went rolling off.

By then I was fully convinced that this was not for me, and I tried to take my leave, but my uncle didn't hear me. He was very preoccupied. We drove along, on the way stopping now one person, now another.

"Nine o'clock at the Yar!" my uncle said briefly to each of them. And the people to whom he said this were all such venerable old men, and they all took their hats off and just as briefly answered my uncle:

"Your honored guest, Fedoseich."

I don't remember how many people we stopped in that fashion, but I think it was some twenty, and just then it turned nine o'clock, and we rolled up to the Yar again. A whole crowd of waiters poured out to meet us and took my uncle under the arms, and on the porch the Frenchman himself brushed the dust off his trousers with a napkin.

"All clear?" asked my uncle.

"One general," he said, "is lingering in a private room, he begged to be allowed to finish . . ."

"Out with him at once!"

"He'll be finished very soon."

"I don't care—I've given him enough time—let him go and finish eating on the grass."

I don't know how it would have ended, but at that moment the general came out with two ladies, got into his carriage, and left, and the guests my uncle had invited to the park began driving up to the entrance one by one.

III

The restaurant was tidied up, clean, and free of customers. Only in one of the rooms sat a giant, who met my uncle silently and, without saying a word to him, took his stick and hid it away somewhere.

My uncle surrendered the stick without the least protest, and also gave the giant his wallet and change purse.

This massive, gray-haired giant was the same Ryabyka of whom I had heard the incomprehensible order given to the restaurateur. He was some sort of "children's teacher," but here he obviously also had some special duties. He was as necessary here as the Gypsies, the orchestra, and the whole get-up, which instantly appeared in full muster. Only I didn't understand what the teacher's role was, but that was still early on in my inexperience.

The brightly lit restaurant was in operation: music thundered, Gypsies strolled about and snacked from the buffet, my uncle inspected the rooms, the garden, the grotto, and the galleries. He looked everywhere to see if there were any "non-belongers," and beside him walked the inseparable teacher; but when they came back to the main dining room, where everyone was gathered, a great difference between them could be noticed. The campaign had not affected them in the same way: the teacher was as sober as when he set out, but my uncle was completely drunk.

How it could have happened so quickly, I don't know, but he was in excellent spirits; he sat in the chairman's place, and the show began.

The door was locked, and, as was said of the whole world, "neither could they pass from them to us, nor from us to them."[4] We were separated by a gulf, a gulf of everything—wine, viands, and, above all, a gulf of carousing—I don't want to say outrageous, but wild, furious, such as I'm unable to describe. And that shouldn't be asked of me, because, seeing myself squeezed in there and cut off from the world, I grew timid and hastened to get drunk the sooner myself. And therefore I will not give an account of how the night went on, because it is not given to my pen to describe *all* of it; I remember only two outstanding battle episodes and the finale, but in them was also contained what was most *dreadful*.

IV

Some Ivan Stepanovich was announced, who, as it turned out later, was a prominent Moscow factory owner and businessman.

That produced a pause.

"But you were told: let nobody in," my uncle replied.

"He begs very much."

"Let him take himself off where he came from."

The man went out, but timidly came back.

"Ivan Stepanovich asked me to tell you," he says, "that he very humbly begs."

"Never mind, I don't want to."

Others said: "Let him pay a fine."

"No! Drive him away. No need for a fine."

But the man reappears and says still more timidly:

"He agrees to pay any fine, because at his age, he says, it's very sad for him to be excluded from your company."

My uncle rose and flashed his eyes, but at the same moment Ryabyka rose to his full height between him and the lackey: with his left hand he flung the servant away, somehow with one tweak, like a chicken, and with his right hand he seated my uncle in his place.

From among the guests voices were heard in favor of Ivan Stepanovich, asking to let him in—take a hundred-rouble fine from him for the musicians and let him in.

"He's one of us, a pious old man, where is he to go now? If he's driven away, he may make a scandal in front of the small fry. We should take pity on him."

My uncle heeded them and said:

"If it won't be my way, it won't be yours either, it will be God's way: I grant Ivan Stepanovich admittance, only he must beat the kettledrum."

The messenger came back:

"He begs to pay a fine instead."

"Devil take him! If he doesn't want to drum, he doesn't have to—let him go wherever he likes."

A little while later Ivan Stepanovich yielded and sent to tell them he *agreed* to beat the kettledrum.

"Let him come here."

A man of great height and respectable appearance enters: stern aspect, extinct eyes, bent spine, and tufty, greenish beard. He tries to joke and greet them all, but is put in his place.

"Later, later, all of that later," my uncle shouts at him. "Now beat the drum."

"Beat the drum!" others join in.

"Music! For the kettledrum!"

The orchestra strikes up a loud piece—the staid old man takes the wooden drumsticks and starts banging on the kettledrum in time and out of time.

Infernal noise and shouting; everybody's pleased and cries out: "Louder!"

Ivan Stepanovich puts more into it.

"Louder, louder, still louder!"

The old man bangs with all his might, like the Black King in Freiligrath,[5] and finally the goal is achieved: the kettledrum gives out a desperate crack, the skin splits, everybody laughs, the noise is unimaginable, and for breaking through the kettledrum Ivan Stepanovich is relieved of a five-hundred-rouble fine to benefit the musicians.

He pays, wipes his sweat, sits down, and while everybody drinks his health, he, to his own no small horror, notices his son-in-law among the guests.

Again laughter, again noise, and so it goes until I lose my senses. In rare moments of lucidity I see Gypsy women dancing, see my uncle pumping his legs while sitting in place; then he gets up in front of someone, but Ryabyka at once appears between them, and somebody goes flying to one side, and my uncle sits down, and before him stand two forks stuck into the table. Now I understand Ryabyka's role.

But here the freshness of a Moscow morning breathed through the window. Once more I was conscious of something, but as if only so as to doubt my own reason. There was combat and the chopping of wood: I heard crashing, thunder, trees were swaying, virgin, exotic trees, behind them some swarthy faces huddled in a corner, and here, at the roots, terrible axes flashed and my uncle chopped, and old Ivan Stepanovich chopped . . . Right out of a medieval picture.

This was the "taking captive" of the Gypsy women hiding in the grotto beyond the trees. The Gypsy men did not defend them and left them to their own devices. There was no sorting out joke from seriousness here: plates, chairs, stones from the grotto flew through the air, yet the cutting of trees went on, and Ivan Stepanovich and my uncle performed most valiantly of all.

At last the fortress was taken: the Gypsy women were seized, embraced, kissed, and each of them had a hundred-rouble note stuck behind her *corsage,*[*] and that was the end of it . . .

Yes, all at once everything quieted down . . . everything ended. No one had interfered, but enough was enough. The feeling was that, as there had been "no life" without it, so now there was enough of it.

There had been enough for everyone, and everyone had had enough. Maybe it was also of importance that the teacher had said it was "time for classes," but anyhow it was all the same: Walpurgis-nacht[6] was over, and "life" was beginning again.

The public did not go driving off, did not say good-bye, but simply vanished; there was no longer any orchestra or Gypsies. The restaurant was a picture of total devastation: not a single drape, not a single intact mirror, even the overhead chandelier lay all in pieces on the floor, and its crystal prisms crunched under the feet of the barely stirring, exhausted waiters. My uncle sat alone on the sofa and drank kvass; now and then he recalled something and pumped his legs. Beside him stood the hurrying-to-class Ryabyka.

They were brought the bill—a short one: "rounded off."

Ryabyka read the bill attentively and demanded a reduction of fifteen hundred roubles. They didn't argue much with him and totted it up: it came to seventeen thousand, and Ryabyka, after a second look, declared it fair. My uncle said monosyllabically: "Pay," and then put his hat on and motioned for me to follow him.

To my horror, I saw that he had not forgotten anything and that it was impossible for me to escape from him. I found him extremely frightening and couldn't imagine remaining alone with him in this state. He had taken me along without saying even two reasonable

---

[*] Bodice. *Trans.*

words, and now he was dragging me with him and I couldn't get away. What would become of me? All my drunkenness disappeared. I was simply afraid of this dreadful wild beast, with his incredible fantasy and terrifying scope. And meanwhile we were already leaving: in the front hall we were surrounded by a throng of lackeys. My uncle dictated, "Five to each"—and Ryabyka paid it out; less was paid to the porters, watchmen, policemen, gendarmes, who had all been of some service to us. That was all satisfied. But it all made up quite a sum, and there were also cabbies standing over the whole visible expanse of the park. There was no end of them, and they were also all waiting for us—waiting for dear old Ilya Fedoseich, "in case His Honor needs to send for something."

We found out how many they were, handed them each three roubles, and my uncle and I got into the carriage, where Ryabyka gave him his wallet.

Ilya Fedoseich took a hundred-rouble bill from the wallet and gave it to Ryabyka.

Ryabyka turned the bill over in his hands and said rudely:

"Too little."

My uncle added two more twenty-fives.

"That's still not enough: there wasn't a single scandal."

My uncle added a third twenty-five, after which the teacher handed him his stick and bowed out.

V

The two of us were left alone and racing back to Moscow, while all that cabby riffraff came whooping and rattling at full speed behind us. I didn't understand what they wanted, but my uncle did. It was outrageous: they wanted to grab some smart money as well, and so, in the guise of paying special honor to Ilya Fedoseich, they exposed his highly esteemed self to shame before the whole world.

Moscow was on our noses and all in view—all in the beautiful morning brightness, in the light smoke of hearths and the peaceful ringing of church bells summoning to prayer.

To right and left of the city gate there were grocery stores. My uncle stopped at the first of them, went to a linden barrel that stood by the door, and asked:

"Honey?"

"Honey."

"How much for the barrel?"

"We sell it by the pound for small change."

"Sell me the whole thing: come up with a price."

I don't remember, I think he came up with seventy or eighty roubles.

My uncle threw him the money.

And our cortège closed in.

"Do you love me, my fine city cabbies?"

"Sure enough, we're always at Your Honor's . . ."

"You feel an attachment?"

"A strong attachment."

"Take the wheels off."

They were puzzled.

"Quickly, quickly!" my uncle commanded.

The most light-footed of them, some twenty men, climbed under the boxes, took out wrenches, and began unscrewing the nuts.

"Good," said my uncle. "Now spread honey on them."

"But sir!"

"Spread it."

"Such a good thing . . . more interesting in the mouth."

"Spread it."

And, without further insistence, my uncle got back into the carriage, and we raced on, and they, many as they were, were all left standing with their wheels off over the honey, which they probably did not spread on the wheels, but just appropriated or sold back to the grocer. In any case they abandoned us, and we found ourselves in a bathhouse. Here I expected my end had come, and I sat neither dead nor alive in the marble bath, while my uncle stretched out on the floor, but not simply, not in an ordinary pose, but somehow apocalyptically. The whole enormous mass of his stout body rested on the floor only by the very tips of his toes and fingers, and on these fine points of support his red body trembled under the spray of the cold water showered on him, and he roared with the restrained roar of a bear tearing the ring from its nose. This lasted for half an hour, during which he went on trembling like jelly on a shaky table, until he finally jumped up all at once, asked for kvass, and we got dressed and went "to the Frenchman" on Kuznetsky.[7]

Here we both had a slight trim, a slight curling and brushing up, and then we crossed the city on foot—to his shop.

With me there was still no talk, no release. Only once he said:

"Wait, not all at once. What you don't understand—you'll understand with the years."

In the shop he prayed, looked everybody over with a proprietary eye, and stood at the counter. The outside of the vessel was clean, but inside there still lurked a deep foulness seeking its own cleansing.

I saw it and now stopped being afraid. It interested me. I wanted to see how he was going to deal with himself: by abstinence or some sort of grace?

At around ten o'clock he became terribly restless, kept waiting and looking for a neighbor, so that the three of us could go for tea—with three it's a whole five kopecks cheaper. The neighbor didn't come: he had died a galloping death.

My uncle crossed himself and said:

"We'll all die."

This did not disconcert him, despite the fact that for forty years they had gone to have tea together at the Novotroitsky Tavern.

We invited a neighbor from across the street and went more than once to sample this or that, but all in a sober way. For the whole day I sat and went about with him, and towards evening my uncle sent for the carriage to go to the All-Glorious.[8]

There they also knew him and met him with the same respect as at the Yar.

"I want to fall down before the All-Glorious and weep for my sins. And this—allow me to introduce him—is my nephew, my sister's son."

"Welcome," said the nuns, "welcome. From whom else if not you should the All-Glorious accept repentance—ever our cloister's benefactor. Now is a very good moment . . . the vigil."

"Let it finish—I like it without people, and so you can make a blessed darkness for me."

They made darkness for him; put out all the icon lamps except one or two and the big green lamp in front of the All-Glorious herself.

My uncle did not fall, but crashed to his knees, then prostrated himself, beat his brow against the floor, sobbed, and lay stock still.

I sat with two nuns in a dark corner by the door. There was a long pause. My uncle went on lying there, unspeaking, unheeding.

It seemed to me that he was asleep, and I even said so to the nuns. The more experienced sister thought a little, shook her head, and, lighting a thin candle, clutched it in her fist and went very, very quietly to the penitent. She quietly tiptoed around him, shook her head negatively, and whispered:

"It's working . . . and with a twist."

"What makes you say so?"

She bent down, gesturing for me to do the same, and said:

"Look straight through the light, where his feet are."

"I see."

"Look, what a struggle!"

I peer closely and indeed notice some sort of movement: my uncle is lying reverently in a prayerful position, but in his feet it's as if there are two cats fighting—now one, now the other attacking, and so rapidly, with such leaps.

"Mother," I say, "where did these cats come from?"

"It only seems to you that they are cats," she replies, "but they are not cats, they are temptation: see, in spirit he burns towards heaven, but his feet are still moving towards hell."

I see that with his feet my uncle is indeed still dancing last night's trepak,[9] but in spirit is he now really burning towards heaven?

As if in reply to that, he suddenly sighs and cries out loudly:

"I will not rise until thou forgivest me! Thou only art holy, and we are all accursed devils!"—and bursts into sobs.

He sobbed so that the three of us began to weep and sob with him: Lord, do unto him according to his prayer.

And we don't notice that he is already standing next to us and saying to me in a soft, pious voice:

"Let's go—we'll manage."

The nuns ask:

"Were you granted, dear man, to see the gleam?"

"No," he says, "I was not granted the gleam, but here . . . here's how it was."

He clenched his fist and raised it, as one raises a boy by his hair.

"You were raised?"

"Yes."

The nuns started crossing themselves, and so did I, and my uncle explained:

"Now," he says, "I'm forgiven! Right from above, from under the coopola, the open right hand gathered all my hair together and lifted me straight to my feet . . ."

And now he's not outcast and is happy. He gave a generous gift to the convent where he had prayed and had been granted this miracle, and he felt "life" again, and he sent my mother her full share of the dowry, and me he introduced to the good faith of the people.

Since then I have become acquainted with the people's taste for falling and rising . . . And this is what's known as the *devil-chase*, "which drives out the demon of wrong-mindedness." One can be granted this, I repeat, only in Moscow, and then only through special luck or the great patronage of the most venerable old men.

Deathless Golovan

Perfect love casteth out fear.

I JOHN 4:18

I

h e himself is almost a myth, and his story a legend. To tell about him, one should be French, because only the people of that nation manage to explain to others what they don't understand themselves. I say all this with the aim of begging my reader's indulgence beforehand for the overall imperfection of my story of a person whose portrayal is worth the efforts of a far better master than I. But Golovan may soon be quite forgotten, and that would be a loss. Golovan is worthy of attention, and though I did not know him well enough to be able to draw his full portrait, I will select and present some features of this mortal man of no high rank who was reputed to be *deathless.*

The nickname "deathless," given to Golovan, did not express mockery and was by no means an empty, meaningless sound—he was nicknamed "deathless" as a result of the strong conviction that he was a special man, a man who did not fear death. How could such an opinion of him have been formed among people who walk under God and are always mindful of their mortality? Was there a sufficient reason for it, which subsequently turned into a convention, or was this sobriquet given him by a simplicity akin to foolishness?

It seemed to me that the latter was more probable, but how others considered it I don't know, because in my childhood I didn't think about it, and when I grew up and could understand things, "deathless" Golovan was no longer in the world. He had died, and in a none-too-tidy manner at that: he perished during the so-called "big fire" in Orel,[1] drowned in a boiling pit, which he fell into saving someone's life or someone's goods. However, "a big part of him, escaping corruption, went on living in grateful memory,"[2] and I want to try to put down on paper what I knew and heard about him, so that his memory, which is deserving of attention, may be prolonged in the world.

II

Deathless Golovan was a simple man. His face, with its extraordinarily large features, was stamped in my memory early on and remained in it forever. I met him at an age when they say children cannot receive lasting impressions and carry the memory of them all their lives, but it happened otherwise with me. This incident was recorded by my grandmother in the following way:

"Yesterday [May 26, 1835], I came from Gorokhov to see Mashenka [my mother], did not find Semyon Dmitrich [my father] at home, him having been sent on a mission to Elets for an inquest into a frightful murder. In the whole house there were just us women and the serving girls. The coachman went with him [my father], there was only the yard porter Kondrat left, and in the evening a watchman came from the office [the government office, where my father was a councilor] to spend the night in the front hall. Today between eleven and twelve Mashenka went to the garden to look at the flowers and water her costmary, and took Nikolushka [me] along with her, carried by Anna [now an old woman, still living]. And when they came back for lunch, Anna was just opening the garden gate when the dog Ryabka tore free of her chain and flung herself straight onto Anna's breast, but at the very moment that Ryabka, raising her paws, threw herself on Anna's breast, Golovan seized her by the scruff of the neck, held her tight, and threw her through the trapdoor into the cellar. There she was shot, but the child was saved."

The child was me, and however accurate the proofs may be that an infant of one and a half cannot remember what happens to him, I nevertheless remember this occurrence.

Of course, I don't remember where the rabid Ryabka came from and what Golovan did with her, after he held her high up in his iron grip, wheezing, flailing her legs, her whole body squirming; but I do remember that moment . . . *only that moment.* It was like a flash of lightning amidst the dark of night, when for some reason you suddenly see an extraordinary multitude of things at once: the bed canopy, the folding screen, the window, the canary fluttering on its perch, and a glass with a silver spoon in it and spots of magnesium on its handle. It is probably the quality of fear to have big eyes. In that one moment I can see before me, as now, a dog's enormous muzzle with little speckles, dry fur, completely red eyes, a gaping maw filled with cloudy foam in a bluish, as if pomaded, gullet . . . bared teeth that already want to snap shut, but suddenly the upper lip is wrenched back over them, the mouth is stretched to the ears, and the thrust-out throat below moves convulsively, like a bared human elbow. Above it all stood an enormous human figure with an enormous head, and he took the rabid dog and carried it off. And the man's face was *smiling* all the while.

The figure I've described was Golovan. I'm afraid I'm quite unable to paint his portrait, precisely because I see him very well and clearly.

Like Peter the Great, he was nearly seven feet tall; he was broadly built, lean and muscular; he was swarthy, had a round face, blue eyes, a very big nose, and thick lips. The hair on Golovan's head and trimmed beard was very thick, the color of salt and pepper. His head was always close-cropped, his beard and mustache were also clipped. The calm and happy smile never left Golovan's face for a minute: it shone in his every feature, but played mostly on his lips and in his eyes, intelligent and kind, but as if slightly mocking. It seemed Golovan had no other expression, at least none that I remember. To supplement this unskillful portrait of Golovan, it is necessary to mention one oddity or peculiarity, which consisted in his gait. Golovan walked very quickly, as if he was always hurrying somewhere, not evenly, though, but with little hops. He didn't limp, but, in a local expression, "hitched"—that is, he stepped firmly on one leg, the right one, but on the left leg he hopped. It seemed as if the leg didn't flex, but had a spring in it somewhere, in a muscle or a joint. People walk that way on an artificial leg, but Golovan's wasn't artificial; however, this peculiarity also did not come from nature; he brought it about himself, and there was a secret in it, which can't be explained straight off.

Golovan dressed as a muzhik—summer and winter, in scorching heat and freezing cold, he always wore a long, raw sheepskin coat, all greasy and blackened. I never saw him in any other clothes, and I remember my father often joked about that coat, calling it "everlasting."

Golovan belted his coat with a strap of white laminated harness, which had turned yellow in many places and in others had flaked off completely, exposing the wax-end and holes. But the coat was kept clean of various little tenants—I knew that better than anyone, because I often sat in Golovan's bosom listening to his talk and always felt myself very comfortable there.

The wide collar of the coat was never buttoned, but, on the contrary, was left wide open to the waist. Here was the "bosom," offering a very ample space for bottles of cream, which Golovan provided to the kitchen of the Orel Assembly of the Nobility.[3] That had been his trade ever since he "went free" and was given a "Ermolov cow" to start out.

The powerful chest of the "deathless" was covered only with a linen shirt of Ukrainian cut, that is, with a standing collar, always white as milk and unfailingly with long, bright-colored ties. These ties were sometimes a ribbon, sometimes simply a strip of woolen cloth or even cotton, but they lent something fresh and gentlemanly to Golovan's appearance, which suited him very well, because he was in fact a gentleman.

III

Golovan was our neighbor. Our house in Orel was on Third Dvoryanskaya Street, and it stood third in from the precipitous bank above the river Orlik. It's a rather beautiful spot. At that time, before the fires, this was the edge of the city proper. To the right, beyond the Orlik, lay the small outlying hovels of the neighborhood adjoining the city center, which ended with the church of St. Basil the Great. To the side was the very steep and uncomfortable descent down the bank, and behind, beyond the gardens, a deep ravine, with open pasture beyond it, on which some sort of storehouse stuck up. In the morning, soldiers' drills and beatings with rods took place there—the earliest pictures I saw and watched more often than anything else. On that same pasture, or, better to say, on the narrow strip that separated our fenced gardens from the ravine, grazed Golovan's six or seven cows and the red bull of the Ermolov breed, which also belonged to him. Golovan kept the bull for his small but excellent herd, and also took him around on a halter to "lend" him to those who had need of him for breeding. That brought him some income.

Golovan's means of livelihood consisted of his milk cows and their healthy spouse. Golovan, as I said above, provided the club of the nobility with cream and milk, which were famous for their high quality, owing, of course, to the good breed of his cattle and his good care of them. The butter supplied by Golovan was fresh, yellow as egg yolk, and fragrant, and the cream "didn't flow"—that is, if you turned the bottle neck down, the cream did not pour out in a stream, but fell out in a thick, heavy mass. Golovan didn't deal in products of inferior quality, and therefore he had no rivals, and the nobility of that time not only knew how to eat well, but also had the means to pay for it. Besides that, Golovan also supplied the same club with excellent big eggs from his especially big Dutch hens, of which he kept a great many, and, finally, he "prepared calves," fattening them expertly and always on time, for instance, for the largest gathering of the nobility or other special occasions in noble circles.

In view of these things, which Golovan depended on as a means of livelihood, it was very handy for him to stick close to the streets of the nobility, where he provided for interesting individuals, whom the Orlovians recognized once upon a time in Panshin, Lavretsky, and other heroes and heroines of *A Nest of Gentlefolk*.[4]

Golovan lived, however, not on the street itself, but "apart." The construction that was known as "Golovan's house" stood not in the row of houses, but on a small terrace of the bank, below the left side of the street. The surface of this terrace was some forty feet in length and about the same in width. It was a ledge of earth that had slid down once, but had stopped on its way, stuck there, and, offering no firm support, hardly constituted anyone's property. Back then it was still possible.

Golovan's construction could be called neither a barn nor a house in the proper sense. It was a big, low shed that took up all the space of the fallen ledge. It may be that this formless building was erected there long before the ledge decided to descend, and at that time was part of the nearest household, whose owner did not chase after it, but ceded it to Golovan for the low price that the mighty man could offer him. I even remember it being said that this shed was given to Golovan for some service, at the rendering of which he was a great and willing master.

The shed was divided in two: one half, plastered and whitewashed, with three windows looking out on the Orlik, served as living quarters for Golovan and the five women who were with him; in the other, stalls were made for the cows and bull. In the low garret lived the Dutch hens and a black "Spanish" cock, who lived for a very long time and was considered a "wizard's bird." In him Golovan was growing a cock's stone, which was useful in a great many cases: to bring happiness, to recover a state fallen into enemy hands, to transform old people into young. This stone ripens for seven years and is fully ripe only when the cock stops crowing.

The shed was so big that both parts—for people and for cattle— were very roomy, but, despite all the care taken over it, it held warmth poorly. However, warmth was needed only for the women, while Golovan himself, being insensible to atmospheric changes, slept both summer and winter on an osier mat in a stall, beside his favorite—the red Tyrolean bull Vaska. Cold didn't get to him, and that constituted one of the peculiarities of this mythical person, which earned him his legendary reputation.

Of the five women living with Golovan, three were his sisters, one was his mother, and the fifth was called Pavla, or sometimes Pavlageyushka. But more often she was called "Golovan's sin." I was used to hearing that since childhood, when I still didn't even understand the meaning of the insinuation. For me this Pavla was simply a very affectionate woman, and I can remember as now her tall stature, pale face with bright red spots on the cheeks, and eyebrows of an extraordinary blackness and regularity.

Such black eyebrows in regular half circles could only be seen in pictures portraying a Persian woman reclining on the knees of an elderly Turk. Our girls knew, however, and explained to me very early on, the secret of those eyebrows: the thing was that Golovan was a potion-maker and, loving Pavla, he anointed her eyes with bear grease while she slept, so that no one would recognize her. After that, naturally, there was nothing remarkable about Pavla's eyebrows, and she became attached to Golovan by a power other than her own.

Our girls knew all that.

Pavla herself was an extraordinarily meek and "ever silent" woman. She was so silent that I never heard more than one word from her, and that the most necessary: "greetings," "sit," "good-bye." But in each of these brief words could be heard no end of welcome, benevolence, and kindness. The same was expressed in the sound of her quiet voice, in the gaze of her gray eyes, and in her every movement. I also remember that she had remarkably beautiful hands, which constitutes a great rarity in the working class, and she was such a worker that her industriousness distinguished her even in Golovan's hardworking family.

They all had a great deal to do there: the "deathless" himself had work at the boil from morning till late at night. He was a herdsman, and a deliveryman, and a cheese-maker. At dawn he drove his herd into the dew beyond our fences, and he kept moving his stately cows from ledge to ledge, choosing where the grass was lusher. When people were just getting up in our house, Golovan would already appear with the empty bottles he had taken from the club in place of the new ones he had brought there that day; with his own hands he would hollow out the ice in our ice house for his jugs of freshly drawn milk, while talking something over with my father, and when I went out to the garden after finishing my lessons, he would already be sitting outside our fence again, tending his cows. There was a small gate in the fence, through which I could go out to Golovan and talk with him. He was so good at telling the hundred and four sacred stories that I knew them from him without ever learning them from a book.[5] Some simple folk also used to come to him there—always seeking advice. One of them would come and begin like this:

"I've been looking for you, Golovan. Give me some advice."

"What is it?"

"This and that: something's going wrong in the household, or there's family discord."

Most often they came with matters of this second category. Golovan would listen, while plaiting osier or shouting to the cows, and smiling all the while, as if paying no attention, and then he would raise his blue eyes to his interlocutor and reply:

"I'm a poor adviser, brother! Ask God's advice."

"How can I do that?"

"Oh, very simple, brother: pray and then do as you would if you had to die at once. Tell me: what would you do in that case?"

The man would think and reply.

Golovan would agree, or else say:

"And if I was the one to die, brother, I'd rather do this."

And he usually said it all quite cheerfully, with his customary smile.

His advice must have been very good, because people always listened to it and thanked him very much.

Could there be a "sin" for such a man in the person of the most meek Pavlageyushka, who at that time, I think, was a little over thirty, a limit she was not to go beyond? I didn't understand that "sin" and in my innocence did not insult her and Golovan by rather general suspicions. Yet there were grounds for suspicion, and very strong grounds, even irrefutable, judging by appearances. Who was she to Golovan? A stranger. Not only that: he had known her once, they had belonged to the same masters, Golovan had wanted to marry her, but it hadn't taken place. He had been sent to serve the hero of the Caucasus, Alexei Petrovich Ermolov,[6] and meanwhile Pavla had been given in marriage to the horse-master Ferapont, or "Khrapon," as the locals said. Golovan had been a needed and useful servant, because he could do everything—he was not only a good cook and confectioner, but a keen-witted and ready servant on campaign. Alexei Petrovich had paid what he owed to his landowner for Golovan, and besides, they say, had lent Golovan the money to buy himself out. I don't know if that's true, but soon after he returned from serving Ermolov, Golovan did indeed buy himself out and always called Alexei Petrovich his "benefactor." And once Golovan was free, Alexei Petrovich gave him a good cow and calf for his farm, from which came Golovan's "Ermolov breed."

IV

Precisely when Golovan settled in the shed on the landslip I don't know at all, but it coincided with the first days of his "freemanship"— when he was faced with major concerns about his kin, who remained in servitude. Golovan bought himself out personally, but his mother, his three sisters, and his aunt, who later became my nanny, remained "in bondage." And their tenderly beloved Pavla, or Pavlageyushka, was in the same position. Golovan made it his first concern to buy them all out, and for that he needed money. His expertise qualified him to become a cook or a confectioner, but he preferred something else, namely dairy farming, which he started with the help of the "Ermolov cow." There was an opinion that he chose that because he himself was a *molokan*.[7] Maybe that simply meant that he always busied himself with milk, but maybe the title aimed directly at his faith, in which he appeared as odd as in his many other doings. It's very possible that he had known molokans in the Caucasus, and had borrowed something from them. But that has to do with his oddities, which we will touch upon below.

The dairy farming went beautifully: in some three years, Golovan already had two cows and a bull, then three, four cows, and he had made enough money to buy out his mother, then each year he bought out a sister, and brought them all together in his roomy but chilly hovel. In that way, after six or seven years, he had freed his whole family, but the beauty Pavla had flown from him. By the time he was able to buy her out as well, she was already far away. Her husband, the horse-master Khrapon, was a bad man—he had not pleased his master in something, and, as an example to others, had been sent as a soldier without conscription.

In the service, Khrapon landed among the "gallopers," that is, as a rider in the Moscow fire brigade, and had his wife sent there; but he soon did something bad there as well and ran away, and his abandoned wife, having a quiet and timid character, feared the whirl of life in the capital and returned to Orel. Here she also didn't find any support in her old place and, driven by need, she went to Golovan. He, naturally, took her in at once and placed her in the same big room where his sisters and mother lived. How Golovan's mother and sisters looked upon the installing of Pavla, I don't know for certain, but it didn't sow any discord in their house. The women all lived in great friendship with each other, and even loved poor Pavlageyushka very much, and Golovan paid equal attention to them all, except for the special respect he showed his mother, who was now so old that in summer he carried her out to the sun in his arms, like a sick child. I remember how she "went off" into terrible coughing fits and kept praying to be "taken."

All of Golovan's sisters were old maids, and they all helped their brother on the farm: they mucked out and milked the cows, tended the hens, and spun an extraordinary yarn, from which they then wove extraordinary fabrics such as I've never seen since. This yarn went by the very unattractive name of "spittings." Golovan brought material for it from somewhere in bags, and I saw and remember that material: it consisted of small, twiggy scraps of various colored cotton thread. Each scrap was from two to ten inches long, and on each such scrap there was sure to be a more or less fat knot or snarl. Where Golovan got these scraps I don't know, but it was obviously factory refuse. That's also what his sisters told me.

"They spin and weave cotton there, dearest," they said to me, "and each time they come upon a knot, they tear it off and *spit it out* on the floor, because it won't go through the reed. My brother gathers them up, and we make warm blankets out of them."

I saw how they patiently sorted these pieces of thread, tied them together, wound the resulting motley, multicolored threads on long spools. Then they spliced them together, spun them into thicker ones stretched along the wall on pegs, sorted those of the same color for stripes, and finally wove these "spittings" through a special reed into "spitting blankets." These blankets looked like today's woolen ones, each with the same two stripes, but the fabric was always marbleized. The knots in them were somehow smoothed out from the spinning, and though they were, of course, very noticeable, that did not keep the blankets from being light, warm, and sometimes even rather pretty. Besides, they were sold very cheaply—at less than a rouble apiece.

This cottage industry in Golovan's family went on nonstop, and he probably had no trouble finding a market for the spitting blankets.

Pavlageyushka also tied and spun the spittings and wove blankets, but, besides that, in her zeal for the family that had given her shelter, she also took on all the heaviest work in the house: went down the steep bank to the Orlik for water, brought in fuel, and so on and so forth.

Firewood in Orel was already very expensive even then, and poor people heated either with buckwheat chaff or with dung, and the latter required big provisions.

All this Pavla did with her slender hands, in eternal silence, looking at God's world from under her Persian eyebrows. Whether she knew that her name was "sin" I am not aware, but that was her name among the people, who stand firmly by the nicknames they invent. And how else could it be? Where a woman, a loving one, lives in the house of a man who loved her and sought to marry her, there is, of course, sin. And indeed, back in my childhood, when I first saw

Pavla, she was unanimously considered "Golovan's sin," but Golovan himself did not lose the least bit of general respect on account of it and kept his nickname of "deathless."

V

People started calling Golovan "deathless" in the first year, when he settled by himself above the Orlik with his Ermolov cow and her calf. The occasion for it was the following wholly trustworthy circumstance, which nobody remembered about in the time of the recent "Prokofy" plague. It was the usual hard times in Orel, and in February, on the day of St. Agafya the Dairymaid,[8] the "cow death" fittingly swept through the villages. It went as it usually does and as it is written in the universal book known as *The Cool Vineyard*:[9] "As summer comes to an end and autumn draws near, the pestilential infection soon begins. And during that time it is needful that every man place his hope in almighty God and in His most pure Mother, and protect himself with the power of the honorable Cross, and hold back his heart from grief, and dread, and painful thoughts, for through these the human heart is diminished, and sores and cankers soon stick to it—seize the brain and heart, overcome the man, and he dies forthwith." All this also went according to the usual pictures of the nature around us, "when the mists in autumn set in thick and dark, with wind from the meridian lands, followed by rain, and the earth steams in the sun, and then it is needful not to go out in the wind, but to sit in the warmth of the cottage and not open the windows, and best would be not to stay in that town, but to leave it and go to clean places." When, that is, in what precise year, the pestilence occurred that gave Golovan his fame for being "deathless," I don't know. There was no great interest then in such trifles, and no noise was made on account of them, as there was on account of Naum Prokofiev.[10] Local woes used to end locally, appeased by hope in God and His most pure Mother alone, and perhaps only in cases of the strong predominance of the sensible "intellectuals" in certain locales were unusual sanitary measures taken: "Build clean bonfires in the yards, of oak wood, so that the smoke disperses, and in the cottages burn wormwood and juniper and rue leaves." But all that could be done only by intellectuals, and only well-to-do ones at that, while death carried off "forthwith" not the educated, but those who had no time to sit in warm cottages and were not up to burning oak wood in open yards. Death went arm in arm with famine, and they supported each other. The famished begged from the famished, the sick died "forthwith," that is, quickly, which was more advantageous for peasants. There was no lengthy languishing, no rumors of recoveries were heard. Whoever fell sick, died "forthwith," *except for one man.* What illness it was has not been scientifically determined, but it was popularly known as "bosom," or "boil," or "oilcake carbuncle," or even just "carbuncle." It started in grain-producing districts, where, for lack of bread, they ate hempseed oilcakes. In the districts of Karachev and Bryansk, where peasants mixed unsifted flour with ground bark, the illness was different, also deadly, but not "carbuncle." "Carbuncle" first appeared in cattle, and was then transmitted to people. "A red sore breaks out on a man's bosom or neck, and he gets stitches all over his body, and an unquenchable burning inside, or a sort of chill in his limbs and heavy breathing, and he cannot breathe—he tries to draw a breath, but lets it out at once; he gets sleepy, cannot stop sleeping; feels a bitterness or sourness in the mouth and starts to vomit; the man's countenance changes, a claylike look comes over him, and he dies forthwith." Maybe it was anthrax, maybe it was some other pest, but in any case it was pernicious and merciless, and its most widespread name, I repeat again, was "carbuncle." A pimple breaks out on your body, a "carbuncle" as simple folk called it, turns yellow-headed, reddens all around, and by morning the flesh begins to rot, and then it's death forthwith. A quick death was seen, however, "in a good light." The end was quiet, not painful, most peasant-like, only the dying all wanted to drink till the last minute. That constituted all the brief and unwearisome care demanded, or, better to say, begged for by the sick. Though caring for them even in this form was not only dangerous, but almost impossible—a man who gave a sick relation a drink today, would fall sick with "carbuncle" himself tomorrow, and it was not rare in a house to have two or three dead people lying next to each other. The last person in these orphaned houses died without help—without that one help our peasant cared about, "that someone give him a drink." Such an orphan would first put a bucket of water by his head and drink from a dipper as long as he could raise his arm, and then he would twist a sleeve or shirttail, wet it, put it in his mouth, and go stiff like that.

Deathless Golovan

A great personal calamity is a poor teacher of mercy. At least it has no good effect on people of ordinary, mediocre morality, which doesn't rise above the level of mere compassion. It dulls the sensitivity of the heart, which suffers painfully itself and is filled with the sense of its own torment. Instead, in such woeful moments of general calamity, the people's milieu brings forth of itself heroes of magnanimity, fearless and selfless. In ordinary times they are not conspicuous and often are in no way distinguishable from the masses: but let "carbuncle" fall upon the people, and the people produce a chosen one for themselves, and he works wonders, which make of him a mythical, legendary, *deathless* person. Golovan was one of these, and during the very first plague he surpassed and eclipsed in people's minds another remarkable local man, the merchant Ivan Ivanovich Androsov. Androsov was an honorable old man, respected and loved for his kindness and fairness, for he was "ready helpful" in all the people's calamities. He also helped during the "plague," because he had a written "treatment," and he "recopied it all in multiples." These copies of his were taken and read in various places, but nobody understood them or "knew how to go about it." It was written: "Should a sore appear on the head or another place above the waist, let much blood from the median; should it appear on the brow, quickly let blood from under the tongue; should it appear by the ears or under the chin, let blood from the cephalic vein, but should it appear under one of the breasts, it means the heart is affected, and then the median should be opened on that side." For each place "where a burden is felt," it was written which vein to open: the "saphena," or "the one opposite the thumb, or the spatic artery, the pulmatic, or the basical," with the recommendation to "let the blood flow, till such time as it turns green and changes aspect." And to treat also "with remedies of athelaea, sealed earth or Armenian earth, Malvasian wine, bugloss vodka, Venetian virian, mithridate, and Manus-Christi sugar."[11] And those who entered the sickroom were advised "to hold Angelica root in their mouths, wormwood in their hands, have their nostrils wetted with wild rose vinegar, and sniff a vinegar-soaked sponge." No one could make anything of it, as in official decrees, which have been written and rewritten, this way and that, and "in foursome thereforesomes." The veins couldn't be found, nor the Malvasian wine, nor the Armenian earth, nor the bugloss vodka, and people read good old Androsov's copies more only so as to "quench my sorrows." All they could apply were the concluding words: "And where there be plague, it behooves you not to go to those places, but to go away." That was what most people followed, and Ivan Ivanovich himself adhered to the same rule and sat in his warm cottage and dispensed his medical prescriptions through a little slot, holding his breath and keeping angelica root in his mouth. The only ones who could enter a sickroom safely were those who had deer's tears or a *bezoar*-stone;[12] but Ivan Ivanovich had neither deer's tears nor a bezoar-stone, and while a bezoar-stone might have been found in the pharmacies on Bolkhovskaya Street, the pharmacists were one a Pole, the other a German, and they had no proper pity for Russian people and saved the bezoar-stones for themselves. This was fully trustworthy, because when one of the Orel pharmacists lost his bezoar, his ears began to turn yellow right there in the street, one eye grew smaller than the other, he started trembling, and though he wanted to sweat and for that asked them at home to put hot bricks to his soles, all the same he didn't sweat, but died in a dry shirt. A great many people searched for the pharmacist's lost bezoar, and somebody did find it, only not Ivan Ivanovich, because he also died.

And so in this terrible time, when the intellectuals wiped themselves with vinegar and did not give up the ghost, the "carbuncle" swept still more fiercely through the poor village huts; people began to die here "wholesale and with no help at all"—and suddenly, there, on the field of death, with astonishing fearlessness, appeared Golovan. He probably knew, or thought he knew, something of medicine, because he put a "Caucasian plaster" of his own making on the sick people's swellings; but this Caucasian, or Ermolov, plaster of his was of little help. Like Androsov, Golovan did not cure the "carbuncle," but his service to the sick and the healthy was great in this respect, that he went dauntlessly into the plague-stricken hovels and gave the infected not only fresh water but also the skim milk he had left after removing the cream for the club. In the early morning, before dawn, he crossed the Orlik on a shed gate he had taken off its hinges (there was no boat there), and went from hovel to hovel, his boundless bosom filled with bottles, moistening the dry lips of the dying from a flask, or putting a chalk cross on the door, if the drama of life was already over there and the curtain of death had been drawn on the last of its actors.

From then on the hitherto little-known Golovan became widely known in all the villages, and a great popular attraction to him began. His name, previously familiar to the servants in noble houses, came to be uttered with respect among simple folk; they began to see him as a man who not only could "replace the late Ivan Ivanovich Androsov, but meant even more than he to both God and men." And they weren't slow in finding a supernatural explanation for the very fearlessness of Golovan: Golovan obviously knew something, and by virtue of such knowledge he was *deathless* . . .

Later it turned out that it was precisely so: the herdsman Panka helped to explain it all, having seen Golovan do something incredible, and it was confirmed by other circumstances.

The pest did not touch Golovan. All the while it raged in the villages, neither he himself nor his Ermolov cow and calf got sick; but that wasn't all: the most important thing was that he deceived and expelled—or, keeping to local speech, "denihilated"—the pest itself, and he did it not sparing his own warm blood for the peasant folk.

The bezoar-stone lost by the pharmacist was with Golovan. How he got it was not known. It was supposed that Golovan had been taking cream to the pharmacist for "daily unction," had spotted the stone and secreted it away. Whether such secreting away is held to be honest or dishonest, there was no strong criticism of it, and there shouldn't have been. If it is no sin to take and secrete away eatables, because God gives eatables to everybody, then still less is it blameworthy to take a healing substance, if it is meant for general salvation. So our people judge, and so say I. Golovan, having secreted away the pharmacist's stone, acted magnanimously with it, letting it be of general benefit to the whole of Christendom.

All this, as I said above, was discovered by Panka, and the general intelligence of the people cleared it up.

VI

Panka, a muzhik with different-colored eyes and sun-bleached hair, was a herdsman's helper, and besides his general herding duties, he also drove the rebaptizers'[13] cows out *to the dew* in the morning. Being thus occupied early one morning, he spied out the whole business that raised Golovan to the height of popular greatness.

It was in springtime, doubtless soon after young St. George,[14] bright and brave, rode out to the emerald Russian fields, his arms in red gold to the elbows, his legs in pure silver to the knees, on his brow the sun, on his nape the crescent moon, on all sides the moving stars, and the honest, righteous people of God drove their cattle big and small to meet him. The grass was still so short that the sheep and goats had barely enough, and the thick-lipped cows could take little. But in the shade under the fences and in the ditches, worm-wood and nettles were already sprouting, which could be eaten at need with the dew.

Panka drove the rebaptizers' cows out early, still in darkness, and led them straight along the bank of the Orlik to a clearing beyond the outskirts, just across from the end of Third Dvoryanskaya Street, where on one sloping side lay the old "city" garden, as it was known, and on the left Golovan's nest clung to its ledge.

It was still cold in the morning, especially before dawn, and to someone who wants to sleep it feels even colder. Panka's clothes, naturally, were poor, orphan-like, some sort of rags with hole upon hole. The lad turned one way, then the other, praying that St. Prokop would warm him up, but instead the cold went on. As soon as he closed his eyes, a little wind would sneak, sneak through a rip and awaken him again. However, young strength held its own: Panka pulled his coat over his head like a tent and dozed off. He didn't hear what hour it was, because the green bell tower of the Theophany church was far away. And there was no one around, not a human soul, only fat merchants' cows huffing, and every once in a while a frisky perch splashed in the Orlik. The herdsman slumbered in his tattered coat. But then it was as if something suddenly nudged him in the side—zephyr had probably found a new hole somewhere. Panka roused himself, looked around half-awake, was about to shout: "What are you up to, hornless!" and stopped. It seemed to him that somebody was going down the steep slope on the other side. Maybe a thief wanted to bury some stolen thing in the clay. Panka became interested: maybe he would sneak up on the thief and catch him red-handed, or shout "Let's go halves," or, better still, try to take good note of the burial place, then swim across the Orlik during the day, dig it up, and take it all for himself without sharing.

Panka began to stare, looking at the steep slope across the Orlik. It was still barely gray outside.

Somebody comes down the slope, steps out on the water, and begins to walk. Just simply walks on the water, as if on dry land, and doesn't row with anything, but only leans on a stick. Panka was dumbfounded. A miracle was expected then in the Orel monastery, and voices had already been heard from under the floor. This began right after "Nikodim's funeral." Bishop Nikodim[15] was a wicked man, who distinguished himself towards the end of his earthly career by this: that, wishing to have yet another decoration, he sought to please by sending a great many clerics as soldiers, among whom there were some only sons and even married deacons and sacristans. A whole party of them was leaving town, pouring out tears. Those seeing them off were also sobbing, and simple folk themselves, for all their dislike of well-stuffed priestly britches, wept and gave them alms. The officer of the party himself felt so sorry for them that, wishing to put an end to the tears, he ordered the new recruits to strike up a song, and when the chorus sang out loud and clear a song they themselves had composed:

Our old bishop Nikodim
Is as cruel as he is mean,

the officer himself supposedly burst out weeping. All this was drowned in a sea of tears and for sensitive souls represented an evil that cried out to heaven. And indeed, just as their cries reached heaven, "voices" came to Orel. At first the "voices" were inarticulate and it was not known who they came from, but when Nikodim died soon after that and was buried under the church, then the talking clearly came from a bishop buried there previously to him (Apollos, it seems[16]). The previously departed bishop was displeased with his new neighbor and, ashamed at nothing, said directly: "Take this carrion out of here, he makes me choke." And he even threatened that, if the "carrion" was not removed, he himself "would go and appear in another town." Many people heard it. They would come to the monastery for the vigil, stand through the service, and on the way out hear the old bishop moan: "Take the carrion away." Everyone wished very much that the request of the kindly deceased be fulfilled, but the authorities, who are not always attentive to the needs of the people, did not throw Nikodim out, and the saint who was clearly revealing himself[17] might at any moment "quit the premises."

None other than that very thing was now happening: the saint was leaving, and no one saw him but one poor little shepherd, who was so bewildered by it that he not only did not hold him back, but did not even notice how the saint vanished from his sight. Dawn was just beginning to break. With light a man's courage grows, and with courage his curiosity increases. Panka wanted to go near the water over which the mysterious being had just passed; but as soon as he came near, he saw a big, wet gate held to the bank by a pole. The matter became clear: meaning it had not been the saint passing over, but simply deathless Golovan floating. He had probably gone to comfort some orphaned children with milk from his bosom. Panka marveled: when did this Golovan sleep! . . . And how could such a huge man as he float on such a vessel—on half a gate? True, the Orlik is not a big river and its water, held back by a dam further down, is quiet as a puddle, but even so, what was this floating on a gate?

Panka decided to try it himself. He stepped onto the gate, took the pole, and, for a lark, crossed to the other side, got off on the bank there to have a look at Golovan's house, because it was already good and bright, and meanwhile Golovan cried out just then from the other side: "Hey! Who made off with my gate! Bring it back!"

Panka was a lad of no great courage and was not used to counting on anybody's magnanimity, and therefore he got frightened and did a foolish thing. Instead of bringing Golovan his raft, Panka went and hid himself in one of the clay pits, of which there were a multitude there. Panka lay in the pit and, no matter how Golovan called from the other side, he did not show himself. Then, seeing that he couldn't get his boat back, Golovan threw off his coat, stripped naked, tied his whole wardrobe up with his belt, put it on his head, and swam across the Orlik. The water was still very cold.

Panka's only care was that Golovan shouldn't see him and give him a beating, but soon his attention was drawn to something else. Golovan crossed the river and began to get dressed, but suddenly he squatted down, looked under his left knee, and paused.

This was so close to the pit Panka was hiding in that he could see everything from behind the hummock that shielded him. And it was already quite light by then, dawn was blushing, and though most of the citizens were still asleep, a young fellow with a scythe appeared by the city garden and started mowing the nettles and putting them in a basket.

Golovan noticed the mower and, standing up in nothing but his shirt, shouted loudly to him:

"Hey, boy, give me that scythe, quick!"

The boy brought him the scythe, and Golovan said to him:

"Go and pick me a big burdock leaf." And when the fellow turned away from him, he took the blade off the handle, squatted down again, pulled at his left calf with one hand, and with one stroke cut it off. He hurled the cut-off hunk of flesh, the size of a peasant flat-cake, into the Orlik, pressed the wound with both hands, and collapsed.

Seeing that, Panka forgot everything, jumped out, and started calling the mower.

The two fellows picked Golovan up and carried him to his house. There he came to his senses, and told them to take two towels from a trunk and bind the wound as tight as they could. They tightened it with all their might, and it stopped bleeding.

Then Golovan told them to set a bucket of water and a dipper beside him, go about their business, and not tell anybody what had happened. They went, shaking with horror, and told everybody. Those who heard about it figured out at once that Golovan hadn't done it just like that, but, out of heartache for the people, had thrown the hunk of his body to the pest, so that this sacrificed hunk would pass down all the Russian rivers from the little Orlik to the Oka, from the Oka to the Volga, all across Great Russia to the wide Caspian Sea, and in that way Golovan suffered for all, and he himself would not die from it, because he possessed the pharmacist's living stone and was a "deathless" man.

This story suited everybody's thinking, and the prophecy also came true. Golovan did not die of his terrible wound. The evil sickness actually stopped after this sacrifice, and days of tranquillity set in: the fields and meadows were lush with green growth, and young St. George, bright and brave, could now freely ride over them, his arms in red gold to the elbows, his legs in pure silver to the knees, on his brow the sun, on his nape the crescent moon, and around him the moving stars. Canvas was bleached by the fresh St. George's dew, and instead of the hero St. George, the prophet Jeremiah rode out to the field with a heavy yoke, dragging ploughs and harrows, nightingales whistled on St. Boris's day, comforting the martyr, sturdy seedlings, owing to the efforts of St. Mavra, showed their bluish sprouts, St. Zosima passed with a long cane bearing a queen bee on its head; the day of St. John the Theologian, "father of St. Nicholas," passed, and Nicholas himself was celebrated, and then came Simon the Zealot, when the earth celebrates its own day.[18] On the earth's day Golovan crept outside to sit by the wall, and after that he began little by little to walk and take up his business again.

His health, evidently, hadn't suffered in the least, only he began to "hitch"—hopping on his left leg.

Of the touchingness and courage of his bloody act upon himself people probably had a high opinion, but they judged it as I've said: they did not seek natural causes for it, but, wrapping it all in their own fantasy, from a natural event composed a fabulous legend, and of simple, magnanimous Golovan made a mythical personage, something like a magician or sorcerer, who possessed an invincible talisman and could venture upon anything and would perish nowhere.

Whether Golovan was aware or not that popular rumor attributed such deeds to him—I don't know. However, I think he was, because people very often turned to him with requests and questions such as one would only turn to a good magician with. And to many such questions he gave "helpful advice," and generally he did not frown at any requests. In the country roundabout he would be now a cow doctor, now a human doctor, or an engineer, or an astrologer, or a pharmacist. He knew how to get rid of mange and scabs, once again with some sort of "Ermolov ointment," the cost of which was one copper kopeck for three people; he removed fever from the head with pickled cucumber; he knew that herbs should be gathered from St. John's to St. Peter-and-Paul's, and was excellent at "dowsing," that is, at showing where a well should be dug. But he couldn't do that all the time, but only from the beginning of June till St. Theodore of the Wells, when "you could hear how the water goes through the joints of the earth."[19] Golovan could also do everything else a man needs, but he had given God a pledge against the rest for stopping the pestilence. He had sealed it then with his blood, and he held firm to it. God loved him for that and had mercy on him, and the people, delicate in their feelings, never asked anything of Golovan that ought not to be asked. According to the people's etiquette—that's how it's done with us.

Golovan, however, was so little burdened by the mystical cloud that popular *fama* shrouded him in, that he made no effort to undo the image people had formed of him. He knew it would be useless.

When I eagerly leafed through Victor Hugo's novel *Toilers of the Sea* and there met Gilliatt, with his brilliantly outlined severity towards himself and indulgence towards others, which reached the point of utter selflessness, I was struck not only by the grandeur of the figure and the power of its portrayal, but also by the similarity of the Guernsey hero to the living person I had known under the name of Golovan. In them lived the same spirit and in both a like heart beat selflessly. They did not differ much in their fates: all their lives some sort of mystery thickened around them, precisely because they were all too pure and clear, and to the lot of the one as of the other there fell not a single drop of personal happiness.

VII

Golovan, like Gilliat, seemed to be "of dubious faith."

He was thought to be some sort of schismatic, but that was not so important, because in Orel at that time there were many different beliefs: there were (and probably still are now) simple Old Believers, as well as not so simple ones—Fedoseevans, "Pilipons," and the rebaptizers, there were even Flagellants and "people of God," all of whom human justice sent far away.[20] But all these people firmly held to their own flock and firmly disapproved of any other faith—they set themselves apart in prayer and eating and considered themselves the only ones on "the right path." Whereas Golovan behaved himself as if he even knew nothing at all for sure about the best path, but shared his hunk of bread indiscriminately with anyone who asked, and himself sat down at any table you like when he was invited. He even gave the Jew Yushka from the garrison milk for his children. But people's love for Golovan found an excuse for the non-Christian aspect of this last act: they perceived that, by cajoling Yushka, Golovan wanted to get from him the "lips of Judas," carefully preserved by the Jews, with which one could lie one's way out of court, or the "hairy vegetable" that the Jews quench their thirst with, so that they can go without drinking vodka. But the most incomprehensible thing about Golovan was that he kept company with the coppersmith Anton, who, in terms of all real qualities, enjoyed the worst of reputations. This man did not agree with anybody on the most sacred questions, but deduced something mysterious from the signs of the zodiac and even did some writing. Anton lived on the outskirts, in an empty little garret room, for which he paid fifty kopecks a month, but kept such frightful things there that nobody visited him except Golovan. It was known that Anton had a chart there called "the zodiac," and a glass that "drew down the sun's fire"; and besides that he had access to the roof, where he went at night, sat by the chimney like a tomcat, and "set up an aggrandizing tube," and, during the sleepiest time, gazed at the sky. Anton's devotion to this instrument knew no bounds, especially on starry nights, when he could see the whole zodiac. He came running from his boss's shop, where he did his copper work, crept at once into his upstairs room, and immediately slipped through the dormer window to the roof, and if there were stars in the sky, he sat all night and gazed. This might have been forgiven him, if he had been a scientist or at least a German, but since he was a simple Russian man—they spent a long time breaking him of it, poked him with poles, threw dung at him and a dead cat, but he paid no attention to any of it and didn't even notice they had poked him. They all laughingly called him "Astronomer," and in fact he was an astronomer.[*] He was a quiet and very honest man, but a freethinker; he insisted that the earth turns and that we are sometimes upside down on it. For this last obvious absurdity, Anton was beaten and recognized as a fool, but then, as a fool, he began to enjoy the freedom of thought that is the privilege of this advantageous title among us, and reached the limits of the unbelievable. He did not acknowledge the seventy-times-seven years of the prophet Daniel[21] as applicable to the Russian tsardom, said that the "ten-horned beast" was only an allegory, and the bear was an astronomical figure, which was found on his charts. Just as unorthodox was his reasoning about the "eagle's wings," about the cups, and about the seal of the Antichrist.[22] But, because he was feebleminded, this was all forgiven him. He wasn't married, because he had no time to get married and would have been unable to feed a wife—and anyway what fool would want to marry an astronomer? Yet Golovan, being of sound mind, not only kept company with the astronomer, but also never made fun of him. They could even be seen together at night, on the astronomer's roof, taking turns looking at the zodiac through the aggrandizing tube. It's understandable what sort of thoughts these two figures standing at the tube by night might inspire, with fanciful superstition, medical poetry, religious

---

[*] My schoolmate, now the well-known Russian mathematician K. D. Kraevich,[23] and I got to know this eccentric at the end of the forties, when we were in the third class of the Orel high school and roomed together in the Losevs' house. "Anton the Astronomer" (then very old) actually had some sort of notion about the luminaries and the laws of their revolution, but the most interesting thing was that he made the lenses for his tubes himself, polishing them from the bases of thick crystal glasses with sand and stone, and he looked all over the heavens through them . . . He lived like a beggar, but he didn't feel his poverty, because he was in constant ecstasy from his "zodiac." *Author.*

raving, and sheer bewilderment milling around them . . . And, finally, circumstances themselves put Golovan in a somewhat strange position: it was not known what parish he belonged to . . . His cold hovel stood out so much on its own that no spiritual strategist could add it to his jurisdiction, and Golovan himself was unconcerned about it and, if pestered too much about his parish, would reply:

"I'm of the parish of the Almighty Creator"—but there was no such church in all Orel.

Gilliatt, in answer to the question about where his parish was, only raised his finger and, pointing to the sky, said: "Up there"—but the essence of both answers was the same.

Golovan liked hearing about any faith, but didn't seem to have his own opinions on the subject, and in cases of persistent questioning about what he believed, recited:

"I believe in one God, the Father Almighty, maker of all things visible and invisible."[24]

That, of course, was evasiveness.

However, it would be wrong for anyone to think that Golovan was a sectarian or avoided the Church. No, he even went to Father Pyotr at the Boris-and-Gleb cathedral "to verify his conscience." He would come and say:

"Cover me with shame, father, I don't like myself these days."

I remember this Father Pyotr, who used to come to visit us, and once, when my father said something to him about Golovan being a man of excellent conscience, Father Pyotr replied:

"Have no doubts: his conscience is whiter than snow."

Golovan liked lofty thoughts and knew the poet Pope,[25] but not as a writer is usually known by people who *have read* his works. No, Golovan, having approved of *An Essay on Man*, given him by the same Alexei Petrovich Ermolov, knew the whole poem *by heart*. And I can remember how he once stood by the doorpost, listening to the story of some sad new event, and, suddenly sighing, replied:

My gentle Bolingbroke, 'tis no surmise,
In pride, in reasoning pride, our error lies.

The reader need not be surprised that a man like Golovan could toss off a line from Pope. Those were harsh times, but poetry was in fashion, and its great word was dear even to men of good blood. From the masters it descended to the plebs. But now I come to the major incident in Golovan's story—the incident which unquestionably cast an ambiguous light on him even in the eyes of people not inclined to believe all sorts of nonsense. Golovan came out as not clean in some remote past time. This was revealed suddenly, but in the most vivid form. There appeared on the squares of Orel a person who meant nothing in anyone's eyes, but who laid the most powerful claims on Golovan and treated him with incredible insolence.

This person and the history of his appearance make a rather characteristic episode from the moral history of the time and a picture from life that is not without some color. And therefore I ask you to turn your attention for a moment slightly away from Orel, to still warmer parts, to a quiet-flowing river between carpeted banks, to the people's "feast of faith," where there is no room for everyday, practical life, where everything, *decidedly everything*, passes through a peculiar religiosity, which imparts to it all its special relief and liveliness. We must attend the revealing of the relics of a new saint—which was an event of the greatest significance for the most various representatives of society in those days. For simple folk it was an epic event, or, as one of the bards of the time used to say, "the accomplishment of the sacred feast of faith."

VIII

Not one of the printed accounts of that time can convey the commotion that set in at the opening of the solemnities. The living but low-life aspect of the thing escaped them. This was not today's peaceful journey by coach or rail, with stops at comfortable inns, where there is everything necessary and at a reasonable price. Travel back then was a great feat, and in this case a feat of piety, which, however, was equal to the expected solemn event in the Church. There was also much poetry in it—once again of a special sort—motley and shot through with various tinges of the Church's everyday life, of limited popular naïveté and the boundless yearnings of the living spirit.

A multitude of people from Orel set out for this solemnity. Most zealous of all, naturally, was the merchant estate, but landowners of the middling sort didn't lag behind, and simple folk in particular came pouring in. They went on foot. Only those who transported the infirm "for healing" dragged along on some wretched nag. Sometimes, however, the infirm were transported *on the back* and were not even counted a burden, because the inns charged them less for everything, and sometimes even let them stay without paying at all. There were not a few who deliberately "invented a sickness for themselves: rolled up their eyes, and two would alternately transport a third on wheels, so as to earn income from donations for wax, and oil, and other rites."

So I read in an account, unprinted but reliable, copied down not from a standard pattern, but from "living vision," and by someone who preferred the truth to the tendentious mendacity of that time.

The movement was so populous that there were no places in the inns or hotels in the towns of Livny and Elets, through which its path lay. It would happen that important and eminent people spent the night in their carriages. Oats, hay, grain—the prices of everything along the high road went up, so that, as noted by my grandmother, whose memoirs I am using, the cost of feeding a man with head cheese, cabbage soup, lamb stew, and kasha at an inn rose from twenty-five kopecks (seven and a half in silver) to fifty-two (fifteen in silver). At the present time, of course, fifteen is still a completely incredible price, but that's how it was, and the revealing of the relics of the new saint had the same significance for the area, in terms of raising the prices of living supplies, as the recent fire on the Mstinsky Bridge in Petersburg. "The prices *soared* and stayed there."

Among other pilgrims setting out from Orel for the revealing was the merchant family S——, very well-known people in their time, "suppliers," that is, to put it simply, rich kulaks,[26] who collected wheat from the peasants' wagons into big granaries, and then sold their supplies to wholesale dealers in Moscow and Riga. This was a profitable business, which, after the emancipation of the peasants,[27] was not scorned even by the nobility; but they liked to sleep late, and soon learned from bitter experience that they weren't capable even of this stupid kulak business. The merchants S—— were regarded as the foremost suppliers, and their importance went so far that their house was known, not by their name, but by an ennobling nickname. The house, to be sure, was a strictly pious one, where they prayed in the morning, oppressed and robbed people all day, and then prayed again in the evening. And by night, watchdogs on cables clanked their chains, and in all the windows it was "icon lamps and brightness," loud snoring, and someone's hot tears.

The ruler of the house, who today would be known as "the founder of the firm," was then simply called *himself*. He was a mild little old man, whom, however, everyone feared like fire. It was said of him that he made for a soft bed, but hard sleeping: he fondly called everybody "my dearest," and then sent them all into the teeth of the devil. A well-known and familiar type, the type of the merchant patriarch.

So this patriarch, too, traveled to the revealing "with full complement"—himself, and his wife, and his daughter, who suffered from "the disease of melancholy" and was to be cured. All the known remedies of folk poetry and creativity had been tried on her: she had been made to drink stimulating elecampane, had had powdered peony root poured all over her for repulsing phantoms, had been given wild garlic to sniff, so as to straighten the brain in her head, but nothing had helped, and now she was being taken to the saint, hurrying to have the first chance, when the very first force is released. Belief in the advantage of the *first force* is very great, and is rooted in the story of the pool of Siloam, where those were cured first who managed to get in first after the troubling of the water.[28]

The Orel merchants traveled through Livny and Elets, enduring great hardships, and were completely worn out by the time they reached the saint. But to seize the "first chance" from the saint turned out to be impossible. Such a host of people had gathered that there was no thought of forcing one's way into the church for the vigil of the "revealing day," when the "first chance," properly speaking, would occur—that is, when the greatest force would issue from the new relics.

The merchant and his wife were in despair—the most indifferent of all was the daughter, who didn't know what she was losing. There was no hope of doing anything about it—there were so many nobility, with such names, while they were simple merchants, who, if they were of some significance in their own place, were totally lost here, in such a concentration of Christian grandeur. And so one day, sitting in grief over tea under their little kibitka[29] at the inn, the patriarch complained to his wife that he no longer had any hope of reaching the holy coffin either among the first or among the second, but only perhaps among the last, along with tillers of the soil and fishermen, that is, generally, with simple people. And by then what would be the good of it: the police would be ferocious and the clergy tired—they wouldn't let you pray your fill, but would just push you by. In general, once so many thousands of people had put their lips to the relics, it wouldn't be the same. In view of which, they could have come later, but that was not what they had striven for: they had traveled, worn themselves out, left the business at home in the assistants' hands, and paid three times the price on the road, and suddenly here's your consolation!

The merchant tried once or twice to get to the deacons; he was ready to show his gratitude, but there was no hope there either—on the one hand there was a hindrance in the form of a gendarme with a white glove or a Cossack with a whip (they, too, had come in great numbers to the revealing of the relics), and on the other, the great danger of being crushed by the good Orthodox folk, who surged like an ocean. There had already been "occasions," and even a great many, both yesterday and today. At the stroke of a Cossack whip, our good Christians would rush aside somewhere in a wall of five or six hundred people, and would push and press together so much that only moans and stink came from inside, and then, when it eased off, you could see women's ears with the earrings torn away and fingers with rings pulled off, and two or three souls gone to their reward altogether.

The merchant was telling about all these difficulties over tea to his wife and daughter, for whom it was necessary to seize the first force, and meanwhile some "wastrel" of no known city or country rank was walking about among all those kibitkas near the barn and seemed to be looking at the Orel merchants with some intention.

There were many "wastrels" gathered here at the time. They not only found their place at the feast of faith, but even found themselves good occupations; and so they came thronging in abundance from various places, especially from towns famous for their thievish folk, that is, from Orel, Kromy, Elets, and from Livny, renowned for its great experts at working wonders. All these "wastrels" rubbing elbows here were looking for some profitable business. The boldest among them acted in concert, placing themselves in groups among the crowds, the more conveniently to produce jostling and confusion, with the aid of a Cossack, and use the turmoil to search people's pockets, tear off watches, belt buckles, and pull earrings from ears; but the more dignified went around the inn yards singly, complained of their poverty, "told dreams and wonders," offered potions to attract and detract, and "secret aids for old men, of whale semen, crow fat, elephant sperm," and other nostrums, which "promoted permanent potency." These nostrums did not lose their value even here, because, to the credit of humankind, conscience did not allow turning to the saint for every sort of healing. No less eagerly did the wastrels of peaceful ways take up simple thievery and on convenient occasions clean out visitors who, for lack of quarters, were living in their carts or under them. There was little space anywhere, and not all the carts could be put under the sheds of the inns; the rest stood outside town in the open fields. Here a still more varied and interesting life went on, and one still more filled with the nuances of sacred and medicinal poetry and amusing chicanery. Shady dealers poked about everywhere, but their home was this outlying "poor wagon train," with ravines and hovels surrounding it, where there was a furious trade in vodka, and two or three carts stood with ruddy soldiers' wives who had pitched together and come there. Here they also fabricated shavings from the coffin, "sealed earth," pieces of rotted vestments, and even "fragments." Occasionally, among the artisans who dealt in these things, very witty people turned up, who pulled interesting tricks remarkable for their simplicity and boldness. To these belonged the man whom the pious family from Orel had noticed. The swindler had overheard their lament about the impossibility of getting near the saint before the first streams of healing grace from the relics were exhausted, went straight up to them, and began speaking frankly:

"I heard your grievances and can help you, and you have no reason to shun me . . . Here, now, in this great and renowned assembly, you won't get the satisfaction you desire without me, but I've been in such situations and know the ways. If you'd like to get the first force from the saint, don't grudge a hundred roubles for your success, and I will provide it."

The merchant looked at the fellow and said:

"Quit lying."

But the man held his ground:

"You probably think that way judging by my nonentity," he says, "but what is nonentity in the eyes of men may be reckoned quite differently with God, and what I undertake to do, I'm firmly able to accomplish. Here you're worrying about earthly grandeur, that so much of it has come here, but to me it's all dust, and if there were no end of princes and kings, they couldn't hinder us in the least, and would even make way for us themselves. And so, if you wish to have a clear and smooth path ahead of you, and see the foremost persons, and give the first kisses to the friend of God, don't stint on what I told you. But if you're sorry about the hundred roubles and don't scorn company, then I'll promptly find two more persons I've already had my eye on, and that will make it cheaper for you."

What did the pious worshippers have left to do? Of course, there was risk in trusting the wastrel, but they didn't want to miss the chance, and the money he was asking wasn't so much, especially with company . . . The patriarch decided to risk it and said:

"Get up a company."

The wastrel took the down payment and ran off, having told the family to dine early and, an hour before the first bell rang for vespers, to take a new hand towel for each of them, go out of town to a designated place in the "poor train," and wait for him there. From there they would immediately set out on their march, which, the entrepreneur assured them, no princes or kings could stop.

These "poor trains," of larger or smaller dimensions, stood in vast camps during all such assemblies, and I myself saw and remember them in Korennaya, outside Kursk, and about the one our narrative has come upon I had heard tell from eyewitnesses to what is about to be described.

IX

The place occupied by the poor encampment was outside town, between the river and the high road, on a spacious and free common which at the end bordered on a big, meandering ravine, overgrown with thick shrubs and with a rivulet running through it. Beyond it began a mighty pine forest where eagles screamed.

On the common stood a multitude of poor carts and wagons, which, however, presented in all their indigence a rather motley diversity of national genius and inventiveness. There were ordinary bast mat hutches, canvas tents covering the whole cart, "bowers" made of fluffy feather grass, and perfectly hideous bast wagons. A whole big piece of bast from a century-old linden is bent and nailed to the sides of the wagon, leaving space enough to lie down underneath: people lie with their feet towards the inside of the vehicle and their heads towards the open air at both ends. The wind passes over them lying there, airing them out, so they don't choke on their own breath. Right there, by the baskets and sacks of hay tied to the shafts, stood the horses, mostly skinny, all of them in collars, and some, owned by thrifty people, under matted "lids." In some carts there were also dogs, which were not supposed to be taken on pilgrimages, but, being "zealous" dogs, had caught up with their owners at the second or third stop and, for all that they were beaten, did not want to be left behind. There was no place for them here, in true conditions of pilgrimage, but they were put up with and, sensing their contraband position, behaved very meekly; they huddled somewhere under a tar barrel by the cart wheel and maintained a grave silence. Modesty alone saved them from ostracism and from the danger posed for them by the baptized Gypsy, who would have "taken their coat off" in a minute. Here, in the poor train, under the open sky, life was merry and good, as at a fair. There was more diversity here than in hotel rooms, which only special chosen ones could get, or under the sheds of the inns, where, in eternal semidarkness, people of the second-best sort found shelter with their carts. True, fat monks and deacons did not come to visit the poor train, and there were also no real, experienced pilgrims to be seen, but instead there were jacks-of-all-trades, and a vast production of various "holy objects" went on. When I happened to read in the Kiev papers about a notorious case of faking relics from sheep bones, I was amazed at the childish methods of these fabricators, compared to the boldness of the artisans I had heard about earlier. Here it was a sort of frank *negligée with valor.* Even the street leading down to the common was already distinguished by a totally unrestrained freedom of the widest enterprise. People knew that such occasions do not occur often, and they didn't waste time: little tables stood by many gateways, displaying little icons, crosses, and paper envelopes supposedly containing rotten wood dust from the old coffin, with shavings from the new one lying next to them. All these materials were, on the assurances of the sellers, of much higher quality than in the actual places, because they had been brought there by the woodworkers, diggers, and carpenters who had done the most important work. At the entrance to the camp, "hurriers and scurriers" ran around with little icons of the new saint, covered for the time being in white paper with a cross drawn on it. These icons were sold very cheaply and could be bought on the spot, but they were not supposed to be uncovered before the first prayer service was held. For many of the unworthy, who bought such icons and opened them beforehand, they turned out to be bare boards.

In the ravine behind the encampment, under overturned sledges, by the stream, a Gypsy lived with his Gypsy wife and Gypsy children. The Gypsy and his wife had a big medical practice there. They kept tied to one sledge runner a big, voiceless cock, who produced stones in the morning that "promoted bedstead potency," and the Gypsy had a catnip that was then quite necessary against "aphedronian sores."[30] This Gypsy was a celebrity of sorts. Word went around about him that when the seven sleeping virgins were "revealed" in infidel lands, he was not a superfluous man there: he could transform old people into young, could heal serfs punished by flogging, could make the pain of soldiers who had run the gauntlet pass out of their insides through the drainage system. His Gypsy wife seemed to know still greater secrets of nature. She gave husbands two kinds of water: one to expose wives who sin by fornication (such wives, when given this water, could not retain it, but passed it right out again); the other a magnetic water, which made an unwilling wife embrace her husband passionately in her sleep, but if she tried to love another man, she would fall out of bed.

In short, things were at the boil here, and the manifold needs of mankind found useful helpers.

When the wastrel caught sight of the merchants, he didn't speak to them, but started beckoning to them to go down into the ravine, and darted down there himself.

Again this seemed a bit frightening: there was the danger of an ambush, in which evildoers could be hiding capable of robbing pilgrims blind, but piety overcame fear, and after some reflection, the merchant, having said a prayer and commemorated the saint, decided to go three steps down.

He moved carefully, holding on to little shrubs, after telling his wife and daughter to shout with all their might if anything happened.

There was indeed an ambush there, but it was not dangerous: the merchant found in the ravine two men like himself, pious men in merchant garb, with whom he was to be "put together." They all had to pay the wastrel the promised sum for taking them to the saint, and then he would reveal his plan to them and take them there at once. There was no point in thinking long about it, and resisting would not have gotten them anywhere: the merchants put together the sum and handed it over, and the wastrel revealed his plan to them, a simple plan, but, in its simplicity, of pure genius. It consisted of there being in the "poor train" a paralytic whom the wastrel knew, who needed only to be picked up and carried to the saint, and nobody would stop them or bar their way with a sick man. All they had to do was buy a litter and a coverlet for the paralytic, and then the six of them would pick him up and carry the litter on towels.

The first part of this idea seemed excellent—with the paralytic, the bearers would, of course, be allowed in, but what would the consequences be? Wouldn't there be embarrassment afterwards? However, they were also set at ease on this account; their guide simply said it wasn't worthy of attention.

"We've already seen such occasions," he said. "You'll be honored with seeing everything to your satisfaction and with kissing the relics during the singing of the vigil, and as for the sick man, it's as the saint wills: if he wishes to heal him, he will heal him, and if he doesn't, again it's as he wills. Now, just chip in quickly for the litter and coverlet, I've got it all ready in a house nearby, I only have to hand over the money. Wait here for me a little, and we'll be on our way."

After some bargaining, he took another two roubles per person for the tackle and ran off, came back ten minutes later, and said:

"Let's go, brothers, only don't step too briskly, and lower your eyes so you look a bit more God-fearing."

The merchants lowered their eyes and walked along with reverence, and in the same "poor train" they came to a wagon where a completely sickly nag stood eating from a sack, and a scrofulous little boy sat on the box amusing himself by tossing the plucked hearts of yellow chamomile from hand to hand. In this wagon, under a bast top, lay a middle-aged man with a face yellower than the chamomile, and his arms were also yellow, stretched out and limp as soft wattle.

The women, seeing such terrible infirmity, began crossing themselves, but their guide addressed the sick man and said:

"Look, Uncle Fotey, these good people have come to help me take you to be healed. The hour of God's will is approaching you."

The yellow man began to turn towards the strangers, looking at them with gratitude and pointing his finger at his tongue.

They guessed that he was mute. "Never mind," they said, "never mind, servant of God, don't thank us, it's God you must thank," and they started pulling him from the wagon, the men taking him under the shoulders and legs, but the women only held up his weak arms, and became still more frightened by the man's dreadful condition, because his arms were completely "loose" in the shoulder joints and were only held on somehow by horsehair ropes.

The litter stood right there. It was a little old bed, the corners thickly covered with bedbug eggs; on the bed lay a sheaf of straw and a piece of flimsy cloth with the cross, the spear, and the reed crudely painted on it.[31] The guide fluffed up the straw with a deft hand, so that it hung over the edges on all sides; they put the yellow paralytic on it, covered him with the cloth, and carried him off.

The guide went ahead with a little clay brazier, censing them crosswise.

Even before they left the train, people began to cross themselves at the sight of them, and as they went down the streets, the attention directed at them became more and more serious: seeing them, everyone realized that this was a sick man being carried to the wonderworker, and they joined in. The merchants hastened on, because they heard the bells ringing for the vigil, and they arrived with their burden just in time, as they started singing: "Praise the name of the Lord, ye servants of the Lord."[32]

The church, of course, had no room for even a hundredth part of the assembled crowd; untold numbers of people stood in a packed mass around it, but as soon as they saw the litter and the bearers, everyone started buzzing: "They're bearing a paralytic, there'll be a miracle," and the crowd parted.

They made a living passageway up to the door of the church, and then everything went as the guide had promised. Even the firm hope of his faith was not put to shame: the paralytic was healed. He stood up and walked on his own feet, "glorifying and giving thanks."[33] Someone took notes about it all, in which the healed paralytic, in the words of the guide, was called a "relative" of the Orel merchant, which made many people envious, and the healed man, owing to the late hour, did not go to his poor train, but spent the night under the shed with his new relatives.

This was all very nice. The healed man was an interesting person, and many came to look at him and left "donations."

But he still spoke little and indistinctly—he mumbled badly from lack of habit and mostly pointed to the merchants with his healed hand, meaning, "Ask them, they're my relatives, they know everything." And willy-nilly they had to say they were his relatives; but suddenly amidst all this an unexpected unpleasantness stole up on them: during the night following the healing of the yellow paralytic, it was noticed that a gold cord with a gold tassel had disappeared from the velvet cover on the saint's coffin.

Discreet inquiries were made, and the Orel merchant was asked if he had noticed anything when he came close, and who were the people who had helped him to bear his sick relative. He answered in good conscience that they were all strangers from the poor train and had helped him out of zeal. He was taken there to identify the place, the people, the nag, and the wagon with the scrofulous boy who was playing with the chamomile, but only the place was in its place, while of the people, the cart, and the boy with the chamomile there was no trace.

The inquiry was abandoned, "so there would be no rumors among the people." A new tassel was attached, and the merchants, after such unpleasantness, quickly made ready to go home. But here the healed relative gratified them with a new joy: he insisted that they take him with them, threatening to make a complaint otherwise, and reminding them of the tassel.

And therefore, when the time came for the merchants to leave for home, Fotey was found on the box beside the driver, and it was impossible to throw him off before they came to the village of Krutoe, which was on their way. In those days there was a very dangerous descent there and a difficult ascent up the other side, and all sorts of incidents occurred with travelers: horses fell, carriages overturned, and other things of that sort. One had to pass through the village of Krutoe while it was light, or else spend the night there. Nobody risked the descent in the dark.

Our merchants also spent the night there, and while ascending the hill in the morning found themselves "at a loss," that is, they had lost their healed relative Fotey. They had "given him a good taste of the flask" in the evening, and in the morning had left without waking him up. But some other good people were found who set this loss to rights and, taking Fotey with them, brought him to Orel.

There he tracked down his ungrateful relatives, who had abandoned him in Krutoe, but he did not meet with a family welcome from them. He went around the town begging and telling how the merchant had not gone to the saint for his daughter, but to pray that the price of wheat would go up. Nobody was so precisely informed of that as Fotey.

X

Not long after the appearance in Orel of the known and abandoned Fotey, the merchant Akulov, from the parish of the Archangel Michael, set up "poor tables." In the courtyard, on boards, stood big, steaming lime-wood bowls of noodles and iron kettles of kasha, and onion tarts and savory pies were handed out from the merchant's porch. A multitude of guests gathered, each with his own spoon in his boot or on his bosom. The pies were handed out by Golovan. He was often invited to such "tables" as the architricline or chief butler, because he was fair, did not hide anything away for himself, and knew very well who deserved what sort of pie—with peas, with carrots, or with liver.

So he stood now and "endowed" each approaching person with a big pie, and if he knew someone had a sick person in the house, he gave them two or more as a "sick ration." And among the various approaching people, Fotey also approached Golovan, a new man, who seemed to surprise Golovan. Seeing Fotey, it was as if Golovan remembered something, and he asked:

"Who are you and where do you live?"

Fotey winced and said:

"I'm God's, that's all, wrapped in a slave's pall, living under the wall."

Others said to Golovan: "The merchants brought him from the saint . . . He's the Fotey who got healed."

Golovan smiled and was starting to say:

"What kind of Fotey is he!" but at that very moment Fotey snatched a pie from him and with the other hand gave him a deafening slap in the face and shouted:

"Don't shoot your mouth off!" and with that sat down at the table. And Golovan suffered it without saying a word. Everybody understood that it had to be so, that the healed man was obviously playing the holy fool, and Golovan knew that it had to be suffered. Only "by what reckoning did Golovan deserve such treatment?" That was a mystery that lasted for many years and established the opinion that Golovan was concealing something very bad, because he was afraid of Fotey.

And there really was something mysterious here. Fotey, who soon fell so low in the general opinion that they called after him "Stole a tassel from the saint and drank it away in the pot-house," treated Golovan with extreme impudence.

Meeting Golovan anywhere at all, Fotey would stand in his way and shout: "Pay your debt." And Golovan, without the least objection, would go to his breast pocket and take out a ten-kopeck piece. If he happened not to have ten kopecks, but had less, Fotey, who was called the Polecat because his rags were so motley, would fling the insufficient money back at Golovan, spit at him, and even beat him, throwing stones, mud, or snow.

I myself remember how once, in the evening, when my father and the priest Pyotr were sitting by the window in the study, and Golovan was standing outside the window, and the three of them were having a conversation, the bedraggled Polecat ran through the gates, which happened to be open, and with the cry "You forgot, scoundrel!" struck Golovan in the face in front of everybody, and he, quietly pushing him away, gave him some copper money from his breast pocket and led him out of the gate.

Such acts were by no means rare, and the explanation that the Polecat knew something about Golovan was, of course, quite natural. Understandably, it also aroused curiosity in many, which, as we shall soon see, had solid grounds.

XI

I was about seven years old when we left Orel and moved to live permanently in the country. I didn't see Golovan after that. Then it came time for me to go and study, and the original muzhik with the big head dropped from my sight. I heard of him only once, during the "big fire." Not only did many buildings and belongings perish at that time, but many people were burned up as well—Golovan was mentioned among the latter. They said he had fallen into some hole that couldn't be seen under the ashes and "got cooked." I didn't inquire about his family, who survived him. Soon after that I went to Kiev and revisited my native parts only ten years later. There was a new tsar, a new order was beginning; there was a breath of new freshness—the emancipation of the peasants was expected, and there was even talk of open courts. All was new: hearts were aflame. There were no implacables yet, but the impatient and the temporizing had already appeared.

On my way to my grandmother's, I stopped for a few days in Orel, where my uncle, who left behind him the memory of an honest man, was then serving as a justice of conscience.[34] He had many excellent sides, which inspired respect even in people who didn't share his views and sympathies: when young he had been a dandy, a hussar, then a horticulturist and a dilettante artist of remarkable abilities; noble, straightforward, an aristocrat, and "an aristocrat *au bout des ongles.*"* Having his own understanding of his duties, he naturally submitted to the new, but wished to treat the emancipation critically and presented himself as a conservative. He wanted only such emancipation as in the Baltic countries. With the young he was protective and kind, but their belief that salvation lay in a steady movement forward, and not backward, seemed erroneous to him. My uncle loved me and knew that I loved and respected him, but he and I did not agree in our views of the emancipation and other questions of the time. In Orel he made me into a purifying sacrifice on those grounds, and though I carefully tried to avoid these conversations, he aimed for them and liked very much to "defeat" me.

Most of all my uncle liked to bring me to cases in which his justice's practice revealed "popular stupidity."

I recall a luxurious, warm evening that I spent with my uncle in the "governor's garden" in Orel, taken up with the—I must confess—by then considerably wearisome argument about the properties and qualities of the Russian people. I insisted, incorrectly, that the people are *very* intelligent, and my uncle, perhaps still more incorrectly, insisted that the people are *very* stupid, that they have no notion of law, of property, and are generally *Asians,* who can astonish anyone you like with their savagery.

"And here, my dear sir," he says, "is an example for you: if your memory has preserved the situation of the town, then you should remember that we have gullies, outskirts, further outskirts, of which the devil knows who fixed the boundaries and to whom the building permits were allotted. That has all been removed by fire in several stages, and in place of the old hovels, new ones of the same sort have

---

* "To his fingertips." *Trans.*

been built, and now nobody can find out who has what right to be sitting there."

The thing was that when the town, having rested from the fires, began to rebuild itself, and some people began to buy lots in the areas beyond the church of St. Basil the Great, it turned out that the sellers not only had no papers, but that these owners and their ancestors considered all papers utterly superfluous. Up to then, houses and land had been changing hands without any declaration to the authorities, and without any taxes or contributions to the treasury, and all this was said to have been written down in some "moatbook," but the "moatbook" had burned up in one of the countless fires, and the one who kept the records in it had died, and along with it all traces of rights of ownership had vanished. True, there were no disputes about rights of ownership, but all this had no legal authority, and was upheld by the fact that Protasov said his father had bought his little house from the Tarasovs' late grandfather, and the Tarasovs did not contest the Protasovs' right of ownership. But since *rights* were now mandatory, and there were no rights, the justice of conscience was faced with resolving the question: did crime call up law, or did law create crime?

"And why did they do it that way?" asked my uncle. "Because these aren't ordinary people, who need good state institutions to safeguard their rights, these are *nomads,* a *horde* that has become sedentary, but is still not conscious of itself."

With that we fell asleep and slept well. Early in the morning I went to the Orlik, bathed, looked at the old places, remembered Golovan's house, and on coming home found my uncle conversing with three "good sirs" unknown to me. They were all of merchant construction—two of them middle-aged, in frock coats with hooks, and one completely white-haired, in a loose cotton shirt, a long, collarless coat, and a tall peasant hat.

My uncle indicated them to me and said:

"Here's an illustration of yesterday's subject. These gentlemen are telling me their case: join our discussion."

Then he turned to those present with a joke that was obvious to me, but, of course, incomprehensible to them, and added:

"This is my relative, a young prosecutor from Kiev, who is going to see a minister in Petersburg and can explain your case to him."

The men bowed.

"Of the three of them, you see," he went on, "this is Mr. Protasov, who wishes to buy a house and land from this man, Tarasov; but Tarasov has no papers. You understand: *none!* He only remembers that his father bought the house from Vlasov, and this man here, the third, is the son of Mr. Vlasov, who, as you see, is also of a certain age."

"Seventy," the old man observed curtly.

"Yes, seventy, and he also has no papers and never did have."

"Never did," the old man put in again.

"He came to certify that it was precisely so and that he doesn't claim any rights."

"I don't—my forefathers sold it."

"Yes, but the ones who sold it to your 'forefathers'—are no more."

"No, they were sent to the Caucasus for their beliefs."

"They could be sought out," I said.

"There's nothing to seek out, the water there was no good for them—they couldn't take it and all passed away."

"Why is it," I said, "that you acted so strangely?"

"We acted as we could. The government clerk was cruel, small landowners didn't have enough to pay the taxes, but Ivan Ivanovich had a moatbook, and we wrote in it. And before him—I don't even remember this—there was the merchant Gapeyev, he kept the moatbook, and after all of them it was given to Golovan, and Golovan got cooked in a foul hole, and all the moatbooks burned up."

"This Golovan, it turns out, was something like your notary?" asked my uncle (who was not an old-timer in Orel).

The old man smiled and said softly:

"Why moatary! Golovan was a just man."

"So everybody trusted him?"

"How could we not trust such a man: he cut his flesh off his living bones for the people."

"There's a legend for you!" my uncle said softly, but the old man heard him and replied:

"No, sir, Golovan's not a liegend, but the truth, and he should be remembered with praise."

"And with befuddlement," my uncle joked. And he didn't know how well his joking answered to the whole mass of memories that awakened in me at that time, to which, with my then curiosity, I passionately wanted to find the key.

And the key was waiting for me, kept by my grandmother.

XII

A couple of words about my grandmother. She came from the Moscow merchant family of the Kolobovs and was taken in marriage into a noble family "not for her wealth, but for her beauty." But her best quality was an inner beauty and lucidity of mind, which always kept its common-folk cast. Having entered the circles of the nobility, she yielded to many of its demands and even allowed herself to be called Alexandra Vassilievna, though her real name was Akilina, but she always thought in a common-folk way and even retained—unintentionally, of course—a certain common-folk quality in her speech. She said "dat" instead of "that," considered the word "moral" insulting, and couldn't pronounce the word "registrar." On the other hand, she never allowed any fashionable pressures to shake her faith in common-folk sense and never departed from that sense herself. She was a good woman and a true Russian lady; she kept house excellently and knew how to receive anyone from the emperor Alexander I to Ivan Ivanovich Androsov. She never read anything except her children's letters, but she liked the renewal of the mind in conversation and for that "summoned people for talks." Her interlocutors of this sort were the bailiff Mikhailo Lebedev, the butler Vassily, the head cook Klim, or the housekeeper Malanya. The talk was never idle, but to the point and useful—they discussed why the girl Feklusha had had "morals fall on her" and why the boy Grishka disliked his stepmother. These conversations were followed by talk of how to protect Feklusha's maidenly honor and what to do so that the boy Grishka would not dislike his stepmother.

For her all this was filled with a living interest perhaps quite incomprehensible to her granddaughters.

When my grandmother came to visit us in Orel, her friendship was enjoyed by the archpriest Father Pyotr, the merchant Androsov, and Golovan, who were "summoned for talks" with her.

It must be supposed that here, too, the talk was not idle, not merely for passing the time, but probably also about some such matters as morals falling on someone or a boy's dislike of his stepmother.

She therefore might have held the keys to many secrets, petty ones for us, perhaps, but quite significant in their milieu.

Now, in this last meeting of mine with my grandmother, she was already very old, but had preserved in perfect freshness her mind, memory, and eyes. She could still sew.

This time, too, I found her at the same worktable, with an inlaid top portraying a harp held up by two cupids.

Grandmother asked me whether I had visited my father's grave, which of our relatives I had seen in Orel, and what my uncle was doing these days. I answered all her questions and enlarged upon my uncle, telling her how he dealt with old "liegends."

Grandmother stopped and pushed her eyeglasses up on her forehead. She liked the word "liegend" very much: she heard in it a naïve alteration in the popular spirit, and laughed:

"That's wonderful," she said, "the way the old man said 'liegend.'"

And I answered:

"I'd like very much to know how it happened in reality, not in liegend."

"What precisely would you like to know?"

"About all that. What sort of man was Golovan? I do remember him a little, and all of it in some sort of liegends, as the old man says, but of course it was a simple matter . . ."

"Well, of course it was simple, but why does it surprise you that our people back then avoided deeds of purchase and just wrote down their transactions in notebooks? There'll be a lot of that uncovered in the future. They were afraid of clerks and trusted their own people, that's all."

"But how," I say, "could Golovan earn such trust? To tell the truth, I sometimes have the impression that he was a bit of a . . . charlatan."

"Why is that?"

"Don't I remember people saying, for instance, that he supposedly had some sort of magic stone, and that he stopped the plague with his blood or flesh, by throwing it into the river? And why was he called 'deathless'?"

"It's nonsense about the magic stone. People made it up, and it wasn't Golovan's fault, and he was nicknamed 'deathless' because, in that horror, when the fumiasms of death hovered over the earth and everybody got frightened, he alone was fearless, and death couldn't touch him."

"And why," I say, "did he cut his leg?"

"He cut off his calf."

"What for?"

"Because he also had a plague pimple on him. He knew there was no salvation from that, quickly grabbed the scythe, and cut the whole calf off."

"Can it be?!" I said.

"Of course it can."

"And what," I say, "are we to think of the woman Pavla?"

Grandmother glanced at me and replied:

"What about her? The woman Pavla was Fraposhka's wife. She was very unhappy, and Golovan gave her shelter."

"But, all the same, she was called 'Golovan's sin.'"

"Each one judges and gives names by his own lights. He had no such sin."

"But, Grandmother, dear, do you really believe that?"

"I not only believe it, I *know* it."

"But how can you *know* it?"

"Very simply."

Grandmother turned to the girl who was working with her and sent her to the garden to pick raspberries, and when the girl left, she looked me in the eye significantly and said:

"Golovan was a *virgin!*"

"How do you know that?"

"From Father Pyotr."

And my grandmother told me how Father Pyotr, not long before his end, spoke to her of what incredible people there are in Russia, and that the late Golovan was a virgin.

Having touched upon this story, Grandmother went into fine detail and recalled her conversation with Father Pyotr.

"Father Pyotr had doubts himself at first," she said, "and began to question him in more detail, and even alluded to Pavla. 'It's not good,' he says. 'You don't repent, and you're in temptation. It's not meet for you to keep this Pavla. Let her go with God.' But Golovan replies: 'It's wrong of you to say that, Father: better let her live with God at my place—I can't let her go.' 'And why is that?' 'Because she has nowhere to lay her head . . .' 'Well,' he says, 'then marry her!' 'That,' he replies, 'is impossible.' Why it was impossible, he didn't say, and Father Pyotr had doubts about it for a long time. But Pavla was consumptive and didn't live long, and before her death, when Father Pavel came to her, she revealed the whole reason to him."

"What was that reason, Grandmother?"

"They lived according to *perfect* love."

"What does that mean?"

"Like angels."

"Excuse me, but why was that? Pavla's husband disappeared, and there's a law that after five years one can marry. Didn't they know that?"

"No, I think they did, but they also knew something more than that."

"What, for instance?"

"For instance, that Pavla's husband survived it all and never disappeared anywhere."

"But where was he?"

"In Orel!"

"Are you joking?"

"Not a bit."

"And who knew about it?"

"The three of them: Golovan, Pavla, and the scoundrelly fellow himself. Maybe you remember Fotey?"

"The healed one?"

"Call him what you like, only now that they're all dead, I can tell you that he wasn't Fotey at all, but the runaway soldier Fraposhka."

"What?! Pavla's husband?"

"Precisely."

"Then how was it . . ." I was about to begin, but was ashamed of my own thought and fell silent, but my grandmother understood me and finished:

"You surely want to ask: how was it that no one else recognized him, and Pavla and Golovan didn't give him away? That's very simple: others didn't recognize him, because he wasn't from this town, and he had grown old and was overgrown with hair. Pavla didn't give him away out of pity, and Golovan out of love for her."

"But in court, according to the law, Fraposhka didn't exist, and they could have married."

"They could have—according to court law they could have, but according to the law of their conscience they couldn't."

"Why, then, did Fraposhka persecute Golovan?"

"The deceased was a scoundrel and thought the same about them as everybody else."

"But on account of him they deprived themselves of all their happiness!"

"That depends on what you consider happiness: there's righteous happiness, and there's sinful happiness. Righteous happiness doesn't step over anybody, sinful happiness steps over everything. They loved the former better than the latter . . ."

"Grandmother," I exclaimed, "these were astonishing people!"

"Righteous people, my dear," the old woman replied.

But all the same I want to add—astonishing, too, and even incredible. They are incredible while they are surrounded by legendary fiction, but they become still more incredible when you manage to take that patina from them and see them in all their holy simplicity. The *perfect* love that alone inspired them placed them above all fear and even subdued their nature, without inducing them to bury themselves in the ground or fight the visions that tormented St. Anthony.

The White Eagle

A Fantastic Story

The dog dreams of bread, of fish the fisherman.

THEOCRITUS (*Idyll*)[1]

I

there are more things in heaven and earth."[2] That is how we usually begin such stories, so as to shield ourselves with Shakespeare from the sharp-witted arrows of those for whom there is nothing unknown. I, however, still think that "there are things" that are very strange and incomprehensible, which are sometimes called supernatural, and therefore I listen willingly to such stories. For the same reason, when, two or three years ago, reducing ourselves to childishness, we began to play at spiritualism,[3] I willingly sat in on one such circle, the rules of which required that at our evening gatherings we not say a word about the authorities or about the principles of the earthly world, but talk only about incorporeal spirits—about their appearances and participation in the destinies of living people. Not even the "preservation and salvation of Russia" was permitted, because on such occasions many "begin with cheers and end with tears."

For the same reason, all taking in vain of "great names" of whatever sort was strictly forbidden, with the sole exception of the name of God, which, as we know, is most often used for beauty of style. Breaches occurred, of course, but those, too, with great caution. Two impatient politicians might step over to the window or the fireplace and whisper a little, but even then they would warn each other: *"Pas si haut!"** And the host already has his eye on them and jokingly threatens to fine them.

Each of us in turn had to tell something fantastic *from his own life*, and since a knack for storytelling is not given to everyone, the story was not picked on from the artistic side. Nor were proofs required. If the storyteller said that the event he told about had actually happened to him, we believed him, or at least pretended to believe. Such was the etiquette.

I was interested most of all in the subjective side of it. That "there are more things than are dreamt of in your philosophy" I do not doubt, but how such things present themselves to someone—that I found extraordinarily interesting. And in fact, the subjectivity here merited great attention. No matter how the storyteller tried to keep to the higher sphere of the incorporeal world, one could not fail to notice that the visitor from beyond the grave comes to earth in color, like a ray of light when it passes through stained glass. And here there is no sorting out lie from truth, and yet it is an interesting thing to follow, and I want to tell you of one such case.

II

The "martyr on duty," that is, the next storyteller, was a rather highly placed and with that a very original person, Galaktion Ilyich, who was jokingly called an "ill-born dignitary." This nickname concealed a pun: he was in fact something of a dignitary, and with that was sickly thin, and moreover was of quite undistinguished parentage. Galaktion Ilyich's father had been a serf butler in a prominent house, then a tax farmer, and, finally, a benefactor and church builder, for which he received a decoration in this mortal life, and in the future life—a place in the kingdom of heaven. He gave his son a university education and set him up in the world, but the "memory eternal"

---

* Not so loud! *Trans.*

which was sung over his grave in the Nevsky Lavra[4] remained and weighed upon his heir. This son of a servant reached a certain rank and was admitted in society, but the joke of the title "ill-born" still dragged after him.

Of the mind and abilities of Galaktion Ilyich scarcely anyone had a clear idea. What he could and could not do—that, too, probably no one knew. His work record was short and simple: at the start of his service, through his father's efforts, he went to work under Viktor Nikitich Panin,[5] who loved the old man for some merits known to himself, and having taken the son under his wing, rather quickly promoted him beyond that limit at which "entries" begin.

In any case, it must be thought that he had some merits for which Viktor Nikitich could promote him. But in the world, in society, Galaktion Ilyich had no success and generally was not spoiled with regard to the joys of life. He was of very poor, frail health and of fatal appearance. As tall as his late patron, Count Viktor Nikitich, he did not, however, possess the count's majestic exterior. On the contrary, Galaktion Ilyich inspired horror, mixed with a certain revulsion. He was at one and the same time a typical village lackey and a typical living corpse. His long, skinny frame was barely enclosed in grayish skin, his excessively high brow was dry and yellow, his temples were tinged with a corpselike greenness, his nose was broad and short like a skull's, there was no trace of eyebrows, his mouth with its long, glittering teeth was eternally half open, and his eyes were dark, dim, totally colorless, set in deep, perfectly black sockets.

To meet him—was to be frightened.

The peculiarity of Galaktion Ilyich's looks was that in his youth he was much more frightening, and towards old age he was getting better, so that one could bear him without being horrified.

He was of mild character and had a kind, sensitive, and even—as we shall see presently—a sentimental heart. He loved to dream and, like the majority of ugly-looking people, hid his dreams deeply. At heart he was more a poet than an official and had a greedy love of life, which he never enjoyed to his full content.

He endured his misfortune and knew it was eternal and would be with him till the grave. His very rise in the service brought with it a deep cup of bitterness: he suspected that Count Viktor Nikitich had kept him as a receptionist mainly in consideration of the fact that he had an oppressive effect on people. Galaktion Ilyich saw that when people waiting to be received by the count had to inform him of the purpose of their visit—their eyes grew dim and their knees gave way . . . Galaktion Ilyich's contribution was that, after seeing him, each of them found a personal conversation with the count easy and even enjoyable.

With the years Galaktion Ilyich went from being an official who announced people to being the one to whom they were announced, and was entrusted with a very serious and ticklish mission in a distant region, where a supernatural event happened to him, his own account of which follows below.

III

About twenty-five years ago (the ill-born dignitary began), rumors started to reach Petersburg about repeated abuses of power by the governor P——v. These abuses were vast and involved almost all parts of the administration. Letters reported that the governor himself supposedly beat and whipped people with his own hands; confiscated, along with the marshal,[6] all the local supplies of spirits for his own mills; arbitrarily took loans from the treasury; insisted on personally inspecting all postal correspondence—sent what was suitable, and tore up and burned what was unsuitable, and then took revenge on the authors; locked people up and left them to languish. With all that, he was a lover of art, maintained a big and very good orchestra, loved classical music, and was himself an excellent cellist.

For a long time only rumors came of his outrages, but then a little official appeared there, who dragged himself to Petersburg, wrote up the whole épopée very thoroughly and in detail, and delivered it personally into the proper hands.

The story turned out to be such as merited an immediate senatorial inspection. Indeed, that should have been done, but the governor and the marshal were in good standing with the late sovereign, and therefore it was not so simple to get at them. Viktor Nikitich first wanted to verify everything more precisely through *his own* man, and his choice fell on me.

He summons me and says:

"Thus and so, such and such sad news has come, and unfortunately it seems there's some substance to it; but before giving this affair the go-ahead, I'd like to verify it more closely, and I've decided to employ you for that."

I bow and say:

"I will be very happy to do it, if I can."

"I'm sure you can," the count replied, "and I'm relying on you. You have this special talent, that people won't go talking nonsense to you, but will lay out the whole truth."

That talent (the storyteller explained, smiling gently) is my lamentable appearance, which spreads gloom before it; but one must get by with what one is given.

"Your papers are all ready," the count continued, "and the money as well. But you're going *only* for our department alone . . . Understand? *Only!*"

"I understand," I say.

"It's as if you're not concerned with any abuses in other departments. But it must only *seem not,* and in fact you must find out *everything.* You'll be accompanied by two capable officials. Go there, get down to business, and make as if you're most attentively examining the bureaucratic order and forms of legal procedure, but personally look into everything . . . Summon local officials for clarifications and . . . look *stern.* And don't hurry back. I'll let you know when to return. What was your last decoration?"

I reply:

"Vladimir, second degree, with coronet."

The count picked up his famous heavy bronze paperweight, "the slain bird," in his enormous hand, took an office memorandum book from under it, and with all five fingers of his right hand grasped a fat giant of an ebony pencil, and, not concealing it from me in the least, wrote down my name and beside it "White Eagle."[7]

Thus I even knew the decoration that would await me for the fulfillment of the mission entrusted to me, and with that I left Petersburg the next day in complete tranquillity.

With me were my servant Egor and two officials from the senate—both adroit men of the world.

IV

We had a safe trip, naturally; having reached the town, we rented an apartment and all settled into it: myself, my two officials, and my servant.

The lodgings were so comfortable that I could perfectly well turn down the more comfortable ones that the governor obligingly offered me.

I, naturally, did not want to owe him the least service, though he and I, of course, not only exchanged visits, but I even went once or twice to his Haydn quartets. However, I'm not a great lover and connoisseur of music, and in general, understandably, I tried not to get closer with him than was necessary—necessary for me to see, not his gallantry, but his dark deeds.

However, the governor was an intelligent and adroit man, and he did not importune me with his attentions. He seemed to leave me in peace to busy myself with incoming and outgoing records and minutes, but nonetheless I kept feeling that something was going on around me, that people were trying to feel out which side to catch me from, and then, probably, to ensnare me.

To the shame of the human race, I must mention that I do not consider even the fair sex totally uninvolved in it. Ladies began to present themselves to me now with complaints, now with petitions, but also, along with that, always with such schemes as could only make me marvel.

However, I remembered Viktor Nikitich's advice—"look stern"—and the gracious visions vanished from my horizon, which was unsuitable for them. But my officials had successes in that sense. I knew it and did not interfere either with their philandering or with their giving themselves out as very big men, which everyone willingly took them for. It was even useful for me that they move in certain circles and have success with certain hearts. I required only that there be no scandal and that I be informed as to which points of their sociability provincial politics was most interested in.

They were conscientious lads and revealed everything to me. What everyone wanted to learn from them was my weaknesses and my particular likings.

The truth is they would never have gotten to that, because, thank God, I have no particular weaknesses, and my tastes, ever since I can remember, have always been quite simple. All my life I've eaten simple food, drunk one glass of simple sherry, and even in sweets, which I've been fond of since I was young, I prefer, to all refined jellies and pineapples, an Astrakhan watermelon, a Kursk pear, or, from childhood habit, a honey cake. I've never envied anyone's wealth, or fame, or beauty, or happiness, and if I've ever envied anything, then, I may say, perhaps it was *health* alone. But even the word "envy" does not go towards defining my feeling. The sight of a man blooming with health never called up in me the vexatious thought: why him and not me? On the contrary, I look at him with sheer rejoicing that such a sea of happiness and blessings is accessible to him, and here I may occasionally dream in various ways about the happiness, impossible for me, of enjoying good health, which I have not been granted.

The pleasure afforded me by the sight of a healthy man developed in me a like strangeness in my aesthetic taste: I never ran after Taglioni or Bosio and was generally indifferent to both opera and ballet, where everything is so artificial, and liked more to listen to the Gypsies on Krestovsky Island.[8] That fire and ardor of theirs, that passionate force of movement, I liked most of all. The man isn't even handsome, he's all askew, but once he gets going—it's as if Satan himself is jerking him, his legs dance, his arms wave, his head twists, his body whirls—it's all a beating and thrashing. And here am I, who know only infirmity, willy-nilly admiring and dreaming. What can such as I taste of the feast of life?

So I said to one of my officials:

"My friend, if you should be asked again what I like most of all, tell them it's health, that most of all I like cheerful, happy, and merry people."

"It seems there's no great imprudence here?" the storyteller asked, pausing.

His listeners thought a little, and several voices replied:

"Of course not."

"Well, excellent, I also thought not, and now kindly listen further."

V

They sent a clerk-on-duty from the office to be at my disposal. He announced visitors, noted down this and that, gave me addresses whenever it was necessary to send for someone or go and inquire about something. This official was my match—elderly, dry, and mournful. The impression he produced was not good, but I paid little attention to him. His name, as I recall, was Ornatsky. A beautiful last name, like a hero from an old novel. But suddenly one day they say: Ornatsky has fallen ill, the executor has sent another official in his place.

"Who's that?" I asked. "Maybe I'd better wait until Ornatsky gets better."

"No, sir," the executor says, "Ornatsky won't be back soon—he went on a drinking binge, and it will last till Ivan Petrovich's mother nurses him back to health, but kindly do not worry about the new official: it's Ivan Petrovich himself who has been appointed in Ornatsky's place."

I look at him and don't quite understand: he's talking to me about some Ivan Petrovich *himself* and has mentioned him twice in two lines.

"Who is this Ivan Petrovich?" I say.

"Ivan Petrovich! . . . the one who sits in the registry—an assistant. I thought you had been pleased to notice him: the handsomest one, everybody notices him."

"No," I say, "I haven't noticed him. What's his name again?"

"Ivan Petrovich."

"And his last name?"

"His last name . . ."

The executor became embarrassed, put three fingers to his forehead in an effort to remember, but instead added with a deferential smile:

"Forgive me, Your Excellency, it was as if a sudden stupor came over me and I couldn't remember. His last name is Aquilalbov, but we all simply call him Ivan Petrovich, or sometimes, jokingly, 'the White Eagle,' for his good looks. An excellent man, in good standing with the authorities, earns a salary of fourteen roubles and fifteen kopecks as an assistant, lives with his mother, who does a bit of fortune-telling and caring for the sick. Allow me to introduce him: Ivan Petrovich is waiting."

"Yes, if it needs must be, please ask this Ivan Petrovich to come in."

"The White Eagle!" I think to myself. "What a strange thing! I'm due for the Order of the White Eagle, and not for Ivan Petrovich."

And the executor half opened the door and called:

"Ivan Petrovich, please come in."

I cannot describe him for you without falling slightly into caricature and making comparisons that you may consider exaggerations, but I warrant you that no matter how I try to describe Ivan Petrovich, my picture cannot convey even half the beauty of the original.

Before me stood a real "White Eagle," a downright *Aquila alba,* as portrayed at the formal receptions of Zeus. A big, tall man, but extremely well proportioned, and of such a healthy look as if he had never ever been ill and knew neither boredom nor fatigue. He was the picture of health, not crudely, but somehow harmoniously and attractively. Ivan Petrovich's complexion was all tender pink, with ruddy cheeks framed in fair, light down, which, however, was on its way to turning into mature growth. He was exactly twenty-five years old; his hair was fair, slightly wavy, *blonde,* and his little beard was the same, with delicate reddish highlights; his eyes were blue under dark eyebrows and framed with dark lashes. In short, the folktale hero Churilo Aplenkovich could not have been better. But add to that a bold, very intelligent, and merrily open gaze, and you have before you a truly handsome fellow. He was wearing a uniform, which sat very well on him, and a scarf of a dark pomegranate color tied into a splendid bow.

People wore scarves then.

I stood there admiring Ivan Petrovich and, knowing that the impression I make on people seeing me for the first time is not an easy one, said simply:

"Good day to you, Ivan Petrovich."

"How do you do, Your Excellency," he replied in a very heartfelt voice, which also sounded extremely sympathetic to me.

Speaking his phrase of response in the military version, he was nevertheless skillful enough to lend his tone a shade of simple and permissible jocularity, and at the same time this response by itself established a character of familial simplicity for the whole conversation.

I was beginning to understand why "everybody loved" this man.

Seeing no reason for keeping Ivan Petrovich from maintaining this tone, I told him that I was glad to make his acquaintance.

"And I, for my part, also consider it an honor for me and a pleasure," he replied, standing, but stepping ahead of his executor.

We made our bows—the executor went to his office, and Ivan Petrovich remained in my anteroom.

An hour later I invited him to my office and asked:

"Do you have good handwriting?"

"I have a firm hand," he replied, and added at once: "Would you like me to write something?"

"Yes, kindly do."

He sat down at my desk and after a minute handed me a page in the middle of which was written with a "firm hand" in clear cursive: "Life is given us for joy.—Ivan Petrovich Aquilalbov."

I read it and couldn't help bursting into laughter: no other expression could have suited him better than what he had written. "Life for joy"—*all* of life was for him a continuous joy!

A man entirely to my taste! . . .

I gave him an insignificant document to copy right there at my desk, and he did it very quickly and without the least mistake.

Then we parted. Ivan Petrovich left, and I remained at home alone and gave myself up to my morbid spleen, and I confess—devil knows why, but several times I was carried in thought to *him*, that is, to Ivan Petrovich. He surely doesn't sigh and mope. To him life is given for joy. And where does he live it with such joy on his fourteen roubles . . . I suppose he must be lucky at cards, or a little bribe may come his way . . . Or maybe merchants' wives . . . It's not for nothing he has such a fresh pomegranate tie . . .

I'm sitting over a multitude of cases and minutes open before me, and thinking about such pointless trifles, which do not concern me at all, and just then my man announces that the governor has come.

I ask him in.

VI

The governor says:

"I'll be having a quintet the day after tomorrow—their playing won't be bad, I hope, and there will be ladies, and you, I hear, are moping in our backwoods, so I've come to visit you and invite you for a cup of tea—maybe it won't hurt to amuse yourself a little."

"I humbly thank you, but why does it seem to you that I'm moping?"

"From a remark of Ivan Petrovich's."

"Ah, Ivan Petrovich! The one who's on duty with me? So you know him?"

"Of course, of course. He's our student, singer, actor—only not a malefactor."

"Not a malefactor?"

"No, he's as lucky as Polycrates,[9] he has no need to be a malefactor. He's the universal town favorite—and an unfailing participant in every sort of merrymaking."

"Is he a musician?"

"He's a jack-of-all-trades: he sings, plays, dances, organizes parlor games—it's all Ivan Petrovich. Where there's a feast, there's Ivan Petrovich: if there's a lottery or a charity performance—again it's Ivan Petrovich. He appoints the winning lots and displays the articles prettily; he paints the sets himself, and then turns at once from painter to actor ready for any role. The way he plays kings, uncles, ardent lovers—it's a feast for the eyes, but he's best at playing old women."

"Not old women!"

"Yes, it's astonishing! For the soirée the day after tomorrow, I confess, I'm preparing a little surprise with Ivan Petrovich's help. There will be *tableaux vivants*—Ivan Petrovich will stage them. Naturally, some will be the kind put on for women desirous of showing themselves, but there will be three of some interest for a real artist."

"Done by Ivan Petrovich?"

"Yes, Ivan Petrovich. The tableaux will present 'Saul and the Witch of Endor.'[10] The subject, as you know, is biblical, and the disposition of the figures is a bit trumped up, what's known as 'academic,' but the whole point is in Ivan Petrovich. He's the one everybody will be looking at—especially when the second tableau opens and our surprise is revealed. I can tell you the secret. The tableau opens, and you see Saul: this is a king, a king from head to foot! He'll be dressed like everybody else. Not the slightest distinction, because in the story Saul comes to the witch disguised, so that she won't recognize him, but it's *impossible not to recognize him*. He's a king, and a real, biblical shepherd-king at that. But the curtain falls, and the figure quickly changes position. Saul lies prostrate before the shade of Samuel, who comes to him. Saul is now as good as gone, but what a sight Samuel is in his shroud! . . . This is a most inspired prophet, on whose shoulders lie power personified, grandeur, and wisdom. This man could '*order the king* to appear in Bethel and Gilgal.'"

"And this will again be Ivan Petrovich?"

"Ivan Petrovich! But that's not the end. If they ask for an encore—which I'm sure of and will see to myself—we're not going to weary you with repetitions, but you will see the sequel of the épopée.

"The new scene from the life of Saul will be with no Saul at all. The shade has vanished, the king and his attendants have gone: through the door you can make out only a bit of the cloak of the last figure withdrawing, and on stage there's the witch alone . . ."

"And again it's Ivan Petrovich!"

"Naturally! But what you see won't be the same as the way they portray witches in *Macbeth* . . . No stupefying horror, no affectation or grimacing, but you'll see a face that knows what philosophy never dreamt of.[11] You'll see how frightening it is to speak to one who comes from the grave."

"I can imagine," I said, being infinitely far from the thought that before three days were out, I would have, not to imagine, but to experience that torment myself.

But that came later, while now everything was filled by Ivan Petrovich alone—that merry, lively man, who suddenly popped up from the grass like a mushroom after warm rain, not big yet, but visible from everywhere—and everybody looks at him and smiles: "See what a firm and pretty one."

VII

I've told you what the executor and the governor said of him, but when I expressed curiosity as to whether either of my officials of worldly tendency had heard anything about him, they both began saying at once that they had met him and that he was indeed very nice and sang well to the guitar and the piano. They, too, liked him. The next day the archpriest stopped by. After I'd gone to church once, he brought me blessed bread every Sunday and sacrotattled on everybody. He said nothing good about anyone and in that regard made no exception even of Ivan Petrovich, but on the other hand, this sacrotattler knew not only the nature of all things, but also their origin. About Ivan Petrovich he began himself:

"They've switched clerks on you. It's all with a purpose . . ."

"Yes," I said, "they've given me some Ivan Petrovich."

"We know him, indeed, we know him well enough. My brother-in-law, to whose post here I've been transferred with the obligation of bringing up the orphans, he baptized him . . . His father was also a man of the cloth . . . rose to a clerkship, and his mother . . . Kira Ippolitovna . . . that's her name—she left home and married his father out of passionate love . . . But soon she also tasted the bitterness of love's potion, and then was left a widow."

"She educated him by herself?"

"As if he's got any education! He went through five grades of school and became a scribe in the criminal court . . . after a while they made him an assistant . . . But he's very lucky: last year he won a horse and saddle at the lottery, and this year he went hunting hares with the governor. A regimental piano left by some transferred officers came as a prize in the lottery, and he took that, too. I bought five tickets and didn't win, while he had just one and got it. Makes music on it himself, and teaches Tatyana."

"Who is Tatyana?"

"They took in a little orphan—not bad at all . . . a swarthy little thing. He teaches her."

We talked all day about Ivan Petrovich, and in the evening I hear something buzzing in my Egor's little room. I call him and ask him what it is.

"I'm doing cut-outs," he replies.

Ivan Petrovich, having noticed that Egor was bored from inactivity, brought him a fretsaw and some little boards from cigar boxes with glued-on designs and taught him to cut out little plaques. Commissioned for the lottery.

VIII

On the morning of the day when Ivan Petrovich was to perform and astonish everybody in tableaux at the governor's banquet, I did not want to keep him, but he stayed through lunchtime and even made me laugh a lot. I joked that he ought to get married, and he replied that he preferred to remain "in maidenhood." I invited him to Petersburg.

"No, Your Excellency," he says, "here everybody loves me, and my mother's here, and we've got the orphan Tanya, I love them, and they're not suited to Petersburg."

What a wonderfully harmonious young man! I even embraced him for this love of his mother and the orphan girl, and we parted three hours before the tableaux.

Taking leave of him, I said:

"I'm waiting impatiently to see you in various forms."

"You'll get sick of me," Ivan Petrovich replied.

He left, and I had lunch alone and took a nap in the armchair, to freshen myself up, but Ivan Petrovich did not let me sleep: he soon and somewhat strangely disturbed me. He suddenly came in very hurriedly, noisily shoved the chairs in the middle of the room aside with his foot, and said:

"So here you see me; but I just want to humbly thank you—you gave me the evil eye. I'll be revenged on you for that."

I woke up, rang for my man, and ordered him to bring my clothes, and kept marveling to myself: how clearly I had seen Ivan Petrovich in my dream!

I arrived at the governor's—it was all lit up and there were many guests, but the governor himself, meeting me, whispered:

"The best part of the program fell through: the tableaux can't take place."

"What's happened?"

"Shh . . . I don't want to speak loudly and spoil the general impression. Ivan Petrovich is dead."

"What? . . . Ivan Petrovich? . . . dead?!"

"Yes, yes, yes—he's dead."

"Merciful heavens—he was at my place three hours ago, as healthy as could be."

"Well, so he came from your place, lay down on the sofa, and died . . . And you know . . . I must tell you, in case his mother . . . she's so beside herself that she may come running to you . . . The unfortunate woman is convinced that you are guilty of her son's death."

"How so? Was he poisoned at my place, or what?"

"That she doesn't say."

"Then what does she say?"

"That you gave Ivan Petrovich *the evil eye*."

"Excuse me . . . ," I say, "but that's nonsense!"

"Yes, yes, yes," replies the governor, "it's all foolishness, of course, but then this is a provincial town—here foolishness is more readily believed than cleverness. Of course, it's not worth paying attention to."

Just then the governor's wife invited me to play cards.

I sat down, but what I endured during that tormenting game I simply cannot tell you. First, I suffered from the consciousness that this nice young man, whom I had admired so, was now laid out on a table,[12] and, second, I kept imagining that everybody was whispering and pointing at me: "He gave him the evil eye," I even heard those foolish words "evil eye, evil eye," and, third, allow me to tell you the truth—I saw Ivan Petrovich himself everywhere! . . . As if I had acquired an eye for him—wherever I looked—there was Ivan Petrovich . . . Now he's walking, strolling about the empty room, to which the doors are open; now two men stand talking—and he's beside them, listening. Then he suddenly appears right next to me and looks into my cards . . . Here, naturally, I play whatever my hand falls on, and my vis-à-vis gets offended. Finally, the others began to notice it as well, and the governor whispered in my ear:

"It's Ivan Petrovich spoiling it for you: he's having his revenge."

"Yes," I say, "I'm indeed upset and feeling very unwell. I beg to be allowed to add up the score and excuse myself."

This favor was granted me, and I went home at once. But I rode in the sleigh, and Ivan Petrovich was with me—now sitting beside me, now on the box with the driver, but with his face turned to me.

I think: maybe I'm coming down with a fever?

I came home—it was still worse. As soon as I lay down and put the light out—Ivan Petrovich is sitting on the edge of the bed, and he even says:

"You really did give me the evil eye, and I died, and there was no need for me to die so early. That's the point! . . . Everybody loved me so, my mother, and Tanyusha—she hasn't finished her studies yet. What terrible grief it is for them!"

I called for my man and, awkward as it was, told him to lie down and sleep on my rug, but Ivan Petrovich wasn't afraid; wherever I turned, he stuck up in front of me, and basta!

I could hardly wait till morning, and first off sent one of my officials to the dead man's mother, to bring three hundred roubles for the funeral and give them to her with all possible delicacy.

The man came back bringing the money with him: they wouldn't take it, he says.

"What did they say?" I asked.

"They said, 'No need: *good people* will bury him.'"

Which meant that I was counted among the *wicked*.

And as soon as I thought of him, Ivan Petrovich was right there.

In the evening I couldn't keep calm: I took a cab and drove to have a look at Ivan Petrovich and to take leave of him. That is a customary thing, and I thought I wouldn't disturb anyone. And I put all I could in my pocket—seven hundred roubles—to persuade them to accept it, at least for Tanya.

IX

I saw Ivan Petrovich: the "White Eagle" lies there as if shot down.

Tanya is walking around. A swarthy little thing indeed, about fifteen years old, in cheap cotton mourning, and she keeps putting things right. She smooths the dead man's hair and kisses him.

What agony to see it!

I asked her if I could talk with Ivan Petrovich's mother.

The girl replied, "Very well," and went to the other room, and a moment later she opened the door and asked me to come in, but as soon as I entered the room where the old woman was sitting, she stood up and excused herself:

"No, forgive me—I was wrong to trust myself, I cannot see you," and with that she left.

I was not offended or embarrassed, but simply dispirited, and I turned to Tanya:

"Well, you're a young being, maybe you can be kinder to me. For, believe me, I did not and had no reason to wish Ivan Petrovich any misfortune, least of all death."

"I believe you," she let fall. "No one could wish him any ill, everybody loved him."

"Believe me, in the two or three days that I saw him, I, too, came to love him."

"Yes, yes," she said. "Oh, those terrible two or three days—why did they have to be? My aunt treated you that way out of grief, but I feel sorry for you."

And she held out both hands to me.

I took them and said:

"Thank you, dear child, for these feelings; they do honor to your heart and your good sense. It really is impossible to believe such nonsense, that I supposedly gave him the evil eye!"

"I know," she replied.

"Then show me your kindness . . . do me a favor *in his name*!"

"What favor?"

"Take this envelope . . . there's a bit of money in it . . . for household needs . . . for your aunt."

"She won't accept it."

"Well, for you then . . . for your education, which Ivan Petrovich was looking after. I'm deeply convinced that he would have approved of it."

"No, thank you, I won't take it. He never took anything from anyone for nothing. He was very, very noble."

"But you grieve me by that . . . it means you're angry with me."

"No, I'm not angry. I'll prove it to you."

She opened Ollendorff's manual of French, which was lying on the table, hastily took a photograph of Ivan Petrovich from between the pages and, handing it to me, said:

"He put it there. We had reached this place in our studies yesterday. Take it from me as a memento."

With that the visit was over. The next day Ivan Petrovich was buried, and afterwards I remained in town for another eight days, still in the same agony. I couldn't sleep at night; I listened to every little noise, opened the vent window so that at least some fresh human voice might come from outside. But it was of little use: two men go by, talking—I listen—it's about Ivan Petrovich and me.

"Here," they say, "lives that devil who gave Ivan Petrovich the evil eye."

Someone is singing as he returns home in the still of the night: I hear the snow crunching under his feet, I make out the words: "Ah, of old I was bold"—I wait for the singer to come even with my window—I look—it's Ivan Petrovich himself. And then the father archpriest kindly drops by and whispers:

"There's such a thing as the evil eye and casting spells, but that works on chickens—no, Ivan Petrovich was poisoned . . ."

Agonizing!

"Who would poison him and why?"

"They had fears that he'd tell you everything . . . They should have gutted him. Too bad they didn't. They'd have found the poison."

Lord, deliver me at least from this suspicion!

In the end, I suddenly and quite unexpectedly received a confidential letter from the director of the chancery, saying that the count orders me to limit myself to what I have managed to do already and return to Petersburg without the slightest delay.

I was very glad of it, made ready in two days, and left.

On the road Ivan Petrovich did not leave me alone—he appeared every once in a while, but now, whether from the change of place or because a man gets used to everything, I grew bolder and even got used to him. He lingers before my eyes, but it's nothing to me: sometimes, while I'm dozing, we even exchange jokes. He wags his finger:

"Got you, didn't I!"

And I reply:

"And you still haven't learned French!"

And he replies:

"Why should I study: I rattle away nicely now on what I've taught myself."

X

In Petersburg I felt that they were not so much dissatisfied with me, but worse, that they looked at me somehow pityingly, somehow strangely.

Viktor Nikitich himself saw me for just a moment and said nothing, but he told the director, who was married to a kinswoman of mine, that to him I seemed *unwell* . . .

There was no explanation. A week later it was Christmas, and then the New Year. Festive turmoil, naturally—the expectation of awards. I was not so greatly concerned, the less so as I knew I would be awarded the White Eagle. On the eve, my kinswoman, the director's wife, sent me a gift of the medal and ribbon, and I put it in a drawer together with an envelope containing a hundred roubles for the couriers who were to bring me the official order.

But during the night Ivan Petrovich suddenly nudged me in the side and made a *fig* right under my nose. He had been much more delicate when alive, such a thing did not suit his harmonious nature at all, but now he stuck a fig at me just like a prankster, and said:

"That's enough for you right now. I must go to poor Tanya," and he melted away.

I got up in the morning. No couriers with the order. I hastened to my in-law to find out what it meant.

"Can't fathom it," he says. "It was there, listed, and suddenly it's like it got cut at the printer's. The count crossed it out and said he'd announce it personally . . . You know, there's some story that's harmful to you . . . Some official, after leaving you, died somehow suspiciously . . . What was it about?"

"Drop it," I say, "do me a favor."

"No, really . . . the count even asked after your health several times . . . Various persons wrote from there, including the archpriest, the father confessor of them all . . . How could you let yourself get mixed up in such a strange business?"

I listen and—like Ivan Petrovich himself from beyond the grave—feel only a desire to stick my tongue out at him or show him a fig.

But Ivan Petrovich, after I was awarded a fig instead of the White

Eagle, disappeared and did not show up again for exactly three years, when he paid me his final and most tangible visit.

XI

Again it was Christmas and the New Year and the same expectation of awards. I had already been passed over repeatedly, and did not trouble myself about it. No give, no care. There was a New Year's party at my cousin's—very merry—lots of guests. The healthy ones stayed for supper, but I was looking for a chance to slip away before supper, and was edging towards the door, when suddenly, amidst the general talk, I hear these words:

"My wanderings are now over: mama's with me. Tanyusha has settled down with a good man. I'll pull my last stunt and zhe mon vay!"* And then suddenly he sang in a drawl:

Farewell, my own,
Farewell, my native land.

"Aha," I think, "he's shown up again, and what's more he's speaking French . . . Well, I'd better wait for somebody, I won't go downstairs alone."

And he deigns to walk past me dressed in the same uniform with the splendid pomegranate tie, and he had just passed by when the front door suddenly slammed so that the whole house shook.

The host and servants ran to see whether anyone had gotten to the guests' fur coats, but everything was in place, and the door was locked . . . I kept mum, so that no one would say "hallucinations" again and start asking about my health. It slammed, and that's that— lots of things can slam . . .

I sat it out so as not to leave alone and returned home safely. My man was no longer the one who had traveled with me and to whom Ivan Petrovich had given lessons in making cut-outs, but another; he met me looking sleepy and lit my way. We passed by the side table and I saw something lying there covered with white paper . . .

---

* I.e., *Je m'en vais*, I'm going away. *Trans.*

The White Eagle

I looked: it was my Order of the White Eagle, of which, you remember, my cousin had made me a gift that time . . . It had always been under lock and key. How could it suddenly appear? Of course, I'll be told: "He probably took it out himself in a moment of distraction." I won't argue about that, but there was something else: on my bedside table there was a small envelope addressed to me, and the hand seemed familiar . . . It was the same hand that had written: "Life is given us for joy."

"Who brought it?" I ask.

And my man points straight at the photograph of Ivan Petrovich, which I keep as a memento from Tanyusha, and says:

"This gentleman."

"Surely you're mistaken."

"No, sir," he says, "I recognized him at first glance."

In the envelope there turned out to be an official stamped copy of the order: I had been awarded the White Eagle. And what was still better, I slept for the rest of the night, though I heard something somewhere singing the stupidest words: "Now's my chaunce, now's my chaunce, zhe allay o contradaunce."*

From the experience of the life of spirits taught me by Ivan Petrovich, I realized that this was Ivan Petrovich "rattling away in self-taught French" as he flew off, and that he would never trouble me again. And so it turned out: he took his revenge and then forgave me. That's clear. But why everything in the world of spirits is so confused and mixed up that human life, which is more valuable than anything, is revenged by frivolous frights and a medal, and flying down from the highest spheres is accompanied by the stupidest singing of "Now's my chaunce, zhe allay o contradaunce"—that I don't understand.

---

* I.e., *je allais au contredanse*, illiterate French for "I'm going to the contradance." *Trans.*

A Flaming Patriot

Of foreign government celebrities, I have seen the late Napoleon III at the inauguration of a boulevard in Paris, Prince Bismarck at a health spa, MacMahon on parade, and the present-day Austrian emperor Franz Joseph over a mug of beer.

The most memorable impression was made on me by Franz Joseph, though at the same time he caused a capital quarrel between two of my lady compatriots.

The story is worth telling.

I have been abroad three times, traveling twice by the Russian "high road" directly from Petersburg to Paris, and the third time, owing to circumstances, making a detour and stopping in Vienna. I wanted, at the same time, to visit a certain Russian lady worthy of respect.

It was the end of May or the beginning of June. The train I was traveling by brought me to Vienna at around four o'clock in the afternoon. I did not have to look for quarters: in Kiev I had been furnished with a reference that saved me any trouble. As soon as I arrived, I settled in, and an hour later I had put myself in order and gone to see my compatriot.

At that hour, Vienna was also doing herself up: a heavy summer shower passed over and then suddenly a radiant sun began to sparkle in the perfectly blue sky. The beautiful city, having washed, looked still more beautiful.

The streets my guide led me along all seemed very elegant, but as we drew nearer to Leopoldstadt, their elegance became still more noticeable. The buildings were bigger, stronger, and more majestic.

My guide stopped by one of them and said that this was the hotel I wanted.

We entered through a majestic archway into a vast hall, decorated in the Pompeian style. To the right and left of this hall were heavy doors of dark oak: the opposite wall was draped luxuriously in red cloth. In the middle of the hall stood a carriage hitched to a pair of live horses, and on the box sat a coachman.

This magnificent hall was simply nothing other than the "gateway." We were standing under such "gates" as I had never yet seen either in Petersburg or in Paris.

To the right was the porter's lodge. It was also remarkable; remarkable, too, was the magnificent porter himself, with his chamberlain's figure: he sat there like a golden beetle displayed behind an enormous plate-glass window. He could see all around him. And next to him, for the sake of pomp or for some other convenience, stood three assistants, all of them wearing aglets. If the necessity arose of putting someone out or not letting him in, such a porter would not, of course, dirty his hands with it.

To my question, "Is my acquaintance here?"—one of the assistants replied: "She is," and when I asked, "Might I see her?"—the assistant told the porter, who moved an eyebrow diplomatically and explained to me *himself*:

"Strictly speaking, I do not think it would be convenient for the princess to receive you now—a carriage has come for her, and her excellency is about to go for a ride. But if it is very necessary . . ."

"Yes," I interrupted, "it is very necessary."

"In that case, I ask you for a moment's patience."

It was clear that I had to do with a real diplomat and to argue over a moment's patience would be out of place.

We bowed to each other.

The porter pushed an electric button on the table, before which stood his papal throne with its high gothic back, and, putting his ear to the receiver, explained to me after a moment:

"The princess is already coming downstairs."

I stood waiting for her.

A moment later, my acquaintance appeared on the white marble steps, accompanied by her elderly Russian maid, Anna Fetisovna, long known to me, who plays a role in this little story.

. . .

The princess met me with the sweet affability that had always distinguished her, and, saying that she was about to go for her after-dinner promenade, invited me to ride with her.

She wanted to show me the Prater. I had nothing against that, and we drove off: I beside the princess on the rear seat, and Anna Fetisovna facing us.

Contrary to what is maintained, that abroad everyone drives much more slowly than in Russia, we raced very quickly down the streets of Vienna. The horses were brisk and spirited, the coachman an expert at his trade. The Viennese drive a pair harnessed to the shafts as handsomely and deftly as the Poles do. Our coachmen don't know how to drive like that. They're very heavy and they fuss with the reins—they don't have that free, ribbon-like movement and all that "elevation," which there is so much of in the Krakower and the Viennese.

Before I could bat an eye, we were already in the Prater.

I am not going to make the slightest attempt to describe this park; I will tell only what is necessary for a proper elucidation of the coming scene.

I remind you that it was about five o'clock in the afternoon and just after a heavy rain. Fresh moisture still lay everywhere: the heavy gravel of the paths looked brown, clear drops sparkled on the leaves of the trees.

It was pretty damp, and I don't know whether the dampness or the rather early hour was the reason for it, but all the best alleys of the park, along which we were driving, were completely deserted. At most we met some gardener in a jacket, with a rake and spade on his shoulder, and no one else; but my kind hostess remembered that, besides this, so to speak, fair part of the park, there was also a *rough* part, called the Kalbs-Prater or "Calf's Park"—the place where the rough Viennese promenaded.

"They say it may be interesting," said the princess, and she told the coachman at once to drive to the Kalbs-Prater.

The coachman turned left, called out his guttural "Hup," snapped his whip, and it was as if the ground began to give way under us, we seemed to be going down somewhere, falling, as though dropping into a lower sphere.

The situation harmonized beautifully with the social reality.

· · ·

The picture was rapidly changing: the alleys were becoming narrower and were kept less clean, scraps of paper flashed here and there on the sand and at the edges of the flowerbeds. Then, too, we began to meet people, all of them on foot, first the vendors of the famous Viennese sausages, then the public. Some trudged along with children. The local public was obviously not afraid of dampness, but only feared losing a moment of precious time.

When a poor man marries, the night's too short for him; still shorter is the hour of rest for such hardworking and parsimonious people as the southern Germans, in whom, however, the need for pleasure is almost as great as in the French.

There was no movement in the opposite direction—we were overtaking everyone. Obviously, the goal of all their striving lay ahead; it was there where we, too, were hurrying and from where some sort of sounds began to reach us, growing louder moment by moment. Strange sounds, like the buzzing of a bee between a window and curtain. But now through the treetops flashed the high pediment of a large wooden building; the carriage bore left again and suddenly came to a stop. We were at the intersection of two paths. Before us opened a rather large lawn, on the other side of which stood a large wooden house in the Swiss style, and before it, on the grass, stretched long tables, and at them sat a multitude of different people. Before each guest stood his mug of beer, and on the open gallery four musicians were playing and a Hungarian couple were whirling in a dance. Here was where the musical sounds had come from, which in the distance had resembled the buzzing of a bee between a window and curtain. That buzzing could be heard now as well, with the difference that now one could hear in the sounds something that kept catching at some nerve and spilling out all around with moaning, with ringing, with defiance.

"They're dancing a czardas: I advise you to pay attention to them," said the princess. "You won't often come across it: no one is able to perform the czardas like the Hungarians. Coachman, drive up closer."

The coachman edged closer, but the horses had barely gone two steps when he stopped them again.

We had advanced, of course, but were still too far away to be able to have the possibility of scrutinizing the dancers, and therefore the princess again told the coachman to move closer. It seemed, however, that he did not hear this repetition, but then, when the princess told him the same thing a third time, the coachman not only touched up the reins, but loudly cracked his whip and all at once brought our carriage out into the middle of the lawn.

Now we could see everything in detail and were ourselves seen by everyone. Several persons among those sitting at the tables turned at the crack of the whip, but at once turned back to the dancers, and only one fat waiter was left looking at us from the steps of the lower terrace, but as if he were waiting for some fitting moment, when a suitable exchange of mutual relations should take place between us.

I tried in the most conscientious way to follow the advice of my lady and wanted to watch the czardas without taking my eyes from it, but a chance occasion drew *my attention* to something else.

We had barely stopped, when the coachman half turned slightly towards the carriage and said:

"Kaiser!"

"Wo ist der Kaiser?"*

Instead of an answer, the driver directed the extended little finger of his glove to the left, towards the opposite end of the lawn, where, at an intersection identical to the one we had just left, there could now be seen two horse heads of a light bay, goldish color.

Only those two fine heads could be seen, in composite bridles studded with turquoise, while the carriage itself remained at the same distance at which our coachman had first wanted to keep us.

"That," I thought to myself, "is indeed very tactful, but then he won't see anything very well from there, nor will he allow us to admire him. And that's vexing."

Only there was no need to be vexed: at that same moment, looking towards where the horses stood, I saw without any difficulty a tall, slightly stooping, but gallant man in a blue Austrian jacket and simple military cap.

This was his apostolic majesty, the senior member of the house of Habsburg, the reigning emperor Franz Joseph. He was quite alone and walked straight to the tables set up on the lawn, where the cobblers of Vienna were sitting. The emperor came up and sat on the end of a bench at the first table, next to a tall worker in a light gray blouse, and the fat waiter in that same second placed a black felt circle on the table before him and set down on it an expertly drawn mug of beer.

---

* *"Where is the kaiser?" Trans.*

A Flaming Patriot

Franz Joseph took the mug in his hand, but didn't drink from it; while the dance lasted, he went on holding it in his hand, but when the czardas was finished, the emperor silently held out his mug to his neighbor. The man understood at once what he must do: he clinked with his sovereign and, immediately turning to his other neighbor, exchanged clinks with him. Thereupon, as many people as were there, they all stood up, all clinked with each other, and breathed out over the whole lawn a concerted, unanimous "Hoch!"* This "hoch" is not shouted loudly and boomingly there, but like a good, heartfelt sigh.

The emperor drained his mug in one breath, bowed, and left.

The bay horses carried him back down the same road that we also took, following after him. But now the considerable power of the impression produced by this incident was riding with us, and it was all lodged chiefly in Anna Fetisovna. The maid, to our no little surprise, was *crying*! . . . She sat before us, covering her eyes with a white handkerchief and pressing it with her hands.

"Anna Fetisovna, what's the matter?" the princess addressed her with a kindly and gentle jocularity.

The woman went on crying.

"What are you crying about?"

Anna Fetisovna uncovered her eyes and said:

"Just like that—about nothing."

"No, really?"

The maid sighed deeply and replied:

"Suchlike simplicity moves me."

The princess winked at me and said jokingly:

"Toujours servile! C'est ainsi que l'on arrive aux cieux."†

But the joke somehow did not come off. Anna Fetisovna's emotion endowed this trifling incident with a different meaning.

We returned to the hotel and found there yet another visitor. This was an Austrian baron who was intending to go to Russia and was studying Russian. We had tea, and Anna Fetisovna served us. We talked of many things: of Russia, of Petersburg acquaintances, of

---

* "[Raise them] high!" *Trans.*

† "Ever servile! That's how one gets to heaven." *Trans.*

our rate of exchange, of who was our best embezzler, and, finally, of our meeting that day with Franz Joseph.

The entire conversation was in Russian, so that Anna Fetisovna must have heard it all word for word.

The princess told me some not entirely "legal" things from court bucolics and political rhapsodies. The baron smiled.

I have no need to recall all this, but one thing I find it appropriate to observe, that my interlocutrice tried to construe many features of the Austrian emperor's character for me in terms of the seeking of *popularity*.

This treatise on popularity, or, more correctly, on popularism, was developed with specific details and examples, among which that day's mug of beer popped up again. And—if I'm mistaken, the fault is mine—it seemed to me that this was done much less for our benefit than for that of Anna Fetisovna, who kept coming in and going out all the time, serving something her mistress needed.

It was some sort of woman's caprice, which carried my compatriot away so much that she went on from the emperor to the nation, or nations, to the Austrians and us. She even admired the way the "Viennese cobblers" had borne themselves *"with dignity,"* and then she quickly switched to the motherland, to our Russian people, to their feasts and amusements, to vodka, and again to the tears and upsets of the impressionable Anna Fetisovna.

This last was spoken in French, but even so the baron only went on smiling.

"We shall ask my esteemed Jeanne her opinion again," said the princess, and when the maid came to take a cup, she said:

"Anna Fetisovna, did you like the local king very much today?"

"Yes, ma'am, very much," Anna Fetisovna answered quickly.

"She's angry," the princess whispered to me, and went on aloud:

"And what would you think if he came to us in Moscow, to the fairground?"

The maid said nothing.

"You don't want to talk with us?"

"What would he come to us in Moscow for?"

"Well, but suppose he just up and came? What do you think: would he go sitting with our muzhiks?"

"Why should he sit with ours when he's got his own?" Anna Fetisovna replied and quickly went to her room carrying an empty cup.

"She's decidedly angry," the princess said in French and added that Anna Fetisovna was a flaming patriot and suffered from a passion for generalizations.

The baron went on smiling and soon left. I left an hour later.

When I was taking my leave, Anna Fetisovna, with a candle in her hand, went to show me the way to the stairs through the unfamiliar passages of the hotel and asked unexpectedly:

"And do you agree, sir, that our kind are all people without dignity?"

"No," I said, "I do not."

"Then why didn't you say anything?"

"I didn't want to argue to no purpose."

"Oh, no, sir, it wouldn't have been to no purpose . . . And in front of a foreign baron at that . . . How come it's always so hurtful when it's about your own! As if we like everything bad and nothing good."

I felt sorry for her, and also ashamed before her.

My wanderings abroad did not last long. By the fall I was back in Petersburg, and one day, in one of the passages of a shopping arcade, I unexpectedly ran into Anna Fetisovna with a basket of knitting. We greeted each other, and I asked her about the princess, and Anna Fetisovna replied:

"I know nothing about the princess, sir—we parted from each other."

"You mean there, abroad?"

"Yes, I came back alone."

Knowing their long-standing habitude—one might almost say, friendship—I expressed my unfeigned astonishment and asked:

"Why did you part?"

"You know the reason: it was in your presence . . ."

"You mean on account of the Austrian emperor?"

Anna Fetisovna was silent for a moment, and then suddenly snapped:

"What have I got to tell you: you saw for yourself . . . He was very polite, and the more honor to him, but I felt pained on account of the princess—on account of her lack of education."

"What does the princess's education have to do with it?"

"It's that *he* is a king, and he knows how to behave, he went and

sat with them all as an equal, while we sat in our carriage like stat-
ues put up for show. They all laughed at us."

"I didn't see anyone laugh at us there," I said.

"No, sir, not there, but in the hotel—the porter, and all the people."

"What did they say to you?"

"They didn't say anything, because I don't understand their language, but in their eyes I saw how they had no respect for our lack
of education."

"Well, ma'am, and that was enough to make you part from the
princess!"

"Yes . . . why . . . what's surprising, when the Lord is like to have
confused our tongues, and we've started not understanding each
other in anything . . . It was impossible to stay, when there was disagreement in all our thoughts, so I asked to come back here. I don't
want to serve anymore: I live by my own dim nature."

In that "nature" a true *dignity* could be felt, which made lack of
education painful for her.

Not for nothing did the princess call her a "flaming patriot."

Lefty

The Tale of Cross-eyed Lefty from Tula and the Steel Flea

I

When the emperor Alexander Pavlovich finished up the Congress of Vienna,[1] he wanted to travel through Europe and have a look at the wonders in the various states. He traveled around all the countries, and everywhere, owing to his amiability, he always had the most internecine conversations with all sorts of people, and they all astonished him with something and wanted to incline him to their side, but with him was the Don Cossack Platov,[2] who did not like such inclinations and, longing for his own backyard, kept luring the sovereign homewards. And the moment Platov noticed that the sovereign was getting very interested in something foreign, while his suite all remained silent, Platov would say at once: "Well, so, we've got no worse at home," and would sidetrack him with something.

The Englishmen knew that, and by the sovereign's arrival they had thought up various ruses so as to charm him with foreignness and distract him from the Russians, and on many occasions they succeeded, especially at large gatherings, where Platov could not speak fully in French; but that was of little interest to him, because he was a married man and regarded all French talk as trifles that were not worth fancying. But when the Englishmen started inviting the sovereign to all sorts of warehouses, ammunition and soap-rope factories, so as to show their advantage over us in everything and glory in it, Platov said to himself:

"Well, that'll do now. I've put up with it so far, but no further. Maybe I can speak or maybe I can't, but I won't let our people down."

And he had only just said these words to himself when the sovereign said to him:

"Well, so, tomorrow you and I will go and have a look at their armory collection. They have such perfections of nature there," he says, "that, once you've seen them, you'll no longer dispute that we Russians, with all our importance, are good for nothing."

Platov made no reply to the sovereign, but only lowered his hooked nose into his shaggy cape and, coming to his quarters, told his servant to fetch a flask of Caucasian vodka from the cellaret, tossed off a good glassful, said his prayers before the folding traveling icon, covered himself with his cape, and set up such a snoring that no Englishman in the whole house was able to sleep.

He thought: "Morning's wiser than evening."

II

The next day the sovereign and Platov went to the collection. The sovereign took no other Russians with him, because the carriage they gave him was a two-sitter.

They pull up to a very big building—an indescribable entry, endless corridors, rooms one after another, and finally, in the main hall, various henormous blustres, and in the middle under a canoply stands the Apollo Belderear.

The sovereign keeps glancing at Platov, to see if he's very surprised and what he's looking at; but the man walks with lowered eyes, as if seeing nothing, and only twists his mustache into rings.

The Englishmen at once start showing them various wonders and explaining what military circumstances they are suited to: sea blowrometers, drench coats for the infantry, and for the cavalry tarred waterprovables. The sovereign is delighted with it all, to him it all seems very good, but Platov holds back his agectation, as if it all means nothing to him.

The sovereign says:

"How is it possible—where did you get such insensitivity? Can it be that nothing here surprises you?"

And Platov replies:

"One thing here surprises me, that my fine lads from the Don fought without any of it and drove off two and ten nations."[3]

The sovereign says:

"That's an imprejudice."

Platov replies:

"I don't know what you're getting at, but I daren't argue and must hold my peace."

And the Englishmen, seeing such exchanges with the sovereign, at once bring him straight to Apollo Belderear and take from his one hand a Mortimer musket[4] and from the other a pistolia.

"Here," they say, "this is what our productivity is like," and they hand him the musket.

The sovereign looked calmly at the musket, because he had one like it in Tsarskoe Selo,[5] but then they handed him the pistolia and said:

"This is a pistolia of unknown, inimitable craftsmanship—an admiral of ours pulled it from the belt of a pirate chief in Candelabria."

The sovereign gazed at the pistol and could not take his eyes from it.

He oh'd and ah'd something awful.

"Ah, oh, ah," he says, "how is it . . . how is it even possible to do such fine work!" And he turns to Platov and says in Russian: "If I had just one such master in Russia, I'd be extremely happy and proud, and I'd make that master a nobleman at once."

At these words, Platov instantly thrusts his right hand into his wide balloon trousers and pulls out a gunsmith's screwdriver. The Englishmen say, "It can't be opened," but, paying no attention, he starts poking at the lock. He turns once, turns twice—and the lock comes out. Platov indicates the trigger to the sovereign, and there, right on the curve, is a Russian inscription: "Ivan Moskvin, town of Tula."

The Englishmen were astonished and nudged each other.

"Oh-oh, we've slipped up!"

And the sovereign says woefully to Platov:

"Why did you embarrass them so? Now I feel sorry for them! Let's go."

They got back into the same two-sitter and drove off, and the sovereign went to a ball that evening, but Platov downed an even bigger glass of vodka and slept a sound Cossack sleep.

He was glad that he had embarrassed the Englishmen and had put the Tula masters in the limelight, but he was also vexed: why did the sovereign feel sorry for the Englishmen in such a case!

"What made the sovereign so upset?" Platov thought. "I just don't understand it." And in such thoughts he got up twice, crossed himself, and drank vodka, until he made himself fall into a sound sleep.

But the Englishmen also did not sleep during that time, because they got all wound up as well. While the sovereign was making merry at the ball, they arranged such a new surprise for him that it robbed Platov of all his fantasy.

III

The next day, when Platov appeared before the sovereign with his good mornings, the latter said to him:

"Have the two-sitter hitched up at once, and we'll go to see some new collections."

Platov even ventured to suggest that they might have had enough of looking at foreign products, and it might be better if they got ready to go back to Russia, but the sovereign said:

"No, I want to see more novelties: they've boasted to me how they make first-rate sugar."

Off they went.

The Englishmen kept showing the sovereign the various first-rate things they had, but Platov looked and looked and suddenly said:

"Why don't you show us your *molvo* sugar factories?"

But the Englishmen don't even know what *molvo* sugar is. They exchange whispers, wink at each other, say "Molvo, molvo" to each other, but cannot understand that this is a kind of sugar we make, and have to confess that they have all kinds of sugar, but not "molvo."

Platov says:

"Well, so there's nothing to boast about. Come and visit us, we'll serve you tea with real molvo sugar from the Bobrinskoy factory."[6]

But the sovereign pulls him by the sleeve and says softly:

"Please, don't spoil the politics on me."

Then the Englishmen invited the sovereign to the last collection, where they have mineral stones and nymphosoria collected from all over the world, starting from the hugest Egyptian overlisk down to the subderminal flea, which cannot be seen with the eye, but causes remorsons between skin and body.

The sovereign went.

They looked at the overlisks and all sorts of stuffed things and were on their way out, and Platov thought to himself:

"There, thank God, everything's all right; the sovereign's not marveling at anything."

But they had only just come to the very last room, and there stood the workmen in their jackets and aprons, holding a tray with nothing on it.

The sovereign suddenly got surprised that they were offering him an empty tray.

"What's the meaning of this?" he asks. And the English masters reply:

"This is our humble offering to Your Majesty."

"What is it?"

"Here," they say, "kindly notice this little speck."

The sovereign looked and saw that there was, in fact, the tiniest little speck lying on the silver tray.

The workmen say:

"Kindly lick your finger and place it on your palm."

"What do I need this little speck for?"

"It is not a speck," they reply, "it is a nymphosoria."

"Is it alive?"

"By no means alive," they reply. "It is the likeness of a flea, fashioned by us of pure English steel, and inside there is a wind-up mechanism and a spring. Kindly turn the little key: it will begin at once to do a *danser*."

The sovereign became curious and asked:

"But where is the little key?"

And the Englishmen say:

"The key is here before your eyes."

"Why, then," says the sovereign, "do I not see it?"

"Because," they reply, "for that you need a meagroscope."

They gave him a meagroscope, and the sovereign saw that there was indeed a little key lying on the tray next to the flea.

"Kindly take it on your palm," they say. "It has a little winding hole in its belly. Turn the key seven times and it will start to *danser* . . ."

With difficulty the sovereign got hold of this little key and with difficulty pinched it between his fingers, and with the other hand he pinched the flea, and as soon as he put in the key, he felt the flea move its feelers, then its legs, and then it suddenly hopped and with one leap broke into a *danser,* with two veritations to one side, then to the other, and thus in three veritations it danced out a whole quandrille.

The sovereign ordered that the Englishmen be given a million at once, in whatever money they liked—silver five-kopeck coins or small banknotes.

The Englishmen asked to be paid in silver, because they had no clue about banknotes; and then at once they produced another of their ruses: they had offered the flea as a gift, but they had not brought its case; and neither the flea nor the key could be kept without the case, lest they get lost and be thrown away with the litter. And the case for the flea was made of a solid diamond nut and had a little place hollowed out in the middle. They had not brought it, because, they said, the case belonged to the state treasury, and there were strict rules about state property, even for a sovereign—it could not be given away.

Platov was very angry, because, he said:

"What's all this skullduggery! They made a gift and got a million for it, and it's still not enough! A thing," he said, "always comes with its case."

But the sovereign says:

"Leave off, please, it's not your affair—don't spoil the politics on me. They have their ways." And he asks: "What's the price of the nut that the flea is kept in?"

The Englishmen asked another five thousand for it.

The sovereign Alexander Pavlovich said, "Pay it," lowered the flea into the nut, and the key along with it, and so as not to lose the nut, he put it into his gold snuffbox, and ordered the snuffbox to be placed in his traveling chest, which was all inlaid with mutter-of-pearl and fish bone. As for the English masters, the sovereign dismissed them with honor, saying: "You are the foremost masters in the whole world, and my people can do nothing up against you."

They were very pleased with that, and Platov could say nothing against the sovereign's words. He only took the meagroscope, without speaking, and dropped it into his pocket, because "it comes with it," he said, "and you've taken a lot of money from us as it is."

The sovereign did not know of it until their arrival in Russia, and they left very soon, because military affairs made the sovereign melancholy, and he wanted to have a spiritual confession in Taganrog with the priest Fedot.* There was very little pleasant talk between him and Platov on the way, because they were having quite different thoughts: the sovereign considered that the Englishmen had no equals in craftsmanship, while Platov argued that ours could make anything shown to them, only they lacked useful education. And he put it to the sovereign that the English masters had entirely different rules of life, learning, and provisioning, and each man of them had all the absolute circumstances before him, and consequently an entirely different understanding.

The sovereign did not want to listen to that for long, and Platov, seeing as much, did not insist. So they drove on in silence, only Platov got out at every posting station and in vexation drank a glass of vodka, ate a salty pretzel, smoked his tree-root pipe, which held a whole pound of Zhukov tobacco at once,[7] then got back into the carriage and sat silently beside the tsar. The sovereign looked out one side, and Platov stuck his pipe out the other window and smoked into the wind. In this way they reached Petersburg, and the sovereign did not take Platov to the priest Fedot at all.

"You," he says, "are intemperate before spiritual conversation and smoke so much that I've got soot in my head because of it."

Platov was left offended and lay at home on a vexatious couchment, and went on lying like that, smoking Zhukov tobacco without quittance.

IV

The astonishing flea of burnished English steel stayed in Alexander Pavlovich's chest inlaid with fish bone until he died in Taganrog, having given it to the priest Fedot, to be given later to the empress when she calmed down. The empress Elisaveta Alexeevna looked at the flea's veritations and smiled, but did not become interested in it.

---

* The "priest Fedot" has not blown in on the wind: before his death in Taganrog, the emperor Alexander Pavlovich confessed to the priest Alexei *Fedotov*-Chekhovsky, who afterwards was referred to as "His Majesty's Confessor" and liked to remind everyone of this completely accidental circumstance. This *Fedotov*-Chekhovsky is obviously the legendary "priest Fedot." *Author.*

"My business now," she says, "is to be a widow, and no amusement holds any seduction for me"—and, on returning to Petersburg, she handed over this wonder, with all the other valuables, to the new sovereign as an heirloom.

The emperor Nikolai Pavlovich also paid no attention to the flea at first, because there were disturbances at his ascension,[8] but later one day he began to go through the chest left him by his brother and took out the snuffbox, and from the snuffbox the diamond nut, and in it he found the steel flea, which had not been wound up for a long time and therefore did not work, but lay quietly, as if gone stiff.

The sovereign looked and wondered.

"What's this gewgaw, and why did my brother keep it here so carefully?"

The courtiers wanted to throw it out, but the sovereign says:

"No, it means something."

They invited a chemist from the opposing pharmacy by the Anichkov Bridge, who weighed out poisons in very small scales, and showed it to him, and he took it, put it on his tongue, and said: "I feel a chill, as from hard metal." Then he nipped it slightly with his teeth and announced:

"Think what you like, but this is not a real flea, it's a nymphosoria, and it's made of metal, and it's not our Russian workmanship."

The sovereign gave orders at once to find out where it came from and what it meant.

They rushed and looked at the files and lists, but there was nothing written down in the files. Then they began asking around— nobody knew anything. But, fortunately, the Don Cossack Platov was still alive and was even still lying on his vexatious couchment smoking his pipe. When he heard that there was such a stir in the palace, he got up from his couchment at once, abandoned his pipe, and appeared before the sovereign in all his medals. The sovereign says:

"What do you need of me, courageous old fellow?"

And Platov replies:

"Myself, Your Majesty, I need nothing from you, because I eat and drink what I like and am well pleased with it all, but," he says, "I've come to report about this nymphosoria that's been found: it happened thus and so, and it took place before my eyes in England—and there's a little key here, and I've got a meagroscope you can see it through, and you can wind up the nymphosoria's belly with the key, and it will leap through any space you like and do veritations to the sides."

They wound it up, and it started leaping, but Platov said:

"This," he says, "is indeed a very fine and interesting piece of work, Your Majesty, only we shouldn't get astonished at it with rapturous feeling only, but should subject it to Russian inspection in Tula or Sesterbeck"—Sestroretsk was still called Sesterbeck then—"to see whether our masters can surpass it, so that the Englishmen won't go putting themselves above the Russians."

The sovereign Nikolai Pavlovich was very confident in his Russian people and did not like yielding to any foreigners, and so he answered Platov:

"You've put it well, courageous old fellow, and I charge you with seeing to this matter. With my present troubles, I don't need this little box anyway, so take it with you, and don't lie on your vexatious couchment anymore, but go to the quiet Don and start up an internecine conversation with my Cossacks there concerning their life and loyalty and likings. And when you pass through Tula, show this nymphosoria to my Tula masters and let them think about it. Tell them from me that my brother marveled at this thing and praised the foreign people who made this nymphosoria more than all, but that I'm relying on our people, that they're no worse than any others. They won't let my word drop and will do something."

V

Platov took the steel flea and, on his way through Tula to the Don, showed it to the Tula gunsmiths, passed on the sovereign's word to them, and then asked:

"What are we to do now, my fellow Orthodox?"

The gunsmiths replied:

"We are sensible of the sovereign's gracious words, good sir, and can never forget that he relies on his people, but what we are to do in the present case we cannot say this minute, because the English nation is also not stupid, but even rather clever, and there is a lot of sense in their craftsmanship. To vie with them," they said, "calls for reflection and God's blessing. But you, if Your Honor trusts in us as the sovereign does, go on your way to the quiet Don, and leave us this flea as it is, in its case and in the tsar's golden snuffbox. Have a good time on the Don, let the wounds heal that you received for the fatherland, and on your way back through Tula, stop and send for us: by that time, God willing, we'll have come up with something."

Platov was not entirely pleased that the Tula masters were asking for so much time and yet did not say clearly just what they hoped to bring off. He questioned them this way and that, and talked in all the manners of a wily Don Cossack, but the Tula men were no less wily than he, because they at once hit on such a scheme that there was even no hope of Platov's believing them, and they wanted to carry out their bold fancy directly, and then give the flea back.

They said:

"We ourselves don't know yet what we're going to make, we'll just trust in God, and maybe the tsar's word won't be disgraced on account of us."

So Platov dodged mentally and the Tula men did likewise.

Platov dodged and dodged, then saw that he could not out-dodge the Tula men, gave them the snuffbox with the nymphosoria, and said:

"Well, no help for it, go on," he said, "have it your way; I know how you are; well, anyhow, no help for it—I trust you, only see that you don't go replacing the diamond, and don't spoil the fine English workmanship, and don't fuss too long, because I travel fast: before two weeks are up, I'll be on my way back from the quiet Don to Petersburg—and then I'll have to have something to show the sovereign."

The gunsmiths fully reassured him:

"We will not spoil the fine workmanship," they said, "and we will not replace the diamond, and two weeks are enough for us, and by the time you go back, you'll have *something* to present worthy of the sovereign's magnificence."

But *precisely what*, they still did not say.

VI

Platov left Tula, and three of the gunsmiths, the most skillful of them, one of them cross-eyed, left-handed, with a birthmark on his cheek and the hair on his temples pulled out during his apprentice-

ship, bid farewell to their comrades and families, and, saying nothing to anyone, took their bags, put into them what eatables they
needed, and disappeared from town.

The only thing people noticed was that they did not go out by the
Moscow Gate, but in the opposite direction, towards Kiev, and it was
thought that they were going to Kiev to venerate the saints resting
there or to consult some of the living holy men, who are always to be
found in Kiev in abundance.

But that was only a near truth, not the truth itself. Neither time
nor space would allow the Tula masters to spend three weeks walking to Kiev, and then also manage to do work that would cover the
English nation with shame. They might better have gone to pray in
Moscow, which was only "twice sixty" miles away, and where there
were not a few saints resting as well. While to Orel, in the opposite
direction, it was the same "twice sixty," and from Orel to Kiev a good
three hundred miles more. Such a journey cannot be made quickly,
and once it is made, one is not soon rested—the feet will be swolt
and the hands will go on shaking for a long time.

Some even thought that the masters had boasted before Platov,
and then, thinking better of it, had turned coward, and had now fled
for good, carrying off the tsar's golden snuffbox, and the diamond,
and, in its case, the English steel flea that had caused them so much
trouble.

However, this conjecture was also totally unfounded and unworthy of such skillful people, in whom the hope of our nation now
rested.

VII

The Tula men, intelligent and experienced in metalwork, are equally
well known as foremost connoisseurs in religion. Their native land
is filled with their glory in this regard, and it has even reached holy
Athos:[9] they are not only masters of singing with flourishes, but they
know how to paint out the picture of "Evening Bells,"[10] and once
one of them devotes himself to greater service and becomes a monk,
such a one is reputed to make the best monastery treasurer and
most successful collector of money. On holy Athos they know that
Tula men are the most profitable people, and if it weren't for them,

the dark corners of Russia would probably never have seen a great many holy relics from the distant East, and Athos would have been deprived of many useful offerings from Russian generosity and piety. Nowadays the "Tula-born Athonites" carry holy relics all over our native land and masterfully collect money even where there's none to be had. A Tula man is filled with churchly piety and is a great practitioner in these matters, and therefore the three masters who undertook to uphold Platov, and the whole of Russia along with him, made no mistake in heading, not for Moscow, but for the south. They didn't go to Kiev at all, but to Mtsensk, the district capital of Orel province, where the ancient "stone-hewn" icon of St. Nicholas is kept, which came floating there in the most ancient times on a big cross, also of stone, down the river Zusha. The icon has a "dread and most fearsome" look—the bishop of Myra in Lycea is portrayed "full-length," all dressed in gilded silver vestments; his face is dark, and in one hand he holds a church and in the other a sword—"for military conquest." This "conquest" was the meaning of the whole thing: St. Nicholas is generally the patron of mercantile and military affairs, and the "Nicholas of Mtsensk" is particularly so, and it was him that the Tula men went to venerate. They held a prayer service before the icon itself, then before the stone cross, and finally returned home "by night" and, telling nobody anything, went about their business in terrible secrecy. All three of them came together in Lefty's house, locked the door, closed the shutters, lit the lamp in front of the icon of St. Nicholas, and set to work.

One day, two days, three days they sat and went nowhere, tapping away with their little hammers. They were forging something, but of what they were forging—nothing was known.

Everybody was curious, but nobody could learn anything, because the workmen didn't say anything and never showed themselves outside. Various people went up to the house, knocked at the door under various pretexts, to ask for a light or for salt, but the three artisans did not open to any demand, and nobody even knew what they fed on. People tried to frighten them, saying that the neighbors' house was on fire, to see if they would get scared and come running out, and whatever they had forged there would be revealed, but nothing worked with these clever masters. Only once Lefty stuck his head out and shouted:

"Burn yourselves up, we have no time," and pulled his plucked head in again, slammed the shutter, and they went back to business.

Through small chinks you could only see that lights were shining in the house and you could hear fine little hammers ringing on anvils.

In short, the whole affair was conducted in such terrible secrecy that it was impossible to find anything out, and it went on like that right up to the Cossack Platov's return from the quiet Don to the sovereign, and in all that time the masters neither saw nor talked with anyone.

VIII

Platov traveled in great haste and with ceremony: himself in the carriage, and on the box two Cossack odorlies with whips sitting on either side of the driver and showering him mercilessly with blows to keep him galloping. And if one of the Cossacks dozed off, Platov poked him with his foot from the carriage, and they would race on even more wickedly. These measures of inducement succeeded so well that the horses could not be reined in at the stations and always overran the stopping place by a hundred lengths. Then the Cossacks would apply the reverse treatment to the driver, and they would come back to the entrance.

And so they came rolling into Tula—at first they also flew past the Moscow Gate by a hundred lengths, then the Cossacks applied their whips to the driver in the reverse sense, and they started hitching up new horses by the porch. Platov did not leave the carriage, and only told an odorly to bring him the masters with whom he had left the flea as quickly as possible.

Off ran one odorly, to tell them to come as quickly as possible and bring the work with them that was to shame the English, and that odorly had not yet run very far, when Platov sent more behind him one after the other, to make it as quick as possible.

He sent all the odorlies racing off and had already started sending simple people from the curious public, and was even impatiently sticking his own legs out of the carriage and in his impatience was about to run off himself, and kept gnashing his teeth—so slow it all seemed to him.

Because at that time it was required that everything be done with great punctuality and speed, so that not a minute would be lost for Russian usefulness.

IX

The Tula masters, who were doing their astonishing deed, were just then finishing their work. The odorlies came running to them out of breath, and as for the simple people from the curious public—they did not reach them at all, because, being unaccustomed, their legs gave out on the way and they collapsed, and then, for fear of facing Platov, they hied themselves home and hid wherever they could.

The odorlies came running, called out at once, and, seeing that they did not open, at once unceremoniously tore at the bolts of the shutters, but the bolts were so strong that they did not yield in the least; they pulled at the door, but the door was held shut from inside by an oaken bar. Then the odorlies took a log from the street, placed it fireman-fashion under the eaves of the roof, and ripped off the whole roof of the little house at one go. But on taking off the roof, they themselves collapsed at once, because the air in the cramped little chamber where the masters had been working without respite had turned into such a sweaty stuffage that for an unaccustomed man, fresh from outdoors, it was impossible to take a single breath.

The envoys shouted:

"What are you blankety-blank scum doing, hitting us with such stuffage! There's no God in you after that!"

And they replied:

"We're just now hammering in the last little nail and, once we're done, we'll bring our work out to you."

And the envoys say:

"He'll eat us alive before that and won't leave enough to pray over."

But the masters reply:

"He won't have time to swallow you, because while you were talking, we hammered that last nail in. Run and tell him we're bringing it."

The odorlies ran, but not confidently: they thought the masters would trick them, and therefore they ran and ran and then looked back; but the masters came walking behind them, and so hurriedly that they were not even fully dressed as was proper for appearing before an important person and were fastening the hooks of their kaftans as they went. Two of them had nothing in their hands, and the third, Lefty, was carrying under a green cover the tsar's chest with the English steel flea.

X

The odorlies came running to Platov and said:

"Here they are!"

Platov says at once to the masters:

"Is it ready?"

"Everything's ready," they say.

"Give it here."

They gave it to him.

And the carriage was already hitched up, and the driver and postillion were in place. The Cossacks were right there beside the driver and had their whips raised over him and held them brandished like that.

Platov tore off the cover, opened the chest, unwrapped the cotton wool, took the diamond nut out of the snuffbox and looked: the English flea was lying there as before, and there was nothing else besides.

Platov says:

"What is this? Where is your work, with which you wanted to hearten our sovereign?"

The gunsmiths reply:

"Our work is here, too."

Platov asks:

"What does it consist in?"

And the gunsmiths reply:

"Why explain? It's all there in front of you—see for yourself."

Platov heaved his shoulders and shouted:

"Where's the key for the flea?"

"Right there," they reply. "Where the flea is, the key is—in the same nut."

Platov wanted to pick up the key, but his fingers were clubbsy; he tried and tried, but could not get hold either of the flea or of the key to its belly-winding, and suddenly he became angry and began to abuse them Cossack-fashion.

He shouted:

"So, you scoundrels, you did nothing, and you've probably ruined the whole thing besides! Your heads will roll!"

The Tula masters replied:

"You needn't abuse us like that. You being the sovereign's emissary, we must suffer all your offenses, but because you have doubted us and thought that we're even likely to let down the sovereign's name, we will not tell you the secret of our work, but kindly take it to the sovereign—he'll see what sort of people he has in us and whether he should be ashamed of us or not."

But Platov shouted:

"Ah, you're talking through your hats, you scoundrels! I won't part with you just like that. One of you is going to ride with me to Petersburg, and there I'll find out just how clever you are."

And with that, he seized cross-eyed Lefty by the scruff of the neck with his clubbsy fingers, so hard that all the hooks of his jacket flew off, and threw him into the carriage at his feet.

"Sit there like a pooble-dog all the way to Petersburg," he says. "You'll answer for all of them. And you," he says to the odorlies, "get a move on! And look sharp, I have to be in Petersburg at the sovereign's the day after tomorrow."

The masters only ventured to say to him about their comrade, "How is it you're taking him away without any dokyment? He won't be able to come back!" But instead of an answer, Platov showed them his fist—terrible, burple, scarred all over and healed any old way—shook it at them, and said: "Here's your dokyment!" And to the Cossacks, he said:

"Get a move on, boys!"

The Cossacks, the driver, and the horses all began working at once, and they carried Lefty off without any dokyment, and in two days, as Platov had ordered, they drove up to the sovereign's palace and, going at a good clip, even rode past the columns.

Platov stood up, pinned on his decorations, and went to the sovereign, and told the Cossack odorlies to guard cross-eyed Lefty by the entrance.

XI

Platov was afraid to show his face to the sovereign, because Nikolai Pavlovich was terribly remarkable and memorable—he never forgot anything. Platov knew that he would certainly ask him about the flea. And so he, who had never feared any enemy in the world, now turned coward: he went into the palace with the little chest and quietly put it behind the stove in the reception room. Having hidden the chest, he presented himself before the sovereign in his office and hastily began to report to him what the internecine conversation was among the Cossacks on the quiet Don. He thought like this: that he would occupy the sovereign with that, and then, if the sovereign himself remembered and began to speak of the flea, he would have to give it to him and answer, but if he didn't begin to speak, he would keep silent; he would tell the office valet to hide the chest and put Lefty in a cell in the fortress with no set term and keep him there until he might be needed.

But the sovereign, Nikolai Pavlovich, never forgot anything, and as soon as Platov finished about the internecine conversation, he asked at once:

"And so, how have my Tula masters acquitted themselves against the English nymphosoria?"

Platov replied in keeping with the way the matter seemed to him.

"The nymphosoria, Your Majesty," he said, "is still in the same place, and I've brought it back, and the Tula masters were unable to do anything more astonishing."

The sovereign replied:

"You're a courageous old fellow, but what you report to me cannot be so."

Platov started assuring him, and told him how the whole thing had gone, and when he reached the point where the Tula masters had asked him to show the flea to the sovereign, Nikolai Pavlovich slapped him on the shoulder and said:

"Bring it here. I know that my own can't let me down. Something supramental has been done here."

XII

They brought the chest from behind the stove, took off the flannel cover, opened the golden snuffbox and the diamond nut—and in it lies the flea, just as it was and as it lay before.

The sovereign looked and said:

"What the deuce!" But his faith in his Russian masters was undiminished, and he sent for his beloved daughter, Alexandra Nikolaevna, and told her:

"You have slender fingers—take the little key and quickly wind up the mechanism in the nymphosoria's belly."

The princess started turning the key, and the flea at once moved its feelers, but not its legs. Alexandra Nikolaevna wound it all the way up, but the nymphosoria still did no *danser* nor any veritations, as it had before.

Platov turned all green and shouted:

"Ah, those doggy rogues! Now I understand why they didn't want to tell me anything there. It's a good thing I took one of those fools along with me."

With those words, he ran out to the front steps, seized Lefty by the hair, and began yanking him this way and that so hard that whole clumps went flying. But once Platov stopped thrashing him, the man put himself to rights and said:

"I had all my hair torn out as an apprentice. What's the need of performing such a repetition on me?"

"It's this," said Platov, "that I trusted you and vouched for you, and you ruined a rare thing."

Lefty said:

"We're much pleased that you vouched for us, and as for ruining anything, that we haven't done: take and look at it through the most powerful meagroscope."

Platov ran back to tell about the meagroscope, and only threatened Lefty:

"You so-and-such-and-so," he said, "you're still going to get it from me."

And he told the odorlies to pull Lefty's elbow still tighter behind his back, while he himself went up the steps out of breath and reciting a prayer: "Blessed Mother of the blessed King, pure and most pure . . ." and so on, in good fashion. And the courtiers standing on the steps all turned away from him, thinking: "That's it for Platov, now he'll be thrown out of the palace"—because they couldn't stand him on account of his bravery.

XIII

When Platov brought Lefty's words to the sovereign, he at once said joyfully:

"I know my Russian people won't let me down." And he ordered a meagroscope brought on a cushion.

The meagroscope was brought instantly, and the sovereign took the flea and put it under the glass, first back up, then side up, then belly up—in short, they turned it all ways, but there was nothing to be seen. But the sovereign did not lose his faith here either, and only said:

"Bring the gunsmith who is downstairs here to me at once."

Platov reported:

"He ought to be smartened up a bit—he's wearing what he was taken in, and he looks pretty vile now."

The sovereign says:

"Never mind—bring him as he is."

Platov says:

"Now come yourself, you such-and-such, and answer before the eyes of the sovereign."

And Lefty replies:

"Well, so I'll go as I am and answer."

He went wearing what he had on: some sort of boots, one trouser leg tucked in, the other hanging out, and his coat is old, the hooks all gone and the collar torn off, but—never mind—he's not embarrassed.

"What of it?" he thinks. "If it pleases the sovereign to see me, I must go; and if I have no dokyment, it's not my fault, and I'll tell how come it happened."

When Lefty entered and bowed, the sovereign said to him at once:

"What does it mean, brother, that we've looked at it this way and that, and put it under the meagroscope, and haven't found anything remarkable?"

And Lefty says:

"Was Your Majesty so good as to look in the right way?"

The courtiers wag their heads at him, as if to say "That's no way to speak!" but he doesn't understand how it's done at court, with flattery and cunning, but speaks simply.

The sovereign says:

"Don't complicate things for him—let him answer as he can."

And he clarified at once:

"We," he says, "put it this way." And he put the flea under the meagroscope. "Look for yourself," he says, "there's nothing to see."

Lefty replies:

"That way, Your Majesty, it's impossible to see anything, because on that scale our work is quite hidden."

The sovereign asked:

"How should we look?"

"Only one leg should be put under the meagroscope," he said, "and each foot it walks on should be examined separately."

"Mercy," says the sovereign, "that's mighty small indeed!"

"No help for it," Lefty replies, "since that's the only way our work can be seen: and then the whole astonishment will show itself."

They put it the way Lefty said, and as soon as the sovereign looked through the upper glass, he beamed all over, took Lefty just as he was—disheveled, covered with dust, unwashed—embraced and kissed him, then turned to his courtiers and said:

"You see, I know better than anyone that my Russians won't let me down. Look, if you please: the rogues have shod the English flea in little horseshoes!"

XIV

They all went up to look: the flea was indeed shod on each foot with real little horseshoes, but Lefty said that that was still not the most astonishing thing.

"If," he said, "there was a better meagroscope, one that magnifies five million times, then," he said, "you'd see that each shoe has a master's name on it—of which Russian master made that shoe."

"And is your name there?" asked the sovereign.

"By no means," Lefty replied, "mine is the only one that's not."

"Why so?"

"Because," he says, "I worked on something smaller than these shoes: I fashioned the nails that hold the shoes on. No meagroscope can see that."

The sovereign asked:

"Where did you get a meagroscope with which you could produce this astonishment?"

And Lefty replied:

"We're poor people and from poverty we don't own a meagroscope, but we've got well-aimed eyes."

Here the other courtiers, seeing that Lefty's case had come off well, began to kiss him, and Platov gave him a hundred roubles and said:

"Forgive me, brother, for yanking your hair."

Lefty replies:

"God forgives—it's not the first time my head's caught it."

And he said no more, nor did he have time to talk with anyone, because the sovereign ordered at once that the shod nymphosoria be packed up and sent back to England—as a sort of present, so that they would understand there that for us this was nothing astonishing. And the sovereign ordered that the flea be carried by a special courier, who had learned all the languages, and that Lefty go with him, so that he himself could show the English his work and what good masters we have in Tula.

Platov made the sign of the cross over him.

"May a blessing be upon you," he said, "and I'll send you some of my vodka for the road. Don't drink too little, don't drink too much, drink middlingly."

And so he did—he sent it.

And Count Nestlebroad[11] ordered that Lefty be washed in the Tulyakovsky public baths, have his hair cut at a barber shop, and be put in the dress kaftan of a court choirboy, so that it would look as if he had some sort of rank.

Once he was shaped up in this fashion, they gave him some tea with Platov's vodka, drew in his belt as tightly as possible, so that his innards wouldn't get shaken up, and took him to London. From then on with Lefty it was all foreign sights.

XV

The courier and Lefty drove very fast, and did not stop to rest anywhere between Petersburg and London, but only tightened their belts a notch at each station, so that their lungs would not get tangled with their innards; but since Lefty, after his presentation to the sovereign, on Platov's orders, had received a plentiful supply of drink from the treasury, he did not eat, but got by on that alone, and sang Russian songs all across Europe, only adding the foreign refrain: *"Ai liu-lee, say tray zhulie."*

As soon as he brought him to London, the courier made his appearance to the right people and handed them the chest, and Lefty he installed in a hotel room, but it quickly became boring for him there, and he wanted to eat. He knocked on the door and pointed at his mouth to the attendant, and the attendant led him at once to the food-taking room.

Lefty seated himself at the table and sat there, but how to ask for something in English—that he did not know. But then he figured it out: again he simply tapped the table with his finger and pointed at his mouth—the Englishmen caught on and served him, not always what he wanted, but he did not take what did not suit him. They served him a hot inflamed puddling the way they make it—he said, "I don't know that such a thing can be eaten," and refused it; they changed it and set something else before him. He also did not drink their vodka, because it was green, as if mixed with vitriol, but chose what looked most natural, and awaited the courier in the cool over a nice noggin.

But the persons to whom the courier delivered the nymphosoria examined it that same minute under the most powerful of meagroscopes and sent the description at once to the *Publice Gazette,* so that the very next day a fooliton for general information came out.

"As for that same master," they said, "we want to see him at once."

The courier brought them to the hotel room, and from there to the food-taking room, where our Lefty was already properly flushed, and said: "Here he is!"

The Englishmen at once gave Lefty a pat-pat on the back and shook hands with him as an equal. "Cumrade," they said, "cumrade—good master—we'll talk with you in due time, and now we'll drink your health."

They ordered many drinks, and offered Lefty the first glass, but he politely refused to drink first. He thought, "Maybe you want to poison me out of envixation."

"No," he says, "that's not proper—guest is not above host—have a go yourselves first."

The Englishmen tried all the drinks before him and then started pouring for him. He stood up, crossed himself with his left hand, and drank the health of them all.

They noticed that he had crossed himself with his left hand, and asked the courier:

"What is he—a Lutheranian or a Protestantist?"

The courier replied:

"No, he's no Lutheranian or Protestantist, he's of Russian faith."

"Why then does he cross himself with his left hand?"

The courier said:

"He's a lefty and does everything with his left hand."

The Englishmen were still more astonished and began pumping both Lefty and the courier full of drink, and it went on like that for a whole three days, and then they said: "Enough now." They drank fuzzy water from a symphon and, quite freshened up, began questioning Lefty: where had he studied and how much arithmetic did he know?

Lefty replied:

"Our science is simple: the Psalter and the Dream Book, and as for arithmetic, we don't know any."

The Englishmen exchanged glances and said:

"That's astonishing."

And Lefty replies:

"With us it's that way everywhere."

"And what," they ask, "is this 'Dream Book' in Russia?"

"That," he says, "is a book which, if you're looking for some fortune-telling in the Psalter and King David doesn't reveal it clearly, then in the Dream Book you get souplemental divinations."

They say:

"That's a pity. It would be better if you knew at least the four rules of addition in arithmetic—that would be much more useful to you than the whole Dream Book. Then you might have realized that for every mechanism there is a calculation of force, while you, though

you have very skillful hands, did not realize that such a small mechanism as in this nymphosoria is calculated with the finest precision
and cannot carry these horseshoes. That's why it no longer leaps or
does a *danser*."

Lefty agreed.

"There's no disputing," he said, "that we haven't gone far in learning, but, then, we're faithfully devoted to our fatherland."

And the Englishmen say to him:

"Stay with us, we'll give you a grand education, and you'll come
out an astonishing master."

But Lefty did not agree to that.

"I've got parents at home," he said.

The Englishmen offered to send money to his parents, but Lefty
did not accept.

"I'm attached to my native land," he says, "and my father's already
an old man, and my mother's an old woman, they're used to going to
their parish church, and I'll be very bored here alone, because I'm
still of the bachelor's estate."

"You'll get used to it here," they say. "Change your religion, and
we'll get you married."

"That," said Lefty, "can never be."

"Why so?"

"Because," he says, "our Russian faith is the most correct one, and
as our anceptors believed, so the descenders should believe."

"You don't know our faith," say the Englishmen. "We're of the
same Christian religion and adhere to the same Gospel."

"The Gospel," says Lefty, "is indeed the same for all, only our
books are thicker next to yours, and our faith has more in it."

"What makes you think so?"

"About that," he says, "we have all the obvious proofs."

"Such as?"

"Such as," he says, "that we have God-working icons and tomb-
exuding heads and relics, and you have nothing, and, except for Sunday, you don't even have any extraneous feast days, and for another
reason—though we might be married legally, it would be embarrass-
ing for me to live with an Englishwoman."

"How come?" they ask. "Don't scorn them: our women also dress
neatly and make good housewives."

And Lefty says:

"I don't know them."

The Englishmen reply:

"That doesn't matter. You can get to know them: we'll arrange a grandezvous for you."

Lefty became abashed.

"Why addle girls' heads for nothing?" he says. And he declined. "A grandezvous is for gentlefolk, it's not fitting for us, and if they find out back home in Tula, they'll make a great laughingstock of me."

The Englishmen became curious:

"And if it's without a grandezvous," they said, "what do you do in such cases, so as to make an agreeable choice?"

Lefty explained our situation to them.

"With us," he says, "when a man wants to display thorough-going intentions regarding a girl, he sends a talker woman, and once she makes a preposition, they politely go to the house together and look the girl over, not in secret, but with all the familiality."

They understood, but replied that with them there were no talker women and no such custom, and Lefty said:

"That's even better, because if you take up such business, it must be with thorough-going intentions, and since I feel none at all towards a foreign nation, why addle girls' heads?"

He pleased the Englishmen with these reasonings of his, and they again set about patting him pleasantly on the shoulders and knees, and then asked:

"We'd like to know just one thing out of curiosity: what reproachable qualities have you noticed in our girls and why are you devoiding them?"

Here Lefty replied quite openly:

"I don't reproach them, and the only thing I don't like is that the clothes on them somehow flutter, and you can't figure out what it is they're wearing and out of what necessity; first there's some one thing, then something else pinned on below, and some sort of socks on their arms. Just like a sapajou ape in a velveteen cape."

The Englishmen laughed and said:

"What obstacle is that to you?"

"Obstacle," replied Lefty, "it's not. Only I'm afraid I'd be ashamed to watch and wait for her to get herself out of it all."

"Can it be," they said, "that your fashion is better?"

"Our fashion in Tula," he replies, "is simple: each girl wears her own lace, and even grand ladies wear our lace."[12]

They also showed him to their ladies, and there they served him tea and asked:

"Why do you wince?"

He replied that we are not used to it so sweet.

Then they gave him a lump of sugar to suck Russian-style.

It seemed to them that it would be worse that way, but he said:

"To our taste it's tastier."

There was nothing the Englishmen could do to throw him off, so as to tempt him by their life, and they only persuaded him to stay for a short time, during which they would take him to various factories and show him all their art.

"And then," they say, "we'll put you on our ship and *deliver you alive to Petersburg.*"

To that he agreed.

XVI

The Englishmen took charge of Lefty and sent the Russian courier back to Russia. Though the courier was a man of rank and knew various languages, they were not interested in him, but in Lefty they were interested—and they started taking him around and showing him everything. He looked at all their industries—metalworking shops and soap-rope factories—and liked all their arrangements very much, especially with regard to the workers' keeping. Each of their workers ate his fill, was dressed not in rags, but in his own good jacket, and was shod in thick boots with iron hobnails, so that his feet would never run up against anything; he worked, not under the lash, but with training and with his own understanding. In plain view before each of them hung the multipeclation table, and under his hand was a rub-out board: whatever a master does, he looks at the multipeclation table and checks it with his understanding, and then writes one thing on the board, rubs out another, and brings it to precision: whatever's written in the numbers is what turns out in reality. And when a holiday comes, they get together in pairs, take their sticks, and go promenading nobly and decorously, as is proper.

Lefty took a good look at their whole life and all their work, but he paid most attention to something that greatly astonished the

Englishmen. He was interested not so much in how new guns were made as in the way the old ones were kept. He goes around and praises it all, and says:

"We can do that, too."

But when he comes to an old gun, he puts his finger into the barrel, moves it around inside, and sighs:

"That," he says, "is far superior to ours."

The Englishmen simply couldn't figure out what Lefty had noticed, and then he asks:

"Might I know whether our generals ever looked at that or not?"

They say:

"Those who were here must have looked at it."

"And how were they," he asks, "in gloves or without gloves?"

"Your generals," they say, "wear dress uniforms, they always go about in gloves, meaning here as well."

Lefty said nothing. But he suddenly felt a restless longing. He languished and languished and said to the Englishmen:

"I humbly thank you for all your treats, and I'm very pleased with everything here, and I've already seen everything I had to see, and now I'd like to go home quickly."

There was no way they could keep him any longer. It was impossible for him to go by land, because he didn't speak any languages, and to go by sea was not so good, because it was autumn and stormy, but he insisted that they let him go.

"We looked at the blowrometer," they say. "A storm's blowing up, you may drown; it's not like your Gulf of Finland, it's the real Firmaterranean Sea."

"That makes no difference," he replies. "Where you die is all the same, it's God's will, and I want to get back to my native land soon, because otherwise I may fetch myself some kind of insanity."

They didn't force him to stay: they fed him up, rewarded him with money, gave him a gold watch with a rebeater as a souvenir, and for the sea's coolness on his late autumn journey they gave him a woolen coat with a windbreaking hood. They dressed Lefty very warmly and took him to a ship that was going to Russia. There they accommodated him in the best way, like a real squire, but he didn't like sitting with other gentlemen in a closed space and felt abashed, so he would go up on deck, sit under a tarpoling, and ask: "Where is our Russia?"

The Englishman whom he asked would point his hand in that

direction or nod his head, and Lefty would turn his face and look impatiently towards his native shore.

Once they left harbord for the Firmaterranean Sea, his longing for Russia became so strong that there was no way to calm him. There was a terrible downflood, but Lefty still would not go below to his room—he sits under the tarpoling, his hood pulled over his head, and looks towards his fatherland.

The Englishmen came many times to call him to the warm place below, but he even began to snap at them, so as not to be bothered.

"No," he replies, "it's better for me here outside; under the roof I may get seaccups from the fluctuations."

And so he never went below in all that time until one special occasion, through a certain bos'man who liked him very much and who, to our Lefty's misfortune, could speak Russian. This bos'man could not help admiring that a Russian landlubber could endure such foul weather.

"Fine fellow, Rus!" he says. "Let's drink!"

Lefty drank.

The bos'man says:

"Another!"

Lefty drank another, and they got drunk.

Then the bos'man asks him:

"What's the secret you're taking from our state to Russia?"

Lefty replies:

"That's my business."

"In that case," replied the bos'man, "let's make an English bet between us."

Lefty asks:

"What sort?"

"This sort: that we don't drink anything on our lonesome, but everything equally; whatever the one drinks, the other's got to drink, too, and whichever out-drinks the other is the winner."

Lefty thought: "The sky's cloudy, my belly's rowdy—the trip's a big bore, it's a long way to shore, and my native land can't be seen beyond the waves—anyhow to make a bet will cheer things up."

"All right," he says, "you're on!"

"Only keep it honest."

"Don't you worry about that," he says.

So they agreed and shook hands.

XVII

They made the bet while still in the Firmaterranean Sea, and they drank till Dünamünde near Riga, but they kept even and did not yield to each other, and were so perfectly matched that when one looked into the sea and saw a devil emerging from the water, the same thing at once appeared to the other. Only the bos'man saw a red-haired devil, while Lefty said he was dark as a Moor.

Lefty says:

"Cross yourself and turn away—it's the devil from the watery deep."

And the Englishman argues that "it's a deep-sea driver."

"Do you want me to toss you into the sea?" he says. "Don't be afraid—he'll give you back to me at once."

And Lefty replies:

"In that case, toss me in."

The bos'man took him on his back and carried him to the bulwarps.

The sailors saw it, stopped them, and reported to the captain, and he ordered them both locked up below and given rum and wine and some cold food, so that they could eat and drink and go on with their bet—but they were not to be given hot inflamed puddling, because the alcohol might cause combustion inside them.

And so they were brought to Petersburg locked up, and neither of them won the bet between them; and there they were laid in different carriages, and the Englishman was taken to the embassy on the English Embankment, while Lefty was taken to the police station.

From then on their fates began to differ greatly.

XVIII

As soon as the Englishman was brought to the embassy, a doctor and an apothecary were called for him. The doctor ordered him put into a warm bath, in his presence, and the apothecary at once rolled a gutta-percha pill and stuck it into his mouth himself, and then they both took him and laid him on a featherbed, covered him with a fur coat, and left him there to sweat, and, so that he wouldn't be disturbed, the order was given to the whole embassy that no one should dare to sneeze. The doctor and the apothecary waited until the bos'man fell asleep, and then prepared another gutta-percha pill for him, put it on his bedside table, and left.

But Lefty was dumped on the floor of the police station and asked:

"Who are you and where from and do you have a passport or any other dokyment?"

But he was so weakened by illness, drinking, and the prolonged fluctations that he didn't answer a word, but only groaned.

Then he was searched at once, his nice clothes were taken off him, the money and the watch with the rebeater were confiscated, and the police chief ordered him dispatched to the hospital for free in the first cab that came along.

A policeman took Lefty out, intending to put him in a sleigh, but he was a long time catching a cabby, because they avoid the police. And all that while Lefty lay on the cold gobbles, and then, when the policeman did catch a cabby, he had no warm fox fur, because on such occasions cabbies hide the warm fox fur under them, so that the policemen will get their feet frozen quickly. They transported Lefty uncovered, and, when changing cabs, they also dropped him each time, and when they picked him up, they pulled his ears so that he would come to his senses. They brought him to one hospital—he could not be admitted without a dokyment; they brought him to another—he was not admitted there either; and the same for the third, and the fourth—they dragged him around the remote by-lanes till morning, and kept changing cabs, so that he got all battered up. Then one doctor told the policeman to take him to the Obukhovsky Charity Hospital, where people of unknown estate were all brought to die.

There he asked for a receipt, and Lefty was left sitting on the floor in the corridor until things were sorted out.

And meanwhile the English bos'man got up the next day, swallowed the other gutta-percha pill, had a light breakfast of chicken and rice, washed it down with fuzzy water, and said:

"Where's my Russian cumrade? I'll go and look for him."

He got dressed and ran off.

XIX

Astonishingly enough, the bos'man somehow found Lefty very quickly, only he was still not lying in bed, but on the floor of the corridor, and he complained to the Englishman.

"There's a couple of words," he says, "that I absolutely must say to the sovereign."

The Englishman ran to Count Kleinmichel[13] and raised a ruckus.

"This is not possible! It's a sheep's hide," he says, "but there's a man's soul inside."

For such reasoning the Englishman was thrown out at once, so that he wouldn't dare mention man's soul. And then someone said to him, "You'd better go to the Cossack Platov—he has simple feelings."

The Englishman got to Platov, who was now lying on his couchment again. Platov heard him out and remembered Lefty.

"Why, of course, brother," he says, "I'm a close acquaintance of his, even pulled his hair once, only I don't know how to help him in this unfortunate case, because I'm no longer in the service at all and got myself a full aperplexy—there's no respect for me now—but run quickly to Commandant Skobelev,[14] he's in power and also has experience in this line, he'll do something."

The bos'man went to Skobelev and told him everything: what Lefty's ailment was and how it came about. Skobelev says:

"I understand that ailment, only a German can't treat it, what's needed is a doctor from the clerical estate, who grew up with such examples and knows what to do. I'll send the Russian doctor Martyn-Solsky[15] there at once."

But by the time Martyn-Solsky arrived, Lefty was already done for, because the back of his head had been bashed against the gobbles, and he could utter only one thing clearly:

"Tell the sovereign that the English don't use bath brick to clean their guns: let us not use it either, otherwise, God forbid there's a war, they'll be no good for shooting."

And with these loyal words, Lefty crossed himself and died.

Martyn-Solsky went at once and reported it to Count Chernyshev,[16] so that the sovereign could be informed, but Count Chernyshev yelled at him:

"Take care of your vomitives and purgatives," he says, "and don't mix in what's not your business: in Russia we've got generals for that."

So the sovereign was not told, and such cleaning went on right up to the Crimean campaign. At that time, they started loading their guns, and the bullets were loose in them, because the barrels had been cleaned with bath brick.

Then Martyn-Solsky reminded Chernyshev about Lefty, but Count Chernyshev only said:

"Go to the devil, anima-tube, don't mix in what's not your business, otherwise I'll deny I ever heard it from you—and then you'll really get it."

Martyn-Solsky thought: "It's true he'll deny it," so he kept quiet.

But if they had made Lefty's words known to the sovereign in time, the Crimean War would have turned out quite differently for the enemy.

XX

Now all this is already "the deeds of bygone days" and "legends of old,"[17] though not very old, but we need not hasten to forget this legend, despite its fabulous makeup and the epic character of its main hero. Lefty's proper name, like the names of many great geniuses, is forever lost to posterity; but, as a myth embodied by popular fantasy, he is interesting, and his adventures may serve as a reminder of that epoch, the general spirit of which has been aptly and rightly grasped.

To be sure, there are no such masters as the fabulous Lefty in Tula nowadays: machines have evened out the inequality of talents and gifts, and genius does not strive against assiduousness and precision. While favoring the increase of earnings, machines do not favor artistic boldness, which sometimes went beyond all measure, inspiring popular fantasy to compose fabulous legends similar to this one.

Workers, of course, know how to value the advantages provided by the practical application of mechanical science, but they remember the old times with pride and love. It is their epos, and, what's more, with "a man's soul inside."

The Spirit of Madame de Genlis

A Spiritualistic Occurrence

It is sometimes much easier to call up a spirit than to get rid of it.

A. B. CALMET[1]

I

The strange adventure I intend to tell took place several years ago, and can now be freely told, the more so as I reserve for myself the right not to use a single proper name in doing so.

In the winter of the year 186–, there came to settle in Petersburg a very prosperous and distinguished family, consisting of three persons: the mother—a middle-aged lady, a princess, reputed to be a woman of refined education and with the best social connections in Russia and abroad; her son, a young man, who that year had set out on his career in the diplomatic corps; and her daughter, the young princess, who was just going on seventeen.

Up to then the newly arrived family had usually lived abroad, where the old princess's late husband had occupied the post of Russian representative at one of the minor European courts. The young prince and princess were born and grew up in foreign parts, receiving there a completely foreign but very thorough education.

II

The princess was a woman of highly strict principles and deservedly enjoyed a most irreproachable reputation in society. In her opinions and tastes she adhered to the views of French women renowned for their intelligence and talents in the time of the blossoming of women's intelligence and talents in France. The princess was considered very well read, and it was said that she read with great discrimination. Her favorite reading was the letters of Mmes de Sévigné, La Fayette, and Maintenon, as well as of Caylus, Dangeau, and Coulanges, but most of all she respected Mme de Genlis,[2] for whom she had a weakness to the point of adoration. The small volumes of the finely made Paris edition of this intelligent writer, modestly and elegantly bound in pale blue morocco, always occupied a beautiful little bookshelf hanging on the wall over a big armchair, which was the princess's favorite place. Over the edge of the bookshelf, inlaid with mother-of-pearl, reaching slightly beyond its dark velvet cushion, rested a miniature hand, perfectly formed from terracotta, which Voltaire had kissed in his Ferney, not suspecting that it was going to let fall on him the first drop of a refined but caustic criticism.[3] How often the princess had reread the little volumes traced by that small hand, I do not know, but she always had them near her, and the princess used to say that they had for her a particular, so to speak, mysterious meaning, of which she would not venture to tell just anyone, because not everyone would believe it. From what she said, it followed that she had never parted from these volumes "since she could remember herself," and that they would go with her to the grave.

"I have instructed my son," she said, "to put these little books into the coffin with me, under the pillow, and I'm certain they will be useful to me even after death."

I cautiously expressed a wish to receive an explanation, however remote, of these last words—and I received it.

"These little books," the princess said, "are suffused with the *spirit* of Felicity" (so she called Mme de Genlis, probably as a sign of the closeness of their relations). "Yes, piously believing in the immortality of the human spirit, I also believe in its ability to communicate freely, from beyond the grave, with those who have need of such communication and are able to appreciate it. I am certain that the fine fluid of Felicity chose itself a pleasant abode under the fortunate morocco that embraces the pages on which her thoughts have found rest, and if you are not a total unbeliever, I should hope that would be understandable to you."

I bowed silently. It evidently pleased the princess that I did not contradict her, and in reward she added that everything she had just told me was not merely a belief, but a real and full *conviction,* which had such a firm foundation that no powers could shake it.

"And that precisely," she concluded, "because I have a multitude of proofs that the spirit of Felicity lives, and lives precisely here!"

At the last word the princess raised her hand above her head and pointed her elegant finger at the shelf on which the pale blue volumes stood.

III

I am slightly superstitious by nature and always listen with pleasure to stories in which there is at least some place for the mysterious. That, it seems, is why perspicacious critics, who kept including me in various bad categories, spoke for a time of my being a spiritualist.

Besides, let it be said, everything we are talking about now took place just at the time when an abundance of news about spiritualist phenomena was coming to us from abroad. It aroused curiosity then, and I saw no reason not to be interested in something people were beginning to believe in.

The "multitude of proofs" the princess mentioned could be heard from her a multitude of times: these proofs consisted in the princess having long since formed the habit, in moments of the most diverse states of mind, of turning to the works of Mme de Genlis as to an oracle, and the pale blue volumes, in their turn, invariably displayed an ability to respond reasonably to her mental questions.

That, in the princess's words, became one of her *habitudes,*[*] which she never changed, and the "spirit" abiding in the books never once told her anything inappropriate.

---

[*] Habits. *Trans.*

I could see that I was dealing with a very convinced follower of spiritualism, who besides was not without her share of intelligence, experience, and education, and therefore I became extremely interested in it all.

I already knew a thing or two about the nature of spirits, and, in what I had happened to witness, I had always been struck by a strange thing common to all spirits, that, appearing from beyond the grave, they behaved themselves much more light-mindedly and, frankly speaking, stupidly, than they had shown themselves in earthly life.

I was already familiar with Kardec's theory of "mischievous spirits"[4] and was now greatly interested in how the spirit of the witty marquise de Sillery, Comtesse Brûlart, would deign to show itself in my presence.

The occasion was not slow in coming, but since in a short story, as in a small household, order ought not to be upset, I ask for another minute of patience before matters are brought to a supernatural moment capable of going beyond all expectations.

IV

The people who made up the princess's small but very select circle were probably aware of her whimsicality; but since they were all well-bred and courteous people, they knew enough to respect another's beliefs, even in cases when those beliefs diverged sharply from their own and could not stand up under criticism. Therefore no one ever argued about it with the princess. However, it might also be that the princess's friends were not sure whether the princess considered her pale blue volumes the abode of their author's "spirit" in a direct and immediate sense, or took these words as a rhetorical figure. Finally, more simply still, they may have taken it all as a joke.

The only one who could not look at the matter in such fashion was, unfortunately, I myself; and I had my reasons for it, which may have been rooted in the gullibility and impressionability of my nature.

V

The attention of this high-society lady, who opened the doors of her respectable house to me, I owed to three causes: first, for some reason she liked my story "The Sealed Angel," which had been published shortly before then in *The Russian Messenger*; second, she was interested in the bitter persecutions, beyond count and measure, to which I had been subjected for a number of years by my good literary brethren, who wished, of course, to correct my misunderstandings and errors; and third, I had been well recommended to the princess in Paris by a Russian Jesuit, the most kindly Prince Gagarin[5]—an old man with whom I had enjoyed many conversations and who had not formed the worst opinion of me.

This last was especially important, because the princess was concerned with my way of thinking and state of mind; she needed, or at least fancied she might need, some small services from me. Strange though it was for a man of such modest significance as myself, it was so. This need was created for the princess by maternal solicitude for her daughter, who knew almost no Russian . . . Bringing the lovely girl to her native land, the mother wanted to find a man who could acquaint the young princess at least somewhat with Russian literature—*good* literature exclusively, to be sure, that is, real literature, not infected by the "evil of the day."

About the latter the princess had very vague notions, and extremely exaggerated ones besides. It was rather difficult to understand precisely what she feared on the part of the contemporary titans of Russian thought—their strength and courage, or their weakness and pathetic self-importance; but having somehow grasped, with the help of suggestions and surmises, the "heads and tails" of the princess's thoughts, I arrived at the conviction, unmistaken in my view, that she most definitely feared the "unchaste allusions" by which, to her mind, all our immodest literature had been utterly corrupted.

To try to dissuade the princess of that was useless, because she had reached the age when one's opinions are already firmly formed, and it is a very rare person who is capable of subjecting them to a new review and testing. She was undoubtedly not one of those, and to make her change her mind about something she believed in, the words of an ordinary man were insufficient, though it might perhaps have been done through the power of a spirit, who deemed it necessary to come from hell or paradise with that aim. But could such petty concerns interest the bodiless spirits of the unknown world? Were not all arguments and concerns about literature too petty for them, like our contemporary ones, which even the vast majority of living people consider the empty occupation of empty heads?

Circumstances soon showed, however, that I was greatly mistaken in reasoning this way. The habit of literary peccadilloes, as we shall soon see, does not abandon literary spirits even beyond the grave, and the reader will be faced with the task of deciding to what extent these spirits act successfully and remain faithful to their literary past.

VI

Owing to the fact that the princess had strictly formed views about everything, my task in helping her to choose literary works for the young princess was very well defined. It was required that the young princess be able to learn about Russian life from this reading, while not coming upon anything that might trouble her maidenly ear. The princess's maternal censorship did not allow the whole of any author, not even Derzhavin or Zhukovsky. None of them seemed fully safe to her. There was, naturally, no speaking of Gogol—he was banished entirely. Of Pushkin, *The Captain's Daughter* and *Evgeny Onegin* were allowed, the latter with considerable cuts, which were marked by the princess's own hand. Lermontov, like Gogol, was not allowed. Of new authors, Turgenev alone was approved without question, but minus the passages "where they talk of love," while Goncharov was banished, and though I interceded for him quite boldly, it did not help. The princess replied:

"I know he's a great artist, but so much the worse—you must admit there are arousing subjects in him."

VII

I wished at all costs to know what precisely the princess meant by the *arousing subjects* she found in the works of Goncharov. How could he, with the mildness of his attitude towards people and the passions that possess them, offend anyone's feelings?

This was intriguing to such a degree that I plucked up my courage and asked outright what the arousing subjects in Goncharov were.

To this frank question I received a frank, terse reply, uttered in a sharp whisper: "Elbows."

I thought I had not heard right or had not understood.

"Elbows, elbows," the princess repeated and, seeing my perplexity, seemed to grow angry. "Don't you remember . . . how that one . . . the hero at some point . . . admires the bare elbows of his . . . of some very simple lady?"

Now, of course, I recalled the well-known episode from *Oblomov* and could not find a word of reply. As a matter of fact, it was more convenient for me to say nothing, since I neither needed nor wished to argue with the princess, who was beyond the reach of persuasion, and whom, to tell the truth, I had long been observing much more zealously than I tried to serve her with my recommendations and advice. And what recommendations could I make to her, since she considered "elbows" an outrageous indecency, and all the latest literature had stepped so far beyond such revelations?

What boldness one had to have, knowing all that, to name even one recent work, in which the coverings of beauty are raised far more resolutely!

I felt that, circumstances being revealed in this way, my role as an adviser should be over—and I resolved not to advise, but to contradict.

"Princess," I said, "it seems to me that you are being unfair: there is something exaggerated in your demands on artistic literature."

I laid out everything that, in my opinion, had to do with the matter.

VIII

Carried away, I not only delivered a whole critique of false purism, but also quoted a well-known anecdote about a French lady who could neither write nor speak the word *culotte,*[*] and when she once could not avoid saying this word in front of the queen, faltered and made everyone burst out laughing. But I simply could not remember in which French writer I had read about this terrible court scandal, which would not have taken place at all if the lady had spoken the word *culotte* as simply as the queen herself did with her august little lips.

My goal was to show that too much delicacy could be detrimental to modesty, and therefore an overly strict selection of reading was hardly necessary.

The princess, to my no little amazement, heard me out without showing the least displeasure, and, not leaving her seat, raised her hand over her head and took one of the pale blue volumes.

"You," she said, "have arguments, but I have an oracle."

"I would be interested to hear it," I said.

"Without delay: I invoke the spirit of Genlis, and it will answer you. Open the book and read."

"Be so kind as to point out where I should read," I asked, accepting the little volume.

"Point out? That's not my business: the spirit itself will do the pointing out. Open it at random."

This was becoming slightly ridiculous for me, and I even felt ashamed, as it were, for my interlocutrice; however, I did as she wanted, and as soon as I glanced at the first sentence of the open page, I felt a vexing surprise.

"You're puzzled?" asked the princess.

"Yes."

"Yes, it's happened to many. I ask you to read it."

---

* Drawers or panties. *Trans.*

IX

"Reading is an occupation far too serious and far too important in its consequences for young people's tastes not to be guided in its selection. There is reading which young people like, but which makes them careless and predisposes them to flightiness, after which it is difficult to correct the character. All this I know from experience." I read that and stopped.

The princess, with a quiet smile, spread her arms and, tactfully triumphant in her victory over me, said:

"In Latin I believe it's known as *dixi*."*

"Quite right."

After that we did not argue, but the princess could not deny herself the pleasure of sometimes speaking in my presence about the ill breeding of Russian writers who, in her opinion, "could not possibly be read aloud without preliminary revision."

To the "spirit" of Genlis, naturally, I gave no serious thought. People say all kinds of things.

But the "spirit" indeed lived and was active, and, in addition, seemed to be on our side, that is, on the side of literature. Literary nature took the upper hand in it over dry philosophizing, and, unassailable on the score of decency, the "spirit" of Mme de Genlis, having spoken *du fond du coeur*,† pulled off (yes, precisely pulled off) such a schoolboy stunt in that strict salon that the consequences of it were filled with deep tragicomedy.

X

Once a week "three friends" used to gather at the princess's in the evening for tea. These were distinguished people, excellently placed. Two were senators, and the third was a diplomat. Naturally, we did not play cards, but conversed.

---

* I have spoken. *Trans.*
† From the bottom of [its] heart. *Trans.*

Usually the older ones, that is, the princess and the "three friends," did the talking, while the young prince, the young princess, and I very rarely put in a word of our own. We were learning, and it must be said to the credit of our elders that we did have something to learn from them—especially from the diplomat, who amazed us with his subtle observations.

I enjoyed his favor, though I do not know why. In fact, I am obliged to think he considered me no better than the others, and in his eyes "littérateurs" all shared "the same root." He said jokingly, "The best of serpents is still a serpent."

This same opinion gave rise to the terrible incident that follows.

XI

Being stoically faithful to her friends, the princess did not want such a general definition to extend to Mme de Genlis and the "women's pléiade" that the writer kept under her protection. And so, when we gathered in this esteemed person's home to quietly see in the New Year, shortly before midnight the usual conversation started among us, in which the name of Mme de Genlis was mentioned, and the diplomat recalled his observation that "the best of serpents is still a serpent."

"There is no rule without its exception," said the princess.

The diplomat understood *who* the exception must be, and said nothing.

The princess could not contain herself and, glancing in the direction of Genlis's portrait, said:

"What kind of serpent is she!"

But the worldly-wise diplomat stood his ground: he gently shook his finger and gently smiled—he believed neither flesh nor spirit.

To resolve the disagreement, proofs were obviously needed, and here the method of addressing the spirit came in pat.

The small company was in an excellent mood for such experiments, and the hostess, first reminding us of what we knew concerning her beliefs, then suggested an experiment.

"I claim," she said, "that the most fault-finding person will not find anything in Genlis that could not be read aloud by the most innocent young girl, and we are going to test it right now."

Again, as the first time, she reached her hand to the bookshelf that was still situated over her *établissement,* took a volume at random— and turned to her daughter.

"My child! Open it and read us a page."

The young princess obeyed.

We all became pictures of earnest expectation.

XII

The writer who begins to describe the appearance of his characters at the end of his story is blameworthy; but I have written this little trifle in such a way that no one in it should be recognized. Therefore I have not set down any names or given any portraits. The portrait of the young princess would in any case have exceeded my powers, because she was fully what is known as "an angel in the flesh." As far as her all-perfect purity and innocence were concerned—they were so great that she could even have been entrusted with resolving the insuperably difficult theological problem posed in Heine's "Bernardiner und Rabiner."[6] Of course, something standing higher than the world and its passions had to speak for this soul not privy to any sin. And the young princess, with that very innocence, charmingly rolling her r's, read Genlis's interesting memoirs about the old age of Mme du Deffand, when she became "weak in the eyes." The text spoke of the fat Gibbon,[7] who had been recommended to the French writer as a famous author. Genlis, as we know, quickly sized him up and sharply derided the French who were made enthusiastic by the inflated reputation of this foreigner.

Here I will quote from the well-known translation of the French original read by the young princess who was capable of resolving the argument between "Bernardiner und Rabiner":

"Gibbon was of small stature, extremely fat, and had a most remarkable face. It was impossible to make out any features on this face. Neither the nose, nor the eyes, nor the mouth could be seen at all; two huge, fat cheeks, resembling the devil knows what, engulfed everything . . . They were so puffed up that they quite departed from all proportion ever so slightly proper even for the biggest cheeks; anyone seeing them must have wondered: why has that place not been put in the right place? I would characterize Gibbon's face with one word, if it were only possible to speak such a word. Lauzun,[8] who was on close terms with Gibbon, once brought him to du Deffand. Mme du Deffand was already blind then and had the habit of feeling with her hands the faces of distinguished people newly introduced to her. In this way she would acquire a rather accurate notion of the features of her new acquaintance. She applied this tactile method to Gibbon, and the result was terrible. The Englishman approached her chair and with especial good-naturedness offered her his astonishing face. Mme du Deffand brought her hands to it and passed her fingers over this ball-shaped face. She tried to find something to stop at, but it was impossible. All at once the blind lady's face expressed first astonishment, then wrath, and at last, quickly pulling her hands away in disgust, she cried: 'What a vile joke!'"[9]

XIII

That was the end of the reading, and of the friends' conversation, and of the anticipated celebration of the New Year, because, when the young princess closed the book and asked, "What was it that Mme du Deffand imagined?" the mother's look was so terrible that the girl cried out, covered her face with her hands, and rushed headlong to another room, from where her weeping was heard at once, verging on hysterics.

The brother rushed to his sister, and at the same moment the princess hastened there on long strides.

The presence of outsiders was now inappropriate, and therefore the "three friends" and I all quietly cleared off that minute, and the bottle of Veuve Clicquot prepared for seeing in the New Year remained wrapped in a napkin, as yet uncorked.

XIV

The feelings with which we left were painful, but did no credit to our hearts, for, while keeping our faces strenuously serious, we could barely refrain from bursting into laughter, and bent down with exaggerated care to look for our galoshes, which was necessary because the servants had also scattered on occasion of the alarm caused by the young lady's sudden illness.

The senators got into their carriages, but the diplomat accompanied me on foot. He wished to take some fresh air and, it seems, was interested in knowing my insignificant opinion about what might have presented itself to the young princess's mental eyes after reading the above passage from the writings of Mme de Genlis.

But I decidedly did not dare to make any suggestions about it.

XV

From the unfortunate day when this incident took place, I saw no more of the princess or her daughter. I could not resolve to go and wish her a Happy New Year, and only sent to inquire after the young princess's health, but even that with great hesitation, lest it be taken in some other sense. Visits of *condoléance* seemed totally out of place to me. The situation was a most stupid one: to suddenly stop visiting acquaintances would be rude, but to appear there also seemed inappropriate.

Perhaps I was wrong in my conclusions, but they seemed right to me; and I was not mistaken: the blow that the princess suffered on New Year's Eve from the "spirit" of Mme de Genlis was very heavy and had serious consequences.

XVI

About a month later I met the diplomat on Nevsky Prospect: he was very affable, and we fell to talking.

"I haven't seen you for a long time," he said.

"We have nowhere to meet," I replied.

"Yes, we've lost the dear house of the esteemed princess: the poor woman had to leave."

"Leave?" I said. "For where?"

"As if you don't know."

"I know nothing."

"They all left for abroad, and I'm very happy that I was able to find a post there for her son. It was impossible not to do so after what happened then . . . So terrible! You know, the unfortunate woman burned all her volumes that same night and smashed the little terracotta hand to smithereens, though one finger, or better say a fig, seems to have survived as a souvenir. Generally, it was a most unpleasant incident, but then it serves as an excellent proof of one great truth."

"Even two or three, in my opinion."

The diplomat smiled and, looking fixedly at me, asked:

"Which, sir?"

"First, it proves that the books we decide to talk about, we should read beforehand."

"And second?"

"And second—that it's not reasonable to keep a young girl in such childish ignorance as the young princess was in before that occurrence; otherwise she would certainly have stopped reading about Gibbon much sooner."

"And third?"

"Third, that spirits are just as unreliable as living people."

"And that's not all: the spirit confirms one of *my opinions,* that 'the best of serpents is still a serpent,' and what's more, the better the serpent, the more dangerous it is, because it *holds its venom in its tail.*"

If we had satire in our country, this would be an excellent subject for it.

Unfortunately, having no satirical ability, I can recount it only in the simple form of a story.

The Toupee Artist

A Story Told on a Grave

(To the sacred memory of the blessed day of February 19, 1861)[1]

Their souls will abide with the blessed.

FUNERAL CHANT

I

many among us think that the only "artists" are painters and sculptors, and then only those who have been granted this title by the Academy, and they refuse to consider others artists. Sazikov and Ovchinnikov are for many no more than "silversmiths." It is not so for other peoples: Heine mentions a tailor who "was an artist" and "had ideas," and Worth made ladies' dresses that are now called "works of art."[2] Of one of them it was written recently that it "concentrates an abyss of fantasy in a basque waist."

In America the artistic sphere is understood still more broadly: the famous American writer Bret Harte tells of the extraordinary fame of an "artist" there who "worked on the dead."[3] He endowed the faces of the deceased with various "comforting expressions," which testified to the more or less happy state of their flown-off souls.

There were several degrees in this art—I remember three: "(1) serenity, (2) lofty contemplation, and (3) the bliss of immediate converse with God." The artist's fame corresponded to the high perfection of his work, that is, it was enormous, but, regrettably, the artist fell victim to the coarse crowd, which did not respect the freedom of artistic creativity. He was stoned to death for giving "the expression of blissful converse with God" to the face of a certain fraudulent banker, who had died after robbing the whole town. The swindler's lucky heirs were moved by the wish to express their gratitude to their departed relation, but the artistic executor paid for it with his life . . .

We also had a master of this extraordinarily artistic sort here in Russia.

II

My younger brother's nanny was a tall, dry, but very shapely old woman whose name was Lyubov Onisimovna. She was a former actress from the onetime theater of Count Kamensky in Orel,[4] and it was in Orel that all I shall tell about further on took place.

My brother is seven years younger than I; consequently, when he was two years old and was being carried in Lyubov Onisimovna's arms, I was already over nine and could easily understand the stories I was told.

Lyubov Onisimovna was not yet very old then, but her hair was snow white; the features of her face were fine and tender, and her tall figure was perfectly straight and astonishingly shapely, like a young girl's.

My mother and my aunt, looking at her, said of her more than once that she had undoubtedly been a beauty in her time.

She was infinitely honest, meek, and sentimental; loved the tragic in life and . . . occasionally got drunk.

She used to take us for walks to the cemetery of the Trinity church, would always sit down on the same simple grave with an old cross, and often told me one thing or another.

It was there that I heard from her the story of the "toupee artist."

III

He had been our nanny's fellow in the theater; the difference was that she "performed on stage and danced dances," while he was a "toupee artist"—that is, a hairdresser and makeup man, who "painted and dressed the hair" of all the count's serf actresses. But he was not a simple, banal workman with a comb behind his ear and a tin of rouge mixed with grease in his hand; he was a man with *ideas*—in short, an *artist*.

In the words of Lyubov Onisimovna, nobody was able "to do impression on a face" so well as he.

I am unable to specify under precisely which of the counts Kamensky these two artistic natures blossomed. There are three known counts Kamensky, and the old-timers of Orel called them all "unheard-of tyrants." Field Marshal Mikhail Fedotovich was murdered by his serfs in 1809 on account of his cruelty, and he had two sons: Nikolai, who died in 1811; and Sergei, who died in 1835.

A child in the forties, I still remember a huge, gray wooden building, with false windows painted crudely in soot and ochre, and surrounded by a long, half-dilapidated fence. This was the theater at the cursed country seat of Count Kamensky. It stood in a place where it could be very well seen from the cemetery of the Trinity church, and therefore when it happened that Lyubov Onisimovna wanted to tell something, she almost always began with the words:

"Look there, my dear . . . See how terrible it is?"

"Terrible, nanny."

"Well, and what I'll tell you now is still more terrible."

Here is one of her stories about the toupee master Arkady, a sensitive and brave young man, who was very close to her heart.

IV

Arkady "did the hair and makeup" only for actresses. For men there was another hairdresser, and Arkady, if he occasionally went to "the men's half," did so only in cases when the count himself gave orders to "paint somebody up in a very noble way." The main particularity of this artist's touch with makeup was that he had certain notions, owing to which he could endow faces with the most subtle and diverse expressions.

"It happened that they would call him," said Lyubov Onisimovna, "and say: 'There should be such and such an impression on the face.' Arkady would step back, tell the actor or actress to stand or sit before him, cross his arms on his chest, and think. And meanwhile he himself was the handsomest of the handsome, because he was of average height, but you couldn't say how well built, a fine and proud little nose, and his eyes—angelic, kind, and a thick lock hung down beautifully over his eyes, so that he used to look as if from behind a misty cloud."

In short, the toupee artist was handsome and "pleased *everybody.*" "The count himself" also liked him and "distinguished him from everybody else, had him charmingly dressed, but kept him in the greatest strictness." Not for anything did he want Arkady to cut, shave, and comb anyone but him, and for that he *always* kept him by his dressing room, and, except for the theater, Arkady could not go anywhere.

He was not even allowed to go to church for confession or communion, because the count himself did not believe in God, and could not bear the clergy, and once at Easter he set his wolfhounds on the priests from the Boris and Gleb cathedral as they carried the cross.[*]

The count, in Lyubov Onisimovna's words, was so terribly ugly from his habitual angrying that he resembled all beasts at once. But Arkady was able to endow even that beastlikeness, at least for a time, with such an impression, that when the count sat in his box in the evening, he even seemed grander than many.

Yet what the count's nature lacked most, to his great vexation, was precisely grandeur and a "military impression."

Thus, so that nobody else could make use of the services of such an inimitable artist as Arkady, he sat "all his life without leave and never in his born days saw money in his hands." And he was then

---

[*] This incident was known to many in Orel. I heard about it from my grandmother Alferyeva and from the merchant Ivan Androsov, known for his unfailing truthfulness, who *saw himself* "the dogs tearing at the clergy," and who saved himself from the count only by "taking sin upon his soul." When the count ordered him brought and asked him, "Do you feel sorry for them?" Androsov replied: "No, Your Serenity, it serves them right: why go hanging about?" For that, Kamensky pardoned him. *Author.*

already over twenty-five, and Lyubov Onisimovna was going on nine-teen. They were acquainted, of course, and there took place between them what happens at that age, that is, they fell in love with each other. But they could not speak of their love otherwise than in front of other people, in distant hints during makeup sessions.

To see each other alone was completely impossible and even unthinkable . . .

"We actresses," Lyubov Onisimovna used to say, "were kept in the same way that *wet nurses* are kept in noble families; we were looked after by older women who had children, and if, God forbid, anything happened with one of us, those women's children were all subjected to a terrible tyrannizing."

The rule of chastity could be violated only by "himself"—the one who had established it.

V

Lyubov Onisimovna was at that time not only in the flower of her virginal beauty, but also in the most interesting moment in the devel-opment of her versatile talent: she "sang in potpourri choruses," danced "the lead part in *The Chinese Farm Girl*," and, feeling a call-ing for the tragic, "knew all the roles *from looking*."

Precisely what years these were, I don't know, but it so happened that the sovereign (whether Alexander Pavlovich or Nikolai Pavlov-ich, I can't say),[5] was passing through Orel and spent the night there, and in the evening was expected to be at Count Kamensky's theater.

The count invited all the nobility to his theater (there was no pay-ing for seats), and the performance put on was the very best. Lyubov Onisimovna was supposed to sing in a "potpourri" and dance in *The Chinese Farm Girl,* and then suddenly, during the last rehearsal, a flat fell and hurt the foot of the actress who was to perform "the duchesse de Bourblan" in the play.

I have never come across a role with that name anywhere, but Lyubov Onisimovna pronounced it in precisely that way.

The carpenters who dropped the flat were sent to the stable to be punished, and the injured actress was carried to her closet, but there was no one to play the role of the duchesse de Bourblan.

"Here," Lyubov Onisimovna told me, "I volunteered, because I liked very much how the duchesse de Bourblan begged forgiveness at her father's feet and died with her hair let down. And I myself had such wonderfully long, light brown hair, and Arkady used to do it up—a lovely sight."

The count was very glad that the girl had unexpectedly volunteered and, on receiving assurances from the director that "Lyuba won't spoil the role," said:

"If she does, your back will answer for it, and take her these camarine[6] earrings from me."

"Camarine earrings" were both a flattering and a repulsive gift. They were a first token of the special honor of being raised for a brief moment to the position of the master's odalisque. Soon after that, and sometimes straightaway, Arkady would be given the order to make the doomed girl up after the theater "with the innocent look of St. Cecilia," and this symbolized innocence, all in white, in a coronet and with a lily in her hand, would be delivered to the count's quarters.

"That," said my nanny, "you can't understand at your age, but it was the most terrible thing, especially for me, because I was dreaming of Arkady. I began to weep. I threw the earrings on the table and wept, and of how I was going to perform that evening I couldn't even think."

VI

And in those same fatal hours another matter—also fatal and trying—stole up on Arkady as well.

The count's brother came from his country estate to present himself to the sovereign. He was still worse looking and had long been living in the country and never put on his uniform or shaved himself, because "his whole face was overgrown and bumpy." Now, on this special occasion, he had to wear a uniform and put himself all in order and "in a military impression," as form required.

And it required a great deal.

"Now nobody even understands how strict it was then," my nanny said. "Form was observed in everything then, and there was a standard for important gentlemen as much in their faces as in their hairstyle, and for some it was terribly unbecoming, and it could happen that, if a man's hair was done according to fashion, with a brushed-up forelock and side-whiskers, the face came out looking exactly like a muzhik's balalaika without strings. Important gentlemen were terribly afraid of that. In these matters, skill in shaving and doing hair counted for a lot—how to clear a path on the face between the side-whiskers and mustache, and how to dispose the curls, and how to brush up—these same small things resulted in a face having a totally different fantasy. It was easier for civilians," in my nanny's words, "because no attentive regard was paid to them—they were only required to have a meek look; but from the military more was required—that they express meekness before their superiors, but before all others flaunt their boundless courage."

It was this that Arkady was able to impart to the count's ugly and insignificant face by means of his astonishing art.

VII

The count's country brother was still uglier than the city one, and on top of that had "got so overgrowned" and "coarse in the face" from country life that he even felt it himself, and there was no one to tend to him, because he was very stingy in all things and had let his barber go to Moscow in exchange for quitrent, and besides, this second count's face was all in big bumps, so that it was impossible to shave him without cutting it all over.

He arrived in Orel, summoned the town barbers, and said:

"If any of you can make me look like my brother, Count Kamensky, I'll give him two gold pieces, but if he cuts me, I'm putting two pistols here on the table. If you do a good job—take the gold and go, but if you cut a single pimple or shave the side-whiskers wrong by a hair—I'll kill you on the spot."

He was just scaring them, because the pistols were loaded with blanks.

In Orel at that time there were few town barbers, and those mostly went around to the bathhouses with bowls, to apply cupping glasses and leeches, but had neither taste nor fantasy. They realized that themselves, and they all refused to "transfigure" Kamensky. "God be with you," they thought, "and with your gold."

"We can't do what you want," they say, "because we're not worthy even to touch a person like you, and we don't have the right razors, because ours are simple Russian razors, and for your face English razors are needed. Only the count's Arkady can do it."

The count ordered the town barbers thrown out on their ears, and they were glad to escape to freedom, while he himself goes to his older brother and says:

"Thus and so, brother, I've come to you with a big request: let me have your Arkashka before evening, so that he can get me into shape good and proper. I haven't shaved for a long time, and the local barbers can't do it."

The count answers his brother:

"The local barbers are sure to be vile. I didn't even know there were any here, because my dogs, too, are clipped by my own people. But as for your request, you're asking an impossible thing, because I gave an oath that, as long as I live, Arkashka will tend to nobody but me. What do you think—can I change my word given before my own slave?"

The other says:

"Why not? You decreed it, you can also repeal it."

The count-master replies that for him such an opinion is even strange.

"If I start acting that way myself," he says, "what can I demand of my people after that? Arkashka has been told that I've decided so, and everybody knows it, and for that he's kept better than any of them, and if he ever dares to touch anyone else but me with his art—I'll have him flogged to death and sent for a soldier."

His brother says:

"It'll be one or the other: either flogged to death or sent for a soldier, you can't do both."

"All right," says the count, "let it be as you say: not to death, but half to death, and then sent."

"And that," the other says, "is your last word?"

"Yes, my last."

"And that's all there is to it?"

"Yes, that's all."

"Well, in that case it's fine, otherwise I'd have thought you hold your own brother cheaper than a bonded serf. Don't change your word, then, but send me Arkashka to *clip my poodle*. And there it's my business what he does."

The count felt awkward denying him that.

"All right," he says, "I'll send him to clip your poodle."

"Well, that's all I need."

He shook the count's hand and left.

VIII

It was that time before evening, at dusk, in winter, when the lamps are lit.

The count summons Arkady and says:

"Go to my brother's house and clip his poodle for him."

Arkady asks:

"Will that be your only order?"

"Nothing more," says the count. "But come back quickly to make up the actresses. Lyuba has to be made up for three roles today, and after the theater present her to me as St. Cecilia."

Arkady staggered.

The count says:

"What's the matter?"

Arkady replies:

"Sorry, I tripped on the rug."

The count hints:

"Look out, that doesn't bode well!"

But Arkady's soul was in such a state that it was all the same to him whether it boded well or ill.

He had heard himself ordered to bring me as St. Cecilia, and, as if seeing and hearing nothing, he took his instruments in their leather case and left.

IX

He comes to the count's brother, who already has candles lit by the mirror and again the two pistols next to it, and there are already not two gold pieces, but ten, and the pistols are loaded, not with blanks, but with Circassian bullets.

The count's brother says:

"I haven't got any poodle, but here's what I want: do me up in the bravest fashion and you get ten gold pieces, but if you cut me, I'll kill you."

Arkady looked and looked, and suddenly—God knows what got into him—started clipping and shaving the count's brother. In one minute he did it all in the best way, poured the gold into his pocket, and said:

"Good-bye."

The other replies:

"Go, only I'd like to know: what made you so reckless that you dared to do it?"

Arkady says:

"Why I dared—only my breast and what's inside it know."

"Or maybe you've got a spell on you against bullets, so that you're not afraid of pistols?"

"Pistols are nothing," Arkady replies. "I wasn't even thinking about them."

"How is that? Did you dare think the count's word is firmer than mine and I wouldn't shoot you for cutting me? If there's no spell on you, your life would have been over."

At the mention of the count, Arkady gave another start, and as if in half sleep, said:

"There's no spell on me, but there's understanding from God: while you were raising your hand with a pistol to shoot me, I'd have cut your throat first with a razor."

And with that he rushed out and came to the theater just on time and began doing my hair, and he was shaking all over. Each time he curled a lock of my hair, he bent down to blow on it, and whispered:

"Don't be afraid, I'll carry you off."

X

The performance went well, because we were all like stone, used to fear and torment: whatever was in our hearts, we did our job so that nothing could be noticed.

From the stage we saw the count and his brother—the one resembling the other. When they came backstage, it was even hard to tell them apart. Only ours was very, very quiet, as if he'd grown kind. That always happened to him before the greatest ferocity.

And we all went numb and crossed ourselves.

"Lord, have mercy upon us and save us! Whoever his bestiality falls upon!"

We didn't know yet about the insanely desperate thing Arkasha had done, but Arkady himself, of course, understood that there would be no merciness for him, and he turned pale when the count's brother glanced at him and quietly murmured something to our count. But I had very keen hearing, and I made it out.

"I advise you as a brother: beware of him when he shaves you."

Ours only smiled quietly.

It seems Arkasha himself heard something, because, when he began making me up as the duchess for the last performance, he—something that never happened to him—put on so much powder that the French *costumier* started shaking me and said:

"*Trop beaucoup, trop beaucoup!*"*—and brushed off the excess.

XI

But once the performance was over, they took the dress of the duchesse de Bourblan off of me and dressed me as Cecilia, in a simple white dress with no sleeves and only caught up in knots at the shoulders—we couldn't stand this costume. And then Arkady comes to do my hair in the innocent way it's done in pictures of St. Cecilia, and to fix a thin coronet around it, and he sees six men standing by the door of my little closet.

That meant that as soon as he does me up and goes back out the door, he'll be seized at once and led off somewhere to be tortured. And the tortures with us were such that it would be a hundred times better to be condemned to death. Racking and drawing and squeezing the head with a twisted rope: there was all that. Punishment by the state authorities was nothing compared to it. There were secret cellars under the whole house where people lived chained up like bears. Going past, you could sometimes hear the chains clank and the fettered people moan. They probably wanted news of them to reach us or for the authorities to hear it, but the authorities did not dare even to think of intervening. And people languished there for a

* "Much too much, much too much!" *Trans.*

long time, sometimes all their lives. One man sat and sat and made up verses:

Snakes—he says—will come slithering and suck out your eyes,
Scorpions will pour poison on your face.[7]

Sometimes you whisper these verses to yourself and get terrified.

And others were even chained with bears, so the bear was only within an inch of getting his paws on them.

Only they didn't do any of that with Arkady Ilyich, because as soon as he sprang into my little closet, he instantly seized the table and smashed out the whole window, and I don't remember anything more after that . . .

I began to come to myself because my feet were very cold. I moved my legs and felt that I was all wrapped up in a wolfskin or bearskin coat, and it was pitcher-dark around, and the troika of horses is dashing along, and I don't know where. And by me are two men in a heap, sitting in a wide sled—one holding me, that was Arkady Ilyich, and the other urging the horses on with all his might . . . Snow sprays from under the horses' hooves, and the sled tilts every second to one side, then to the other. If we hadn't been sitting right in the middle on the floor and holding each other with our arms, nobody could possibly have stayed whole.

And I hear their worried conversation, in agictation as always—all I can understand is: "They're coming, they're coming! Faster, faster!" and nothing more.

Arkady Ilyich, when he noticed that I was coming to myself, bent over to me and said:

"Lyubushka, my dove! We're being pursued . . . Do you agree to die if we can't get away?"

I replied that I even agreed with joy.

He was hoping to get to Turkish Rushchuk,[8] where many of our people had escaped from Kamensky.

And suddenly we flew cross the ice of some river, and ahead something like dwellings showed gray and dogs were barking; and the driver whipped up the troika, and the sled all at once heaved to one side, and Arkady and I tumbled out onto the snow, but he, and the sled, and the horses all vanished from sight.

Arkady says:

"Don't be afraid, it has to be this way, because I don't know the driver who brought us here, and he doesn't know us. He hired out for three gold pieces to take you away, and he's saved his own life. Now we're in the hands of God: this is the village of Dry Orlitsa—a brave priest lives here who marries desperate couples and has helped many of our people. We'll give him a gift, he'll hide us till next evening and marry us, and in the evening the driver will come back, and then we'll disappear."

XII

We knocked at the door and went into the front hall. The priest himself opened, old, stocky, one front tooth missing, and his little old wife lit a candle. We both fell down at his feet.

"Save us, let us get warm and hide till next evening."

The priest asks:

"What is it, my bright lights, have you come with stolen goods or are you just fugitives?"

Arkady says:

"We haven't stolen anything, we're running away from Count Kamensky's ferocity and want to escape to Turkish Rushchuk, where not a few of our folk are living already. And we have our own money with us, and if we're not found, we'll give you a gold piece for one night's lodging and three for marrying us. Marry us if you can, and if you can't, we'll get hitched in Rushchuk."

The priest says:

"No, what do you mean, can't? I can. Why do it in Rushchuk? Give me five gold pieces in all—I'll hitch you here."

Arkady gave him the money, and I took the camarine earrings from my ears and gave them to his wife.

The priest took the money and said:

"Ah, my bright lights, it would all be nothing—I've happened to hitch all sorts, what's bad is that you're the count's. Though I'm a priest, his ferocity frightens me. Well, all right, let it be as God grants—just add one more, even if it's a clipped one, and hide here."

Arkady gave him a sixth gold piece, a whole one, and the priest then said to his wife:

"Why stand there, old woman? Give the girl a skirt at least, or some coat, it's shameful to look at her—she's all but naked."

And then he wanted to take us to the church and hide us in a trunk of vestments. But the priest's wife had just started dressing me behind a screen, when we suddenly heard someone ring the bell.

XIII

Our hearts both froze. But the priest whispered to Arkady:

"Well, my bright light, you clearly won't get as far as the trunk of vestments, but quickly get under the featherbed."

And to me he says:

"And you, my bright light, go here."

He took and put me into the case of the clock, and locked it, and put the key in his pocket, and went to open the door. And we can hear there are many folk, and some are standing by the door, and two are already looking in the windows from outside.

Seven of the pursuers came in, all from the count's hunters, with bludgeons, and hunting crops, and rope leashes in their belts, and with them an eighth one, the count's majordomo, in a long wolfskin coat and a high peaked cap.

The case I was hiding in was all lattice-like openwork in front, hung with thin old cambric, and I could see through it.

And the old priest was in a fright, seeing how bad things were. He trembled before the majordomo, crossing himself and crying out all in a patter:

"Ah, my bright lights, oh, my shining lights! I know, I know what you're looking for, only I'm not guilty of anything before the most serene count, truly, not guilty, not guilty!"

And he crosses himself and points his finger over his left shoulder at the clock case where I'm locked up.

"I'm done for," I thought, seeing him perform this wonder.

The majordomo also saw it and says:

"It's all known to us. Give me the key to that clock there."

But the priest waved his hands again:

"Oh, my bright lights, oh, my shining ones! Forgive me, have mercy: I forget where I put the key, I forget, by God, I forget!"

And all the while he's patting his pocket with the other hand.

The majordomo noticed that wonder as well, took the key from his pocket, and unlocked me.

"Get out, my dove," he says, "and your mate will soon show himself."

But Arkasha already showed himself: he threw the priest's blanket on the floor and stood up.

"Yes," he says, "there's clearly nothing to do, the game is yours—take me to be tortured, but she's not to blame for anything: I abducted her."

As for the priest, all Arkady did was turn and spit in his face.

The priest says:

"Do you see, my bright lights, what profanation is done to my dignity and my fidelity? Report it to the most serene count."

The majordomo replies:

"Never mind, don't worry, it will all be accounted to him," and he ordered that Arkady and I be led away.

We were put in three sleds, in the first the bound Arkady and some hunters, and me under the same escort in the last, and the rest of them went in the middle one.

Wherever we met folk, they all made way for us, thinking maybe it was a wedding.

XIV

We galloped very quickly, and when we spilled into the count's courtyard, I couldn't even see the sled Arkasha was taken in, but me they took to my former place and kept putting question after question to me about how long a time I had found myself alone with Arkady.

To all of them I said:

"Oh, no time at all!"

Then what had been assigned to me by fate—not with my dear, but with my worst fear—I did not avoid, but when I came to my little closet and had just buried my head in the pillow to weep over my misfortune, I suddenly heard terrible moaning from under the floor.

In our wooden building it was arranged that we, the girls, lived on the second floor, and downstairs was a big, high-ceilinged room where we studied singing and dancing, and everything from there could be heard upstairs. And the fiendish king Satan put it into those cruel men's heads to torture Arkasha right under my room . . .

When I realized that it was him they were torturing . . . I rushed . . .

threw myself against the door, so as to run to him . . . but the door was locked . . . I don't know myself what I wanted to do . . . I fell down, but on the floor I could hear still more clearly . . . And there was no knife, no nail, nothing to finish myself off with somehow . . . I took my own braid and wound it around my throat . . . I kept twisting and twisting, and only began to hear a ringing in my ears and to see circles, and then it all stopped . . . And I came to my senses in an unfamiliar place, in a big, bright shed . . . There were little calves there . . . many little calves, as much as ten—they'd come and lick my hand with their cold lips, thinking they were sucking at their mother . . . I woke up because it tickled . . . I looked around, wondering "Where am I?" I see a woman come in, an older woman, tall, all in blue calico, with a clean calico kerchief on her head, and her face is gentle.

The woman noticed that I was showing signs of life, and she was gentle with me and told me that I was in the calves' shed on the count's estate . . .

"It was there," Lyubov Onisimovna explained, pointing towards the farthest corner of the half-dilapidated gray fence.

XV

She wound up in the cattle yard, because there were suspicions that she might have gone a bit crazy. People who became like beasts were tested among beasts, because cattlemen were elderly and sedate, and it was thought they could "look after" psychoses.

The old woman in calico with whom Lyubov Onisimovna had recovered herself was very kind, and her name was Drosida.

When she was ready for bed in the evening (my nanny continued), she herself made my bed from fresh oat chaff. She fluffed it up soft as down and says: "I'll reveal everything to you, my girl. What will be will be, if you tell on me, but I'm just like you, and I didn't dress in this calico all my life, but saw other things, only God forbid I should remember it, but I'll tell you: don't be distressed that you're exiled to the cattle yard—it's better in exile, only beware of this terrible falask."

And she took a white glass vial from under her shawl.

I ask:

"What is it?"

And she answers:

"This is the terrible falask, and in it is the poison of oblivion."

I say:

"Give me this oblivious poison: I want to forget everything."

She says:

"Don't drink—it's vodka. I couldn't help myself once, I drank it . . . good people gave me some . . . Now I can't do without it, I need it, but don't you drink for as long as you can, and don't judge me for sipping a bit—I hurt very much. And there's still a comfort for you in the world: the Lord has delivered *him* from tyranny! . . ."

I cried out: "He's dead!" and seized my hair, but I see that it's not my hair—it's white . . . What is this!

And she says to me:

"Don't be frightened, don't be frightened, your hair was already white when they untangled you from your braid; but he's alive and safe from all tyranny: the count showed him such mercy as he never did anybody—when night comes, I'll tell you everything, and now I'll have another little sip . . . I have to sip it away . . . my heart's on fire."

And she kept sipping and sipping, and fell asleep.

At night, when everybody was asleep, Auntie Drosida got up again very quietly, went to the window without any light, and I saw her standing there and sipping again from the falask, and putting it away again, and she asked me softly:

"Is grief sleeping or not?"

I answer:

"Grief is not sleeping."

She came over to my bed and told me that, after the punishment, the count summoned Arkady to him and said:

"You had to go through everything I said you would, but since you were my favorite, I will now show you my mercy: tomorrow I will send you for a soldier without conscription, but because you were not afraid of my brother, a count and a nobleman, with his pistols, I will open a path to honor for you—I don't want you to be lower than you have placed yourself with your noble spirit. I will send a letter asking that you be sent straight to war at once, and you will serve not as a simple soldier, but as a regimental sergeant, and show your courage. Then it will not be my will over you, but the tsar's."

"For him," the old woman in calico said, "it's easier now and there's nothing more to fear: over him there is just one power—to fall in battle—and not the master's tyranny."

So I believed, and for three years I dreamed of the same thing every night, of how Arkady Ilyich was fighting.

Three years went by that way, and all that time God's mercy was upon me, that I was not brought back to the theater, but stayed on in the calves' shed with Auntie Drosida as her helper. And it was very good for me there, because I pitied the woman, and when she happened not to drink too much at night, I liked to listen to her. And she still remembered how our people, and the head valet himself, had killed the old count—because they could no longer suffer his infernal cruelty. But I still didn't drink at all, and I did a lot for Auntie Drosida, and with pleasure: those little brutes were like children to me. I got so used to the little calves that, when they took one I had milk fed to be slaughtered for the table, I'd make a cross over him and weep for three days afterwards. I was no good for the theater anymore, because my feet had gone bad on me, they hobbled. Before, I'd had a very light step, but after Arkady Ilyich carried me off unconscious in the cold, I probably chilled my feet and no longer had any strength in the toes for dancing. I put on the same calico as Drosida, and God knows how long I'd have lived in such dreariness, when suddenly one time I was there in the shed before evening: the sun was setting and I was unreeling yarn by the window, and suddenly a small stone falls through my window, and it's all wrapped in a piece of paper.

XVI

I looked this way and that, I looked out the window—nobody was there.

"Most likely," I thought, "somebody beyond the fence outside threw it and missed, and it landed here with me and the old woman." And I thought to myself: "Should I unwrap the paper or not? Seems better to unwrap it, because something's surely written on it. And maybe somebody or other needs it, and I could figure it out and keep the secret, and throw the note with the stone to the right person in the same way."

I unwrapped it and began to read, and couldn't believe my eyes . . .

XVII

There was written:

"My faithful Lyuba! I fought and served the sovereign and shed my blood more than once, and for that I was raised to officer's rank and granted nobility. Now I have come as a free man on leave to recover from my wounds. I am staying at an inn in the Pushkarsky quarter, and tomorrow I will put on my medals and crosses and appear before the count and bring all the money given me for treatment, five hundred roubles, and I will ask to buy you out, in hopes that we can be married before the altar of the Most High Creator."

"And further," Lyubov Onisimovna continued, always with suppressed emotion, "he wrote that 'whatever calamity may have befallen you and whatever you have been subjected to, I count it as your suffering, and not as sin or weakness, and leave it to God, feeling nothing but respect for you.' And it was signed: 'Arkady Ilyich.'"

Lyubov Onisimovna burned the letter at once in the stove and did not tell anyone about it, not even the old woman in calico, but only prayed to God all night, without uttering a word about herself, but all for him, because, she said "though he wrote that he was now an officer, with crosses and wounds, all the same I couldn't possibly imagine that the count would treat him differently than before.

"To put it simply, I was afraid they'd flog him again."

XVIII

Early in the morning, Lyubov Onisimovna took the calves out into the sun and began to feed them with milk-soaked crusts at the tubs, when it suddenly came to her hearing that "in the open," outside the fence, people were hurrying somewhere and talking loudly among themselves as they ran.

"I didn't hear a word of what they were talking about," she said, "but it was as if their words cut my heart. And just then the dung collector, Filipp, drove through the gate, and I said to him: 'Filyushka, dear! Did you hear what these people passing by are talking about so curiously?'

"And he replies: 'It's them going to the Pushkarsky quarter, to see how the innkeeper murdered a sleeping officer during the night. Slit his throat right through,' he says, 'and took five hundred roubles in cash. They caught him all bloody with the money on him.'

"As soon as he told me that, I fell down bang on the spot . . .

"Here's what happened: the innkeeper murdered Arkady Ilyich . . . and they buried him here, in this same grave where we're sitting now . . . Yes, he's now here under us, lying under this ground . . . And why do you think I keep going for walks here with you . . . I don't want to look there," she pointed to the gloomy and gray ruins, "but to sit here next to him and . . . take a little drop to commemorate his soul . . ."

XIX

Here Lyubov Onisimovna stopped and, considering her story told, took a small vial from her pocket and "commemorated," or "sipped," but I asked her:

"And who buried the famous toupee artist here?"

"The governor, dearest, the governor himself was at the funeral. What else! He was an officer. At the liturgy both the deacon and the priest called Arkady 'bolyarin'[9] and once the coffin was lowered down, the soldiers fired blanks into the air with their guns. And later, a year after, the innkeeper was punished by the executioner on the Ilyinka square with a knout. They gave him forty and three knouts for Arkady Ilyich, and he endured it—was left alive and went branded to hard labor. Our men, those who could get away, came to watch, and the old men, who remembered the sentence for murdering the cruel count, said it was as little as forty and three because Arkasha was of simple origin, but for the count the sentence had been a hundred and one knouts. By law you can't stop at an even number of strokes, it always has to be an odd number. That time, they say, an executioner was brought on purpose from Tula, and before the business they gave him three glasses of rum to drink.

Then he flogged him, a hundred strokes just for the torture, and the man was still alive, but then, at the hundred and first crack, he shattered his whole backbone. They started to lift him from the board, but he was already going . . . They covered him with sacking and took him to jail—he died on the way. And this Tula man, the story goes, kept crying out: 'Give me somebody else to flog—I'll kill all you Orel boys.'"

"Well, but you," I say, "were you at the funeral, or not?"

"I went. I went with everybody else: the count ordered all the theater people to be brought, to see how one of us could earn distinction."

"And you said your last farewells?"

"Yes, of course! Everybody went up to him, and I did, too . . . He was so changed I wouldn't have recognized him. Thin and very pale—they said he lost all his blood, because he was murdered at midnight . . . He shed so much of his blood . . ."

She became silent and fell to thinking.

"And you," I say, "how did you bear up after that?"

She seemed to come to her senses and passed a hand over her forehead.

"To begin with," she says, "I don't remember how I got home . . . I was with them all—somebody must have brought me . . . And in the evening Drosida Petrovna says: 'Well, you can't do that—you don't sleep, and meanwhile you lie there like a stone. It's no good—weep, pour your heart out.'

"I say: 'I can't, auntie—my heart's burning like a coal, and there's no pouring it out.'

"And she says: 'Well, that means there's no avoiding the falask now.'

"She poured for me from her little bottle and says: 'Before, I myself wouldn't let you do it and I told you not to, but now there's no help for it: take a sip—pour it on the coal.'

"I say: 'I don't want to.'

"'Little fool,' she says, 'nobody wants to at first. Grief is bitter, but this poison is bitterer still. If you pour this poison over the coal—it goes out for a minute. Sip it quickly, sip it!'

"I drank the whole falask at once. It was disgusting, but I couldn't sleep without it, and the next night also . . . I drank . . . and now I can't fall asleep without it, and I have my own falask, and I buy vodka . . . You're a good boy, you'll never tell that to your mother, you'll never betray simple folk: because simple folk ought to be spared, simple folk are all sufferers. And when we go home, I'll knock again at the window of the pot-house around the corner . . . We won't go in, but I'll give them my empty little falask, and they'll hand me a new one."

I was touched and promised that I would never tell about her "falask."

"Thank you, dearest—don't go talking: I need it."

And I can see her and hear her as if it was right now: at night, when everyone in the house is asleep, she sits up in bed, quietly, so that even a little bone won't crack; she listens, gets up, walks stealthily to the window on her long, chilled legs . . . She stands for a moment, looks around, listens for whether mama is coming from the bedroom; then she softly knocks the neck of the "falask" on her teeth, tips it up, and "sips" . . . One gulp, two, three . . . She quenches the coal and commemorates Arkasha, and goes back to bed again—quickly slips under the covers, and soon begins whistling away very, very softly—phwee-phwee, phwee-phwee, phwee-phwee. She's asleep!

Never in my life have I seen such a terrible and heartrending commemoration.

The Voice of Nature

I

The well-known military writer General Rostislav Andreevich Fad-deev, long attached to the late Field Marshal Baryatinsky,[1] told me of the following amusing incident.

Once, traveling from the Caucasus to Petersburg, the prince felt unwell on the way and sent for a doctor. It happened, if I am not mistaken, in Temir-Khan-Shura.[2] The doctor examined the patient and found that there was nothing dangerous in his condition, but that he was simply tired and needed to rest for a day without rocking and jolting along the road in a carriage.

The field marshal obeyed the doctor and agreed to stop in the town; but the station house there was quite vile, and private quarters, given the unforeseen nature of the occasion, had not been prepared. An unexpected predicament presented itself: where to lodge such a renowned visitor for a day.

There was much bustling and rushing about, and for the time being the unwell field marshal settled in the posting station and lay down on a dirty divan, which was covered just for him with a clean sheet. Meanwhile, news of this event, of course, quickly flew around the whole town, and all the military hastened to scrub and dress themselves up, and the civil authorities polished their boots, pomaded their whiskers, and they all crowded together across the street from the station. They stood and looked out for the field marshal, in case he should show himself in the window.

Suddenly, unexpected and unforeseen by anybody, a man pushed them all aside from behind, sprang forward, and ran straight to the station, where the field marshal lay on the dirty divan covered with a sheet, and began to shout:

"I can't bear it, the voice of nature rises up in me!"

Everyone looked at him and marveled: what an impudent fellow! The local inhabitants all knew this man, and knew he was not of high rank—since he was neither in civil nor in military service, but was simply a minor supervisor in some local supply commissariat and had been chewing on government rusks and boot soles along with the rats, and in that fashion had chewed himself up a pretty little house with a mezzanine right across from the station.

II

This supervisor came running to the station and asked Faddeev to announce him to the field marshal without fail.

Faddeev and all the others started protesting to him.

"Why? There's no need for that, and there won't be any formal reception—the field marshal is tired and is here only for a temporary rest, and once he's rested, he'll be on his way."

But the commissary supervisor stood his ground and became even more inflamed—asking that they announce him to the prince without fail.

"Because," he says, "I'm not looking for glory or for honors, and I stand before you precisely as you've said: not out of duty, but in the zeal of my gratitude to him, because I am indebted to him for everything in the world and, in my present prosperity, moved by the voice of nature, I wish to gratefully repay my debt."

They asked him:

"And what does your debt of nature consist in?"

And he replied:

"This is my grateful debt of nature, that it is wrong for the prince to be resting here in institutional untidiness, when I have my own house with a mezzanine just across the street, and my wife is of German stock, the house is kept clean and tidy, and I have bright, clean rooms in the mezzanine for the prince and for you, with white, lace-trimmed curtains on all the windows and clean beds with fine linen sheets. I wish to receive the prince in my house with the greatest cordiality, like my own father, because I'm indebted to him for everything in my life, and I will not leave here before you tell him that."

He so insisted on it and refused to leave, that the field marshal heard it from the next room and asked:

"What's this noise? Will nobody tell me what all this talk is about?"

Then Faddeev told him everything, and the prince shrugged his shoulders and said:

"I decidedly do not remember who this man is and how he's indebted to me; but in any case, have a look at the rooms he's offering, and if they're better than this hovel, I'll accept the invitation and pay him for his trouble. Find out how much he wants."

Faddeev went to look at the commissary's mezzanine and reported:

"The place is very quiet and of an extraordinary cleanliness, and the owner will not hear of any payment."

"What? Why not?" asked the field marshal.

"He says he owes you a great deal and the voice of nature prompts him to the happiness of expressing his debt of gratitude to you. 'Otherwise,' he says, 'if you want to pay, then I cannot open my doors.'"

Prince Baryatinsky laughed and praised this official.

"Still," he says, "I see he's a fine fellow and has character—that has become rare among us, and I like such people: how he's indebted to me, I can't recall, but I'll move to his place. Give me your arm and let's leave here."

III

They went across the street and . . . into the yard; and at the gate the supervisor himself is already greeting the field marshal—pomaded, sleek, all his buttons buttoned, and with the most joyful face.

The prince looked around and saw that everything was clean, shining brightly, in the front garden cheerful green and blossoming roses. The prince himself cheered up.

"What is my host's name?"

The latter replies something like Filipp Filippovich Filippov.

The prince goes on talking with him and says:

"Your place is very nice, Filipp Filippych, I like it—there's just one thing I simply can't remember: where and when did I meet or see you, and what sort of favor could I have done you?"

And the supervisor replies:

"Your Excellency certainly did see me, but when—if you've forgotten—will become clear later."

"Why later, if I want to remember you now?"

But the supervisor did not say.

"I beg Your Excellency's pardon," he said. "If you don't remember that yourself, I dare not tell you, but the voice of nature will tell you."

"Nonsense! What 'voice of nature'? And why do you not dare to tell me yourself?"

The supervisor replied, "I just don't dare," and dropped his eyes.

And meanwhile they had come to the mezzanine, and here it was still more clean and tidy: the floor washed with soap and rubbed with mare's tail till it gleamed, white runners laid all down the middle of the clean stairway, in the living room a divan, a round table before it with a big, glazed water jug, and in it a bouquet of roses and violets, further on—the bedroom, with a Turkish carpet over the bed, and again a table, a carafe of clean water and a glass, and another bouquet of flowers, and, on a special little desk, a pen, an ink stand, paper and envelopes, wax and a seal.

The field marshal took it all in at a glance, and it pleased him very much.

"It's clear," he says, "that you, Filipp Filippych, are a polished man, that you know how things ought to be, and it seems I really did see you somewhere, but I can't recall it."

And the supervisor only smiles and says:

"Please don't worry: it will all be explained by the voice of nature."

Baryatinsky laughed.

"In that case, brother," he says, "you are not Filipp Filippovich, but the 'voice of nature' yourself"—and he became very intrigued by the man.

IV

The prince lay down on the clean bed, stretched out his legs and arms, and it felt so good that he dozed off at once. He woke up an hour later in an excellent state of mind, and before him already stood a cool cherry sherbet, and that same host asking him to taste it.

"Don't rely on doctors' medications, Your Excellency," he says. "Here with us nature and the breathing of the atmosphere are beneficial."

The prince cheerfully answers him that that is all very well, "but I must confess to you—I slept splendidly here, but, devil take me, even in my sleep I kept thinking: where did I see you, or maybe I never did?"

But the man replies:

"No," he says, "you saw me very well, if you please, only in a completely different natural guise, and therefore you don't recognize me now."

The prince says:

"Very well, let it be so: there's no one here now besides you and me, and if there's anybody there in the next room, send them all out, let them stand on the stairs, and tell me frankly, without hiding anything, who you were and what your criminal secret is—I can promise to solicit for your pardon, and I'll keep my promise, as I am the true Prince Baryatinsky."

But the official even smiled and replied that there was not and never had been any guilty secret whatever concerning him, and that he simply did not dare to "abash" the prince for his forgetfulness.

"So you see," he says, "I constantly remember Your Excellency for your goodness and commemorate you in my prayers; and our sovereign and all the royal family, once they've seen and noticed someone, constantly remember him all their lives. Therefore allow me," he says, "not to remind you of myself verbally, but in due time I will reveal it all to you by clear signs through the voice of nature—and then you will remember."

"And what means do you have for revealing it all through the voice of nature?"

"In the voice of nature," he replies, "there is every means."

The prince smiled at the odd fellow.

"True for you," he said, "it's bad to forget, and our sovereign and the royal family do indeed have very good memories, but my memory is weak. I do not override your will, do as you think best, only I would like to know when you are going to reveal your voice of nature to me, because I'm now feeling very well in your house, and I want to leave after midnight, once it cools off. And you must tell me how I can reward you for the rest I've had myself here—because that is my custom on such occasions."

The supervisor says:

"Before midnight I will have time to reveal the voice of nature fully to Your Excellency, if only, in the matter of my reward, you will not deny me something that I hold most precious."

"Very well," says the prince, "I give you my word that I will do everything you ask, only don't ask the impossible."

The supervisor replies:

"I will not ask the impossible, but I wish more than anything in the world that you would show me this favor—to come to my rooms downstairs and sit at the table with us, and eat something, or even just simply sit for a while, because tonight I am celebrating my silver wedding anniversary, it being twenty-five years since, by your grace, I married Amalia Ivanovna. It will be at eleven o'clock tonight; and at midnight, once it cools off, you may be well pleased to go."

The prince agreed and gave his word, but all the same he was again simply unable to recall what this man was and where from, and why it was that twenty-five years ago, by his grace, he had married Amalia Ivanovna.

"It will even be a pleasure for me to have supper with this odd fellow," said the prince, "because he intrigues me very much; and, to tell the truth, I do remember something either about him or about Amalia Ivanovna, but precisely what—I can't recall. Let us wait for the voice of nature!"

V

By evening the field marshal had quite recovered and even went for a walk with Faddeev, to see the town and admire the sunset, and when he came back to the house at ten o'clock, the host was already waiting for him and invited him to the table.

The prince said:

"Very gladly, I'll come at once."

Faddeev said jokingly that it was even opportune, because he had a good appetite after their walk and wanted very much to eat whatever Amalia Ivanovna had cooked up for them.

Baryatinsky was only afraid that the host would seat him in the place of honor and start pouring a lot of champagne and regaling him. But these fears were all quite unfounded: the supervisor showed as much pleasant tact at the table as in all the previous hours the prince had spent in his house.

The table was laid elegantly but simply in a spacious room, with a neat but modest service, and two black cast-iron candlesticks of excellent French workmanship, each with seven candles. And the wines were of good sorts, but all local—and among them were some fat-bellied little bottles with handwritten labels.

These were liqueurs and cordials, and of excellent taste— raspberry, cherry, gooseberry.

The supervisor started seating the guests and here also showed his adroitness: he did not lead the prince to the head of the table, to the host's place, but seated him where the prince himself wanted, between his adjutant and a very pretty little lady, so that the field marshal would have someone to exchange a few words with and could amuse himself paying compliments to the fair sex. The prince at once fell to talking with the little lady: he was interested in where she came from, and where she had been educated, and what she did for diversion in such a remote provincial town.

She answered all his questions quite boldly and without any mincing, and revealed to him that she was, it seems, mainly occupied with reading books.

The prince asked what books she read.

She replied: the novels of Paul de Kock.[3]

The prince laughed.

"That," he said, "is a merry writer," and he asked: "What precisely have you read? Which novels?"

She replied:

"*The Confectioner, Moustache, Sister Anne,* and others."

"And you don't read our Russian writers?"

"No," she says, "I don't."

"And why not?"

"There's too little high society in them."

"And you like high society?"

"Yes."

"Why is that?"

"Because we know all about our own life, and those things are more interesting."

And here she said that she had a brother who was writing a novel about society life.

"That's interesting!" said the prince. "I don't suppose I could see a little something he's written?"

"You may," the lady replied, and she left the table for a moment and came back with a small notebook, in which Baryatinsky glanced only at the first page, became all merry, and, handing it to Faddeev, said:

"How's that for a pert beginning!"

Faddeev looked at the first lines of the society novel and also became merry.

The novel began with the words: "I, as a man of society, get up at noon and do not take my morning tea at home, but go around the restaurants."

"Wonderful, eh?" asked Baryatinsky.

"Very good," replied Faddeev.

By then everyone had grown merry, and the host stood up, raised a glass of sparkling Tsimlyanskoe, and said:

"Your Excellency, I beg your permission, for the general good pleasure and for my own, on this day so precious for me, to be allowed to explain who I am, and where I am from, and to whom I am indebted for all the prosperity I have. But I cannot explain it in the cold words of the human voice, because I was educated on very little money, and so allow me by the whole law of my being to emit in all solemnity the voice of nature."

Here it came time for the field marshal himself to be abashed, and he was so confused that he bent down as if to pick up his napkin, and whispered:

"By God, I don't know what to tell him: what is it he's asking of me?"

But the little lady, his neighbor, chirps:

"Don't be afraid, just allow him: Filipp Filippovich won't think up anything bad."

The prince thinks: "Ah, come what may—let him emit the voice!"

"I'm here as a guest," he says, "like everyone else, and you are the host—do whatever you want."

"I thank you and everyone," replies the supervisor, and, nodding to Amalia Ivanovna, he says: "Go, wife, bring you know what with your own hands."

VI

Amalia Ivanovna went and came back with a big, brightly polished brass French horn and gave it to her husband. He took it, put the mouthpiece to his lips, and in an instant was utterly transformed. As soon as he puffed his cheeks and gave one crackling peal, the field marshal cried:

"I know you, brother, I know you now: you were the musician in the chasseur regiment whom I sent, on account of his honesty, to keep an eye on that crooked commissary."

"Just so, Your Excellency," replied the host. "I didn't want to remind you of it, but nature herself has reminded you."

The prince embraced him and said:

"Ladies and gentlemen, let us join in drinking a toast to an honest man!"

And they drank well, and the field marshal recovered completely and left feeling extremely merry.

A Little Mistake

A Moscow Family Secret

I

One evening, at Christmastime, a sensible company sat talking about faith and lack of faith. The talk, however, had to do not with the loftier questions of deism and materialism, but with faith in people endowed with special powers of foresight and prophecy, and perhaps even their own sort of wonderworking. Among the listeners was a staid man from Moscow, who said the following:

"It's not easy, my good sirs, to judge about who lives with faith and who is without faith, for there are various applications of that in life: it may happen in such cases that our reason falls into error."

And after that introduction he told us a curious story, which I shall try to convey in his own words:

My uncle and aunt were both equally devoted to the late wonderworker Ivan Yakovlevich.[1] Especially my aunt—she wouldn't undertake anything without asking him. First she would go to him in the madhouse and get his advice, and then she would ask him to pray for her undertaking. My uncle kept his own counsel and relied less on Ivan Yakovlevich, though he also confided in him occasionally and did not hinder his wife's bringing him gifts and offerings. They were not rich people, but quite well-to-do—they sold tea and sugar from a shop in their own house. They had no sons, but there were three daughters: Kapitolina Nikitishna, Katerina Nikitishna, and Olga Nikitishna. They were all quite pretty and were good at house-keeping and all sorts of handwork. Kapitolina Nikitishna was married, only not to a merchant, but to a painter—though he was a very good man and earned money enough: he took profitable commissions for decorating churches. One unpleasant thing for the whole family was that, while he worked on godly things, he was also versed in some sort of freethinking from Kurganov's *Pismovnik*.² He liked to talk about Chaos, about Ovid, about Prometheus, and was fond of comparing fables with sacred history. If not for that, everything would have been fine. Another thing was that they had no children, and my uncle and aunt were very upset about it. They had seen only their first daughter married, and suddenly she remained childless for three years. Owing to that, suitors started avoiding the other sisters.

My aunt asked Ivan Yakovlevich how it happened that her daughter did not have children: "They're both young and handsome," she said, "yet there are no children?"

Ivan Yakovlevich began to mutter:

"There's a heaven of heavens, a heaven of heavens."

His women prompters translated for my aunt: "The dear father says to tell your son-in-law to pray to God, for it must be that he's of little faith."

My aunt simply gasped: "Everything's revealed to him," she said. And she started badgering the painter to go to confession; but to him it was all horsefeathers! He treated it all very lightly . . . even ate meat on fast days . . . and besides that, they heard indirectly, he supposedly ate worms and oysters. Yet they all lived in the same house and were often distressed that in their merchant family there was such a man of no faith.

II

So my aunt went to Ivan Yakovlevich to ask him to pray that the servant of God Kapitolina's womb be opened and that the servant of God Lary (that was the painter's name) be enlightened by faith.

My uncle and aunt asked it together.

Ivan Yakovlevich began to babble something that couldn't be understood at all, and the attendant women sitting around him explained:

"He's not very clear today," they said, "but tell us what you're asking, and we'll give him a little note tomorrow."

My aunt began to tell them, and they wrote down: "Servant of God Kapitolina to have womb opened, and servant of God Lary to have faith increased."

The old folk left this petitionary little note and went home stepping lightly.

At home they said nothing to anyone except Kapochka alone, and then only so that she shouldn't tell her husband, the faithless painter, but simply live with him as tenderly and harmoniously as possible, and watch to see if he would get closer to faith in Ivan Yakovlevich. But he was a terrible man for cursing and as full of little sayings as a clown from Presnya.[3] Everything was jokes and quips with him. He'd come to his father-in-law of an evening: "Let's go and read the fifty-two-page prayer book," he'd say, meaning play cards . . . Or he'd sit down and say: "On condition that we play till the first swoon."

My aunt simply couldn't listen to such words. My uncle said to him, "Don't upset her so: she loves you and has made a promise for you." He started laughing and said to his mother-in-law:

"Why do you make unwitting promises? Or don't you know that because of such a promise John the Baptist had his head cut off?[4] Watch out, there may be some unexpected misfortune in our house."

This frightened his mother-in-law still more, and every day, in her anxiety, she went running to the madhouse. There they calmed her down—said things were going well: the dear father read their note each day, and what was now written there would soon come true.

And suddenly it did come true, but how it came true I'm reluctant to say.

III

My aunt's second daughter, Katechka, comes to her, and falls right at her feet, and sobs, and weeps bitterly.

My aunt asks:

"What's wrong—has someone offended you?"

The girl answers through her tears:

"Dearest mama, I myself don't know what it is or why . . . it's the first and last time it's happened . . . Only conceal my sin from papa."

My aunt looked at her, poked her finger right into her belly, and said:

"Is it here?"

Katechka replies:

"Yes, mama . . . how did you guess . . . I myself don't know why . . ."

My aunt only gasped and clasped her hands.

"My child," she says, "don't even try to find out: it may be that I'm guilty of a mistake, I'll go at once and find out," and she flew off at once in a cab to Ivan Yakovlevich.

"Show me the note," she says, "with our request that the dear father ask the fruit of the womb for the servant of God: how is it written?"

The hangers-on found it on the windowsill and handed it to her.

My aunt looked and nearly went out of her mind. What do you think? It all actually came about through a mistaken prayer, because instead of the servant of God Kapitolina, who was married, there was written the servant of God Katerina, who was still unmarried, a maiden.

The women say:

"Just imagine, what a sin! The names are very similar . . . but never mind, it *can be set right*."

But my aunt thought: "No, nonsense, you can't set it right now: Katya's been prayed for," and she tore the note into little pieces.

IV

The main thing was their fear of telling my uncle. He was the sort of man who was hard to calm down once he got going. Besides, he loved Katya least of all, and his favorite daughter was the youngest, Olenka—it was to her he had promised the most.

My aunt thought and thought and saw that her mind alone could not think over this calamity—she invited her painter son-in-law to a council and revealed everything to him in detail, and then begged:

"Though you have no faith," she says, "there may be some feeling in you—please take pity on Katya, help me to conceal her maidenly sin."

The painter suddenly scowled and said sternly:

"Excuse me, please, but first of all, though you're my wife's mother, I resent being considered a man of no faith, and, second of all, I don't understand what can be counted as Katya's sin here, if Ivan Yakovlevich has been pleading so long for her. I have all a brother's feelings for Katechka, and I'll stand up for her, because she's not to blame for anything here."

My aunt bit her fingers and wept, saying:

"Well . . . how not for anything?"

"Of course, not for anything. It's your wonderworker who made a mess of it, and he's got to answer for it."

"How can he answer for it? He's a righteous man."

"Well, if he's righteous, then keep quiet. Send me Katya with three bottles of champagne."

My aunt asked him to repeat himself:

"What's that?"

And again he answers:

"With three bottles of champagne—one right now to me in my rooms, and two later, I'll tell you where, but keep them ready here at home and on ice."

My aunt looked at him and only shook her head.

"God help you," she said. "I thought you only had no faith, though you paint holy images, but it turns out you have no feelings at all . . . That's why I cannot venerate your icons."

And he replied:

"No, leave off about faith: it seems it's you who have doubts and keep thinking about nature, as if Katya had her own reasons here, but I firmly believe that Ivan Yakovlevich alone is the cause of it all; and you'll see my feelings when you send Katya to my studio with champagne."

V

My aunt thought and thought, and did send the wine to the painter with Katechka herself. She came in with the tray, all in tears, but he jumped up, seized her by the arms, and wept himself.

"My little dove," he said, "I grieve at what's happened to you, but there's no time for nodding over it—quickly let me in on all your secrets."

The girl confided her mischief to him, and he locked her in his studio with a key.

My aunt met her son-in-law with teary eyes and said nothing. But he embraced her and kissed her and said:

"Now, don't be afraid, don't weep. Maybe God will help."

"Tell me," my aunt whispered, "who's to blame for it all?"

But the painter tenderly shook his finger at her and said:

"That's not nice: you yourself constantly reproach me with having no faith, and now, when your faith is being tested, I see you haven't any faith at all. Isn't it clear to you that there's no one to blame, and the wonderworker simply made a little mistake?"

"But where is my poor Katechka?"

"I charmed her with a fearsome painter's charm and—poof!—she disappeared."

And he showed his mother-in-law the key.

My aunt realized that he had hidden the girl from her father's first wrath, and she embraced him.

She whispered:

"Forgive me—there are tender feelings in you."

VI

My uncle came, had his tea as usual, and said:

"Well, shall we read the fifty-two-page prayer book?"

They sat down. And the family closed all the doors around them and went about on tiptoe. My aunt now moved away from the door, then went up to it again—listening and crossing herself.

Finally, something clanked in there . . . She ran off and hid.

"He's revealed it," she says, "he's revealed the secret! Now there'll be a hellish performance."

And just so: all at once the door opened, and my uncle cried out:

"My overcoat and my big stick!"

The painter holds him back by the arm and says:

"What is it? Where are you going?"

My uncle says:

"I'm going to the madhouse to give the wonderworker a thrashing!"

My aunt moaned behind the other door.

"Quick," she says, "run to the madhouse, have them hide our dear Ivan Yakovlevich!"

And indeed my uncle would have thrashed him for certain, but his painter son-in-law kept him from it by frightening him with his own faith.

VII

The son-in-law started reminding his father-in-law that he had one more daughter.

"Never mind," my uncle says, "she'll have her portion, but I want to thrash Koreisha. Let them take me to court afterwards."

"But I'm not frightening you with court," says the painter. "Look at what harm Ivan Yakovlevich can do Olga. No, it's terrible, what you're risking!"

My uncle stopped and pondered:

"Well," he says, "what harm can he do?"

"Exactly the same harm he's done to Katechka."

My uncle glanced up and replied:

"Stop pouring out drivel! As if he could do that!"

The painter replies:

"Well, if, as I see, you're an unbeliever, do as you know best, only don't grieve afterwards and blame the poor girls."

My uncle stopped at that. And his son-in-law dragged him back into the room and began persuading him.

"In my opinion," he says, "it's better to leave the wonderworker out of it and try to set this matter straight by domestic means."

The old man agreed, only he did not know how to set it straight himself, but his son-in-law helped him here as well. He says:

"Good thoughts must be sought not in wrath, but in joy."

"What joy can there be, brother, in a case like this?"

"Here's what," says the painter. "I've got two bottles of fizzy, and until you drink them with me, I won't say a single word to you. Agree to it. You know my character."

The old man looked at him and said:
"Go on, go on. What next?"
But all the same he agreed.

VIII

The painter marched off briskly and came back, followed by his assistant, a young artist, with a tray bearing two bottles and glasses.

As soon as they came in, the son-in-law locked the door behind him and put the key in his pocket. My uncle looked and understood everything, and the son-in-law nodded towards the assistant—the lad stood there in humble petition.

"I'm to blame—forgive me and give us your blessing."
My uncle asks his son-in-law:
"Can I thrash him?"
The son-in-law says:
"You can, but you needn't."
"Well, then at least let him kneel before me."
The son-in-law whispered:
"Well, kneel before the father for the sake of the girl you love."
The lad knelt.
The old man began to weep.
"Do you love her very much?" he asked.
"I do."
"Well, kiss me."
So Ivan Yakovlevich's little mistake was covered up. And it all remained safely hidden, and suitors began to pursue the youngest sister, because they saw that the girls were trustworthy.

The Pearl Necklace

I

In a certain cultivated family, some friends were sitting over tea and talking about literature—about invention, plot. They regretted that with us all this was getting poorer and paler. I remembered and recounted a characteristic observation of the late Pisemsky,[1] who said that the perceived impoverishment of literature was connected first of all with the multiplication of railroads, which are very useful for commerce, but harmful for artistic literature.

"Today man travels a lot, but quickly and painlessly," said Pisemsky, "and therefore he doesn't accumulate any strong impressions, he has no time to observe anything—everything slips by. Hence the poverty. Once upon a time you went from Moscow to Kostroma 'the slow way,' in a public tarantass or a hired coach—and happened upon a scoundrelly coachman, and insolent companions, and the postmaster was a rogue, and his 'cooky' was a sloven—so much diversity for the eyes. And if your heart can't bear it—you fish some sort of vileness from the cabbage soup and start cursing the 'cooky' and she answers back tenfold—then there's simply no getting away from impressions. And they sit thick in you, like yesterday's kasha stewing—well, naturally, it came out thick in the writing as well; but nowadays it's all railroad-like—take your plate, don't ask anything; eat—no time for chewing; ding-ding-ding and that's it: you're off again, and the only impression you're left with is that the waiter cheated you on the change, and there's no time to curse him to your heart's content."

To this, one guest observed that Pisemsky was original, but wrong, and he held up the example of Dickens, who wrote in a country where they traveled very fast, yet saw and observed a great deal, and the plots of his stories do not suffer from poverty of content.

"The only exception is perhaps his Christmas stories. They're wonderful, too, of course, but they have a certain monotony; however, the author can't be blamed for that, because this is a kind of literature in which the writer feels himself the prisoner of a much too narrow and strictly organized form. It is unfailingly demanded of a Christmas story that it be timed to the events of the evenings from Christmas Eve to Epiphany; that it be at least to some degree fantastic, that it have some sort of moral, if only such as disproving a harmful superstition, and finally—that it unfailingly have a happy ending. In life such events are few, and therefore the author forces himself to think up and compose a plot that fits the program. Which is why Christmas stories are notable for their great artificiality and uniformity."

"Well, I don't entirely agree with you," replied a third guest, a respectable man, who was often able to put in an appropriate word. Therefore we all wanted to hear him.

"I think," he went on, "that a Christmas story, while staying within all its limits, can still be modified and show an interesting variety, reflecting in itself both its time and morals."

"But how can you prove your opinion? For it to be persuasive, you must show us one such event from the contemporary life of Russian society, in which the present age does stand, and the contemporary man,[2] and which at the same time answers to the form and program of a Christmas story—that is, it should be slightly fantastic, and should eradicate some superstition, and should have not a sad, but a happy ending."

"And why not? I can present you with such a story, if you like."

"Please do! Only remember that it must be a *real incident*!"

"Oh, rest assured—I'll tell you about the realest of incidents, and about persons who are very near and dear to me at that. It concerns my own brother, who, as you probably know, has a decent job and enjoys a good reputation, which he fully deserves."

Everyone confirmed that it was so, and many added that the narrator's brother was indeed a worthy and excellent man.

"Yes," he said, "and so I shall speak of this, as you say, excellent man."

II

Some three years ago, my brother came to me at Christmastime from the province where he was working then, and, as if some fly had bitten him, accosted me and my wife with a persistent request: "Get me married."

At first we thought he was joking, but he badgered us seriously and in no few words: "Kindly get me married! Save me from the unbearable boredom of solitude! I hate bachelor life, I'm sick of provincial gossip and nonsense—I want to have my own hearth, I want to sit in the evening with my dear wife by my lamp. Get me married!"

"Now, wait a minute," we say, "that's all very fine, and let it be your way—God bless you—get married, but it takes time, you've got to have a nice girl in mind, a girl after your own heart, and one who also finds herself disposed towards you. That all takes time."

And he replies:

"So what—there's plenty of time: for the two weeks of Christmastime there's no marrying—you find me a match during that time, and on Epiphany, in the evening, we'll get married and leave."

"My dear man," I say, "you must have gone a bit out of your mind from boredom." (The word "psychopath" was not yet in use among us.) "I have no time to play the fool with you, I'm going to work at the court right now, and you can stay here with my wife and fantasize."

I thought, naturally, that it was all trifles, or, at least, that the undertaking was very far from fulfillment, and yet I come home for dinner and see that the matter has already ripened for them.

My wife tells me:

"Mashenka Vasilieva came by, asked me to go and help her choose a dress, and while I was changing, they"—that is, my brother and the girl—"sat over tea, and your brother says: 'What a fine girl! Why look further—get me married to her!'"

I reply to my wife:

"Now I see my brother's really gone foolish."

"No, excuse me," my wife replies, "what makes it necessarily 'foolish'? Why deny what you yourself have always respected?"

"What is it that I've respected?"

"Unaccountable sympathies, inclinations of the heart."

"Well, my dear wife," I say, "you won't hook me with that. That's all very well in due time, very well when these inclinations proceed from some clear awareness, from recognition of obvious excellencies of soul and heart, but this—what is it . . . they see each other for a minute and they're ready to get hitched for life?"

"Yes, and what do you have against Mashenka? She's precisely as you say—a girl of clear mind, noble character, and a beautiful and faithful heart. Besides, she also liked him very much."

"What!" I exclaimed. "So you've already managed to secure her acceptance as well?"

"Acceptance or not," she replied, "isn't it obvious? Love is in our women's line—we notice it and see it in the bud."

"You're all disgusting matchmakers," I say. "All you want is to get somebody married, and what comes of it doesn't concern you. Beware the consequences of your light-mindedness."

"I won't beware anything," she says, "because I know them both and know that your brother is an excellent man and Masha the dearest of girls, and since they've given their word to look after each other's happiness, that's what they'll do."

"What!" I cried, forgetting myself. "They've already given each other their word?"

"Yes," my wife replies. "So far it's just allegorical, but clear enough. Their tastes and aspirations are the same, and in the evening I'll take your brother to them—the old parents are sure to like him, and then . . ."

"What, what then?"

"Then—let them do as they like; only don't you interfere."

"Very well," I say, "very well, I'll be glad not to interfere in such silliness."

"There won't be any silliness."

"Splendid."

"And everything will be fine; they'll be happy!"

"Very glad! Only it won't do any harm," I say, "for my brother and you to know and remember that Mashenka's rich father is a notorious wealthy skinflint."

"What of it? I can't dispute that, unfortunately, but it doesn't keep Mashenka in the least from being a wonderful girl, who is going to make a wonderful wife. You've probably forgotten what we've lingered over more than once: remember that all the best women in Turgenev, as if by design, had very unrespectable parents."

"I'm not talking about that at all. Mashenka really is an excellent girl, but her father, in giving her two older sisters in marriage, deceived both sons-in-law and gave them nothing—and he'll give Masha nothing."

"Who knows? He loves her most of all."

"Well, my dear wife, hope springs eternal: we know all about this 'special' love for daughters who are getting married. He'll deceive everybody! And he can't help deceiving them—he stands on that, and they say he laid the foundation of his fortune by lending money on pledges at high interest. You want love and magnanimity from such a man. But I'm telling you that his first two sons-in-law are both sly foxes themselves, and if he duped them and they're now big enemies of his, then all the more will my brother, who from a young age has suffered from the most exaggerated delicacy, be left beanless."

"How do you mean," she says, "left beanless?"

"Well, my dear wife, there you're playing the fool."

"No, I'm not."

"Do you really not know what it means to be 'left beanless'? He won't give Mashenka anything—that's the long and short of it."

"Ah, so that's it!"

"Well, of course."

"Of course, of course! That all may be," she says, "only I never thought that, in your opinion, to get a sensible wife, even without a dowry, was what's known as 'being left beanless.'"

You know that sweet female habit and logic: she's already wandered off, but you get a neighborly dig in the side . . .

"I'm not speaking of myself at all . . ."

"No, really? . . ."

"Well, that's strange, *ma chère!*"

"Why strange?"

"Strange, because I wasn't saying it on my own account."

"Well, you were thinking it."

"No, I was by no means thinking it."

"Well, you were imagining it."

"No, devil take it, I wasn't imagining anything!"

"Why are you shouting?!"

"I'm not shouting."

"And these 'devils' . . . 'the devil' . . . What's that?"

"Because you try my patience."

"Well, so that's it! And if I'd been rich and had brought you a dowry . . ."

"Oh, ho, ho! . . ."

That I couldn't bear, and, in the words of the late poet Tolstoy,[3] "having begun like a god, I ended like a swine." I assumed an offended look—because I indeed felt myself unjustly offended—and, shaking my head, I turned and went to my study. But as I was closing the door behind me, I felt an invincible thirst for revenge—opened the door again and said:

"That's swinishness!"

And she replies:

"*Merci,* husband dear."

III

Devil knows, what a scene! And don't forget—that was after four years of the happiest married life, never for a moment troubled by anything! . . . I was annoyed, offended—it was unbearable! What rubbish! And for what? . . . It was all my brother's mischief-making. And what was it to me, that I was so upset and seething? Isn't he in fact an adult, doesn't he have the right to decide whom he likes and wishes to marry? . . . Lord—nowadays you can't even guide your own son in these matters, so why on earth should a brother listen to his brother? . . . And by what right, finally? . . . And can I in fact be such a prophet as to firmly predict how this matchmaking will end? . . . Mashenka is indeed an excellent girl, and isn't my wife a lovely woman? . . . And, thank God, no one has ever called me a scoundrel, and yet here we are, she and I, after four years of happy life, never troubled for a moment by anything, now squabbling like a tailor and his wife . . . And all over a trifle, over someone else's clownish whim . . .

I was terribly ashamed of myself and terribly sorry for her, because I now took no account of her words and blamed myself for everything, and in this sad and displeased mood I fell asleep on the sofa in my study, wrapped in a soft quilted robe, made by my dear wife's own hands . . .

It's a winning thing—a comfortable piece of clothing, made for

a husband by his wife's own hands! It's so good, so sweet, and such
a reminder, timely or untimely, both of our faults and of those precious little hands, which one suddenly wants to kiss and ask forgiveness for something.

"Forgive me, my angel, that you have finally tried my patience. In
future it won't happen."

And, I'll confess, I wanted so much to go quickly with that request
that I woke up, rose, and left my study.

I look—all through the house it's dark and quiet.

I ask the maid:

"Where is the lady?"

"She went with your brother to see Marya Nikolaevna's father,"
she replied. "I'll make your tea at once."

"What a woman!" I think. "So she won't give up her stubbornness—
she really wants my brother to marry Mashenka . . . Well, let them
do as they like, and let Mashenka's father dupe them as he did his
older sons-in-law. And even more, because they're shysters themselves, and my brother—the embodiment of honesty and delicacy.
So much the better—let him cheat them—both my brother and my
wife. Let her get burnt by her first lesson in matchmaking!"

I received a glass of tea from the maid's hand and sat down to
read the case that was to begin the next day in our court and which
presented me with no little difficulty.

This work occupied me long past midnight, and at two o'clock my
wife and brother returned, both in the merriest spirits.

My wife says to me:

"Would you like some cold roast beef and a glass of water with
wine? We had supper at the Vasilievs'."

"No," I say, "I humbly thank you."

"Nikolai Ivanovich waxed generous and gave us an excellent meal."

"Well now!"

"Yes—we passed the time most merrily and drank champagne."

"Lucky you!" I say, while thinking to myself: "So that slyboots,
Nikolai Ivanovich, saw through my mooncalf of a brother at once,
and gave him some swill—not without reason. Now he'll coddle him
till the end of the engagement period, and then—a short tether."

And my feeling against my wife became embittered again, and,
being innocent, I did not ask her forgiveness. And even if I had been
free and had had leisure to enter into all the details of the love game
they had started, it would have been no surprise if again I had lost

patience—had interfered in some way, and we'd have arrived at some sort of psychosis; but, fortunately, I had no time. The case I told you about occupied us so much at court that we had no hope of getting free of it even by the holiday, and therefore I came home only to eat and sleep, and spent all my days and part of my nights before the altar of Themis.[4]

But at home things did not wait for me, and when I appeared under my own roof on Christmas Eve, pleased to be free of my court duties, I was met by an invitation to examine a magnificent basket of expensive gifts that my brother was offering to Mashenka.

"What might this be?"

"These are the groom's gifts to the bride," explained my wife.

"Aha! So it's come to that now! Congratulations."

"How else! Your brother didn't want to make a formal proposal without talking it over with you once more, but he wants to hasten his wedding, and you, as ill luck would have it, went on sitting in your disgusting court. It was impossible to wait, and they've become engaged."

"Well, splendid," I say. "There was no reason to wait for me."

"You're being witty, it seems?"

"Not in the least."

"Or ironic?"

"Not ironic either."

"It would all be useless anyway, because, in spite of your croaking, they'll be very happy."

"Of course," I say, "if you guarantee it, they will be . . . There's a proverb: 'Take three days to choose, and you'll always lose.' It's safer not to choose."

"You know," replied my wife, closing the basket of gifts, "it's you who think you choose us, but essentially that's all nonsense."

"Why is it nonsense? I hope it's not the girls who choose their suitors, but the suitors who do the wooing."

"Yes, they do the wooing, that's true, but there's no such thing as a circumspect or reasonable choice."

I shook my head and said:

"You should think before you say such a thing. I, for instance, chose you—precisely out of respect for you and being conscious of your merits."

"Rubbish."

"Why rubbish?!"

"Rubbish—because you didn't choose me for my merits at all."

"For what, then?"

"Because you liked me."

"So you even deny that you have merits?"

"Not in the least—I do have merits, but all the same you wouldn't have married me if you hadn't liked me."

I felt that what she said was true.

"However," I said, "I waited a whole year and visited your house. Why did I do that?"

"In order to look at me."

"Not true—I was studying your character."

My wife burst out laughing.

"What's this senseless laughter?!"

"It's not senseless at all. You, my dear, were not studying anything in me, and you couldn't have been."

"Why not?"

"Shall I tell you?"

"Kindly do!"

"Because you were in love with me."

"Maybe so, but that didn't prevent me from seeing your inner qualities."

"Yes, it did."

"No, it didn't."

"It did, and it will always prevent anyone, and therefore this prolonged studying is useless. You think that when you're in love with a woman you *look at her in a reasoning way,* but in fact you only *gaze in wonder all the day.*"

"Well . . . after all," I said, "you make it somehow . . . very real."

And I thought to myself: "In fact it's true!"

And my wife said:

"Enough thinking—there's no harm done, and now change quickly and we'll go to Mashenka's: we're celebrating Christmas with them tonight, and you should congratulate her and your brother."

"I'll be very glad to," I said. And we went.

IV

Gifts were offered there and congratulations exchanged, and we all drank a fair amount of the merry nectar of Champagne.

There was no more time for thinking and persuading or dissuading. It remained only to uphold in everyone a faith in the happiness that awaited the betrothed couple and to drink champagne. That is how the days and nights were spent, sometimes at our house, sometimes at the house of the bride's parents.

In such spirits can the time drag out long?

Before we looked twice, New Year's Eve was upon us. The joyful expectation increased. The whole world wished for joy—and we didn't lag behind the rest. We ushered in the New Year at Mashenka's parents' again, with such "wetting of the whistle," as our grandfathers used to say, that we also justified the grandfatherly saying: "The joy of Rus' is to drink."[5] Only one thing was wrong. Mashenka's father said nothing about a dowry, but instead he gave his daughter a very odd and, as I later understood, a totally inadmissible and ill-omened present. He himself, in front of everyone at supper, put on her a rich pearl necklace . . . We men, looking at the thing, even gave it some good thought.

"Oh-ho-ho, just how much might that be worth? A little thing like that has probably been stored away here since the good old days, when rich people of the nobility did not yet send things to the pawnbroker, but, in great need of money, preferred to entrust their valuables to secret usurers like Mashenka's father."

The pearls were big, well-rounded, and extraordinarily alive. The necklace was made in the old style, what's known as *refid*—strung starting at the clasp with small but perfect Black Sea pearls, then larger and larger Persian Gulf pearls, then further down came pearls as big as beans, and in the very center three black pearls of remarkable size and the finest brilliance. The beautiful, valuable gift entirely outshone and put to shame my brother's gifts. In a word, we crude men all found Mashenka's father's gift beautiful, and we also liked the words the old man spoke in presenting the necklace. Mashenka's father, giving her this treasure, said: "Here, my dear daughter, is a little thing with a spell on it: rot will never rot it, nor a thief steal it, and if he does, he won't be glad of it. It is eternal."

But women have their own point of view on everything, and Mashenka, on receiving the necklace, burst into tears, and my wife, unable to help herself, found a convenient moment and even reprimanded Nikolai Ivanovich at the window, and by family right he heard her out. He deserved to be reprimanded for the gift of pearls, because pearls signify and foretell *tears*. And therefore pearls are never used as New Year's gifts.

However, Nikolai Ivanovich deftly laughed it off.

"First of all," he said, "that is an empty superstition, and if anyone can give me the pearl that Princess Yusupov bought from Gorgibus,[6] I'll take it at once. I, madam, also studied these subtleties in my time, and I know what should not be given. Girls should not be given turquoise, because turquoise, in the Persian notion, comes from the bones of people who died of love, and married women should not be given amethysts *avec flèches d'Amour*,* and yet I have ventured to makes gifts of such amethysts, and ladies have taken them . . ."

My wife smiled. And he said:

"I'll also venture to give them to you. And with regard to pearls, it should be known that there are pearls and pearls. Not all pearls are obtained with tears. There are Persian pearls, there are pearls from the Red Sea, and there are pearls from fresh water—*d'eau douce,* which are obtained without tears. The sentimental Mary Stuart wore only these *perles d'eau douce* from Scotland's rivers, but they did not bring her happiness. I know what should be given—and that is what I gave my daughter, but you frighten her. For that I will give you nothing *avec flèches d'Amour*, I will give you a cold-blooded 'moonstone.' But you, my child, don't cry and put it out of your head that my pearls bring tears. These aren't like that. I'll reveal the secret of these pearls to you the day after your wedding, and you'll see that you needn't fear any superstitions . . ."

So it quieted down, and my brother and Mashenka were married after Epiphany, and the next day my wife and I went to visit the young couple.

---

* With Cupid's darts (gems made from rutilated quartz). *Trans.*

V

We found them already up and in a remarkably cheerful state of mind. My brother himself opened the door to the lodgings he had rented in a hotel for the wedding day, and met us beaming all over and rocking with laughter.

This reminded me of an old novel in which the new husband went out of his mind with happiness, and I mentioned it to my brother, to which he replied:

"And what do you think, such a thing has actually happened to me as could make a man doubt his reason. My family life, having begun today, has brought me not only the expected joys from my dear wife, but quite unexpected prosperity from my father-in-law."

"What on earth has happened?"

"Come in, I'll tell you."

My wife whispers:

"Must be the old scoundrel duped them."

I reply:

"That's none of my business."

We went in and my brother handed us an opened letter, which had come addressed to them early in the morning by the city post, and in the letter we read the following:

"The superstition concerning pearls can in no way threaten you: those pearls are *false*."

My wife sank into a chair.

"What a scoundrel!" she said.

But my brother nodded his head in the direction of the bedroom, where Mashenka was finishing her toilette, and said:

"You're wrong: the old man has acted quite honestly. I received this letter, read it, and burst out laughing . . . What was sad for me here? I wasn't looking or asking for a dowry, I was only looking for a wife, and so there was nothing distressing to me in the fact that the pearls of the necklace weren't real but false. Let the necklace be worth not thirty thousand but a mere three hundred roubles—isn't it all the same to me, so long as my wife is happy? . . . Only one thing worried me—how to break it to Masha? I fell to thinking about that and sat down facing the window, and so I didn't notice that I'd forgotten to bolt the door. A few minutes later I turned and suddenly saw that my father-in-law was standing behind me and holding something wrapped in a handkerchief.

"'Greetings, my dear son-in-law!' he says.

"I jumped up, embraced him, and said:

"'How nice! We were to go to you in an hour, and here you . . . It's against all the customs . . . How nice and how precious.'

"'Well,' he replies, 'who's counting! We're family. I went to the liturgy—prayed for you, and here I've brought you a prosphora.'[7]

"Again I embraced him and kissed him.

"'Did you get my letter?' he asks.

"'I certainly did,' I say.

"And I burst out laughing.

"He looks at me.

"'Why are you laughing?' he says.

"'And what should I do? It's very amusing.'

"'Amusing?'

"'Certainly.'

"'Give me those pearls.'

"The necklace was right there in a case on the table—I gave it to him.

"'Do you have a magnifying glass?'

"I say: 'No.'

"'In that case, I do. Out of old habit, I always have it with me. Please look at the clasp under the dog.'

"'Why should I look?'

"'No, have a look. Maybe you think I'm deceiving you?'

"'Not at all.'

"'No—look, look!'

"I take the glass and see—on the clasp, in the least conspicuous place, there are microscopic letters in French: 'Bourguignon.'[8]

"'Are you convinced,' he says, 'that these really are *false* pearls?'

"'I see it.'

"'And what do you say to me now?'

"'The same thing as before. That is: this does not concern me, and I will only ask you for one thing . . .'

"'Ask, ask!'

"'Allow me not to speak of it to Masha.'

"'Why is that?'

"'Just so . . .'

"'No, to precisely what end? You don't want to upset her?'

"'Yes—that among other things.'

"'And what else?'

"'I also don't want anything in her heart to be stirred against her father.'

"'Against her father?'

"'Yes.'

"'Well, for her father she's now a cut-off slice, which can't be stuck back on the loaf, and the main thing for her is her husband . . .'

"'Never,' I say, 'is the heart a roadside inn: there's no lack of space in it. One love goes to the father, and to the husband another, and besides that . . . a husband who wishes to be happy should see to it that he can respect his wife, and for that he must cherish her love and esteem for her parents.'

"'Aha! What a practical one you are!'

"And he started silently drumming his fingers on the seat, then got up and said:

"'I, my gentle son-in-law, have made my fortune by my own labor, but by various means. From a lofty point of view, it may be that they are not all very laudable, but such was my time, and I didn't know how to make it any other way. I don't have much faith in people, and of love I've heard only what you read about in novels, but in fact all I saw was that everybody wants money. I gave no money to my two sons-in-law, and right enough: they're angry with me and won't let their wives see me. I don't know who is more noble—they or I? I don't give them money, and they corrupt living hearts. So I won't give them money, but you I'll go and give it to! Yes! And here, I'll even give it to you right now!'

"And kindly look at this!"

My brother showed us three fifty-thousand-rouble banknotes.

"Can all that be for your wife?" I say.

"No," he replies, "he gave Masha fifty thousand, and I said to him:

"'You know, Nikolai Ivanovich—it will be ticklish . . . Masha will feel awkward that she received a dowry from you and her sisters didn't . . . It's sure to cause envy and hostility towards her in her sisters . . . No, forget the money—let it stay with you and . . . someday, when a favorable chance comes for you to be reconciled with your other daughters, you'll give to *all of them* equally. And then it will bring us all joy . . . But to us alone . . . *better not!*'

"Again he got up, again he paced the room, and, stopping outside the bedroom door, called:

" 'Marya!'

"Masha was already in her peignoir and came out.

" 'I congratulate you,' he says.

"She kissed his hand.

" 'Do you want to be happy?'

" 'Of course I do, papa, and . . . I hope to be.'

" 'Very good . . . You've chosen yourself a good husband, old girl!'

" 'I didn't choose, papa. God gave him to me.'

" 'Very good, very good. God gave, and I'll *give on top*. I want to add to your happiness. Here are three banknotes, all the same. One for you, and two for your sisters. Give them to them yourself—say it's *your gift* . . .'

" 'Papa!'

"Masha first threw herself on his neck, then suddenly lowered herself to the ground and, weeping joyfully, embraced his knees. I looked—he was weeping, too.

" 'Get up, get up!' he says. 'Today, in the words of the people, you are a "princess"—it's not proper for you to bow down to me.'

" 'But I'm so happy . . . for my sisters! . . .'

" 'Well, there . . . And I'm happy, too! . . . Now you can see there was nothing for you to be afraid of in the pearl necklace. I've come to tell you the secret: the *pearls* I gave you are *false*; a bosom friend of mine duped me with them long ago—and not a simple friend, but one blended from the races of Rurik and Gediminas.[9] While you have a husband with a simple but *genuine* soul: to dupe such a one is impossible—the soul can't bear it.' "

"There you have the whole of my story," our interlocutor concluded, "and I truly think that, despite its modern origin and its nonfictional character, it answers to the program and form of a traditional Christmas story."

The Spook

Fear has big eyes.

A SAYING

I

my childhood was spent in Orel. We lived in Nemchinov's house, somewhere not far from the "little cathedral." Now I can't make out exactly where this tall wooden house stood, but I remember that from its garden there was an extensive view over the wide and deep ravine with its steep sides crosscut by layers of red clay. Beyond the ravine spread a big field on which the town warehouses stood, and near them soldiers always drilled in the summer. Every day I watched how they drilled and how they were beaten. That was common practice then, but I simply couldn't get used to it and always wept over them. To keep that from being repeated too often, my nanny, Marina Borisovna, an elderly soldier's widow from Moscow, took me for walks in the town garden. There we would sit over the shallow Oka and watch little children swimming and playing in it. I envied their freedom very much then.

The main advantage of their unfettered condition, in my eyes, lay in their wearing neither shoes nor shirts, because they took their shirts off and tied the sleeves to the collar. Adapted like that, the shirts turned into little sacks, and by holding them against the current, the boys caught tiny, silvery fish in them. They were so small it was impossible to clean them, and that was considered sufficient grounds for cooking them and eating them uncleaned.

I never had the courage to find out how they tasted, but the fishing performed by those diminutive fishermen seemed to me the height of happiness that freedom could afford a boy of the age I was then.

My nanny, however, knew some good reasons why such freedom would be completely improper for me. Those reasons consisted in my being the child of a noble family and my father being known to everyone in town.

"It would be a different matter," my nanny said, "if we were in the country." There, among simple, boorish muzhiks, I too might be allowed to enjoy something of that sort of freedom.

I think it was precisely because of those restrictive arguments that I began to feel an intense yearning for the countryside, and my rapture knew no bounds when my parents bought a small estate in the Kromy district. That same summer we moved from the big house in town to a very cozy but small village house with a balcony and a thatched roof. Woods in the Kromy district were costly and rare even then. This was an area of steppes and grain fields, well irrigated besides by small but clean streams.

II

In the country I at once struck up a wide and interesting acquaintance with the peasants. While my father and mother were intensely occupied with setting up the estate, I lost no time in becoming close friends with the grown-up lads and the little boys who pastured horses on the "kuligas."* The strongest of all my attachments, however, was to an old miller, Grandpa Ilya—a completely white-haired old man with huge black mustaches. He was more available for conversation than all the others because he didn't go away to work, but either strolled about the dam with a dung fork or sat over the trembling sluice-gate, pensively listening to whether the wheels were turning regularly or water was seeping in somewhere under the gate. When he got tired of doing nothing, he fashioned spare maple shafts

---

* *Kuliga*—a place where the trees have been cut down and burned, a clearing, a burn. *Author.*

or spindles for the cogwheel. But in all the situations I've described, he easily left off work and entered willingly into conversation, which he conducted in fragments, without any connection, but with his favorite system of allusions, and in the process making fun maybe of himself, maybe of his listeners.

Through his job as a miller, Grandpa Ilya had rather close connections with the water demon who was in charge of our ponds, the upper and the lower, and of two swamps. This demon had his main headquarters under an unused sluice-gate at our mill.

Grandpa Ilya knew everything about him and used to say:

"*He* likes me. Even when *he* comes home angry over some disorder, he does me no harm. If anybody else is lying in my place here on the sacks, he pulls at him and throws him off, but he won't ever touch me."

All the young people assured me that the relations I've described between Grandpa Ilya and the "old water demon" really existed, but that they held out not at all because the water demon liked him, but because Grandpa Ilya, being a real, true miller, knew a real, true miller's word, which the water demon and all his little devils obeyed as unquestioningly as did the grass snakes and toads that lived under the sluiceways and on the dam.

I went fishing with the boys for the gudgeons and loaches that abounded in our narrow but clear little river Gostomlia; but, because of the seriousness of my character, I kept company more with Grandpa Ilya, whose experienced mind opened to me a world full of mysterious delight that was completely unknown to a city boy like me. From Ilya I learned about the house demon, who slept on a counter, and the water demon, who had fine and important lodgings under the mill wheel, and the kikimora,[1] who was so skittish and changeable that she hid from any immodest gaze in various dusty corners—now in the threshing barn, now in the granary, now at the pounding mill, where hemp was pounded in the fall. Grandpa knew least of all about the wood demon, because he lived somewhere far away by Selivan's place and only occasionally visited our thick willow grove, to make a new willow pipe and play on it in the shade by the soaking tubs. Anyhow, Grandpa Ilya saw the wood demon face-to-face only once in all his richly adventurous life, and that was on St. Nicholas's day, which was the feast day of our church. The wood demon came up to Ilya pretending to be a perfectly quiet little muzhik and asked for a pinch of snuff. And when Grandpa said, "Here, devil take you!" and opened the snuffbox, the demon could no longer keep up his good behavior and played a prank: he hit the snuffbox from underneath, so that the good miller got an eyeful of snuff.

All these lively and interesting stories seemed fully probable to me then, and their dense imagery filled my fantasy to the point that I almost became a visionary myself. At least when I once peeked, at great risk, into the pounding shed, my eye proved so keen and sharp that I saw the kikimora, who was sitting there in the dust. She was unwashed, wearing a dusty headdress, and had scrofulous eyes. And when, frightened by this vision, I rushed out headlong, another of my senses—hearing—discovered the presence of the wood demon. I can't say for sure exactly where he was sitting—probably on some tall willow—but when I fled from the kikimora, the wood demon blew into his green pipe with all his might and held my foot so fast to the ground that the heel of my boot tore off.

Nearly out of breath, I told about it all at home, and for my candor I was put in my room to read the Holy Scriptures, while a barefoot boy was sent to a soldier in the nearby village who could mend the damage the wood demon had done to my boot. But by then even reading the Holy Scriptures didn't protect me from belief in the supernatural beings, to whom, it might be said, I had grown accustomed through Grandpa Ilya. I knew well and loved the Holy Scriptures—to this day I willingly read them over—and yet the dear, childish world of the fairy-tale creatures Grandpa Ilya told me about seemed indispensable to me. The forest springs would have been orphaned if they had been deprived of the spirits popular fantasy attached to them.

Among the unpleasant consequences of the wood demon's pipe was that my mother reprimanded Grandpa Ilya for the course in demonology he had given me, and he avoided me for a while, as if unwilling to continue my education. He even pretended to drive me away.

"Get away from me, go to your nanny," he said, turning me around and applying his broad, calloused palm to my seat.

But I could already pride myself on my age and considered such treatment incompatible with it. I was eight years old and by then had no need to go to my nanny. I let Ilya feel that by bringing him a basin of cherries left over from making liqueur.

Grandpa Ilya liked cherries. He took them, softened, stroked my head with his calloused hand, and very close and very good relations were restored between us.

"I tell you what," Grandpa Ilya said to me. "Always respect the muzhik most of all, and listen to him, but don't go telling everybody what you hear. Otherwise I'll chase you away."

After that I kept secret all that I heard from the miller, and I learned so many interesting things that I was now afraid not only at night, when all the house and forest demons and kikimoras become very bold and insolent, but even in the daytime. This fear seized me because it turned out that our house and our whole area were under the sway of a really scary brigand and bloodthirsty sorcerer named Selivan. He lived only four miles from us, "at the fork," that is, where the big high road divided in two: one, the new road, went to Kiev, and the other, the old one, with hollow willows "of Catherine's planting,"[2] led to Fatezh. That road was now abandoned and gone to waste.

Half a mile beyond that fork was a fine oak forest, and by the forest a most wretched inn, completely exposed and half fallen down, in which they said nobody ever stayed. That was easy to believe, because the inn offered no comforts for a stay, and because it was too close to the town of Kromy, where, even in those half-savage times, one could hope to find a warm room, a samovar, and second-rate white rolls. It was in this terrible inn, where *nobody* ever stayed, that the "empty innkeeper" Selivan lived, a terrible man whom nobody was glad to meet.

III

The story of the "empty innkeeper" Selivan, in Grandpa Ilya's words, was the following. Selivan was of Kromy tradesman stock; his parents died early, and he lived as an errand boy at the baker's and sold white rolls at a tavern outside the Orel gate. He was a good, kind, and obedient boy, but people kept telling the baker that he ought to be careful with Selivan, because he had a fiery red mark on his face—and that was never put there for nothing. There were such people as knew a special proverb for it: "Beware of him whom God hath marked." The baker praised Selivan highly for his zeal and trustworthiness, but everybody else, as his sincere well-wishers, said that all the same real prudence called for wariness and warned against trusting him too much—because "God hath marked" him. If a mark had been put on his face, it was precisely so that all overly trusting people would be wary of him. The baker didn't want to lag behind intelligent people, but Selivan was a very good worker. He sold his rolls assiduously and each evening conscientiously poured out for his master from a big leather purse all the ten- and five-kopeck pieces he had earned from passing muzhiks. However, the mark was not on him for nothing, but waiting for a certain occasion (it's always like that). A "retired executioner" named Borka came to Kromy from Orel, and they said to him: "An executioner, Borka, so you was, and now you'll have a bitter life with us," and everybody tried the best they could to make these words come true for the man. When the executioner Borka came from Orel to Kromy, he had with him a daughter of about fifteen who had been born in jail—though many thought it would have been better for her not to have been born at all.

They came to live in Kromy by assignment. It's incomprehensible now, but the practice then was to assign retired executioners to some town, and it was done just like that, without asking anyone's wishes or consent. So it happened with Borka: some governor ordered that this old executioner be assigned to Kromy—and so he was, and he came there to live and brought his daughter with him. Naturally, the executioner was not a desirable guest for anybody in Kromy. On the contrary, being spotless themselves, they all scorned him, and decidedly nobody wanted to have either him or his daughter around. And the weather was already very cold when they came.

The executioner asked to be taken into one house, then another, and then stopped bothering people. He could see that he aroused no compassion in anybody, and he knew that he fully deserved it.

"But the child!" he thought. "The child's not to blame for my sins—somebody will take pity on the child."

And Borka again went knocking from house to house, asking them to take not him, but only the girl . . . He swore that he would never even come to visit his daughter.

But that plea was also in vain.

Who wants to have anything to do with an executioner?

And so, having gone around the little town, these ill-fated visitors asked to be taken to jail. There they could at least warm up from the autumnal wetness and cold. But the jail did not take them either, because they had already served their term and were now free people. They were free to die by any fence or in any ditch they liked.

Occasionally people gave the executioner and his daughter alms, not for their own sake, but for Christ's, of course, but no one let them in. The old man and his daughter had no shelter and spent their nights in clay pits under the riverbank or in empty watchmen's huts by the kitchen gardens along the valley. Their hard lot was shared by a skinny dog who had come with them from Orel.

He was a big, shaggy dog, whose fur was all matted. What he ate, having beggarly owners, no one knew, but they finally figured out that he had no need to eat, because he was "gutless," that is, he was only skin and bones and yellow, suffering eyes, but "in the middle" he had nothing and therefore required no food at all.

Grandpa Ilya told me how this could be achieved "in the easiest way." Take any dog while it's still a pup and make it drink melted tin or lead, and it will become *without guts* and have no need to eat. But, naturally, for that you had to know "a special magic word." And since the executioner obviously knew that word, people of strict morals killed his dog. This had to be done, of course, so as not to give indulgence to sorcery; but it was a great misfortune for the beggars, because the girl slept with the dog, who shared with her some of the warmth he had in his fur. However, there naturally could be no pandering to magic for the sake of such trifles, and everyone was of the opinion that destroying the dog was perfectly right. Sorcerers should not be allowed to fool right-minded people.

IV

After the destruction of the dog, the executioner himself kept the girl warm in the huts, but he was already old and, luckily for him, did not have to keep up this care, which was beyond his strength, for very long. One freezing night, the child felt that her father was colder than she, and she was so frightened that she moved away from him and even fainted from terror. Till morning she remained in the embrace of death. When the sun rose and people on their way to church peeked into the hut out of curiosity, they saw the father and daughter frozen stiff. They somehow managed to warm up the girl, and when she saw her father's strangely immobile eyes and wildly bared teeth, she realized what it meant and burst into sobs.

The old man was buried outside the cemetery, because he had lived badly and died without repentance, and his girl they more or less forgot about . . . Not for long, it's true, just for a month or so, but when they remembered her a month later, she was nowhere to be found.

One might have thought that the orphan girl had run away to some other town or gone begging in the villages. Far more curious was another strange circumstance connected with the girl's disappearance: even before she turned up missing, it was noticed that the baker's boy Selivan had vanished without a trace.

He vanished quite unexpectedly, and more heedlessly, besides, than any other runaway before him. Selivan took absolutely nothing from anybody. All the rolls given him to sell even remained on his tray, and all the money for those he had sold was there as well. But he himself did not return home.

These two orphans were regarded as lost for a whole three years.

Suddenly one day a merchant came back from a fair, the man who also owned the long-abandoned inn "at the fork," and said he had had an accident: he was driving along a log road, misguided his horse, and was nearly crushed under his cart, but an unknown vagabond saved him.

He recognized this vagabond, and it turned out he was none other than Selivan.

The merchant Selivan had saved was not the sort to be insensitive to a service rendered him: to avoid being accused of ingratitude at the Last Judgment, he wished to do the vagabond a good turn.

"I want to be your benefactor," he said to Selivan. "I have a vacant inn at the fork: go and settle there as the innkeeper, sell oats and hay, and pay me only a hundred roubles a year in rent."

Selivan knew that four miles from town on an abandoned road was no place for an inn, and whoever kept it could not possibly expect any travelers; but all the same, since this was the first time he had been offered a place of his own, he accepted.

The merchant let him have it.

V

Selivan arrived at the inn with a small, one-wheeled dung cart in which he had placed his belongings, and on top of which a sick woman, dressed in pitiful rags, lay with her head thrown back.

People asked Selivan:

"Who is she?"
He replied:
"She's my wife."
"What parts is she from?"
Selivan meekly replied:
"God's parts."
"What ails her?"
"Her legs hurt."
"What caused the hurt?"
Frowning, Selivan grunted:
"The cold earth."

He didn't say another word, picked up the ailing cripple in his arms, and carried her inside.

There was no talkativeness or general social affability in Selivan; he avoided people and even seemed afraid of them; he never appeared in town, and nobody saw his wife at all after he brought her there in the dung cart. Since then many years had gone by, the young people of that time had already aged, and the inn at the fork had fallen further into decrepitude and ruin; but Selivan and his poor cripple still lived in it and, to the general amazement, paid some rent to the merchant's heirs.

Where did this strange man earn all that was necessary for his own needs and what he had to pay for the completely ruined inn? Everybody knew that *not one* traveler had *ever* stopped at it, that *not one* driver had fed his horses there, and yet Selivan, while he lived in want, had not yet died of hunger.

That was the question the neighboring peasants puzzled over, though not for very long. Soon they all realized that Selivan kept company with the unclean powers . . . These unclean powers set up all sorts of profitable deals for him, which for ordinary people were even impossible.

It's a known thing that the devil and his helpers have a great eagerness to do people all sorts of evil; but they especially like taking people's souls out of them unexpectedly, so that they have no time to purify themselves by repentance. If some human being helps them in their schemes, all the unclean powers—that is, all the wood demons, water demons, and kikimoras—willingly do him various favors, though on very stiff conditions. A man who helps demons must follow them to hell himself—sooner or later, but inevitably. Selivan found himself precisely in that fatal situation. In order to live somehow in his ruined little house, he had long since sold his soul to several devils at once, and after that they had begun to use the strongest measures to drive travelers to his inn. No one ever came out of Selivan's again. It was done in such a way that the wood demons, in collusion with the kikimoras, would suddenly raise a storm or blizzard towards evening, so that the man on the road would get confused and hurry to hide wherever he could from the raging elements. Selivan would at once pull a clever trick: he would put a light in his window, and by that light would draw in merchants with fat moneybags, noblemen with secret strongboxes, and priests in fur hats all lined with banknotes. It was a trap. Of those who went through Selivan's gates, not one ever came back out. What Selivan did with them nobody knew.

Grandpa Ilya, having come to that point, would just move his hand through the air and say imposingly:

"The owl flies, the hawk glides . . . nothing to be seen: storm, blizzard, and . . . mother night—all's out of sight."

Not to lower myself in Grandpa Ilya's opinion, I pretended to understand what the words "The owl flies and the hawk glides" meant, but I understood only one thing, that Selivan was some sort of all-around spook, whom it was extremely dangerous to meet . . . God forbid it should happen to anybody.

I tried, nevertheless, to verify the terrible stories about Selivan with other people, but they all said the same thing word for word. They all looked upon Selivan as a fearful spook, and, like Grandpa Ilya, they all sternly warned me "not to tell anybody about Selivan at home." Following the miller's advice, I observed this muzhik commandment until one especially frightening occasion when I myself fell into Selivan's clutches.

VI

In winter, when the storm windows were put up, I couldn't see Grandpa Ilya and the other muzhiks as often as before. I was protected from the frosts, while they were all left to work in the cold, during which one of them got into an unpleasant episode that brought Selivan onstage again.

At the very beginning of winter, Ilya's nephew, the muzhik Nikolai, went to celebrate his name day in Kromy and didn't come back, and two weeks later he was found at the edge of Selivan's forest. Nikolai was sitting on a stump, his chin propped on his stick, and, by the look of it, resting after such great fatigue that he didn't notice how a blizzard had buried him up to the knees in snow and foxes had taken bites from his nose and cheeks.

Nikolai had obviously lost his way, gotten tired, and frozen to death; but everybody knew it had happened with some hidden purpose and Selivan was behind it. I learned of it from the maids, of whom there were many in our house, almost all of them named Annushka. There was big Annushka, little Annushka, pockmarked Annushka, round Annushka, and also another Annushka nicknamed "Snappy." This last one was a sort of journalist and reporter among us. She received her pert nickname for her lively and playful character.

There were only two maids who weren't called Annushka—Neonila and Nastya, whose position was somewhat special, because they were specially educated in Madame Morozova's fashion shop in Orel; and there were also three errand girls in the house—Oska, Moska, and Roska. The baptismal name of one was Matrena, of another Raïssa, and what Oska's real name was I don't know. Moska, Oska, and Roska were still in their nonage and were therefore treated scornfully by everybody. They ran around barefoot and had no right to sit on chairs, but sat low down, on footstools. Their duties included various humiliating tasks, such as cleaning basins, taking out washtubs, walking the lapdogs, and running errands for the kitchen staff and to the village. Nowadays there is no such superfluous servantry in country households, but back then it seemed necessary.

All our maids and errand girls, naturally, knew a lot about the fearful Selivan, near whose inn the muzhik Nikolai froze to death. On this occasion they now remembered all of Selivan's old pranks, which I hadn't known about before. It now came to light that once, when the coachman Konstantin had gone to town to buy beef, he had heard a pitiful moaning coming from the window of Selivan's place and the words: "Aie, my hand hurts! Aie, he's cutting my finger off!"

Big Annushka, the maid, explained that during a blizzard Selivan had seized a carriage with a whole family of gentlefolk, and he was slowly cutting off the fingers of all the children one by one. This horrible barbarism frightened me terribly. Then something still more horrible, and inexplicable besides, happened to the cobbler Ivan. Once, when he was sent to town for shoemaking supplies and, having tarried, was returning home in the evening darkness, a little blizzard arose—and that gave Selivan the greatest pleasure. He immediately got up and went out to the fields, to blow about in the darkness together with Baba Yaga,[3] the wood demons, and kikimoras. And the cobbler knew it and was on his guard, but not enough. Selivan leaped out right in front of his nose and barred the way . . . The horse stopped. But the cobbler, luckily for him, was brave by nature and highly resourceful. He went up to Selivan, as if amiably, and said, "Hi there," and at the same time stuck him right in the stomach with his biggest and sharpest awl, which he had in his sleeve. The stomach is the only place where a sorcerer can be mortally wounded, but Selivan saved himself by immediately turning into a stout milepost, in which the cobbler's sharp tool stuck so fast that the cobbler couldn't pull it out, and he had to part with the awl, much though he needed it in his work.

This last incident was even an offensive mockery of honest people, and everyone became convinced that Selivan was indeed not only a great villain and a cunning sorcerer, but also an impudent fellow, who must be given no quarter. They decided to teach him a harsh lesson; but Selivan was also no slouch and learned a new trick: he began to "shapeshift," that is, at the slightest danger, even simply at each encounter, he would change his human look and turn before everyone's eyes into various animate and inanimate objects. True, thanks to the general uprising against him, he suffered a bit despite all his adroitness, but to eradicate him proved impossible, and the struggle against him even assumed a somewhat ridiculous aspect, which offended and angered everyone still more. Thus, for instance, after the cobbler pierced him as hard as he could with his awl, and Selivan saved himself only by managing to turn into a milepost, several people saw the awl stuck into a real milepost. They even tried to pull it out, but the awl broke off, and they brought the cobbler only the worthless wooden handle.

After that, Selivan walked about the forest as if he hadn't been stuck at all, and turned himself so earnestly into a boar that he ate acorns with pleasure, as if such fruit were suited to his taste. But most often he came out on his tattered black roof in the guise of a red rooster and from there crowed "Cock-a-doodle-doo!" Everybody knew, naturally, that he was not interested in crowing "Cock-a-doodle-doo," but was spying out whether anyone was coming, so as to prompt the wood demon or kikimora to stir up a good storm and worry him to death. In short, the local people figured out all his tricks so well that they never got caught in the villain's nets and even took good revenge on Selivan for his perfidy. Once, having turned himself into a boar, he ran into the blacksmith Savely, who was returning on foot from a wedding in Kromy, and they had a real fight, but the blacksmith came out victorious, because, luckily, he happened to have a heavy cudgel in his hand. The were-boar pretended he had no wish to pay the slightest attention to the blacksmith and, grunting heavily, chomped his acorns; but the keen-witted blacksmith saw through his stratagem, which was to let him go by and then attack him from the rear, knock him down, and eat him instead of the acorns. The blacksmith decided to forestall trouble; he raised his cudgel high above his head and whacked the boar on the snout so hard that it squealed pitifully, fell down, and never got up again. And when, after that, the blacksmith began making a hasty getaway, Selivan assumed his human form again and looked at him for a long time from his porch—obviously having the most unfriendly intentions towards him.

After this terrible encounter, the blacksmith even came down with a fever, and only cured himself by taking the quinine powder sent to him from our house as a treatment and scattering it to the winds.

The blacksmith passed for a very reasonable man and knew that neither quinine nor any other pharmaceutical medication could do anything against magic. He waited it out, tied a knot in a thick string, and threw it onto the dung heap to rot. That put an end to it all, because as soon as the string and the knot rotted, Selivan's power was supposed to end. And so it happened. After this incident, Selivan never again turned into a pig, or at least decidedly no one since then ever met him in that slovenly guise.

With Selivan's pranks in the form of a red rooster things went even more fortunately: the cross-eyed mill hand Savka, a most daring young lad, who acted with great foresight and adroitness, took up arms against him.

Having been sent to town once on the eve of a fair, he went mounted on a very lazy and obstinate horse. Knowing his character, Savka brought along on the sly, just in case, a good birch stick, with which he hoped to imprint a souvenir on the flanks of his melancholy Bucephalus. He had already managed to do something of the sort and had broken the character of his steed enough so that, losing patience, he began to gallop a little.

Selivan, not expecting Savka to be so well armed, jumped out on the eaves as a rooster the moment he arrived and began turning around, rolled his eyes in all directions, and sang "Cock-a-doodle-doo!" Savka wasn't cowed by the sorcerer, but, on the contrary, said to him: "Eh, brother, never fear—you won't get near," and without thinking twice he deftly hurled the stick at him, so that he didn't even finish his "cock-a-doodle-doo" and fell down dead. Unfortunately, he didn't fall outside, but into the courtyard, where, once he touched the ground, it cost him nothing to go back to his natural human form. He became Selivan and, running out, took off after Savka brandishing the same stick with which Savka had given him the treatment when he sang as a rooster on the roof.

According to Savka, Selivan was so furious this time that it might have gone badly for him; but Savka was a quick-witted fellow and knew very well one extremely useful trick. He knew that his lazy horse forgot his laziness at once the moment he was turned towards home, to his trough. That was what he did. The moment Selivan rushed at him armed with the stick, Savka turned the horse around and vanished. He came galloping home, his face distorted by fear, and told about the frightful incident that had befallen him only the next day. And thank God he started to speak, because they feared he might be left mute forever.

VII

Instead of the cowed Savka, another braver ambassador was dispatched, who reached Kromy and came back safely. However, this one, too, on completing the trip, said it would have been easier for him to fall through the earth than to go past Selivan's inn. Other people felt the same: the fear became general; but to make up for it they all combined their efforts to keep an eye on Selivan. Wherever and whatever shape he took, he was always found out, and they strove to cut off his harmful existence in all its guises. Let Selivan appear by his inn as a sheep or a calf—he was recognized and beaten anyway, and he couldn't manage to hide in any of his guises. Even when he rolled out to the road one time as a new, freshly tarred cart wheel and lay in the sun to dry, his ruse was discovered and smart people smashed the wheel to bits, so that both the hub and the spokes flew in all directions.

The Spook

Of all these incidents that made up the heroic epopee of my childhood, I promptly received quick and highly trustworthy intelligence. The swiftness of the news was owing in large part to the fact that there was always an excellent itinerant public that came to do their grinding at our mill. While the millstones ground the grain, their mouths with still greater zeal ground out all sorts of drivel, and from there all the interesting stories were brought to the maids' room by Moska and Roska, and were then conveyed to me in the best possible versions, and I would set to thinking about them all night, creating very amusing situations for myself and Selivan, for whom, despite all I had heard about him, I nursed in the depths of my soul a most heartfelt attraction. I believed irrevocably that the time would come when Selivan and I would meet in some extraordinary way—and would even love each other far more than I loved Grandpa Ilya, in whom I disliked it that one of his eyes, namely the left one, always laughed a little.

I simply couldn't believe for long that Selivan had done all his supernatural wonders with evil intent towards people, and I liked very much to think about him; and usually, as soon as I began to doze off, I dreamed about him—quiet, kind, and even hurt. I had never yet seen him, and was unable to picture his face to myself from the distorted descriptions of the talebearers, but I saw his eyes as soon as I closed my own. They were big eyes, perfectly blue and very kind. And while I slept, Selivan and I were in the most pleasant harmony: we found various secret little burrows in the forest, where we kept a lot of bread and butter and warm children's coats stashed away, which we would take, run to cottages we knew in the village, place them in a dormer window, knock to get somebody's attention, and run away.

I think those were the most beautiful dreams of my life, and I always regretted that when I woke up, Selivan turned back into a brigand, against whom every good man had to take every measure of precaution. I admit, I had no wish to lag behind the others, and while I had the warmest friendship with Selivan in my dreams, on waking I considered it not superfluous to protect myself from him even at a distance.

To that end, by way of no little flattery and other humiliations, I talked the housekeeper into giving me my father's old and very big Caucasian dagger, which she kept in the larder. I tied it to the chinstrap I had taken from my uncle's hussar shako and cleverly hid this weapon under the mattress at the head of my little bed. If Selivan had appeared at night in our house, I would certainly have confronted him.

Neither my father nor my mother knew of this secret armory, and that was absolutely necessary, otherwise the dagger would, of course, have been taken from me, and then Selivan would have disturbed my peaceful sleep, because I was still terribly afraid of him. And meanwhile he was already making approaches to us, but our pert young girls recognized him at once. Selivan dared to appear in our house as a big red-brown rat. At first he simply made noise in the larder at night, but then he got down into a big tub made from a hollowed linden trunk, at the bottom of which, covered by a sieve, lay sausages and other good things set aside for receiving guests. Here Selivan wanted to cause us serious domestic trouble—probably to pay us back for the troubles he had suffered from our muzhiks. Turning into a red-brown rat, he jumped to the bottom of the tub, pushed aside the stone weight that lay on the sieve, and ate all the sausages. But then there was no way he could jump back out of the high tub. This time, by all appearances, Selivan couldn't possibly escape the well-deserved punishment that Snappy Annushka, the quickest of the girls, volunteered to mete out to him. For that she appeared with a kettle full of boiling water and an old fork. Annushka's plan was first to scald the were-rat with the boiling water, and then stab him with the fork and throw the dead body into the weeds, to be eaten by crows. But in carrying out the execution, Round Annushka made a clumsy move: she splashed boiling water on Snappy Annushka's hand. The girl dropped the fork from pain, and at the same moment the rat bit her finger and, running up her sleeve with remarkable agility, jumped out, and, having put a general fright into all those present, made himself invisible.

My parents, who looked upon this incident with ordinary eyes, ascribed the stupid outcome of the hunt to the clumsiness of our Annushkas; but we, who knew the secret springs of the matter, also knew that it was impossible to do any better here, because it was not a simple rat, but the were-rat Selivan. However, we didn't dare tell that to the adults. As simple-hearted folk, we feared criticism and the mockery of something we ourselves considered obvious and unquestionable.

Selivan didn't dare to cross the front doorstep in any of his guises, as it seemed to me, because he knew something about my dagger.

And to me that was both flattering and annoying, because, as a matter of fact, I was tired of nothing but talk and rumors and was burning with a passionate desire to meet Selivan face-to-face.

That finally turned into a languishing in me, in which I spent the whole long winter with its interminable evenings, but when the first spring torrents came down the hills, an event took place that upset the whole order of our life and unleashed the dangerous impulses of unrestrained passions.

VIII

The event was unexpected and sad. At the height of the spring thaw, when, according to a popular expression, "a puddle can drown a bull," a horseman came galloping from my aunt's far-off estate with the fateful news of my grandfather's dangerous illness.

A long journey over such bad spring roads presented a great danger; but that didn't stop my mother and father, and they set out on their way at once. They had to go seventy miles, and in nothing but a simple cart, because it was impossible to make the trip in any other kind of carriage. The cart was accompanied by two horsemen carrying long poles. They went ahead and felt out the depth of the potholes. The house and I were left in the care of a special interim committee composed of various persons from various departments. Big Annushka was in charge of all persons of the female sex, down to Oska and Roska; but the high moral supervision was entrusted to Dementievna, the headman's wife. Our intellectual guidance—in the sense of the observing of feasts and Sundays—was confided to Apollinary Ivanovich, the deacon's son, who, having been expelled from the class of rhetoric in the seminary,[4] had been attached to my person as a tutor. He taught me the Latin declensions and generally prepared me so that the next year I could enter the first class of the Orel school not as a complete savage likely to show surprise at the Latin grammar of Beliustin and the French grammar of Lhomond.

Apollinary was a young man of worldly tendency and planned to enter the "chancellery," or, in modern parlance, to become a clerk in the Orel provincial office, where his uncle served in a most interesting post. If some police officer or other failed to observe some regulation or other, Apollinary's uncle was sent as a one-horse "special envoy" at the expense of the culprits. He rode about without paying anything for his horse, and, besides that, received gifts and offerings from the culprits, and saw different towns and many different people of different ranks and customs. My Apollinary also set his sights on achieving such happiness in time, and could hope to do much more than his uncle, because he possessed two great talents that could be very pleasing in social intercourse: Apollinary could play two songs on the guitar, "A Girl Went to Cut Nettles," and another, much more difficult one, "On a Rainy Autumn Evening," and—what was still more rare in the provinces at that time—he could compose beautiful verses for the ladies, which, as a matter of fact, was what got him expelled from the seminary.

Despite our difference in age, Apollinary and I were on a friendly footing, and, as befits faithful friends, we kept each other's secrets. In this case, his share came out a bit smaller than mine: all my secrets were limited to the dagger under my mattress, while I was obliged to keep deeply hidden two secrets entrusted to me: the first concerned the pipe hidden in his wardrobe, in which of an evening Apollinary smoked sour-sweet white Nezhin roots into the stove,[5] and the second was still more important—here the matter had to do with verses composed by Apollinary in honor of some "light-footed Pulcheria."

The verses seemed very bad, but Apollinary said that to judge them correctly, it was necessary to see the impression they produced when read nicely, with feeling, to a tender and sensitive woman.

That posed a great and, in our situation, even insurmountable difficulty, because there were no little ladies in our house, and when grown-up young ladies came to visit, Apollinary didn't dare suggest that they be his listeners, because he was very shy, and among the young ladies of our acquaintance there were some great scoffers.

Necessity taught Apollinary to invent a compromise—namely, to declaim the ode to "Light-footed Pulcheria" before our maid Neonila, who had adopted various polished city manners in Madame Morozova's fashion shop and, to Apollinary's mind, ought to have the refined feelings necessary in order to feel the merits of poetry.

Being very young, I was afraid to give my teacher advice in his poetic experiments, but I considered his plan to declaim verses before the seamstress risky. I was judging by myself, naturally, and though I did take into account that young Neonila was familiar with some subjects of city circles, it could hardly be that she would understand the language of lofty poetry in which Apollinary sang of Pulcheria. Besides, in the ode to "Light-footed Pulcheria" there were such exclamations as "Oh, you cruel one!" or "Vanish from my sight!" and the like. By nature Neonila was of a timid and shy character, and I was afraid she would take it personally and most certainly burst into tears and run away.

But worst of all was that, with the usual strict order of our domestic life, this poetic rehearsal thought up by the rhetorician was absolutely impossible. Neither the time, nor the place, nor even all the other conditions favored Neonila's listening to Apollinary's verses and being their first appreciator. However, the anarchy that installed itself with my parents' departure changed all that, and the student decided to take advantage of it. Now, forgetting all difference in our positions, we played cards every evening, and Apollinary even smoked his Nezhin roots around the house and sat in my father's chair in the dining room, which offended me a little. Besides that, at his insistence, we played blind man's buff several times, from which my brother and I wound up with bruises. We also played hide-and-seek, and once even organized a formal fête with lots of food. It seems all this was done "on the house," as many thoughtless carousers reveled in those days, down whose ruinous path we were drawn by the rhetorician. To this day I don't know who then made the suggestion that we gather a whole sack of the ripest hazelnuts, extracted from the mouse holes (where one usually finds only nuts of the highest quality). Besides the nuts, we had three gray paper bags of yellow sugar lollipops, sunflower seeds, and candied pears. These last really stuck to your hands and were hard to wash off.

Since this last fruit enjoyed special attention, pears were given only as prizes in the game of forfeits. Moska, Oska, and Roska, being essentially insignificant, got no candied fruit at all. The game of forfeits included Annushka, and me, and my tutor Apollinary, who proved to be very clever and inventive. All this took place in the drawing room, where only very honored guests used to sit. And there, in the daze of passionate merriment, some desperate spirit got into Apollinary, and he conceived a still bolder undertaking. He decided to declaim his ode in a grandiose and even terrifying setting, where the strongest nerves would be subjected to the highest tension. He began inciting us all to go together the next Sunday to pick lily of the valley in Selivan's forest. And in the evening, when he and I were going to bed, he revealed to me that the lily of the valley was only a pretext, while the main goal was to read the verses in that terrible setting.

On one side would be the effect of the fear of Selivan, on the other the fear of the terrible verses . . . How would it turn out, and could anyone bear it?

And, imagine, we did venture to do it.

In the animation that gripped us all on that memorable spring evening, it seemed to us that we were all brave and could pull off the desperate stunt safely. In fact, there would be a lot of us, and besides I would, naturally, bring along my huge Caucasian dagger.

I admit, I wanted very much for all the others to be armed according to their strength and possibilities, but I didn't meet with any due attention or readiness for that. Apollinary took only his pipe and guitar, and the girls went with trivets, skillets, a kettle of eggs, and a cast-iron pot. In the pot they intended to boil wheat porridge with lard, and in the skillets to fry eggs, and in that sense they were excellent; but in the sense of defending ourselves in case of possible mischief on Selivan's part, they meant decidedly nothing.

To tell the truth, however, I was displeased with my companions for something else as well—namely, that I didn't feel on their part the same consideration for Selivan that I myself was imbued with. They did fear him, but somehow light-mindedly, and even risked some critical bantering about him. One Annushka said she would take a rolling pin and kill him with it, and Snappy laughingly said she could bite him, and with that she bared her extremely white teeth and bit off a piece of wire. All this was somehow unserious; but the rhetorician surpassed them all. He denied the existence of Selivan altogether—said that there had never even been such a person, and that he was simply a figment of the imagination, like the Python, Cerberus, and their ilk.[6]

I saw then for the first time how far a man was capable of being carried away by negation! What was the use, then, of any rhetoric, if it allowed one to put on the same level of probability the mythological Python and Selivan, the reality of whose existence was confirmed by a multitude of manifest events?

I did not yield to that temptation and preserved my belief in Selivan. More than that, I believed that the rhetorician was certain to be punished for his unbelief.

However, if one did not take this philosophizing seriously, then the projected outing in the forest promised much merriment, and no one either wished or was able to make himself prepare for occurrences of another sort. And yet good sense should have made us highly cautious in that cursed forest, where we would be, so to speak, in the very jaws of the beast.

They all thought only of what fun it would be to wander about in the forest, where everybody was afraid to go, but they were not. They reflected on how we would go through the whole dangerous forest, hallooing and calling to each other, and leaping over holes and gullies where the last snow was crumbling away, and never thought whether all this would be approved of when our higher authorities returned. On the other hand, however, we did have in mind making two big bouquets of the best lily of the valley for mama's dressing table, and using the rest to make a fragrant extract, which would serve for the whole coming summer as an excellent lotion against sunburn.

IX

The impatiently awaited Sunday came, we left Dementievna, the headman's wife, to look after the house, and set out for Selivan's forest. The whole public went on foot, keeping to the raised shoulders, which were already dry and where the first emerald-green grass was sprouting, while the train, which consisted of a cart hitched to an old dun horse, followed on the road. In the cart lay Apollinary's guitar and the girls' jackets, taken along in case of bad weather. I was the driver, and behind me, in the quality of passengers, sat Roska and the other little girls, one of whom carefully cradled a bag of eggs on her knees, while the other had general charge of various objects, but mainly supported with her hand my huge dagger, which I had slung over my shoulder on an old hussar cord from my uncle's saber, and which dangled from side to side, interfering considerably with my movements and distracting my attention from guiding the horse.

The girls, walking along the shoulder, sang: "I plough the field, I sow the hemp," and the rhetorician doubled them in the bass. Some muzhiks we met on the way bowed and asked:

"What's up?"

The Annushkas replied:

"We're going to take Selivan prisoner."

The muzhiks wagged their heads and said:

"Besotted fools!"

We were indeed in some sort of daze, overcome by an irrepressible, half-childish need to run, sing, laugh, and do everything recklessly.

But meanwhile an hour's driving on a bad road began to have an adverse effect on me—I was sick of the old horse, and the eagerness to hold the rope reins in my hands had gone cold in me; but nearby, on the horizon, Selivan's forest showed blue, and everything livened up again. My heart pounded and ached as Varus's had when he entered the forest of Teutoburg.[7] And just then a hare leaped out from under the melting snow on the shoulder and, crossing the road, took off over the field.

"Phooey on you!" the Annushkas shouted after him.

They all knew that meeting a hare never portends anything good. I also turned coward and seized my dagger, but, in the effort of drawing it from the rusty scabbard, I didn't notice that I had let go of the reins, and I quite unexpectedly found myself under the overturned cart, which the horse, who pulled towards the shoulder to get some grass, turned over in the most proper fashion, so that all four wheels were up, and Roska and I and all our provisions were underneath.

This misfortune befell us in a moment, but its consequences were countless: Apollinary's guitar was smashed to bits, and the broken eggs ran down and plastered our eyes with their sticky content. What's more, Roska was howling.

I was utterly overwhelmed and abashed, and so much at a loss that I even wished they would rather not free us at all, but I already heard the voices of all the Annushkas, who, while working to free us, explained the reason for our fall very much to my advantage. Neither I nor the horse was the reason: it was all Selivan's doing.

This was his first ruse to keep us from coming to his forest, but it didn't frighten anyone very much; on the contrary, it filled us all with great indignation and increased our resolve to carry out at all costs the whole program we had conceived.

It was only necessary to lift the cart and turn it right side up, wash off the unpleasant egg slime in some brook, and see what remained after the catastrophe of the things we had brought as the day's provisions for our numerous group.

All this got done somehow. Roska and I were washed in a brook that ran just at the edge of Selivan's forest, and when my eyes opened, the world seemed very unsightly to me. The girls' pink dresses and my new blue cashmere jacket were good for nothing: the dirt and egg that covered them ruined them completely and couldn't be washed off without soap, which we had not brought with us. The pot and the skillet were cracked, the trivet's legs were broken off and lay about, and all that was left of Apollinary's guitar was the neck with strings twined around it. The bread and other dry goods were covered with mud. At the very least, we were threatened with a whole day of hunger, to say nothing of the other horrors that could be felt in everything around us. The wind whistled over the stream in the valley, and the black forest, not yet covered with green, rustled and ominously waved its branches at us.

Our spirits sank considerably—especially in Roska, who was cold and wept. But still we decided to enter Selivan's kingdom, and let come what might.

In any case, the same adventure could not repeat itself without some sort of change.

X

We all crossed ourselves and began to enter the forest. We entered timidly and hesitantly, but each of us concealed his timidity from the others. We all simply agreed to call out to each other as often as we could. However, there was no great need for that, because nobody went very far in, and, as if by chance, we all kept crowding towards the edge and strung ourselves out along it. Only Apollinary proved braver than the rest and went a little further into the depths; he was concerned with finding the most remote and frightening spot, where his declaiming could produce the most terrible impression on the listening girls. But Apollinary had no sooner disappeared from sight than the forest resounded with his piercing, frenzied cry. No one could imagine what danger Apollinary had met with, but everybody abandoned him and ran headlong out of the forest to the clearing, and then, without looking back, ran further down the road home. All the Annushkas fled, and all the Moskas, and after them, still crying out from fear, sped our pedagogue himself; and my little brother and I were left alone.

There was no one left of all our company: not only the people, but even the horse, following the inhuman example of the people, abandoned us. Frightened by their cries, it tossed its head and, turning away from the forest, raced home, scattering over the potholes and bumps whatever was still left in the cart.

This was not a retreat, it was a full and most shameful rout, because it was accompanied by the loss not only of the train, but of all good sense, and we children were thrown on the mercy of fate.

God knows what we would have to endure in our helplessly orphaned condition, which was the more dangerous because we couldn't find the way home by ourselves, and our footgear consisted of soft goatskin boots with thin soles, not at all convenient for walking three miles over sodden paths, on which there were still cold puddles in many places. To complete the disaster, before my brother and I had time to fully realize all the horror of our situation, something rumbled through the forest and then a breath of cold dampness blew from the direction of the stream.

We looked across the hollow and saw, racing through the sky from the direction where our road lay and where our retinue had shamefully fled, a huge cloud laden with spring rain and the first spring thunder, when young girls wash themselves from silver spoons, so as to become whiter than silver themselves.

Seeing myself in this desperate situation, I was ready to burst into tears, and my little brother was already crying. He was all blue and trembling from fear and cold, and, with his head bent under a little bush, was fervently praying to God.

It seems God heeded his childish prayer and invisible salvation was sent to us. At the same moment when the thunder rumbled and we were losing our last courage, we heard a crunching in the forest behind the bushes, and from the thick branches of a tall hazel the broad face of a muzhik unknown to us peeked out. That face seemed so frightening that we cried out and rushed headlong towards the stream.

Beside ourselves, we crossed the hollow, tumbled down the wet, crumbling bank, and straightaway found ourselves up to the waist in the turbid water, our legs sunk knee-deep in mire.

It was impossible to run any further. The stream further on was too deep for our small size; we couldn't hope to cross it, and, besides, zigzags of lightning were now flashing terribly on its water—they quivered and meandered like fiery serpents, as if hiding among last year's reeds.

Finding ourselves in the water, we seized each other's hands and stood frozen there, while from above us heavy drops of rain were already beginning to fall. But this frozenness saved us from great danger, which we could in no way have avoided if we had gone one step further into the water.

We might easily have slipped and fallen, but fortunately we were embraced by two dark, sinewy arms, and the same muzhik who had looked at us so frighteningly from the hazel said gently:

"Ah, you silly boys, look where you've gotten to!"

And with that he picked us up and carried us across the stream.

Coming out on the other bank, he lowered us to the ground, took off his short jacket, which was fastened at the collar by a round brass button, and wiped our wet feet with it.

We looked at him all the while in complete bewilderment and felt ourselves wholly in his power, but—wondrous thing—the features of his face were quickly changing before our eyes. Not only did we see nothing frightening in them now, but, on the contrary, his face seemed to us very kind and pleasant.

He was a sturdy, thickset muzhik with some gray in his hair and mustache—his beard was a clump and also graying, his eyes were lively, quick, and serious, but on his lips there was something close to a smile.

Having wiped as much as he could of the dirt and slime from our feet with the skirt of his jacket, he smiled outright and spoke again:

"You just . . . never mind . . . don't be scared . . ."

With that he looked around and went on:

"Never mind. There's a big rainstorm coming!" (By then it had already come.) "You boys won't make it on foot."

We only wept silently in reply.

"Never mind, never mind, don't howl, I'll carry you!" he said and wiped my brother's tear-stained face with his palm, which immediately left dirty streaks on it.

"See what dirty hands the muzhik's got," our deliverer said and passed his palm over my brother's face again in the other direction, which didn't decrease the dirt, but only added shading in the other direction.

"You won't make it . . . I'll take you . . . No, you won't make it . . . and you'll lose your little boots in the mud. Do you know how to ride?" the muzhik went on again.

I got up enough courage to utter a word and said:

"Yes."

"Well, all right then!" he said, and in a trice he hoisted me up on one shoulder and my brother on the other, told us to hold hands behind the back of his head, covered us with his jacket, held tight to our knees, and carried us with quick, long strides over the mud, which spread and squelched under his firmly treading feet, shod in big bast shoes.

We sat on his shoulders, covered with his jacket. That must have made for a giant figure, but we were comfortable: the jacket got soaked from the downpour and turned stiff, and we were dry and warm under it. We rocked on our bearer's shoulders like on a camel, and soon sank into some sort of cataleptic state, but came to ourselves by a spring on our farmstead. For me personally this had been a real, deep sleep, from which I did not awaken all at once. I remember that same muzhik taking us out of the jacket. He was surrounded now by all our Annushkas, and they were all tearing us from his hands and at the same time cursing him mercilessly for something, him and his jacket, which had protected us so well and which they now flung on the ground with the greatest contempt. Besides that, they also threatened him with my father's arrival, and with running to the village at once to call out the farm people with their flails and set the dogs on him.

I decidedly did not understand the reason for such cruel injustice, and that was not surprising, because at home, under the now ruling interim government, they had formed a conspiracy not to reveal anything to us about the man to whom we owed our salvation.

"You owe him nothing," our protectresses said. "On the contrary, it was he who caused it all."

From those words I guessed at once that we had been saved by none other than *Selivan* himself!

XI

And so it was. The next day, in view of our parents' return, the fact was revealed to us, and we swore an oath that we would say nothing to our father and mother about the incident that had occurred with us.

In those days when there were still serfs, it sometimes happened that landowners' children nursed the most tender feelings for household serfs and kept their secrets faithfully. That was so with us. We even concealed as well as we could the sins and transgressions of "our people" from our parents. Such relations are mentioned in many works describing the landowner's life of that time. As for me, our childhood friendship with our former serfs still constitutes my warmest and most pleasant memory. Through them we knew all the needs and cares of the poor life of their relations and friends in the village, and we learned to *pity the people*. But, unfortunately, those good people were not always fair themselves and were sometimes capable of casting a dark shadow on their neighbor for no important reason, regardless of the harmful consequences it might have. That is how "the people" acted with Selivan, of whose true character and principles they had no wish to know anything substantial, but boldly, not afraid of sinning against justice, spread rumors about him, which in the eyes of all made him into a *spook*. And, surprisingly, everything that was said about him not only seemed probable, but even had some visible tokens which could make one think that Selivan was in fact a bad man and that horrible villainies took place near his solitary dwelling.

That was what happened now, when we were scolded by those whose duty it was to protect us: not only did they shift all the blame onto Selivan, who had saved us from the storm, but they even heaped a new accusation on him. Apollinary and all the Annushkas told us that, when Apollinary noticed a pretty hill in the forest, which he thought it would be good to declaim from, he ran to that hill across a little gully filled with last year's fallen leaves, and stumbled there over something soft. This "something soft" turned under Apollinary's feet and he fell, and as he got up he saw that it was the corpse of a young peasant woman. He noticed that the corpse was dressed in a clean white sarafan with red embroidery, and . . . its throat was cut, and blood was pouring from it . . .

Such a terrible unexpectedness could, of course, frighten a man and make him cry out—which was what he did; but the incomprehensible and surprising thing was that Apollinary, as I said, was far from all the others and the only one to stumble over the corpse of the murdered woman, yet all the Annushkas and Roskas swore to God that they had also *seen* the corpse . . .

"Otherwise," they said, "why would we be so frightened?"

And I'm convinced to this day that they weren't lying, that they were deeply convinced that they had seen a murdered woman in

Selivan's forest, in a clean peasant dress with red embroidery, with her throat cut and blood flowing from it . . . How could that be?

Since I'm not writing fiction, but what actually happened, I must pause here and add that this incident remained forever unexplained in our house. No one but Apollinary could have seen the murdered woman, who, according to his own words, was lying in a hollow under the leaves, because no one but Apollinary was there. And yet they all swore that they had all seen the dead woman appear in the twinkling of an eye wherever any of them looked. Besides, had Apollinary himself actually seen this woman? It was hardly possible, because it had happened during the thaw, when not all the snow had melted yet. The leaves had lain under the snow *since autumn*, yet Apollinary saw a body dressed in a clean, white, embroidered dress, and blood was still flowing from the wound . . . Nothing like that could actually be, and yet they all crossed themselves and swore that they had seen the woman just as she's been described. And afterwards we were all afraid to sleep at night, and we were all horrified, as if we had committed a crime. Soon I, too, became persuaded that my brother and I had also seen the murdered woman. A general fear set in among us, which ended with the whole affair being revealed to my parents, and my father wrote a letter to the police chief—and he came to us wearing the longest saber and secretly questioned everybody in my father's study. Apollinary was even called in twice, and the second time the police chief reprimanded him so severely that, when he came out, both his ears were fiery red and one was even bleeding.

That, too, we *all saw*.

But however it was, our tall tales caused Selivan much grief: his place was searched, his whole forest was combed, and he himself was kept under guard for a long time, but nothing suspicious was found, and no traces of the murdered woman we had all seen turned up either. Selivan went back home again, but that didn't help him in public opinion: after that, everybody knew he was an undoubted, though elusive, villain, and nobody would have anything to do with him. As for me, so that I wouldn't be exposed to the strong influence of the poetic element, I was taken to a "noble boarding school," where I began to acquire a general education in perfect tranquillity, until the approach of the Christmas holidays, when it was time for me to go home, again inevitably passing Selivan's inn, and seeing great horrors in it with my own eyes.

XII

Selivan's bad repute earned me great prestige among my boarding school comrades, with whom I shared my knowledge of this horrible man. None of my schoolmates had yet experienced such horrific sensations as I could boast of, and now, when I was faced with driving past Selivan again—to that no one could remain unconcerned and indifferent. On the contrary, most of my comrades pitied me and said straight out that they wouldn't want to be in my place, though two or three daredevils envied me and boasted that they would like very much to meet Selivan face-to-face. But two of them were inveterate braggarts, while the third could very well not fear anyone, because, according to him, his grandmother had an *antique Venetian ring* with a *tavousi stone* in it, which made a man "inaccessible to any trouble."* In my family there was no such jewel, and, besides, I was supposed to make my Christmas journey not with our own horses, but with my aunt, who had sold her house in Orel just before the holidays and, having received thirty thousand roubles for it, was coming to us to buy an estate in our parts that my father had long ago negotiated for her.

To my vexation, my aunt's departure had been delayed a whole two days by some important business matters, and we left Orel only on the morning before Christmas.

We traveled in a roomy bast-covered sleigh hitched to a troika, with the coachman Spiridon and the young footman Boriska. In the sleigh were my aunt, myself, my boy cousin, my little girl cousins, and the nanny Lyubov Timofeevna.

With decent horses on a good road, one could reach our estate from Orel in five or six hours. We arrived in Kromy at two o'clock and stopped at a merchant's we knew, to have tea and feed the horses. This was a usual stopover for us, and it was also necessary for the toilette of my little cousin, who was still in diapers.

The weather was good, close to being a thaw; but while we were

---

* A "tavousi stone"—a light sapphire with *peacock feather* reflections, in olden times considered a lifesaving talisman. Ivan the Terrible had such a stone in a ring. "A gold finger-ring, and in it a tavousi stone, and in that a look of cloudiness and a sort of effervescence." *Author.* (*Tavousi* is Persian for "peacock." *Trans.*)

feeding the horses, a slight chill set in, and then it began to "smoke"—
that is, a fine snow blew low over the ground.

My aunt hesitated whether to wait until it was over or, on the
contrary, to hurry up and start sooner, so as to get home before
the real storm broke.

We had some fourteen miles left to go. The coachman and the
footman, who wanted to see in the holiday with their families and
friends, assured us that we had time to make it safely, as long as we
didn't dawdle and set out soon.

My own wishes and my aunt's also corresponded fully to what
Spiridon and Boriska wanted. No one wanted to see in the holiday
in a strange house in Kromy. Besides, my aunt was mistrustful and
suspicious, and she now had a considerable sum of money with her,
placed in a little mahogany box, covered with a slipcase of thick
green frieze.

To spend the night in a strange house with such a large sum of
money seemed very unsafe to my aunt, and she decided to heed the
advice of our faithful servants.

At a little past three, our sleigh was hitched up and left Kromy
in the direction of the schismatic village of Kolchevo;[8] but we had
only just crossed the river Kroma over the ice when we felt as if we
suddenly didn't have enough air to take a deep breath. The horses
ran quickly, snorting and wagging their heads, which was a sure sign
that they also felt a lack of air. Meanwhile the sleigh raced along
with a peculiar lightness, as if it were being pushed from behind.
The wind was at our backs, and seemed to be urging us on with
redoubled speed towards some predestined boundary line. Soon,
however, our brisk path began to "stammer"; soft snowdrifts already
appeared along the road—they became more and more frequent,
and soon enough our former brisk path couldn't be seen at all.

My aunt peeked worriedly out of the window to ask the coachman
whether we had kept to the right road, but drew back at once, all
showered with fine, cold dust, and before we managed to catch the
attention of the men on the box, snow came rushing past in thick
flakes, the sky turned dark in an instant, and we found ourselves in
the grip of a real blizzard.

XIII

To go back to Kromy was as dangerous as to go on. It was probably more dangerous behind us, because there was the river, with several ice holes near the town, and we might easily not see them in the snowstorm and fall through the ice, while ahead there was the level steppe and only Selivan's forest at the fifth mile, which was no more dangerous in a storm, because it must even have been quieter in the forest. Besides, the road didn't go deep into the forest, but ran along the edge of it. The forest could only serve us as an indication that we were halfway home, and therefore the coachman Spiridon drove the horses more quickly.

The road kept getting more difficult and snowy: the former merry noise of the runners was forgotten; on the contrary, the sleigh crawled over crumbly snowdrifts and soon began lurching now this way, now that.

We lost our calm state of mind and began asking the footman and the coachman all the time about our situation, receiving uncertain and hesitant replies from them. They tried to instill in us a confidence in our safety, while feeling no such confidence themselves.

After half an hour of quick driving, with Spiridon whipping up the horses more and more often, we were cheered by the outcry:

"There's Selivan's forest coming in sight!"

"Is it far off?" asked my aunt.

"No, we've almost reached it."

That was as it should have been—we had already been driving for about an hour since Kromy, but another good half hour went by—we kept driving, and the whip snapped over the horses more and more often, but there was no forest.

"What's wrong? Where's Selivan's forest?"

No reply from the box.

"Where's the forest?" my aunt asked again. "Have we passed it?"

"No, we haven't," Spiridon replied in a muffled voice, as if from under a pillow.

"What does it mean?"

Silence.

"Come down here! Stop! Stop!"

My aunt stuck herself out from behind the flap, desperately cried "Stop!" with all her might, and fell back into the sleigh, bringing with her a whole cloud of snowy swirls, which, under the influence of the wind, did not settle at once, but trembled like hovering flies.

The coachman stopped the horses, and it was well he did, because their bellies were heaving heavily and they were staggering from fatigue. If they hadn't been given a rest at that moment, the poor animals would probably have collapsed.

"Where are you?" my aunt asked Boris, who had climbed down from the box.

He was unrecognizable. Before us stood not a man, but a pillar of snow. The collar of Boris's wolfskin coat was turned up and tied with a scrap of something. All this was plastered with snow and stuck together in a single lump.

Boris did not know the road and replied timidly that it *seemed* we had lost our way.

"Call Spiridon here."

To call vocally was impossible: the blizzard shut all mouths and itself roared and howled abroad with terrible violence.

Boriska climbed up on the box to pull Spiridon by the arm, but . . . he spent a very long time there, before he appeared beside the coach again and explained:

"Spiridon is not on the box!"

"Not on the box! Where is he then?"

"I don't know. He must have gone looking for the way. Let me go, too."

"Oh, Lord! No, don't—don't go. You'll both perish, and we'll all freeze to death."

On hearing those words, my cousin and I started to cry, but just then another pillar of snow appeared by the carriage beside Borisushka, still bigger and scarier.

This was Spiridon, who had put on a spare bast bag, which stood up around his head all packed with snow and frozen.

"Where did you see the forest, Spiridon?"

"I did see it, madam."

"Then where is it now?"

"You can see it now, too."

My aunt wanted to look, but she didn't see anything, it was all dark. Spiridon assured her that that was because her eyes were "unfamiliarized," but that he had seen the forest looming up for a very long time, but . . . the trouble was that, as we moved towards it, it moved away from us.

"Like it or not, it's all Selivashka's doing. He's luring us somewhere."

Hearing that, in such terrible weather, we had fallen into the hands of the villain Selivashka, my cousin and I cried even louder, but my aunt, who was born a country squire's daughter and was later a colonel's wife, was not so easily disconcerted as a town lady, for whom various adversities are less familiar. My aunt had experience and know-how, and they saved us in a situation which, in fact, was very dangerous.

XIV

I don't know whether my aunt believed or not in Selivan's evil enchantments, but she understood perfectly well that right now the most important thing for our salvation was that our horses not over-strain themselves. If the horses got exhausted and stopped, and if the cold intensified, we would all certainly perish. We'd be smoth-ered by the storm and frozen to death. But if the horses kept enough strength to plod on somehow, step by step, then we could nurse some hope that, going by the wind, they would somehow come out on the road and bring us to some dwelling. Let it be just an unheated hut on chicken's legs in a gully, still the blizzard wouldn't rage so fiercely in it, there'd be none of this jerking that we felt each time the horses tried to move their weary legs . . . There we could fall asleep . . . My cousin and I wanted terribly to sleep. In that respect the only lucky one among us was the baby girl, who slept on the nanny's breast under a warm hare coat, but the two of us weren't allowed to fall asleep. My aunt knew it was dangerous, because a sleeping person freezes sooner. Our situation was becoming worse by the minute, because the horses could barely walk, the coachman and the foot-man on the box began to freeze and to speak inarticulately, but my aunt stopped paying attention to me and my cousin, and we snuggled up to each other and fell asleep at once. I even had cheerful dreams: summer, our garden, our servants, Apollinary, and suddenly it all skipped over to our outing for lily of the valley and to Selivan, about whom I either heard something, or merely recalled something. It was all confused . . . I couldn't tell what was happening in dream and what in reality. I feel cold, hear the howling of the wind and the heavy flapping of the bast mat on the sleigh's roof, and right in front of my eyes stands Selivan, his jacket over his shoulder, and holding a lantern towards us in his outstretched hand . . . Is this an apparition, a dream, or a fantastic picture?

But it was not a dream, not a fantasy, but fate had in fact seen fit to bring us on that dreadful night to Selivan's dreadful inn, and we couldn't seek salvation anywhere else, because there was no other dwelling close by. And meanwhile we had with us my aunt's box, in which lay her thirty thousand roubles, constituting her entire fortune. With such tempting riches, how could we stay with such a suspicious man as Selivan?

Of course, we were done for! However, the choice could only be of which was better—to freeze in the blizzard, or die under the knife of Selivan and his evil accomplices?

XV

As in the brief moment when lightning flashes, the eye that was in darkness suddenly makes out a multitude of objects at once, so at the appearance of Selivan's lantern shining on us, I saw terror on all the faces in our disaster-stricken sleigh. The coachman and footman all but fell on their knees and remained transfixed in that position; my aunt drew back as if she wanted to push through the rear of the sleigh. The nanny pressed her face to the baby and suddenly shrank so much that she became no bigger than a baby herself.

Selivan stood there silently, but . . . in his unhandsome face I did not see the slightest malice. Only now he seemed more concentrated than when he had carried me on his shoulder. After looking us over, he asked quietly:

"Want to warm up?"

My aunt came to her senses sooner than the rest of us and answered:

"Yes, we're freezing . . . Save us!"

"Let God save you! Drive in—the cottage is heated."

And he stepped off the porch and lit the way for the sleigh.

Between the servants, my aunt, and Selivan there was an exchange of curt little phrases, betraying mistrust and fear of the host on our

side, and on Selivan's side a deeply concealed peasant irony and perhaps also a sort of mistrust.

The coachman asked whether there was any food for the horses.
Selivan replied:

"We'll look for some."

The footman Boris tried to find out if there were any *other* travelers.

"Come in—you'll see," replied Selivan.

The nanny said:

"Isn't it scary to stay with you?"

Selivan replied:

"If you're scared, don't go in."

My aunt stopped them, saying to each of them as softly as she
could:

"Stop it, don't squabble—it won't help anything. It's impossible to
go further. Let's stay, and God be with us."

And meanwhile, as this exchange was going on, we found ourselves in a plank-walled room, partitioned off from the rest of the
spacious cottage. My aunt went in first, and Boris brought her box in
after her. Then came my cousin and I with the nanny.

The box was placed on the table, and on the box was placed a
tallow-spattered tin candlestick with a small candle end, which
might last an hour, not more.

My aunt's practical quick-wittedness turned immediately to this
object—that is, to the candle.

"First of all, my dear," she said to Selivan, "bring me a new candle."

"There's a candle here."

"No, give me a new, whole candle!"

"A new, whole one?" Selivan repeated, resting one hand on the
table and the other on the box.

"Give me a new, whole candle at once."

"What do you need a whole one for?"

"That's none of your business—I won't be going to bed very soon.
Maybe the blizzard will pass and we'll go on."

"The blizzard won't pass."

"Well, it doesn't matter—I'll pay you for the candle."

"I know you'd pay, but I don't have a candle."

"Look for one, my dear!"

"No point looking for what's not there!"

An extremely weak, high voice unexpectedly mixed into this conversation from behind the partition.

"We have no candle, dear lady."

"Who is that speaking?" asked my aunt.

"My wife."

My aunt's face and the nanny's brightened a little. The nearby presence of a woman seemed to have something cheering about it.

"Is she sick or something?"

"Yes."

"With what?"

"An ailment. Go to bed, I need the candle end for the lantern. To bring the horses in."

And no matter what they said to him, Selivan stood his ground: he needed the candle end, and that was that. He promised to bring it back—but meanwhile he took it and left.

Whether Selivan kept his promise to bring the candle end back—I didn't see, because my cousin and I fell asleep again, though I kept being troubled by something. Through my sleep I heard the occasional whispering of my aunt and the nanny, and in that whispering I most often heard the word "box."

Obviously, the nanny and our other people knew that this coffer concealed a great treasure, and everybody had noticed that from the first moment it had caught the greedy attention of our untrustworthy host.

Possessed of great practical experience, my aunt clearly saw the necessity of submitting to circumstances, but then she at once gave orders that suited our dangerous situation.

To keep Selivan from murdering us, it was decided that no one should sleep. Orders were given to unharness the horses, but not to remove the collars, and the coachman and footman both had to sit in the sleigh: they mustn't separate, because Selivan would kill them one by one, and then we would be helpless. Then he would also murder us and bury us all under the floor, where he had already buried the numerous victims of his fiendishness. The footman and coachman couldn't stay in the cottage with us, because Selivan could then cut the tugs of the shaft horse, so that it would be impossible to harness up, or else simply hand the whole troika over to his comrades, whom he meanwhile kept hidden somewhere. In that case we would be quite unable to escape, but if the storm let up soon, as might very well happen, then the coachman would start hitching up, Boris would rap three times on the wall, and we would all rush to the yard, get in, and drive off. So as to be constantly at the ready, none of us got undressed.

I don't know whether the time went quickly or slowly for the others, but for us, the two sleeping boys, it flew by like a single moment, which suddenly ended in a most terrible awakening.

XVI

I woke up because I found it unbearably hard to breathe. When I opened my eyes, I saw precisely nothing, because it was dark all around me, but in the distance something seemed to show gray: that was the window. As in the light of Selivan's lantern I had at once seen the faces of all the people in that terrible scene, so now I instantly recalled everything—who I was, and where, and why I was there, and who were all my near and dear people in my father's house—and I felt pity, and pain, and fear for everything and everybody, and I wanted to cry out, but that was impossible. My mouth was tightly covered by a human hand, and a trembling voice was whispering to me:

"Not a sound, quiet, not a sound! We're lost—somebody's trying to break in."

I recognized my aunt's voice and pressed her hand as a sign that I had understood her request.

A rustling could be heard outside the door to the front hall . . . Someone was softly stepping from one foot to the other and feeling the wall with his hands . . . Obviously, the villain was looking for the door but couldn't find it . . .

My aunt pressed us to herself and whispered that God might still help us, because she had fortified the door. But at that same moment, probably because we had betrayed ourselves with our whispering and trembling, behind the plank partition where the rest of the cottage was and from where Selivan's wife had told us about the candle, someone ran and fell upon the one who was softly stealing up to our door, and they both started breaking it down; the door cracked, the table, bench, and suitcases my aunt had piled against it fell to the floor, and in the flung-open doorway appeared the face of Borisushka, with Selivan's powerful hands around his neck . . .

Seeing that, my aunt shouted at Selivan and rushed to Boris.

"Dear lady! God has saved us!" wheezed Boris.

Selivan took his hands away and stood there.

"Quick, quick, let's get out of here," said my aunt. "Where are our horses?"

"The horses are at the porch, dear lady, I was just going to call you . . . And this brigand . . . God has saved us, dear lady!" Boris babbled quickly, seizing my and my cousin's hands and gathering up all he could on his way. We all rushed out the door, jumped into the carriage, and went galloping off as fast as the horses could go. Selivan seemed painfully disconcerted and followed us with his eyes. He obviously knew that this would not go without consequences.

Outside it was now getting light, and before us in the east glowed the red, frosty Christmas dawn.

XVII

We reached home in no more than half an hour, talking incessantly all the way about the frights we had lived through. My aunt, the nanny, the coachman, and Boris kept interrupting each other and constantly crossing themselves, thanking God for our amazing salvation. My aunt told us she hadn't slept all night, because she kept hearing someone approaching the door and trying to open it. That had prompted her to block it with whatever she could find. She had also heard some suspicious whispering behind Selivan's partition, and it had seemed to her that he had quietly opened his door more than once, come out to the front hall, and quietly touched the latch of our door. Our nanny had also heard all that, though she, by her own admission, had fallen asleep on and off. The coachman and Boris had seen more than anyone else. Fearing for the horses, the coachman had never left them for a moment, but Borisushka had come to our door more than once, and each time he had come, Selivan had appeared in his doorway at the same moment. When the blizzard had died down towards dawn, the coachman and Boris had quietly harnessed the horses and quietly driven out through the gate, having opened it themselves; but when Boris had just as quietly come to our door again to lead us out, Selivan, seeing that the booty was slipping through his fingers, had fallen upon Boris and begun to choke him. Thank God, of course, he had not succeeded, and now he was no longer going to get off with suspicions alone, as he had so far: his evil intentions were all too clear and all too obvious, and everything had taken place not eye to eye with some one person, but before six witnesses, of whom my aunt alone was worth several owing to her importance, because the whole town knew her for an intelligent woman, and, despite her modest fortune, the governor visited her, and our then police chief owed her the arranging of his family happiness. At one word from her, he would, of course, immediately start investigating the matter while the trail was hot, and Selivan would not escape the noose he had thought to throw around our necks.

The circumstances themselves seemed to fall together so that everything pointed to immediate revenge for us on Selivan and to his punishment for the brutal attempt on our lives and property.

As we approached our house, beyond the spring on the hill, we met a fellow on horseback, who was extremely glad to see us, swung his legs against his horse's flanks, and, taking off his hat while still some distance away, rode up to us with a beaming face and began reporting to my aunt about the worry we had caused everybody at home.

It turned out that father, mother, and the entire household as well had not slept that night. They had expected us without fail, and ever since the snowstorm had broken out in the evening, there had been great anxiety as to whether we had lost our way, or some other misfortune had befallen us: we might have broken a shaft in a pothole, we might have been attacked by wolves . . . Father had sent several men on horseback with lanterns to meet us, but the storm had torn the lanterns from their hands and extinguished them, and neither men nor horses could get very far from the house. A man trudges on for a long time—it seems to him that he's going against the storm, and suddenly—halt, the horse refuses to move from the spot. The rider urges it on, though he is so choked he can hardly breathe, but the horse doesn't move . . . The horseman dismounts, so as to take the bridle and lead the frightened animal on, and suddenly, to his surprise, he discovers that his horse is standing with its forehead leaning against the wall of the stable or the shed . . . Only one of the scouts made it a little further and had an actual encounter on his way: this was the harness-maker Prokhor. They gave him an outrunner, a postillion's horse, who used to take the bit between his teeth, so that the iron didn't touch his lips, and as a result became insensible to any restraint. He carried Prokhor off into the very hell of the snowstorm, and galloped for a long time, kicking up his rump and bobbing his head down to his knees, until finally, during one of these capers, the harness-maker went flying over the horse's head and landed right in the middle of some strange heap of living people, who, however, at first did not show him any friendliness. On the contrary, one of them straightaway fetched him a whack on the head, another made corrections to his back, and a third set about trampling him with his feet and poking him with something cold, metallic, and extremely uncomfortable for his senses.

Prokhor was nobody's fool: he realized he was dealing with special creatures and started shouting furiously.

The terror he felt probably lent his voice special force, and he was immediately heard. For his salvation, right there, a couple of steps away from him, a "fiery glow" appeared. This was the light that had been placed in the window of our kitchen, by the wall of which huddled the police chief, his secretary, his messenger, and a coachman with a troika of horses, stuck in a snowdrift.

They, too, had lost their way and, ending up by our kitchen, thought they were somewhere in a field by a haystack.

They were dug out and taken, some to the kitchen, some to the house, where the police chief was now having tea, hoping to get back to his family in town before they woke up and started worrying about his absence after such a stormy night.

"That's splendid," said my aunt. "The police chief is the one we need most of all now."

"Yes, he's a plucky fellow—he'll give it to Selivashka!" people chimed in, and we raced on at a gallop and drove up to the house while the police chief's troika was still standing at our porch.

They would at once tell the police chief everything, and half an hour later the brigand Selivan would already be in his hands.

XVIII

My father and the police chief were struck by what we had endured on the way and especially in the house of the brigand Selivan, who had wanted to kill us and take our things and money . . .

By the way, about the money. At the mention of it, my aunt at once exclaimed:

"Ah, my God! Where is my box?"

The Spook

Where, indeed, was that box and the thousands that were in it?

Just imagine, it wasn't there! Yes, yes, it was the one thing that wasn't there, either among the things brought inside, or in the sleigh—in short, not anywhere . . . The box had obviously remained there and was now in the hands of Selivan . . . Or . . . maybe he had even stolen it during the night. It would have been possible for him; as the owner, he would know all the cracks in his wretched house, and there were probably not a few of them . . . He might have a removable floorboard or a loose plank in the partition.

And the police chief, with his experience in tracking down robberies, had only just uttered this last suggestion about the loose plank, which Selivan might quietly have removed at night and reached through to make away with the box, when my aunt covered her face with her hands and collapsed into an armchair.

Fearing for her box, she had hidden it precisely in the corner under the bench that stood against the partition separating our night lodgings from the part of the cottage where Selivan and his wife lived . . .

"Well, there you are!" exclaimed the police chief, glad of the correctness of his experienced reasoning. "You put the box there for him yourself! . . . But all the same I'm surprised that neither you, nor your people, nor anybody missed it when it came time for you to leave."

"My God, we were all so frightened!" my aunt moaned.

"That's true, that's true, too; I believe you," said the police chief. "There was reason to be afraid, but still . . . such a large sum . . . such good money. I'll gallop there, I'll gallop there right now . . . He's probably hiding out somewhere already, but he won't get away from me! It's lucky for us that everybody knows he's a thief, and nobody likes him: they're not going to hide him . . . Although—he's got money in his hands now . . . he can divvy it up . . . I'll have to hurry . . . People are plain scoundrels . . . Good-bye, I'm going. And you calm yourself, take some drops . . . I know their thievish nature, and I assure you he'll be caught."

And the police chief was buckling on his saber, when suddenly an unusual stir was heard among the people in the front hall and . . . Selivan stepped across the threshold into the big room where we all were, breathing heavily and holding my aunt's box.

Everybody jumped up and stood as if rooted to the spot . . .

"You forgot your little coffer—here it is," Selivan said in a muffled voice.

He couldn't say any more, because he was completely out of

breath from the excessively quick pace and, perhaps, from strong inner agitation.

He put the box on the table and, without being invited, sat down on a chair and lowered his head and arms.

XIX

The box was perfectly intact. My aunt took a little key from around her neck, unlocked it, and exclaimed:

"All, all just as it was!"

"Kept safe . . ." Selivan said softly. "I ran after you . . . tried to catch up . . . couldn't . . . Forgive me for sitting down in front of you . . . I'm out of breath."

My father went to him first, embraced him, and kissed his head.

Selivan didn't move.

My aunt took two hundred-rouble notes from the box and tried to put them into his hands.

Selivan went on sitting and staring as if he understood nothing.

"Take what's given you," said the police chief.

"What for? There's no need!"

"For having honestly saved and brought the money that was forgotten at your place."

"What else? Shouldn't a man be honest?"

"Well, you're . . . a good man . . . you didn't think of keeping what wasn't yours."

"Keeping what wasn't mine! . . ." Selivan shook his head and added: "I don't need what isn't mine."

"But you're poor—take it to improve things for yourself!" my aunt said tenderly.

"Take it, take it," my father tried to persuade him. "You have a right to it."

"What right?"

They told him about the law according to which anyone who finds and returns something lost has a right to a third of what he has found.

"What kind of law is that?" he replied, again pushing away my aunt's hand with the money. "Don't profit from another's misfortune . . . There's no need! Good-bye!"

And he got up to go back to his maligned little inn, but my father wouldn't let him: he took him to his study, locked himself in with him, and an hour later ordered a sleigh hitched up to take him home.

A day later this incident became known in town and all around it, and two days later my father and aunt went to Kromy, stopped at Selivan's, had tea in his cottage, and left a warm coat for his wife. On the way back they stopped by again and brought him more presents: tea, sugar, flour.

He accepted it all politely, but reluctantly, and said:

"What for? It's three days now that people have begun stopping here . . . money's coming in . . . we made cabbage soup . . . They're not afraid of us like they used to be."

When I was taken back to boarding school after the holidays, things were again sent with me for Selivan, and I had tea at his place and kept looking in his face and thinking:

"What a beautiful, kind face he has! Why is it that for so long he looked to me and others like a *spook*?"

This thought pursued me and would not leave me in peace . . . Why, this was the same man whom everyone had found so frightening and considered a sorcerer and an evildoer. And for so long it had seemed that all he did was plot and carry out evil deeds. Why had he suddenly become so good and nice?

XX

I was very lucky in my childhood, in the sense that my first lessons in religion were given me by an excellent Christian. This was the Orel priest Ostromyslenny[9]—a good friend of my father's and a friend to all of us children, who was able to teach us to love truth and mercy. I told my comrades nothing of what had happened to us on Christmas Eve at Selivan's, because there was nothing in it all that flattered my courage, while, on the contrary, they might have laughed at my fear, but I revealed all my adventures and doubts to Father Efim.

He stroked me with his hand and said:

"You're very lucky. Your soul on Christmas Day was like a manger for the holy infant, who came to earth to suffer for the unfortunate. Christ lit up for you the darkness in which the empty talk of dark-minded folk had shrouded your imagination. It was not Selivan who was the spook, but you yourselves—your suspiciousness of him, which kept all of you from seeing his good conscience. His face seemed dark to you, because your eye was dark.[10] Take note of that so that next time you won't be so blind."

This was intelligent and excellent advice. In later years of my life I became close with Selivan and had the good fortune to see how he made himself a man loved and honored by everyone.

On the new estate which my aunt bought there was a good inn at a much-frequented point on the high road. She offered this inn to Selivan on good terms, and Selivan accepted and lived there until his death. Then my old childhood dreams came true: I not only became closely acquainted with Selivan, but we felt full confidence and friendship for each other. I saw his situation change for the better—how peace settled into his house and he eventually prospered; how instead of the former gloomy expressions on the faces of people who met Selivan, everyone now looked at him with pleasure. And indeed it happened that, once the eyes of the people around Selivan were enlightened, his own face also became bright.

Among my aunt's servants, it was the footman Borisushka who disliked Selivan the most—the one whom Selivan had nearly strangled on that memorable Christmas Eve.

This story was sometimes joked about. That night's incident could be explained by the fact that, as everyone suspected that Selivan might rob my aunt, so Selivan himself had strong suspicions that the coachman and the footman might have brought us to his inn on purpose in order to steal my aunt's money during the night and then conveniently blame it all on the suspicious Selivan.

Mistrust and suspicion on one side provoked mistrust and suspicion on the other, and it seemed to everyone that they were all enemies of each other and they all had grounds for considering each other as people inclined towards evil.

Thus evil always generates more evil and is defeated only by the good, which, in the words of the Gospel, makes our eye and heart clean.

XXI

It remains, however, to see why, ever since Selivan left the baker, he became sullen and secretive. Had anyone back then wronged and spurned him?

My father, being well disposed towards this good man, nevertheless thought that Selivan had some *secret,* which he stubbornly kept to himself.

That was so, but Selivan revealed his secret only to my aunt, and that only after he had lived for several years on her estate and after his ever-ailing wife had died.

When I came to see my aunt once, already as a young man, and we started recalling Selivan, who had died himself not long before then, my aunt told me his secret.

The thing was that Selivan, in the tender goodness of his heart, had been touched by the woeful fate of the helpless daughter of the retired executioner, who had died in their town. No one had wanted to give this girl shelter, as the child of a despised man. Selivan was poor, and besides he didn't dare to keep the executioner's daughter with him in town, where everyone knew them both. He had to conceal her origin, which was not her fault, from everyone. Otherwise she could not avoid the harsh reproaches of people who were incapable of mercy and justice. Selivan concealed her, because he constantly feared she would be recognized and insulted, and this secretiveness and anxiety pervaded his whole being and partly left their mark on him.

Thus everyone who called Selivan a "spook" was in fact far more of a "spook" for him.

The Man on Watch

1839

I

The event an account of which is offered to the reader's attention below is touching and terrible in its significance for the main heroic character of the piece, and the denouement of the affair is so original that its like is even hardly possible anywhere but in Russia.

It consists in part of a court, in part of a historical anecdote, which characterizes rather well the morals and tendencies of the very curious, though extremely poorly chronicled, epoch of the thirties of the current nineteenth century.

There is no trace of fiction in the following story.

II

In the winter of 1839, around Theophany, there was a big thaw in Petersburg. The weather was so sodden, it was as if spring were coming: the snow melted, drops fell from the roofs all day, and the ice on the rivers turned blue and watery. On the Neva, there were deep pools just in front of the Winter Palace. A warm but very strong wind was blowing from the west: it drove the water back from the sea, and warning cannon were fired.

The guard at the palace was mounted by a company of the Izmailovsky Regiment, commanded by a young officer of brilliant education and very good standing in society, Nikolai Ivanovich Miller (later a full general and director of the *lycée*).[1] He was a man of the so-called "humane" tendency, a fact which had long been noted by his superiors and which had been slightly detrimental to his career.

In fact, Miller was a good and trustworthy officer, and the palace guard at that time presented no danger. It was a most quiet and untroubled period. Nothing was required of the palace guard except a punctual standing at their posts, and yet right then, during Captain Miller's turn on guard at the palace, there took place a highly extraordinary and alarming incident, which is now barely remembered by its few surviving contemporaries.

III

At first everything went well in the guard: the posts were distributed, people were placed in them, and everything was in perfect order. The sovereign, Nikolai Pavlovich,[2] was in good health, took a drive in the evening, returned home, and went to bed. The palace, too, fell asleep. A most quiet night set in. The guardroom was silent. Captain Miller pinned his white handkerchief to the high and always traditionally greasy morocco back of the officer's chair and sat down to while away the time over a book.

N. I. Miller had always been a passionate reader, and therefore he was not bored, but read and did not notice how the night slipped by; but suddenly, towards two o'clock in the morning, he was roused by a terrible disturbance: before him the sergeant on duty appears, all pale, gripped by fear, and babbles rapidly:

"Disaster, sir, disaster!"

"What is it?!"

"A terrible misfortune has befallen us!"

N. I. Miller leaped up in indescribable alarm and was barely able to find out clearly what the "disaster" and "terrible misfortune" consisted in.

IV

The matter consisted in the following: a sentry, a private of the Izmailovsky Regiment by the name of Postnikov, standing watch outside of what is now the Jordan entrance,[3] heard a man drowning in a pool filled by the Neva just opposite that place and desperately calling for help.

Private Postnikov, a former house serf, was a very nervous and very sensitive man. He had long been listening to the distant cries and moans of the drowning man and was petrified by them. In terror he looked this way and that over the whole expanse of the embankment visible to him, and neither here, nor on the Neva, as ill luck would have it, did he catch sight of a single living soul.

There was no one who could help the drowning man, and he was sure to go under . . .

And yet the sinking man was putting up a terribly long and stubborn struggle.

It seemed there was only one thing left for him—not to waste his strength, but to go to the bottom—and yet no! His exhausted moans and cries for help first broke off and ceased, then began to ring out again, and each time closer and closer to the palace embankment. It was clear that the man was not lost yet and was moving in the right direction, straight towards the light of the streetlamps, though, of course, all the same he would not save himself, because the Jordan ice hole lay precisely in his way. There he would duck under the ice and—the end . . . Now he is quiet again, and a moment later he is splashing and moaning once more: "Help, help!" And now he is already so close that you can even hear the lapping of the waves as he splashes . . .

Private Postnikov began to realize that it would be extremely easy to save this man. If he runs out onto the ice now, the drowning man is sure to be right there. Throw him a rope, or reach him a pole, or hand him his gun, and he's saved. He's so close that he can take hold of it and climb out. But Postnikov remembers his duty and his oath: he knows that he is a sentry, and a sentry dare not desert his sentry box for anything or under any pretext.

On the other hand, Postnikov's heart is very recalcitrant: it aches, it pounds, it sinks . . . He'd like to tear it out and throw it under his own feet—so troubled he is by the moans and howls . . . It is a dreadful thing to hear another man perishing, and not give the perishing one help, when, as a matter of fact, it is perfectly possible to do so, because the sentry box is not going to run away and nothing else harmful is going to happen. "Shouldn't I run down there, eh? . . . They won't see me . . . Ah, Lord, only let it be over! Again he's moaning . . ."

During the half hour that this went on, Private Postnikov's heart was quite torn, and he began to feel "doubt of his reason." He was an intelligent and disciplined soldier, with a clear mind, and he understood perfectly well that for a sentry to leave his post is such an offense that it would lead at once to court-martial, and to running the gauntlet of rod-wielders, and then to hard labor and maybe even the firing squad. But from the direction of the swollen river the moaning again comes drifting closer and closer, and a spluttering and desperate floundering can be heard.

"I'm drowning! . . . Help, I'm dro-o-owning!"

The Jordan ice hole is right there now . . . The end!

Postnikov glanced around once or twice more. Not a soul anywhere, only the streetlamps shaking in the wind and glimmering, and the wind intermittently carrying this cry . . . maybe the last cry . . .

There was another splash, another brief howl, and a gurgling in the water.

The sentry could not bear it and deserted his post.

V

Postnikov rushed to the gangway, ran with a violently beating heart down onto the ice, then to the water-filled pool and, quickly spotting where the drowning man was still struggling to stay afloat, held out the stock of his gun to him.

The drowning man seized the butt, and Postnikov pulled him by the bayonet and dragged him out onto the bank.

The saved man and his savior were thoroughly soaked, and since of the two of them the saved man was in a state of extreme exhaustion and kept trembling and falling down, his savior, Private Postnikov, could not bring himself to abandon him on the ice, but led him to the embankment and began looking around for someone to hand him over to. And meanwhile, as all this was going on, a sleigh appeared on the embankment, in which sat an officer of the then-existing Palace Invalid Command (later abolished).

This gentleman arriving at just the wrong moment for Postnikov was, it must be supposed, a man of very light-minded character, and somewhat muddleheaded besides, and also a rather impudent fellow. He leaped out of the sleigh and began asking:

"Who is this man . . . Who are these people?"

"He was drowning, going under," Postnikov tried to begin.

"Drowning? Who was drowning? You? Why in such a place?"

The other man only spluttered, and Postnikov was no longer there: he had shouldered his gun and gone back to the sentry box.

Whether or not the officer grasped what had happened, he did not go into it any further, but at once picked up the saved man and drove with him to the Admiralty police station on Morskaya Street.

There the officer made a declaration to a policeman that the wet man he had brought in had been drowning in a pool opposite the palace and he, mister officer, had saved him at the risk of his own life.

The man who had been saved was all wet, chilled, and worn out. From fright and terrible exhaustion he fell into unconsciousness, and it made no difference to him who had saved him.

Around him bustled a sleepy police doctor, and in the office they were writing up a report from the verbal declaration of the invalid officer, and, with the suspiciousness peculiar to policemen, were wondering how he had come out of the water perfectly dry. The officer, who was itching to get himself the medal for lifesaving, explained it by a lucky concurrence of circumstances, but his explanation was incoherent and incredible. They went to awaken the police chief and sent to make inquiries.

And meanwhile in the palace this matter was already generating other swift currents.

VI

In the palace guardroom, all the just-mentioned turns after the officer took the saved drowned man in his sleigh were unknown. The officers and soldiers of the Izmailovsky Regiment knew only that one of their soldiers, Postnikov, had abandoned his sentry box and run to save a man, and since this was a grave violation of military duty, Private Postnikov would now certainly be tried and sent under the rods, and all high-ranking persons, from the company to the regimental commander, would get into terrible trouble, against which they could in no way either protest or vindicate themselves.

The wet and trembling Private Postnikov was, naturally, replaced at his post at once and, having been brought to the guardroom, candidly told N. I. Miller everything known to us, and in all its details, up to the point when the invalid officer put the saved drowned man in the sleigh with him and told the driver to gallop to the Admiralty police station.

The danger was growing greater and more inevitable. Naturally, the invalid officer would tell the police chief everything, and he would at once bring the matter to the attention of the superintendant of police, Kokoshkin, who would report it to the sovereign in the morning, and things would get "hot."

There was no time for lengthy discussions, it was necessary to call in their seniors.

Nikolai Ivanovich Miller immediately sent an alarmed note to his battalion commander, Lieutenant Colonel Svinyin,[4] in which he asked him to come to the palace guardroom as soon as possible and take all measures to remedy the horrible disaster.

By then it was around three o'clock, and Kokoshkin appeared with his report to the sovereign quite early in the morning, so there was very little time for any thinking or acting.

VII

Lieutenant Colonel Svinyin did not have that compassion and soft-heartedness which had always distinguished Nikolai Ivanovich Miller. Svinyin was not heartless, but before all and above all he was a "serviceman" (a type that is nowadays remembered with regret). Svinyin was distinguished by his strictness and even liked to flaunt his exactingness in discipline. He had no taste for evil, and never sought to cause anyone needless suffering; but if a man violated any duty of the service whatsoever, Svinyin was implacable. He considered it irrelevant to get into a discussion of the motives that guided the actions of the guilty man in a given case, but held to the rule that in the service all guilt is guilt. And therefore in the guards company everybody knew that, whatever Private Postnikov was going to suffer for having abandoned his post, he was going suffer, and Svinyin was not going to grieve over it.

That was how this staff officer was known to his superiors and comrades, among whom were people who did not sympathize with Svinyin, because back then "humanism" and other such delusions had not yet been entirely rooted out. Svinyin was indifferent to whether the "humanists" blamed or praised him. To beg and beseech Svinyin, or even to appeal to his sense of pity, was a totally useless thing. He was hardened against all that with the firm hardening of the career men of that time, but, like Achilles, he had his weak spot.

Svinyin also had a well-launched career in the service, which he, of course, carefully protected and cared for, so that not one speck of dust should settle on it, as on a dress uniform; and yet the unfortunate escapade of a man from a battalion entrusted to him must unfailingly cast a bad shadow on the discipline of his entire unit. Whether the battalion commander was or was not responsible for what one of his soldiers had done under the influence of the most noble compassion—that was not going to be sorted out by those upon whom Svinyin's well-launched and carefully maintained career in the service depended, and many would even willingly roll the log under his feet, in order to clear the way for a relative or promote some fine fellow patronized by the current favorites. The sovereign would, of course, get angry and would unfailingly tell the regimental commander that he had "weak officers" and "undisciplined people" under him. And who was the cause of it? Svinyin. And so it would go on being repeated that "Svinyin is weak," and so the reproach of weakness might well remain as an indelible blot on his, Svinyin's, reputation. He was not, then, to become anything noteworthy in the ranks of his contemporaries, and was not to leave his portrait in the gallery of historical personages of the Russian State.

Though history was little studied back then, people believed in it, and were especially eager to participate in its making themselves.

VIII

As soon as Svinyin received the alarming note from Captain Miller, at around three o'clock in the morning, he jumped out of bed, put on his uniform, and, under the influence of fear and wrath, arrived in the guardroom of the Winter Palace. There he immediately carried out the questioning of Private Postnikov and convinced himself that the incredible incident had taken place. Private Postnikov again quite candidly confirmed to his battalion commander all that had happened during his watch and that he, Postnikov, had told earlier to his company captain, Miller. The soldier said that he was "guilty before God and his sovereign without mercy," that he had been standing watch and, hearing the moans of a man drowning in a pool, had suffered for a long time, had struggled for a long time between duty to the service and compassion, and, finally, temptation had come over him, and he had been unable to keep up the struggle: he had abandoned the sentry box, had jumped down onto the ice, and had pulled the drowning man to the bank, and there, as ill luck would have it, he had run into the officer of the Palace Invalid Command driving by.

Lieutenant Colonel Svinyin was in despair; he gave himself the only possible satisfaction by venting his wrath on Postnikov, whom he at once sent under arrest straight from there to the punishment cells, and then said a few sharp words to Miller, accusing him of "humaneering," which was good for nothing in military service; but all that was not enough to set things straight. To find, if not a justification, then at least an excuse for such an act as a sentry's abandoning his post, was impossible, and there remained only one way out: to conceal the whole affair from the sovereign . . .

But was it possible to conceal such an occurrence?

By the look of it, it appeared impossible, since the saving of the perishing man was not only known to all the guards, but was known to that detestable invalid officer as well, who by then, of course, had managed to bring it all to the knowledge of General Kokoshkin.

Where gallop off to now? Rush to whom? Seek help and protection from whom?

Svinyin wanted to gallop to the grand duke Mikhail Pavlovich[5] and tell him everything candidly. Such maneuvers were current then. Let the grand duke, with his fiery character, get angry and shout at him, but his temper and habits were such that, the more harsh and even painfully offensive he was at first, the sooner he would become merciful afterwards and even intercede on his own. There had been not a few occasions like that, and sometimes they were sought out on purpose. "Names can never hurt," and Svinyin wanted very much to bring the matter to that favorable state, but was it possible to gain access to the palace at night and disturb the grand duke? Yet if he waited until morning and appeared before Mikhail Pavlovich after Kokoshkin had come to the sovereign with his report, it would be too late. While Svinyin was fretting amidst such difficulties, he softened, and his mind began to perceive one more way out, which until then had been hidden in the mist.

IX

In the number of well-known military maneuvers there is one which holds that, at the moment when the greatest danger threatens from the walls of a besieged fortress, do not withdraw from it, but go straight up to its walls. Svinyin decided not to do any of the things that had first come into his head, but immediately to go straight to Kokoshkin.

Many horrific and preposterous things were said about the superintendent of police Kokoshkin at that time in Petersburg, but, among others, it was maintained that he possessed an astonishingly many-sided tact and with the aid of this tact was not only "able to make a mountain out of a molehill, but, with equal ease, was able to make a molehill out of a mountain."

Kokoshkin was indeed very stern and forbidding and inspired great fear in everyone, but he sometimes indulged pranksters and good fun-lovers among the military, and there were many such pranksters then, and more than once they chanced to find in his person a powerful and zealous protector. Generally, he could do much and knew how to do it, if only he wanted to. Svinyin and Captain Miller both knew this about him. Miller also strengthened his battalion commander's resolve to go immediately to Kokoshkin and trust in his magnanimity and "many-sided tact," which would probably dictate to the general how to wriggle out of this vexing incident without provoking the sovereign's wrath, which Kokoshkin, to his credit, always made great efforts to avoid.

Svinyin put on his overcoat, raised his eyes aloft, and, exclaiming "Lord, Lord!" several times, drove off to Kokoshkin.

It was now past four o'clock in the morning.

X

Superintendent of Police Kokoshkin was awakened, and it was announced to him that Svinyin had come on an important matter that would brook no delay.

The general immediately got up and came out to Svinyin in a house robe, rubbing his forehead, yawning, and shivering. Kokoshkin listened to everything that Svinyin told him with great attention, but calmly. During all these explanations and requests for leniency, he said only one thing:

"The soldier left his sentry box and saved a man?"

"That's right," replied Svinyin.

"And the sentry box?"

"Remained empty during that time."

"Hm . . . I know it remained empty. Very glad it wasn't stolen."

At that Svinyin became even more convinced that everything was already known to him and that he had, of course, already decided how he was going to present it in his morning report to the sovereign, and that the decision was not to be changed. Otherwise such an event as a sentry's abandoning his post in the palace guard should

undoubtedly have caused much greater alarm in the energetic superintendent of police.

But Kokoshkin knew nothing. The police chief to whom the
invalid officer had come with the saved drowned man saw no particular importance in this matter. In his eyes it was even not at all such
a matter as called for troubling the weary superintendent during the
night, and, besides, the event itself appeared rather suspicious to the
police chief, because the invalid officer was completely dry, which
could not possibly have been so if he had saved a drowning man at
the risk of his own life. The police chief saw in this officer only an
ambitious man and a liar, itching to have a new medal on his chest,
and therefore, while his man on duty was drawing up the report, the
police chief kept the officer with him and tried to extort the truth
from him through inquiries into small details.

The police chief was also not pleased that such an occurrence
had taken place in his precinct and that the drowning man had been
pulled out, not by a policeman, but by a palace officer.

As for Kokoshkin's calm, it could be explained simply, first, by the
terrible fatigue he felt at that time, after a whole day's bustling about
and a nighttime participation in the extinguishing of two fires, and,
second, by the fact that for him, mister superintendent of police, the
sentry Postnikov's doings were of no direct concern.

However, Kokoshkin at once gave the appropriate orders.

He sent for the police chief of the Admiralty precinct and ordered
him to appear immediately, along with the invalid officer and the
saved drowned man, and Svinyin he asked to wait in the small anteroom outside his office. Thereupon Kokoshkin retired to his office
and, without closing the door behind him, sat at his desk and set
about signing papers; but his head sank onto his arms at once, and
he fell asleep in the chair behind his desk.

XI

Back then there were as yet neither city telegraphs nor telephones,
and to rapidly transmit the orders of the authorities, "forty thousand messengers" went galloping in all directions, the long-lasting
memory of which would be preserved in Gogol's comedy.[6]

That, naturally, was not as speedy as the telegraph or telephone, but on the other hand it imparted to the city a considerable animation and testified to the unremitting vigilance of the authorities.

By the time the breathless police chief and the officer-savior, as well as the saved drowned man, arrived from the Admiralty police station, the nervous and energetic General Kokoshkin had had a nap and refreshed himself. That could be seen in the expression on his face and in the manifestation of his mental faculties.

Kokoshkin summoned all the new arrivals to his office and invited Svinyin to join them.

"The report?" Kokoshkin asked the police chief tersely in a refreshed voice.

The man silently handed him a folded sheet of paper and whispered softly:

"I must ask permission to add a few words to Your Excellency in private . . ."

"Very well."

Kokoshkin stepped into the embrasure of the window, and the police chief followed him.

"What is it?"

The indistinct whispering of the police chief and the distinct grunting of the general were heard:

"Hm . . . Yes! . . . Well, what about it? . . . That could be . . . Insists he came out dry . . . Nothing else?"

"Nothing, sir."

The general stepped away from the embrasure, sat down at his desk, and began to read. He read the report to himself, betraying neither fear nor doubt, and then turned immediately to the saved man with a loud and firm question:

"How is it, brother, that you wound up in a pool in the ice opposite the palace?"

"I'm sorry," replied the saved man.

"Well, so! You were drunk?"

"I'm sorry, I wasn't drunk, but I'd had a drop."

"Why did you wind up in the water?"

"I wanted to take a short cut across the ice, lost my way, and wound up in the water."

"Meaning it was dark ahead of you?"

"Dark, it was dark all around, Your Excellency!"

"And you couldn't make out who pulled you out?"

"I'm sorry, I couldn't make anything out. It was him, it seems."

He pointed to the officer and added: "I couldn't make out, I was too afeared."

"There it is. You gad about when you should be asleep! Take a good look now and remember forever who your benefactor is. This noble man risked his life for you!"

"All my life I'll remember."

"Your name, mister officer?"

The officer gave his name.

"Do you hear?"

"I hear, Your Excellency."

"Are you Orthodox?"

"Yes, Your Excellency."

"Write his name down and remember him in your prayers."

"I will, Your Excellency."

"Pray to God for him and be on your way: you're no longer needed."

The man made a low bow and darted off, immeasurably pleased that they had let him go.

Svinyin stood and wondered how, by the grace of God, everything could have taken such a turn!

XII

Kokoshkin turned to the invalid officer:

"So you risked your own life to save this man?"

"That's right, Your Excellency."

"There were no witnesses to this occurrence, and given the lateness of the hour there couldn't have been?"

"Yes, Your Excellency, it was dark, and there was no one on the embankment except the sentries."

"There's no cause to mention sentries: a sentry guards his post and shouldn't be distracted by anything extraneous. I believe what's written in the report. So it's in your own words?"

Kokoshkin uttered these words with special emphasis, as if he were threatening him or berating him.

But the officer did not quail, and, with his eyes goggling and his chest puffed out, replied:

"In my own words and perfectly correct, Your Excellency."

"Your action deserves a reward."

The man began to bow gratefully.

"There's nothing to be grateful for," Kokoshkin continued. "I will report on your selfless action to the sovereign emperor, and your chest may be decorated with a medal this very day. You can go home now, drink something warm, and don't go out anywhere, because you may be needed."

The invalid officer beamed, bowed out, and left.

Kokoshkin followed him with his eyes and said:

"It's possible the sovereign himself will want to see him."

"Yes, sir," the quick-witted police chief replied.

"I no longer need you."

The police chief went out and, having closed the door behind him, at once, out of pious habit, crossed himself.

The invalid officer was waiting for him downstairs, and they left the place together, in much warmer relations than when they had entered it.

In the superintendent's office there remained only Svinyin, on whom Kokoshkin at first fixed a long, intent gaze and then asked:

"You haven't gone to the grand duke?"

At that time, when there was mention of a grand duke, everyone knew it referred to the grand duke Mikhail Pavlovich.

"I came straight to you," replied Svinyin.

"Who is the officer of the guard?"

"Captain Miller."

Kokoshkin again looked Svinyin over and then said:

"It seems you were saying something different to me earlier."

Svinyin did not even understand what this had to do with, and kept silent. Kokoshkin added:

"Well, never mind: I bid you good night."

The audience was over.

XIII

At one o'clock in the afternoon, the invalid officer was indeed summoned again to Kokoshkin, who very affably announced to him that the sovereign was highly pleased that among the officers of his palace's invalid command there were such vigilant and selfless people, and that he was bestowing on him the medal for lifesaving. At that,

Kokoshkin handed the medal to the hero with his own hands, and the man went off to flaunt it. The affair, therefore, could be considered over and done with, yet Lieutenant Colonel Svinyin felt some sort of inconclusiveness in it and considered himself called upon to put *le point sur les i*.*

He was so alarmed that he lay ill for three days, but on the fourth he got up, went to Peter's Little House,[7] had prayers of thanksgiving offered before the icon of the Savior, and, returning home with a quieted soul, sent to ask Captain Miller to come to him.

"Well, thank God, Nikolai Ivanovich," he said to Miller, "now the storm that has been hanging over us is quite gone, and our unfortunate affair with the sentry is completely settled. Now, it seems, we can breathe easy. We owe it all, without doubt, first to God's mercy, and then to General Kokoshkin. They may say he's unkind and heartless, but I'm filled with gratitude for his magnanimity and with esteem for his resourcefulness and tact. With astonishing skill he made use of the boasting of that shifty invalid, who, in truth, should have been rewarded for his insolence not with a medal, but with a thorough thrashing behind the woodpile, but there was no other choice: he had to be made use of for the salvation of many, and Kokoshkin turned the whole affair so intelligently that no unpleasantness came of it for anybody—on the contrary, everybody's very glad and pleased. Just between us, it has been conveyed to me through a trustworthy person that Kokoshkin himself is also *very pleased* with me. He liked it that I did not go anywhere else, but came straight to him and didn't argue with that rascal who got the medal. In short, no one has suffered, and everything has been done with such tact that there's nothing to fear in the future. But there's one small omission on our part. We should also tactfully follow Kokoshkin's example and finish the matter on our side, so as to protect ourselves in any case later on. There is one more person whose position has not been regularized. I'm speaking of Private Postnikov. He's still in the punishment cell under arrest, and he's no doubt tormented, waiting for what will happen to him. We must put an end to his racking torment."

"Yes, it's high time!" Miller put in happily.

"Well, of course, you are in the best position to do that: please go to the barracks at once, gather your company, release Private

---

* *The dots on the i's. Trans.*

Postnikov from arrest, and punish him before the ranks with two hundred strokes of the birch."

XIV

Miller was dumbfounded and made an attempt to persuade Svinyin, for the joy of all, to spare and pardon Private Postnikov altogether, since he had already suffered much without that, waiting in the punishment cell for the decision on what was to be done with him; but Svinyin flared up and did not even let Miller continue.

"No," he interrupted, "drop that: I've just been talking about tact, and right away you start your tactlessness! Drop it!"

Svinyin changed his tone to a more dry and official one and added firmly:

"And since you yourself are also not entirely in the right in this affair, and are even very much to blame, because there's a softness in you unbecoming to a military man, and this defect in your character is reflected in the subordination of the men under you, I order you to be personally present during the execution of the sentence and to insist that the flogging be performed in earnest . . . as severely as possible. To that end, kindly see to it that the birching is done by young soldiers newly arrived from the army, because in this respect our old-timers have all been infected by the guardsmen's liberalism: they don't whip a comrade as they should, but just scare the fleas off his back. I'll stop by and see for myself how the culprit's been done."

Deviation from any official orders given by superiors could not, of course, take place, and the softhearted N. I. Miller had to carry out with precision the order he had received from his battalion commander.

The company was lined up in the courtyard of the Izmailovsky barracks, the birch rods were brought from the reserve in sufficient quantity, and Private Postnikov, led out from the punishment cell, was "done" with the zealous assistance of his young comrades newly arrived from the army. These men, uncorrupted by the guardsmen's liberalism, made a perfect job of putting all the *points sur les i* on him, in the full measure prescribed by the battalion commander. Then the punished Postnikov was picked up and immediately carried, on the same greatcoat on which he had been flogged, from there to the regimental infirmary.

XV

Battalion commander Svinyin, on receiving notice of the carried-out punishment, at once paid Postnikov a fatherly visit in the infirmary, and was convinced to his satisfaction that his order had been carried out to perfection. The tenderhearted and nervous Postnikov had been "done properly." Svinyin remained pleased and ordered that the punished Postnikov be given on his behalf a pound of sugar and a quarter pound of tea, to sweeten his recovery. Postnikov, lying on his cot, heard this order about the tea and replied:

"Very pleased, sir, thanks for your fatherly kindness."

And indeed he was "pleased," because, while sitting for three days in the punishment cell, he had been expecting something much worse. Two hundred strokes, in those harsh times, amounted to very little compared with the punishments people endured under sentencing from the courts-martial; and that was precisely the sort of punishment Postnikov would also have received, if, luckily for him, all those bold and tactical evolutions recounted above had not taken place.

But the number of all who were pleased by the incident we have recounted was not limited to these.

XVI

On the quiet, Private Postnikov's exploit spread through various circles of the capital, which at that time of voiceless print lived in an atmosphere of endless gossip. In oral transmissions, the name of the real hero—Private Postnikov—was lost, but to make up for it the épopée itself was blown up and acquired a very interesting, romantic character.

It was said that some extraordinary swimmer came swimming towards the palace from the direction of the Peter-and-Paul Fortress,[8] that one of the sentries standing watch by the palace shot at the swimmer and wounded him, and that a passing invalid officer threw himself into the water and saved him, for which they received, the one his due reward, the other his deserved punishment. This absurd rumor even reached patriarchal quarters, where at that time a certain bishop was living, a cautious man and not indifferent to "secular events," who was benevolently disposed towards the pious Moscow family of the Svinyins.[9]

To the perspicacious bishop the story of the shot seemed unclear. What was this night swimmer? If he was an escaped prisoner, why had they punished the sentry, who had only done his duty by shooting at him as he swam across the Neva from the fortress? If, however, he was not a prisoner, but some other mysterious person who had had to be saved from the waves of the Neva, then why should the sentry have known about him? And then again, it cannot be that it was the way the idle talk of the world had it. In the world there is a great deal of light-mindedness and "idle talk," but those who live in cloisters and in church precincts treat everything much more seriously and know the very truth about secular matters.

XVII

Once, when Svinyin happened to be at the bishop's to receive his blessing, his reverend host began talking with him "incidentally about that shot." Svinyin told him the whole truth, in which, as we know, there was nothing resembling the story made up "incidentally about that shot."

The bishop heard out the true story in silence, slightly moving his white prayer beads and not taking his eyes off the storyteller. When Svinyin finished, the bishop uttered in softly burbling speech:

"Wherefore it is incumbent upon us to conclude that not always and everywhere has this affair been set forth in accordance with the full truth?"

Svinyin faltered and then answered evasively that the report was made not by him, but by General Kokoshkin.

The bishop ran his beads through his waxen fingers several times in silence, and then said:

"A distinction must be made between what is a lie and what is an incomplete truth."

Again the beads, again the silence, and, finally, the softly flowing speech:

"An incomplete truth is not a lie. But the less said . . ."

"That is indeed so," began the encouraged Svinyin. "For me, of course, the most disturbing thing is that I had to subject that soldier to punishment, for, though he violated his duty . . ."

The beads and then a softly flowing interruption:

"The duties of the service must never be violated."

"Yes, but he did it out of magnanimity, out of compassion, and with such a struggle and such danger besides: he realized that, by saving another man's life, he was destroying himself . . . This was a lofty, a holy feeling!"

"The holy is known to God, while punishment of the flesh is never injurious for the simple man and contradicts neither national custom nor the spirit of the Scriptures. The rod is far easier for the coarse body to bear than refined suffering is for the soul. In this justice has not suffered from you in the least."

"But he was also deprived of the reward for saving a life."

"Saving a life is not a merit, but rather a duty. He who could save a life and does not is punishable by law, and he who does has performed his duty."

A pause, the beads, and the soft flow:

"For a soldier to suffer humiliation and wounds for his exploit may be far more salutary than to be exalted by some mark. But the major thing here is—to observe caution about this whole affair and by no means mention anywhere those to whom by some chance or other it has been recounted."

Evidently the bishop was also pleased.

XVIII

If I had the daring of those lucky ones chosen by heaven, to whom, for the greatness of their faith, it is given to penetrate the mysteries of divine providence, I might be so bold as to allow myself to suppose that God himself was probably pleased with the behavior of

Postnikov's humble soul, which He created. But I have little faith; it does not give my mind the power to contemplate such loftiness: I am of the earth, earthy.[10] I am thinking of those mortals who love the good simply for the sake of the good itself and expect no reward for it anywhere. These straightforward and reliable people, it seems to me, should also be perfectly pleased by the holy impulse of love and the no less holy patience of the humble hero of my faithful and artless story.

A Robbery

I

the conversation got onto the embezzlement in the Orel bank, the case of which was tried in the fall of 1887.

It was said that this one was a good man, and that one seemed like a good man, but, nevertheless, they all turned out to be thieves.

An old Orel merchant, who happened to be in the company, said:

"Ah, gentlemen, when the thieves' time comes, even honest people turn robber."

"Well, there you're joking."

"Not in the least. Otherwise why is it said: 'With the pure thou wilt show thyself pure; and with the froward thou wilt show thyself froward'?[1] I know of an occasion when an honest man robbed another man in the street."

"That can't be."

"On my word of honor—he robbed him, and if you like, I can tell you about it."

"Please be so kind."

Then the merchant told us the following story, which had taken place some fifty years ago in that same Orel, not long before the famous fires that devastated the town. It happened under the late governor of Orel, Prince Pyotr Ivanovich Trubetskoy.[2]

Here is how he told it.

A Robbery

II

I'm an Orel old-timer. Our whole family—we weren't among the least of people. We had our own house on Nizhnaya Street, by the Plautin Well, and our own granaries, and our own barges; we kept a fulling works, traded in hemp, and handled the grain collection. Our fortune wasn't desperately big, but we never pinched pennies, and we passed for being honest people.

My father died when I was going on sixteen. The business was managed by my mother, Arina Leontyevna, and an old clerk, and at the time I only looked on. In everything, by paternal will, I was totally obedient to my mother. I never got up to any mischief or naughtiness, and I was zealous and fearful towards the Church of the Lord. Mama's sister, my aunt, the venerable widow Katerina Leontyevna, also lived with us. She was a most pious, saintly woman. We were of churchly faith, as father had been, and belonged to the parish of the Protection, served by the reverend Father Efim, but Aunt Katerina Leontyevna adhered to the old ways: she drank from her own special glass and went to the Old Believers in the fish market to pray.[3] My mama and aunt were from Elets, and there, in Elets and in Livny, they had very good kin, but they rarely saw them, because the Elets merchants like to boast before the Orel merchants and often get belligerent in company.

Our house by the Plautin Well wasn't big, but it was very well appointed, merchant-style, and our way of life was the strictest. Having lived in the world for nineteen years, I knew my way only to the granaries or the barges on the riverbank, when they were being loaded, and on Sundays to the early service in the Protection—and from the service straight back home, so as to give proof to my mama by telling her what the Gospel reading was about and whether Father Efim gave any sermon; and Father Efim had a degree in divinity, and when he applied himself to a sermon, there was no understanding it. After Kamensky, our theater was kept by Turchaninov and then by Molotkovsky,[4] but not for anything would mama allow me to go to the theater, or even to the Vienna tavern to drink tea. "You'll hear nothing good there in the Vienna," she'd say. "You'd better sit at home and eat pickled apples." Only once or twice a winter was a full pleasure allowed me: to go out and see how Constable Bogdanov and the archdeacon turned their fighting geese loose or how the towns-folk and seminarians got into fistfights.

At that time many people in our town kept fighting geese and turned them loose on Kromskaya Square; but the foremost goose was Constable Bogdanov's: he'd tear the wing off another fighter alive; and so that nobody would feed his goose soaked peas or harm him in some other way, the constable used to carry him on his back in a basket—he loved him so much. The archdeacon's goose was clay-colored and gabbled and hissed terribly when he fought. A numer-ous public would gather. And for fistfights the townsfolk and the seminarians gathered on the ice, on the Oka, near the monastery, or at the Navugorskaya Gate; they got together there and went, wall against wall, across the whole street. It was often quite desperate. There was only this one rule, to hit in the belly and not in the face, and not to put big copper coins in your mittens. But, anyhow, this rule wasn't obeyed. It often happened that they'd drag a man home in their arms and he'd pass away before he had time to confess. A lot of them were left alive, but then wasted away. Mama gave me per-mission only to watch, but not to stand in the wall myself. I sinned, though, by disobeying my late parent in that: my strength and daring urged me on, and if the townsfolk's wall wavered, and the seminary wall really piled onto it and drove it back—then I sometimes couldn't help myself and joined in. From early on my strength was such that, as soon as I jumped onto the driven-back wall and cried: "God bless us, boys! Beat the clericals!" and lit into the seminarians facing me, they'd all just scatter. But I wasn't seeking glory for myself, and I used to ask for just one thing: "Please, brothers, be so kind, don't mention my name!"—because I was afraid my mama would find out.

I lived like that until I was nineteen, and was so terribly healthy that I began to have fainting fits and nosebleeds. Then mama began thinking of getting me married, so that I wouldn't start visiting the Sekerens' brewery or playing around with rebaptized girls.[5]

III

On account of that, matchmakers in sack coats started coming to us from Nizhnaya, Kromskaya, and Karachevskaya Streets, offering my mother various brides for me. All this was carried out in secret from me, so that everybody knew more than I did. Even our fullers in the shed used to say:

"Your mama's going to get you married, Mikhailo Mikhailych. How agreeable are you to that? Watch out—you know, your wife's going to tickle you after the wedding, but don't be timid—tickle her sides all you can, or else she'll out-tickle you."

I'd only blush. I figured out, naturally, that it somehow had to do with me, but I never heard what brides mama and the matchmakers were talking about. One matchmaker or another would come— mama would shut herself up with her in the icon room, they'd sit under the crosses, have the samovar served, and talk all by themselves, and then the matchmaker would come out, pat me on the head, and encourage me:

"Don't worry, Mishenka, my boy: soon now you won't sit bored and alone, soon we'll gladden you up."

And mama even used to get angry at that and say:

"He needn't know anything about it; whatever I decide over his head, that's how it must be for him. It's like in the scriptures."

I didn't worry about it. It was all the same to me: if I'm to marry, I'll marry, and when it comes to tickling, we'll see who out-tickles who.

But Aunt Katerina Leontyevna went against mama's wish and instructed me against her.

"Don't marry an Orel girl, Misha," she said, "not for anything. Just you look: the local Orel girls are all haywire—not merchants, not gentry. They marry officers. Ask your mother to take you a wife from Elets, where she and I come from. Among the merchants there, the men are carousers, but the marriageable girls are real maidens: pious, modest—don't look at officers, but wear kerchiefs when they go to pray and cross themselves in the old Russian way. If you marry one like that, you'll bring blessings on your house, and start praying with your wife in the old way, and then I'll leave you all my property, and to her I'll give my God's blessing, and my round pearls, and silver, and beads, and brocade jerkins, and warm jackets, and all my Bolkhovo lace."

And there was quiet displeasure between my mother and my aunt on that score, because by then mama had quit the old faith entirely and read the akathist to the great martyr Barbara by the new Church calendar.[6] She wanted to take a wife for me from the Orel girls, so as to renew the family.

"At least," she said, "on the days of forgiveness before Lent, we'll have somebody to go to with bread for forgiveness, and they'll also have someone to bring braided loaves to."

Mama liked to cut these loaves up afterwards for rusks and dunk them in tea with honey during Lent, but for my aunt their ancient faith had to be placed above everything.

They argued and argued, but the whole thing came out differently.

IV

A most unexpected incident suddenly occurred.

Once, during Christmastime, my aunt and I were sitting by the window after dinner, talking about something religious and eating pickled apples, and suddenly we notice a troika of hired horses standing outside in the snow by our gate. We look—a tall man gets out from under the felt flap of the kibitka, dressed in a Kalmyk coat of dark broadcloth lined with fleece, tied with a red belt, a green worsted scarf wrapped around the raised collar, its long ends twisted on his chest and tucked into his bosom, a felt hat on his head, and on his feet calfskin boots with the fur side out.

The man stood up and shook the snow off himself like a poodle, and then, together with the driver, pulled from under the flap of the kibitka another man, in a beaver hat and a wolfskin coat, and held him under the arms so that he could keep his feet, because it was slippery for him in his leather-soled felt boots.

Aunt Katerina Leontyevna was very worried, not knowing who these people were or why they had gotten out by our gate, but when she saw the wolfskin coat, she crossed herself:

"Lord Jesus Christ, have mercy on us, amen!" she said. "It's my brother Ivan Leontych, your uncle, come from Elets. What's happened to him? He hasn't been here for three years, not since your father's funeral, and suddenly he turns up at Christmastime. Quick, fetch the key for the gate, run to meet him."

I rushed to look for mama, and mama started looking for the key and finally found it in the icon chest, but by the time I ran to the gate, unlocked the lock, and drew the bolt, the troika had already gone, and the man in the Kalmyk coat had gone with the kibitka, and my uncle was standing there alone, holding on to the gate pull, and angry.

"What's this?" he says. "You lock yourselves up in the daytime like scaredy-cats?"

Mama greeted him and replied:

"Don't you know, brother, what a situation we have in Orel? There's constant thievery, and we lock ourselves in day and night from the police."

My uncle replied that the situation was the same everywhere: Orel and Kromy are thieving cronies, Karachev's another, and Elets is their father. "We also lock ourselves in from the police," he says, "but only at night—why in the daytime? I'm displeased that you left me outside the gate in the daytime: my felt boots have leather soles, it's slippery to walk—and I've come on a church necessity, not empty-handed. God forbid some Orelian should snatch it from me and run off, and me unable to catch up with him."

V

We all apologized to my uncle and brought him to a room where he could change his traveling clothes. Ivan Leontych changed his felt boots for leather ones, put on a frock coat, and sat down by the samovar, and mother began asking him what sort of church business he had come on, that he should go to the trouble even during the feast days, and where his companion by our gate had disappeared to.

Ivan Leontych replied:

"It's big business. You must understand that I'm now the church warden, and our deacon tore something on the very first day of the feast."

Mama says:

"We hadn't heard."

"As if you ever hear anything interesting! Your town's such a backwater."

"But how was it that your deacon tore something?"

"Ah, my dear, he suffered it on account of his zeal. He began serving nicely on the occasion of our deliverance from the Gauls,[7] and kept singing louder, and louder, and still louder, and suddenly, as he exclaimed 'for the salvation'—a vein burst on him. They went to take him from the ambo, and he already had a boot full of blood."

"He died?"

"No. The merchants didn't let that happen: they called in a doctor. Would our merchants just abandon him? The doctor says he may yet recover, but he won't have any voice. So I came here with our fore-most parishioner to make sure our deacon gets sent to the nuns in some convent or other, and here we must choose ourselves the best one from all you've got."

"And who is this foremost parisher of yours and where did he go off to?"

"Our foremost parishioner is named Pavel Mironych Mukomol. He's married to a rich Moscow woman. The wedding celebration went on for a whole week. He's very devoted to the church and knows all the church services better than any archdeacon. So everybody begged him: go, and look, and choose; the one you like will be to our liking, too. Everybody, old and young, honors him. And he, with his enormous capital, owner of three houses, and a candle factory, and a flour mill, obeyed at once and dropped it all for the church necessity and came flying. He'll take a room in the Repinskaya Inn now. Are they tricksters there, or honest?"

Mama replied:

"I don't know."

"There you have it, you live here and don't know anything."

"We're afraid of inns."

"Well, never mind. Pavel Mironych is also not easily offended: there's no stronger fistfighter in Elets or in Livny. Whenever there's a fight, two or three men fall by his hand. Last year, during Lent, he went on purpose to Tula, and though he's a miller, he up and left two of the foremost samovarniks there with ruptures."[8]

Mama and my aunt crossed themselves.

"Lord!" they said. "Why have you brought such a man to us at Christmastime?"

But my uncle laughs:

"What are you women afraid of?" he says. "Our parishioner's a good man, and for this church business I can't do without him. He and I came on the spur of the moment to snatch what suits us and leave."

Mama and my aunt gasp again.

"What are you doing, brother, making such frightful jokes!"

My uncle laughs even more merrily.

"Eh," he says, "you lady-crows, you Orel merchant-wives! Your town's maybe a town, maybe a burnt-down place—it doesn't resemble anything, and you yourselves sit in it like smoked sardines stuffed in a box! No, your town's a far cry from our Elets, never mind that it's a provincial capital. Our Elets is a little district town, but in a Moscow gown, and you can't even appreciate what you've got that's good here. And that's just what we'll take away from you."

"What is it?"

"We need a good deacon for our parish, and they say you've got two deacons with voices: one at the Theophany in the marketplace, the other in the clerks' quarter, at St. Nicetas. We'll give them a listen in all styles, and we'll choose whichever one Pavel Mironych decides is more suited to our Elets taste, and we'll lure him away and make a deal with him; and the one who doesn't suit us we'll call number two: he'll get money for a new cassock for his trouble. Pavel Mironych has already gone now to gather them for a tryout, and I must go at once to the Boris and Gleb cathedral; they say you've got an innkeeper there whose inn is always empty. So we'll take three connecting rooms in this empty inn and hold the audition. You, Mishutka my lad, will have to come now and take me there."

I ask:

"Are you speaking to me, uncle?"

He replies:

"Obviously. Who else but you, Mishutka? Well, if you're offended, then allow me to call you Mikhailo Mikhailovich. Do us a family service—kindly lead your uncle through this strange land."

I cleared my throat and answered politely:

"Uncle, dear, it's not on account of that: I'm not offended at anything, and I'm ready and glad to do it, but I'm not my own man and do as mama tells me."

Mama didn't like it at all:

"Why, dear brother, should you take Misha with you to such company?! You can have someone else lead you."

"I find it more proper to go with my nephew."

"But what does he know?!"

"He most likely knows everything. Mishutka, do you know everything?"

I got embarrassed.

"No," I say, "I can't know everything."

"Why's that?"

"Mama won't allow it."

"Just look at that! And what do you think: can an uncle always guide his nephew in everything, or not? Of course he can. Get dressed at once and let's be gone before trouble comes on."

I started to go, then stood there like a post: I listened to him, but saw that mama didn't want to let me go for anything.

"Our Misha," she said, "is still young, he's not used to going out anywhere at night. Why do you insist on having him? It will be dark before you notice, and the thieves' time will come."

But here my uncle even yelled at them:

"Enough playing the fool, really! What are you stewing him in your women's skirts for! The boy's grown so big he can kill an ox, and you still coddle him like a baby. It's all nothing but your female foolishness, and he'll be the worse off for it because of you. He has to have his life forces developed and his character firmed up, and I need him because, God forbid, in the darkness or in some back street your Orel thieves may actually fall upon me or I may run into a police patrol—you see, I have all our money for the business with me . . . There's enough to dump our torn deacon on the nuns and lure your mighty one to us . . . Can it be that you, my own sisters, are so unfamilial that you want me, your brother, to be bashed on the head or picked up by the police, and end up there with nothing?"

My mother says:

"God save us from that—families aren't only respected in Elets! But take our clerk with you, or even two sturdy fullers. Our fullers are from Kromy, they're terribly strong, they eat some eight pounds a day of bread alone, besides other things."

My uncle didn't want to.

"What good are your hired people to me?" he says. "You sisters even ought to be ashamed to say it, and I'd be ashamed and afraid to go with them. Kromy men! And you call them good people! They'd go with me and be the first to kill me, but Misha's my nephew—with him at least it will be brave and proper."

He stood his ground and wouldn't give way:

"You can't possibly refuse me this," he says. "Otherwise I renounce you as my family."

My mother and aunt became frightened at that and exchanged glances, meaning "What on earth should we do?"

A Robbery

Ivan Leontych persisted:

"And understand that it's not just a family matter! Remember, I'm not taking him for my own amusement or pleasure, but on a Church necessity. Can you refuse me that? Consider well. To refuse that is the same as refusing God. The boy's a servant of God; God's will is upon him: you want him to stay with you, but God just won't let him stay."

He was an awfully persuasive one with words.

Mama became frightened.

"Enough talk, please, of such horrors."

But my uncle again burst into merry laughter.

"Ah, you lady-crows! You don't understand the power of words! Who isn't a servant of God? But now I can see that you won't decide on anything yourselves, so I'm just going to knock him from under your wing . . ."

And with that he seized me by the shoulder and said:

"Up you get now, Misha, and put on your visiting clothes—I'm your uncle, and a man who has lived into gray-haired old age. I have grandchildren, and I'm taking charge of you and order you to follow me."

I looked at mama and my aunt, and I myself felt all merry inside, and this Elets free-and-easiness of my uncle's pleased me greatly.

"Who should I listen to?" I ask.

My uncle answers:

"You must listen to the eldest one—that's me. I'm not taking you forever, but only for an hour."

"Mama!" I cry. "What do you tell me to do?"

Mama replies:

"Why . . . if it's only for an hour, it's all right—put on your visiting clothes and go with your uncle; but don't stay one minute beyond an hour. If you're a minute late—I'll die of fear!"

"Well," I say, "that's a good one! How can I know so precisely that an hour has already gone by and a new minute's beginning—and meanwhile you'll have started worrying . . ."

My uncle burst out laughing.

"You can look at your watch," he says, "and see what time it is."

"I don't have a watch," I reply.

"Ah, you still don't even have your own watch! Things are bad with you!"

But mama answers back:

"What does he need a watch for?"

"To know what time it is."

"Well . . . he's still young . . . he wouldn't know how to wind it . . . Outside you can hear it strike the hours in the Theophany and in the Devichy Convent."

I reply:

"Maybe you don't know it, but a weight fell off the Theophany clock yesterday and it stopped striking."

"Well, there's the Devichy clock."

"We never hear the Devichy clock."

My uncle intervenes and says:

"Never mind, never mind: get dressed quickly and don't worry about being late. We'll stop at the watchmaker's, and I'll buy you a watch as a present for going with me. That will give you something to remember your uncle by."

When I heard about the watch, I got all excited: I smacked a kiss on my uncle's hand, put on my visiting clothes, and was ready.

Mama gave me her blessing and said several more times:

"Only for an hour!"

VI

My uncle was a gentleman of his word. The moment we stepped out, he said:

"Quickly whistle for a cabby, we'll go to the watchmaker's."

But back then, in Orel, decent people didn't ride around town in cabs. Only some sort of carousers did that, but most cabbies waited for the hirelings who were sent off as soldiers in place of local recruits.

I said:

"I know how to whistle, dear uncle, but I can't, because here only hirelings ride in cabs."

He said: "Fool!"—and whistled himself. And when a cab drove up, he said again:

"Get in without talking! On foot, we won't make it back to your women within an hour, but I gave them my word, and my word is adamant."

But I was beside myself with shame and kept leaning out of the cab.

"What are you fidgeting for?" he says.

"For pity's sake," I say, "they're going to think I'm a hireling."

"With your uncle?"

"They don't know you here. They'll say: look, he's driving him around now, he'll take him to all the bad places, and then whisk him away. It will bring shame on mama."

My uncle started swearing.

No matter how I protested, I had to sit beside him to avoid a scandal. I ride along and don't know where to turn—I'm not looking, but it's as if I see and hear everybody around saying: "Look at that! Arina Leontyevna's Misha is riding in a cab—must be a fine place he's going to!" I couldn't stand it!

"Do as you like, uncle," I say, "but I'm jumping off."

He held me back and laughed.

"Can it be," he says, "that they're a whole string of fools here in Orel, to go thinking your old uncle would take you to any bad places? Where's your best watchmaker here?"

"Our best watchmaker is considered to be the German Kern; in his window a Moor with a clock on his head winks his eyes in all directions. Only the way to him is across the Orlitsky Bridge to Bolkhovskaya Street, and merchants we know there will be looking out their windows. I won't drive past them in a cab for anything."

But my uncle wasn't listening.

"Cabby," he says, "drive to Kern's on Bolkhovskaya Street."

We arrived. I persuaded him to dismiss the cabby here at least—I said I wouldn't drive back down those same streets again for anything. That he agreed to. He called me a fool one more time, gave the cabby fifteen kopecks, and bought me a silver watch with a gold rim and a chain.

"Such watches," he says, "are now all the fashion among us in Elets; once you get accustomed to winding it, and I come again, I'll buy you a gold watch with a gold chain."

I thanked him and was very glad of the watch, only I begged him all the same not to ride in cabs with me anymore.

"Very well, very well," he says. "Now take me quickly to the Boris and Gleb Inn; we have to have three connecting rooms there."

I say:

"It's a stone's throw from here."

"Let's go, then. We have no time to idle away with you here in Orel. What have we come for? To choose a full-throated deacon for ourselves; and that we must do now. There's no time to lose. Take me to the inn and go home to your mother."

I took him there and hurried home.

I ran so quickly that an hour hadn't passed since I left, and at home I showed them my uncle's gift—the watch.

Mama looked and said:

"Why . . . it's very nice—hang it on the wall over your bed, otherwise you'll lose it."

But my aunt regarded it critically:

"Why is it," she says, "that the watch is silver, but the rim is yellow?"

"That," I reply, "is all the fashion in Elets."

"What silly things they think up in Elets," she says. "The old men of Elets used to be smarter—they wore everything of the same kind: if it's a silver watch, it's silver; if gold, it's gold. What's the point of forcing together what God put separately on earth?"

But mama said peaceably that you don't look a gift horse in the mouth, and told me again:

"Go to your room and hang it over your bed. On Sunday I'll tell the nuns to make you a little cushion for it embroidered with beads and fish scales, so that you won't somehow crush the glass in your pocket."

I said cheerfully:

"That can be repaired."

"When it needs repairing, the watchmaker will replace the magnetized needle with a stone one inside, and the watch will be ruined. Better go quickly and hang it up."

So as not to argue, I hammered in a nail over my bed and hung up the watch, and I lay back on the pillow and looked at it admiringly. I was very pleased to have such a noble thing. And how nicely and softly it ticked: tick, tick, tick, tick . . . I listened and listened, and fell asleep. I was awakened by loud talk in the drawing room.

VII

I hear my uncle's voice and some other unknown voice behind the wall; and I also hear that mama and my aunt are there.

The unknown man tells them that he has already been to the

Theophany and heard the deacon there, and he has also been to St. Nicetas, but, he says, "they must be placed on an equal level and listened to under our own tuning fork."

My uncle replies:

"Do it, then. I've prepared everything at the Boris and Gleb Inn. All the doors between the rooms will be open. There are no other guests—shout as much as you like, there's nobody to get annoyed. An excellent inn: only government clerks come there with petitioners during office hours; but in the evening there's nobody at all, and there are shafts and bast sleighs standing like a forest blocking the windows on Poleshskaya Square."

The unknown man replies:

"That's what we need, because they've also got some brazen amateurs, and they'll undoubtedly gather to hear my voice and make fun of it."

"You don't mean you're afraid?"

"I'm not afraid, but their insolence will make me angry, and I'll beat them."

He himself has a voice like a trumpet.

"I'll freely explain to them," he says, "all the examples of what's liked in our town. We'll listen to what they can do and how they perform in all tones: a low growl when vesting a bishop, middle and upper notes when singing 'Many Years,' how to let out a cry for 'In the blessed falling asleep . . .' and a howl for 'Memory Eternal.'[9] That's the long and short of it."

My uncle agreed.

"Yes," he says, "we must compare them and then quite inoffensively make a decision. Whichever of them suits our Elets fashion better we'll work on and lure over to us, and to the one who comes out weaker we'll give a cassock for his trouble."

"Keep your money on you—they've got thieves here."

"And you keep yours on you."

"All right."

"Well, and now you go and set out some refreshments, and I'll fetch the deacons. They asked to do it in the evening—'because,' they say, 'our people are rascals, they may get wind of it.'"

My uncle answers in the affirmative, only he says:

"It's these evenings here in Orel that I'm afraid of, and soon now it will be quite dark."

"Well," the unknown man says, "I'm not afraid of anything."

"And what if one of these Orelian priggers strips your fur coat off you?"*

"Oh, yes! As if he'll strip it off me! He'd better not cross paths with me, or I may just strip everything off him!"

"It's a good thing you're so strong."

"And you go with your nephew. Such a fine lad, he could fell an ox with his fist."

Mama says:

"Misha's weak—how can he protect him!"

"Well, have him put some copper coins in his gloves, that'll make him strong."

My aunt says:

"What an idea!"

"Why, did I say something bad?"

"Well, it's clear you have your own rules for everything in Elets."

"And what else? You've got a governor for setting up rules, but we haven't got one—so we make our own rules."

"On how to beat people?"

"Yes, we also have rules on how to beat people."

"Well, you'd better come back before the thieves' time, that way nothing will happen to you."

"And when is the thieves' time in your Orel?"

My aunt answered from some book:

"'Once folk have their dinner and, after praying, go to sleep, that is the time when thieves arise and set about to rob.'"

My uncle and the unknown man burst out laughing. Everything mama and my aunt said seemed unbelievable or unreasonable to them.

"In that case," they say, "where are your police looking?"

My aunt again answers from the scriptures:

"'Except the Lord guard the house—the watchman waketh but in vain.'[10] We have a police chief by the name of Tsyganok. He looks after his own business, he wants to buy property. And when somebody gets robbed, he says: 'Why weren't you asleep at home? You wouldn't have been robbed.'"

"He'd do better to send out patrols more often."

"He already did."

---

* *Podlyot*, in old Orel speech, was the same as the Moscow word *zhulik* or the Petersburg word *mazurik* ("rogue, swindler, cheat"). *Author.* (We translate it by the old thieves' word "prigger." *Trans.*)

"And what happened?"

"The robberies got worse."

"Why is that?"

"Nobody knows. The patrol goes by, the priggers follow after it and rob."

"Maybe it's not the priggers, but the patrolmen themselves who rob?"

"Maybe it is."

"Call in the constable."

"With the constable it's even worse—if you complain about him, you have to pay him for the dishonor."

"What a preposterous town!" cried Pavel Mironych (I figured it was him), and he said good-bye and left, but my uncle went on pacing and reasoning:

"No, truly," he says, "it's better with us in Elets. I'll take a cab."

"Don't go in a cab! The cabby will bilk you and dump you out of the sleigh."

"Well, like it or not, I'll take my nephew Misha with me again. Nobody will harm the two of us."

At first mama wouldn't even hear of letting me go, but my uncle began to take offense and said:

"What is this: I give him a watch with a rim, and he won't show gratitude by rendering me a trifling family service? I can't upset the whole business now. Pavel Mironych left with my full promise that I'd join him and prepare everything, and now, what, instead of that I should listen to your fears and stay home, or else go alone to a certain death?"

My aunt and mama quieted down and said nothing.

And my uncle persists:

"If I had my former youth," he says, "when I was, say, forty years old, I wouldn't fear the priggers, but I'm an elderly man, going on sixty-five, and if they strip my fur coat off me when I'm far from home, then, while I'm walking back without my fur coat, I'm bound to catch an inflammation in my shoulders, and then I'll need a young leech to draw the blood off, or else I'll croak here with you. Bury me here, then, in your church of John the Baptist, and people can remember over my coffin that in your town your Mishka let his own uncle go without a family service and didn't accompany him this one time in his life . . ."

Here I felt such pity for him and such shame that I jumped out at once and said:

"No, mama, say what you like, but I won't leave my uncle without this family service. Am I to be ungrateful like Alfred, whom the soldier mummers perform in people's houses?[11] I bow down to your feet and beg your permission, don't force me to be ungrateful, allow me to accompany my uncle, because he's my relation and he gave me the watch and I will be shamed before all people if I leave him without my service."

Mama, however put out, had to let me go, but even so she ordered me very, very strictly not to drink, and not to look to the sides, and not to stop anywhere, and not to come home late.

I reassured her in all possible ways.

"Really, mama," I say, "why look to the sides when there's a straight path? I'll be with my uncle."

"All the same," she says, "though you're with your uncle, come back before the thieves' time. I won't sleep until you're back home."

Outside the door she started making crosses over me and whispered:

"Don't look too much to your uncle Ivan Leontyevich: they're all madcaps in Elets. It's even frightening to visit them at home: they invite officials for a party, and then force them to drink, or pour it behind their collars; they hide their overcoats, lock the gate, and start singing: 'He who won't drink—stays in the clink.' I know my brother on that score."

"All right, mama," I reply, "all right, all right. Rest easy about me in everything."

But mama goes on with her refrain:

"I feel in my heart," she says, "that you'll both come to no good."

VIII

At last my uncle and I went out the gate and set off. What could the priggers do to the two of us? Mama and my aunt were notorious homebodies and didn't know that I alone used to beat ten men with one fist in a fistfight. And my uncle, too, though an elderly man, could also stand up for himself.

A Robbery

We ran here and there, to the fish stores and wine cellars, bought everything, and sent it to the Boris and Gleb Inn in big bags. We ordered the samovars heated at once, laid out the snacks, set up the wine and rum, and invited the innkeeper of the Boris and Gleb to join our company:

"We won't do anything bad, our only desire and request is that no outsiders hear or see us."

"That I grant you," he said. "A bedbug on the wall may hear you, but nobody else."

And he was so sleepy himself, he kept yawning and making crosses over his mouth.

Soon Pavel Mironych arrived and brought both deacons with him: the one from the Theophany and the one from Nicetas. We had a little snack to begin with, a bit of sturgeon and caviar, then crossed ourselves and straightaway got down to the business of the tryout.

In three upstairs rooms, all the connecting doors stood open. We put our coats on the bed in one, in another, the far one, the snacks were set up, and in the middle one we tried out the voices.

First, Pavel Mironych stood in the middle of the room and showed what the merchants in Elets liked most from a deacon. His voice, as I said to you, was quite terrifying, as if it beat us on the face and shattered the glass in the windows.

Even the innkeeper woke up and said:

"You yourself should be the first deacon."

"Tell me another!" Pavel Mironych replied. "With my capital, I can get along as I am. It's just that I like to hear loudness in holy services."

"Who doesn't!"

And right after Pavel Mironych did his shouting, the deacons began to display themselves, first one and then the other, intoning the same things. The deacon from the Theophany was dark and soft, as if all quilted with cotton, while the one from Nicetas was redheaded, dry as a horseradish root, and his beard was small, upturned; but once they got to shouting, it was impossible to pick the better one. One kind came out better with one, but the other did another more pleasingly. Pavel Mironych began by presenting the way they liked it in Elets, so that the growling comes as if from far off. He growled out "It is meet and right," and then "Pierce, Master" and "Sacrifice, Master," and then both deacons did the same. The redhead's growl came out better. For the Gospel reading, Pavel Mironych took such a low note that it was lower than the lowest, as if carried on the wind from far away: "In those da-a-ays." Then he began rising higher and higher, and in the end gave such an exclamation that the window-panes jingled. And the deacons didn't lag behind him.

Well, then the rest all went the same way, how to conduct the litany and how it must be kept in tune with the choir, then the joy-ful "and for the salvation" in "Many Years," then the mournful "Rest Eternal."[12] The dry deacon from St. Nicetas pleased everyone so much with his howling that my uncle and Pavel Mironych started weeping and kissing him and asking him whether it might not lie within his natural powers to make it still more terrible.

The deacon says:

"Why not? It's allowed me by religion, but I'll have to fortify myself with pure Jamaican rum—it expands the resounding in the chest."

"Help yourself—that's what the rum is there for: you can drink it from a shot glass, swill it from a tumbler, or, better still, upend the bottle and down it all at once."

The deacon says:

"No, more than a tumbler at a time is not to my liking."

They fortified themselves—and the deacon began "Rest eternal in blessed repose" from low down and went on climbing ever higher and with an ever denser howling all the way to "the deceased bishops of Orel and Sevsk, Apollos and Dosiphey, Iona and Gavriil, Nikodim and Innokenty," and when he reached "make their memory e-ter-r-r-nal," his whole Adam's apple stuck out of his throat and he pro-duced such a howl that we were horrorstruck, and my uncle began crossing himself and shoving his feet under the bed, and I did the same. And under the bed, suddenly, something whacked us on the anklebones—we both cried out and all at once leaped into the mid-dle of the room and stood trembling . . .

My uncle said in fright:

"To blazes with it all! Stop them . . . don't name them anymore . . . they're here already, shoving us from under the bed."

Pavel Mironych asked:

"Who could be shoving you from under the bed?"

My uncle replied:

"Those dead ones."

Pavel Mironych, however, did not turn coward: he seized a burning candle, thrust it under the bed, but something blew out the candle, and knocked the candlestick from his hand, and emerged looking like one of our merchants from the Meat Market near St. Nicholas.

All of us, except the innkeeper, rushed in various directions and repeated the same word:

"Begone! Begone!"

And after that another merchant crawled out from under the other bed. And it seemed to us that this one, too, was from the Meat Market.

"What's the meaning of this?"

And the merchants both say:

"Please, it doesn't mean anything . . . We simply like to hear bass voices."

And the first merchant, who had struck my uncle and me on the legs and knocked the candle out of Pavel Mironych's hand, apologized, saying that we ourselves had kicked him with our boots, and Pavel Mironych had nearly burned his face with the candle.

But Pavel Mironych got angry at the innkeeper and started accusing him, saying that since money had been paid for the rooms, he should not have put strangers under the beds without permission.

The innkeeper, who seemed to have been sleeping, turned out to be quite drunk.

"These gentlemen," he says, "are both my relations: I wanted to do them a family service. I can do whatever I like in my own house."

"No, you can't."

"Yes, I can."

"And what if you've been paid?"

"So what if I've been paid? It's my house, and my relations are dearer to me than any payment. You stay here and you'll leave, but they're permanent: you've got no call to go poking your heels at them or burning their eyes with candles."

"We didn't poke our heels at them on purpose, we just tucked our feet under," says my uncle.

"You shouldn't have tucked your feet under, you should have sat upright."

"We did it from fear."

"Well, there's no harm done. But they're devoted to lerigion and wanted to listen . . ."

Pavel Mironych boiled over.

"What kind of lerigion is that?" he says. "It's only a sample for education: lerigion's in the Church."

"That makes no difference," says the innkeeper. "It all comes to the same thing."

"Ah, you incendiaries!"

"And you're rioters."

"How come?"

"You dealt in dead meat. You locked up the assessor!"

And endless stupidities of the same sort followed. And suddenly everything was in an uproar, and the innkeeper was shouting:

"Away with all you millers, get out of my establishment, me and my butchers will carry on by ourselves."

Pavel Mironych shook his fist at him.

But the innkeeper replies:

"If you threaten me, I'll shout up such Orelian stalwarts right now that you won't bring a single unbroken rib home to Elets."

Pavel Mironych, being the foremost strongman in Elets, got offended.

"Well, no help for it," he says, "call for them, if you can still stand up, but I'm not leaving this room; we laid out money for the drink."

The butchers wanted to leave—they had obviously decided to call people.

Pavel Mironych herded them back and shouted:

"Where's the key? I'll lock them all up."

I said to my uncle:

"Uncle! For God's sake! See what we're coming to! There may be a murder here! And mama and auntie are waiting at home . . . What must they be thinking! . . . How they'll worry!"

My uncle was frightened himself.

"Grab your coat," he says, "while the door's still open, and let's get away."

We leaped into the next room, grabbed our coats, and gladly came barreling out into the open air; only the darkness around us was so thick you couldn't see an inch, and a wet snow was slapping big flakes in our faces, so that our eyes were blinded.

"Lead me," says my uncle. "I've somehow suddenly forgotten all about where we are, and I can't make anything out."

"Just run for it," I say.

"It's not nice that we left Pavel Mironych."

"But what could we do with him?"

"That's so . . . but he's our foremost parishioner."

"He's a strong man; they won't hurt him."

A Robbery

The snow blinded us, and once we leaped out of that stuffiness, we fancied God knows what, as if somebody were coming at us from all sides.

IX

Naturally, I knew the way very well, because our town isn't big and I was born and grew up in it, but it was as if this darkness and wet snow right after the heat and light of the room dimmed my memory.

"Wait, uncle," I said, "let me figure out where we are."

"You mean you don't know the landmarks of your own town?"

"No, I know them. The first landmarks for us are the two cathedrals, the one new and big, the other old and small, and we have to go between them and turn right, but in this snow I don't see either the big one or the small one."

"How about that! They may really take our fur coats or even strip us naked, and we won't know where to run. We could catch our death of cold."

"Maybe, God willing, they won't strip us naked."

"Do you know those merchants who came out from under the beds?"

"Yes."

"Both of them?"

"Both of them. One is named Efrosin Ivanovich, and the other Agafon Petrovich."

"And what—are they real true merchants?"

"They are."

"I didn't like the mug on one of them at all."

"What about it?"

"Some sort of Jesovitic expression."

"That's Efrosin: he frightened me once, too."

"How?"

"In my imagination. Once I was walking past their shops in the evening after the vigil, and I stopped across from St. Nicholas to pray that God would let me pass, because they have vicious dogs in the market; and this merchant Efrosin Ivanych had a nightingale whistling in his shop, and the light of an icon lamp was coming through a crack in the fence . . . I put my eye to the crack and saw him standing knife in hand over a bullock. The bullock at his feet has its throat cut and is kicking its bound feet and tossing its head; the head is dangling from the cut throat and blood is gushing out; and there's another calf in the dark corner awaiting the knife, maybe mooing, maybe trembling, and over the fresh blood the nightingale in its cage is whistling furiously, and far across the Oka a thunderstorm is rumbling. Fear came over me. I was frightened and cried out: 'Efrosin Ivanych!' I wanted to ask him to accompany me to the pontoon bridge, but he suddenly gave such a start . . . I ran away. And I've only just remembered it."

"Why are you telling me such a frightening thing now?"

"And what of it? Are you afraid?"

"No, I'm not, but better not talk about frightening things."

"But it ended well. The next day I told him: thus and so—I got scared of you. And he says: 'And you scared me, because I was standing there listening to the nightingale, and you suddenly cried out.' I say: 'How is it you listen so feelingly?' 'I can't help it,' he says, 'my heart often swoons in me.'"

"Are you strong, or not?" my uncle suddenly interrupted.

"I wouldn't boast of any special strength," I said, "but if I put three or four old coppers in my fist, I can send any prigger you like to an early grave."

"That's fine," he says, "if he's alone."

"Who?"

"The prigger, that's who! But if there's two of them, or a whole company? . . ."

"Never mind: if there's two, we'll manage—you can help. And priggers don't go around in big companies."

"Well, don't rely much on me: I've grown old, my lad. Formerly, it's true, I gave such beatings for the glory of God that they were known all over Elets and Livny . . ."

Before he finished saying it, we suddenly thought we heard somebody coming behind us and even hastening his steps.

"Excuse me," I said, "but it seems to me somebody's coming."

"Ah, yes! I also hear somebody coming," my uncle replied.

A Robbery

I kept silent. My uncle whispered to me:

"Let's stop and let him go past us."

And this was just on the slope of the hill where you go down to the Balashevsky Bridge in summer, and across the ice between the barges in winter.

It was a godforsaken place from old times. There were few houses on the hill, and those were closed up, and below, to the right, on the Orlik, there were seedy bathhouses and an empty mill, and up from there a sheer cliff like a wall, and to the right a garden where thieves always hid. The police chief Tsyganok had built a sentry box there, and folk started saying that the sentry helped the thieves . . . I thought to myself, whoever's coming—prigger or not—in fact it's better to let him go past.

My uncle and I stopped . . . And what do you think: the man who was walking behind us must also have stopped—his footsteps were no longer heard.

"Maybe we were mistaken," said my uncle. "Maybe there wasn't anybody."

"No," I replied, "I clearly heard footsteps, and very close."

We stood there a little longer—nothing to be heard; but as soon as we went on—we heard him hurrying after us again . . . We could even hear him hustling and breathing hard.

We slackened our pace and went more quietly—and he also went more quietly; we speeded up again—and he again came on more quickly and was nearly stepping in our tracks.

There was nothing more to talk about: we clearly understood that this was a prigger following us, and he'd been following us like that all the way from the inn; which meant that he was lying in wait for us, and when I lost my way in the snow between the big cathedral and the small—he caught sight of us. Which meant that now there was no avoiding some run-in. He couldn't be alone.

And the snow, as if on purpose, poured down still more heavily; you walk as if you're stirring a pot of curds: it's white, and wet, and sticks to you all over.

And now the Oka is ahead of us, we have to go down on the ice;

but on the ice there are empty barges, and in order to reach home on the other side, we have to make our way through the narrow passages between these barges. And the prigger who is following us surely has some fellow thieves hidden there somewhere. It would be handiest for them to rob us on the ice between the barges—and kill us and shove us underwater. Their den was there, and in the daytime you could always see them around it. They fixed up their lairs with mats of hemp stalks and straw, on which they lay smoking and waiting. And special pot-house wives hung out with them there. Rascally wenches. They'd show themselves, lure a man and lead him away, and he'd get robbed, and they'd be there on the lookout again.

Most of all they attacked those returning from the vigil in the men's monastery, because people liked the singing, and back then there was the astounding bass, Strukov, of terrifying appearance: all swarthy, three tufts of hair on his head, and a lower lip that opened like the folding front flap of a phaeton. While he bellowed, it stayed open, and then it slammed shut. Anybody who wanted to return home safely from the vigil invited the clerks Ryabykin or Korsunsky to go with him. They were both very strong, and the priggers were afraid of them. Especially of Ryabykin, who was wall-eyed and was put on trial when the clerk Solomka was killed in the Shchekatikhino grove during the May fête . . .

I'm telling all this to my uncle so that he won't think about himself, but he interrupts:

"Stop it, you'll really be the death of me. It's all about killing. Let's rest at least, before we go down on the ice. Here, I've still got three coppers on me. Take them and put them in your glove."

"Do please give them to me—I've got room in my mitten, I can take three more coppers."

And I was just going to take these three coppers from him, when somebody emerged from the darkness right next to us and said:

"So, my good fellows, who have you robbed?"

I thought: that's it—a prigger, but I could tell by the voice that it was that butcher I told you about.

"Is that you, Efrosin Ivanych?" I say. "Come along with us, brother."

But he hurries by, as if blending with the snow, and answers on his way:

"No, brothers, we're no birds of a feather: divide up your own booty, but don't touch Efrosin. Efrosin's just been listening to voices, his heart's swooning in his breast . . . One flick—and there'll be no life left in you."

"Impossible to stop him," I say. "You see, he's mistaken on our score: he takes us for thieves."

My uncle replies:

"God keep him and his bird feathers. With him, too, you don't know if you'll be left alive. We'd better take what God grants and go with God's help alone. If God doesn't desert you, pigs won't hurt you. Now that he's gone, I feel brave. . . . Lord have mercy! Nicholas, protector of Mtsensk, Mitrophany of Voronezh, Tikhon and Josaf . . . Scat! What is it?"

"What?"

"Didn't you see?"

"What can anybody see here?"

"Something like a cat under our feet."

"You imagined it."

"Just like a watermelon rolling."

"Maybe somebody's hat got torn off."

"Aie!"

"What's wrong?"

"It's the hat."

"What about it?"

"Why, you yourself said 'torn off' . . . They must be trouncing somebody up there on the hill."

"No, it must be the wind tore it off."

And with those words we both started going down towards the barges on the ice.

The barges, I repeat, were simply standing there then, without any order, one beside the other, just as they had put in. They were piled terribly close together, with only the narrowest little passageways between them, where you could barely get through and had to keep twisting and turning this way and that.

"Well, uncle," I say, "I don't want to conceal it from you: here lies the greatest danger."

My uncle froze—he even stopped praying to the saints.

"Now, uncle," I say, "you go on ahead."

"Why ahead?" he whispers.

"It's safer ahead."

"Why safer?"

"Because, if a prigger attacks you, you can immediately fall back towards me, and then I'll support you, and give him one. But behind I won't see you: the prigger may cover your mouth with his hand or some slippery bast—and I won't hear . . . I'll keep walking."

"No, don't keep walking . . . And what sort of bast is it?"

"Slippery. Their women pick it up around the bathhouses and bring it to them for stopping people's mouths so they can't shout."

I could see that my uncle kept talking like this because he was afraid to go ahead.

"I'm apprehensive about going ahead," he says, "because he may hit me on the forehead with a weight, and then you won't have time to defend me."

"Well, but behind is still more frightening, because he may swat you on the head with a svaika."

"What svaika?"

"Why do you ask? Don't you know what a svaika is?"

"No, I do know: a svaika's used in a game—made of iron, sharp."

"Yes, sharp."

"With a round head?"

"Yes, a three- or four-pound ball-shaped head."

"Back home in Elets they carry bludgeons for that; but this is the first I hear about a svaika."

"Here in Orel it's the most favorite fashion—on the head with a svaika. The skull splits right open."

"Better, though, if we walk arm in arm beside each other."

"It's too narrow for two between the barges."

"Still . . . this svaika, really! . . . Better if we squeeze together somehow."

XI

But as soon as we locked elbows and started squeezing through those passageways between the barges—we hear that one from behind us, again not hanging back, again pressing close on our heels.

"Tell me, please," says my uncle, "maybe the other one wasn't the butcher?"

I just shrugged my shoulders and listened.

A scraping could be heard as he squeezed through sideways, and he was just about to seize me from behind with his hand . . . And another one could be heard running down the hill . . . Well, it was obvious these were priggers—we had to get away. We tore ahead, but it was impossible to go quickly, because it was dark, and narrow, and ice stuck up everywhere, and this nearest prigger was already right on my back . . . breathing.

I say to my uncle:

"Anyhow there's no avoiding it—let's turn around."

I thought, either let him go on past us, or better if I meet him in the face with my fist full of coppers than have him strike from behind. But as soon as we turned to face him, the good-for-nothing bent down and shot between us like a cat! . . .

My uncle and I both went sprawling.

My uncle shouts to me:

"Catch him, catch him, Mishutka! He snatched my beaver hat!"

And I can't see a thing, but I remember about my watch and clutch myself where it should be. And just imagine, my watch is gone . . . The beast snatched it!

"Same for me," I answer. "He took my watch!"

And, forgetting myself, I went hurtling after the prigger as fast as I could, and was lucky enough to catch him in the dark just behind a barge, hit him on the head as hard as I could with my coppers, knocked him down, and sat on him:

"Give me back the watch!"

He didn't say a word in reply, the scoundrel, but he nipped my hand with his teeth.

"Ah, you dog!" I say. "See how he bites!" And I gave him a good belt in the jaw, then stopped his mouth with the cuff of my sleeve, and with the other hand went straight for his breast pocket, found the watch at once, and yanked it out.

Just then my uncle ran up:

"Hold him, hold him," he says, "I'll give him a drubbing . . ."

And we started drubbing him Elets-fashion and Orel-fashion. We pummeled him cruelly, so much so that when he tore away from us, he didn't even cry out, but dashed off like a hare; and only when he had fled as far as the Plautin Well did he shout "Help"; and at once somebody on the other side, on the hill, also shouted "Help."

"What brigands!" says my uncle. "They rob people, and then shout 'Help' themselves on both sides! . . . Did you take your watch back from him?"

"Yes."

"Why didn't you take back my hat as well?"

"Your hat," I reply, "went clean out of my head."

"And I'm cold now. I've got a bald spot."

"Put on my hat."

"I don't want yours. My hat cost fifty roubles at Faleev's."

"Never mind," I say, "nobody can see it now."

"What about you?"

"I'll simply go bareheaded like this. We're already close—we'll turn that corner in a moment, and it'll be our house."

My hat, however, was too small for my uncle. He took a handkerchief from his pocket and tied it over his head.

And so we came running home.

XII

Mama and my aunt had not gone to bed yet: they were both knitting stockings and waiting for us. When they saw my uncle come in all covered with snow and his head tied with a handkerchief like a woman's, they both gasped at once and began talking.

"Lord! What's the matter! . . . Where's the winter hat you were wearing?"

"Farewell, good old winter hat! . . . It's no more," my uncle replied.

"Our Lady, most holy Mother of God! Where did it go?"

"Your Orelian priggers took it on the ice."

"So that's why we heard you cry 'Help.' I said to my sister, 'Let's send our fullers—I think I hear Misha's innocent voice.'"

"Oh, yes! By the time your fullers woke up and came out, there wouldn't even have been a name left to us . . . No, it wasn't us crying 'Help,' it was the thieves; and we defended ourselves."

Mama and my aunt boiled up.

"What? Can Misha have shown his strength?"

"Yes, our Misha played the main part—he may have let my hat slip, but he did take back his watch."

I can see mama is glad that I've done so well, but she says:

"Ah, Misha, Misha! And I begged you so not to drink anything and not to stay out late, till the thieves' time. Why didn't you listen to me?"

"Forgive me, mama," I say, "but I didn't drink anything, and I didn't dare leave uncle there alone. You can see for yourself, if he'd come home alone, he might have gotten into some big trouble."

"He's had his hat taken as it is."

"Well, so what! . . . You can always get yourself a hat."

"Of course—thank God you took back your watch."

"Yes, mama, I took it. And, oh, how I took it! I knocked him down in a trice, stopped his mouth with my sleeve so that he wouldn't cry out, put my other hand into his breast pocket and pulled out my watch, and then uncle and I started pummeling him."

"Well, that was pointless."

"Not at all! Let the rascal remember it."

"The watch wasn't damaged?"

"No, I don't think so—only the chain seems to be broken . . ."

And with those words I took the watch from my pocket and examined the chain, but my aunt looks closely and asks:

"Whose watch might that be?"

"What do you mean, whose? It's mine, of course."

"But yours had a rim."

"Well, so?"

And I look myself and suddenly see: in fact, this watch doesn't have a gold rim, but instead of that it has a silver face with a shepherd and shepherdess on it, and little sheep at their feet . . .

I started shaking all over.

"What is this??! It's not my watch!"

And they all just stood there, not comprehending.

My aunt says:

"How about that!"

My uncle reassures us:

"Wait," he says, "don't be frightened. The thief must have made off with Mishutka's watch, and this one he took earlier from somebody else."

But I flung the filched watch on the table and, so as not to see it, rushed to my room. And there I hear my watch on the wall above my bed ticking away: tick-tock, tick-tock, tick-tock.

I jump up to it with a candle and see—that's it, my watch with the rim . . . Hanging there quite nicely, where it belongs!

Here I slapped myself on the forehead as hard as I could and started, not crying, but howling . . .

"Lord God! Who have I robbed?"

XIII

Mama, my aunt, my uncle—everybody got frightened, came running, shook me.

"What's the matter? What's the matter? Calm down!"

"Please," I say, "leave me alone! How can I calm down if I've robbed a man?"

Mama started crying.

"He's gone mad," she says. "He must have seen something horrible!"

"I certainly did, mama! . . . What do I do now!!"

"What was it that you saw?"

"That there. Look for yourself."

"What? Where?"

"That, that there! Look! Don't you see what it is?"

They looked at the wall where I was pointing and saw the silver watch with the gold rim that my uncle had given me, hanging on the wall and ticking away quite calmly . . .

My uncle was the first to recover his reason.

"Holy God," he says, "isn't that your watch?"

"Yes, of course it is!"

"So it must be you didn't take it with you, but left it here?"

"You can see I did."

"And that one . . . that one . . . Whose is that one you took?"

"How should I know?"

"What is this! My little sisters, my dear ones! Misha and I have robbed somebody!"

Mama's legs gave way under her: she cried out as she stood there and sat down on the floor right where she was.

I rushed to pick her up, but she said wrathfully:

"Away, robber!"

My aunt just made crosses in all directions and muttered:

"Holy God, holy God, holy God!"

But mama clutched her head and whispered:

"They beat somebody, they robbed somebody, and they don't know who!"

My uncle picked her up and tried to calm her:

"Calm yourself now, it wasn't a good man we beat."

"How do you know? Maybe he was; maybe it was somebody going to fetch a doctor for a sick man."

My uncle says:

"And what about my hat? Why did he snatch my hat?"

"God knows about your hat and where you left it."

My uncle was offended, but mama paid no attention to him and turned to me again.

"I've kept my boy in the fear of God for so many years, and this is what he prepared himself for: thief or none, but he looks like one . . . After this no sensible girl in Orel will marry you, because now everybody, everybody, will know you're a prigger."

I couldn't help myself and said loudly:

"For pity's sake, mama, what kind of a prigger am I? It's all a mistake!"

But she didn't want to listen, and kept rapping me on the head with her knuckles and wailing woefully:[13]

"I taught you: my child, live far from wickedness, do not go gambling and merrymaking, do not drink two cups in a single gulp, do not fall asleep in a secluded place, lest your costly trousers be taken off you, lest great shame and disgrace overtake you, and through you your family suffer idle reproach and revilement. I taught you: my child, do not go to dicers and taverners, do not think how to steal and rob, but you did not want to heed your mother. Now take off your fine clothes and put on pot-house rags, and wait till the watchmen knock at our gates and Tsyganok himself comes barging into our honest house."

She kept wailing like that and rapping me on the head with her knuckles.

But when my aunt heard about Tsyganok, she cried out:

"Lord, save us from bloody men and from Arid!"[14]

My God! In other words, our house turned into a veritable hell.

My aunt and mama embraced each other and, in that embrace, withdrew weeping. Only my uncle and I remained.

I sat down, leaned on the table, and I don't remember how many hours I went on sitting there. I kept thinking: who was it that I robbed? Maybe it was the Frenchman Saint-Vincent coming from a lesson, or the secretary from the office who lives in the house of Strakhov, the marshal of the nobility[15] . . . I was sorry for each of them. And what if it was my godfather Kulabukhov coming from the other side after visiting the treasury secretary! . . . He wanted to pass by quietly, so as not to be seen with a little sack, and I up and worked him over . . . A godson! . . . his own godfather!

"I'll go to the attic and hang myself. There's nothing else left for me."

And my uncle was just fiercely drinking tea, and then he comes up to me somehow—I didn't even see how—and says:

"Enough sitting and moping, we must act."

"Why, yes," I reply, "of course, if we can find out whose watch I took . . ."

"Never mind. Get up quickly, and we'll go together and declare everything ourselves."

"Who are we going to declare it to?"

"To your Tsyganok himself, naturally."

"How shameful to confess it!"

"What can we do? Do you think I'm eager to go to Tsyganok? . . . But all the same, it's better to own up to it ourselves than to have him come looking for us: take both watches and let's go."

I agreed.

I took both my own watch, which my uncle had given me, and the one I had brought home that night, and, without saying good-bye to mama, we left.

XIV

We went to the police station, and Tsyganok was already sitting in his office before the zertsalo,[16] and at his door stood a young constable, Prince Solntsev-Zasekin. The family was notable, the talent unremarkable.

My uncle saw that I bowed to this prince, and said:

"Is he really a prince?"

"By God, it's true."

"Flash something at him in your fingers, so that he'll pop out to the stairs for a minute."

And that's just how it went: I held up a twenty-five-kopeck piece— the prince popped out to the stairs.

My uncle put the coin in his hand and asked that we be let in to the office as soon as possible.

The constable started telling us that a great many incidents had taken place here in town last night.

"And with us an incident also occurred."

"Well, but what sort? You both look yourselves, but down on the river there's a man sunk under the ice; two merchants on Poleshskaya Square scattered all the shafts, frames, and sleigh bodies about; a man was found unconscious under a tub, and two had their watches stolen. I'm the only one left on duty, all the rest are running around looking for the priggers . . ."

"All right, all right, you go and report that we've come to explain a certain matter."

"Have you had a fight or some family trouble?"

"No, just report that we're here on a secret matter; we're ashamed to explain it in front of people. Here's another."

The prince pocketed the fifty-kopeck piece and five minutes later called us:

"Come in, please."

XV

Tsyganok was a thickset Ukrainian—exactly like a black cockroach; bristling mustaches, and the crudest Ukrainian-style conversation.

My uncle, in his own way, his Elets way, wanted to go up to him, but he shouted:

"Speak from a distance."

We stopped.

"What's your business?"

My uncle says:

"First of all—this."

And he placed a sweetener on the table, wrapped in paper. Tsyganok covered it up.

Then my uncle began his story:

"I'm a merchant and a church warden from Elets, I came here yesterday on a church necessity; I'm staying with my relations beyond the Plautin Well . . ."

"So it was you who got robbed last night, was it?"

"Exactly. My nephew and I were on our way home at eleven o'clock, and an unknown man was following us, and as we started to cross the ice between the barges, he . . ."

"Wait a minute . . . And who was the third one with you?"

"There was no third one with us, besides this thief, who rushed . . ."

"But who got drowned there last night?"

"Drowned?"

"Yes!"

"We know nothing about that."

The police chief rang and said to the constable:

"Take them to the clink!"

My uncle pleaded:

"For pity's sake, Your Honor! Why? . . . We ourselves came to tell . . ."

"Wasn't it you who drowned the man?"

"We never even heard anything about any drowning. Who got drowned?"

"Nobody knows. A mucked-up beaver hat was found by a hole in the ice, but who was wearing it—nobody knows."

"A beaver hat!?"

"Yes. Show him the hat, let's see what he says."

The constable took my uncle's hat from the closet.

My uncle says:

"That's my hat. A thief snatched it off me yesterday on the ice."

Tsyganok batted his eyes.

"What thief? Stop blathering! The thief didn't take a hat, the thief stole a watch."

"A watch? Whose watch, Your Honor?"

"The Nicetas deacon's."

"The Nicetas deacon's!"

"Yes, and he was beaten badly, this Nicetas deacon."

We were simply astounded.

So that's who we worked over!

Tsyganok says:

"Must be you know these crooks."

"Yes," my uncle replies, "it's us."

And he told how it all happened.

"Where is this watch now?"

"If you please—here's the one watch, and here's the other."

"And that's all?"

My uncle slips him another sweetener and says:

"Here's more for you."

He covers it up and says:

"Bring the deacon here!"

XVI

The lean deacon comes in, all beaten up and his head bandaged.

Tsyganok looks at me and says:

"See?!"

I bow and say:

"Your Honor, I'm ready to endure anything, only please don't send me to some far-off place. I'm my mother's only son."

"No, tell me, are you a Christian or not? Is there any feeling in you?"

I see the conversation isn't going right and say:

"Uncle, give him a sweetener for me, they'll pay you back at home."

My uncle gives it.

"How did this happen to you?"

The deacon began telling how "the whole company of us were in the Boris and Gleb Inn, and everything was very good and noble, but then, for a bribe, the innkeeper put strangers under the bed so they could listen, and one of the Elets merchants got offended, and a fight came of it. I quietly put my coat on and left, but when I went around the office building, I see two men on the lookout ahead of me. I stop to let them go further, and they stop; I go on—so do they. And suddenly I hear somebody else from far away overtaking me from behind . . . I got completely frightened, rushed ahead, and the first two turned towards me in the narrow passage between the barges and blocked my way . . . And the one from the hill behind had almost caught up with me. I prayed in my mind: 'Lord bless me!' and bent down to slip between these two, and so I did, but they ran after me, knocked me down, beat me, and snatched my watch . . . Here's what's left of the chain."

"Show me the chain."

He put the piece of chain together with the one attached to the watch and said:

"There you are. Look, is this your watch?"

The deacon says:

"It's mine all right, and I'd like to have it back."

"That's impossible, it has to stay here till the investigation."

"And what did I get beaten for?" he says.

"That you can ask them."

Here my uncle intervened.

"Your Honor! There's no point in asking us. We are indeed to blame, it was we who beat the father deacon, and we'll make up for it. We're taking him to Elets with us."

But the deacon was so offended that he didn't see things that way at all.

"No," he says, "God forbid I ever agree to go to Elets. Forget it! I was just about to accept, and right off you give me this treatment."

My uncle says:

"Father deacon, this is all a matter of a mistake."

"A fine mistake, when I can't turn my head anymore."

"We'll get you cured."

"No," he says, "I don't want your cures, I always go to the attendant at Finogeich's bathhouse to get cured, but you can pay me a thousand roubles to build a house."

"That we'll do."

"It's no joke. I'm not to be beaten . . . I have my clerical dignity."

"We'll satisfy your dignity, too."

And Tsyganok also started helping my uncle:

"The Elets merchants will satisfy you . . . ," he says. "Is there anybody else there in the clink?"

XVII

They brought in the Boris and Gleb innkeeper and Pavel Mironych. Pavel Mironych's frock coat was in shreds, and so was the innkeeper's.

"What was the fight about?" asks Tsyganok.

They both lay sweeteners on the desk for him and reply:

"It was nothing, Your Honor. We're on perfectly good terms again."

"Well, splendid, if you're not angry about the beating, that's your business; but how dared you cause disorder in town? Why did you scatter all the troughs and sleighs and shafts on Poleshskaya Square?"

The innkeeper said it was accidental.

"I wanted to take him to the police last night, and he me; we pulled each other by the arm, but the butcher Agafon supported me; we got lost in the snow, wound up on the square—no way to get through . . . everything got scattered . . . We started shouting from fear . . . The patrol picked us up . . . a watch got lost . . ."

"Whose?"

"Mine."

Pavel Mironych says:

"And mine, too."

"What proofs have you got?"

"Why proofs? We're not looking for them."

"And who put the butcher Agafon under the washtub?"

"That we can't say," says the innkeeper. "The tub must have fallen on him and knocked him down, and he, being drunk, fell asleep under it. Let us go, Your Honor, we're not looking for anything."

"Very well," says Tsyganok, "only we've got to finish with the others. Bring in the other deacon."

The swarthy deacon comes in.

Tsyganok says to him:

"Why did you smash up the sentry box last night?"

The deacon replies:

"I was very frightened, Your Honor."

"What were you frightened of?"

"Some people on the ice started shouting 'Help' very loud. I rushed back and asked the sentry to hide me from the priggers, and he chased me away: 'I can't stand up, I sent my boot soles to be mended.' Then I pressed myself against the door in fright, and it broke. It's my fault—I forced my way into the box and fell asleep there, and in the morning I got up, looked: no watch, no money."

Tsyganok says:

"So you see, Eletsians? This deacon also suffered through you, and his watch disappeared."

Pavel Mironych and my uncle replied:

"Well, Your Honor, we'll have to go home and borrow from acquaintances, we've got nothing more on us."

So we all went out, but the watch stayed there, and soon we were all consoled for that, and there was a lot of joking and laughing, and I drank with them then in the Boris and Gleb Inn till I got drunk for the first time in my life, and I rode down the street in a cab, waving my handkerchief. After that they borrowed money in Orel and left, but they didn't take the deacon along with them, because he was too afraid of them. Insist as they might—he wouldn't go.

"I'm very glad," he says, "that the Lord granted that I get a thousand roubles from you for my offense. I'll build myself a little house now, and talk the secretary into giving me a good post here. You Eletsians, I can see, are just too brassy."

For me, however, a terrible trial began. Mama got so ill from her anger at me that she had one foot in the grave. There was dejection all through the house. Doctor Dépiche was not called in: they were afraid he would ask all kinds of questions about her health. They turned to religion. Mother Evnikeya was living in the convent then, and she had a Jordanian sheet, which she had wiped herself with after bathing in the Jordan River. They wrapped mama in this sheet. It didn't help. They blessed the water with seven crosses in seven churches every day. That didn't help. There was a layabout peasant, Esafeika—he lay about all the time and never worked. They sent him a hatful of cut-up apples and asked him to pray. That didn't help either. Only when she and her sister finally went to Finogeich's bathhouse and had her blood let with leeches, only then did she pull herself together somewhat. She ordered the Jordanian sheet sent back to Evnikeya and started looking for an orphan to raise at home.

This was the matchmaker's teaching. The matchmaker had many children of her own, but she was also very fond of orphans—she kept taking them in, and so she started saying to my mother:

"Take some poor people's child into your home. Everything at home will change for you at once: the air will become different. Gentlefolk set out flowers for the air—of course, there's nothing wrong with that; but the main thing for the air is children. There's a spirit that breathes from children, and the angels rejoice at it, but Satan gnashes his teeth . . . There's a girl now in the Pushkarny quarter: she's had such a hard time with her baby, she even took her to the Orlik mill to drown her."

Mama said:

"Tell her not to drown her, but to leave her with me."

That same day the little girl Mavrutka started squealing in our house and sucking her little fist. Mama busied herself with the girl, and a change came over her. She became caustic with me.

"You don't need any new clothes for the feast day: now that you're a drunkard, pot-house rags are enough for you."

A Robbery

At home I endured it all, but I also couldn't show my face outside, because as soon as they saw me, the market folk started teasing me:

"He's the one who took the deacon's watch."

No living at home, no going out.

Only the orphan girl Mavrutka smiled at me.

But the matchmaker Matryona Terentyevna saved me and helped me out. She was a simple woman, but a kindly one.

"My fine lad," she says, "would you like to have your head put back on your shoulders? I'll do it so that, if anybody laughs at you, you won't feel it."

I say:

"Please do, I'm disgusted with life."

"Well, then," she says, "listen to me alone. You and I will go to Mtsensk, pray zealously to St. Nicholas, and offer him a candle big as a post; and I'll marry you to a picture of beauty, whom you'll live with all your life, thanking God and remembering me, and protecting poor orphans, because I have a soft spot for orphans."

I replied that I myself felt pity for orphans, but that no decent sort of girl would marry me now.

"Why not? That's all nonsense. This girl's intelligent. You didn't take from your own household, you brought to it. That makes a difference. I'll tell her how to understand it, and she'll see it clearly, and she'll marry you all right. And we'll travel so nicely to St. Nicholas with full satisfaction: the horse will pull a little cart with our load, with a samovar, with provisions, and we three will go by foot along the roadside, we'll take that trouble for the saint's sake: you, and me, and her, and I'll take an orphan girl to keep me company. And she, my swan, Alyonushka, also pities orphans. They'll let her go to Mtsensk with me. And you and she will walk and walk, then sit down, and sit and sit, and then take to the road again and get to talking, and the talking will lead to loving, and once you've tasted love, you'll see that in it is all our life and joy, and our desire is to live in family quietude. And then you'll just spit on all people's talk, and not even look their way. So all will be well, and your former pranks will be forgotten."

I obtained mama's leave to go to St. Nicholas and heal my soul, and the rest all went as the matchmaker Matryona Terentyevna had said. I became friends with the girl Alyonushka, and I forgot about all those happenings; and once I married her and a children's spirit came to our house, mama also calmed down, and to this day I live and keep saying: Blessed art thou, O Lord!

Notes

Biblical quotations, unless otherwise noted, are from the King James Version.

The Lady Macbeth of Mtsensk (1865)

1. **the lives of the Kievan saints:** A collection of writings about monks from the Monastery of the Caves in Kiev (founded in 1015) and the history of the monastery, based on letters exchanged in the early thirteenth century by Simon, bishop of Suzdal, and the monk Polycarp.

2. **include him in the communion:** That is, write his name down on a list of those to be prayed for by the priest during the preparation of the bread and wine for communion.

3. **the feast of the Entrance:** The full title is "The Feast of the Entrance of the Mother of God into the Temple," commemorating Mary's first entrance as a child into the temple of Jerusalem, where she was met by the high priest Zacharias. It is celebrated on November 21.

4. **St. Feodor Stratilatos:** Theodore Stratilatos, or Stratelates ("the General"), military commander of the city of Heraclea Pontica, a fourth-century Greek martyr, executed by the Roman emperor Licinius for declaring himself a Christian and refusing to take part in a pagan celebration.

5. **the social-democratic communes of Petersburg:** The first experiments by Russian nihilists in alternative social organization. In the early 1860s, the nihilists took Leskov for their ideological opponent and vilified him in their writings—hence the sarcasm here.

6. **an Old Believer:** In 1656–58, Nikon, patriarch of the Russian Orthodox Church, introduced certain reforms to bring the Church into conformity with current Greek Orthodox practice, and also made corrections in the translation of liturgical texts. These changes were rejected by some, who held to the old ways and thus became known as Old Believers (also *Raskolniki,* "Schismatics"). In 1666, the Old Believers were anathematized by the Church and deprived of civil rights. Some renounced having priests and sacraments (apart from baptism), as a consequence of their break with the apostolic church; others ordained their own priests and maintained the sacraments; still others even practiced the "rebaptism" of those who joined them. Leskov was especially interested in the Old Believers, who figure prominently in a number of his stories.

7. **Curse the day . . . die**: Job's wife actually says, ". . . curse God, and die" (Job 2:9). In Job 3:3, Job himself curses the day he was born.
8. **A blond head . . . none can see**: Lines from the poem "The Call" (1844), by the Russian poet and prose writer Yakov Polonsky (1819–98).

The Sealed Angel (1873)

1. **the eve of St. Basil's**: The feast day of St. Basil the Great of Caesarea in Cappadocia (ca. AD 330–379) falls on January 1.
2. **on the stove**: The Russian peasant stove was a large and elaborate structure that served not only for heating and cooking, but also for sleeping and even for bathing, as will be seen later.
3. **the old Russian faith**: See note 6 to "Lady Macbeth." "The Sealed Angel" deals in particular with the maintaining of the tradition of icon painting among the Old Believers. Icon painting was beginning to be revived in Leskov's time and interested him deeply. He claimed to have written "The Sealed Angel" while sitting in the studio of an icon painter in an Old Believers' quarter in Petersburg.
4. **granary**: In the Old and New Testaments, granaries symbolize wealth in general (see, for instance, Luke 12:16–20, the parable of the rich man).
5. **Novgorod or Stroganov icon painters**: After the Mongol invasion of Russia in the thirteenth century and the fall of the capital Kiev, the center of Russian artistic culture shifted to the city of Novgorod, where the art of icon painting reached a high point in the fourteenth and fifteenth centuries. The Stroganovs were wealthy merchants from Novgorod who moved further north and brought Novgorod icon painters with them. The Stroganov school was known in particular for its use of bright colors and for its miniature icons, such as the one painted by Sevastian later in "The Sealed Angel."
6. **Deisises . . . wet hair**: The Deisis, the central section in the iconostasis, is a triple icon representing Christ in majesty between the Virgin and St. John the Baptist. The Savior-not-made-by-hands is an icon depicting the face of Christ imprinted on a towel or cloth. According to legend, Abgar, king of Edessa, wishing to be healed of leprosy, sent his court painter to make an image of Christ, but the painter could not get close enough to do it. Christ then took a towel, wiped his face, imprinting his image on it, and had the towel sent to Abgar, who was healed by it. On some icons of this type, Christ is portrayed with wet-looking hair and beard.
7. **the Indictus . . . Palekh**: The Indictus is the icon of the first feast of the ecclesiastical year, which begins on September 1. The Council of Angels usually portrays the archangel Michael and/or Gabriel holding a round icon of the infant Emmanuel (Christ), surrounded by a host of angels. The Paternity portrays God the Father with the Christ Child on his lap holding a dove. The Six Days usually has six parts illustrating the six days of the creation; another type has six days of the week identified with certain feasts, and sometimes the two are combined. The Healers is a late type of icon (eighteenth or early nineteenth century) portraying various saints and indicating which one heals

which disease. The Trinity illustrates the episode in Genesis 18:1–16 in which three angels visit Abraham, considered the first manifestation of God as the Trinity. The town of Palekh was an important center of icon painting from the sixteenth to the mid-nineteenth century.

8. **Bezaleel:** See Exodus 35:30–35. Bezaleel was one of two men called by God and Moses to build and decorate the sanctuary for the ark of the covenant.

9. **famous stone bridge:** Leskov has in mind the suspension bridge over the Dniepr River in Kiev, built in 1849–53, while he himself was living in Kiev.

10. **Amalthea's horn:** That is, the horn of plenty. In Greek mythology, the goddess or goat-goddess Amalthea saved the infant Zeus from being devoured by his father Cronus by hiding him and nursing him on goat's milk in a cave. Zeus accidentally broke off the goat's (or goddess's) horn, which then became a source of perpetual abundance.

11. **an old antlion:** A fantastic animal described in the medieval Russian *Physiologist* as having the front parts of a lion and the rear parts of an ant—probably a fanciful misinterpretation of the Latin *myrmeleontid*.

12. **Belial:** In the Old and New Testaments, Belial is one of the four princes of Hell, a demon of wickedness or impurity, or sometimes Satan himself.

13. **passports:** Russians were, and still are, required to have "internal passports" when moving from their registered place of residence.

14. **Herodias:** See Mark 6:17–29 and Matthew 14:1–12. Herodias was the wife of the tetrarch Herod Antipas; when John the Baptist condemned their marriage, she contrived by means of her daughter Salome to have his head brought to her on a platter.

15. **the prophet Amos:** ". . . they sold the righteous for silver, and the poor for a pair of shoes" (Amos 2:6).

16. **the prophets . . . earth:** "And they that dwell upon the earth shall rejoice over them, and make merry, and shall send gifts one to another; for these two prophets tormented them that dwelt on the earth" (Revelation 11:10).

17. **prayer book of Pyotr Mogila:** Pyotr (Petro, or Peter) Mogila (1596–1646), bishop and then metropolitan of Kiev, was a major figure in the history of the Orthodox Church under Polish domination and among other things undertook an important printing program. His *Trebnik* ("Prayer Book"), published in 1646, contained the texts of all the Orthodox rites and services.

18. **Ushakov . . . Rublev . . . Paramshin:** Semyon Ushakov (1626–86), icon painter and theorist, was the most well-known of the newer "proto-Baroque" painters from the time of Nikon's reforms (see note 6 to "Lady Macbeth") and enjoyed the favor of the royal family. He was also a secular artist. Andrei Rublev (ca. 1360–ca. 1430) is considered the greatest Russian icon painter and the glory of the Moscow school. He was canonized by the Orthodox Church in 1988. Paramshin (or Paramsha) was a well-known silver- and goldsmith of the fourteenth century; in 1356 he made a gilded icon and cross for the grand prince of Moscow, which was remembered for several generations afterwards in the wills of the ruling family.

19. **folding icons . . . he sold it:** Folding icons were mainly intended for travelers. In Leskov's time, this particular folding icon was wrongly dated to the thirteenth century; later it was shown to have been painted no earlier than the

second half of the seventeenth century. It was actually bought by an Italian archaeologist from a relative of the father confessor of Peter the Great, who had given it to him.

20. **Prince Potemkin . . . as a Jew:** Grigory Potemkin (1739–91) was a Russian general and statesman, a favorite of the empress Catherine the Great, who made him governor general of the newly acquired southern provinces of Russia and gave him the title of Prince of Taurida. The reference to "Christ . . . depicted as a Jew" is probably to the painting *Christ in the Desert* (1872), by Ivan Kramskoy (1837–87), one of the founders of the group known as the Peredvizhniki ("Wanderers"), who broke with the conventions of academic painting in the 1860s.

21. **Joseph's lament:** The lines that follow are from an anonymous spiritual song of the same title belonging to Russian oral tradition and dating approximately to the sixteenth century. The story of Joseph is told in Genesis 37–45.

22. **with one mouth and one heart:** These words come from the prayer preceding the reciting of the Creed in the Orthodox liturgy. Levonty suffers because he feels separated from the "one holy, catholic, and apostolic Church" mentioned in the Creed.

23. **the gates of Aristotle . . . the same view as theirs:** *The Gates of Aristotle* was the title of a collection of apocryphal sayings, which was condemned by the Church in 1551, but continued to circulate in Russia until the eighteenth century. Remphan is mentioned in Acts 7:43 ("Yea, ye took up the tabernacle of Moloch and the star of your god Remphan, figures which you made to worship them"). The words, with slight changes, come from Amos 5:26.

24. **All the earth . . . dwell in it:** A slightly altered version of Psalm 24:1 ("The earth is the Lord's, and the fulness thereof; the world, and they that dwell therein").

25. **Creed . . . the old way:** The Old Believers (see note 6 to "Lady Macbeth") rejected the patriarch Nikon's revision, which removed two words from the Nicene Creed.

26. **the spirit of God . . . nostrils:** Slightly altered from Job 27:3–4 ("All the while my breath is in me, and the spirit of God is in my nostrils, my lips will not speak wickedness, nor my tongue utter deceit").

27. **the slaughter of the innocents . . . comforted:** The event and some of the words are from Matthew 2:16–18, which in turn quotes Jeremiah 31:15.

28. **heron . . . forbidden to eat:** In Leviticus 11:13–19, the heron is included among the fowl that the Jews are forbidden to eat.

29. **the spirit bloweth where it listeth:** See John 3:8 ("The wind bloweth where it listeth, and thou hearest the sound thereof, but canst not tell whence it cometh, and whither it goeth: so is every one that is born of the Spirit"). The Greek word *pneuma* can mean wind, breath, or spirit.

30. **the great prokeimenon:** The prokeimenon (*graduale* in Latin) is composed of verses sung responsively before the reading of the Gospel, approximately midway through the "all-night vigil," which may last from two to six hours or even longer.

31. **Prepare yourself . . . morning:** The Old Believers in this story have no priests and no sacraments apart from baptism; thus, receiving communion is a part of their reintegration into the sacramental unity of the Church.

The Enchanted Wanderer (1873)

1. **Konovets . . . Valaam . . . Korela:** Konovets, an island off the southwest shore of Lake Ladoga, in northern Russia near Finland, is the location of a monastery founded in the fourteenth century. Sixty miles north of Konovets is Valaam, a group of islands also famous for its monastery, probably founded at the same time. Korela was a fortress on the shore of Ladoga, first mentioned as early as the twelfth century.

2. **Ilya Muromets . . . Tolstoy:** Ilya Muromets is a *bogatyr* ("mighty man") in the anonymous Russian medieval epic poems known as *byliny*, who defeats various enemies and monsters. Vassily Petrovich Vereshchagin (1835–1909) painted his *Ilya Muromets at the Banquet of Prince Vladimir* in 1871, and in that same year the poet Alexei K. Tolstoy (1817–75) published his ballad "Ilya Muromets" in *The Russian Messenger*.

3. **the metropolitan Filaret:** Filaret Drozdov (1781–1867) was one of the most influential Orthodox churchmen of his time. In 1826 he became metropolitan of Moscow (i.e., metropolitan archbishop, head bishop of a "metropolia"—a major city area, a region, or a province). Leskov was critical of his conservatism.

4. **a husband . . . feed my family:** In perpetuation of the clerical estate, the daughter's husband would be a seminarian eligible to replace his father-in-law at the latter's death or retirement and to continue serving the same parish.

5. **St. Sergius:** St. Sergius of Radonezh (1314?–92), one of the most highly revered saints of Russia, was the founder of the Trinity Monastery (later known as the Trinity–St. Sergius Monastery) in Zagorsk, sixty miles from Moscow. He was canonized in 1452.

6. **stratopedarchos:** New Testament Greek for military leader or camp commandant.

7. **because of the "knock":** See Matthew 7:7 and Luke 11:9 ("Ask, and it shall be given you; seek, and ye shall find; knock, and it shall be opened unto you").

8. **the Trinity . . . the Holy Spirit:** The Sunday of Pentecost, celebrating the descent of the Holy Spirit fifty days after Easter, is also known as the feast of the Trinity. The Monday following it is the day of the Holy Spirit. Traditionally, prayers for suicides were forbidden by the Orthodox Church except on the Saturday before Pentecost or in private prayer at home. This interdiction was lifted by the patriarch Kirill at a council of the Russian Orthodox Church in 2011.

9. **hieromonk . . . hierodeacon:** A hieromonk is a monk who has been ordained a priest or a priest who has become a monk; a hierodeacon is a monk who has become a deacon.

10. **a cantonist:** From 1721 to 1856, the sons of conscripted soldiers in Russia were educated in "canton schools" (from "canton" or recruiting district) and were obliged to serve in the army.

11. **the Englishman Rarey:** John Rarey (1827–66) was in fact an American horse tamer, or "horse whisperer," who developed a gentle technique for rehabilitating mistreated or vicious horses. He came to Europe to demonstrate his method and visited Russia in 1857.

12. **St. Vsevolod-Gavriil of Novgorod:** Prince Vsevolod, baptized Gavriil (?1103–38), the patron saint of the city of Pskov, was prince of Novgorod from 1117 to

1136, and prince of Pskov from 1137 to 1138. He was buried in Pskov and later canonized there. His relics were said to protect the city, and his sword bore the inscription (in Latin) that Ivan Severyanych has embroidered on his belt.

13. **Count K—— of Orel province:** That is, Count Kamensky, of whom there were several. Leskov deals more fully with them in "The Toupee Artist." Given the date, this would be Count Sergei Mikhailovich Kamensky (1771–1835).

14. **an old-style blue banknote:** Blue banknotes, first issued in 1786, were worth five roubles, a considerable sum for a peasant at that time.

15. *Kaffeeschenks:* A court position supervising coffee and tea supplies.

16. **Voronezh . . . relics there:** St. Mitrofan of Voronezh (1623–1703) was the first bishop of Voronezh, in southwestern Russia. Relics are "revealed" when they prove to be either miracle-working or incorrupt. In 1831, Bishop Mitrofan's relics were unearthed and found to be incorrupt; in 1832 he was canonized.

17. **wanderers:** The Russian word *strannik* ("wanderer"), as in the title of the present work, can mean anything from a real pilgrim to a simple vagabond.

18. **passport:** See note 13 to "The Sealed Angel."

19. **St. Mitrofan's:** Both a church and a monastery in Voronezh (see note 16 above).

20. **Saracens . . . Prince Bova:** The term "Saracen" is synonymous with "Muslim" in Russian folk tales. Eruslan Lazarevich and Prince Bova are heroes of such tales.

21. **Tartars in kibitkas:** In Russia, a kibitka (from the Tartar *kibit*) was a covered carriage or sleigh; among nomads of the steppe it was a round felt tent, sometimes mounted on a wheeled platform.

22. **Ryn Sands . . . Khan Dzhangar:** The Ryn Sands are a territory of approximately 25,000 square miles of long hummocky dunes between the lower Volga and Ural Rivers north of the Caspian Sea. Khan Dzhangar or Zhangir (d. 1845) was the last khan of the Bukey or Inner Horde of Kazakhs that moved about on the Ryn Sands. He carried on an important trade in horses and entered Russian government service in 1824.

23. **from the apostle Paul:** See Galatians 3:28 ("There is neither Jew nor Greek, there is neither bond nor free, there is neither male nor female: for ye are all one in Christ Jesus"). Also Colossians 3:11.

24. **Holy God:** The chant known as the Trisagion ("Holy God, Holy Mighty, Holy Immortal, have mercy on us"), sung during the Orthodox liturgy and in the burial procession.

25. **from Khiva:** The Khivan khanate, on the territory of present-day Uzbekistan and Tajikistan, was hostile to Russia during the earlier nineteenth century. Its capital, the city of Khiva, fell to the Russian army in 1873, after which it was made a "protectorate."

26. **Nicholas the Wonderworker:** St. Nicholas (ca. 270–343), bishop of Myra in Lycia (Asia Minor), is one of the most widely venerated saints in Christendom, and obviously not a Russian.

27. **the Keremet:** Among the peoples of the Volga-Ural region, the Keremet or Kiremet were generally evil spirits, but the word also refers to the sacred groves the spirits lived in, where sacrifices to them were performed.

28. **the Menaion:** The Menaion, from the Greek word for "month," is a collection

of Orthodox liturgical texts and saints' lives for each day of the month throughout the year.

29. **banknotes . . . missing:** Russian banknotes were distinguished by color: five-rouble notes were blue, ten-rouble notes gray, twenty-five-rouble notes red, and one-hundred- or two-hundred-rouble notes white.

30. **"The Skiff":** A popular song to words by the soldier-poet Denis Davydov (1784–1839), a hero of the Napoleonic Wars.

31. **Go away . . . burning coal?:** Words from the popular song "Go Away, Don't Look," by Alexander Beshentsov (ca. 1811–82), first published in 1858.

32. **the dragon Gorynych:** A three-headed green dragon from Russian epic songs (*byliny*), who walks on his hind legs and spits fire.

33. **Nizhny:** That is, Nizhny Novgorod, a major Russian city. The fair in Nizhny, world-famous in the nineteenth century, attracted millions of visitors every year. It was also known as the Makary Fair, because it originally took place outside the walls of the monastery of St. Macarius in the Nizhny region. In 1816 a fire destroyed the buildings that housed the fair, and in 1817 it moved to Nizhny proper.

34. **the marshal of the nobility:** In 1785 the empress Catherine the Great issued a Charter of the Gentry, organizing the Russian nobility into provincial assemblies, each headed by a marshal chosen by his peers.

35. **Alyonushka . . . called out to her:** "Sister Alyonushka and Brother Ivanushka" is a Russian folktale in which a little brother turned into a white kid saves his sister from a wicked witch.

36. **Suvorov:** Field Marshal Alexander Vasilievich Suvorov (1729–1800), reputed never to have lost a battle, was one of only three Russian military men to bear the title of generalissimo. He was something of an eccentric and was much loved by his troops.

37. **crown peasants:** The category of "crown peasant" was created by the emperor Peter the Great, designating peasants who lived on land belonging to the crown, paid rent, but were personally free, though restricted in their movements.

38. **a show-booth on Admiralty Square:** Until 1873, popular shows similar to the medieval mystery and morality plays were staged in wooden booths on Admiralty Square in Petersburg during the Christmas and Easter seasons.

39. **a messenger . . . in the flesh:** A misquotation of 2 Corinthians 12:7: "there was given to me a thorn in the flesh, the messenger of Satan to buffet me, lest I should be exalted above measure."

40. **"Resist . . . flee from you":** James 4:7.

41. **the Wet Savior:** Also known in Russia as the "First Savior" or the "Honey Savior," this is the feast of the Presentation of the Cross, celebrated on August 1.

42. **St. Tikhon of Zadonsk:** Tikhon of Zadonsk (1724–83) was made bishop of Voronezh in 1763, but in 1769 he retired to the monastery in Zadonsk where he spent the rest of his life. An important spiritual writer and a wonderworker, Tikhon was canonized in 1861 and his "life" was published in 1862.

43. **Solovki . . . Zosima and Sabbatius:** That is, to the monastery on the Solovetsky Islands founded in the fifteenth century by Sts. Zosima and Sabbatius.

Singlemind (1879)

1. **the reign of Catherine II**: Catherine II, the Great, born in Pomerania in 1729, married the Russian emperor Peter III and became empress of Russia after his assassination in 1762. She ruled until her death in 1796.

2. **Prince Gagarin's dictionary**: *A Universal Geographical and Statistical Dictionary*, by Prince S. P. Gagarin, published in 1843.

3. **"in trouble . . . hut on fire"**: Frequently quoted lines from the poem "Red-Nosed Frost" (1863), by Nikolai Nekrasov (1821–78).

4. **memorial notices for old women**: That is, lists of names of the living or dead to be prayed for during the liturgy.

5. **Burns or Koltsov**: The Scottish poet Robert Burns (1759–96) and Alexei Koltsov (1809–42), often called the Russian Burns, were both close to simple country life and wrote stylized peasant songs.

6. **Neither . . . frightened him**: Words remarkably close to Herodotus's praise of the Persian couriers in his *Histories* (8:98): "Neither snow nor rain nor heat nor gloom of night stays these couriers from the swift completion of their appointed rounds," which became the unofficial motto of the U.S. Post Office.

7. **The ox . . . against my fury**: The passage is a quotation from Isaiah 1:3–24, with some modifications and a number of omissions.

8. **the "dry bones" of Ezekiel's vision**: The reference is to Ezekiel 37:1–10, the prophecy on the dry bones, which is read during the Orthodox service of Holy Friday.

9. **the Voltaireans . . . against it**: An allusion to words spoken by the mayor in act 1, scene 1, of *The Inspector General* (1836), by Nikolai Gogol (1809–52): "That's how God Himself made it, and the Voltaireans shouldn't go talking against it."

10. **"In the sweat . . . bread"**: Part of God's curse on Adam (Genesis 3:17–19).

11. **a beshmet . . . hooks**: A beshmet is a man's knee-length jacket, of Turkic origin, belted at the waist, open below, and fastened up to the neck with hooks or buttons.

12. **The Great Lent . . . approaching**: In the Orthodox Church, the Great Lent is the forty-day fast period preceding Holy Week and Easter.

13. **that the spirit may be saved**: See 1 Corinthians 5:5 ("To deliver such an one unto Satan for the destruction of the flesh, that the spirit may be saved in the day of the Lord Jesus").

14. **The Solovetsky Monastery**: See note 43 to "The Enchanted Wanderer." The monastery was sometimes used as a place of banishment and "re-education." Under the Soviets it was turned into one of the harshest hard-labor camps.

15. **Lanskoy . . . Kostroma**: Sergei Stepanovich Lanskoy (1787–1862) was governor of Kostroma province from 1831 to 1834, and later served as minister of the interior (1855–61). In that office he was instrumental in bringing about the emancipation of the serfs in 1861, the same year in which he was made a count.

16. **the zertsalo**: A three-sided pyramid of mirrored glass topped by a two-headed eagle, which stood on the desk of every Russian official. It was introduced by Peter the Great as a symbol of law and order, each face of the zertsalo being engraved with words from one of his decrees.

17. **my garment . . . wedding feast:** See Matthew 22:11–12, the parable of the wedding feast ("And when the king came to see the guests, he saw there a man which had not on a wedding garment: and he saith unto him, Friend, how camest thou in hither not having a wedding garment?").

18. **principalities and powers:** Words used by St. Paul in Ephesians 1:21 and Colossians 1:16 referring to the angelic hierarchy, here applied ironically to government authorities.

19. **Theophany water . . . inheritance:** The feast of Theophany (Epiphany), celebrated on January 6, includes the blessing of water for church and home use by immersing a cross in it with accompanying prayers. The quoted words, however, come from the troparion (a short hymn) for the two feasts of the Holy Cross, and ultimately from Psalm 28:9.

20. **the Offenbachian mood:** Meaning a frivolous spirit, from Jacques Offenbach (1819–80), the well-known French composer, author of nearly a hundred operettas full of risqué humor and contemporary satire.

21. **Blessed . . . Lord:** Words from Psalm 118:26, repeated in Luke 13:35 and Matthew 11:9 in reference to Christ, and also used in the Orthodox liturgy.

22. **for a wicked servant it's little:** See the parable of the master and his three servants in Matthew 25:14–30 and Luke 19:12–27.

23. **Voltaire . . . empress . . . Chrysostom . . . Pavel Petrovich:** The empress Catherine the Great (see note 1 above) corresponded with Voltaire for fifteen years. St. John Chrysostom (349–407), archbishop of Constantinople and one of the most important Byzantine theologians, was called *Chrysostomos* (Greek for "golden mouthed") in tribute to the eloquence of his preaching. Pavel Petrovich Romanov (1754–1801), the son of Catherine the Great and Peter III, became emperor in 1796 and reigned for five years before he was assassinated. In 1773, he was married to Wilhelmina of Hesse-Darmstadt (1755–76), who died in childbirth three years later.

24. **stump duties . . . tax on timber:** The newly imposed tax on timber was calculated by the number of stumps. Maria, the first daughter of the emperor Alexander I (1777–1825), lived for only a year.

25. **St. Vladimir's Cross . . . nobility:** The Order of St. Vladimir was established in 1782 by Catherine the Great, in honor of Grand Prince Vladimir of Kiev (ca. 958–1015), the "baptizer" of Russia. It was one of only two orders that granted the bearer the rights of hereditary nobility.

26. **"three righteous men":** The first book publication of "Singlemind" in 1880 included the following foreword:

> *Without three righteous men no city can stand.*

A certain great Russian writer was dying before me for the forty-eighth time. He is still alive, just as he went on living after his forty-seven previous deaths, observed by other people and in other circumstances.

He lay before me, alone, splayed out on the boundless sofa and preparing to dictate his last will to me, but instead he began to curse.

I can relate unabashedly how it went and what consequences it led to.

The writer was threatened by death through the fault of the theatrical-literary committee, which was just then killing his play with an unflinching hand. No pharmacy had any medicine against the racking pains this inflicted upon the author's health.

"My soul is wounded and my guts are all twisted inside me," said the sufferer, gazing at the ceiling of the hotel room, and then, shifting his gaze to me, he suddenly shouted:

"Why are you silent, as if your mouth's stuffed with devil knows what? You Petersburgers all have some kind of nastiness in your hearts: you never say anything to console a man; he could just as well give up the ghost right in front of your eyes."

It was the first time I had been present at the death of this extraordinary man and, not understanding his mortal anguish, I said:

"How can I console you? I can only say that everybody will be extremely sorry if the theatrical-literary committee cuts your precious life short with its harsh decision, but . . ."

"Not a bad beginning," the writer interrupted. "Kindly keep talking and maybe I'll fall asleep."

"As you wish," I replied. "So, are you sure that you're now dying?"

"Am I sure? I tell you, I'm almost gone!"

"Splendid," I said, "but have you thought well about whether this grief is worth your expiring on account of it?"

"Of course it's worth it; it's worth a thousand roubles," the dying man moaned.

"Right. Unfortunately," I replied, "the play would hardly bring you more than a thousand roubles, and therefore . . ."

But the dying man did not let me finish: he quickly raised himself on the sofa and cried:

"What a vile way to reason! Kindly give me a thousand roubles and then you can reason all you like."

"Why should I pay for someone else's sin?" I said.

"And why should I be the loser?"

"Because, knowing how things go in our theaters, you described all sorts of titled persons in your play and presented them as each one worse and more banal than the other."

"Ahh, so that's your consolation! According to you, one must describe nothing but good people, but I describe what I see, brother, and all I see is filth."

"Then something's wrong with your eyesight."

"Maybe so," the dying man replied, now thoroughly angry, "but what am I to do if I see nothing but abomination in my own soul and in yours? And thereupon the Lord God will now help me turn from you to the wall and sleep with a peaceful conscience, and I'll leave tomorrow despising all my native land and your consolations."

And the sufferer's prayer was answered: he "thereupon" had an excellent night's sleep, and the next day I took him to the station; but then, as a result of his words, I myself was overcome by a gnawing anxiety.

"Can it be," I thought, "that in my or his or any other Russian soul there really is nothing to be seen but trash? Can it be that all the goodness and kindness ever noticed by the artistic eye of other writers is simply stuff and nonsense? That is not only sad, it's frightening. If, according to popular belief, no city can stand without three righteous men, how can the whole earth stand with nothing but the trash that lives in my soul and yours, dear reader?"

That was terrible and unbearable to me, and I went in search of righteous men, vowing that I would not rest until I had found at least that small number of three righteous men without whom "no city can stand." But wherever I turned, whoever I asked, everyone answered me in the same way, that they had never seen any righteous men, because all men are sinful, but one or another of them had occasionally met good people. I began taking notes. Whether they're righteous or unrighteous, I thought, I must collect all this and then try to see "what in it rises above the level of simple morality" and is therefore "holy to the Lord."

These are some of my notes.

The number of righteous men in Leskov's work went well beyond three, as the reader will see, but the cycle as such was never published and Leskov cut the foreword in later printings.

The Devil-Chase (1879)

1. **bread and salt . . . metropolitan's . . .** : The offering of bread and salt was the traditional way of greeting important persons on their arrival. A metropolitan is an Orthodox bishop or archbishop in charge of churches in a major city or regional capital.

2. **Filaret's catechism:** See note 3 to "The Enchanted Wanderer." Metropolitan Filaret's catechism, written in the strict manner of Roman Catholic catechisms and first published in 1823, presented the fundamentals of Orthodox teaching. It was continually reprinted until 1917 and has been republished, to the dismay of many, since the collapse of the Soviet regime in the 1990s.

3. **the Yar:** A famous restaurant, founded in 1826 and still in existence, located in the Petrovsky Park, which was then a suburb of Moscow.

4. **neither . . . them:** See the parable of the rich man and Lazarus, Luke 16:26 ("And beside all this, between us and you there is a great gulf fixed: so that they which would pass from hence to you cannot; neither can they pass to us, that would come from thence").

5. **the Black King in Freiligrath:** Ferdinand Freiligrath (1810–76) was a German poet and liberal activist. In his poem "A Negro Chieftain," a captured black chieftain, when forced to beat a drum at a fair, beats so furiously that he breaks the head.

6. **Walpurgisnacht:** The eve of May 1, the day of St. Walburga, an eighth-century English missionary and martyr. On that night, according to German tradition going back to the seventeenth century, witches hold their sabbath on Mount Brocken, the highest of the Harz Mountains.

7. **Kuznetsky:** Since the eighteenth century, Kuznetsky Most (literally "Black-smith's Bridge") has been one of the most fashionable and expensive shopping streets in Moscow.
8. **the All-Glorious:** An icon of the All-Glorious Mother of God in one of Moscow's convents.
9. **the trepak:** A fast Cossack dance in 2/4 time.

Deathless Golovan (1880)

1. **"big fire" in Orel:** There were several major fires in Orel during the first half of the nineteenth century. The "big fire" referred to here is probably the one in 1848, which destroyed much of the town.
2. **"a big part . . . memory":** A paraphrase of lines from the poem "Monument," by Gavrila Derzhavin (1743–1816), which is in turn a paraphrase of the *Exegi monumentum* ("I have built a monument") of Horace (65–8 BC), the closing poem of his third book of odes.
3. **Orel Assembly of the Nobility:** See note 34 to "The Enchanted Wanderer."
4. *A Nest of Gentlefolk:* A novel by Ivan Turgenev (1818–83), published in 1859. Turgenev, like Leskov, was born in Orel, but unlike Leskov he belonged to the wealthy landed gentry.
5. **the hundred and four sacred stories . . . book:** *One Hundred and Four Sacred Stories from the Old and New Testaments,* a popular eighteenth-century collection of biblical stories, translated from the German.
6. **Alexei Petrovich Ermolov:** General Ermolov (1777–1861) distinguished himself in the Napoleonic Wars (1805–1814) and was then sent to the Caucasus, where he was made commander in chief of Russian forces. He retired in 1831 and spent the last thirty years of his life on his estate near Orel.
7. **molokan:** The word comes from *moloko* ("milk"). It was applied derisively to a Christian sect that emerged in seventeenth-century Russia, because its members drank milk on fast days, contrary to Orthodox teaching. They called themselves "Spirit Christians" and rejected all churches, not only the Orthodox.
8. **St. Agafya the Dairymaid:** An eighteenth-century martyr, patron saint and protector of cattle, who died on February 5, 1738.
9. *The Cool Vineyard:* A handwritten book of medical advice translated from the Polish at the end of the seventeenth century. It became very popular and spread among the Russian people until the early nineteenth century. Leskov quotes from a printed edition of 1879.
10. **Naum Prokofiev:** Despite the author's claim here, Russian scholars have been unable to identify the man.
11. **athelaea . . . Manus-Christi sugar:** A list of partly fanciful, partly authentic medicaments. "Sealed earth" is *terra sigillata,* a medieval medicinal earth; "Malvasian wine" is made from the Malvasian varieties of grapes, originally grown in the Mediterranean basin; "mithridate" is an ancient remedy made up of as many as sixty-five different ingredients, used in treatment of the plague; "Manus-Christi sugar" is a cordial made by boiling sugar with violet or rose water, thought to give enfeebled people "a hand" (*manus*).

12. **bezoar-stone:** A gray or black stone from the stomach of a goat or other herbivorous animal, much used in popular medicine and believed to cure many diseases.

13. **rebaptizers:** Leskov may be referring to the Anabaptists (literally "rebaptizers"), who had come to southern Russia from Germany in the later eighteenth century, but more likely he means Old Believers who practiced rebaptism (see note 6 to "Lady Macbeth").

14. **young St. George:** The feast of St. George is celebrated on April 23.

15. **Bishop Nikodim:** Nikodim (d. 1839) was bishop of Orel from 1828 to 1839.

16. **Apollos:** Apollos Baibakov (1745–1801) was bishop of Orel from 1788 to 1798.

17. **the saint . . . revealing himself:** See note 16 to "The Enchanted Wanderer." The saint in this case uses more radical methods to "reveal himself." Reference will be made to the "revealing of relics" at the end of chapter 7.

18. **the prophet Jeremiah . . . its own day:** The prophet Jeremiah is commemorated on May 1, St. Boris on May 2, St. Mavra on May 3, St. Zosima (of Volokolamsk) on May 8, St. John the Theologian (the Evangelist) likewise on May 8, St. Nicholas on May 9, and Simon the Zealot on May 10, which is also the pagan Slavic feast day of Mother Earth.

19. **St. John's . . . the joints of the earth:** The birth of St. John the Baptist is celebrated on June 24, the feast of Sts. Peter and Paul on June 29. The feast day of St. Theodore of the Wells is June 8.

20. **simple Old Believers . . . sent far away:** A list of various sectarians. For Old Believers, see note 6 to "Lady Macbeth." The Fedoseevans were a branch of the Old Believers who rejected marriage because they thought the end of the world was at hand; the "Pilipons" (Philippians) preached suicide as a way of preserving the true faith; the "rebaptized" were those who had originally been baptized in the Orthodox Church and accepted a second baptism from the Old Believers. The Flagellants (*Khlysty*) held ecstatic group rituals that included flagellation; "people of God" may refer to holy fools, pilgrims, or simple vagabonds.

21. **the prophet Daniel:** See Daniel 9:24 ("Seventy weeks are determined upon thy people and upon thy holy city, to finish the transgression, and to make an end of sins . . ."), where the "weeks" stand for years.

22. **the "eagle's wings" . . . the Antichrist:** See the prophetic visions in Daniel 7:4 ("The first was like a lion, and had eagle's wings . . .") and Revelation 12:14 ("And to the woman were given two wings of a great eagle . . ."). For the "seal of the Antichrist," see Revelation 13:16–18 ("And he causeth all, both small and great, rich and poor, free and bond, to receive a mark in their right hand, or in their foreheads . . . and his number is Six hundred threescore and six").

23. **K. D. Kraevich:** Konstantin Dmitrievich Kraevich (1833–92) was a noted physicist and the author of widely used school textbooks.

24. **"I believe . . . invisible":** An abbreviated but perfectly correct version of the first section of the Orthodox (Nicene) Creed.

25. **the poet Pope:** The English neoclassical poet Alexander Pope (1688–1744). His philosophical poem, *An Essay on Man,* was published between 1732 and 1734. The poem is dedicated to Henry St. John, Lord Bolingbroke. In the couplet that follows, the second line is line 123 of Epistle I.

26. **rich kulaks:** *Kulak* is the Russian word for "fist." It was commonly used to refer to rich peasants.

27. **the emancipation of the peasants:** In 1861—the first and most important of the reforms carried out by the "tsar-liberator" Alexander II (1818–81).

28. **first . . . troubling of the water:** The narrator is mistaken: cures in the troubled water occurred at the pool of Bethesda (John 5:2–9); in the pool of Siloam the man born blind goes to wash and be healed (John 9:7).

29. **kibitka:** See note 21 to "The Enchanted Wanderer."

30. **"aphedronian sores":** Probably hemorrhoids, from the Greek *aphedron* ("toilet").

31. **the cross, the spear, and the reed . . . :** That is, the instruments of Christ's passion.

32. **"Praise the name of the Lord . . .":** The opening words of Psalm 135, sung at the vigil in the first part of matins.

33. **the paralytic was healed . . . "glorifying and giving thanks":** The reference is to Luke 5:18–25, where the healed man "departed to his own house, glorifying God."

34. **a justice of conscience:** A local court function established by Catherine the Great in 1775 under the influence of Montesquieu's *The Spirit of the Laws* (1748). The court was made up of a justice plus six representatives, two from the nobility, two from the townspeople, and two from the peasants.

The White Eagle (1880)

1. **Theocritus (Idyll):** The line comes from Idyll XXI, "The Fisherman," by Theocritus, the father of Greek bucolic poetry, who lived in the third century BC.

2. **"There are more things in heaven and earth":** *Hamlet,* act 1, scene 5, lines 166–167 ("There are more things in heaven and earth, Horatio, / Than are dreamt of in your philosophy").

3. **to play at spiritualism:** The vogue for spiritualistic mediums and séances came to Russia in the 1870s, where it spread among members of the aristocracy in Moscow and Petersburg. Tolstoy made fun of it in part 7 of *Anna Karenina,* which was published in those same years.

4. **the Nevsky Lavra:** That is, in the graveyard of the Trinity–St. Alexander Nevsky Monastery in Petersburg, founded by Peter the Great in 1710.

5. **Viktor Nikitich Panin:** Count Panin (1801–74) served as minister of justice from 1841 to 1862. He was exceptionally tall.

6. **marshal:** See note 34 to "The Enchanted Wanderer."

7. **"White Eagle":** The Order of the White Eagle, founded in 1705, was the highest Polish decoration for military or civil service. In 1798, following the partition of Poland by Russia, Prussia, and Austria, it was taken over by the Russian royal family. Abandoned after the Russian revolution, it was revived in Poland in 1921 and is still awarded. For the order of St. Vladimir, see note 25 to "Singlemind."

8. **Taglioni . . . Bosio . . . Krestovsky Island:** Maria Taglioni (1804–84), an Italian-Swedish ballet dancer, first came to Russia in 1827 on a three-year contract with the imperial ballet theater in Petersburg and last danced there in

1842. Angelina Bosio (1830–59) was an Italian soprano and prima donna who enjoyed great success in Europe, America, and Russia, where she first sang in 1853 and where she died of a cold while traveling from Moscow to Petersburg. Krestovsky Island, in the Neva delta in Petersburg, was home to various amusements in the nineteenth century, including open-air restaurants with Gypsy singers.

9. **Polycrates:** Polycrates, tyrant of Samos in the sixth century BC, was extremely lucky in all his endeavors, which made people predict a bad end for him. The prediction came true when he was murdered by his ally, Oroetes, satrap of Sardis.

10. **"Saul and the Witch of Endor":** See I Samuel 28:3–35. Saul, the first king of Israel, goes secretly to ask the witch of Endor to consult the shade of the late prophet Samuel. She does so, and Samuel predicts his fall and the kingship of David.

11. **What philosophy never dreamt of:** See note 2 above.

12. **laid out on a table:** It was customary in Russia to lay a dead person out on a table until the body could be put in a coffin.

Lefty (1881)

1. **Alexander Pavlovich . . . the Congress of Vienna:** Alexander Pavlovich is the emperor Alexander I. The Congress of Vienna was a conference of representatives of Austria, Great Britain, Russia, Prussia, and France, held in Vienna from September 1814 to June 1815, to decide the future organization of Europe after the Napoleonic Wars and the breakup of the Holy Roman Empire.

2. **the Don Cossack Platov:** Count Matvei Ivanovich Platov (1757–1818) was a distinguished Russian general and ataman (commander) of the Don Cossacks under Field Marshal Suvorov (see note 36 to "The Enchanted Wanderer") and later during the Napoleonic Wars. At the conclusion of the peace, he indeed accompanied the emperor to England. However, Leskov's narrator grants him a mythical longevity well into the reign of Nicholas I.

3. **two and ten nations:** Napoleon's army was referred to in Russia as "the army of twelve nations."

4. **a Mortimer musket:** Harvey Walklate Mortimer (1753–1819) and his brothers and descendants were well-known English gunsmiths for several generations.

5. **Tsarskoe Selo:** The imperial country estate, fifteen miles south of Petersburg. The name means "Tsar's Village."

6. **molvo sugar . . . Bobrinsky factory:** Y. N. Molvo ran a sugar refinery in Petersburg during the early nineteenth century. Count Alexei Alexeevich Bobrinsky (1800–68) was also one of the first sugar refiners in Russia. William B. Edgerton, in *Satirical Stories of Nikolai Leskov* (New York, 1969) suggests that "Molvo" was a Russified form of the French name Mollevaut and comments, "If this supposition is true, then the irony of Platov's Russian defense of 'Mollevaut' sugar becomes all the sweeter."

7. **Zhukov tobacco . . . :** Vasily Zhukov produced pipe tobacco in his Petersburg factory from the 1820s to the 1850s.

8. **The emperor Nikolai Pavlovich . . . at his ascension:** Nikolai Pavlovich is the emperor Nicholas I (1796–1855). The "disturbances at his ascension" were the events of the Decembrist uprising of December 14, 1825, when young officers in Petersburg mutinied during the confusion following the death of Alexander I and demanded democratic reforms in Russia.

9. **holy Athos:** The mountain and peninsula of Athos is home to twenty Orthodox monasteries, among them the Russian Orthodox monastery of St. Panteleimon.

10. **"Evening Bells":** "Evening Bells" is a song by the Irish poet Thomas Moore (1779–1852), published in 1818, with the subtitle "The Bells of St. Petersburg." Moore claimed it was based on a Russian original, but the source is unknown. In 1828, the Russian poet Ivan Kozlov (1779–1840) translated Moore's poem into Russian. His version became immensely popular and is still widely sung. The musical setting by Alexander Alyabyev (1787–1851) is indeed "painted out."

11. **Count Nestlebroad:** That is, Count Karl Vasilievich Nesselrode (1780–1862), of Baltic German birth, who entered the Russian navy and then the diplomatic service under Alexander I, becoming foreign minister in 1816 and remaining in that capacity for more than forty years.

12. **our lace:** The city of Tula had four specialties: firearms, samovars, gingerbread, and lace.

13. **Count Kleinmichel:** Count Pyotr Andreevich Kleinmichel (1793–1869) served from 1842 to 1855 as chief administrator of highways and public buildings under Nicholas I.

14. **Commandant Skobelev:** In 1839, General Ivan Nikitich Skobelev (1778–1849) was commandant of the Peter-and-Paul Fortress in Petersburg, which served as a prison.

15. **Martyn-Solsky:** The narrator's variant on the name of Martyn Dmitrievich Solsky (1793–1869), doctor in a guards regiment and member of the medical council of the ministry of internal affairs.

16. **Count Chernyshev:** Count Alexander Ivanovich Chernyshev (1786–1857), cavalry general and statesman, served as minister of war under Nicholas I from 1826 to 1852.

17. **"deeds . . . of old":** A reference to lines from *Ruslan and Lyudmila* (1820), a narrative poem by Alexander Pushkin (1799–1837).

The Spirit of Madame de Genlis (1881)

1. **A. B. Calmet:** Leskov is mistaken about the middle initial. Antoine Augustin Calmet (1672–1757) was a Benedictine monk. His most well-known work, *Dissertations on Apparitions, Angels, Demons, and Spirits, and on Ghosts and Vampires in Hungary, Bohemia, Moravia, and Silesia* (Paris, 1746; re-edited in 1951), was published in Russia in 1867.

2. **Mmes de Sévigné . . . de Genlis:** Leskov gives a list of six famous letter writers or memoirists of the reign of Louis XIV, all ladies, before he comes to Mme de Genlis. He misspells most of the names, but we give them in their correct form. Mme de Genlis (Stéphanie Félicité Ducrest de St. Aubin Brûlart, marquise de Sillery, comtesse de Genlis, 1746–1830) first entered the royal palace as lady-in-

waiting to the duchesse de Chartres and became the governess of her children, one of whom, Louis Philippe d'Orléans (1773–1850), later became king. She wrote verse, novels, plays, treatises, and some important memoirs.

3. **Voltaire . . . criticism:** Mme de Genlis met Voltaire at his estate in Ferney, near Geneva, and noted in her memoirs that he was a tasteless, ill-bred man with a love of crude flattery.

4. **Kardec's theory of "mischievous spirits":** Allan Kardec was the pen name of Hippolyte Léon Denizard Rivail (1808–69), a French schoolteacher and a prime mover of the spiritualist vogue in the mid-nineteenth century (see note 3 to "The White Eagle"). Among other things, he coined the word "spiritism" and produced a five-volume theoretical synthesis, *The Spiritual Codification*.

5. **Prince Gagarin:** Prince Ivan Sergeevich Gagarin (1814–82) was serving as secretary of the Russian legation in Paris when, in 1842, he converted to Catholicism and became a Jesuit. He lived the rest of his life in Paris, where Leskov met him in 1875.

6. **Heine's "Bernardiner und Rabiner":** The reference is to the poem "Disputation," from *Romanzero* (1851), by Heinrich Heine (1797–1856). The poem, which is set in medieval Toledo, presents a dispute between a Capuchin friar and a rabbi about whose God is the true God. It is resolved by the young Doña Blanka, who says "I don't know which of them is right, but they both stink."

7. **Mme du Deffand . . . Gibbon:** Marie Anne de Vichy-Chamrond, marquise du Deffand (1697–1780), was a prolific letter writer who corresponded with many notable people of her time, including Voltaire and Horace Walpole, with whom she formed an enduring attachment. The English historian Edward Gibbon (1737–94) is most famous for his *Decline and Fall of the Roman Empire* (1776–88).

8. **Lauzun:** Armand Louis de Gontaut, duc de Lauzun (1747–1793), took part in the American War of Independence on the side of the colonists and in the French revolutionary wars. He was arrested and guillotined during the Reign of Terror.

9. **Gibbon was . . . "vile joke"!:** Leskov quotes this passage, with cuts and alterations, from the Russian edition of the memoirs of Mme de Genlis, *Memoirs of Felicia L****, published in Moscow in 1809.

The Toupee Artist (1883)

1. **February 19, 1861:** The date of the imperial manifesto proclaiming the emancipation of the serfs.

2. **Sazikov and Ovchinnikov . . . Heine . . . Worth . . . :** Pavel Ignatyevich Sazikov (d. 1868) and Pavel Akimovich Ovchinnikov (1830–88) were well-known gold- and silversmiths with shops in Moscow and Petersburg. In his late prose work *Lutezia* (1854), Heine speaks not of a tailor but of a Parisian shoemaker named Sakosky, describing him as "an artist in leather footwear." The Englishman Charles Frederick Worth (1825–95) became a famous Parisian couturier, inventor of the *défilé de mode* ("fashion show").

3. **Bret Harte . . . :** The reference is to the story "A Sleeping-Car Experience,"

by Francis Brett Harte (1836–1902), published in the collection *Drift from Two Shores* (1878), but Leskov's recounting of it has little to do with the original.

4. **Count Kamensky in Orel:** Field Marshal Count Mikhail Fedotovich Kamensky (1738–1809) retired from the army to his estate in Orel in 1806. He was notorious for mistreating his serfs and was murdered by one of them three years later. He had two sons, both generals, Sergei (1771–1836) and Nikolai (1776–1811). Sergei retired from the army in 1822, returned to the Kamensky estate, and threw himself into running the serf theater started by his father. The troupe, including actors, dancers, and musicians, numbered about four hundred souls. Kamensky treated them quite tyrannically. Serf theaters arose in Russia in the late seventeenth century; by the nineteenth century there were more than 170 of them.

5. **Alexander Pavlovich or Nikolai Pavlovich . . . :** See notes 1 and 8 to "Lefty."

6. **camarine:** That is, aquamarine, or blue beryl. Some of the best aquamarines come from Russia. Ironically, aquamarine is said to symbolize love, harmony, and marital happiness.

7. **Snakes . . . your face:** A somewhat inaccurate quotation from the Serbian song "Prince Marco in Prison."

8. **Turkish Rushchuk:** The town of Ruse, on the Danube in Bulgaria, was called "Rushchuk" ("Little Ruse") by the Ottomans, who made it a major fortress and city. It was liberated from Ottoman control in 1878.

9. **"bolyarin":** The Church Slavonic equivalent of the Russian *boyarin*, equivalent to the medieval "baron."

The Voice of Nature (1883)

1. **Faddeev . . . Baryatinsky:** Field Marshal Prince Alexander Ivanovich Baryatinsky (1814–1879) was made commander of Russian forces in the Caucasus and then governor of the region, a post he held until his retirement in 1862. Rostislav Andreevich Faddeev (1824–83), a general and a writer on military subjects, was attached to the governor of the Caucasus from 1859 to 1864.

2. **Temir-Khan-Shura:** A settlement in what is now Dagestan, founded as a fortress in 1834 and granted the status of a town in 1866.

3. **Paul de Kock:** (1793–1871). A prolific French novelist, author of crude but spicy and often amusing novels about Parisian life.

A Little Mistake (1883)

1. **Ivan Yakovlevich:** Ivan Yakovlevich Koreisha (1780–1861) was an inmate of a Moscow psychiatric clinic for over forty years. His bizarre verbosity earned him the reputation of a seer, and people of all classes came to have him "prophesy" for them. Koreisha was Dostoevsky's model for the holy fool Semyon Yakovlevich in *Demons* (1872).

2. *Pismovnik:* Nikolai Gavrilovich Kurganov (1726–96), mathematician, teacher,

and member of the St. Petersburg Academy, published his *Pismovnik,* a collection of writings for self-education in Russian language and literature, in 1793.

3. **a clown from Presnya:** In the late eighteenth to nineteenth century, the Presnya district of Moscow was a park and picnic area with ponds and entertainments.

4. **promise . . . head cut off:** See note 14 to "The Sealed Angel." The tetrarch Herod Antipas was so taken with his stepdaughter Salomé's dancing that he promised to give her whatever she asked for. At the prompting of her mother, Herodias, she asked for John the Baptist's head.

The Pearl Necklace (1885)

1. **the late Pisemsky:** Alexei Feofilaktovich Pisemsky (1826–81), distinguished novelist and playwright, was a realist of a dark turn of mind, skeptical of the liberal reforms of the 1860s.

2. **in which . . . man:** A slightly altered quotation from Pushkin's *Evgeny Onegin,* chapter 7, stanza 22.

3. **the late poet Tolstoy:** See note 2 to "The Enchanted Wanderer." The line is from stanza 35 of Tolstoy's satirical poem "The Dream of Councilor Popov" (1873), which spread widely through Russia in handwritten copies.

4. **the altar of Themis:** Themis was an ancient Greek titaness, an oracle at Delphi, the goddess of divine order and justice.

5. **"The joy of Rus' is to drink":** The *Primary Chronicle,* compiled in Kiev around 1113, attributes these words to Prince Vladimir, who supposedly rejected Islam because it prohibits alcohol.

6. **Princess Yusupov . . . Gorgibus:** Princess Tatyana Vasilievna Yusupov (1769–1848) indeed had a famous collection of precious gems, but the "pearl of Gorgibus," a 126-carat pear-shaped pearl, was brought from the Indies by Gorgibus of Calais and sold to King Philip IV of Spain (1605–65).

7. **a prosphora:** A small, round bread especially blessed for holy communion.

8. **'Bourguignon':** The firm of Bourguignon, on the boulevard des Capucines in Paris, specialized in making imitation jewelry.

9. **Rurik and Gediminas:** That is, the ancient ruling dynasties of Russia and Lithuania, respectively.

The Spook (1885)

1. **the kikimora:** A female house spirit in Slavic folklore, sometimes married to the house demon (*domovoi*).

2. **"of Catherine's planting":** That is, planted in the time of Catherine the Great (see note 1 to "Singlemind").

3. **Baba Yaga:** A wicked witch in Russian folklore, who lives in the forest in a hut on chicken's legs and rides around in an enormous mortar, steering it with a broom.

4. **the class of rhetoric in the seminary:** Seminaries were the only educational

institutions open to children of the peasant and merchant classes in Russia. Their students were not necessarily preparing for the priesthood.

5. **white Nezhin roots . . . :** That is, crude local tobacco. Nezhin, in Chernigov province to the west of Orel, was a center of the tobacco industry.

6. **the Python, Cerberus, and their ilk:** In Greek mythology, the Python was the gigantic serpent that guarded the oracle at Delphi and Cerberus was the three-headed hound that guarded the entrance to the underworld.

7. **Varus . . . Teutoburg:** Publius Quintilius Varus (46 BC–9 AD), a Roman patrician and general under Augustus Caesar (63 BC–19 AD), was defeated by a confederation of Germanic troops under the general Arminius at the battle of Teutoburg in Germany, where his three legions were annihilated.

8. **the schismatic village of Kolchevo:** That is, a village inhabited by Old Believers (see note 6 to "Lady Macbeth").

9. **the Orel priest Ostromyslenny:** Father Efim Ostromyslenny (or Ostromyslensky) was a priest in Orel and taught religion in the Orel high school. Leskov was one of his grateful students and mentions him a number of times in his work.

10. **because your eye was dark:** See Matthew 6:22–23: "The eye is the lamp of the body. So, if your eye is sound, your whole body will be full of light; but if your eye is not sound, your whole body will be full of darkness" (Revised Standard Version). Also Luke 11:34.

The Man on Watch (1887)

1. **Nikolai Ivanovich Miller . . . :** Lieutenant General Nikolai Ivanovich Miller (d. 1889), after retiring from the army, was first an inspector then the director of the Alexandrovsky Lycée, founded by Alexander I for the education of the elite of the nobility.

2. **Nikolai Pavlovich:** See note 8 to "Lefty." The emperor Nicholas I was known for the military strictness of his rule.

3. **the Jordan entrance:** The entrance to the imperial palace from the Neva embankment, where the "Jordan" ice hole was located, cut in the ice for the blessing of the waters on the feast of Theophany (see note 19 to "Singlemind").

4. **Kokoshkin . . . Svinyin:** Sergei Alexandrovich Kokoshkin (1795–1861), formerly an infantry general, served as superintendent of police in Petersburg from 1830 to 1847. He was a favorite of Nicholas I. By 1839 Nikita Petrovich Svinyin had already been a lieutenant colonel in the Izmailovsky Regiment for six years.

5. **the grand duke Mikhail Pavlovich:** Mikhail Pavlovich Romanov (1798–1849), the fourth son of the emperor Paul I (see note 23 to "Singlemind"), was at that time a colonel of the guards.

6. **in Gogol's comedy:** See note 9 to "Singlemind." The reference is to act 3, scene 6, where the number of messengers is actually thirty-five thousand.

7. **Peter's Little House:** The oldest building in Petersburg, a small wooden house on the Petrovskaya Embankment, built for Peter the Great in 1703 and now a museum. During the reign of Nicholas I, the dining room was turned into a

chapel and the icon of the Savior that Peter the Great used to take with him on campaign was placed in it.

8. **the Peter-and-Paul Fortress:** See note 14 to "Lefty."
9. **a certain bishop . . . :** The bishop in question is thought to be Metropolitan Filaret Drozdov (see note 3 to "The Enchanted Wanderer").
10. **of the earth, earthy:** See 1 Corinthians 15:47 ("The first man is of the earth, earthy: the second man is the Lord from heaven").

A Robbery (1887)

1. **"With the pure . . . froward":** Psalm 18:26.
2. **the famous fires . . . Trubetskoy:** Pyotr Ivanovich Trubetskoy (1798–1871), governor of Orel province, is mentioned frequently in Leskov's work. For the "famous fires," see note 1 to "Deathless Golovan."
3. **churchly faith . . . Father Efim . . . Old Believers:** For "churchly faith" and Old Believers, see note 6 to "Lady Macbeth." For Father Efim, see note 9 to "The Spook."
4. **Kamensky . . . Turchaninov . . . Molotkovsky:** For Kamensky, see note 4 to "The Toupee Artist." After Kamensky's death, the theater was taken over by the entrepreneurs Turchaninov and Molotkovsky.
5. **rebaptized girls:** See note 13 to "Deathless Golovan."
6. **the great martyr Barbara . . . :** Little is known about the third-century St. Barbara, known as "the Great Martyr Barbara" in the Orthodox Church. An akathist is a special prayer service.
7. **our deliverance from the Gauls:** That is, from the Grande Armée of Napoleon, which was driven out of Russia in 1812.
8. **Tula . . . samovarniks . . . :** See note 12 to "Lefty."
9. **'Many Years' . . . 'Memory Eternal':** Well-known Orthodox hymns wishing long life for the living and peace and God's memory for the dead.
10. **'Except the Lord . . . but in vain':** A conflated variant of Psalm 127:1 ("Except the Lord build the house, they labour in vain that build it; except the Lord keep the city, the watchman waketh but in vain").
11. **Alfred . . . in people's houses:** The reference is probably to the eighteenth-century folk drama *Of King Maximilian and His Disobedient Son Adolph.* Either Misha or Leskov has mistaken the name.
12. **"It is meet and right" . . . "Rest Eternal":** Various phrases from the preparation of communion, the reading of the Gospel, and the commemoration of the dead.
13. **wailing woefully:** An imprecise quotation from the seventeenth-century "Tale of Woe and Grief and How Woeful-Grief Drove a Young Man to Monkhood."
14. **"Lord, save us . . . Arid":** See Psalm 59:2 ("Deliver me from the workers of iniquity, and save me from bloody men"). It is not clear whom the aunt means by Arid. It has been suggested that she means Jared, a fifth-generation descendant of Adam, but he is distinguished only by his longevity. She may mean Herod.
15. **the marshal of the nobility:** See note 34 to "The Enchanted Wanderer."
16. **zertsalo:** See note 16 to "Singlemind."

A NOTE ABOUT THE AUTHOR

Nikolai Leskov was born in 1831 in the village of Gorokhovo in Russia. He began his writing career as a journalist living in Kiev, and later settled in St. Petersburg. He published his first piece of fiction in 1862, and went on to write and publish many short stories and novellas, including *The Lady Macbeth of Mtsensk* (1865), *The Enchanted Wanderer* (1873), and *Lefty* (1881). He died in February 1895.

A NOTE ABOUT THE TRANSLATORS

Together, Richard Pevear and Larissa Volokhonsky have translated works by Tolstoy, Dostoevsky, Chekhov, Gogol, Bulgakov, and Pasternak. They were twice awarded the PEN/Book-of-the-Month Club Translation Prize (for their versions of Dostoevsky's *The Brothers Karamazov* and Tolstoy's *Anna Karenina*), and their translation of Dostoevsky's *Demons* was one of three nominees for the same prize. They are married and live in France.

A NOTE ON THE TYPE

This book was set in Fairfield, a typeface designed by the distinguished American artist and engraver Rudolph Ruzicka (1883–1978) In its structure Fairfield displays the sober and sane qualities of the master craftsman whose talents were dedicated to clarity. Ruzicka was born in Bohemia and came to America in 1894. He designed and illustrated many books, and was the creater of a considerable list of individual prints in a variety of techniques.

Typeset by
Scribe, Philadelphia, Pennsylvania

Printed and bound by
Berryville Graphics, Berryville, Virginia

Designed by
Iris Weinstein